Raves for Tanya Huff's *Blood* Books:

"If you enjoy contemporary fantasy, Tanya Huff has a distinctive knack, one she gives full vent in her detective mystery, *Blood Trail*. There's a strong current of romance that's as interesting . . . as the current investigation . . . a carefully thought out pattern of nonhuman family life . . . an unexpected serious theme that helps raise it above the crowd . . . funny, often lighthearted and highly entertaining . . . more than just another 'light' fantasy."
—*Locus*

"Explores the borders of death and beyond with an intensity that is only partially lightened by touches of ironic humor. Written with the author's usual flair for realistic fantasy."
—*Library Journal*

"This story is a gruesome romp through mystery, horror, and the occult. The author takes it seriously enough that it succeeds, but she also injects some delightful humor."
—*Voya*

"A suspenseful story that deals with the emotional content of the situation, and with a real surprise ending for fans of the series."
—*Science Fiction Chronicle*

"Tanya Huff brews up a yummy concoction of equal parts fantasy and mystery, throwing in a splash of humor and a dash of romance to beguile the palate quite delightfully. In a prodigious feat of inticate choreography, Ms. Huff manages to develop all her different plot threads to marvelous effect. How could anyone resist this vastly entertaining pastiche?"
—*Romantic Times*

D0018008

THE BLOOD BOOKS, VOLUME 2

BLOOD LINES

BLOOD PACT

Tanya Huff

DAW BOOKS, INC.

DONALD A. WOLLHEIM, FOUNDER

375 Hudson Street, New York, NY 10014

ELIZABETH R. WOLLHEIM
SHEILA E. GILBERT
PUBLISHERS

http://www.dawbooks.com

Introduction

My favorite part of *Blood Lines*, the third Blood book, was doing the research for it. Over the two or three months leading up to the actual writing, I essentially taught myself Egyptology 101. I bought all kinds of fascinating books and took pages and pages of notes, wallowing in the incredible history of one of the oldest and most elaborate civilizations on the planet. But that wasn't all, thanks to the kind offices of Dr. Roberta Shaw; I got to go behind the scenes at the Royal Ontario Museum in Toronto.

When Vicki is hiding in the sarcophagus—I saw that very sarcophagus. The bit about the cleaning lady being upset about mummified heads wearing the headgear of various Toronto sports teams; true story. I got to wander around peering at the many shelves of catalogued items and to very gently touch a piece of three-thousand-year-old faience.

I have the coolest job in the world.

Vicki, Mike, and Henry are, of course, less thrilled since I took the information I'd gathered and used it to create the latest in a long and honorable line of ambulatory mummies. A small digression to wonder just what was supposed to be so scary about those shambling, shedding, early versions? A poorly motivated couch potato could not run them. Now, someone who can threaten a four-hundred-and-fifty-year-old vampire and put some bite in the threat—that's scary.

That said, I think I've managed to make at least some of the people significantly scarier than the walking dead.

Oh, and I also got to hang around on top of the CN tower for a while.

Coolest job *in the world*.

For a while in *Blood Pact* I thought I was writing a zombie story until I got going on it and realized it was actually a thematic retelling of Frankenstein, about how crossing the line between science and responsibility can come back to bite you on the ass. Some of the science is even accurate—for the time and within certain broad values of accurate. Just as I was starting the book, I read an article about the possibilities of bacteria being used as a type of nanotechnology to repair damaged organs and the rest, as we say, is rising up off the laboratory slab.

This is also the first book I set in Kingston, a city where the downtown core is dominated by Queens, one of the top universities in Canada. Where shambling half-dead hulks appear wandering the streets every year at exam time.

It might distress you to learn that I don't actually make everything up . . .

The other books in the Blood series are dark fantasy—there are scary bits, yes, but they aren't at the emotional heart of the story I'm telling. *Blood Pact*, however, is horror. Not the kind of hack and slash, blood all over, high body count that a lot of horror has become of late (although there is blood and a relatively high body count) but more the deep visceral fear that arises when the horror being hunted is someone you loved. For the first time, I have pages of notes detailing emotional reaction at various points in the story.

Blood Pact is the most personal of the Blood Books. My mother died when I was very young and many of Vicki's nightmares are mine. After I read "The Monkey's Paw" at an impressionable age, I'd lay awake at night and try to work out how long it would take my mother's corpse to walk from Halifax, Nova Scotia, where she was buried, to Kingston, Ontario, where I was growing up. As I got older, I realized it was a bit far for a dead woman to hike and stopped worrying quite so much.

This book ends the emotional story arc begun in *Blood Price* and begins the one explored in *Blood Debt* and most of the short stories.

—Tanya Huff
March 2006

BLOOD LINES

For Mother Bowen, who taught me that a book lasts because it touches the heart and soul. She not only gave me ancient Greece but Middle Earth as well and while I might have found Tolkien without her, I would've been the poorer for Homer's loss. She also put up with more spelling mistakes in a single semester than one woman should have to deal with in a lifetime. For both of these, for Christmas sherry and gingerbread, for Adeste Fideles and wine-dark seas, thank you. (Oh, and by the way: "Ab, cum, de, ex, in, pro, sina, sub, all take the ablative case. All others take accusative. Go team!")

I'd also like to take this time to thank Ms. Roberta Shane, Curatorial Assistant, Egyptology, at the Royal Ontario Museum for taking the time to show me around behind the scenes and for helping me to work out just how an undiscovered mummy could be, well, discovered. For those interested, the Egyptology Exhibit at the ROM is fantastic.

One

He had been almost aware for some time. Nothingness had shattered when they removed him from the chamber long concealed behind the centuries empty tomb of a forgotten priest. The final layer of the binding spell had been written on the rock wall smashed to gain access and, with that gone, the spell itself had begun to fray.

Every movement frayed it further. The surrounding ka, more souls than had been near him in millennia, called him to feed. Slowly, he reached for memory.

Then, just as he brushed against self and had only to reach out and grasp it and draw home the key to his freedom, the movement stopped and the lives went away. But the nothingness didn't quite return.

And that was the worst of all.

Sixteenth Dynasty, thought Dr. Rax running his finger lightly along the upper surface of the plain, unadorned rectangle of black basalt. Strange, when the rest of the collection was Eighteenth. He could now, however, understand why the British were willing to let the artifact go; although it was a splendid example of its type, it was neither going to bring new visitors flocking to the galleries nor was it likely to shed much light on the past.

Besides, thanks to the acquisitiveness of aristocracy with more money than brains, Great Britain has all the Egyptian antiquities it can hope to use. Dr. Rax was careful not to let that thought show on his face, as a member of said aristocracy, albeit of a more recent vintage, fidgeted at his shoulder.

Too well bred to actually ask, the fourteenth Baron Montclair leaned forward, hands shoved into the pockets of his crested blazer.

Dr. Rax, unsure if the younger man was looking worried or merely vacant, attempted to ignore him. *And I thought Monty Python created the concept of the upper-class twit,* he mused as he continued his inspection. *How foolish of me.*

Unlike most sarcophagi, the artifact Dr. Rax examined had no lid but rather a sliding stone panel in one narrow end. Briefly, he wondered why that feature alone hadn't been enough to interest the British museums. As far as he knew the design survived on only one other sarcophagus, an alabaster beauty found by Zakaria Goneim in the unfinished step pyramid of Sekhem-khet.

Behind him, the fourteenth baron cleared his throat.

Dr. Rax continued to ignore him.

Although one corner had been chipped, the sarcophagus was in very good condition. Tucked away in one of the lower cellars of the Monclairs' ancestral home for almost a hundred years, it seemed to have been ignored by everything including time.

And excluding spiders. He brushed aside a dusty curtain of webbing, frowned, and with fingers that wanted to tremble, pulled a penlight out of his suit pocket.

"I say, is something wrong?" The fourteenth baron had an excuse for sounding a little frantic. The very exclusive remodeling firm would be arriving in a little under a month to turn the ancestral pile into a very exclusive health club and that great bloody stone box was sitting right where he'd planned to put the women's sauna.

The thudding of Dr. Rax's heart almost drowned out the question. He managed to mutter, "Nothing." Then he knelt and very carefully played the narrow beam of light over the lower edge of the sliding plate. Centered on the mortared seam, six inches above the base of the sarcophagus, was an oval of clay—a nearly perfect intact clay seal stamped with, as far as Dr. Rax could tell through the dust and the spiderwebs, the cartouche of Thoth, the ancient Egyptian god of wisdom.

Just for a moment, he forgot to breathe.

An intact seal could mean only one thing.

The sarcophagus wasn't—as everyone had assumed—empty.

For a dozen heartbeats, he stared at the seal and struggled with his conscience. The Brits had already said they didn't want the artifact. He was under no obligation to let them know what they were giving away. On the other hand . . .

He sighed, switched off the penlight, and stood. "I need to make a call," he told the anxious peer. "If you could show me to a phone."

"Dr. Rax, what a pleasant surprise. Still out at Haversted Hall are you? Get a look at his lordship's 'bloody-great-black-stone-box'?"

"As a matter of fact, yes. And that's why I've called." He took a deep breath; best to get it over with quickly, the loss might hurt less. "Dr. Davis, did you actually send one of your people out here to look at the sarcophagus."

"Why?" The British Egyptologist snorted. "Need some help identifying it?"

Abruptly, Dr. Rax remembered why, and how much, he disliked the other man. "I think I can manage to classify it, thank you. I was just wondering if any of your people had seen the artifact."

"No need. We saw the rest of the junk Montclair dragged out of his nooks and crannies. You'd think that with all the precious bits and pieces leaving Egypt at the time, his Lordship's ancestor could have brought home something worthwhile, even by accident, wouldn't you?"

Professional ethics warred with desire. Ethics won. "About the sarcophagus . . ."

"Look, Dr. Rax . . ." On the other end of the line, Dr. Davis sighed explosively. ". . . this sarcophagus might be a big thing for you, but trust me, we've got all we need. We have storerooms of important, historically significant artifacts we may never have time to study." *And you don't,* was the not too subtly implied message. "I think we can allow one unadorned hunk of basalt to go to the colonies."

"So I can send for my preparators and start packing it up?" Dr. Rax asked quietly, his tone in severe contrast to the white-knuckled grip that twisted the phone cord.

"If you're sure you don't want to use a couple of my people . . ."

Not if my only other option was to carry the sarcophagus

on my lap all the way home. "No, thank you. I'm sure all your people have plenty of historically significant things to do."

"Well, if that's the way you want it, be my guest. I'll have the paperwork done up and sent down to you at the Hall. You'll be able to get your artifact out of the country as easily as if it were a plaster statue of Big Ben." *Which,* his tone said clearly, *is about its equivalent value.*

"Thank you, Dr. Davis." *You pompous, egocentric ass-hole,* Dr. Rax added silently as he hung up. *Oh, well,* he soothed his lacerated conscience, *no one can say I didn't try.*

He straightened his jacket and turned to face the hovering baron, smiling reassuringly. "I believe you said that 50,000 pounds was your asking price . . . ?"

"Uh, Dr. Rax . . ." Karen Lahey stood and dusted off her knees. "Are you sure the Brits don't want this?"

"Positive." Dr. Rax touched his breast and listened for a second to the comforting rustle of papers in his suit pocket. Dr. Davis had been as good as his word. The sarcophagus could leave England as soon as it was packed and insurance had been arranged.

Karen glanced down at the seal. That it held the cartouche of Thoth and not one of the necropolis symbols was rare enough. What the seal implied was rarer still. "They knew about . . ." She waved a hand at the clay disk.

"I called Dr. Davis right after I discovered it." Which was true, as far as it went.

She frowned and glanced over at the other preparator. His expression matched hers. Something was wrong. No one in his right mind would give up a sealed sarcophagus and the promise that represented. "And Dr. Davis said . . . ?" she prodded.

"Dr. Davis said, and I quote, 'This sarcophagus might be a big thing for you, but we've got all we need. *We* have storerooms of important, historically significant artifacts we may never have time to study.' " Dr. Rax hid a smile at the developing scowls. "And then he added, 'I think we can let one unadorned hunk of basalt go to the colonies.' "

"You didn't tell him about the seal, did you, Doctor?"

He shrugged. "After that, would you?"

Karen's scowl deepened. "I wouldn't tell that patronizing son of a bitch, excuse my French, the time of day. You leave this with us, Dr. Rax, and we'll pack it up so that even the spiderwebs arrive intact."

Her companion nodded. "Colonies," he snorted. "Just who the hell does he think he is?"

Dr. Rax had to stop himself from skipping as he left the room. The Curator of Egyptology, Royal Ontario Museum, did not skip. It wasn't dignified. But *no one* mortared, then sealed, an empty coffin.

"Yes!" He allowed himself one jubilant punch at the air in the privacy of the deserted upper cellar. "We've got ourselves a mummy!"

The movement had begun again and the memories strengthened. Sand and sun. Heat. Light. He had no need to remember darkness; darkness had been his companion for too long.

As the weight of the sarcophagus made flying out of the question, a leisurely trip back across the Atlantic on the grand old lady of luxury ocean liners, the QE II, would have been nice. Unfortunately, the acquisitions budget had been stretched almost to the breaking point with the purchase and the packing and the insurance and the best the museum could afford was a Danish freighter heading out of Liverpool for Halifax. The ship left England on October 2nd. God and the North Atlantic willing, she'd reach Canada in ten days.

Dr. Rax sent the two preparators back by plane and he himself traveled with the artifact. It was foolish, he knew, but he didn't want to be parted from it. Although the ship occasionally carried passengers, the accommodations were spartan and the meals, while nourishing, were plain. Dr. Rax didn't notice. Refused access to the cargo hold where he could be near the sarcophagus and the mummy he was sure it contained, he stayed as close as he could, caught up on paperwork, and at night lay in his narrow bunk and visualized the opening of the coffin.

Sometimes, he removed the seal and slid the end panel up in the full glare of the media; the find of the century, on every news program and front page in the world. There'd

be book contracts, and speaking tours, and years of research as the contents were studied, then removed to be
studied further.

Sometimes, it was just him and his staff, working slowly
and meticulously. Pure science. Pure discovery. And still
the years of research.

He imagined the contents in every possible form or combination of forms. Some nights expanding on the descrip-
tions, some nights simplifying. It wouldn't be a royal
mummy—more likely a priest or an official of the court—
and so hopefully would have missed the anointing with aromatic oils that had partially destroyed the mummy of
Tutankhamen.

He grew so aware of it that he felt he could go into the
hold and pick its container out of hundreds of identical
containers. His thoughts became filled with it to the exclu-
sion of all else; of the sea, of the ship, of the sailors. One
of the Portuguese sailors began making the sign against the
evil eye whenever he approached.

He started to speak to it each night before he slept.

"Soon," he told it. "Soon."

*He remembered a face, thin and worried, bending over
him and constantly muttering. He remembered a hand, the
soft skin damp with sweat as it brushed his eyes closed. He
remembered terror as he felt the fabric laid across his face.
He remembered pain as the strip of linen that held the spell
was wrapped around him and secured.*

But he couldn't remember self.

*He could sense only one ka, and that at such a distance
he knew it must be reaching for him as he reached for it.*

"Soon," it told him. "Soon."

He could wait.

The air at the museum loading dock was so charged with
suppressed excitement that even the driver of the van, a
man laconic to the point of legend, became infected. He
pulled the keys out of his pocket like he was pulling a
rabbit out of a hat and opened the van doors with a flourish
that added a silent *Tah dah* to the proceedings.

The plywood packing crate, reinforced with two by twos
and strapping, looked no different from any number of

other crates that the Royal Ontario Museum had received over the years, but the entire Egyptology Department— none of whom had a reason to be down in Receiving— surged forward and Dr. Rax beamed like the Madonna must have beamed into the manger.

Preparators did not usually unload trucks. They unloaded this one. And as much as he single-handedly wanted to carry the crate up to the workroom, Dr. Rax stood aside and let them get on with it. His mummy deserved the best.

"Hail the conquering hero comes." Dr. Rachel Shane, the assistant curator, walked over to stand beside him. "Welcome back, Elias. You look a little tired."

"I haven't been sleeping well," Dr. Rax admitted, rubbing eyes already rimmed with red.

"Guilty conscience?"

He snorted, recognizing she was teasing. "Strange dreams about being tied down and slowly suffocating."

"Maybe you're being possessed." She nodded at the crate.

He snorted again. "Maybe the Board of Directors has been trying to contact me." Glancing around, he scowled at the rest of his staff. "Don't you lot have anything better to do than stand around watching a wooden box come off a truck?"

Only the newest grad student looked nervous, the others merely grinned and collectively shook their heads.

Dr. Rax grinned as well; he couldn't help himself. He was exhausted and badly in need of something more sustaining than the coffee and fast food they'd consumed at every stop between Halifax and Toronto, but he'd also never felt this elated. This artifact had the potential to put the Royal Ontario Museum, already an internationally respected institution, on the scientific map and everyone in the room knew it. "As much as I'd like to believe that all this excitement is directed at my return, I know damned well it isn't." No one bothered to protest. "And as you can now see there's nothing to see, why don't the lot of you head back up to the workroom where we can all jump about and enthuse in the privacy of our own department?"

Behind him, Dr. Shane added her own silent but emphatic endorsement to that suggestion.

It took more than a few last, lingering looks at the crate, but, finally, Receiving emptied.

"I suppose the whole building knows what we've got?" Dr. Rax asked as he and Dr. Shane followed the crate and the preparators onto the freight elevator.

Dr. Shane shook her head. "Surprisingly enough, considering the way gossip usually travels in this rabbit warren, no. All of our people have been very closemouthed." Dark brows drew down. "Just in case." *Just in case it does turn out to be empty, the less people know, the less our professional reputations will suffer. There hasn't been a new mummy uncovered in decades.*

Dr. Rax chose to ignore the subtext. "So Von Thorne doesn't know?" While the Department of Egyptology didn't really resent the Far East's beautiful new temple wing, they did resent its curator's more-antiquarian-than-thou attitude concerning it.

"If he does," Dr. Shane said emphatically, "he hasn't heard about it from us."

As one, the two Egyptologists turned to the preparators who worked, not just for them, but for the museum at large.

One hand resting lightly on the top of the crate, Karen Lahey drew herself up to her full height. "Well he hasn't heard about it from *us*. Not after accusing us of creating a nonexistent crack in that porcelain Buddha."

Her companion grunted agreement.

The freight elevator stopped on five, the doors opened, and Dr. Van Thorne beamed genially in at them.

"So, you're back from your shopping trip, Elias. Pick up anything interesting?"

Dr. Rax managed a not very polite smile. "Just the *usual* sorts of things, Alex."

Stepping nimbly out of the way as the preparators rolled the crate from the elevator, Dr. Von Thorne patted the wood as it passed; a kind of careless benediction. "Ah," he said. "More broken bits of pottery, eh?"

"Something like that." Dr. Rax's smile had begun to show more teeth. Dr. Shane grabbed his arm and propelled him down the hall.

"We've just received a new Buddha," the curator of the Far East Department called after them. "Second century BC. A beautiful little thing in alabaster and jade without a mark on it. You must come and see it soon."

"Soon," Dr. Shane agreed, her hand still firmly holding

her superior's arm. Not until they were almost at the work-room did she let go.

"A new Buddha," he muttered, flexing his arm and watching the preparators maneuver the crate through the double doors of the workroom. "Of what historical significance is that? People are still *worshiping* Buddha. Just wait, just wait until we get this sarcophagus open and we'll wipe that smug temple-dog smile off his face."

As the doors of the workroom swung closed behind him, the weight of responsibility for the sarcophagus lifted off his shoulders. There was still a lot to do, and any number of things that could yet go wrong, but the journey at least had been safely completed. He felt like a modern day Anubis, escorting the dead to eternal life in the Underworld, and wondered how the ancient god had managed to bear such an exhausting burden.

He rested both hands on the crate, aware through the wood and the packing and the stone and whatever interior coffin the stone concealed, of the body that lay at its heart. "We're here," he told it softly. "Welcome home."

The ka that had been so constant was now joined by others. He could feel them outside the binding, calling, being, driving him into a frenzy with their nearness and their inaccessibility. If he could only remember . . .

And then, suddenly, the surrounding ka began to fade. Near panic, he reached for the one he knew and felt it moving away. He hung onto it as long as he could, then he hung onto the sense of it, then the memory.

Not alone. Please, not alone again.

When it returned, he would have wept if he'd remembered how.

Refreshed by a shower and a good night's sleep plagued by nothing more than a vague sense of loss, Dr. Rax stared down at the sarcophagus. It had been cataloged—measured, described, given the card number 991.862.1—and now existed as an official possession of the Royal Ontario Museum. The time had come.

"Is the video camera ready?" he asked pulling on a pair of new cotton gloves.

"Ready, Doctor." Doris Bercarich, who took care of most

of the departmental photography, squinted through the view finder. She'd already taken two films of still photography— one black and white, one color—and her camera now hung around the neck of the more mechanically competent of the two grad students. He'd continue to take photographs while she shot tape. If she had anything to say about it, and she did, this was going to be one well documented mummy.

"Ready, Dr. Shane?"

"Ready, Dr. Rax." She tugged at the cuffs of her gloves, then picked up the sterile cotton pad that would catch the removed seal. "You can start any time."

He nodded, took a deep breath, and knelt. With the sterile pad in place, he slid the flexible blade of the palette knife behind the seal and carefully worked at the centuries old clay. Although his hands were sure, his stomach tied itself in knots, tighter and tighter as the seconds passed and his fear grew that the seal, in spite of the preservatives, could be removed only as a featureless handful of red clay. While he worked, he kept up a low-voiced commentary of the physical sensations he was receiving through the handle of the knife.

Then he felt something give and a hairline crack appeared diagonally across the outer surface of the seal.

For a heartbeat the only sound in the room was the soft whir of the video camera.

A heartbeat later, the seal, broken cleanly in two, halves held in place by the preservative, lay on the cotton pad.

As one, the Department of Egyptology remembered how to breathe.

He felt the seal break, heard the fracture resonate throughout the ages.

He remembered who he was. What he was. What they had done to him.

He remembered anger.

He drew on the anger for strength, then he threw himself against his bonds. Too much of the spell remained; he was now aware but still as bound as he had been. His ka howled in silent frustration.

I will be free!

"Soon," *came the quiet answer.* "Soon."

*   *   *

It took the rest of the day to clear the mortar. In spite of mounting paperwork, Dr. Rax remained in the workroom.

"Well, whatever they sealed up in here, they certainly didn't make it easy to get to." Dr. Shane straightened, one hand rubbing the small of her back. "You're sure that his lordship had no idea of where the venerable ancestor picked this up?"

Dr. Rax ran one finger along the joint. "No, none." He had expected to be elated once work finally began but he found he was only impatient. Everything moved so slowly—a fact he was well aware of and shouldn't even be considering as a problem. He scrubbed at his eyes and tried to banish the disquieting vision of taking a sledge to the stone.

Dr. Shane sighed and bent back to the mortar. "What I wouldn't give for some contextual information."

"We'll know everything we need to when we get the sarcophagus open."

She glanced up at him, one raised brow disappearing under a curl of dark hair. "You seem very sure of that."

"I am." And he was very sure. In fact he *knew* that they would have all the answers they needed when the sarcophagus was finally opened although he had no idea where that knowledge came from. He wiped suddenly sweaty palms on his trousers. No idea . . .

By the time they finished removing the mortar, it was too late to do any further work that day—or more exactly, that night. They would see what their stone box contained in the morning.

That night, Dr. Rax dreamed of a griffinlike animal with the body of an antelope and the head of a bird. It peered down at him with too-bright eyes and laughed. He got up, barely rested, at dawn and was at the museum hours before the rest of the department arrived. He intended to avoid the workroom, to use the extra time for the administrative paperwork that threatened to bury his desk, but his key was in the lock and his hand was pushing open the door before his conscious mind registered the action.

"I almost did it," he said as Dr. Shane came in some time later. He was sitting in an orange plastic chair, hands clasped so tightly that the knuckles were white.

She didn't have to ask what he meant. "Good thing you're too much of a scientist to give way to impulse," she

told him lightly, privately thinking that he looked like shit.
"As soon as the others get here, we'll get this over with."

"Over with," he echoed.

Dr. Shane frowned, then shook her head, deciding not
to speak. After all, what could she say? That just for a
moment the Curator of the Department of Egyptology had
neither sounded nor looked like himself? Maybe he wasn't
the only one not getting enough sleep.

Five hours and seven rolls of film later, the inner coffin
lay on padded wooden supports, free of its encasing stone
for the first time in millennia.

"Well," Dr. Shane frowned down at the painted wood,
"that's the damnedest thing I've ever seen."

The rest of the department nodded in agreement; except
for Dr. Rax who fought not to step forward and throw off
the lid.

The coffin was anthropomorphic but only vaguely. There
were no features either carved into or painted on the wood,
nor any symbols of Anubis or Osiris as might be expected.
Instead, a mighty serpent coiled its length around the coffin,
its head, marked with the cartouche of Thoth, resting above
the breast of the mummy. At the head of the coffin was a
representation of Setu, a minor god who stood guard in the
tenth hour of Tuat, the underworld, and used a javelin to
help Ra slay his enemies. At the foot of the coffin was a
representation of Shemerthi, identical in all ways to the
other guardian save that he used a bow. Small snakes,
coiled and watchful, filled in the spaces that the great serpent left bare.

In Egyptian mythology, serpents were the guardians of
the underworld.

As a work of art, it was beautiful; the colors so rich and
vibrant that the artist might have finished work three hours
instead of three millennia ago. As a window on history, the
glass was cloudy at best.

"If I have to hazard a guess," Dr. Shane said thoughtfully, "I'd say, based on the cartouche and the workman-
ship, that this is Eighteenth Dynasty, not Sixteenth. In spite
of the sarcophagus."

Dr. Rax had to agree with her even though he seemed
incapable of forming a coherent observation of his own.

It took them the rest of the day to photograph it, catalog it, and remove the seal of cedar gum that held the lid tightly in place.

"Why this stuff hasn't dried to a nice, easily removable powder, I have no idea." Dr. Shane shook the kinks out of one stiff leg, and then the other. This had been the second day she'd spent mostly on her knees and, while it *was* a favored position of archaeologists, she'd never been a great believer in crippling herself for science.

"It looks," she added slowly, her hand stretching out but not quite touching one of the small serpents, "like something interred in this coffin was not supposed to get out."

One of the graduate students laughed, a high-pitched giggle quickly cut off.

"Open it," Dr. Rax commanded, through lips suddenly dry.

In the silence that followed, the soft whir of the video camera sounded intrusively loud.

Dr. Rax was not completely unaware of his subordinates' shocked glances, both at each other and at him. He spread his hands and managed a smile. "Will any of us sleep tonight if we don't?"

Will any of us sleep tonight if we do? Dr. Shane found herself thinking, and wondered where the thought came from. "It's late. We've all been working hard and now we've got a whole weekend ahead of us; why don't we start fresh on Monday?"

"We'll only lift the lid." He was using the voice he used to get funds out of the museum board, guaranteed to charm. Dr. Shane didn't appreciate it being used on her. "And I think all that hard work deserves a look inside."

"What about X-rays?"

"Later." He pulled on a clean pair of gloves as he spoke, the action serving to hide the trembling of his hands. "As the handles that were used to lower the lid into place appear to have been removed, I will take the head. Ray," he motioned to the largest of the researchers, "you will take the feet."

It could have stopped there, but when it came down to it, they *were* all anxious to see what the artifact held. As the assistant curator offered no further objections, Ray shrugged, pulled on a pair of gloves, and went to his place.

"On three. One, two, three!"

The lid lifted cleanly, heavier than it looked.

"Ahhh." The sound came involuntarily from half a dozen throats. Placing the lid carefully on another padded trestle, Dr. Rax, heart slamming painfully against his ribs, turned to see what might lie revealed.

The mummy lay thickly swathed in ancient linen and the smell of cedar was almost overpowering—the inside of the casket had been lined with the aromatic wood. Someone sneezed although no one noticed who. A long strip of fabric, closely covered in scarlet hieroglyphs was wrapped around the body following the path the serpent had taken around the coffin. The mummy wore no death mask, but features were visible in relief through the cloth.

The dry air of Egypt was good to the dead, preserving them for the future to study by leeching all the moisture from even protected tissue. Embalming was only the first step and, as sites that predated the pharaohs proved, not even the most necessary one.

Desiccated was the only word to describe the face beneath the linen, although other, more flattering words might have been used once, for the cheekbones were high and sharp, the chin determined, and the overall impression one of strength.

Dr. Rax let out a long breath he hadn't been aware of holding and the tension visibly left his shoulders.

"You were expecting maybe Bela Lugosi?" Dr. Shane asked dryly, pitched for his ears alone. The look he turned on her—half horror, half exhaustion—made her regret the words almost instantly. "Can we go home now?" she asked in a tone deliberately light. "Or did you want to cram another two years of research into this evening?"

He did. He saw his hand reach out and hover over the strip of hieroglyphs. He snatched it back.

"Pack it up," he said, straightening, forcing his voice to show no sign of how he had to fight to form the words. "We'll deal with it Monday." Then he turned and, before he could change his mind, strode from the workroom.

He would have laughed aloud had it been possible, unable to contain the rush of exaltation. His body might still be bound, but with the opening of his prison his ka was free. Free . . . freed . . . feed.

TWO

"My name is Ozymandias, King of Kings: Look on my works, ye Mighty, and despair!"

Detective-Sergeant Michael Celluci frowned at his companion. "What the hell are you babbling about?"

"Babbling? I was not babbling. I was ruminating on the monuments that man builds to man." Pushing her glasses securely into place, Vicki Nelson bent, stiff-legged, and laid both palms against the concrete at her feet.

Celluci snorted at this blatant display of flexibility—obviously intended to remind him of his limitations—tilted his head back and gazed up the side of the CN Tower. From their position at its base, foreshortening made it appear simultaneously infinite and squat, the radio antennae that extended its height hidden behind the bulge of the restaurants and observation deck. "Cows ruminate," he grunted. "And I assume you mean man in the racial sense rather than the genetic."

Vicki shrugged, the motion almost lost in her position. "Maybe." She straightened and grinned. "But they don't call it the world's tallest free-standing phallic symbol for nothing."

"Dream on." He sighed as she grasped her left ankle and lifted the leg up until it rose into the air at a better than forty-five-degree angle. "And quit showing off. You ready to climb this thing yet?"

"Just waiting for you to finish warming up."

Celluci smiled. "Then get ready to eat my dust."

A number of charitable organizations used the one thousand seven hundred and ninety steps of the CN Tower as a means of raising money, climbers collecting pledges per step from friends and business associates. The Heart Fund was sponsoring the current climb; as well as a starting time, both Vicki and Celluci had starting pulses measured.

"You'll find the run pretty clear," the volunteer told them as he wrote Vicki's heart rate down on a slip of paper. "You're like the six and seventh up and the others have been serious racers."

"What makes you think we aren't?" Celluci asked belligerently. With his last birthday, he'd started on the downhill run to forty and was finding himself a little sensitive about it.

"Well . . ." The younger man swallowed nervously—very few people do belligerent as well as the police. "You're like both wearing sweats and normal running shoes. Climbers one to five were seriously aerodynamic."

Vicki snickered, knowing full well what had prompted Celluci's question. He glared but, recognizing he'd probably come out the worse for any comment, kept his mouth shut. With their time stamped, they ran for the stairs.

The volunteer had been both right and wrong. Neither of them cared about racing the other climbers or the tower itself, but they couldn't have been more serious about racing each other. Competition had been the basis of their relationship from the day they first met, two very intense young police constables both certain that they were the answer regardless of the question. Michael Celluci, with four years' seniority, an accelerated promotion, and a citation, had some reason for believing that. Vicki Nelson, just out of the academy, took it on faith. Four years later, Vicki had become known as "Victory" around the force, they'd discovered a number of mutual interests, and the competition had become so much a part of the way they operated that their superiors used it to the force's advantage. Four years after that, when Vicki's deteriorating eyesight compelled her to choose between a desk or leaving, the system broke down. She couldn't stay and become less than what she was, so she left. He couldn't just let her go. Words were said. It took months for the wounds left by those words to heal and more months where pride on both sides refused to make the first move. Then a threat to the city they'd both sworn to serve threw them together and a new relationship had to be forged out of the ruins of the old.

"Blocking me is cheating, you long-armed bastard!"

It turned out not to be significantly different.

The yellow metal steps switchbacking up the side of the CN Tower were no more than three and a half feet wide—easy enough for a tall man to keep one hand on each banister and use his arms to take some of the strain on the muscles of his upper body. And, incidentally, make it impossible for anyone behind to pass.

Six landings up, Vicki put on a burst of speed and slid between Celluci and the inner wall, the damp concrete scraping against her shoulder blades. She pulled out ahead, two stairs at a time, feeling Celluci climbing right on her heels. At five ten it was almost easier for her to climb taking double strides. Unfortunately, it was definitely easier for Celluci at six four.

Neither of them paused at the first water station.

The lead switched back and forth twice more, the sound of high tech rubber soles pounding down on the metal stairs reverberating throughout the enclosed space like distant thunder. Later in the day, the plexiglass sheets that separated the climbers from the view would begin to cloud over with the accumulated moisture panted out of hundreds of pairs of lungs, but this early in the morning, the skyline of Toronto fell away beside them with vertigo-inducing clarity.

Giving thanks in this one instance that she had almost no peripheral vision and therefore no idea of how high they actually were from the ground, Vicki charged past the second water station. Three hundred feet to go. No problem. Her calves were beginning to protest, her lungs to burn, but she'd be damned if she'd slow and give Celluci a chance to get past.

The stairs turned from yellow to gray, although the original color showed through where countless feet had rubbed off the second coat of paint. They were into the emergency exit stairs for the restaurant level.

Almost there . . . Celluci was so close she could feel his breath hot against her back. He hit the last landing seconds behind her. One, two strides to the open door. On level ground, his longer legs brought them even. Vicki made a desperate grab at the edge of the doorway and exploded out into the carpeted hall.

"Nine minutes, fifty-four seconds. Nine minutes, fifty-five seconds."

As soon as I have enough breath, I'll rub it in. For the moment, Vicki leaned against the wall, panting, heart pounding with enough force to vibrate her entire body, sweat collecting and dripping off her chin.

Celluci collapsed against the wall beside her.

One of the Heart Fund volunteers approached, stopwatch in hand. "Now then, I'll just get your finishing heart rates. . . ."

Vicki and Celluci exchanged identical glances.

"I don't think," Vicki managed to gasp, "that we really want . . . to know."

Although the timed portion of the climb was over, they had another four flights to go up before they reached the observation deck and were officially finished.

"Nine minutes and fifty-four seconds." Celluci scrubbed at his face with the lower edge of his T-shirt as they moved back into the stairwell. "Not bad for an old broad."

"Who are you calling old, asshole? Let's just keep in mind that I can give you five years."

"Fine." He held out his hand. "I'll take them now."

Vicki pulled herself up another step, quadriceps visibly trembling under the fleece of her sweatpants. "I want to spend the rest of the day submerged in hot water."

"Sounds good to me."

"Mike?"

"Yeah?"

"Next time I suggest we climb the CN Tower, remind me of how I feel right now."

"Next time . . ."

His kind never dreamed, or so he'd always believed— they lost dreaming as they lost the day—but in spite of this, for the first time in over four hundred and fifty years, he came to awareness with a memory that had no connection to his waking life.

Sunlight. He hadn't seen the sun since 1539 and he had *never* seen it as a golden disk in an azure sky, heat spreading a shimmering shield around it.

Henry Fitzroy, bastard son of Henry VIII, romance writer, vampire, lay in the darkness, stared at nothing, and wondered what the hell was going on. Was he losing his mind? It had happened to others of his kind. They grew so that they couldn't stand the night and finally they gave themselves to the sun and death. Was this *memory,* then, the beginning of the end?

He didn't think so. He felt sane. But would a madman recognize his condition?

"This is going nowhere." Lips tight, he swung his legs off the bed and stood. He certainly had no conscious wish to die. If his subconscious had other ideas, it would be in for a fight.

But the memory lingered. It lingered in the shower. It lingered as he dressed. A blazing circle of fire. When he closed his eyes, he could see the image on his lids.

His hand was on the phone before he remembered; she was with *him* tonight.

"Damn!"

In the last few months Vicki Nelson had become a necessary part of his life. He fed from her as often as it was safe, and blood and sex had pulled them closer into friendship if not something stronger. At least on his side of the relationship.

"Relationship, Jesu! Now *that's* a word for the nineties." Tonight, he only wanted to talk to her, to discuss the dream—if that's what it was—and the fears that came with it.

Running pale fingers through short, sandy-blond hair, he walked across the condo to look out at the lights of Toronto. Vampires hunted alone, prowled the darkness alone, but they had been human once and perhaps at heart were human still, for every now and then, over the long years of their lives, they searched for a companion they could trust with the truth of what they were. He had found Vicki in the midst of violence and death, given her his truth, and waited for what she would give him in return. She'd offered him acceptance, only that, and he doubted she ever realized how rare a thing acceptance was. Through her, he'd had more contact with mortals since last spring than he'd had in the last hundred years.

Through her, two others knew his nature: Tony, an uncomplicated young man who, on occasion, shared bed and blood, and Detective-Sergeant Michael Celluci, who was neither young nor uncomplicated and while he hadn't come right out and said *vampire,* he was too intelligent a man to deny the evidence of his eyes.

Henry's fingers curled against the glass, forming slowly into a fist. She was with Celluci tonight. She'd as much as warned him of it when they'd last spoken. All right. Maybe he was getting a bit possessive. *It was easier in the old days.* She'd have been his then, no one else would have had a claim on her. How *dared* she be with someone else when he needed her?

The sun burned down in memory, an all-seeing yellow eye.

He frowned down at the city. He was not used to dealing with fear, so he fed the dream to his anger and allowed, almost forced, the Hunger to rise. He *did not* need her. He would hunt.

Below him, a thousand points of light glowed like a thousand tiny suns.

Reid Ellis preferred the museum at night. He liked being left alone to do his work, without scientists or historians or other staff members asking him stupid questions. "You'd think," he often proclaimed to his colleagues, "that a guy with four degrees would know when a floor was wet."

Although he didn't mind working the public galleries, he preferred the long lengths of hall linking offices and workrooms. Within the assigned section, he was his own boss; no nosy supervisor hanging over his shoulder checking up on him; free to get the job done properly, his way. Free to consider the workrooms his own private little museums where the storage shelves were often a hell of a lot more interesting than the stuff laid out for the paying customers.

He rolled his cart out onto the fifth floor, patted one of the temple lions for luck, and hesitated with his hand on the glass door to the Far East Department. Maybe he should do Egyptology first? They usually had some pretty interesting things on the go.

Maybe he should do their workroom first. Now.

Nah, that'd leave the heelmarks on the floor outside Von Thorne's office for end of shift and I'm not up to that. He pulled out his passkey and maneuvered his cart through the door. *As my sainted mother used to say, get your thumb out of your butt and get to work. I'll save the good stuff for last. Whatever they've got out isn't going anywhere.*

The ka pulled free of his tenuous grasp and began to move away. He was still pitiably weak, too weak to hold it, too weak to draw it closer. Had he been able to move, hunger would have driven him to desperate measures, but bound as he was, he could only wait and pray that his god would send him a life.

On a Sunday night in Toronto the good, the streets were almost deserted, municipal laws against Sunday shopping forcing the inhabitants of the city to find other amusements.

Black leather trench coat billowing out behind him, Henry made his way quickly down Church Street, ignoring the occasional clusters of humanity. He wanted more than just a chance to feed; his anger needed slaking as much as his Hunger. At Church and College, he paused.

"Hey, faggot!"

Henry smiled, turned his head slightly, and tested the breeze. Three of them. Young. Healthy. Perfect.

"What's the matter, faggot, you deaf?"

"Maybe he's got someone's pecker stuffed in his ear."

Hands in his pockets, he pivoted slowly on one heel. They were leaning against the huge yellow bulk of Maple Leaf Gardens, suburban boys in lace-up boots and strategically ripped jeans downtown for a little excitement. With odds of three to one, they'd probably be after him anyway, but just to be certain . . . the smile he sent them was deliberately provocative, impossible to ignore.

"Fuckin' faggot!"

They followed him east, yelling insults, getting braver and coming closer when he didn't respond. When he crossed College at Jarvis Street, they were right on his heels and, without even considering why he might be leading them there, they followed him into Allen Gardens Park.

"Faggot's walking like he's still got a prick shoved up his ass."

There were lights scattered throughout the small park, but there were also deep pockets of shadow that would

provide enough darkness for his needs. Hunger rising,
Henry led them away from the road and possible discovery,
fallen leaves making soft, wet noises under his feet. Finally,
he stopped and turned.

The three young men were barely an arm's length away.
The night would never be the same for them again.

They moved to surround him.

He allowed it.

"So, why aren't you fucking dead like the rest of the
fucking queers?" Their leader, for all packs have a leader
of sorts, reached out to shove a slender shoulder, the first
move in the night's entertainment. He looked surprised
when he missed. Then he looked startled as Henry smiled.
Then he looked frightened.

A heartbeat later, he looked terrified.

The double doors to the Egyptology workroom had been
painted bright orange. As Reid Ellis put his passkey into
the lock, he wondered, not for the first time, why. All the
doors in this part of the hallway had been painted yellow
or orange and while he supposed it looked cheerful it didn't
exactly look dignified. Not that the folks in the Egyptology
Department were exactly sticklers for dignity. Three
months ago, when the Blue Jays had lost six ball games in
a row he'd gone in to find one of the mummified heads set
up on the table with a baseball cap perched jauntily on its
desiccated brow.

Now that baseball season was over, he wondered if anyone in the department owned a hockey helmet, *rest in peace*
being the kindest epitaph one could give the Leafs even
this early in the season.

"And what've you got for me tonight?" he asked as he
hooked one of the doors open to make way for his cart—
they weren't actually scheduled to have the floors done, but
he liked to keep up with the high traffic areas by the desk
and the sink—then he turned and got his first look at the
new addition to the room. "Holy shit."

Palms suddenly wet, mouth suddenly dry, Reid stood and
stared. The head had been unreal, like a special effect in a
movie, evoking a shudder but easy to laugh at and dismiss.
A coffin though, with a body in it, was another thing alto-

gether. This was a person, a dead person, lying there shrouded in plastic and waiting for him.

Waiting for me? His nervous laugh went no further than his lips, doing nothing to displace the silence that filled the huge room like fog. *Maybe I should just go, come back another night.* But he stepped forward; one pace, two. He'd forgotten to turn on the lights and now the switch was behind him. He'd have to turn his back on the coffin to reach it and he couldn't, he just couldn't. The spill of light from the hall would have to be enough even though it barely chased the shadows from around the body.

The breeze created by his approach stirred the edges of the plastic sheet, setting it fluttering in anticipation.

"Jesus, this is too weird. I'm out of here."

But he kept walking toward the coffin. Eyes wide, he watched his fingers grab the plastic and drag it off the artifact.

Man, I am going to be in deep shit. Maybe if he put the plastic back the way it had been, no one would ever know that he . . . that he . . . *What the fuck am I doing?*

He was bending over the coffin, breath slamming faster and faster against the back of his throat. His eyes stung. He couldn't blink. His mouth opened. He couldn't scream.

And then it started.

He lost his most recent self first: the night's work, all the other nights of work before it, his wife, their daughter, her birth, red-faced and screaming—*"Honestly, Doc, is she supposed to look like that? I mean, she's beautiful but she's kind of squashed . . ."*—the wedding where he'd gotten pissed and almost fallen over while dancing with an elderly aunt. He lost nights drinking with his buddies, cruising up and down Yonge Street—*"Lookit the melons on that one!"*—The Grateful Dead blaring out of the car speakers, the smell of beer and grass and sweat soaking into the upholstery.

He lost his high school graduation, a ceremony he'd made by the skin of his teeth—*"Think maybe now you can get off your ass and get a job? Now you got your fancy piece of paper with your name on it?" "I think so, Dad."* He lost the humiliation of not making the basketball team—*They're not going to call my name. I'm the only guy who tried out they didn't want. Oh, God, I wish I could sink through the floor.*—and he lost the pain when football broke his nose. He tasted again his first kiss and felt again for the first time the explosive results of masturbation, which did not grow hair on his palms or make him blind. And then he lost them.

In quick succession he lost his mother, his father, too many siblings, the house he'd grown up in, the smell of a winter's worth of dog turds melting on the lawn in the spring, a teddy bear with all the fur chewed off, the sweet taste of a nipple clutched between frantically working lips.

He lost his first step, his first word, his first breath.

His life.

Yes.

With iron control, Henry drew his mouth back from the soft skin of the young man's wrist and laid the arm down almost gently, pulling the jacket cuff forward until it covered the small wound. Although he preferred to feed from desire—it had natural parameters for the Hunger that anger lacked—it was, on occasion, good to remember his strength. He rose slowly to his feet, brushing at the decayed leaves on his coat. The coagulant in his saliva would ensure that the bleeding had stopped and all three would regain consciousness momentarily, before the damp and cold had time to do any damage.

He glanced down to where they sprawled in the darker shadow of a yew hedge and licked a drop of blood from the corner of his mouth. As well as the bruises, he'd given them a reason to fear the night, a reminder that the dark hid other, more powerful hunters and that they, too, could be prey. He was in no danger of discovery for their memories of the incident would be of essence, not appearance, and intensely personal. Whether or not he'd changed their attitudes or opinions, he neither knew nor cared.

I am vampire. The night is mine.

His mood broke under the weight of that pronouncement and he left the quiet oasis of the park, smiling at the newsreel quality of the voice in his head—*And thanks to the vampire vigilante, the streets are safe to walk again*—the dream and his earlier disquiet washed away by the blood.

*   *   *

Ceiluci sighed and stuffed the parking ticket into his jacket pocket. From midnight to seven the street outside Vicki's apartment building was permit parking only. The time on the ticket said five thirty-three; if he'd gotten up five minutes earlier, he could have avoided a twenty-dollar fine.

It had been hard to drag himself away. He must've lain in the darkness for a good twenty minutes listening to her breathe. Wondering if she was dreaming. Wondering if she was dreaming about him. Or about Henry. Or if it mattered.

"What I mean, Celluci, is no commitments beyond friendship."

"We're going to be buddies?"

"That's right."

"You don't ball your buddies, Vicki."

She'd snorted and run a bare foot up his inner thigh until she could grab the soft skin of his scrotum with her toes. "Wanna bet?"

So it had been from the beginning. . . .

He scratched at his stubble and got into the car. Their friendship was solid, he knew that; the scars they'd both inflicted when she'd left the force had faded into memory. The sex was still terrific. But lately, things had gotten complicated.

"Henry's not competition, Mike. Whatever happens between him and me doesn't affect us. You're my best friend."

He'd believed her then, he believed her now. But he still thought Henry Fitzroy was a dangerous man for her to get involved with. Not only was he physically dangerous, and that had been proven last August beyond a doubt, but he had the kind of personal power it would be easy to get lost in. *Christ, I could get lost in it.* No one with that kind of power should be, could be, trusted.

He trusted Vicki. He didn't trust Henry. That's what it came down to. Henry Fitzroy made up the rules as he went along, and for Detective-Sergeant Michael Celluci that was the sticking point. More than supposedly supernatural, undead powers of darkness. There were a number of very definite rules surrounding his and Vicki's relationship, and Celluci knew damned well Fitzroy wouldn't honor them.

Except he had so far . . .

"Maybe what it all comes down to," he mused, maneuvering through the maze of one-way streets south of College, "is that I'm ready to settle down."

It took a few seconds for the implications of that to sink in, and he had a sudden vision of what Vicki's response would be if he brought up marriage. He couldn't stop himself from ducking. The woman was more commitment shy than any man he'd ever met.

He frowned as he guided the car around the Queen's Park circle. It was too early in the morning for deep philosophical questions on the nature of his relationship with Vicki Nelson—things were going well, he shouldn't fuck with that. Gratefully noticing the ambulance and the police car pulled up in front of the museum, he made a U-turn across the empty six-lane road and dumped the problems of his love life for more immediate concerns.

"Detective-Sergeant Celluci, homicide." He flipped his badge at the approaching constable as he got out of the car, forestalling a confrontation about the less than legal U-turn. "What's going on?"

The young woman snapped her mouth shut around what she'd been about to say and managed, "Constable Trembley, sir. They sent homicide? I don't understand."

"No one sent me, I was just driving past." The attendants were loading a body into the ambulance, face covered. Obviously D.O.A. "Thought I'd stop and see if there was anything I could do."

"Nothing I can think of, Sergeant. Paramedics say it was a heart attack. They figure it was because of the mummy."

A year ago, eight months ago even, Celluci would have repeated the word mummy, sounding intrigued or amused or both, but after having busted his ass last April tracking down a minion of hell and part of August associating with a pack of werewolves, not to mention time spent with Mr. Henry Fitzroy, his reaction was a little more extreme. He no longer took reality for granted.

"Mummy?" he growled.

"It was, uh, in the Egyptology workroom." Constable Trembley took a step back, wondering why the detective had gone for his gun. "Just laying there in its coffin. Too much for one of the janitors apparently." He still looked weirdly suspicious. "It *had* been dead for a long time." She tried a grin. "I don't think they'll need you on that case either . . ."

The joke fell flat, but the grin worked and Celluci let his hand fall to his side. Of course a museum would have a mummy. He felt like a fool. "If you're sure there's nothing I can do . . ."

"No, sir."

"Fine." Muttering under his breath, he headed back to his car. What he really needed was a hot shower, a large breakfast, and a nice simple murder.

Snapping his occurrence book closed, Trembley's partner wandered over to her side. "Who was that?" he asked.

"Detective-Sergeant Celluci. Homicide. He was driving by, stopped to see if he could help."

"Yeah? He looked like he could use some more sleep. What was he muttering as he walked away?"

"It sounded like," PC Trembley frowned, "lions, and tigers, and bears. Oh, my."

Three

"Hi, Mom."

"Good morning, dear. How did you know it was me?"

Vicki sighed and hiked the towel up more securely under her arms. "I'd just gotten into the shower. Who else could it be?" Her mother had an absolute genius for calling at the worst possible times. Henry had almost died once because of it or, conversely, she'd just missed getting killed because of that same call—Vicki had never quite settled the question to her own satisfaction.

"It's twenty to nine, dear, don't tell me you're just getting up?"

"All right."

There was a long pause while Vicki waited for her mother to work that last comment through. She heard her sigh and then she heard, faintly in the background, the staccato sound of her nails against the desk.

"You're working for yourself now, Vicki, and that doesn't mean you can lie about all day."

"What if I was up all night on a case?"

"Were you?"

"Actually, no." Vicki put her bare foot up on one of the kitchen chairs and massaged her calf with the heel of one hand. Yesterday's climb up the tower had begun to make itself felt. "Now, as I was home two weeks ago for Thanksgiving . . ." *Which is going to have to hold you until Christmas.* ". . . to what do I owe the pleasure of this call?"

"Do I have to have a reason to call my only daughter?"

"No, but you usually do."

"Well, no one else is in the office yet . . ."

"Mom, some day the Life Sciences Department is going to expect you to start paying for these long distance calls."

"Nonsense, Vicki. Queens University has lots of money and it's not like it costs a fortune to call from Kingston to Toronto, so I thought I'd take the opportunity to see how your visit to the eye doctor went."

"Retinitis pigmentosa doesn't get any better, Mom. I still have no night sight and bugger all in the way of peripheral vision. What difference does it make how the visit to the eye doctor went?"

"Victoria!"

Vicki sighed and pushed her glasses up her nose. "Sorry. Nothing's changed."

"Then it hasn't gotten any worse." Her mother's tone acknowledged the apology and agreed to drop the subject. "Have you managed to line up any work?"

She'd finished an insurance fraud case the last week of September. There hadn't been anything since. If she were a better liar . . . "Nothing yet, Mom."

"Well, what about Michael Celluci? He's still on the force. Can't he find you something?"

"Mother!"

"Or that nice Henry Fitzroy." He'd answered the phone once when she called and she'd been very impressed. "He found you something last summer."

"Mother! I don't need them to find me work. I don't need anyone to find me work. I am *perfectly* capable of finding work on my own."

"Don't grind your teeth, dear. And I know you're perfectly capable of finding work, but . . . oops, Dr. Burke just walked in, so I should go. Remember you can always come live with me if you need to."

Vicki managed to hang up without giving in to the urge for violence but only because she knew it would be her phone that suffered and she couldn't afford to buy another new one right now. Her mother could be so . . . so . . . *Well, I suppose it could be worse. She has a career and a life of her own and she* could *be after me for grandchildren.* She wandered back to the shower, shaking her head at the thought; motherhood had never been a part of her plans.

She'd been ten when her father left, old enough to decide

that motherhood had caused most of the problems between her parents. While other children of divorce blamed themselves, she laid the blame squarely where she felt it belonged. Motherhood had turned the young and exciting woman her father had married into someone who had no time for him, and after he left, the need to provide for a child had governed all her choices. Vicki had grown up as fast as she could, her independence granting a mutual independence for her mother—which had never quite been accepted in the spirit in which it was offered.

Vicki sometimes wondered if her mother wouldn't prefer a pink and lacy sort of a daughter who wouldn't mind being fussed over, but she didn't lose any sleep worrying about it, given that her decidedly non-pink and non-lacy attitudes had no effect on her mother's fussing as it was. While proud of the work that Vicki did, she fretted over potential dangers, public opinion, the men in Vicki's life, her eating habits, her eyes, and her caseload.

"Not that my caseload doesn't need fussing over," Vicki admitted, working up a lather on her hair. Money was beginning to get tight and if something didn't turn up soon. . . .

"Something'll turn up." She rinsed and turned the water off. "Something always does."

"This is absolutely ridiculous! I won't stand for it!" Dr. Rax threw himself down into his desk chair, slamming the upper edge back into the wall. "How dare they keep us out!"

"Calm down, Elias, you'll give yourself an ulcer." Dr. Shane stood in the office doorway, arms crossed. "It's only until the autopsy comes back and we know for sure it was a heart attack that killed that poor janitor."

"Of course it was a heart attack." Dr Rax rubbed at his eyes. Trapped in a cycle of frighteningly realistic dreams about being buried alive, he'd welcomed the phone call that'd freed him in the early hours of the morning. "The police officer I talked to said you could tell just from looking at him. Said the mummy had probably scared him to death." He snorted, his opinion of anyone who could be scared to death by a piece of history clear.

Dr. Shane frowned. "Mummy . . . ?"

"Oh, for God's sake, Rachel. You can't have forgotten the baron's little souvenir."

"No, of course not . . ." Except that for a moment, she had.

Dr. Rax rubbed at his eyes again; they felt as though bits of sand had jammed up under the lids. "Funny thing is, I knew young Ellis. Talked to him on a number of occasions when I'd stayed late. He had a good mind, all things considered, but not what I'd call much of an imagination and I'd have expected him to take anything he ran into in the workroom in stride." He surprised himself with a dry chuckle. "Unlike Ms. Taggart."

Although she continued to clean the department offices, Ms. Taggart would not go into the workroom alone since the incident last summer with the mummified head. No one had ever admitted placing the Blue Jays cap on the artifact, but as Dr. Rax had made no real effort to find the culprit and had been more than vocal about the lack of depth in the bull pen, the rest of the department had its suspicions.

"You realize this is only going to encourage her." Dr. Shane sighed. "She'll probably transfer to Geology or somewhere else without bone and we'll lose the best cleaning lady we've ever had. I'll never again be able to leave papers on my desk overnight." Escorting her into the workroom was a small price to pay when measured against the knowledge that Ms. Taggart was the only cleaning lady in the building who *never* disturbed office work in progress. "Speaking of papers . . ." She waved a hand at the curator's overloaded desk. "Why don't you use this time as a chance to catch up?"

"The moment we can get back to work . . ."

"I'll let you know." She pulled the door closed behind her and walked slowly across to her own office, brows drawn down into a worried vee. Her memories of the mummy slid over and around each other as though they'd been run through a blender and she just couldn't believe that for one moment she'd forgotten its existence entirely. *Obviously, I've been more affected by that young man's death than I thought.*

The ka he had taken in the night told him of wonders greater than even Egypt in all her glory had known. The great pyramids had been dwarfed not by monuments to the glory of kings but by gleaming anthills of metal and glass built for fat-assed yuppies. *Chariots had been replaced by* four cylinder shit-boxes with no more pickup than a sick duck. *Although he was unclear on many of the other concepts, beer and bureaucracy, at least, seemed to have endured. He was halfway around the world from the Mother Nile in a country that fought with sticks upon frozen water. Its queen sat in state many leagues away, no longer Osiris incarnate, although he who ruled for her here seemed to think himself some* kind of tin-plate, big-chinned god.

Most importantly, the gods he had known and who had known him appeared to be no more. No longer would he have to hide from the all-seeing eye of Thoth in the night sky but, more importantly, there were none to replace the priest-wizards who had bound him. The gods of this new world were weak and had claimed few souls. He would go among them as a lion among the goats, able to feed where he willed.

He recognized that the one known as Reid Ellis had belonged to the lower classes, a common laborer, and that the information he had absorbed was tainted by this lack of position. That mattered little, for he had long since chosen the one who would feed him with what he needed—the history of the time that had passed and the way to prosper in the time that was now.

The life had also given him strength. Although his physical form remained bound, his ka had been able to wander throughout the minds that knew of him.

And how pitifully little they knew.

With each touch, he took bits of the knowledge away; it was knowledge of him after all and thus he could control it. Those with the weakest wills forgot in a single passing, the stronger lost memories a piece at a time. Soon, there would be none left who knew how to bind him again.

He would be released; he had not touched the one who would ensure it, except to strengthen the bond between them, and he left the other enough to assist. They would peel the binding spell away and he would rise, magic restored, ready to claim his place in this strange new world.

He would deal with them then.

"Where is everybody?"

"Well, as no one knew when we were going to be al-

lowed back into the workroom, I told them they might as
well finish up any paperwork and then head home."

Dr. Rax turned to stare at his assistant curator. *You told
them what?* he wanted to shout. *We have the first new
mummy in decades and you dismissed* my *staff?* But somewhere between thought and speech, the words changed.
"That seems reasonable. No point in them hanging around
with nothing to do." He frowned, confused.

Reaching the door to the workroom, Dr. Shane peeled
off the six-inch strip of bright yellow and black police tape
that had been pasted over the lock. "I'm glad you agree."
She hadn't been sure he would. In fact, now that she
thought about it, she wondered how she could have . . .
could have . . . "And it's not like we'll need them for what
we're about to do."

"No . . ." He had the strangest feeling that they were
walking into deadly danger and half expected the door to
creak open like a bad special effect. *We should get out of
here now, while there's still time.* Then they were in the
workroom with the mummy and nothing else mattered.

Together they removed the plastic shroud, bundling it
carelessly to one side.

"I do feel a bit guilty about young Ellis though," Dr.
Shane sighed as she pulled two pairs of cotton work gloves
out of the cardboard box marked *Wear these or die!* "Heart
failure might have been the cause, but our mummy certainly contributed to the effect."

"Nonsense." Dr. Rax worked his fingers into the gloves.
"As dreadful as it was, as sad as it was, we are in no way
responsible for that young man's fears." He picked up a
pair of broad-tipped tweezers and bent over the coffin,
breathing through his mouth to minimize the almost overpowering smell of cedar. Very, very gently, he caught hold
of the hieroglyphic strip at the point where the winding
ended on the mummy's chest. "I think we'll need some
solvent. It appears to be attached to the actual wrappings."

"Cedar gum?"

"I think so."

He continued to apply a gentle pull on the ancient linen
while Dr. Shane carefully moistened the end with a solvent-
soaked cotton swab.

"It's amazing how little the fabric has deteriorated over

the centuries," she observed. "I send a shirt to the dry
cleaner twice and it begins to fall apar . . . !" The hand
holding the swab jerked back.

"What is it?"

"The chest, where I touched it, it felt warm." She
laughed a little nervously, knowing how ridiculous it
sounded. "Even through the glove."

Dr. Rax snorted. "Probably the heat from the lights."

"They're fluorescent."

"All right, it was a by-product of the slow and continuing
process of decay."

"Felt through the wrapping and the glove?"

"How about pure imagination brought on by misdirected
guilt over that janitor?"

She managed a doubting smile. "I suppose I'll settle for
that."

"Good. Now, can we get back to work?"

Deliberately not touching the body, Dr. Shane stroked
on a little more of the solvent. "This is the damnedest
funereal setup I've ever seen," she muttered. "No Osiran
symbols, no tutelary goddesses, no *Ded*, no *Thet*, no hieroglyphs at all except on this strip." Her brows drew down.
"Shouldn't we . . . shouldn't we be studying the strip before
we remove it?"

"It'll be easier to study once it's off."

"Yes, but . . ." But what? She couldn't seem to hang
onto the thought.

Suddenly Dr. Rax smiled. "It's lifting. Stand back."

*He could feel the end of the linen lifting, each separate
hieroglyph a weight of stone rising off his chest. The spell
stretched and tore as it was pulled more and more out of
alignment. Then, with a silent shriek that cut through bone
and blood and sinew, it ripped apart.*

*He welcomed the pain. It was his first physical sensation
in three millennia and a joyous agony. Nothing came without
price and for his freedom, no price was too high. Had his
limbs been capable of movement, he would have writhed,
but movement would come slowly, over time, and so he
could only endure the waves of red that raced the length of
his body pushing all else before them, pounding all else beneath them. He only wished that he could scream.*

Finally, the last wave began to ebb, leaving behind it a stinging of nettles in his flesh and the red glow of two eyes in the darkness.

My lord? He should have known that if he survived his god would have survived as well.

The eyes grew brighter until by their light his ka could see the birdlike head of his god.

The others are dead, it said.

This confirmed what the taste of the laborer's ka had told him.

There are gods, but not the ones we knew. *Its beak wasn't built for smiling, but it cocked its head to one side and he remembered that meant it was pleased.* I was wise when I created you; through you I survived. The new gods have been strong in the past, but they are not now. Few souls are sworn. Build me a temple, gather me acolytes until I am strong enough to make others like you. We can do what we wish with this world.

Then he was alone again in the darkness.

Nothing held him now except millennia-old fabric already beginning to rot under the pressure of accumulated time, but he would remain for a little longer where he was. His ka had one more short journey to make and then he would gather his strength before he confronted his . . . savior.

Build a temple. Gather acolytes. We can do what we wish with this world. *Indeed.*

He had not really planned beyond gaining his freedom, but it seemed he would have much to do.

Rachel Shane stepped out of the elevator on the ground floor, the rubber soles of her shoes making very little sound against the tile floor. She was worried about Elias. He'd always been an intense man, determined to make the Egyptology Department at the ROM one of the best in the world despite budgets and bureaucrats, but in all the years she'd known him—*and they were a good many years,* she admitted silently to herself—she'd never seen him this obsessed.

She paused just inside the security door to pull her trench coat closed. Although the looming bulk of the planetarium limited the lines of sight from the staff entrance, water glistened on the pavement between the two buildings. If it wasn't raining at this moment, it had been in the recent past.

Recent past . . . She thought back to the workroom and the almost dreamlike way they'd unwrapped the linen strip from around the mummy. No documentation. No photographs. Not even a notation of the hieroglyphs. It was very stra . . .

The sudden pain snapped her head forward and exploded red lights behind her eyes. She sagged against the security door, the smooth glass pulling against the damp skin of her cheek as she fought to stay on her feet. *Is it a stroke?* And with that thought came a terrifying vision of complete and utter helplessness, so much worse than death. *Oh, God, I'm too young.* She couldn't catch her breath, couldn't remember how her lungs worked, couldn't remember anything but the pain.

As if from a great distance, she saw the guard run for the other side of the door and manage to open it without throwing her to the ground. He slipped an arm around her waist and half guided, half carried her over to a chair.

"Dr. Shane? Dr. Shane, are you all right?"

She grabbed desperately onto the sound of her name. The pain began to recede, leaving her feeling as though she'd been scoured from within by a wire brush. Nerve endings throbbed and for just an instant a great golden sun blotted out the security area, the guard, everything.

"Dr. Shane?"

Then it was gone and the pain was gone as if it had never been. She rubbed at her temples, trying to remember how it had felt, and couldn't.

"Should I call an ambulance, Dr. Shane?"

An ambulance? That penetrated. "No, thank you, Andrew. I'm fine. Really. Just a little faint."

He frowned. "You sure?"

"Positive." She took a deep breath and stood. The world remained as it always had been. The tension went out of her shoulders.

"Well, if you're sure. . . ." He still looked a little dubious. "I guess you must've been working too hard, what with the cops keeping you away from your stuff until this afternoon." He went back behind his desk, still watching her with a wary eye. "So, they gonna take the mummy away?"

"Mummy?"

"Yeah. They say Reid Ellis bumped into a mummy up there in the dark and it scared him to death."

"Oh, *that* mummy . . ." It was amazing how rumors got started. She smiled and shook her head. With the police in and out of the workroom there was no real point in the department keeping quiet to save face. They'd just have to convince the scientific community that they'd meant to buy an empty sarcophagus. "There never was a mummy, Andrew. Just an empty coffin. Which I suppose is frightening enough in the middle of the night."

Andrew looked a little disappointed. "No mummy?"

"No."

He sighed. "Well, that certainly makes the story less interesting."

"Sorry." Dr. Shane paused with one hand on the outside door and fixed the security guard with a look she kept just on the edge of intimidating. "I'd appreciate you spreading the *real* story around."

He sighed again. "Sure thing, Dr. Shane. There never was a mummy. . . ."

His fingers had torn through the bottom sheet and his heartbeat echoed off the walls of the bedroom. He'd woken again to the memory of a brilliant white-gold sun centered in an azure sky.

"I don't want to die!"

But then, why the sun?

One night he could force himself to ignore; wash it away in the hunt, in blood. Two nights made it real.

He fought himself free of the sheet and sat up on the edge of the bed, hands turned up on his thighs. His palms were moist. He stared at them for a moment, then frantically scrubbed them dry, trying to remember if in over four hundred and fifty years he'd ever sweated.

The stink of his fear filled the room. He had to get away from it.

Naked, he padded out into the condo and over to the plate glass window that looked down on Toronto. Pressing palms and forehead against the cool glass, he forced himself to take long, slow breaths until he calmed. He traced the flow of traffic down Jarvis Street; marked the blaze of glory

a few streets over that was Yonge; flicked his gaze over
the bands of gold in nearby office towers marking where
conscientious employees worked late; knew that as dusk
deepened to full dark, the other, still human, children of
the night would emerge. This was his city.

Then he found himself wondering how it would look with
dawn reflected rose and yellow in the glass towers, the in-
terlacing ribbons of asphalt pearly gray instead of black,
the fall colors of the trees like gems scattered across the
city under the arcing dome of a brilliant blue sky . . . and
wondering how long he would last, how much he would
see, before the golden circle or the sun ignited his flesh and
he died for the second and very final time.

"Jesu, Lord of Hosts, protect me."

He jerked himself back off the glass and sketched a sign
of the cross with trembling fingers.

"I don't *want* to die." But he couldn't get that image of
the sun out of his head. He reached for the phone.

"Nelson."

"Vicki, I . . ." He what? He was having hallucinations?
He was losing his mind?

"Henry? Are you all right?"

I need to talk to you. But he suddenly couldn't get the
words out.

Apparently, she heard them anyway. "I'm on my way
over." Her tone left no room for argument. "You're at
home?"

"Yes."

"Then stay put. I'll grab a taxi. I'll be right there. Whatever it is, we can work it out."

Her certainty leeched some of the tension out of his
white-knuckled grip on the phone and his mouth twisted
up into a parody of a smile. "No hurry," he told her, attempting to regain some control. "We've got until dawn."

Although guilt was a part of the reason that Dr. Rax
remained at his desk plugging away at the despised paperwork long after Dr. Shane had gone home—he *had* let
the pile achieve mammoth proportions—it was more a
vague sense of something left unfinished that kept him in
his office, almost anxiously waiting for the other shoe to
drop. He scrawled his initials at the bottom of a budget

report, slammed the folder closed, and tossed it into his out basket. Then he sighed and began to doodle aimlessly on his desk calendar. *If only it wasn't so damned hard to concentrate. . . .*

Suddenly, he frowned, realizing his doodle hadn't been that aimless. Under the day and date—Monday, October 19th—he'd sketched a griffinlike animal with the body of an antelope and the head of a bird crowned with three uraei and three sets of wings. He'd sketched the creature who had been watching his dreams.

"And now that I think of it," he pushed his chair back so that he could reach the bookcase behind the desk, "you look awfully familiar. Yes . . . here we are . . ." His drawing matched the illustration almost line for line. "Amazing what the subconscious remembers." Ignoring a cold feeling of dread, he skimmed the text. "Akhekh, a predynastic god of upper Egypt absorbed into the conqueror's religion to become a form of the evil god Set . . ." The book slid out of hands gone limp and crashed to the floor. The eyes of Akhekh, eyes printed in black, had, for an instant, burned red.

Heart in his throat, Dr. Rax bent forward and gingerly picked up the book. It had closed as it fell and he had no desire to open it again.

Elias. Come. It is time.

"Time for what?" he called before he realized the voice he answered was in his head.

He carefully put the book on the desk then rubbed at his temples with trembling fingers. "Right. First I'm seeing things. Now I'm hearing things. I think it's time I went home and had a large Scotch and a long sleep."

The weakness in his legs surprised him when he stood. He held onto the back of his chair until he was sure he could walk without his knees buckling, then made his way slowly across the room. At the door, he grabbed his jacket and flicked off the light, trying not to think of two eyes glowing red in the darkness behind him as he made his way across the outer office.

"This is ridiculous." He squared his shoulders and took a deep breath as he started down the hallway to the elevators. "I'm a scientist, not some superstitious old fool frightened of the dark. I've just been working too hard." The dim quiet of the hall laid balm on his jangled nerves and by the time he reached the door to the workroom his heart-beat and breathing had almost returned to normal.

Elias. Come.

He turned and faced the door, unable to stop himself. From a distance, he felt his hand go into his pocket for his keys, saw them turn in the lock, heard the quiet movement of air as the door opened, smelled the cedar that had been filling the room with its scent since they'd opened the coffin, tasted fear. His legs carried him forward.

The plastic over the coffin had been thrown aside.

The coffin itself was empty save for a pile of linen wrappings already beginning to decay.

The physical compulsion left him and he sagged against the ancient wood. A man stooped with age, eyes deep sunk over ax blade cheekbones, flesh clinging to bone and skin stretched tight, walked out of the shadows. Somehow, he had known that it would come to this and that knowledge kept the terror just barely at bay. From the moment he had first seen the seal, he had felt this moment approaching.

"Des . . . troy those." The voice creaked like two pieces of old wood rubbing together.

Dr. Rax looked down at the linen wrappings and then up at the man who had so recently worn them that the marks still showed imprinted on his skin. "Do what?"

"There must be . . . no evi . . . dence."

"Evidence? Of what?"

"Of me."

"But *you're* evidence of you."

"Des . . . troy them."

"No." Dr. Rax shook his head. "You may be . . ." And then it hit him, finally broke through the cocoon of fate or destiny or whatever had been insulating him from what was actually going on. This man, this creature, had been entombed in the Eighteenth Dynasty, over three thousand years ago. Only his white-knuckled grip on the coffin kept him standing. "How . . . ?"

Something that might have been a smile twisted the ancient mouth. "Magic."

"There's no such . . ." Except obviously there was, so he let the protest die.

The smile flattened into an expression much more unpleasant. "Des . . . troy them."

As he had been while opening the workroom door, Dr. Rax found himself shunted off into an enclosed section of his mind while his body obeyed another's will. Only this time, he was conscious of it. The fog was gone.

He watched himself gather up the linen wrappings and carry them over to the sink.

"That . . . too."

Fighting to stop himself, he lifted the strip of hieroglyphs from the worktable and added it to the rest. When he went into the darkroom, he knew the creature was using his mind—fire would have been an Eighteenth Dynasty solution, chemicals were not. A bottle of concentrated ascorbic acid dissolved the rotting fabric sufficiently to wash the entire mess down the drain and although his hands trembled, he couldn't prevent them from pouring it. His heart ached at the destruction of the artifacts and the anger gave him strength.

Slowly he jerked his body around and met eyes so dark there was no telling where the pupil ended and the iris began. "That wasn't necessary," he managed to gasp.

The eyes narrowed, then widened. "A good thing for me . . . your god has not recognized . . . its power."

"What the hell . . ." He had to stop to breathe. *We sound like a couple of badly tuned transistor radios.* ". . . are you talking about. My god?"

"Science." The ancient voice grew stronger. "Still only an aspect. Not strong enough . . . to save your ass."

Dr. Rax frowned, his thoughts tumbling over themselves in an attempt to pull order out of the impossible—that was not a phrase a dynastic Egyptian would use. "You speak English. But English didn't exist when you were . . ."

"Alive?"

"If you like." *The son of a bitch is enjoying this. He's allowing me to talk to him.*

"I learn from the ka I take."

"From the ka . . . ?"

"So many questions, Dr. Rax."

"Yes . . ." A hundred, a thousand questions, each fighting to be first. Perhaps the loss of the artifacts could be made up. He began to shake with barely suppressed excitement. Perhaps the holes in history could be filled. "There's so much you can tell me."

"Yes." Just for an instant, something very like regret passed over the ancient face. "I'd enjoy . . . shooting shit with you. But, unfortun . . . ately, I need what you can tell . . . me."

Dr. Rax started as an ancient hand wrapped around his wrist, the grip almost painfully tight. *I learn from the ka I take.* And the ka was the soul and a young man had died this morning and English hadn't existed . . . "No!" He began to slide into the black depths of ebony eyes. "But I freed you!" *There's still so much I don't know!* And that gave him the strength to fight.

The grip tightened.

His free arm flailed, slamming his elbow into the cupboards, knocking the empty bottle off the counter, accomplishing nothing.

But he fought all the way down.

He lost the fight question by question.

How and why and where and what? And finally, who?

"I don't think you're crazy."

"But how can you know?"

Vicki shrugged. "Because I know crazy and I know you."

Henry threw himself down beside her on the couch and caught up both her hands in his. "Then why do I keep dreaming of the sun?"

"I don't know, Henry." He desperately wanted reassurance, but she didn't know how much she had to give; this was going to take more than a "poor sweet baby" and a kiss on the nose. He looked, not frightened exactly, but vulnerable, and his expression sat in a knot at the base of her throat, making it hard to swallow, hard to breathe. The only comfort she had to offer was the knowledge that he wouldn't face whatever this turned out to be alone. "But I do know this, we aren't going down without a fight."

"We?"

"You asked me for help, remember?"

He nodded.

"So." She traced a pattern on the back of his hand with her thumb. "You said this has happened to others of your kind . . . ?"

"There've been stories."

"Stories?"

"We hunt alone, Vicki. Except for during the time of changing we almost never associate with other vampires. But you hear stories. . . ."

"Vampiric gossip?"

He shrugged, a little self-consciously. "If you like."

"And these stories say that . . . ?"

"That sometimes when we get too old, when the weight of all those centuries becomes too much to bear, we get so we can no longer stand the night and finally give ourselves to the sun."

"And before that happens, the dreams come?"

"I don't know."

She closed her hand around his. "All right. Let's take this one step at a time. Have you gotten tired of living?"

"No." That, at least, he was sure of and the reason for it stared at him intently from less than an arm's length away. "But, Vicki, as much as I have changed, the body, the mind is still basically human. Perhaps . . ."

"Perhaps the equipment is wearing out?" she interrupted, tightening her grip. "Planned obsolescence? You start heading toward your fifth century and the system starts breaking down?" Her brows drew in and her glasses slid down her nose. "I don't believe that."

Henry reached over and pushed her glasses back into place. "You can't disbelieve the dreams," he said softly.

"No," she admitted, "I can't." She sighed deeply and one side of her mouth quirked up. "It'd be useful if you lot did a little more communicating, so we weren't approaching this blind—maybe put out a newsletter or something." He smiled at that, as she knew he would, and he relaxed a little. "Henry, less than a year ago I didn't believe in vampires or demons or werewolves or myself. Now I know better. You *aren't* crazy. You *don't* want to die. You are therefore *not* going to give yourself to the sun. Q.E.D."

He had to believe her. Her no-nonsense mortal attitude slapped aside the specter of madness. "Stay till morning?" he asked. For a moment he couldn't believe the words had come from his mouth. He might as well have said, *"Stay until I'm helpless."* It meant the same thing. Did he trust her that much? He saw that she understood and by her hesitation gave him time to take back the request. He suddenly realized he didn't want to take it back. That he did, indeed, trust her that much.

Four hundred and fifty years ago he'd asked, *"Can we love?"*

"Can you doubt it?" had been the answer.

The silence stretched. He had to break it before it pulled them apart; pulled her apart, forced her to hear what he knew she wasn't ready to hear. "You can tie me to the bed if I start to do anything stupid."

"My definition of stupid or yours?" Her voice was tight.

In for a penny in for a pound. "Yours." He smiled, planted a kiss on her palm, and turned to face the window. If Vicki thought him sane, then he had to think so, too. Perhaps why he dreamed of the sun was of less immediate concern than how he dealt with the dreams. "More things in heaven and earth . . ." he mused.

Vicki sagged back against the sofa cushions. "Christ, I'm getting tired of that quote."

Four

Vicki had seen a thousand dawns and seen none of them the way she saw this one.

"Can you feel it?"

"Feel what?" Half asleep, she lifted her head off Henry's lap.

"The sun."

A sudden shot of adrenaline snapped her awake and she jerked forward, peering into his face. He looked very intent, brows drawn down, eyes narrowed. She glanced at the window. Although it faced south, not east, the sky had definitely begun to lighten. "Henry?"

He blinked, focused, and shook his head when he saw her expression, his smile both reassuring and slightly embarrassed. "It's all right, this happens every morning. It's like a warning." His voice took on the mechanical tones of a dozen science fiction movie computers. "You have fifteen minutes to reach minimum safe darkness."

"Fine." Vicki stood, still holding his wrist. "Fifteen minutes. Let's go."

"I was making a joke," he protested as she pulled him to his feet. "As warnings go, it's not really that definite. It's just a feeling."

Vicki sighed and shot an anxious glance out the window at the streaks of pink she was sure she could see touching the edges of the city. "Okay. It's just a feeling. What do you usually do when you feel it?"

"Go to bed."

"Well?"

He studied her face for a moment—his intent expression back—sighed in turn, and nodded. "You're right." Then he pulled his hands free, spun on his heel, and walked across the living room.

"Henry?"

Although he stopped, he didn't turn, merely looked back over his shoulder.

I don't have to stay if you're sure you're all right. Except he wasn't sure. That was why she was there. And while he might be regretting making the offer—she recognized second thoughts in his hesitation—the reason he'd made it still existed. It seemed that if they were to both get through sunrise, she'd have to treat this like any other job. *The client fears that under certain conditions he may attempt suicide. I'm here to stop him.* With a start, she realized he was still waiting for her to say something. "Uh, how do you feel?"

Henry watched the parade of emotions cross Vicki's face. *This isn't any easier for you, is it?* he thought. "I feel the sun," he said softly and held out his hand.

She took it with what he'd come to recognize as her working expression and together they made their way to the bedroom.

The first time Vicki had seen Henry's bed, she'd been irrationally disappointed. By that time she'd known he didn't spend the day locked in a coffin atop a pile of his native earth, but she'd been secretly hoping for something a little exotic. A king-size bed—*"I bet your father would have loved to have one of those . . ."*—with white cotton sheets and a dark blue blanket was just too definitively normal looking.

This morning, she shook free of his hand and stopped just inside the closed door. The soft circle of light from the lamp on the bedside table left her effectively blind, but she knew, because he'd told her on that first visit, that the heavy blue velvet drapery over the window covered a layer of plywood painted black and caulked around the edges. Another curtain just inside the glass hid the wood from the prying eyes of the world. It was a barrier designed to keep the sun safely at bay and a barrier, Vicki knew, that Henry could rip down in seconds if he chose. Her body became the barrier before the door.

Standing by the bed, Henry hesitated, fingers on shirt buttons, surprised to find himself uncomfortable about undressing in front of a woman he'd been making love to—and feeding from—for months. *This is ridiculous. She probably can't even see you from there, the light's so dim.* Shaking his head, he stripped quickly, reflecting that helplessness brought with it a much greater intimacy than sex.

He could feel the sun more strongly now, more strongly than he could remember feeling it before. *You're sensitive to it this morning. That's all.* God, he hoped it was all.

For Vicki, watching the flicker of pale skin as Henry moved in and out of the circle of light, standing guard at the door suddenly made less than no sense. "Henry? What the hell am I doing here?" She walked forward until his face swam into focus and then reached out and laid her hand gently on his bare chest, halting his movement. "I can't stop you . . ." She scowled, recognizing the words as inadequate. "I can't even slow you down."

"I know." He covered her fingers with his, marveling as he always did at the heat of her, at the feel of her blood pulsing just under the skin.

"Great." She rolled her eyes. "So what am I supposed to do if you make a run for the sun?"

"Be there."

"And watch you die?"

"No one, not even a vampire, wants to die alone."

It could have sounded facetious. It didn't. Hadn't she realized only hours before that was all she had to give him? But she hadn't realized, not then, that it might come to this.

Breathing a little heavily, wishing the light was strong enough for her to see his expression, Vicki managed not to yank her hand free. *Be there.* Bottom line, it was no more than Celluci had ever asked of her. Only the circumstances were different. "Jesus H. Christ, Henry." It took an effort, but she kept her voice steady, "You're not going to fucking die, okay? Just get your jammies on—or your tuxedo or whatever it is the undead sleep in—and get into bed."

He released her and spread his arms, his meaning plain.

"Fine." She pointed at the bed and glared at him while he did as he was told. Then, pushing her glasses hard against the bridge of her nose, she perched on the edge of the mattress. If she squinted, she could make out his features. "Are you okay?"

"Are you daring me not to be?"

"Henry!"

"I can feel the sun trembling on the horizon, but the only thing in my mind is you."

"You're just a bundle of clichés this morning." But the relief in his voice had made it sound like truth. "What's going to happen? I mean to you?"

He shrugged, his shoulders whispering against the sheets. "From your side, I don't know. From mine, I go away until sunset. No dreams, no physical sensation." His voice began to slow under the weight of dawn. "Nothingness."

"What should I do?"

He smiled. "Kiss me . . . good-bye."

Her lips were on his when the sun rose. She felt the day claim him. Slowly, she pushed herself back up into a sitting position.

"Henry?"

He looked so dreadfully young. So dreadfully vulnerable. She grabbed his shoulders and shook him, hard.

"Henry!"

His heart had always beat slowly; now, her ear pressed tight against his chest, she couldn't hear it beat at all.

He couldn't stop her from doing whatever she wanted to him. He had just put himself completely and absolutely in her hands.

Be there. Bottom line, that was all Celluci had ever asked of her. Bottom line, that was all she'd ever asked of Celluci in return.

Be there. Bottom line, it meant a lot more when Henry Fitzroy asked it.

"Henry, you shit." She shoved her glasses out of the way and scrubbed her knuckles across her eyes. "What the hell can I give you to match this?"

A few moments later, she pulled herself together with a more prosaic question. "Now what? Do I leave? Or do I stay and keep watch over you all day?" A massive yawn threatened to dislocate her jaw; she hadn't gotten much sleep during the long wait for morning. "Or do I climb in with you?"

She ran one finger lightly down his cheek. The skin felt cool and dry. It always had, but without the night to give it animation it had never felt so . . . unalive. "All right, scratch that last idea." Not even as tired as she was could she sleep next to the body—to the absence of Henry—that the day had created. Scooping his discarded pants off the floor, she rummaged in the pockets for his keys.

"I'm going home," she said, needing to hear herself just to offset his absolute stillness. "I'll get some sleep and be back before dark. Don't worry, I'll lock up on my way out. You'll be safe."

The lamp by the bed switched off at the door. Vicki took one look back then extinguished the pale island of light, plunging the room into complete and utter darkness.

She had her hand on the knob and had actually begun to turn it when a sudden realization stopped her cold. "How the hell do I get out of here?" Her fingers traced the rubber seals that edged the door, blocking any possible intrusion of light. Could she leave without destroying Henry? *This is just great.* The door boomed a hollow counterpoint to her thoughts as she beat her head gently against it. *I stay to save him from suicide and end up committing murder.*

Go or stay?

There'd be light spilling into the hall through the open door of his office and if she opened this door here . . . How direct did the sun have to be? How diffuse?

We should have covered this earlier, Henry. She couldn't believe that neither of them had considered anything past sunrise. Of course, they'd both been dealing with other things.

She couldn't risk it. The entrance door to the condo had been locked and the security chain fastened. He was as safe in here as he ever was. He just had company.

Eyes closed—voluntary lack of sight seemed to help— she stumbled back to the bed and lay down on top of the covers as far from Henry's inert body as she could get.

All her senses told her she was alone. Except she knew she wasn't. The entire room had become a coffin of sorts. She could feel the darkness pressing against her, becoming a six by three by one foot box, and tried not to think of Edgar Allan Poe and premature burials.

"How did he die?"

"His heart stopped." The assistant coroner peeled off his

gloves. "Which, in fact, is what kills us all in the end. You want to know why he died, ask me after I've had him on the table for a couple of hours."

"Thank you, Dr. Singh."

He smiled, completely unaffected by the sarcasm. "I live to serve. Don't keep him too long." He paused on his way out the door and threw back, "Offhand, given the position, I'd say he was dead before he hit the floor."

Waving an acknowledgment that he'd heard, Mike Celluci knelt by the body and frowned.

His partner, Dave Graham, leaned over his shoulder and whistled through his teeth. "Someone's got quite the grip."

Celluci grunted in agreement. Purple and green bruises circled the left wrist, brilliantly delineating the marks of four fingers and a thumb. The left arm lay stretching away from the body.

"He got dropped when he died," Dave said quietly.

"That'd be my guess. Check out the face."

"No expression."

"Right first time. No fear; no pain; no surprise; no nothing. No record of the last few minutes of life at all."

"Drugs?"

"Maybe. Nice jacket." Celluci got to his feet. "Wonder why it wasn't taken with the shoes."

Stepping back out of the way, Dave shrugged. "Who the hell can tell these days? They took the cash but not the credit cards or ID. Even left him his transit pass."

Carefully stepping around both the chalk lines and the bits of broken glass on the floor, the two men made their way over to the sink. Where the stainless steel had been previously scored, the acid poured into it had eaten into the metal. A vague ammonia smell still drifted up from the drain.

"No sign of what he dumped . . ."

Celluci snorted. "Or of who dumped it. Kevin!" The ident man looked up from his position at the side of the corpse. "I want prints lifted off the glass."

"Off the glass?" Only the base and the section of the neck protected by the screw-on cap had survived in anything large enough to even be considered pieces. "Shall I cure the common cold while I'm at it?"

"Suit yourself, but I want those prints first. Harper!"

The constable who'd been staring into the coffin started and jerked around. "Detective?"

"Get someone in here to drain the trap . . . the curved pipe under the sink," he added when Harper looked blank. "There's water in it, maybe enough to dilute the acid and give us some indication of what was dumped. Where's the guy who found the body?"

"Uh, in the departmental offices. His name's . . ." Harper frowned and glanced down at his notes. ". . . Raymond Thompson. He's a researcher, been here about a year and a half. Some of the rest of the staff have arrived and they're in there, too. My partner's with them."

"The offices are?"

"End of the hall on the right."

Celluci nodded and started for the door. "We're finished with the body. As soon as all and sundry have got their pound of flesh, you can get it out of here."

"Charming as always," Dave murmured, grinning. He followed his partner out into the hall and asked, "How come you know so much about plumbing?"

"My father was a plumber."

"Yeah? You bastard, you never told me you were independently wealthy."

"Didn't want you borrowing money." Celluci jerked his head back toward the workroom. "What do you think?"

"The good doctor interrupted an intruder?"

"And the janitor they pulled out of here yesterday?"

"I thought you said he saw a mummy and had a heart attack."

"So what happened to the mummy?"

Dave's forehead furrowed. The coffin had definitely been empty and, while the workroom was crowded with all kinds of ancient junk, he'd bet his last loonie that there hadn't been a body tucked into a back corner. "The intruder walked off with it? Dr. Rax broke it into chunks, poured acid over it and washed it down the sink? It came to life and is lurching about the city?" He caught sight of Celluci's expression and laughed. "You've been working too hard, buddy."

"Maybe." Celluci pushed open the door marked Department of Egyptology a little more forcefully than necessary. *Maybe not.*

Besides the uniformed police constable, there were half a dozen people sitting in the large outer office, all exhibiting various forms of shock and/or disbelief. Two of them were crying quietly, a half empty box of tissues on the desk between them. Two were arguing, their voices a constant background drone. One sat, his head buried in his hands. Dr. Shane, her expression wavering between grief and anger, stood as the detectives came into the room and walked toward them.

"I'm Dr. Rachel Shane, the assistant curator. What's going on? No, wait . . ." Her hand went up before either of them could speak. "That's a stupid question. I know what's going on." She took a deep breath. "What's going to happen now?"

Celluci showed her his badge—from the corner of his eye he saw Dave do the same—and continued to hold it out while she focused first on it and then back on him. "Detective-Sergeant Celluci. My partner, Detective-Sergeant Graham. We'd like to ask Raymond Thompson a few questions."

The young man with his head in his hands jerked erect, eyes wide and face pale.

"We'd like to leave Dr. Rax's office as it is for the moment," Celluci continued, carefully using the matter-of-fact tones most people found calming. "Dr. Shane . . . ?"

"Yes, yes, of course. Use mine." She gestured at the door, then laced her fingers together so tightly the tips darkened under the pressure.

"Thank you."

She started a little at the warmth in his voice, then visibly relaxed. Not for the first time, Dave marveled at Celluci's ability to load *"I know you're hurting, but we're counting on you. If you fall apart, they'll all go."* onto two small words.

Raymond Thompson was a tall, thin, intense man who couldn't seem to hold still; he kept a foot or a hand or his head constantly moving. He'd come in early to do catch up on a little of the work the sarcophagus had disrupted and found Dr. Rax sprawled on the floor of the workroom. "I didn't touch him or anything else except the phone. I called 911, said I'd found a body and went into the hall to wait. Christ, this is so . . . so . . . I mean, hell, did somebody kill him?"

"We don't know yet, Mr. Thompson." Dave Graham perched on the edge of the desk, one foot swinging lazily. "We'd appreciate it if you could remember how the workroom looked. Did it appear to be the way you'd last seen it?"

"I didn't really look at it. I mean, jeez, my boss was lying dead on the floor!"

"But after you saw the body, you must have taken a quick look around. Just to make sure there was no one else there."

"Well, yeah . . ."

"And the workroom . . . ?"

The younger man bit his lip, trying to remember, trying to see past the sprawled corpse of a man he'd both liked and respected. "There was glass on the floor," he said slowly, "and the plastic had been pulled off the new coffin—looks like Eighteenth Dynasty in a Sixteenth Dynasty sarcophagus, really strange—but nothing seemed to be missing. I mean, we had a pretty valuable faience and gold pectoral out on the counter being restored and it was still there."

Dave raised a brow. "Faience? Pectoral?"

"Faience is, well, a kind of ceramic and a pectoral is a . . ." long fingers sketched incomprehensible designs in the air. "Well, I guess you could think of it as a fat necklace."

"More than historically valuable?"

Ray Thompson shrugged. "More than half of it is better than eighteen karat gold."

Celluci turned from the window where he'd been watching traffic go by on Queen's Park Road, content to let his partner ask the questions. Whatever the reasons were behind the death of Dr. Rax, he was willing to bet robbery hadn't been a motive. "What about the mummy?"

"There never was one."

"Oh?" He took a step forward. "I talked to one of the officers on the scene yesterday morning as they were carrying that janitor out of the building. She told me he'd seen a mummy and had a heart attack. Essentially, died of fright."

"*Thought* he saw a mummy. Someone had popped an empty coffin back into a stone box and resealed it. We thought we were getting a new piece of history and all we got was air." Ray's laugh was short and bitter. "Maybe that's what killed Dr. Rax; scientific disappointment."

"So there wasn't a mummy?"

"No."

"You're sure?"

"Trust me, Detective, I'd have noticed."

Celluci caught a speaking glance from his partner and, scowling, closed his lips around what he'd been about to say. For the moment, he was willing to believe he'd misunderstood Trembley's explanation.

The rest of the department had even less to offer. They'd all liked Dr. Rax. Sure, occasionally he disagreed with his colleagues, but get twelve Egyptologists in a room and they'd have a dozen different opinions. No, there never had been a mummy. Professional jealousy?

Dr. Shane sighed and pushed her hair back off her forehead. "He was the curator of an underfunded department in a provincial museum. A good job, even a prestigious job compared to many but not one worth killing over."

"I suppose as his assistant curator you're next in line for the position." The words were an observation only, carefully nonweighted.

"I suppose I am. Damn him anyway, I'm the only person I can think of who hates paperwork more than he did." She pressed her fists against her mouth and squeezed her eyes tightly shut. "Oh, God . . ." A moment later she looked up, lashes in damp clumps. "I'm sorry. I'm not usually a watering pot."

"It's been an unusual kind of a day," Celluci said gently, handing her a tissue. "Dave, why don't you tell the others that anyone who wants to go home can. But point out that once the lab people are done, we'll need a complete inventory of that workroom. Maybe some'll stay. The sooner we know for sure if anything's missing the better."

Dr. Shane blew her nose as Dave left. "You're pretty high-handed with my staff, Detective."

"Sorry. If you'd rather tell them yourself . . . ?"

"No, that's all right. You're doing fine." *I bet when he was eighteen he looked like Michelangelo's David.* She closed her eyes again. *God, I don't believe this. Elias is dead and I'm sitting here thinking about how good-looking this cop is.*

"Dr. Shane? Are you all right?"

"I'm fine." She opened her eyes again and managed a watery smile. "Really."

Celluci nodded. He couldn't help but notice that Dr. Rachel Shane had a very attractive smile, even twisted as it was with grief. He wondered how it would look when she actually had something to smile about.

"So." She tossed the soggy tissue in the wastebasket. "You've taken care of my staff, what do you have planned for me?"

For no good reason, Celluci could feel his ears turning red. He cleared his throat and gave thanks he hadn't gone in for that haircut. "If you could check Dr. Rax's office? You'd be in the best position to know if any thing's been disturbed."

The curator's office was on the other side of the large common room. When PC Harper motioned him over to the hall door, Celluci waved Dr. Shane on alone.

"What?"

"It's the press."

"Yeah. So?"

"Shouldn't somebody make a statement; just to keep them from breaking the doors down?"

Celluci snorted. "I'll give them a statement."

As he watched the detective stride off down the corridor, shoulders up and fingers curled into fists, PC Harper wondered if maybe he should've waited for Sergeant Graham to finish with those staff members he'd taken off to the workroom. He had a feeling the press were about to get a statement they wouldn't be able to print.

A number of the reporters milling about in the security lobby recognized the detective as a museum guard let him through the door.

"Oh, great," muttered one. "It's homicide's Mr. Congeniality."

Questions flew thick and fast. Celluci waited, glaring the pack into silence. When the noise subsided enough so that he could be heard, he cleared his throat and began, his tone making his opinion of his audience plain. "In the early hours of this morning, a male Caucasian was found dead of causes unknown in the Department of Egyptology's workroom. Obviously we suspect foul play; I wouldn't be here if we didn't. You want anything else, you'll have to wait for it."

"What about the mummy?" A reporter near the front of the crowd shoved a microphone forward. "We heard there was talk of a mummy being involved."

Yes, what about the mummy? Although still uneasy about its accuracy, Celluci repeated the party line. "There never was a mummy, only an empty coffin being studied by the Department of Egyptology."

"Is there any possibility that the coffin could have caused both the recent deaths in the museum?"

"And how would it do that?" Celluci asked dryly. "Fall on them?"

"What about some kind of an ancient curse?"

Ancient Curse Kills Two. He could see the headlines now. "Don't be an asshole."

The reporter snatched the microphone to safety just in time and, smiling pleasantly, asked, "Can I quote you on that, Detective?"

Celluci's smile was just as sincere. "You can tattoo it on your chest."

Back upstairs, he found Dr. Shane and his partner standing just outside Dr. Rax's office.

Dave turned as he came in. "The doctor's got something for us, Mike."

Dr. Shane pushed her hair back off her face and rubbed at her forehead. "It might not be anything . . ." She looked over at Celluci, who nodded reassuringly, and went on. "It's just that Elias always kept a suit in his office, for board meetings and official business. He won't wear . . ." She paused, closed her eyes briefly, then continued. *"Wouldn't* wear one any longer than he had to. Anyway, when I left yesterday evening, his gray suit, a white shirt, and a burgundy silk tie were all hanging on the door. They're gone."

The two detectives exchanged identical looks. Celluci spoke first. "What about extra shoes?"

"No, he used to say that anywhere you couldn't get to

in a pair of loafers wasn't worth going to in the first place."
Her lower lip began to tremble but with a visible effort
she maintained control. "Damn, but I'm really going to
miss him."

"If you want to go home now, Dr. Shane . . . ?"

"Thanks, but I think I'd rather be doing something useful. If you don't need me any longer, I'll go help with the
inventory." Head high, she walked across the room, paused
at the door, and said, "When you catch the son of a bitch
who did this, I hope you rip out his living heart and feed
it to the crocodiles."

"We don't, uh, do that anymore, Doctor."

"Pity."

When they were alone, Dave sighed deeply and perched
on a corner of the closest desk. "The lab'll have to go over
that office. This case is getting weirder all the time." He
tugged at his beard. "It's beginning to look like Dr. Rax
interrupted a *naked* intruder. What kind of a nut case wanders around a museum starkers?"

Deep in thought, Celluci ignored him. He was remembering a pentagram and the human-seeming creature it had
contained; remembering a man who stripped and changed
and went for his throat with a wolf's fangs in a wolf's body;
remembering Henry Fitzroy who wasn't human now even
if he had been once. Remembering that things weren't always as they seemed.

Wondering what kind of a creature would emerge after
centuries spent in darkness, locked immobile inside a box.

Except there never had been a mummy.

He had twisted the mind of the guard so that she'd
opened the outer door for him and wished him a good
morning without ever wondering why an elderly man in an
ill-fitting suit was leaving the museum hours before it
opened. Once outside, he had turned, smiled, and brushed
away her memory of the entire incident. Then he had
crossed the street and lowered himself onto a bench, resting
and rejoicing in the amount of space around him and his
ability to move; waiting until the memories he absorbed
told him it was time.

The first ka he had devoured had served to reanimate
him and cover his tracks. The second had provided vital

knowledge but little life force as the years remaining to Dr. Rax would have been barely a third of those he had already lived. To restore his youth and replenish his power, he needed a young ka with an almost unrealized potential.

Moving carefully, for this new country was bitterly cold and he had used a great deal of power just remaining warm while he waited, he descended underground into what both sets of stolen memories referred to as *morning rush hour.* He paid the fare, more for novelty than necessity, and moved out onto the subway platform. Which was when the walls started closing in. His heart slammed up against his chest and he thrust up a hand to stop the ceiling from falling. He would have run if he'd been able, but his bones had turned to water and he could only endure. Three trains passed before he calmed, realizing the space was not so small as he had first assumed, that if such monstrous metal beasts could move about freely, there would be room for him to move about as well.

One more train passed while he watched it in amazement— the memories of men used to such things had not done credit to the size or the speed or noise or the sheer presence of the machine—and a second followed before he found what he wanted. He almost balked at the door to the car when he saw how little space remained, but the need for more power was stronger than his fear and, at the last moment, he squeezed himself in.

The schoolboys wearing identical uniforms under fall coats were jammed so tightly up against each other by the crowds that the jerk and sway of the train couldn't move them. They were laughing and talking, even those able to reach a support not bothering to hang on, secure in the knowledge that it was impossible to fall.

He got as close as he could and began to search frantically for the youngest. He didn't know how much longer he could take being so confined.

To his surprise, one of the boys carried a protection that slapped his ka back and caused him to gasp in pain. Murmuring a spell under his breath, he stared in annoyance at the nimbus of golden light. The gods of this new age might be weak but one of them had touched this child—even if the child himself was not yet aware of the vocation—and he would not be permitted to feed.

No matter. There were plenty of others who lived with no protection at all.

It took a very long moment for him to meet the gray/blue eyes of the boy he finally chose; his gaze kept jumping around, looking for a way out. The boy, seeing only a harmless old man who looked distressed, smiled, a little confused but willing enough to be friendly. The smile remained until the end and was the last bit of life lost.

The surrounding mass of people would keep the body upright until he was long away.

At the next stop, he allowed himself to be caught up in the surging crowd and swept from the train, the power from this new ka burning away his fear with his age as he strode across the platform. Those who saw the outward changes—back straightening, hair darkening—refused to believe and he marveled at how everything outside a narrow perception of "possible" simply slid from the surface of their minds. From these people, these malleable bits of breathing clay, he would build an empire that would overshadow all empires of the past.

As he had for the last two nights, Henry awoke with the image of a great golden sun seared into his mind. But for the first time, it didn't bring the fear of madness; the blood scent lay so heavily in his sanctuary that madness became an inconsequential thing beside the Hunger.

"Well, thank God, you're awake at last."

It took a moment for coherent thought to break through. "Vicki?" Her voice had a tight, strained edge to it that made it difficult to recognize. He sat up, saw her for a moment, back pressed up against the door, then had to shield his eyes from the sudden glare as she switched on the light.

When he could see again, the door was open and she was gone. He followed the blood trail to the living room and found her leaning on the back of the couch, fingers dug deep into the upholstery. All the lights that she'd passed had been switched on. The Hunger thrummed in time to her heartbeat.

She looked up as he started toward her. "Henry, don't."

Had he been younger, he might not have been able to

stop, but four hundred and fifty years had taught him control if nothing else. "What's wrong?"

"I spent the day locked in that room with you, that's what's wrong!"

"You what?"

"How could I leave? I couldn't open the door without letting at least a little sunlight in and as I was supposed to be preventing you from incinerating yourself, it would definitely defeat the purpose if I fried you instead. So I was stuck." Her laugh sounded ragged. "At least you've got a master bathroom."

"Vicki, I'm sorry . . ." He stepped forward, but she raised both hands and he stopped again although the blood moving under the delicate skin of her wrists beckoned him closer.

"Look, it's not your fault. It's something we both should've considered." She took a deep breath and settled her glasses more firmly on the bridge of her nose. "I can't stay with you tonight. I've got to get out of here."

He needed to feed and he knew he could convince her to stay; convince her in such a way that she'd think it was her idea. Although he didn't really understand, he took hold of the Hunger and nodded. "Go, then."

Vicki snatched up her jacket and purse and almost ran for the door, then she paused one hand on the knob and turned back to face him, managing a shaky smile. "I'll give you two things as a bed partner, Fitzroy: you don't snore and you don't steal the covers." Then she was gone.

As the day had claimed him and all he could feel was the press of her lips and the life behind them, Henry had envisioned how this new intimacy would change things between them.

Reality hadn't even come close.

Vicki sagged against the stainless steel wall of the elevator and closed her eyes. She felt like such a git. *Running away's a big help to Henry, isn't it?* But she just couldn't stay.

Exhaustion had kept her asleep until mid-afternoon, but the hours between waking and sunset had been some of the longest she'd lived through. Henry had been more alien to her, lying there, completely empty, than he'd ever been while drinking her blood. A hundred times she'd made her way to the door, and a hundred times she'd decided against opening it. *It's a bedroom on Bloor Street,* she'd kept telling herself. But a trembling streak of imagination she hadn't known existed kept answering, *It's a crypt.*

When the elevator reached the ground floor, she straightened and strode across the lobby as though overstretched nerves didn't twang with every movement. She nodded at the security guard as she passed his station and for the first time in over a year went gladly into a night she couldn't see.

"Yo, Victory!"

Some things she didn't need to see. "Hi, Tony. Good night, Tony." She felt him touch her arm and she stopped. Squinting, she could just make out the pale oval of his face under the streetlight.

He clicked his tongue. "Whoa, you look like shit. What happened?"

"Long day." She sighed. "What are you doing around here?"

"Well, uh . . ." He cleared his throat, sounding embarrassed. "I got this feeling that Henry needs me, so . . ."

In order to be here now, he had to have gotten the feeling before Henry had the need. Wonderful. Prescient ex-street punks. Just what *she* needed to make the day's experience complete. "And if Henry needs you, you come running?" Even to her own ears her voice appeared sharp, and she was embarrassed in turn to realize that its edge sounded very much like jealousy. Henry had needed her and she'd left.

"Hey, Victory, don't sweat it." As though he'd read her mind, Tony's voice softened. "It's easier for me. I didn't really have a life till he showed up. He can remake me any way he wants. You've been you for a long time. It makes it harder to fit the two of you together."

You've been you for a long time. She felt some of the tension begin to leave her shoulders. If anyone could understand *that,* it would be Henry Fitzroy. "Thanks, Tony."

"No problem." The cocky tone returned. "You want me to hail you a cab?"

"No."

"Then I better get upstairs."

"Before you split your jeans?"

"Jeez, Victory," she could hear the grin in his voice, "I thought you couldn't see in the dark."

She listened to him walk away, heard the door to the building open and close behind him, then made her way carefully out to the sidewalk. In the distance, she could make out the glow of Yonge and Bloor and decided to walk. City streets had enough light for her to maneuver, even if she couldn't exactly see and at the moment she didn't think she could handle being enclosed in another dark space.

A dozen steps away from the building she stopped. She'd been so caught up in getting out of Henry's apartment that she hadn't even asked him about the dream. For a moment she considered going back, then she grinned and shook her head, willing to bet that he'd be incapable of thinking coherently, let alone worrying, for the rest of the night. Tony had picked up a number of interesting skills during his years on the street, not the least of those being distraction.

Five

He gazed over the breakfast table—a bowl of strawberries and melon, three eggs over easy, six slices of rare roast beef, corn muffins, a chilled glass of apricot nectar, and a pot of fresh brewed coffee—nodded a satisfied dismissal at the young woman who delivered it, and snapped open his copy of the national paper. While he'd had the morning editions of all three Toronto papers delivered, it had been easy to tell which he should read first. Only one had more text than pictures.

After devouring the child's ka, he had spent the rest of the day acquiring suitable garments and a place to stay. The shopkeepers in the small and very exclusive men's wear stores along Bloor Street West had been so concerned with status that they'd been almost embarrassingly easy to enchant and later the manager of the Park Plaza Hotel had responded so well to appearance and arrogance that he'd barely needed to use power at all.

He had registered as Anwar Tawfik, a name he'd pulled from the ka of Elias Rax. Not since the time of Meri-nar, the first Pharaoh, had he used his true name and by the time the priests of Thoth trapped and bound him, he'd been called so many things that they could place only what he was, not who, on their binding spell. If they'd had his true name, he'd not have gotten free so easily.

He'd chosen the Park Plaza because it overlooked both the museum and, a little farther south, the provincial seat of government. He could, in fact, see both from the windows of his corner suite. The museum held only a certain amount of sentimental significance. Queen's Park he would take as his own.

In the old days, when those who had held secular power had also wielded religious might, when there had been no division between the two and the Pharaoh had been the living Horus, he had had to build his power structure from the bottom up, from the disenfranchised and the discontented. In this age, Church and State were kept forcibly separate and that left the State ripe for his plucking.

Often in those days, he found only enough unsworn ka to extend his own life and had hoarded what power he had lest he and his god ultimately perish. Now, with so few sworn, he had no need to conserve power. He could use what magic he wished, bend the mighty to his will, knowing that a multitude existed for him to feed from.

Akhekh, he knew, would not properly appreciate the situation. His lord had . . . simple tastes. A temple, a few acolytes, and a little generated despair kept Akhekh happy.

Folding the paper into quarters, he poured himself a cup of coffee and sat back, allowing the October sun to brush warmth across his face. He had awoken in a cold, gray land where leaves the color of blood lay damply underfoot. He missed the clean golden lines of the desert, the presence of the Nile, the smell of spice and sweat but, as the world he missed no longer existed, he would make this world his own.

And frankly, he didn't see how anyone could stop him.

"Homicide. Detective-Sergeant Celluci. You sure? Caused by what?"

Dave Graham watched his partner scowl and took bets with himself as to who was on the other end of the phone. There were a number of reports still outstanding although they had already received the photographs and an analysis from the lab on the contents of the trap.

"You're sure there's nothing else?" Celluci drummed on the desktop with his fingertips. "Yeah. Yeah, thanks." Although obviously annoyed, he hung up the phone with exaggerated care—the department had refused to replace any more receivers. "Dr. Rax died because his heart stopped."

Ah, the coroner. He owed himself a quarter. "And why did the good doctor's heart stop?"

Celluci snorted. "They don't know." He picked up his coffee, swirled it around to break the scum that had formed over the last two hours, and drank. "Apparently, it just stopped."

"Drugs? Disease?"

"Nada. There were signs of a struggle, but no evidence of a blow to the chest. He'd had a sandwich, a glass of milk, and a piece of blueberry pie about four hours before he died. He was, according to fatigue buildup in the muscles, a bit tired." Celluci shoved an overly long curl of hair back off his forehead. "Dr. Rax was a healthy fifty-two-year-old. He caught a naked intruder in the Egyptology workroom and his heart stopped."

"Well," Dave shrugged. "I suppose it happens."

"*What* happens?"

"Hearts stop."

"Bullshit." Celluci crumbled his cup and tossed it at the garbage basket. It hit the rim, sprayed a few drops of coffee on the side of the desk, and dropped in. "Two deaths by unexplained heart failure in the same room in less than twenty-four hours is . . ."

"A gruesome coincidence." Dave shook his head at his partner's expression. "This is a high stress world we live in, Mike. Any little extra can tip you over. Ellis saw something that frightened him, his heart couldn't take it, he died. Dr. Rax interrupted an intruder, they fought, his heart couldn't take it, *he* died. As I said, it happens. Cardiovascular failure, occurring not as a direct result of violence, doesn't come under our jurisdiction."

"Big words," Celluci grunted.

"Well, *I'm* ready to conclude this wasn't a homicide and toss it over to the B and E boys."

Celluci swung his legs off the desk and stood. "I'm not."

"*Why* not?"

He thought about it for a moment and finally shrugged. He couldn't really come up with a reason, even for himself. "Call it a hunch."

Dave sighed. He hated police work based solely on intuition, but Celluci's arrest record was certainly good enough to allow him to ride a hunch or two. He surrendered. "So, where're you going?"

"Lab."

Watching his partner stride away, Dave considered phoning the lab and warning them. His hand was on the receiver when he changed his mind. "Nah." He settled back in his chair and grinned. "Why should I have all the fun?"

"*This* is a piece of linen?" Celluci stared into the mylar envelope and decided to take Doreen's word for it. "What's it off of?"

"An ancient Egyptian ceremonial robe, probably a size sixteen extra long. It had an empire waist, pleated sleeves, and how the blazes should I know?" Doreen Chui folded her arms and stared up at the detective. "You bring me twenty-two milliliters of sludge that's just had an acid bath and I pull out a square millimeter of linen. More miracles than that you shouldn't ask for."

Celluci took a step back. Small women always made him feel vaguely intimidated. "Sorry. What *can* you tell me about it?"

"Two things. One, it's old." She raised a cautionary hand. "I don't know *how* old. Two, there's a bit of pigment on one of the fibers that's about fifty/fifty blood and a type of vegetable paint. Also old. Nothing to do with last night's body. At least not as far as precious bodily fluids are concerned."

He took a closer look at the fleck of grayish-brown substance. Raymond Thompson had said that the coffin was Eighteenth Dynasty. He wasn't sure when exactly that was, but if the bit of linen could be placed in the same time period . . . he'd be building a case against a mummy that everyone insisted didn't exist. That should go over like a visit from a civil rights lawyer. "You couldn't find out how old this is, could you?"

"You want me to carbon date it?"

"Well, yes."

"Drop dead, Celluci. You want that kind of an analysis done—provided I had a big enough sample which I don't— you get the city to stop cutting my budget so I can get the equipment and the staff." She slapped her palm down on the desk. "Until then, you got a scrap of linen with a bloody paint stain on it. Capìce?"

"So, you're finished with it?"

Doreen sighed. "Don't make me explain it to you again, Detective. I've had a hard morning."

"Right." He carefully slid the envelope into his inside jacket pocket, and tried an apologetic smile. "Thanks."

"You really want to thank me," she muttered, turning back to her work, the smile apparently having no effect, "put a moratorium on murder until I take care of my backlog."

Dr. Shane held the mylar envelope up to the light, then, shaking her head, laid it back down on the desk. "If you say that's a piece of linen, Detective, I believe you, but I'm afraid I can't tell you what it's from or how old it is. When we get the inventory finished and find out what's missing, well, maybe we'll know what went down the sink . . ."

"It had to be something that the intruder felt would give him away," Celluci mused.

"Why?" The detective had a very penetrating gaze, Dr. Shane realized as he turned it on her. And very attractive brown eyes with the sort of long, thick lashes most women would kill for. With an effort she got her train of thought back on track. "I mean, why couldn't it have just been senseless vandalism?"

"No, too specific and too neat. A vandal might have dumped acid on some of your artifacts, but they wouldn't have rinsed down the sink afterward. And," he sighed and brushed the curl of hair back off his forehead, "they wouldn't have started with that. They'd have knocked a few things over first. What about the blood/paint mixture?"

"Well, that's unusual." Dr. Shane frowned down at the linen. "Are you sure that the blood was actually mixed with the pigment and hadn't just been splashed on at some later date?"

"I'm sure." He sat forward in his chair and leaned his forearms across his knees, then had to shift as his holster jabbed him in the small of the back. "Our lab is very good with blood. They get a lot of practice."

"Yes, I suppose they do." She sighed and pushed the sample toward him. "Well, then, the only historical explanation that comes to mind is that this is a piece of a spell." She settled back and steepled her fingers, her voice taking on a lecturing tone. "Most Egyptian priests were also wizards and their spells were not only chanted but written on strips of linen or papyrus when the matter was deemed serious enough to need physical representation. Occasionally, when very powerful spells were needed, the wizard would mix his blood with the paint in order to tie his life force to the magic."

Celluci laid his hand down on the envelope. "So this is a part of a very powerful spell."

"It seems that way, yes."

Powerful enough to keep a mummy locked in its coffin? he wondered. He decided not to ask. The last thing he wanted was Dr. Shane thinking he was some kind of a nut case who'd gotten his training from old Boris Karloff movies. *That* would definitely slow down the investigation. He slid the envelope back into his jacket pocket. "They mentioned carbon dating at the lab . . . ?"

Dr. Shane shook her head. "Too small a sample; they need at least two square inches. It's why the Church objected to dating the Shroud of Turin for so long." Her gaze focused somewhere in memory, then she shook her head and smiled. "It's one of the reasons anyway."

"Dr. Shane?" The tapping on the door and the entry were pretty much simultaneous. "Sorry to disturb you, but you said you wanted that inventory the moment we finished." At the assistant curator's nod, Doris crossed the room and laid a stack of papers on the desk. "Nothing's missing, nothing even looks disturbed, but we did find a whole pile of useless film in the darkroom. Every single frame's been overexposed on about thirty rolls and we've got a stack of video tapes that show nothing but basic black."

"Do you know what was on them?" Celluci asked, getting to his feet.

Doris looked chagrined. "Actually, I haven't the faintest. I've accounted for everything I've shot over the last little while."

"If you could put them to one side, I'll have someone come and pick them up."

"I'll leave them where they are, then." Doris paused on her way out the door and glanced back at the police officer. "If they're still usable though, I'd like them back. Video tape doesn't grow on trees."

"I'll do my best," he assured her. When the door had closed behind her, he turned back to Dr. Shane. "Budget cuts?"

She laughed humorlessly. "When isn't it? I just wish I had more for you. I went over Dr. Rax's office again after your people left and I couldn't find anything missing except that suit."

Which at least gave them the relative size of the intruder—if there had even been an intruder. The ROM had excellent security and there'd been no evidence of anyone entering or leaving. It could have been an inside job; a friend of the dead janitor maybe, up poking around, who'd panicked when Dr. Rax had his heart attack. The name Dr. Von Thorne had come up a couple of times during yesterday's questioning as one of Dr. Rax's least favorite people. Maybe he'd been poking around and panicked—except that they'd already questioned Dr. Von Thorne and he had an airtight alibi, not to mention an extremely protective wife. Still, there were a number of possibilities that had nothing to do with an apparently nonexistent mummy.

While various theories were chasing each other's tails in Celluci's head, part of him watched appreciatively as Dr. Shane came around from behind her desk.

"You mentioned on the phone that you wanted to see the sarcophagus?" she said, heading for the door.

He followed her out. "I'd like to, yes."

"It wasn't in the workroom, you know. We'd already moved it across the hall."

"To the storage room." He could feel the stare of the departmental secretary as they crossed the outer office. *"What are you doing hanging around here?"* it said. *"Why aren't you out catching the one who did this?"* It was a stare he could identify at fifty paces just by the way it impacted with his back. Over the years, he'd learned to ignore it. Mostly.

"You'll find it's just a little large to maneuver around." Dr. Shane stopped across from the workroom and pulled out her keys. "That's why we moved it."

While the workroom doors were bright yellow, the storeroom doors bordered on day-glo orange.

"What's with the color scheme?" Celluci asked.

Dr. Shane's head swiveled between the two sets of doors. "I haven't," she said at last, forehead slightly puckered, "the faintest idea."

To Celluci's eyes the sarcophagus looked like a rectangular box of black rock. He had to actually run his fingers along the edge before he could find the seam where the top had been fitted into the sides. "How can you tell that something like this is Sixteenth Dynasty?" he asked, crouching down and peering in the open end.

"Mostly because the only other one ever found in this particular style was very definitely dated Sixteenth."

"But the coffin was Eighteenth?" He could see faint marks where the coffin had rested.

"No doubt about it."

"Is that unusual? Mixing time periods?"

Dr. Shane leaned on the sarcophagus and crossed her arms. "Well, we've never run into it before, but that may be because we've run into very few undisturbed grave sites. Usually, if we find a sarcophagus, the coffin is missing entirely."

"Hard to run away with one of these," Celluci muttered, straightening and having a look at the end panel. "Any theories?"

"On why this one was mixed?" Dr. Shane shrugged. "Maybe the family of the deceased was saving money."

Celluci looked up and smiled. "Got a good deal on it secondhand?"

Dr. Shane found herself smiling back. "Perhaps."

Moving the sliding panel into its grooves, Celluci let it gently down, then just as gently eased it up again. There was a three-inch lip on the inside that blocked the bottom edge. He frowned.

"What's the matter?" Dr. Shane asked, leaning forward a little anxiously. Pretty much indestructible or not, this was still a three-thousand-year-old artifact.

"They might also have chosen this style because once inside, it'd be the next thing to impossible to get out. There's no way to get a grip on this door and because it slides, brute force would do bugger all."

"Yes. But that's usually not a factor . . ."

"No, of course not." He released the panel and stepped back. Maybe Dave was right. Maybe he was fixating on this nonexistent mummy. "Just a random observation. You, uh, get used to throwing strange details together in this job."

"In my job, too."

She really did have a terrific smile. And she smelled great. He recognized Chanel No. 5, the same cologne Vicki used. "Look, it's . . ." He checked his watch. ". . . eleven forty-five. How about lunch?"

"Lunch?"

"You do eat, don't you?"

She thought about it for a moment, then she laughed. "Yes, I do."

"Then it's lunch?"

"I guess it is, Detective."

"Mike."

"Rachel."

His grandmother had always said food was the fastest way to friendship. Of course, his grandmother was old country Italian and believed in no less than four courses for breakfast while what he had in mind was a little closer to a burger and fries. Still, he could ask Dr. Shane— Rachel—her opinion on the undead while they ate.

The second time Celluci left the museum that day, he headed for the corner and a phone. Lunch had been . . . interesting. Dr. Rachel Shane was a fascinating woman; brilliant, self-assured, with a velvet glove over an iron core. *Which made a nice change,* he observed dryly to himself, *because with Vicki the gloves were usually off.* He liked her wry sense of humor; he enjoyed watching her hands sketch possibilities in the air while she talked. He'd gotten her to tell him about Elias Rax, about his often single-minded pursuit of an idea, about his dedication to the museum. She'd touched on his rivalry with Dr. Von Thorne and Celluci made a mental note to look into it. He hadn't brought up the mummy.

The closest they'd actually gotten to an analysis of the undead had been an animated discussion of old horror films. Her opinion of those had decided him against mentioning, in even a theoretical way, the idea that seemed to have possessed him.

Possessed . . . He shoved his hands deep into his jacket pockets and hunched his shoulders against the chill wind. *Let's come up with another word, shall we. . . .*

When it came right down to it, there was only one person he could tell who'd listen to everything he had to say before she told him that he'd lost his mind.

"Nelson. Private investigations."

"Christ, Vicki, it's one seventeen in the afternoon. Don't tell me you're still asleep."

"You know, Celluci . . ." She yawned audibly and stretched into a more comfortable position in the recliner. ". . . you're beginning to sound like my mother."

She heard him snort. "You spend the night with Fitzroy?"

"Not exactly." When she'd finally gone to bed, having slept most of the day, she'd had to leave the bedroom light on. Lying there in the dark, she couldn't shake the feeling that he was beside her again, lifeless and empty. What sleep she'd managed to eventually get, had been fitful and dream filled. Just before dawn, she'd called Henry. Although he'd convinced her—and at the same time, she suspected, himself—that this morning at least he had no intention of giving his life to the sun, guilt about not actually being there had kept her awake until long after sunrise. She'd been dozing off and on all day.

"Look, Vicki," Celluci took a deep breath, audible over the phone lines, "what do you know about mummies?"

"Well, mine's a pain in the butt." The silence didn't sound all that amused, so she continued. "The ancient embalmed Egyptian kind or the monster movie matinee kind?"

"Both."

Vicki frowned at the receiver. Missing from that single word had been the arrogant self-confidence that usually colored everything Mike Celluci said. "You're on the ROM case." She knew he was; all three papers had mentioned him as the investigating officer.

"Yeah."

"You want to tell me about it?" Even at the height of their competitiveness, they'd bounced ideas off each other, arguing them down to bare essentials, then rebuilding the case from the ground up.

"I think . . ." He sighed and her frown deepened. ". . . I'm going to need to see your face."

"Now?"

"No. *I* still work for a living. How about dinner? I'll buy."

Shit, this is *serious.* She pushed her glasses up on her nose. "Champion House at six?"

"Five thirty. I'll meet you there."

Vicki sat for a moment, staring down at the phone. She'd never heard Celluci sound so out of his depth. "Mummies . . ." she said at last and headed for the pile of "to be recycled" newspapers in her office. Spreading them out on her weight bench, she scanned the articles on the recent deaths at the museum. Forty minutes later, she picked up a hand weight and absently began doing biceps curls. Her memory hadn't been faulty; according to Detective-Sergeant Michael Celluci, *there was no mummy.*

It was cold and it was raining as he walked from Queen's Park back to his hotel, but then, it was October and it was Toronto. According to the ka of Dr. Rax, when the latter conditions were met, the former naturally followed. He decided that, for now, he would treat it as a new experience to be examined and endured, but that later, when his god had acquired more power, perhaps something could be done about the weather.

It had been a most productive day and the day was not yet over.

He had spent the morning sitting and weighing the currents of power eddying about the large room full of shouting men and women. Question period they called it. The name seemed apt, for although there were plenty of questions there seemed to be very few answers. He had been pleased to see that government—and those who sought positions in it—had not changed significantly in millennia. The provinces of Egypt had been very like the provinces of this new land, essentially autonomous and only nominally under the control of the central government. It was a system he understood and could work with.

Amazed at how little both adult ka he had devoured knew of politics, he had convinced a scribe—now called a press secretary—to join him for food. After using barely enough power to ripple the surface of the man's mind, he had sat and listened to an outpouring of information, both professional and personal, about the Members of the Provincial Parliament that lasted almost two and a half hours. Taking the man's ka would have been faster, but until he consolidated his power he had no wish to leave a trail of bodies behind him. While he couldn't be stopped, neither did he wish to be delayed.

Later this afternoon, he would meet with the man now called the Solicitor General. The Solicitor General controlled the police. The police were essentially a standing army. He would prepare the necessary spells and begin his empire from a position of strength.

And then, having set the future in motion, there were loose ends that needed tying off; two ka still carried thoughts of him that must be erased.

Vicki pushed a congealing mushroom around her plate and squinted at Celluci. The light levels in the restaurant were just barely high enough for her to see his face but nowhere near high enough if she actually wanted to pick up nuances of expression. She should have thought of that when she suggested the place and it infuriated her that she hadn't. *Next time it's MacDonalds, right under the biggest block of fluorescent lights I can find.*

He'd told her about the case while they ate, laying out the facts without opinions to color them; the groundwork had been laid and now it was time to cut to the chase.

She watched him play with his teacup for a moment longer, the ceramic bowl looking absurdly small in his hand, then reached across the table and smacked him on the knuckle with one of her chopsticks. "Shit or get off the pot," she suggested.

Celluci grabbed for the chopstick and missed. "And they say after dinner conversation is dead," he muttered, wiping sesame-lemon sauce off his hand. He stared down at the crumpled napkin, then up at her.

It might have been the lack of light, but Vicki could've sworn he looked tentative, and as far as she knew, Michael Celluci had never looked tentative in his life. When he started to speak, he even sounded tentative and Vicki got a cold feeling in the pit of her stomach.

"I told you how PC Trembley said there'd been a mummy when I talked to her that morning?"

"Yeah." Vicki wasn't sure she liked where this was heading. "But everyone else said there wasn't, so she must've been wrong."

"I don't think she was." He squared his shoulders and laid both palms flat on the table. "I think she did see a mummy, and I think that it's responsible for both of the deaths at the museum."

A mummy? Lurching around downtown Toronto, trailing rotting bandages and inducing heart attacks? In this day and age the entire concept was ludicrous. Of course, so was a nerd with a pentagram in his living room, a family of werewolves raising sheep outside London, and, when you got right down to it, so was the concept of Henry Fitzroy, bastard son of Henry the VIII, vampire and romance writer. Vicki adjusted her glasses and leaned forward, elbows propped, chin on hands. Life used to be so much simpler. "Tell me," she sighed.

Celluci began ticking points off on his fingers. "Everyone we talked to, and I mean everyone, was surprised that an empty sarcophagus had been resealed. The only item that the intruder destroyed has been identified as part of a powerful spell. The only items stolen were a suit of clothes and a pair of shoes." He took a deep breath. "I don't think the sarcophagus was empty. I think Reid Ellis was poking around where he shouldn't have, woke something up, and died for it. I think the creature took a little time to regain its strength and then got up out of the coffin and destroyed its wrapping and the spell that had held it. I think Dr. Rax interrupted, was overpowered, and killed. I think that the naked mummy then dressed itself in the doctor's suit and shoes and left the building. I think I'm losing my mind and I want you to tell me I'm not."

Vicki sat back, caught their waiter's attention, and indicated they wanted the bill. Then she adjusted her glasses again although they didn't really need it. "I think," she said slowly, fighting a strong sense of déjà vu—it had to be coincidence that *both* of the men in her life currently thought they were going crazy, "that you're one of the sanest people I've ever met. But are you positive that your recent . . . experiences aren't causing you to jump to supernatural conclusions?"

"I don't know."

"Why doesn't anyone at the museum remember a mummy?"

"I don't know."

"And if there *is* a mummy, how and why is it killing people?"

"Goddamnit, Vicki! How the hell am I supposed to know that?" He scowled down at the bill, threw two twenties on the table, and stood. The waiter beat a hasty retreat. "I'm working on a gut feeling, circumstantial evidence, and I don't know what the fuck to do."

At least he didn't sound tentative anymore. "Talk to Trembley."

He blinked. "What?"

Vicki grinned and got to her feet. "Talk to Trembley," she repeated. "Go down to 52 Division and see if she actually saw a mummy. If she did, then you've got yourself a case. Although," she added after a moment's thought, "God only knows where you're going to go with it." She tucked her hand in the crook of his elbow, less for togetherness than because she needed a guide out of the dimly lit restaurant.

"Talk to Trembley." Shaking his head, he steered her around a Peking duck and toward the door. "I can't believe I didn't think of that."

"And if *she* says she didn't see a mummy, check her occurrence reports. Even if this thing of yours is playing nine ball with memories, it probably knows bugger all about police and procedure."

"And if the report's negative?" he asked as they went out onto Dundas Street.

"Mike." Vicki dragged him to a stop, the perpetual Chinatown crowds breaking and swirling around them. "You sound like you *want* to believe there's a mummy loose in the city." She slapped him gently on the face with her free hand. "Now we both know better than to deny the possibility but sometimes, Sigmund, a cigar is just a cigar."

"What the hell are you talking about?"

"Maybe it's a mummy, maybe it's a slight Oedipal complex."

He caught her hand and dragged her back into motion. "I don't know why I even brought it up. . . ."

"I don't know why you didn't think of talking to PC Trembley."

"You're going to be smug about that for a while, aren't you?"

She smiled up at him. "You bet your ass I am."

Six

"Did you have the dream?"

Henry nodded, his expression bleak. "A yellow sun blazing in a bright blue sky. No change." He leaned back against the window, hands shoved deep into the front pockets of his jeans.

"Still no voice-over?"

"No what?"

"Voice-over." Vicki dropped her purse and a bulging shopping bag on the floor and then flopped down onto the couch. "You know, some kind of narrative that explains what's going on."

"I don't think it works that way."

Vicki snorted. "I don't see why it shouldn't." She could tell from his tone that he wasn't amused and she sighed. So much for easing stress with humor. "Well, it still seems essentially harmless. I mean, it's not actually compelling you to do anything."

She didn't see him move. One moment he was at the window, the next leaning on the arm of the couch, his face inches from hers.

"For over four hundred and fifty years I have not seen the sun. Now I see it in my mind every night when I wake."

She didn't exactly meet his eyes; she knew better than to hand him that much power when he was in a mood to use it. "Look, I sympathize. It's like a recovering alcoholic waking every morning with the knowledge that there'll be an open bottle of booze on the doorstep that evening and having to live all day wondering if he'll be strong enough not to end the day with a drink. I think *you're* strong enough."

"And if I'm not?"

"Well, you can stop with the fucking defeatist attitude for starters." She heard the arm of the couch creak under his grip, and kept going before he could speak. "You told me you didn't want to die. Fine, you're not going to."

Slowly, he straightened.

"I wasn't here for you this morning and I'm sorry about that, but I spent most of the day thinking about this whole thing." Celluci's phone call had given her confidence a boost when it had needed it most. She'd always managed to keep up her half of *that* relationship and she'd be damned if *this* one would defeat her. *And in return for your trust, Henry, I'm going to give you your life.* She pulled her purse up onto her lap and dug a hammer and a handful of u-shaped nails out of its depths. "I've got a blackout curtain in here." She prodded the shopping bag with the toe of her shoe. "I bought it this afternoon from a theatrical supply house. We'll hang it over the door to the bedroom. After you go out, I leave. The curtain will block the sunlight coming in from the hall. From now on, until your personal little sun sets, I tuck you in every morning and if the time comes when you can't stop yourself from heading for the pyre, I stop you."

"How?"

Vicki reached into the shopping bag. "If you go for the window," she said, "I figure I've got about a minute, maybe two, before you get through the barrier. You proved rather definitively last summer that though you heal quickly you can be hurt."

"And if I should try for the door?"

She smacked the aluminum baseball bat against the palm of her left hand. "Then I'm afraid it's a frontal assault."

Henry stared at the bat for a moment, brows drawn down into a deep vee, then he raised his head and gazed intently at Vicki's face. "You're serious," he said at last.

She met his eyes then. "Never more so."

A muscle jumped in his jaw and his brow smoothed out. Then the corners of his mouth began to twitch. "I think," he told her, "that the solution is as dangerous as the problem."

"That's the whole idea."

He smiled then, a softer smile than she'd ever seen him

use. It made him look absurdly young and it made her feel strong, protective, necessary. "Thank you."

She felt her own lips curve and the knots of tension slip out of her shoulders. "You're welcome."

Henry set the points of the last nail against the curtain and pushed it into the wall without bothering to use the hammer. Behind him, he heard Vicki mutter, "Show-off." The curtain was an inspired idea. He wasn't so sure about the baseball bat although clubbing him senseless had a certain brutal simplicity to it he could appreciate in the abstract. When it came right down to it, he still felt Vicki's presence would be enough to remind him that he didn't want to die.

Stepping down off the chair, he twitched the edge of the curtain into place. It extended about three feet past the door, similar, in form at least, to the tapestries that used to hang in his bedchamber at Sheriffhuton to block the drafts. Hopefully, it would be more effective.

Vicki had laid the bat on the bureau where it gleamed dully against the dark wood like a modern mace awaiting the hand of a twenty-first century warrior. There had been a lord at his father's court, a Scot if memory served, whose preferred weapon had been a mace. Just after his investiture as the Duke of Richmond, he had watched in open-mouthed awe as the man—who mostly certainly *had* to have been a Scot—reduced a wooden door to kindling and then defeated the three men behind it with identical strokes. Even his majesty had been impressed, clapping a beefy hand on his bastard's slender shoulder and declaring heartily, *"You can't do* that *with a sword, boy!"*

His royal father and that half-remembered lord had long since returned to dust. Although the mace quite probably still hung over a lowland mantel between the stag heads and the claymores, it no doubt had been centuries since it had been lifted in battle. Henry ran one finger down the smooth, cool length of aluminum.

"Penny for your thoughts?"

He could feel Vicki's unease in spite of her matter-of-fact tone. He could almost hear her thinking, *What do I do if he decides to get rid of the bat?* Or more likely, knowing Vicki, *Would a kidney punch break his grip if he decides to hold on?* "I was just considering," he told her, turning slowly, "how battle has become a stylized ritual with forms that change to fit the seasons."

Both her brows arced above the upper edge of her glasses. "Oh, there's still plenty of real battles going on," she drawled.

"I know that." Henry spread his hands, searching for the words that would help her to understand the difference. "But all the honor and the glory seem to have been taken from reality and given to games."

"Well, I'll admit there's very little honor and less glory in having your head bashed in by some biker with a length of chain or having a junkie in an alley go for you with a knife or even in having to take your nightstick to some drunk trying to do you first, but you're going to have to go a long way to convince me that honor and glory ever went along with violence of any kind."

"It wasn't the violence," he protested, "it was the . . ."

"Victory?"

"Not exactly, but at least you used to know when you won."

"Maybe that's why they've given the honor and glory to games—you can fight for victory without leaving an unsightly mound of bodies behind."

He frowned. "I hadn't actually thought of it like that."

"I know." She ducked under the curtain and out into the hall. "Honor and glory mean bugger all to the losers. Prince, vampire; you've always been on the winning side."

"And what side are you on?" he asked a little testily as he followed her. She hadn't so much missed the point of what he'd been trying to say as completely changed its direction.

"The side of truth, justice, and the Canadian way."

"Which is?"

"Compromise, for the most part."

"Funny, I've never thought of you as a person who compromises well."

"I don't."

He reached out and took hold of her wrist, pulling her to a stop and then around to face him. "Vicki, if I said I was tired, that I've lived six times longer than the natural human span and I've had enough, would you let me walk out into the sun?"

Not bloody likely. She bit back the immediate emotional

response. He'd asked her the question seriously; she could hear that in his voice and see it in his face, and it deserved more than a gut reaction. She'd always believed that a person's life was his own and that what he did with it was his business, no one else's. That worked fine in general, but would she let *Henry* choose to walk out into the sun? Friendship meant responsibility or it didn't mean much and, come to think of it, they'd settled that once already tonight. "If you want me to let you kill yourself, you'd damn well better be able to convince me that dying does more for you than living."

She'd gotten angry just thinking about it. He heard her heart speed up, saw muscles tense beneath clothes and skin. "*Could* I convince you?"

"I doubt it."

He lifted her hand and placed a kiss gently on the palm. "Has anyone ever told you that you're a very pushy person?" he murmured against the soft skin at the base of her thumb, inhaling the blood-rich scent of her flesh.

"Frequently." Vicki snatched her hand away and rubbed it against the front of her sweatshirt. Great, just what she needed, more stimulus. "There's no point in starting something you're not going to finish," she muttered a little shakily. "You fed last night from Tony."

"True."

"You don't *need* to feed tonight."

"True."

It always annoyed her that he could read her physical reaction so easily, that he always *knew* and she could only guess. Occasionally, however, the question became moot.

"I am too old for frenzied fucking in the hall," she informed him a moment later. "Stop that." Walking backward, she towed him toward the bedroom.

Henry's eyes widened. "Vicki, be careful . . ."

She tightened her grip and grinned. "After four hundred and fifty years, you should know that it won't pull off."

"I had dinner with Mike Celluci tonight."

Henry sighed, and lightly traced the shadow of a vein in the soft hollow below Vicki's ear. Although he'd taken only a few mouthfuls of blood he felt replete and lazy. "Do we have to talk about him now?"

"He thinks there's a mummy walking around Toronto."

"Lots of mummies," Henry murmured against her neck. "Daddies, too."

"Henry!" She caught him just under the solar plexus with an elbow. He decided to pay attention. "Celluci seriously believes that an ancient Egyptian has risen from his coffin and killed two people at the museum."

"The two people who died of heart attacks?"

"That's right."

"And you *believe* him?"

"Look, if Mike Celluci called me up and told me aliens had him trapped in his house, I might not believe him, but I'd show up with a flamethrower just in case. And as you're the closest thing to an expert on rising from the dead I know, I'm asking you. Is this possible?"

"Let me get this straight." Henry rolled over on his back and laced his fingers behind his head. "Detective-Sergeant Michael Celluci came to you and said, *There's a mummy loose in Toronto, murdering janitors and Egyptologists.* And let me guess, he can't tell anyone else because no one else will believe him."

"Essentially."

"Are you sure this isn't just an elaborate April Fool's prank?"

"Too complicated. Celluci's a salt in the sugar bowl kind of guy, and besides, it's October."

"Good point. I assume he gave you his reasoning behind this stu . . . ouch, unusual idea."

"He did." Tapping out the points on Henry's chest, Vicki repeated everything Celluci had told her.

"And if PC Trembley confirms that there was a mummy, what then?"

She wound a short, red-gold curl around her finger. "I was hoping you could tell me."

"We help him stop it?"

"How?"

"I haven't the faintest idea." He heard her sigh, felt her breath against his chest, and lightly kissed the top of her head. "Did he ask you to speak to me about it?"

"No. But he said he didn't mind if I did." He'd actually said, *Use a ghoul to find a ghoul? Why not?* But under his sneer there'd been a sense of relief and Vicki had gotten the feeling that he'd been waiting all evening for her to ask, unwilling to bring it up himself. "He had to go to a hockey practice or I'd have suggested he tell you all this firsthand."

"That *would* have been a fun evening."

Vicki grinned. Celluci's reaction would have been louder and more profane but essentially similar.

Henry sat down at his desk and turned on his computer. Over the hum of the fan he could hear deep, slow breathing coming from the living room and, under that, the measured beat of a heart at rest.

"Don't expect me to stay around every night," Vicki had warned him, yawning. *"I expect most of the time I'll show up just before dawn to tuck you in. But, as long as I'm here, you might as well do some writing and I might as well get some sleep."* She'd led the way out of the bedroom, pillow tucked under one arm, blanket under the other. *"I'll sack out on the couch. The airflow's better out there and you won't have to sleep surrounded by blood scent."*

It was a plausible, even a considerate reason, but Henry didn't believe it. He'd seen the lines of tension smooth out of her back as they'd left the room. He listened to her sleep for a moment longer, then shook his head and turned his attention to the monitor. The book was due the first of December and he figured he was still a chapter away from happily ever after.

Veronica paced the length of her room in the Governor's mansion, silk skirts whipping around her shapely ankles. Captain Roxborough would hang on the morrow unless she could find some way to prevent it. She knew he wasn't a pirate but, even though the Governor had been more than kind, would her word mean anything once everyone discovered that she'd made her way to the islands disguised as a cabin boy? That Captain Roxborough had discovered her and that he'd . . .

She stopped pacing and raised slender fingers to cover her heated cheeks. None of that mattered now. "He must not die," she vowed.

"I can't seem to get away from dying at dawn," Henry muttered, pushing back from the desk.

Last spring, the dawn had caught him away from safety

and he'd raced the sun for his life. He still bore the puckered scar on the back of his hand where the day had
marked him. Would it happen as quickly as that had, he
wondered, or more slowly? Would it be instantaneous as
his flesh ignited and turned to ash, or would he burn slowly
in agony, screaming his way to the final death?

He forced his mind away from the thought, listening to
the even tempo of Vicki's breathing until he calmed. There
had to be something else he could think about.

*"Celluci seriously believes that an ancient Egyptian has
risen from his coffin and killed two people at the museum."*

He'd been to Egypt once; just after the turn of the century; just after the death of Dr. O'Mara when England had
seemed tainted and he'd had to get away. He hadn't stayed
long.

He'd met Lady Wallington on the terrace at Shepheard's.
She'd been sitting alone, drinking tea and watching the
crowds of Egyptians making their way up Ibrahim Pasha
Street when she'd felt his gaze and called him over. A recent widow in her early forties, she had no objection to
keeping company with an attractive, well-bred young man.
Henry, for his part, had found her candor refreshing.
"Don't be ridiculous," she'd told him, when he'd expressed
his sympathy on her loss, *"the nicest thing his Lordship ever
did for me was to drop dead before I was too old to enjoy
my freedom."* And then she'd stroked the inside of his thigh
under the cover of the damask tablecloth.

Publicly, they were as discreet as the society of 1903 demanded. Privately, she was just what Henry needed after
the incident with the grimoire. He never told her what he
was and she accepted the time he spent away from her with
the same aplomb as the time he spent with her. He rather
suspected she had another lover for the daylight hours and
found himself admiring her stamina.

On the nights he had to feed from others, he stayed away
from the English and American tourists and slipped into
the dark and twisting streets of old Cairo where sloe-eyed
young men never knew they paid for their pleasure with
blood.

And then he began to feel watched. Although he could

identify no obvious threat—dark eyes watched all the visitors and certainly seemed to watch him no more than the rest—the skin between his shoulder blades continued to crawl. He began to take more care moving to and from his sanctuary.

A moonlight climb to the top of the Great Pyramid had become "the thing to do" and it took little pleading for Henry to agree to accompany Lady Wallington on her expedition. The city had started to feel like it was closing around him, as if it were some large and complicated trap. Perhaps a few hours away from it would clear his head.

They stepped out of the carriage onto moon-silvered sand that drifted up against the base of the monuments like new fallen snow, its purity broken by the pits that marked vandalized tombs or sunken shrines. The light had erased the patina of age from the pyramids and they in turn cast dark bands of shadow across the features of the Sphinx so that he looked both more and less human as he gazed enigmatically down on the night. Unfortunately, flaring torches and crawling bodies marred the pale sides of the Great Pyramid and the sounds of their progress carried clearly on the desert air.

"Hot damn, ain't we there yet?"

"While I admire Americans as a breed," Lady Wallington sighed, tucking her hand in the crook of Henry's elbow, "there are a few individuals I could gladly do without."

As they approached the pyramid, they braced themselves for the charge of self-styled guides, antiquities peddlers, and assorted beggars who stood clustered around the base waiting for the chance to part foreigners from their money.

"How strange," Lady Wallington murmured, as the men remained where they were, peering out at them from under their turbans and muttering to themselves in Arabic. "Although, I suppose we can manage quite well without them." But she looked rather dubiously at the monument as she spoke, for in full evening dress the three to three and a half foot steps would not be easy to navigate without assistance. Most of the women already climbing had two men pulling from above and another pushing from below.

Henry frowned. Under the scent of dirt and sweat and

spice, he could smell fear. As he leapt up onto the first
block and reached down for Lady Wallington's hand, one
of them made the sign against the evil eye.

Lady Wallington followed his gaze and laughed. "Don't
mind that," she explained as he lifted her easily up onto
the next level, "it's just that in the torchlight your hair
looks redder than it generally does and red hair is the mark
of Set, the Egyptian version of the devil."

"Then I won't mind it," he reassured her with a smile.
But the smile would have meant more if he hadn't seen
the knot of men melt away the moment he'd climbed beyond the range of a normal man's vision.

Over the years, the top of the pyramid had been removed, leaving a flat area about thirty feet square at the
summit. Breathing a little heavily, Lady Wallington collapsed onto one of the scattered blocks and was immediately surrounded by natives who tried to sell her everything
from bad reproductions of papyrus scrolls, guaranteed genuine, to the finger of a mummy, undeniably genuine. Henry,
they ignored. He left her to her purchases and wandered
closer to the eastern edge where, past the obsidian ribbon
that was the Nile, he could see the twinkling lights of Cairo.

They came from upwind, moving so quietly that mortal
ears would not have heard them. Henry caught the sound
of hearts pounding in a half dozen chests and turned long
before they were ready.

One man moaned, grimy fist shoved up to cover his
mouth. Another stepped back, whites showing all around
his eyes. The remaining four only froze where they stood
and over the stronger stink of fear, Henry caught the smell
of steel and saw moonlight glint on edged weapons.

"An open place for thieves," he remarked conversation-
ally, hoping he wouldn't have to kill them.

"We are not here to steal from you, *afreet*," their leader
said softly, his voice pitched so that none of the other foreigners on the pyramid would hear, "but to give you a
warning. We know what you are. We know what you do
in the night."

"I don't know what you're talking about." The protest was
purely instinctive; Henry didn't expect to be believed. Even
as he spoke, he realized from their bearing that they did know

what he was and what he did and that the only option left was to find out what they intended to do about it.

"Please, *afreet* . . ." The leader spread his hands, his meaning plain.

Henry nodded, once, and allowed the persona of slightly vapid Englishman to drift away. "What do you want?" he asked, the weight of centuries giving his voice an edge.

The leader stroked his beard with fingers that trembled slightly and all six carefully kept from meeting Henry's gaze. "We want only to warn you. Leave. Now."

"And if I don't?" The edge became more pronounced.

"Then we will find where you hide from the day, and we will kill you."

He meant it. In spite of his fear, and the greater fear of the men behind him, Henry had no doubt they would do exactly as they said. "Why warn me?"

"You have proven yourself to be a neutral *afreet,*" one of the other men spoke up. "We do not wish to make you angry, so we try a neutral path to be rid of you."

"Besides," the leader added dryly, "our young men insisted."

Henry frowned. "I gave them dreams . . ."

"Our people had a civilization when these people were savages." A wave of his hand indicated the tourists, Lady Wallington among them, still haggling over souvenirs. "We have forgotten more than they have yet learned. Dreams will not hide your nature, *afreet.* Will you take our warning and go?"

Henry studied their faces for a moment and saw, under the dirt and malnutrition, a remnant of the race that had built the pyramids and ruled an empire that had included most of northern Africa. To that remnant he bowed, the bow of a Prince receiving an ambassador from a distant, powerful land, and said, "I will go."

We have forgotten more than they have yet learned.

Henry drummed his fingers on the edge of his desk. Somehow he doubted that much more had been learned in the ninety odd years since. If Celluci was right and a mummy did walk the streets of Toronto, a mummy who brought with it the power of ancient Egypt, then they were all in a great deal of danger.

                              *   *   *

"Slumming, Detective?"

"Just seeing how the other half lives." Celluci leaned on the counter at 52 Division and scowled at the woman on the other side. "Trembley and her partner in yet? I need to talk to them."

"Good God, don't tell me one of you boys from homicide is actually working at six fifty in the a.m.? Just let me circle the date . . ."

"Bruton . . ." It wasn't quite a warning. "Trembley?"

"Jee-zus, take a man out of uniform and he loses his sense of humor. Not," she reflected, "that you ever had much of one. And you always were a son of a bitch in the morning. Come to think of it, you were a son of a bitch in the evening, too." Staff-Sergeant Heather Bruton had shared a car with Celluci for a memorable six months back when they'd both been constables, but the department had wisely separated them before any permanent damage had been done. "Trembley's not in yet. You want to wait or you want me to have her give you a shout?"

"I'll wait."

"Be still my beating heart." She blew him a sarcastic kiss and returned to her paperwork.

Celluci sighed and wondered if Vicki had known who'd be on duty when she suggested he talk to Trembley. Just the sort of thing she'd think was funny. . . .

". . . so then she says, 'Aren't you going to arrest him, Mommy?' "

Trembley's partner laughed. "How old is Kate now?"

"Just about three. Her birthday's November." She turned from Harbord Street onto Queen's Park Circle. "And can you believe it, for Halloween she wants . . . oh, fuck!"

"What?"

"The accelerator, it's stuck!"

The patrol car sped over the bridge and into the curve, picking up speed. Trembley swerved around a tiny import, fighting to keep control. She pumped the brakes once, twice, and then the pressure was gone.

"Shit!"

She stamped the emergency brake into the floor. Abused metal shrieked under the car.

Trembley's partner, the fingers of one hand dug deep into the dash, grabbed for the radio. "This is 5239! The car . . . Jesus, Trembley!"

"I see it! I see it!"

She yanked the wheel hard to the left. Tires squealed against asphalt. They passed behind the College streetcar with only a prayer between them.

"Throw it into reverse!"

"That'll fuse the engine!"

"So?"

The world slowed as PC Trembley suddenly realized that the car was not going where she steered it. The wheels had turned, but the car, drawing dark lines of rubber behind it, continued to head for the concrete memorial at the corner of the Toronto General Hospital.

The world resumed its normal speed just before they hit. Trembley's last feelings were relief. She didn't think she could stand dying in slow motion.

Upwind from the clouds of greasy black smoke, Celluci stared at the wreck of the patrol car, the heat from the fire lapping at his face. If by any miracle either officer had survived the impact, the explosion when the engine ignited would have finished them off. The blaze was so intense that the fire department could only let the flames burn out, concentrating on keeping them contained.

In spite of the early hour, a small crowd had gathered and the flower seller, who had been just about to set up on that corner, was having strong hysterics under the care of two paramedics.

"Funny thing," rasped a voice by Celluci's shoulder.

He turned and glared down at the filthy man swaying beside him. Even over the smell of the accident, he stank.

"I seen it," the man continued. "Told the cops. They don't believe me."

"Told them what?" Celluci growled.

"I am *not* drunk!" He staggered and clutched at Celluci's jacket. "But if you could spare some change . . ."

"Told them what?" Celluci repeated in a tone honed over the years to cut through alcoholic haze.

"What I seen." Still holding the jacket, he turned and

pointed a filthy finger at the car. "Wheels was goin' one way. Car was goin' nuther way."

"It's barely light now, how could you have seen that then?"

"Was layin' in the park. Had a wheels-eye view."

It wasn't much of a park, more a garden planted on the median strip, but the trail of black rubber scorched onto the road passed right by it. Celluci followed the line to the wreck and then followed the smoke until it became a part of the overcast sky, spreading over the entire city.

The wheels were going one way.

The car was going another.

With a cold hand closing around his heart, Celluci ran for his car. It had suddenly become very important he see Trembley's occurrence reports for Monday morning.

"Jesus Christ, Celluci," Staff-Sergeant Bruton snapped, phone receiver cradled under her chin and three people clambering for her attention, "this is *not* the time to bother me with a missing fucking occurrence report, you . . . What?" She turned her attention back to the phone. "No. I don't want to call back. I want you to find him! Do *not* put me on ho . . . damnit!" She scrawled her signature on a preferred form, glared through the chaos and shouted, "Takahashi! Get that other line! Now then," she jabbed a finger in Celluci's direction, "if you need that report for a case, you call later. You hear me? Later."

"Sarge?" PC Takahashi held out the phone, his hand tightly over the mouthpiece. "It's Trembley's husband."

The hieroglyphs that had been etched into the paint of the toy police car had been completely obliterated and the small piece of paper folded three times toward the heart and then slipped into the front seat was no more than ash. He slid a magazine under the smoldering remains and lifted it out of the tub with a trembling hand. It had been a very long time since he'd worked that spell and, as burning down the hotel had not been part of his intention, he'd carefully set it up so that any random power would be contained. Because he'd forgotten that the fuel these cars relied upon was highly flammable, his foresight proved fortunate. As it was, the shower curtain appeared a little singed. He would have to have it replaced.

Dumping the nearly unidentifiable bit of metal into a crystal ashtray in the living room of the suite, he collapsed, exhausted, into a chair. Although there existed easier and less draining ways to accomplish the same purpose, the morning's work had, while removing the last two memories of his mummified form, proven that all his old skills were still intact. A quick trip to the station and a short chat with the young man on the desk had taken care of the written records last night.

In the old days, he wouldn't have dared to take his power as low as he had this morning. But in the old days with the gods gathering up souls almost at birth, he wouldn't have been able to feed with the ease he now could. Later, perhaps around lunch, he'd take a walk. According to Dr. Rax's ka, there was a school of sorts for very young children not so far away.

"You're late."

"I was down at 52 when the accident call came in." Celluci shrugged out of his jacket and dropped into his chair. The accident had happened at College and University, three short blocks from Headquarters; everyone in the building knew about it; half of the arriving day shift had been there.

"Was it as bad as they say?"

"Worse."

"Jesus. What do you think happened?"

Celluci glared across the desk at his partner. "The team who died in that crash were the uniforms on the scene Monday morning at the museum."

"Christ, Mike!" Dave leaned forward and lowered his voice. "We are not in some bad monster movie here! There never was a mummy, but if there had been it wouldn't be getting up and killing people and it sure as shit wouldn't be causing car accidents. I don't know where you're coming from with this, but could you just drop the bullshit so we can get on with our work?"

"Look, you don't know . . ."

"Know what? That there's a lot of strange things going

on in this city? Sure I know, I've arrested some of them. But there's plenty of perfectly normal, human slime out there so don't go borrowing trouble." He studied Celluci's expression and shook his head. "Like money through a whore's hands . . . You haven't listened to a thing I said."

"I heard you," Celluci growled. He realized that nothing he said in turn could convince the other man that another world existed outside—or more frighteningly, inside—the boundaries he'd lived with all his life.

"Hey, you two; Cantree wants to see you in his office."

"Why?" Celluci scowled at the messenger even as Dave was getting to his feet.

She shrugged. "How the hell should I know? He's the Inspector, I'm just a detective." She skipped back out of the way as Celluci stood. "Maybe he just got a look at your last expense report. I told you that you should've kept receipts."

Inspector Cantree glanced up as the two detectives came in and indicated with a jerk of his head that they were to close the door. "It's about those deaths at the museum," he said without preamble. "I've looked at the reports. I've had a talk with the Chief. Leave it."

"Leave it?" Celluci took a step forward.

"You heard me. A heart attack isn't a homicide. Leave it to the B & E team. I want you helping Lackey and Dixon on the Griffin case."

Celluci felt his hands curl into fists, but because it was Cantree, probably the one cop in the city he respected without reservation—and *that* carried a lot more weight than the man's rank or position as his immediate superior—he kept a tight hold on his temper. "I have a hunch about this . . ." he began, but the Inspector interrupted.

"I don't care. It isn't a homicide, therefore it isn't any business of yours. Or your hunches."

"But I think it *is* a homicide."

Cantree sighed. "All right. Why? Give me some facts."

Celluci's lips narrowed. "No facts," he muttered, while Dave stared at the ceiling, his expression carefully neutral. "Just a feeling."

"All right." Cantree pulled a pile of folders across his desk. "I'll give *you* some facts. We've had seventy-seven homicides in this city so far this year. A teenage girl found dismembered in the lake. A man knifed behind a bar. A doctor killed in the stairwell of her apartment building. Two women bludgeoned to death in a parking garage in middle of the fucking afternoon!" His voice rose and he surged up out of his seat, slamming his palm down on the folders. "I don't need you making murders where there aren't any. As far as you are concerned, the case is closed. Do I make myself clear?"

"Perfectly," Celluci told him through clenched teeth.

"As a bell," Dave added, pulling his partner toward the door and keeping a tight grip on his elbow until they were back in the outer office. "Well, I guess that's that," he said, caught sight of Celluci's face, and rolled his eyes. "Or maybe not . . ."

"Nelson. Investigations."

"Cantree pulled me off the case."

Vicki dropped her bag and, balancing the receiver under her chin, shrugged out of her jacket. She'd barely gotten in the door when the phone rang. "Did he say why?"

"He said, and I quote, *'I've looked at the reports. I've had a talk with the Chief. A heart attack isn't a homicide.'* "

"And you said?"

"What the hell could I say? If I told him I thought there was a mummy involved, he'd think I was crazy. My partner *already* thinks I'm crazy."

In her mind's eye she could see him shoving the curl of hair back off his forehead and forcing his fingers up through his hair. "You still think there's a mummy involved?"

"Trembley's occurrence report for Monday morning is missing."

"And Trembley?"

"Is dead."

Vicki sat down. "How?"

"Car accident on the way back to the station this morning."

"I passed the site coming home, but I had no idea Trembley was . . . involved." Emergency teams had just managed to get close to the slag. The bodies had been burned beyond even retrieval. "I talked to a couple of the uniforms. They said the car went out of control."

"I have a witness who saw the wheels pointing one way while the car continued to go another." Celluci took a deep breath and she could hear the tension in it humming over the wires. "I want to hire you."

"You what?"

"Cantree tied my hands. You don't work for him anymore. Find that mummy."

She recognized the obsession in his voice. She'd heard it there before and as often in her own. Obsession made a good cop. It had also broken a few. "All right. I'll find it."

"Keep me informed every step of the way."

"I will."

"Be careful."

She saw again the melted remains of Trembley's car. "You, too."

Hanging up the phone, she frowned, remembering. *I've looked at the reports and I've had a talk with the Chief.* "Now why," she asked of the empty apartment, "would Inspector Cantree have talked to the Chief about a departmental matter?"

Seven

". . . No one is available to take your call at this moment. If you leave a message after the tone, I'll get back to you as soon as possible. Please don't assume I can remember where I put your phone number."

"Henry? Vicki. I want to check out that workroom tonight. The Department of Egyptology is on the fifth floor at the south end of the museum; meet me there as soon as you can." She thought for a second, then added, "There'll be a single guard on the desk. I assume you can get in without any trouble." Brow furrowed, Vicki put down the receiver. As it was still a couple of hours to sunset, she hadn't actually expected to speak to Henry, but she suddenly doubted the wisdom of putting that message on the machine.

"You're being ridiculous," she sneered at herself. "The odds of Celluci's alleged mummy randomly tapping phone lines or gaining access to Henry's answering machine are about as likely as . . ." She sighed and redialed Henry's number. ". . . as it existing at all."

"Henry? Vicki. Erase this tape once you've listened to it."

"I'm probably just being paranoid," she told a piece of cold pizza a moment later, picking a slice of salami off the congealed cheese. But as four people were already dead and they had no idea of the enemy's strength or its capabilities, she had no intention of being body number five or setting Henry up as number six.

It took less than fifteen minutes to walk to the Royal Ontario Museum from Vicki's apartment, but by the time she ducked down the alley between the McLaughlin Planetarium and the museum's main building, she was wishing she'd taken a cab. Everything below the angle of the umbrella had gotten soaked and the wind had blown cold rain up into her face at every opportunity.

"I hate October," she muttered, using the narrow band of shelter under the second floor walkway to shake some of the excess water off the bottom of her trench coat. As she straightened, a cold dribble ran off her chin, down the inside of her collar, along the side of her neck, and into the hollow of her collarbone where it finally surrendered and was soaked up by her shirt. "On second thought, I can live with October, I hate *rain.*"

At the staff entrance, she paused and peered through the outer set of glass doors. The only way to the inner set, and then into the museum, passed by a manned security station. A large sign instructed staff that security badges *must* be worn at all times and that visitors *must* check in at the desk.

Vicki smiled, peeled off her leather gloves and stuffed them in her pockets, then opened the door.

"Hello." She extended her smile to include the guard and he willingly returned it. Her clothing said, respectable and her attitude said, nice person—just the sort security guards preferred to deal with. "My name's Celluci. I'm here to see Dr. Rachel Shane in Egyptology." She figured it was the one name guaranteed to get her upstairs and if the guard recognized it, she'd merely use the same story she planned on giving Dr. Shane.

"Is Dr. Shane expecting you?"

"Not at this precise moment, no."

"I'll have to call up."

"Oh, yes, of course."

A moment later she was in the elevator, a small pink badge pinned to her trench coat with *Celluci* and the number forty-two written on it. To her surprise, an attractive dark-haired woman met the elevator on the fifth floor.

"Mike. Is it . . ." she began, stepping forward as the doors opened. Then she stopped, flushed, and stepped back as Vicki moved out into the hall. "I'm sorry. I thought you were someone else."

"Detective-Sergeant Celluci?" Vicki guessed. She had a pretty good idea of who this must be from Celluci's description, but she wondered just how much, exactly, the detective in question *hadn't* told her about the good doctor. Why would she be coming to meet him at the elevator?

"That's right, but . . ."

"You must be Dr. Shane."

"Yes. However . . ." Then she managed to read the name on the badge and her cheeks darkened. "You're not his wife are you?"

Vicki felt herself flush in turn. "Not hardly." Dr. Shane looked relieved but still embarrassed and again Vicki found herself wondering what Mike hadn't told her. And whether she really wanted to know. "I'm his cousin," she continued. "He thought he left some papers here and, as I just work around the corner on Bloor Street, he asked me to come by."

"Papers? Oh." Dr. Shane turned and started down the hall. "Well, if he left them, the departmental secretary, Ms. Gilbert, will know. I don't think she's left for the day."

As they walked down the hall, Vicki noted doorways, locks, lines of sight, and Dr. Rachel Shane. Celluci could, of course, eat lunch with anyone he chose—their relationship had always been nonexclusive—but Vicki had to admit to being curious. He'd been so completely neutral when talking about the assistant curator that she'd known right away he was interested. Celluci wasn't that neutral about anything. Cursory observation showed Rachel Shane to be above average in height, attractive, self-assured, pleasant, polite . . . *And obviously intelligent or she couldn't do her job. Christ, the perfect woman of the 90s. What do you want to bet she cooks, composts, and reads nonfiction?* A muscle jumped in her jaw and, surprised, Vicki unclenched her teeth.

"So why didn't Detective Celluci come himself?"

"I don't know." Dr. Shane's question had been asked in a tone as aggressively noncommittal as any Vicki had ever heard. *That must've been some lunch, Celluci.*

There were, of course, no papers to find, although Ms. Gilbert, tying a plastic rain hat over permed hair, promised to keep an eye out.

"Thanks for looking." As the older woman hurried out of the office, Vicki glanced down at her watch. Time for her to be leaving as well. This next bit had to be tightly choreographed. She held out her hand. "I appreciate you taking the time to see me, Dr. Shane."

"I'm just sorry we couldn't find the detective's papers."

She had a firm handshake and a dry palm. Another two points in her favor. "Time he started remembering where he leaves things anyway. But if they do turn up, will you call him?"

"Yes, of course I will."

I'll bet. All of a sudden it was an effort to sound pleasant. "Did he give you his home number?"

"Yes, he did."

And just what does that Mona Lisa smile mean? "Well, thanks again. I'll find my own way back to the elevator. I mean, it's a straight length of hall, I can hardly get lost."

Back on the first floor, a steady stream of staff members moved through the security area, leaving for the day. Vicki, with one eye on the clock, made sure the guard noticed her sign out and return her badge. Shift change would be in two minutes.

"Oh, blast, I left my umbrella upstairs." She shot a panicked look at the outer doors where sheets of rain were slapping against the glass, then turned to the guard. "Mind if I run up and get it?"

"Nah, go ahead." He shot a disgusted look of his own at the rain.

The best lie isn't a lie at all, Vicki mused retrieving her umbrella from behind one of the temple dogs at the door to the Far East Department. She hurried down the hall to a small supply cupboard, just past the photocopy machine. The door had been open earlier and it had seemed like the perfect hiding place. Unfortunately, the door was now locked and she'd be in plain sight of anyone approaching from either direction while she worked on it.

"Damn."

The open orange doors had to belong to the workroom; Vicki could hear Dr. Shane discussing the restoration of a mural. The double yellow doors across from them were ajar. Vicki slipped inside as the voices from the workroom grew louder.

". . . so we'll take another look at that plaster patch tomorrow."

They were in the hall now.

Vicki turned. Obviously, she was in the storeroom; the black stone sarcophagus Celluci had mentioned sat barely an arm's length away. Just as obviously, someone would be arriving momentarily to turn off the lights and lock the door. After a quick glance at the lock—being trapped inside was low on her list of useful ways to spend the night—Vicki scanned the room for a hiding place. Unfortunately, the sheer volume of stuff made quiet movement impossible and the sarcophagus stood so close to the door that hiding behind it would be useless.

But in it?

She scrambled inside seconds before the storeroom door opened.

"Did you hear something, Ray?"

"Not a thing, Dr. Shane."

"Must've been my imagination . . ."

She didn't sound convinced and Vicki held her breath. A moment later, there was a soft click and the lights went out, then the door closed and Vicki heard keys in the lock.

The interior of the sarcophagus was actually quite roomy, having been built to hold a full-sized coffin, but Vicki had no intention of remaining inside. She crawled out and set both bag and umbrella on the top of the stone box. As far as the new guard knew, she'd signed out and was gone. The odds were slim to none that the old guard had told him she'd gone back inside. If the mummy was messing with people's heads—and as no one remembered it, it certainly looked like it was—there was nothing in anyone's head to incriminate her.

She was actually quite proud of the way she'd gotten past security. With the paranoia caused by two deaths, plain old sneaking in would have been impossible. That what she had done—and was doing—was illegal, bothered her a little, but as she wasn't going to hurt anything, or even disturb anything, her conscience would just have to roll with the punches. Actually, it had gotten pretty good at that since meeting Henry.

She fished her flashlight out of her bag by touch and checked her watch. Sunset would be in fifteen minutes. She'd give Henry half an hour to clear his head and get over to the museum, then she'd start working on the lock.

"Meanwhile," she turned the tight beam on the sarcophagus, "let's see what I can find out here."

* * *

Henry stood for a moment watching Vicki work. Although emergency lights put the hall in twilight rather than true darkness, he knew that for Vicki they were one and the same. She could no more see the lock, inches in front of her face, than she could see him, yet her touch was sure as she probed at the mechanism. Silently, he moved a little closer and smiled as he realized her eyes were tightly shut.

"Well done," he said softly as, with a sound only he could hear, the lock disengaged.

Heart pounding, Vicki fought the urge to leap to her feet and spin around. "Thank you very much, Henry," she muttered, aware that no matter how low her voice he could pick it up, "you've just cost me a good six years of my life and almost made me shit my drawers." Running her hand lightly up the door so as not to become disoriented, she stood. "Now, if we could get out of the hall before someone comes along . . ."

He reached past her, turned the knob, and pulled one of the double doors partway open. Before he had a chance to act as guide, Vicki slipped through the narrow space and into the room beyond. Puzzled, he followed, pulling the door shut behind him. "Can you see?" he asked.

"Not a damn thing." Although she was still bitter about her night blindness, a certain amount of pride colored her voice. "But I could feel the difference in the air where the door wasn't. Now then, be useful and find the lights. The doors fit tightly enough, there'll be no spill into the hall. Or not much anyway," she amended as the multiple banks of fluorescents came on. Eyes streaming from the sudden glare, she turned to face Henry and found him slipping on a pair of dark glasses.

She grinned. "You look like a spy." The black leather trench coat and sunglasses made an exotic contrast with the red-gold hair and pale skin.

His brows rose. "Isn't that what we're doing? Spying?"

"Not really. If we get caught, it's breaking and entering."

Henry sighed. "Wonderful. Vicki, why are we here? All the evidence has certainly been cleared away."

"Maybe. Maybe not. I wanted to get a look at the scene of the crime." Taking one final swipe at her eyes, Vicki glanced around the workroom. It had to be at least fifty feet square, perhaps larger; the high beige walls tended to draw the eye up. Rows of chest-high wooden cabinets covered half the room and floor-to-ceiling metal shelves—filled with stone, and pottery, and sculpture—the other half. They stood in an area obviously used for paperwork beside a buried desk and a number of laden bookshelves. To their left, a camera stood on a tripod before a neutral background and to their right a small kitchenette—fridge, counter, cupboards, and sink—ran along one wall. A lime green door just at the end of the counter led to the darkroom. Two padded sawhorses stood between the desk and the cabinets in the only open space of any size. Resting on them was the coffin, its lid on the closest cabinet. "Besides, I wanted you to take a look at that."

Henry sighed again. He was willing to help, but he honestly didn't see how this . . . excursion . . . was going to do any good. "Are you sure that's the right coffin?"

Vicki's mouth twisted as she studied the artifact. Even without Celluci's description, she would have recognized it. The hair on the back of her neck rose and although she shrugged the feeling away, she was beginning to see why Celluci had been so willing to believe in his mummy. "I'm sure."

Hands shoved deep in his pockets, Henry walked over to the coffin. His dark lenses somehow gave it an unreal appearance and painted the snakes covering it the color of blood. Very ominous—but he had no idea what he was supposed to be looking for. His nose twitched at the still overpowering smell of cedar, then he frowned and lowered his head toward the cavity. So faintly that only one of his kind could pick it up, he caught the scent of a life.

Eyes closed, he breathed in the signature of centuries. Not merely flesh and blood but terror, pain, and despair . . .

Not stone above him, but rough wood embracing him so closely that the rise and fall of his chest brushed against the boards. All around the smell of earth. Screaming until his throat was raw, he twisted and thrashed through the little movement he had . . .

His eyes snapped open and Henry jerked back, away from the coffin, away from the memory of his own burial, trembling fingers sketching the sign of the cross. He turned to find Vicki watching him, her expression saying clearly that his reaction had been observed.

"Well?" she asked.

"Something spent a long time trapped in there."

"Something human?"

He shrugged, more affected by the experience than he wanted to admit. "It was when they closed the lid. If it was aware for all those years, only God knows what it is now."

Vicki nodded thoughtfully and Henry realized that his reaction had not only been observed but anticipated. "That was why you wanted me here." He'd told her of his burial the night he'd told her of his creation.

She nodded again, not noticing his rising anger. "You keep going on about how your senses are more acute, so I figured if there'd been something, someone, in there for three thousand years you'd be able to tell."

"You used me."

Vicki's jaw dropped at the fury in his voice and she took an involuntary step back. "What are you talking about?" She forced the words past a sudden throat tightening rush of fear. "I just assumed you'd be able to sense . . ." Then she remembered.

"You know there's a very good reason most vampires come from the nobility, a crypt is a lot easier to get out of. I'd been buried good and deep and it took Christina three days to find me and dig me free."

She wet her lips and in spite of every instinct that told her to run as he advanced, she held her ground. "Henry, I didn't even think about you being buried. I didn't want an emotional reaction, just a physical one. Jesus Christ, Henry!" She brought her hands up and laid them flat against his chest, beginning to grow angry herself. "I wouldn't mess with my worst enemy's mind that way, let alone a friend's!"

The words penetrated through the red haze and he found he had to believe her. He was left shaken, aghast at how close he had come to loosing the beast. "Vicki . . . I'm sorry."

"It's okay." His cheek felt smooth and cool under her palm. He looked as though he'd frightened himself as much as he had frightened her. "We've all got triggers that cause us to act without thinking."

"And what are yours?" he asked, firmly jamming a civilized mask and a patina of control back into place.

"We haven't got time to go into *that* right now," Vicki snorted. "People'll be coming back in about twelve hours." She jerked her head toward the door, remembering the strain he was under lately, willing to forget the whole incident and go on. "We'd better go check out the offices. This place has told us everything it can."

Henry stood by the office window and looked down at the traffic. He should have known that Vicki would never use him in such a way—use his abilities, yes, but not his fears. Waking every evening to an image of the sun had him on edge and it seemed that the reminder of his burial had shoved him over. How many other reminders would there be, he wondered. Four hundred and fifty odd years of life supplied a great many things to be reminded of.

Perhaps the image *was* an indication that his time had run out, an invitation to a cleaner end than one of gradual loss of self. And if it came to a choice, he would take the fire.

"Ouch! Son of a bitch!"

Henry hid a smile as Vicki careened off a corner of Dr. Rax's desk, thoughts of death temporarily banished by the current condition of his life. As Vicki flicked on the desk lamp, he moved away from the window. "Are you sure that's safe?"

"Of course I'm sure," Vicki told him, rubbing the front of her thigh and blinking owlishly. "If anyone sees the light they'll assume someone's working late, but if they see the flashlight beam," she snapped it off and dropped it into the cavernous depths of her purse as she spoke, "they'll assume a break-in."

"They teach you that at the police academy?"

"Not likely. Back when I was in uniform, a habitual criminal named Weasel took it on himself to further my education."

"Isn't that a little counterproductive on his part?" Henry asked, walking over to the desk. "Letting the cops know his secrets?"

"Oh, Weasel wasn't a bad fellow. His definition of personal property was just a bit loose." She sat down and scanned the desktop. "Now then, what have we here . . ."

"What are you looking for?"

"I'll tell you when I . . . hello." The large book sitting half on and half off the blotter had a number of pages crumpled and folded under as though the book had been dropped and then hastily shut without any regard for its condition. *"Ancient Egyptian Gods and Goddesses, Third Edition."* She opened it to the folds and pulled it directly under the pool of light, scowling at the unpronounceable names. "I wonder if Dr. Rax was looking something up the night he died."

"Is there an illustration in there that looks like this?" Henry handed her the desk calendar. The top page still read Monday, October 19th. Dr. Rax hadn't seen October 20th.

Vicki squinted at the sketch under the date. It looked like some weird combination of a deer's body and a bird's head. Then she turned back to the book.

"Here it is. Pretty good likeness, too, if he was doing it from memory. Akhekh? This guy needs another vowel . . ." She rubbed a hand over the back of her neck and found herself looking up at Henry for reassurance. She felt like a fool when she realized he stood beyond her severely limited range of vision and bent her head to continue reading. "Akhekh, a predynastic god of upper Egypt absorbed into the conqueror's religion to become a form of the evil god Se . . . Fuck!" Slamming the book closed she sat panting, eyes wide, staring at something Henry couldn't see.

"Vicki?" He grabbed her shoulders and shook her, hard enough to break through the blank expression. "What happened?"

She blinked, frowned, and checked to make sure she could still move her head. "Whiplash, I think."

"Vicki!" He shook her again, not as hard but a little more emphatically.

Wetting her lips, she shot a glance at the book. "The eyes on the diagram, they were red. Glowing. They looked right at me."

He moved his shoulders under the silk shirt and smiled at his reflection. The feeling pleased him. This century had much to offer those with the ability to appreciate it. When he finished his restructuring, it would truly be a paradise.

Missing the institution of slavery, and its simplicity of service, he had effectively enslaved the hotel manager and two of his assistants. Their ka had submitted so completely to his, they had very little independence left. It was only a small beginning, but he had plenty of time.

The Solicitor General, with whom he had spent another productive afternoon, was under a similar depth of control. As it was necessary—at least for a time—that the man be able to function independently without arousing suspicion, the application of that control worked on a number of very subtle levels and responded to a myriad of external clues. He was to provide the men and women who would be sworn to Akhekh, their ka going to build power in the heavens even as they gathered power on Earth.

He saw the red glow in the mirror a heartbeat before his reflection faded and he stared instead at the image of his god.

High priest of my new order, it said.

Arms crossed over his breast, he bowed, centuries of practice keeping his distaste from showing. "My lord?"

Open your ka to me. I have marked the first of those who will provide me with sustenance.

Vicki ducked out from behind the blackout curtain and pulled the bedroom door closed, suppressing a shudder as she thought of Henry, stretched out immobile on the bed. Although she wasn't usually inclined to dwell on the past, the afternoon spent waiting for him to wake had made an impression that showed no signs of fading. He seemed to show no desire to immolate himself this morning, but she recognized—last night's little adventure had forced her to recognize—that his nerves were stretched to the breaking point.

"Vampires shouldn't have nerves," she muttered, stepping into the living room and lifting her face to the dawn. It infuriated her that she could do nothing for him but watch and wait.

Yawning, she pulled off her glasses and rubbed at her eyes. Getting out of the museum had been a lot less complicated than getting in; Henry had simply caught the guard's eye, then the two of them had walked right on by. Vicki hadn't been able to stop herself from muttering, *"These are not the droids you're looking for."* Unfortunately, she hadn't managed much sleep after they got back to Henry's condo. Dreams of ancient Egyptian gods and human sacrifice kept jerking her awake. Promising herself a good long nap later in the day, she collapsed into a red velvet armchair and reached for the phone. If Celluci wasn't awake by now, he should be.

He answered on the second ring.

"Celluci."

"Morning, Detective. You awake enough to hear some news?"

She heard him swallow and in her mind's eye could see him standing rumpled and unshaven in the tiny kitchen of his house in Downsview. "Good news or bad?"

"I got both. Which do you want first?"

"Give me the good news, I could use some."

"You aren't crazy. There *was* a mummy in that coffin and it now seems to be roaming around Toronto."

"Great." He swallowed again. "And the bad news?"

"There was a *mummy* in that coffin and it now seems to be roaming around Toronto."

"Very funny. When I want to know who's on first, I'll ask. How are you going to find it?"

Vicki sighed. "I don't know," she admitted. "But I'll think of something. Maybe I should find a reason for Trembley and her partner being killed when the staff at the ROM were only . . . uh, mind-wiped."

"Maybe I should have another talk with Dr. Shane."

"Well, why not. She already seems to be mistakenly impressed." *Idiot! I don't believe I said that.* Vicki smacked herself in the head with her free hand. *Brain first, mouth second!*

She could hear his eyebrows rise. "When did you meet Dr. Shane?"

"Yesterday at the museum." Not telling him would only cause him to jump to the asinine conclusion she'd been checking up on him. "During my investigation of your mummy."

"Right."

The smile in his voice set her teeth on edge. "Fuck off, Celluci. It's too early in the morning for that shit. Call me if she has anything useful to say." She hung up before he could answer.

"He thinks I'm jealous," she told her reflection in the glossy black side of Henry's stereo cabinet. "Why should I be jealous of Rachel Shane when I haven't been jealous of any of the busty bimbettes he's bounced over the years?"

"Because Dr. Shane is a lot like you?" her reflection suggested.

She flipped it the finger and dragged herself up out of the chair. "It is *really* too early in the morning for this."

It had stopped raining, but the sky looked low enough to touch and a cold west wind had chased Vicki all the way down College Street to Police Headquarters. After a long nap and a leisurely breakfast of canned ravioli, she'd realized that Inspector Cantree's speaking to the Chief about a routine departmental matter still bothered her.

"And it's not like I have any other leads," she reminded herself, waiting for the light at Bay. Across the street, Headquarters loomed like an art deco Lego set. A number of people hated it, but Vicki thought it looked cheerful and had always appreciated the image/reality contrast.

She paused for a moment on the steps. Although she'd been back a couple of times in the fourteen months since she'd left the force, it had always been to one of the safe areas, like the morgue or forensics, never to homicide. To get to Inspector Cantree's office, she'd have to run the gauntlet through the entire homicide department. Where someone else would be using her desk. Where old friends and colleagues would still be fighting to keep the city from going down the sewer.

Where none of them can do the job you're doing now against a threat just as real. That helped. She glanced at her watch—twelve twenty-seven. "Oh, hell." She squared her shoulders and reached for the door. "Maybe they'll all be out for lunch."

They weren't, but the big office was empty enough that Vicki, her visitor's pass hanging off her lapel like a scarlet letter, only saw two people she knew—and one of them barely had time to call a greeting before he had to turn his attention back to the phone. Unfortunately, person number two had time on his hands.

"Well, well, well. If it isn't Victory Nelson, returning to the fold."

"Hey, Sid." Although a number of the other women on the force had complained that he was a bit of a tomcat, Vicki had nothing personal against Detective Sidney Austen. Professionally, she thought he didn't take his job seriously enough and was a little surprised to see him still in homicide. "How's it going?"

He perched on the edge of his desk and grinned at her. "You know the drill; overworked and underpaid." She saw him noting the thickness of her glasses, wondering how much she could see. "So, what did you do with your seeing eye dog?"

"I made stew."

His shout of laughter drowned out the grinding of her teeth. "Seriously, Victory, how's life as a private investigator?"

"Not so bad."

"Yeah? Celluci says you're doing pretty good."

Trust Celluci to issue bulletins. "I'm managing."

"I hear a couple of the others have tossed a few cases your way, too." He recognized her expression and hurriedly spread his hands. "Hey, I didn't mean that the way it sounded."

"I'm sure you didn't." Her smile felt tight.

Sid shook his head. "Jesus. It doesn't seem like you've been gone more than a year. You could come back right now and it'd be like you were never away. Speaking of which," he pulled his brows down in an exaggerated frown, "how come you haven't been back more often? You know, just dropping in and touching base?"

Because it sticks a knife in my heart and twists it, you asshole. But she couldn't say that to him. Instead, she shrugged and asked, "If you got out of this shithole, would you come back?" knowing he'd misunderstand the edge on her voice. "I've got to go. The Inspector's expecting me."

Stepping into Inspector Cantree's office was like stepping into the past. How many times had she gone through that door? A hundred? A thousand? A hundred thousand? The last time, just before she left, they'd both been painfully polite. The memory hurt but not so much as she'd feared. She had a new life now and the place where they'd amputated the old had pretty much scarred over.

"Welcome back, Nelson." Cantree covered the mouthpiece of the phone and jerked his head toward the coffee maker on the filing cabinet. "Get yourself something to drink, I'll be with you in a minute."

The coffee had the thick, black, iridescent look of an oil slick. Vicki half-filled a pressed cardboard cup and added two large spoonfuls of powdered whitener, past experience having taught her that after the first couple of mouthfuls her taste buds would surrender and she'd be able to get the rest down without gagging. Someone had suggested once that offering the Inspector's coffee to suspects might convince them to confess, but the idea had to be abandoned as a potential human rights violation.

"So." Cantree hung up the phone as Vicki pulled a chair closer to the desk and sat down. "It's good to see you again, Nelson." He sounded like he meant it. "I've been following your new career when I can. You've been responsible for a couple of nice convictions along with the lost dogs and cheating husbands. I'm sorry we had to lose you."

"Not as sorry as I was to be lost." She managed a wry smile as she said it.

The Inspector nodded acknowledgment, of both the statement and the delivery. "How *are* the eyes?"

"Still in my head." But as he was one of the four people in the world who she felt was owed an honest answer, she continued, "Piss useless after dark but fully functional in bright light, as long as I'm willing to face the world square on. Peripheral's closed in another twenty-five percent in the last year."

"Could be worse."

"Could be raining!" she snapped and savagely swallowed a mouthful of coffee but, after it seared a trail the length of her esophagus, the pressure of his gaze forced her to add, "All right, it could be worse."

Cantree smiled. "You know you're welcome back any time, but as this is the first you've darkened my door since you turned in your badge, I assume there's a reason for the visit."

"I've been hired to look into the deaths at the ROM and I wondered what you could tell me about them."

"Hired by who?"

Vicki smiled in turn. "I can't tell you that."

"All right, tell me this: Why aren't you picking Celluci's brain."

"Picked clean. And, as he tells me you've taken him off the case, I just wondered why."

"You've never *just wondered* anything in your life, Nelson, but, in view of past services and because I'm a nice guy, I'll tell you what I told him . . ."

As he spoke, Vicki hid a frown. He was telling her *exactly* what he told Celluci, word for word, as though it were something he'd memorized and now repeated by rote. And try as she would, she couldn't get him to expand on it. Finally, she gave up and stood. "Well, thanks for the time and the coffee, but I've got to be . . ." A thick cream-colored envelope, its return address done in embossed gold ink caught her eye. "You going to a wedding?" she asked, picking it up.

"I'm going to a Halloween party at the Solicitor General's." Cantree snatched it out of her hand and Vicki stared at him.

"You're bullshitting me?"

"Wouldn't dream of it." He slapped the envelope down on his blotter. "Apparently the Honorable Member's got some hot new adviser he wants everyone from department heads on up to meet."

"Who?"

"How should I know? I haven't met him yet. Some new guy in town with a lot of big ideas no doubt."

Vicki reached down and twitched the invitation free. "The thirty-first. Next Saturday. Halloween. How nice, it's a costume party." She had an image of Inspector Cantree—who did look remarkably like James Earl Jones—dressed as Thulsa Doom, the villain of the first Conan movie, and hid a smile.

"Sure, nice for you, you haven't been ordered to attend." He grimaced and Vicki barely managed to save her fingers as he swept both invitation and envelope into the top drawer of his desk. "The Chief says we're going, no excuses, and I hear the local OPP boys'll be there as well.

Not to mention the goddamned Solicitor General's entire goddamned department." The grimace hardened into a scowl. "Just the way I look forward to spending a Saturday night, talking shop with a bunch of politicians and political cops."

"And very powerful people . . ." She caught the Inspector's expression and grinned, masking a sudden rush of apprehension. "I see you at least got enough notice to get your loins properly girded."

"You leave my loins out of this. And the damn thing came by special courier this morning."

"Special courier? Don't you find that a little strange?"

He snorted. "Ours is not to reason why . . ." The rest of the quote got lost in the shrilling of the phone and she mouthed, *I'll see myself out,* as she backed toward the door.

Out on the street, Vicki looked back at Headquarters and shook her head. *I've got a bad feeling about this.*

Sometimes, only a cliché seemed adequate.

Eight

"Did you ever find those papers you misplaced?"

"Papers?" Celluci asked, holding open the restaurant door.

"The papers your cousin came over to the museum for." Dr. Shane shook her head at his blank expression. "You called her yesterday, asked her to check for them at the museum after work . . . ?"

All at once, Celluci understood. "Oh, that cousin. Those papers." He wondered if Vicki had left him in the dark on purpose or if it just hadn't occurred to her to fill him in on their new relationship. "They turned up this afternoon at the office. I guess I should've called to let you know." He tried a charming smile and made a mental note to take care of Vicki later. "I *did* call to ask you to dinner."

"So you did."

She didn't appear particularly charmed, but neither did she appear completely immune.

Celluci was having a little trouble deciding how to approach the evening. Rachel Shane could have information that would help them find and capture the mummy, which meant he'd have to question her and, to complicate matters, he couldn't question her directly or she'd want to know why. He couldn't *tell* her why.

"Look, this is where things stand: the mummy that killed Dr. Rax is now rampaging through the city and we need your knowledge to catch it."

"And where did this mummy come from?"

"The sarcophagus in your workroom."

"But I told you that was empty."

"The mummy messed with your mind."

"Excuse me, waiter, could you call 911? I'm having dinner with a crazy man."

No. Telling her would merely cut off the only source of information they had. A scientist trained to pull knowledge out of bits of old bone and pottery simply wouldn't believe that a few of those old bones got up and committed murder on the say-so of a homicide detective, a smart-mouthed PI, and a . . . a romance writer. She'd need proof and he simply didn't have any.

Telling her would also ensure that he'd never see her again, but with four people dead what she thought of him personally became significantly less important.

When it came right down to it, he needed the information and he'd have to use her interest in him—or, more exactly, her perception of his interest in her—to get it. He'd once watched Vicki pump a man dry by spending two hours batting her eyelashes and interjecting a breathless "Oh really?" into every pause in the conversation. He wouldn't have to sink that low, but even so, Rachel Shane deserved better. God willing, he'd get a chance to make it up to her another time.

As dinner progressed, he had no trouble getting her to talk about herself and her work. The police had long since learned to exploit the human fondness for self-exposure and an amazing number of crimes were solved every year when the perpetrator just couldn't keep quiet any longer and told all. Nor was it difficult to steer the conversation sideways into ancient Egypt.

"I have the feeling," she said as the waiter set desert and coffee on the table, "that I should only have given you my name, rank, and serial number. I haven't been so thoroughly interrogated since I defended my thesis."

Celluci pushed the curl of hair back off his forehead and searched for something to say. He had, perhaps, been probing a little deeply. And he had, perhaps, not been as subtle as he could have been. The desire to be honest kept fighting with the need to be devious. "It's just that it's a relief not to be talking about police work," he told her at last.

A chestnut brow rose. "Now, why don't I believe that," she mused, stirring cream into her coffee. "You're trying to find something out, something important to you." Lifting her chin, she looked him squarely in the eye. "You'd find out a lot faster if you'd come right out and asked me. And then you wouldn't have wasted an evening."

"I don't consider the evening to be a waste," he protested.

"Ah. Then you found out what you needed to know."

"Damnit, Vicki, don't twist my words!"

Both brows rose, their movement cutting the silence to shreds. "Vicki?"

He *did* say Vicki. Oh, shit. "She's an old colleague. We argue a lot. It just seems natural that a protest like that would have her name attached."

The brows remained up.

Celluci sighed and spread his hands in surrender. "Rachel, I'm sorry. You were right, I did need information, but I can't tell you why."

"Why not?" The brows were down, but the tone was decidedly cool.

"It would put you in too much danger." He waited for her protest, and when it didn't come he realized he was waiting for Vicki's protest.

"Does this have anything to do with Dr. Rax's death?"

"Only indirectly."

"I thought you were taken off the case."

He shrugged. Anything he said at this point could give her ideas and telling her about hiring Vicki—not to mention Vicki's supernatural sidekick—would only complicate things further.

"You know I'll help in any way I can."

Most of the people Celluci met divided the man and the cop into two very neat and separate packages. Certain subtle differences in tone and bearing indicated Rachel Shane had just closed the first package and opened the second.

She kept him in police officer mode for the rest of the evening, and when he dropped her off at her condo he had to admit that, although he felt like he'd just finished Archaeology 101, as far as dates went, it hadn't been exactly a success. She obviously had no intention of inviting him in.

"Thank you for dinner, Mike."

"You're welcome. Can I call you again?"

"Well, I tell you what." She looked up at him, her expression speculative. "You decide you want to see me and not the Assistant Curator of the Royal Ontario Museum's Department of Egyptology *and* you dump the hidden agendas and I'll think about it." Tossing a half smile back over her shoulder, she went into the building.

Celluci shook his head and slid back into his car. In a number of ways Rachel reminded him of Vicki. Only not quite so . . . so . . .

"So Vicki," he decided at last, pulling out of the driveway and turning east toward Huron Street without really thinking. It wasn't until he was searching for a parking space, which was, as usual, in short supply around Vicki's apartment, that he wondered what the hell he was doing.

He drove twice more around the block before a space opened up and he decided he didn't need an excuse for being here; he didn't even particularly need a reason.

When Vicki heard the key in the lock, she knew it had to be Celluci and, for one brief moment, she entertained two completely opposing reactions. By the time he got the door open, she'd managed to force order on the mental chaos and was ready for him.

If he thinks he's going to get sympathy after Dr. Shane dumped him early, he can think again. "What the hell are you doing here?"

"Why?" He threw his jacket over the brass hook in the hall. "Are you expecting Fitzroy?"

"What's it to *you?*" She pushed up her glasses and rubbed at her eyes. "As a matter of fact, I'm not. He's writing tonight."

"Good for him. How long has this coffee been sitting here?"

"About an hour." Settling her glasses back on her nose, she watched him fill a mug and rummage in the fridge for cream. He seemed, well, if she had to put a name to it, she'd say melancholy came closest. *Christ, maybe Dr. Shane broke his heart.* Her own heart gave a curious twist. She ignored it. "So. How went the date?"

He took a swallow of coffee. Two strides brought him across the tiny kitchen and up against the back of Vicki's chair. "It went. What's with all the books?"

"Research. Believe it or not, a history degree is appallingly short on coverage of ancient Egypt."

Behind her, Celluci snorted. "You're not going to find much help from historians."

Vicki tilted her head back and smiled smugly up at him. "That's why I'm researching myths and legends. So, uh, Dr. Shane didn't respond to the celebrated Celluci charm? Guaranteed to get a confession at fifty paces?"

He pushed her head forward, put down the coffee cup, and dug his fingers into her shoulders. "I didn't turn it on."

She sucked in a sudden breath; part pain, part pleasure. "Why not?" *This is kind of like picking a scab,* she decided. *Once you get started, it's hard to stop.*

"Because she deserved better. Bad enough I spent the evening under false pretenses. I had no intention of compounding it. Christ, you're tense."

"It's not tension, it's muscle tone. What do you mean, she deserved better? You've got a lot of faults, Celluci, but I never thought false modesty was—ouch—one of them."

"She deserved honesty. She deserved to have me thinking of her, not of how much she could tell me."

Well, as my mother always says, if you don't want to know, don't ask. "You liked her."

"Don't be an ass, Vicki. I wouldn't have asked her out to dinner if I didn't like her—I could have picked her brains in her office a hell of a lot more cheaply. I find her attractive, intelligent, self-confident . . ."

Of course, the trouble with picking scabs is when you get deep enough they start to bleed.

". . . and, as a result, I found I spent most of the evening thinking about you." He gave her shoulders a final dig, picked up his coffee, and went into the living room.

Vicki opened her mouth, closed it, and tried to sort out some kind of response. From the beginning, they'd never talked about their relationship; they'd accepted it; they'd left it alone. When they got back together last spring, it had been under those same parameters. *That son of a bitch is changing the rules . . .* But beneath the protest she recognized a surge of relief. *He spent most of the evening thinking about me.* And beneath the relief, a hint of panic. *Now what?*

He was waiting for her to say something but she didn't know what to say. *Oh, God, please, send a distraction!*

The knock on the door jerked her around so fast her glasses slid down her nose. "Come in."

"I asked for a distraction, not a disaster," she muttered a moment later.

Celluci snapped the recliner forward. "I thought you were supposed to be writing tonight," he growled, standing and scowling down the hall.

Henry smiled, deliberately provoking. He had known Celluci was in the apartment before he knocked; he could hear his voice, his movements, his heartbeat. But the mortal had the days; he would not have the darkness as well. "I was writing. I finished."

"Another book?" The word book came out as if it were something that turned up on the soles of shoes after a brisk walk through a barnyard.

"No." He hung his trench coat up beside Celluci's jacket. "But I finished the work I intended to do tonight."

"Must be nice as it isn't quite midnight. Still, it's not like it's real work."

"Well, I'm sure it's not as strenuous as taking someone out to dinner, then maintaining the illusion that you're interested in her when you're really only interested in what she knows."

Celluci shot a furious look at Vicki, who winced and said hurriedly, "Low blow, Henry. Mike had to do that, he didn't want to."

Henry moved into the kitchen, which put the two men, although in separate rooms, less than ten feet apart with Vicki, still sitting at the table, squarely between them. He inclined his head graciously. "You're quite right. It was a low blow. And I apologize."

"The fuck you do."

"Are you calling me a liar?" Henry's voice had gone deceptively soft; the voice of a man who had been raised to command, the voice of a man with centuries of experience behind him.

Celluci couldn't help but respond. His anger didn't have a snowflake's chance in hell of making an impression against the other man and he knew it. "No." he forced the words out through clenched teeth. "I'm not calling you a liar."

Vicki looked from one to the other and had a strong desire to go out for pizza. The currents running between the two were so strong that when the phone rang she felt she had to fight against their pull to answer it.

"Hi, honey. It's after eleven and the rates are down so I thought I'd give you a call before I turned in."

Just what the evening needed. "Bad timing, Mom."

"Why? What's wrong?"

"I've, uh, got company."

"Oh." While not exactly disapproving, the two letters carried a disproportionate amount of conversational weight. "Michael or Henry, dear?"

"Uh . . ." Vicki knew the moment she paused that it was a mistake. Her mother excelled at reading silence.

"*Both* of them?"

"Trust me, Mom, it wasn't my idea." She frowned. "Are you laughing?"

"I wouldn't think of it."

"You *are* laughing."

"I'll call you tomorrow, dear. I can't wait to hear how this comes out."

"Mother, don't hang . . ." Vicki glared at the receiver, then slammed it back down onto the phone. "Well, I hope you're happy." She shot up out of the chair and kicked it back out of her way. "I'm going to be hearing about this for the rest of my life." Glaring from Celluci to Henry and back, she raised her voice an octave. "*Don't say I didn't warn you, dear. Well, what do you expect when you're seeing two young men . . .* I'll tell you what I expect, I expect you both to act like intelligent humans beings and not like two dogs squabbling over a bone. I can't see any reason why all three of us can't get along!"

"You can't?" Henry asked, mildly incredulous.

Vicki, recognizing sarcasm, turned on him and snapped, "Shut up, Henry!"

"She always was a lousy liar," Celluci muttered.

"And you can shut up, too!" She took a deep breath and shoved her glasses up her nose. "Now then, seeing as we're all here together, I think we should be discussing the case. Do either of you have any problems with that?"

Celluci snorted. "I wouldn't dare."

Henry spread his hands, his meaning plain.

They moved into the living room, all three of them aware this was only a postponement. That was fine with Vicki; if they had things to work out between them, they could do it without her in the line of fire.

". . . so there's no obvious reason why it murdered Trembley and her partner but only mind-wiped the people at the museum." Celluci took another swallow of coffee, grimaced at the taste, and continued. "The only difference between the two cases is that the people at the museum spent three days close to it while Trembley saw it for maybe three minutes."

"So maybe it takes time and proximity to mess with someone's head." Vicki chewed thoughtfully on the end of her pencil for a moment then spit it out and added, "I wonder why it killed that custodian?"

Celluci shrugged. "Because it could? Maybe it was just flexing its muscles after being cooped up for so long."

"Maybe it was hungry." Henry leaned forward to make his point. "The custodian just happened to be closest when it came fully awake."

"Then what did it eat?" Celluci sneered. "There wasn't a mark on that body and there sure as shit wasn't anything missing."

Henry sat back and let the shadows in the corner of the living room cover him again. "That's not quite accurate. When the custodian was found, he was missing his life."

"And you think this mummy *ate* it?"

"Mortals have always had legends of those who extend their own lives by devouring the lives of others."

"Yeah, and those are *legends.*"

The shadows couldn't hide Henry's pointed smile. "So am I. So, for that matter, are mummies who walk. And demons. And werewolves . . ."

"All right, all right! I get the idea." Celluci shoved one hand up through his hair. He really hated all this supernatural bullshit. Why him? Why not Detective Henderson? Henderson wore a crystal on a leather thong, for Christ's sake. And how come before Vicki got mixed up with Fitzroy the closest thing to a supernatural occurrence in the city was when the Leafs managed to win two in a row? *Just because* you *don't see something doesn't mean it's not there.*

Okay, so he knew the answer to that one. He sighed and wondered how many previously unsolved crimes could be attributed to ghoulies and ghosties and things that went bump in the night. As much as he might want to, he couldn't blame this whole mess on Fitzroy. "So, why did it kill Dr. Rax?"

"It was still hungry and Dr. Rax came into the workroom alone."

"But it must've known that two bodies dying in the same place the same way would start an investigation. Why go to all the trouble to hide its tracks and then do something so stupid?"

"Dr. Rax discovered it as it was leaving and it overreacted."

"Oh, great," Vicki rolled her eyes, "an impulsive mummy." She yawned and resettled her glasses with the end of her pencil. "At least we know it can make mistakes. Unfortunately, it looks like its god survived as well."

Celluci's brows climbed for his hairline. "And how do we know that?"

"Last night at the museum . . ."

"Wait a minute," Celluci held up his hand. "You went to the museum last night? After closing? You broke into the Royal Ontario Museum. . . . *He* might not be aware of this," Celluci jabbed a finger at Henry then swung around to glare at Vicki, "but *you* know damn well that's against the law."

Vicki sighed. "Look, we didn't break in anywhere; we didn't disturb anything; we had a quick look around. It's late, I'm tired. If you're not going to arrest me, just drop it." She paused, knowing there wasn't a thing Celluci could do but accept it, smiled, and continued. "We found a sketch on Dr. Rax's desk, then found a corresponding illustration in a book of ancient gods and goddesses, also on Dr. Rax's desk.

"So?"

"The illustration looked at me." She swallowed and tucked the pencil behind an ear so she could wipe palms gone suddenly damp on her jeans. "Its eyes glowed red and it looked at me."

Celluci snorted. "How much light was in the room?"

"I know what I saw, Mike." Her eyes narrowed. "And RP does *not* cause hallucinations."

He studied her face for a moment, then he nodded. "Does this god have a name?"

"Yeah. Akh. . . ."

Henry's hand was tightly clamped over her mouth before either of them saw him move. "When you call the gods by name," he said softly, "you attract their attention. *Not* a good idea."

He dropped his hand and Celluci waited for the explosion; Vicki, more than most, didn't take well to being summarily silenced. When no explosion occurred, he could only assume that she felt Fitzroy's action justified and a shiver of disquiet ran down his spine. If this ancient god had Victory Nelson spooked, he didn't want to run into it.

Vicki, her fingers still wrapped around Henry's wrist, wet her lips and tried not to think of those burning eyes taking a longer look. After a moment, she let go. "I think we can safely assume, that . . . this god and the mummy are connected."

"The mummy is probably the god's high priest," Celluci suggested. When Vicki and Henry both turned to stare, he shrugged. "Hey, I watch horror movies."

"Not exactly a credible source for research," Henry pointed out as he returned to his chair in the shadows.

"Yeah, well, we don't all have Count Dracula as a close personal friend."

"Gentlemen, it's going on two in the morning; can we get on with this before I fall over?" Vicki yawned and leaned back in the recliner. "As it happens, I think Celluci's right."

"Oh, joyous day," he muttered.

She ignored him. "The wheels on Trembley's car were turned, but the car continued to move in a straight line. That only happens if some outside force is applied. There *was* no visible outside force. According to the books I've been reading, priests of ancient Egypt were also wizards."

"You're saying the mummy killed Trembley with magic?" Celluci asked incredulously.

"All the pieces fit."

In the silence that followed, the sound of the kitchen tap dripping away the seconds could be clearly heard.

"Oh, what the hell," Celluci sighed. "I've already believed seven impossible things before breakfast, what's one more."

"So," Vicki ticked the points off on her fingers as she listed them, "what we're trying to find is the reanimated wizard-priest of a god who may or may not live on the life force of others, who can twist the minds of those near to it, and who can magically kill at a distance."

"Great." Celluci yawned into his fist. "And in this corner, the Three Stooges."

"Nyuk, nyuk, nyuk," Henry agreed.

Vicki jerked forward and stared at Henry in horror while Celluci gave him something close to a nod of approval. "I don't believe this," she muttered. Vicki had a theory that the Three Stooges did sex-linked comedy as she'd never known a woman who thought they were funny. This just proved her theory as Y chromosomes were about the only thing Henry and Celluci had in common. *Vampires are supposed to have more taste!* "If we could get back on topic, maybe you two would like to hear the rest of it."

Celluci, who dearly wanted to do one routine just to provoke a reaction from Vicki, decided against it when he realized who he'd have to do the routine with. The Stooges were something you did with your buddies, not with . . . romance writers. "Go on," he growled.

Henry merely nodded. He no more wanted something in common with Celluci than Celluci wanted with him. *Except, of course, the one thing that neither of us is willing to give up . . .*

"Okay . . ." A yawn cut her off and, although she'd slept for a while in the early evening, Vicki knew that if she didn't fall over soon there'd be no way she'd be conscious for dawn. *Let's wrap this up fast and get to bed.* "Okay, ignoring the wizard aspect for the moment, what is it that priests want? Congregations. Because their gods want followers. And I think I know the congregation this god's trying for." While Celluci's face grew dark, she outlined her meeting with Inspector Cantree. "It's after the police force, not just in Toronto but across the province. Its own private little army and the perfect start to a secular power base."

"Why would a god have any interest in acquiring a secular power base?" Henry asked.

Vicki snorted. "Don't ask me, ask the Catholic Church.

·Look, the god wants the congregation, the *priest* wants the power base—somehow, all things considered, I can't see this guy as altruistic—and the police provide both."

"Then why across the province? Why not begin with just the city?"

"Cities aren't autonomous enough, they're too tightly controlled by higher levels of government. But if you control a province, you control a country within a country. Look at Quebec . . ."

"Weak, Vicki, very weak," Celluci snarled, finally giving his anger voice, unsure which infuriated him more, that the mummy would dare to subvert the police or that Vicki thought it could be done. "You have no proof that this new adviser is the mummy."

"I have a hunch," Vicki told him, her voice edged. "That's what you started with and look where it's gotten us. Cantree's repeating messages from the Chief like they were holy writ. You know that's not like him." They locked gazes. When Celluci looked away, Vicki continued. "One of us has to go to the Solicitor General's party on Saturday."

"One of us?" Henry asked quietly.

"All right, you." Snapping the recliner upright, Vicki laid her forearms across her knees. "Over half the people there would know Mike or me, so neither of us can do it. Besides, it's invitation only and you're good at getting past . . ."

"Social obstacles," he supplied when she paused. "You're right. I'll have to do it."

"What if Vicki's wrong and the mummy isn't there?"

Henry shrugged. "Then I'll leave early, no harm done."

"And if she's right?"

Henry smiled. "Then I'll take care of it."

Celluci remembered a dark barn and pale fingers closing around the throat of a man with only seconds to live. He averted his eyes from the smile. "You think you're up to this wizard-priest?"

Actually, he had no idea, but he wasn't about to let Celluci know that. "I am not without resources."

"Then it's settled." Vicki stood and stretched, snapping the kinks out of her spine. "This little session has been very useful. We'll all get together after the party and talk again. Thank you both for coming. Go home." She made it pretty obvious who she meant.

"I'll be there just before dawn," she told Henry at the door, dropping her voice too low for Celluci to hear. "Don't start without me."

He lifted her hand and lightly kissed the inside of her wrist. "I wouldn't dream of it," he told her softly and was gone.

Celluci came out of the bathroom and reached for his jacket. "I'm on stakeout for the next few nights, so I won't be around, but when this is over you and I have to talk."

"What about?"

He reached over and with one finger, gently slid her glasses up her nose. "What do you think?" The same finger dropped down to trace the line of her jaw.

"Mike, you know . . ."

"I know." He moved out into the hall. "But we're still going to talk."

The door closed behind him and Vicki collapsed against it, fumbling for the lock. For the next few hours, all she wanted was a chance to sleep. For the next few days, she'd concentrate on stopping the mummy. And after that . . .

"Oh, hell," she stumbled into the bedroom, yanking her sweatshirt off over her head. "After that, maybe something'll come up . . ."

He wanted the dawns he remembered where a great golden disk rose into an azure sky, burning the shadows away from the desert until each individual grain of sand blazed with light. He wanted to feel the heat lapping against his shoulders and the stone still cool from the darkness against the soles of his feet. This northern dawn was a pallid imitation, a pale circle of a sun barely showing through a leaden sky. He shivered and walked in off the balcony.

Soon he would have to deal with the woman his god had chosen. Over the next few days he would use the key to her ka that he had been given and lift the manner of her despair off the surface of her mind.

His lord never demanded death, feeding instead on the lesser, self-perpetuating energies generated by the darker aspects of life. In time, of course, the chosen ones usually prayed for an ending. Occasionally, they achieved it.

Nine

Those outside of political circles who thought about the Ontario government at all thought only of Queen's Park, the massive red sandstone, copper-roofed building anchoring the north end of University Avenue. Although it *was* the building where the provincial parliament actually sat, the real work got done in the blocks of office towers to the east. At 25 Grosvenor Street, between Bay and Yonge, the Office of the Solicitor General was about as far east as the government went.

Vicki squinted up at the building with distaste. It wasn't that she disliked the pink concrete tower—even though from the east or west it looked like it had been extruded from a Play-Doh modern architecture toy set—it was just that the three extra blocks from Queen's Park, while not far enough to take transit, had been long enough for her right foot to find a puddle and get soaked.

"Toronto in October. Christ. Any mummy in its right mind would hop the first Air Egyptian flight home." She sighed as she passed the sculpture outside the main entrance. It looked like a set of giant, aluminum prison bars, bent out of shape, and she'd never understood the symbolism.

Nodding at the special constable on duty at the information desk, she crossed the lobby to the cul de sac that held the elevators. Of the half dozen spotlights in the ceiling, only two were working, dropping the area into an amber-hued twilight. As far as Vicki was concerned, they might as well all have been off.

Some fair-haired wunderkind probably thought this up as a way of saving money—just before his monthly raise. She dragged her hand along the marble facing on the wall, across the stainless steel door, and finally to the plastic plate that held the call button. *Let's hope they left the lights on inside the cars or I'll never know when one arrives.*

They had. Although her eyes watered violently in the sudden glare, the reaction was preferable to groping her way into an elevator shaft. Besides, after a ten-block walk in pissing rain, she was already wet.

The Solicitor General's suite was on the eleventh floor and, as government offices went, bordered on palatial. Power colors and a conservative/modern design were intended to both offend the least number of voters and impress the most. Vicki recognized symbolic decorating when she saw it and knew full well that behind closed doors on this floor and others, utilitarian cubicles carried the workload.

"Can I help?"

The young woman at the desk served the same function as the decor—to impress and reassure. Vicki, who hated being pleasant to strangers, wouldn't have had her job for twice the money. "I hope so. My name is Nelson, I have an appointment with Mr. Zottie at one-thirty." She checked her watch. "I'm a little early."

"No problem, Ms. Nelson. Please, go on in."

She's good, Vicki mused, passing through the indicated double doors. *Even watching for it, I barely saw her check the list.*

The woman at the inner desk, while still impressive, was not the least bit reassuring. "Mr. Zottie will see you in a moment, Ms. Nelson. Please, have a seat."

It was considerably more than a moment before the door to the Solicitor General's office opened. Vicki tried not to fidget while she waited. The weekend had passed as a non-event, their only leads unavailable. Each morning she'd tucked Henry in—unsure if she should worry that the dream continued or be grateful that it remained only a dream and he still showed no sign of seeking the sun—then went home and did laundry, a little grocery shopping, called her mother, and marked time. First thing this morning, she'd pulled a few strings to get this appointment.

"Ms. Nelson?" Solicitor General George Zottie was a

not very tall, not very slim, middle-aged man with a full head of dark hair, heavy dark brows, and long dark eyelashes. "Sorry to keep you waiting."

He had the firm, quick handshake of someone who'd spent time out from behind a desk and Vicki, who despised politicians on principle, considered him to be one of the best. A combination of personal integrity and a sincere respect from the combined police forces he was responsible for had kept him in this top cabinet position for his last two terms of office. If the current government won the next election, which seemed certain, his third term was pretty much assured.

Vicki had met him three times while she'd been on the force, the last occasion only eight months before her failing eyesight forced her to quit. They'd spoken for a few moments after the presentation ceremony and that conversation had given Vicki the idea that had gotten her in to see him today; a plan to raise the profile of the police force in both elementary and high schools. In fact, it was such a good idea that she was half convinced to pursue it once the mummy threat had been taken care of. Provided, of course, that the good guys won.

That conversation would also give her a basis for judging his—stability? reality? For judging how much of a hold the mummy already had. Or if it had any kind of a hold at all. Anything she found out today would help to arm Henry for Saturday night.

Following the Solicitor General into his office, she had a quick look around. With next to no peripheral vision she couldn't be subtle about it, but she figured he should be used to first time visitors rubbernecking. Unfortunately, if the mummy had been visiting, it had left no easily discernible signs. No bits of rotting bandage, no little piles of sand, not even a statue of the sphinx with a clock in its tummy.

"Now then," he settled himself behind his desk and waved her into a chair, "about this proposal of yours . . ."

Vicki pulled a pair of file folders out of her bag and handed him one. As she spoke she watched his eyes, his hands, his overall bearing, trying to spot some indication that he was being influenced, if not controlled, by a millennia-old wizard-priest. He didn't seem nervous. If anything, he seemed calmer than he had at the police reception where he'd spent the evening twitching at the collar of his jacket.

I suppose giving up your conscious will might calm you down, she allowed as she finished up the presentation. *But then, so would cutting back the caffeine.*

"Very interesting." The Solicitor General nodded thoughtfully and made a quick notation across the top of the first page. Vicki's eyes weren't up to reading his reversed handwriting although she squinted down at it while he continued. "Have you discussed this with public relations?"

"No, sir. I thought I'd try to get your support first."

"Well," he stood and came around the desk, "I'll have a look at your written proposal and get back to you say, late next week?"

"That would be fine, sir." Vicki stood as well and slid her own copy back into her bag. *Let's just hope we haven't all had our lives sucked out our noses by then.* "Thank you for taking the time to listen."

"Always willing to listen to a good idea." He paused at the door to smile up at her. "And that *was* a good idea. A little visible law and order at an early age might tarnish the appeal of petty crime. I'm very interested in raising the police profile in the province's schools."

"Yes, sir, I know." She slipped past him. "That's why I'm here."

His smile broadened. "It was a pity you had to leave the force, Ms. Nelson; you were one of the best. How many citations was it? Two?"

"No, sir. Three."

"Yes, good job. I can't imagine civilian life suits you as well."

"Not as well, no." She adjusted her glasses and forced the corners of her mouth up. "But it's been . . . interesting."

"Glad to hear it."

Vicki let the closing door cut off her smile and, shrugging her bag onto her shoulder, she crossed the outer office, conscious of disapproving eyes on her back. *Give it a break, lady,* she thought upon safely reaching the reception area, *before I forget which side I'm on and stuff my white hat up your nose.*

The visit could pretty much be considered a wasted effort; if George Zottie *was* being controlled by the mummy, she couldn't see it. *Which may mean nothing more than it's a subtle son of a bitch. God, what I wouldn't give for a nice simple divorce case right about now, one where you start out with a photograph of the bad guy* . . .

The elevator chimed and she hurried to catch it before someone called it away. At first, she thought the man who pushed his way out as the doors opened was drunk, but an instant later she realized he was actually unwell. His skin had a grayish cast, sweat beaded his upper lip and forehead. One long-fingered, exquisitely manicured hand crushed his cashmere overcoat toward his stomach, the other groped blindly at the air.

Vicki ducked under the moving arm and deftly guided him toward a chair. Fortunately he wasn't much larger than she was as, during the moment between standing and sitting, his entire weight came down on her shoulders. He murmured something in a language she didn't know, but as his looks placed his ethnic background in north Africa, Vicki assumed it was Arabic.

Recognizing his condition could be adding years to her estimate, she placed his age at somewhere between thirty and forty. His facial features were uninspiring—two eyes, a nose, and a rather thin-lipped mouth in the usual arrangement—but even sick and unfocused as he was, he had a perceptible force of personality.

Attempting to hold him steady, Vicki jerked around at an unfamiliar noise behind her and saw that the receptionist had just finished pulling back the thick maroon curtains that covered a wall of windows. With a convulsive shudder, the stranger fixed his gaze on the view—gray skies, the Coroner's Building, made of more pink extruded concrete, and a little farther on Police Headquarters—and seemed to relax.

Frowning, Vicki let the receptionist adroitly take her place as ministering angel. As far as she could see, there wasn't anything especially comforting out the . . . Then she had it. "He's claustrophobic, isn't he?"

"Very." The young woman had undone the top two buttons of the overcoat. "The elevator is sheer terror for him."

"Yet he still uses it . . ."

"He's *very* brave." Her expression grew slightly misty.

"That will be enough, Ms. Evans." The older woman from the inner office advanced purposefully across the dark gray carpet, lowered brows demanding to know what Vicki was doing so close to such an important visitor. "Please, Mr. Tawfik, allow *me*."

Vicki left before she threw up. *Although*, she mused, as she rode down in an elevator that suddenly seemed a lot smaller than it had, *if this thing causes that violent a reaction and he keeps using it, he is very brave. Or moderately masochistic.* While she had no idea of what sort of diplomatic position the stranger held, she wasn't surprised at the reactions he'd evoked. Something about him, in spite of his condition, reminded her of Henry.

"Is there *anything* I can get you, Mr. Tawfik."

"No. Thank you." Keeping his gaze firmly locked on the window and the space beyond it, he forced his breathing to calm. Gradually his heartbeat slowed and the spasms that twisted his gut into knots eased and finally stopped. He pulled a linen handkerchief from the pocket of his suit, fingers still slightly trembling, and wiped the sweat from his face.

Then he frowned at the two women hovering an arm's length away. "There was a third . . ."

"Merely a visitor, Mr. Tawfik. No one for *you* to concern yourself about."

"I shall be the judge of that." Even in his distress her ka had held a certain familiarity. A flavor he had not quite been able to identify. "Her name?"

"Nelson," the younger woman offered. "Victoria Nelson. Mr. Zottie knew her from when she was on the police force."

No. Her name meant nothing to him. But he couldn't shake the feeling that he had touched her ka before.

"May I inform Mr. Zottie that you've arrived?"

"You may." He had made it very clear, right from the beginning, that the Solicitor General was not to be called until he had completely recovered. Control must come from strength and a personal weakness would weaken the whole. The women of this culture were trained to nurture weakness, not despise it, and, while in theory he disapproved, he would, in practice, use the attitude. By the time George Zottie had hurried out to the reception area, anxious to escort his newest adviser into the inner sanctum, he had all but recovered from the effects of the elevator. The mild nausea that remained could not be seen, so it did not matter.

Leading the way toward the double doors, he could feel the heat of the younger woman's gaze. She had created her desire from the merest brush across her ka, intended only to ensure her loyalty; he had not placed it there nor did he welcome it. If truth be told, he found the whole concept vaguely distasteful and had found it so for centuries before he'd been interred. The older woman had responded to a show of power—*that* he understood.

His plans for the Solicitor General had required a more thorough remaking.

Once they were alone inside the office with the doors tightly closed behind them, he held out his hand. Zottie, with remarkable grace for a man of his bulk, dropped to one knee and touched his lips to the knuckles. When he rose again, his expression had become almost beatifically calm.

The scribe—the press secretary—had given him the key to Zottie and fifteen hundred years of dealing with bureaucracy had enabled him to use it. He had gone to their first meeting with a spell of confusion ready on his palm. He had passed it through the ceremonial touching, activated it, and with it gained access to the ka. In the past, a man with this much power would have had powerful protections, would have most likely kept a wizard in his employ solely to prevent exactly this sort of manipulation. At times, he still found it difficult to believe that it could be so easy.

There wasn't much of George Zottie left.

With Zottie, he could go one by one to the others he needed to build a base for his power but, with Zottie, that was no longer necessary; they would come to him.

"Has it been done?"

"As you commanded." The Solicitor General lifted a handwritten list off his desk and offered it with a slight bow. "These are the ones who will be in attendance. In spite of the short notice, most of those invited have agreed to come. Shall I *reinvite* the others?"

"No. I can acquire them later." He scanned the list. Only a few of the titles were familiar. That would not do.

"I need a man, an elderly man, one who has spent his life in government but not as a politician. One who knows not only the rules and regulations, but one who knows . . ." The first ka he had taken supplied a phrase and he smiled as he used it. ". . . where the bodies are buried."

"Then you need Brian Morton. There isn't anything or anyone around Queen's Park he doesn't know."

"Take me to him."

". . . an unfortunate occurrence at Queen's Park this afternoon as senior official Brian Morton was found dead at his desk of a heart attack. Morton had been employed by the Ontario Government for forty-two years. Solicitor General George Zottie, in whose ministry Morton was serving at the time of his death, said that he had been an inspiration to younger men and that his knowledge and experience will be missed. Morton's widow expressed the belief that her husband had not been looking forward to his retirement in less than a year and, if given a choice, he would have preferred to die, as he did, with his boots on. Funeral services will be held Monday at Our Lady of the Redeemer Church in Scarborough.

"And now, here's Elaine with the weather."

Vicki frowned and switched off the television. Reid Ellis and Dr. Rax had died of heart failure at the museum. The mummy had come from the museum. Brian Morton died of a heart attack while in the employ of the Solicitor General. She believed the mummy was using the Solicitor General to gain control of the police and build its own private army. Morton was an older man, his death could be coincidence. She didn't think so.

Henry thought the mummy might be feeding. It had been free for a week now; how often did it have to feed?

She pulled the papers for the last week off the "to be recycled" pile to the left of her desk and sat down on her weight bench to read them. *Sudden deaths in public places . . . makes sense to check the tabloids first.*

It took her less than ten minutes to find the first article. Two inches square on the bottom right-hand corner of page twenty-two, it would have been easy to miss except for the headline. "BOY DIES MYSTERIOUSLY ON SUBWAY." The body had been removed from the University Subway line at Osgoode Station, Queen Street, and had been pronounced dead on arrival at Sick Children's Hospital. Cause of death, heart failure. Osgoode was three stops south of Museum. The date was October 20th. The time, nine forty-five. Only hours after Dr. Rax had died and everyone began declaring that the coffin was and always had been empty.

Vicki's hands closed into fists and her fingers punched through the newsprint. The boy had been twelve years old. Teeth clenched, she clipped the article, then slowly and methodically ripped the paper into a thousand tiny pieces.

It was almost three a.m. before she found the second death buried in a story about child care facilities under investigation. On Thursday, October 22nd, a three-year-old had plunged off the top of a play structure at the Sunny view Co-op Daycare and, according to the autopsy, had been dead before hitting the ground. Only one long block along Bloor Street separated the Sunnyview Co-op Daycare from the museum.

Tuesday afternoon, after seeing Henry safely into the day and catching a few hours of sleep, Vicki stood with one hand resting on the chain link fence that surrounded the Daycare Center where the second child had died. *Not much of a barrier,* she thought, rubbing at a wire pebbled with rust. *Not when you add a reanimated evil to all the other dangers of the city.* Although the sky was gray and heavy with moisture, no rain fell and the playground seethed with small people. Here, half a dozen assaulted a tower made of wood and tires and rope while its four defenders shrieked defiance. There, two used the empty cement wading pool as the perfect racetrack. Here, one squatted in rapt contemplation of a puddle. There, three argued the rights of a slide. And through it all, in the spaces between the scenes where Vicki's limited vision couldn't take her, children ran and jumped and played.

There should be one more. She followed the fence up the driveway and, lips tight, entered the building.

". . . all right, the death of a child under her care might drive the rest of the day out of her mind—I'll give her that, I've seen it happen before—but it's the *way* she didn't remember things, Henry. It just didn't ring true."

Henry looked up from the pair of clippings, his face expressionless. "So what do you think happened?"

"She was in the playground, not ten feet from where the child fell. I think she saw it. I think she saw it and it wiped the memory from her mind, just like it did at the museum."

"By *it* you mean . . . ?"

"The mummy, Henry." Vicki finished stamping down another length of the living room and whirled around to start back. "I mean the goddamned mummy!"

"Don't you think you're jumping to conclusions?" He asked the question as neutrally as he could, but even so, it brought her shoulders up and her brows down.

"What the hell do you mean?"

"I mean, children die. For all sorts of reasons. It's sad and it's horrible, but it happens. I was the only one of my mother's children to make it out of early childhood."

"That was the fifteenth century!"

"And in this century children have stopped dying?"

She sighed and her shoulders dropped. "No. Of course not. But Henry . . ." A half dozen quick strides took her across the room to his chair where she dropped to her knees and laid her hands over his. ". . . these two were taken by the mummy. I know that. I don't know how I know it, but I know. Look, cops are trained to observe. We, they, do it all the time, everywhere. They may not consciously recognize everything they see or hear as important, but the subconscious is constantly filtering information until all the bits and pieces add up to a whole." She tightened her grip and lifted her eyes to meet his. "I *know* the mummy took out these two kids."

He held her gaze until her eyes began to water. She felt naked, vulnerable—worth the price if he believed her.

"Perhaps," Henry said thoughtfully at last, finally allowing her to look away, "there are those few who take observing one step further, who can see to the truth. . . ."

"Oh, Christ, Henry." She retrieved the newspaper clippings and stood. "Don't give me any of that New Age metaphysical bullshit. It's training and practice, nothing more."

"If you wish." Over the centuries he'd seen a number of

things that "training and practice" couldn't have accounted for, but as he doubted Vicki would react well to a discussion of those experiences, he let it drop. "So if you're right about the mummy and the children," he said, spreading his hands, "what difference does it make? We're no closer to finding it."

"Wrong." She jabbed the word into the air with a finger. "We know it's staying around the museum and Queen's Park. That gives us an area in which to concentrate a search. We know it's continuing to kill, not just to protect itself from discovery but for other reasons. Feeding, if you wish. We know it's killing children. And that," she snarled, "gives us an incentive to find it and stop it. Quickly."

"Are you going to tell all this to the detective?"

"To Celluci? No." Vicki leaned her forehead against the glass and stared down at the city. She couldn't see a damned thing but darkness; since she'd entered Henry's building, the city might as well have disappeared. "It's my case now. This'll only upset him."

"Very considerate," Henry said dryly. He saw a muscle in her cheek move and the corner of her mouth twitch up a fraction. Her inability to lie to herself was one of the traits he liked best about her. "What do you want me to do?"

"Find it."

"How?"

Vicki turned from the window and spread her arms. "We *know* what area to search. You're the hunter. I thought you got its scent from the coffin."

"Not one I could use." The stink of terror and despair had all but obscured any physical signature. Henry hurriedly pushed the memory, and the shadows that flocked behind it, away. "I'm a vampire, Vicki. Not a bloodhound."

"Well, it's a magician. Can't you track power surges and stuff?"

"If I am nearby when it happens, I'll sense it, yes, as I sensed the demonic summonings last spring. But," he raised a cautioning hand, "if you'll remember, I couldn't track them back to their source either."

Vicki frowned and began to pace again. "Look," she said after a moment, "would you know it if you saw it?"

"Would I recognize a creature of ancient Egypt reanimated after being entombed alive for millennia? I think so." He sighed. "You want me to stake out the area around the museum, don't you? Just in case it wanders by."

She stopped pacing and turned to face him. "Yes."

"If you're so sure it'll be at this party on Saturday night, why can't we wait until then?"

"Because today's Tuesday, and in four days who knows how many more children may die."

Henry shoved his hands deep into the pockets of his leather overcoat and sat down on one of the wood and cement benches scattered out in front of the museum. A cold, damp wind skirted the building, dead leaves rising up and performing a dance macabre in the gusts and eddies. The occasional car appeared to be scurrying for cover, fragile contents barely barricaded against the night.

This wasn't going to work. The odds of him running into the mummy, even in Vicki's limited search area, because it just happened to be casting a spell as he wandered by were astronomical. He pulled a hand free and checked his watch. Three twelve. He'd still be able to get in a good three hours of writing if he went home now.

Then a wandering breeze brought a familiar scent. He stood and had anyone been watching it would have seemed he disappeared.

A lone figure walked east on Bloor, jacket collar turned up against the cold, chin and elbows tucked in tight, eyes half closed. Ignoring the red light at Queen's Park Road, he started across the intersection, following the silver plume of his breath.

"Good morning, Tony."

"Jesus Christ, man." Tony scrambled to regain his footing as his purely instinctive sideways dive was jerked into a non-event by Henry's precautionary grip on his arm. "Don't do that!"

"Sorry. You're out late."

"Nah, I'm out early. You're out late." They reached the curb and Tony turned to peer at Henry's face. "You hunting?"

"Not exactly. I'm waiting for a series of incredible coincidences to occur so I can be a hero."

"This Victory's idea?"

Henry smiled at the younger man. "How could you tell?"

"Are you kidding?" Tony snickered. "It has Victory written all over it. You've got to watch her, Henry. Give her a chance, give any cop a chance—or any ex-cop," he amended, "and they'll try to run your life."

"My life?" Henry asked, allowing the civilized mask to slip a little.

Tony wet his lips, but he didn't back down. "Yeah," he said huskily, "your life, too."

Henry played with the Hunger a little, allowing it to rise as he traced the line of jaw, then forcing it back down again as he admitted he had no real desire to feed. "You should get some sleep," he suggested over the wild pounding of Tony's heart. "I think you've already had enough excitement for one night."

"Wha . . . ?"

"I can smell him all over you." Henry heard the blood rush up into Tony's face, saw the smooth curve of cheek flush darkly. "It's all right." He smiled. "No one else can."

"He wasn't like you . . ."

"I should certainly hope not."

"I mean, he wasn't . . . it wasn't . . . well, it was but . . . I mean . . ."

"I know what you mean." He made the smile a promise and held it until he saw that Tony understood. "I'd walk you home, but I have an assignment to complete."

"Yeah." Tony sighed, tugged at his jeans, and began to walk away. A few paces down the road, he turned. "Hey, Henry. Those crazy ideas that Victory gets? Well, most times they turn out not to be so crazy after all."

It was Henry's turn to sigh as he spread his arms. "I'm still out here."

". . . leave a message after the tone."

"Vicki? Celluci. It's four o'clock, Wednesday afternoon. One of the uniforms just told me they saw you poking around the drains behind the museum this morning. What the fuck do you think you're doing? You're looking for a mummy, not a goddamned Ninja Turtle.

"By the way, if you find anything—and I mean anything—and you don't immediately let me know, I'm going to kick your ass from here to Christmas."

* * *

The house and garden looked vaguely familiar, like a childhood memory too far in the past to put a name or a place to. Remaining a cautious distance away, she walked around to the back, knowing before she saw them that there'd be hollyhocks by the kitchen door, that the patio would be made of irregular gray flagstones, that the roses would be in bloom. It was sunny and warm and the lawn smelled like it had just been mowed—in fact, there against the garage was the old push lawn mower that she'd used every Monday evening on their handkerchief-sized lawn in Kingston.

The baseball glove she'd inherited from an older cousin lay by the back step, the lacing she'd repaired standing out against the battered leather in a way she didn't think it really had. Her fringed denim jacket, the last thing her father bought her before he left, swayed from the clothesline.

The garden seemed to go on forever. She began to explore, moving slowly at first, then faster and faster, suddenly aware that something followed close behind. She circled the house, raced up the front path, leapt up onto the porch, and came to a full stop with her hand on the doorknob.

"No."

It wanted her to go in.

The knob began to turn and her hand turned with it. She could see her reflection in the door's window. It had to be her reflection, although for a moment she thought she saw herself inside the house looking out.

Whatever had been following her in the garden came up onto the porch. She could feel the worn boards move under its tread and in the window she saw the reflected gleam of glowing red eyes.

"No!"

She dragged her fingers off the doorknob and, almost incapacitated by fear, forced herself to turn around.

Vicki shoved her glasses at her face and peered at the clock. Two forty-six.

"I don't have time for this," she muttered, settling back against the pillows, heart still slamming against her ribs. In barely two hours she'd be heading over to Henry's, which made sleep the priority of the moment. Although that incident at the museum had obviously spooked her more than she'd thought, dream analysis would just have to wait. She dropped her glasses back where they belonged, stretched up a long arm, and switched off the light. "I'm going to blacken the next set of glowing red eyes that wakes me up," she promised her subconscious.

A few moments later, lying awake in the dark, she frowned. She hadn't thought of that jacket in years.

Thursday night, the house stood alone on a gray plain and the dream began by the front door. The compulsion to open it was too strong to resist and she walked in, closely followed. She caught just a glimpse of the contents of the first room when the light dimmed and she fought to hold it down.

It wanted to see what was in the house. Well, it could just take a flying fuck.

Although her head felt as if it had been slammed repeatedly between two large rocks, Vicki woke feeling smug.

She was giving him more of a fight than he'd anticipated. His lord would not be pleased. As she had no protecting gods, merely a strongly developed sense of self, the failure would be perceived as being his.

Akhekh did not tolerate failure and his punishments were such that anything became preferable to facing them.

He needed more power.

In spite of the cold and the damp, a Friday afternoon spent in the park beat the hell out of a Friday afternoon spent with the Riel Rebellion and grade ten chemistry. Brian tightened his grip across Louise's shoulders and turned her face up to meet his.

Now this is what I call getting an education! he thought as her lips parted and she flicked at his tongue with hers. *I wonder if she'll let me slip my hand up under her . . . ouch. Guess not.*

He opened his eyes, just to see what another person looked like from that angle, and frowned as he saw a well-dressed man watching them from no more than five feet away. *Oh, great. A pervert. Or a cop. Maybe we should . . . we should . . .*

"Brian?" Louise pulled back as he went limp. "Cut it out." His head flopped forward onto her shoulder. "I mean it, Brian. You're scaring me. Brian?

"Oh, my God."

He settled back on the bed, throwing the bags of feathers to the floor. Someday soon he'd have a proper headrest made.

It was eleven forty-three—this culture's preoccupation with the division of time into ridiculously small units never failed to amuse him—and she would be asleep by now, her ka at its most vulnerable. Tonight she would not be able to stand against him; he would throw all the power from the ka he had absorbed this afternoon at her defenses.

He closed his eyes and sent his ka forth, following the path his lord had laid out, entering through the image of his lord's eyes.

It was as if something held her elbow and walked her through the house, observing, discarding, searching. She couldn't shake free. She couldn't dim the lights.

She couldn't let it find what it needed.

Except she had no idea of what that was.

They climbed a staircase and started down a long corridor with a multitude of doors off to either side. As they reached for the knob of the second door, she saw the pencil lines and the dates, realized who waited within, and thought—or spoke, she wasn't sure—"Not the third door, anything but the third door," and tried to push them forward.

It stopped her, turned her, walked her down the hall, and into the third room. When they came out, it moved her on. It never came back to the second room.

Obviously, it had never read Aesop's fables.

She managed to protect her mother, Celluci, and Henry. It found everything else.

Everything.

He knew how she would suffer. It would take a while to arrange, even with some of the necessary influences already in place, but his lord could not help but be pleased with the result.

"You don't look so good. Are you all right?"

Vicki shifted her grip on the aluminum baseball bat and managed a smile. "I'm okay. I'm just a little tired."

"I'm sorry I haven't turned up any leads these last couple of nights but, to be honest, I never expected to."

"That's all right. It was a long shot. Henry . . ." She sat down on the edge of the bed and with one finger stroked the patch of red-gold hair in the center of his chest. ". . . are you still dreaming?"

Henry pulled the sheet aside to expose a ragged clutch of multiple holes in the mattress. "I drove my fingers through here this morning," he said dryly. He flicked the sheet back, then covered her hand with his. "If I hadn't caught a hint of your scent on the pillow, I don't know how much more damage I might have done." She looked away and he decided not to say the rest, not to tell her that she gave him reason to hold onto his sanity. Instead, he asked, "Why?"

"I just wondered if they were getting worse."

"They haven't changed. You getting tired of standing guard?"

"No. I just . . ." She couldn't tell him. The dream had seemed so important while it was going on, but now, faced with Henry's basic terror, it seemed stupidly abstract and meaningless.

"You just?" Henry prodded, knowing full well from her expression that she wasn't going to tell him.

"Nothing."

"Look at the bright side." He brought her hand to his mouth and kissed the scars on the inside of her wrist. "Tonight's the night of the party. One way or another, something's bound to . . ."

". . . happen." Vicki drew her hand away and straightened Henry's arm. Sliding her glasses back up her nose, she leaned the bat against the end of the bed. "One way or another."

Ten

"Oh, my God."

"What's wrong?"

Vicki wet her lips. "Absolutely nothing. You look . . . uh, good." Henry's costume had been made traditional in a score of movies—turn-of-the-century formal wear with a broad scarlet ribbon cutting diagonally across the black and a full-length opera cloak falling in graceful folds to the floor. The effect was amazing. And it wasn't the contrast between the black and the white and the sculptured pale planes of face and the sudden red/gold brilliance that was Henry's hair. No, Vicki decided, the attraction was in the way he wore it. Few men would have the self-assurance, the well-bred arrogance to look comfortable in such an outfit; Henry looked like, well, like a vampire. *The kind you'd like to run into in a dark alley. Several times.* "In fact, you look better than good. You look amazing."

"Thank you." Henry smiled and smoothed the sleeve of his jacket down until only a quarter inch of white cuff showed. A heavy gold ring gleamed on his right hand. "I'm glad you approve."

He could feel the years settling on him with the clothing, feel the Henry Fitzroy who wrote romance novels and was occasionally permitted to play detective submerge into the greater whole. Tonight, he would walk among mortals; a shadow amid their bright lights and gaiety, a hunter in the night. *Good lord, I'm beginning to sound as melodramatic as one of my own books.*

"I still think you've got a lot of chutzpah going to this party as a vampire. Aren't you taking a big chance?"

"And what chance is that? Discovery?" He draped the cloak over his arm and peered at her in the classic Hammer Films Dracula pose. "What you're looking at here is the purloined letter trick; hiding in plain sight." Dropping the pose, he smiled down at her. "And it isn't the first time I've done it. Think of it as a smoke screen. Halloween calls for a disguise. If Henry Fitzroy is a vampire on Halloween, then obviously he isn't the rest of the year."

Vicki draped one leg over the arm of the chair and smothered a yawn. "I'm not sure about that logic," she muttered. Early mornings and late nights were beginning to take their toll and a four-hour nap in the afternoon hadn't done much beyond throwing her internal clock even further out of whack. Barely more than a year away from the twenty-four hour aspect of police work, she was amazed at how quickly she'd lost her ability to adapt. The evening spent with her weights had gotten the blood flowing a little, washing away some of the fatigue. Henry's appearance had started things moving faster yet.

Henry's nose twitched as he picked up the sudden intensifying of her scent and he lifted one eyebrow, murmuring softly, "I know what you're thinking."

She felt herself flush but managed to keep her voice tolerably casual even as she shifted position in the chair and crossed her legs. "Don't start anything you can't finish, Henry. You've already eaten."

The Hunger had been blunted earlier, a necessity if he was to spend the evening in close proximity to mortals and be able to think of anything except the life that flowed beneath clothes and skin, but Vicki's interest had resharpened an edge or two. "I haven't started anything," he pointed out, not bothering to hide his smile. "I'm not the one squirming in my . . ."

"Henry!"

". . . seat," he finished quietly as the phone rang. "Excuse me a moment. Good evening. Henry Fitzroy speaking. Oh, hello, Caroline. Yes, it *has* been a while. Working on my latest book for the most part."

Caroline. Vicki recognized the name. While Henry was no more her exclusive possession than she was his, she couldn't help but feel . . . well, smug. She not only shared

Henry's bed, which the other woman no longer did, but she shared the mysteries of Henry's nature, which the other woman never had.

"Unfortunately, I have plans for tonight, but thank you for asking. Yes. Perhaps. No, I'll call you."

As he hung up the phone, Vicki shook her head. "You know, of course, that there's a special circle in hell for those people who make promises to call, then don't."

"They'll probably run out of room long before my time." Henry's voice trailed off. *And then again, maybe not.* While he continued to dream of the sun, every dawn might be his last. For the first time, he looked beyond the possibility of his death to all the things it would leave undone. He stood quietly for a moment, hand resting lightly on the phone, then came to a decision.

Vicki watched him curiously as he came around and knelt, capturing her hands, opera cloak pooling around his legs. While she had no objection to having handsome men at her feet, she had an uneasy feeling that the situation was about to get uncomfortable.

"You're right, I'm not going to call," he began. "But I think you need to know why. I can feed from a chance encounter with a stranger and not feel I'm betraying anything, but when I feed from Caroline I feel I'm betraying you both. Her, because I can give her so little of what I am and you because I have given you all of me."

Suddenly more frightened than smug, Vicki tried to pull her hands free. "Don't . . ."

Henry let them go but stayed where he was. "Why not? Tomorrow's dawn might be the one I've been waiting for."

"Well, it isn't!"

"You don't know that." At this moment, his death had become less important than what he had to say. "What will it change if I say it?"

"Everything. Nothing. I don't know." She took a deep breath and wished the light were dimmer, so she couldn't see his face so clearly. So he couldn't see hers. "Henry, I can sleep with you. I can feed you. I can be your friend and your guardian, but I can't . . ."

"Love me? Don't you?"

Did she?

"Is it because of how you feel about Mike?"

"Celluci?" Vicki snorted. "Don't be a fool. Mike Celluci is my best friend and, yes, I love him. But I don't *love* him and I don't *love* you."

"Don't you? Not either of us? Or both of us?"

Both of them . . . ?

"I'm not asking you to choose, Vicki. I'm not even asking you to admit the way you feel." Henry stood and twitched the cloak back over his shoulders. "I just thought you should know that I love you."

It almost hurt to breathe, everything felt so tight. "I know. I've known since last Thursday. Here." She touched herself lightly on the chest. "You gave yourself to me completely, with no strings. If that's not love, it's a damned close approximation." She got to her feet, moved a careful distance away, then turned to face him. "I can't do that. I come with too many strings. If I cut them all, I'll—I'll fall apart."

He spread his hands. "I'm not demanding a commitment. I just wanted to tell you while I could."

"You have an eternity, Henry."

"The dream of the sun . . ."

"You told me you've almost gotten used to it." If the effects had gotten stronger and he hadn't told her, she was going to wring his neck.

"I'm sure Damocles got used to the sword, but it's still only a matter of time."

"Time! Jesus Christ, look at the time! That party started half an hour ago. We'd better get moving." Vicki grabbed up her bag and headed for the door.

Henry arrived long before she did, teetering between anger and amusement at her sudden change of subject as he blocked the exit with a swirl of satin. "We?"

"Yeah, we. I'll be waiting in the car as backup."

"No, you won't."

"Yes, I will. Get out of the way."

"Vicki, in case you've forgotten, it's dark out there and you can't see anything."

"So?" Her brows drew down and her tone grew heated. "I can hear. I can smell. I can sit in the fucking car for hours and not do anything. But I'm coming with you. *You* are not trained in this sort of thing."

"I am not *trained* in this sort of thing?" Henry repeated

slowly. "For hundreds of years I have fit myself into society, been the unseen hunter in their midst." As he spoke he allowed the civilized mask to slip. "And you *dare* to tell me I am not trained in this sort of thing."

Vicki wet her lips, unable to look away, unable to move away. She thought she'd become used to what Henry was; she realized, now, she seldom saw it. A trickle of sweat ran down her side and she suddenly, desperately, had to go to the bathroom. *Right. Vampire. I keep forgetting.* Half of her mind wanted to run like hell and the other half wanted to kick his feet out from under him and beat him to the floor. *Oh, for Chrissakes, Vicki, get your goddamned hormones under control.*

"All right," her voice shook only a little, "you've had more training than I could ever hope to have. Your point. But I'm still going to go with you and wait in the car." She managed to raise a cautionary hand as he opened his mouth. "And *don't* tell me it's too dangerous," she warned. "I won't face anything tonight that's more dangerous than what I'm facing right now."

Henry blinked, then started to laugh. After four hundred and fifty years, he could recognize when he'd been outmaneuvered.

"This is good. This is very good." He looked out into the room filled with powerful men and women and in his mind's eyes saw them bowing before the altar of Akhekh, giving their power and those it commanded into the hands of his god.

George Zottie bowed his head, pleased that his master was pleased.

"I will move amongst them for a time. You may introduce me as you see fit. Later, when they hold thoughts of me and I can touch their ka, you will bring them to the room I have prepared, so I may speak with them one at a time."

Henry had no need to use any persuasion to get into the Solicitor General's large house on Summerside Drive nor did he expect to have to use much to stay. Arrival at this type of party implied the right to attend. He nodded at the young man who opened the door and swept past him toward the greatest concentration of sound. Servants did not require an explanation, something modern society tended to forget.

The huge formal living/dining room had been decorated in subdued Halloween. Black and orange candles glowed in a pair of antique silver candelabra, the table had been covered by a brilliant orange cloth, the flowers both in vases and in the large centerpiece were black roses and the wine glasses were black crystal—Henry assumed the wine had not been colored orange. Even the waiters, who moved gracefully among the crowd with trays of canapes or drinks, wore orange and black plaid cummerbunds and ties.

He took a glass of mineral water, smiled in a way that set the server's pulse pounding, and moved further into the room. Many of the women wore floor-length gowns from a variety of periods and just for an instant he saw his father's court at Windsor, the palace of the Sun King at Versailles, the Prince Regent's ballroom in Brighton. Smoothing a nonexistent wrinkle from the front of his jacket, he wondered if perhaps he shouldn't have taken the opportunity to indulge in the peacock colors this age normally denied to men.

The costumes on the men ranged from flamboyant to minor variations on street wear—unless the brown tweed suit stood for something or someone Henry didn't recognize. Two additional vampires glared at each other across the broad shoulders of a Keystone Cop. Having joined their various police departments before the height requirements had been relaxed, all the police present were large, usually both tall and burly. A couple, after years of patrolling a desk, had added an insulating layer of fat. The politicians scattered throughout the crowd were easily spotted by their lack of functional bulk.

Henry was not only the shortest man in the room, by some inches, but he also appeared to be the youngest. Neither mattered. These were people who recognized power, height and age came a distant second.

"Hello, I'm Sue Zottie."

The Solicitor General's wife was a tiny woman with luminous dark eyes and a coil of chestnut hair piled regally upon her head. Her dark green velvet Tudor gown added majesty to what had been labeled more than once in society pages as a quiet beauty. Instinct took over and Henry raised the offered hand to his lips. She didn't seem to mind.

"Henry Fitzroy."

"Have—have we met before?"

He smiled and her breathing grew a little ragged. "No, we haven't."

"Oh." She meant to ask him what police force he was with or if, perhaps, he was a junior member of her husband's staff, but the questions got lost in his eyes. "George is in the library with Mr. Tawfik, if you need to speak with him. The two of them have been in there for most of the evening."

"Thank you."

She'd never felt quite so completely thanked before and walked away wondering why George had never invited that lovely young man over for dinner.

Henry took a sip of his mineral water. Tawfik. His quarry, it seemed, was in the library.

It was cold in the car with the window open, but sightless, Vicki couldn't afford to block off her other senses. The wind smelled of woodsmoke and decaying leaves and expensive perfume—she supposed the latter was endemic to the neighborhood—and brought her the noise of distant traffic; a door, fairly close, opening and closing; a phone, either very close or beside an open window, demanding to be answered; a late trick-or-treater imploring his mother to cover just one more block. Two teenaged girls, too old for candy, reviewed the day as they walked down the other side of the street. As her eyes got steadily worse, her hearing seemed to be getting better—or maybe she just had to pay more attention to what she heard.

Vicki had no doubt that based on sound alone, she'd be able to pick these girls out of a lineup. One pair of flats, one pair of heels; the soft shirk, shirk of polyester sleeves rubbing against the body of a polyester jacket; the almost musical chime of tiny, metal bangles, chiming in counterpoint so they each must be wearing a set. One sounded as if she had a mouth full of gum, the other as if she had a mouth full of braces.

". . . and like she was just pressing her breasts up against him."

"You mean she was pressing her padding up against him."

"No!"

"Uh-huh, and then she has the nerve to say she really loves *Bradley* . . ."

And what do you children know about love? Vicki wondered, as they moved out of earshot. *Henry Fitzroy, the bastard son of Henry VIII, the Duke of Richmond, says he loves me. What do you think of that?* She sighed. *What do I think of that?*

She dragged her fingernail against the vents in the dashboard of the BMW, then sighed again. *Okay, so he's afraid of dying, I can understand that. When you've lived in darkness for over four hundred years and then start dreaming about daylight . . .* A sudden thought struck her. *Jesus, maybe he's afraid of dying tonight. Maybe he thinks he can't deal with the mummy.* She fumbled for the door handle but stopped herself before she actually got the door open. *Don't be ridiculous, Vicki. He's a vampire, a predator, a proven survivor. A friend. And he loves me.*

And I'm going to drag up that goddamned non sequitur every goddamned time I think about him from now on. She raised her eyes to the heavens she couldn't see. *First Celluci and his wanting to have a "talk" and now Henry and his declarations. It isn't enough we have a mummy rampaging around the city? Do I need this?*

It's just like a man to want to complicate a perfectly good relationship.

Sliding down on the leather seat until her head was even with the lower edge of the window, she closed her eyes and settled down to wait. But only because there wasn't anything else she could do.

With the lights in the hall turned down to a dim orange glow—extending the Halloween motif out of the actual party area—the curve of the stairs threw a pool of deep shadow just outside the library door. Shrouded by the pocket of darkness, Henry wrapped himself in his cloak and leaned back against the raw silk wallpaper to consider his next move.

According to Sue Zottie, the Solicitor General and Mr. Tawfik were in the library—but he could sense three lives on the other side of the wall and there was nothing to suggest that any of the three had just broken free after millennia of confinement. All three hearts beat to the same rhythm and . . .

No. To an *identical* rhythm.

The hair rose on the back of Henry's neck as he pressed himself farther away from the light. Hearts did not beat so completely in sync by accident. He had, in fact, heard it happen only once before, in 1537 when, faint and dizzy with loss of blood, he had pressed his mouth to the wound in Christina's breast and drunk, conscious of nothing save the heat of her touch and the painful throbbing of his heart in time with hers.

What was happening in that room?

For the first time, Henry felt a faint unease at the thought of actually facing the creature who had been so long entombed. The time of change had been the most powerful, all encompassing experience in his life, not only in the seventeen years before but in the four hundred and fifty-three years since, and if the mummy could call that kind of power to its control . . .

"You think you're up to this wizard-priest?" Celluci had asked.

His answer had been scornful. *"I am not without resources."*

He had defeated wizards in the past, relying on strength and speed and force of will, but they had followed rules he recognized and had not come with their own dark god.

"You think you're up to this wizard-priest?"

The voice of memory had grown sarcastic and Henry's brows drew down. He certainly wasn't going to give Celluci the pleasure of seeing him give up without a fight.

The three hearts paused, then two began again in tandem and one beat to a rhythm all its own.

He had to get into that library. Perhaps through the gardens . . .

Then the single heartbeat approached the door and Henry froze. The knob turned, the door opened, and a woman with close-cropped salt-and-pepper hair stepped out into the hall. Henry recognized the Chief Justice of the Supreme Court of Ontario from a recent newspaper photograph although the picture had not managed to capture either her very obvious self-assurance or her sense of humor. The cavalier costume she wore suited both.

As Henry watched, she brushed the feather in her hat against the floor in a credible bow and said, "You'll have my complete support in this, George. Mr. Tawfik. I'll see you both at the ceremony and I'll tell Inspector Cantree you want to see him now." Then, grinning, she replaced the hat and headed down the hall toward the party. She didn't appear to be enchanted.

There were now only two heartbeats sounding in the library—Tawfik's and the Solicitor General's—and they sounded as one. Through the open door, Henry heard a low voice ask thoughtfully, "And what is Inspector Frank Cantree like?"

"He won't be easy to convince."

"Good. We prefer, my lord and I, to work with the strong; they last longer."

"Cantree believes that independence yields greater results than conformity."

"Does he now."

"They say he's incorruptible."

"That in itself can be used."

Used for what? Henry wondered. There was something in the tone that reminded Henry of his father. He didn't find that at all comforting. His father had been a cruel and Machiavellian prince who could play tennis with a courtier in the morning and have him executed for treason before sunset. Still motionless, he frowned as he watched a large man in a pirate costume walk down the hall on the balls of his feet, carrying himself as though he were perpetually ready for a fight, his expression just to one side of suspicious. Bearing and attitude both said "Cop" so strongly that Henry doubted the man had ever been of any use undercover.

The newcomer paused in the doorway, one beefy hand dropping to the pommel of the plastic cutlass that hung at his hip. Instinct seemed to be warning him of a threat within the room and his tone was carefully, aggressively neutral. "Mr. Zottie? You wanted to speak with me?"

"Ah, Inspector Cantree. Please, come in."

As Cantree stepped over the threshold, Henry raced forward, letting the heavy folds of the cape slip from his shoul-

ders to the floor. Over short distances, he could move
almost faster than mortal eyes could register but not while
dragging meters of fabric behind him. Sliding between the
burly Inspector and the door, he sped shadow silent into
the room, along a book-covered wall, and behind a floor-
to-ceiling barrier of heavy curtain.

Convenient, he thought, his back pressed against glass,
his feet turned to either side so as not to protrude, his
entire body motionless again. Over the sound of three
heartbeats, he heard the door close, the hardwood floor
contract beneath the Inspector's weight, but no hue and
cry. His entry had gone unnoticed.

He felt something. It brushed against his ka with all the
innocent strength of a desert storm, almost dragging him
from the light trance he'd been maintaining for most of the
evening. Before he could begin to react, the barrier wards,
set up more from old habit than perceived necessity, di-
verted the touch and only by lowering them could he hope
to find it again.

For an instant, he weighed what he did tonight against
such tantalizing potential and, regretfully, left the wards in
place. His lord perceived this evening as the initial gathering of a core of acolytes—which it was, in addition to an
initial gathering of a more secular power—and his lord
would not look kindly upon personal indulgences during
such a time.

The touch had been undirected, accidental, therefore it
would have to wait.

But the glorious memory of it lingered in the back of his
mind and he vowed it would not have to wait long.

"Inspector Frank Cantree, Mr. Anwar Tawfik."

Henry slid the curtains apart a centimeter, movement
masked by the quiet sound of flesh touching flesh.

"Please take a seat, Inspector. Mr. Tawfik has a proposal
that I think you'll find very interesting."

He watched the Inspector lower himself onto an expensive leather sofa and saw Solicitor General Zottie move
across the room to stand beside a wing chair, its high back
barely a meter from his hiding place, completely hiding
Anwar Tawfik from Henry's line of sight.

This is beginning to feel like some cheap horror movie, Henry mused, *where the creature rises out of the chair to face the camera at the end of the scene. I guess I wait for my cue.* He'd make his move after Cantree left the room and before another high ranking official took the Inspector's place. Zottie was merely mortal and could be quickly dealt with. As for the mummy—if Tawfik *was* the mummy—it had proven itself to be a taker of innocent lives. Henry didn't particularly care what its reasons were. The time for it to die was millennia past.

From where he stood, he could see Cantree's gaze flicking constantly over the room, observing, noting, remembering. It was apparently a habit all police officers acquired, for Henry had seen both Vicki and Celluci perform variations on the theme.

Then Tawfik began to talk, his voice low and intense. To Henry it sounded like law and order generalities, but obviously Cantree heard something more. The movement of his gaze began to slow until it locked on the man—on the creature—in the chair. Certain words began to be repeated and after each the Inspector nodded and his expression grew blank. A rivulet of sweat—the library was at least ten degrees warmer than the rest of the house—ran unnoticed down his face.

Unease danced icy fingers along Henry's spine as Tawfik's cadence grew more and more hypnotic and the key words occurred more and more frequently. It was magic, Henry could sense that, however much it looked like something less arcane, but magic completely outside his understanding. A working for good or evil he could have sensed, but this was neither. It just was.

When all three hearts beat to an identical rhythm, Tawfik paused, then said, "His ka is open."

"Frank Cantree. Can you hear me?"

"Yes."

"From this moment on, your primary concern is to obey me. Do you understand?"

"Yes."

"You will protect my interests above all else. Do you understand?"

"Yes."

"You will protect me. Do you understand?"

"Yes." But this time after the single syllable of assent, Cantree's mouth continued to work.

"What is it?"

Although independent movement should have been impossible under the conditions of the spell, Cantree's lips curled slightly as he answered. "There is someone standing behind the curtains behind your chair."

For a heartbeat, the scene hung in limbo, then Henry threw the curtains aside, charged forward, came face-to-face with the creature rising from the chair, and froze.

He got a jumbled impression of gold leather sandals, a linen kilt, a wide belt, a necklace of heavy beads that half covered a naked chest, hair too thick and black to be real, and then the kohl-circled eyes under the wig caught his and all he saw was a great golden sun centered in an azure sky.

In blind panic, he wrenched his gaze away, turned, and dove through the window.

Although she knew it was impossible, that the night for her was as dark as it would ever get, Vicki suddenly felt that it had grown darker still; as if a cloud had covered the moon she couldn't see and the shadows had thickened. Senses straining, she slowly got out of the car, allowing the door to close but not to latch. A quick tug would turn on the interior light and enable her to at least find her way back again.

They pay high enough taxes in this neighborhood, you'd think they could manage a few more streetlights.

The night seemed to be waiting, so Vicki waited with it. Then, from not so far away, came the sound of breaking glass, the violent snapping of small branches, and, approaching more quickly than possible, leather soles slapping out a panicked flight against concrete.

There was no time to think, to weigh her move. Vicki stepped away from the car directly into the path of the sound.

They both went down.

The impact drove the breath out of her lungs and her jaw slammed up with enough force so every tooth in her head shuddered with the impact. She took a moment to thank any gods who might be listening that her tongue had been tucked safely out of the way even as she grabbed onto what felt like expensive lapels. During the landing, her head bounced off the pavement, the glancing blow creating an impressive fireworks display on the inside of her lids. Somehow she managed to keep her grip. Not until cold hands grabbed her wrists and yanked them effortlessly away did she realize who she held. Or more accurately, had held.

"Henry? Damnit, it's me, Vicki!"

Sanctuary. The sun was rising. He must reach sanctuary.

Vicki twisted and, barely in time, wrapped herself around Henry's right leg. If she couldn't stop him, maybe she could slow him down.

"Henry!"

A weight clung to his leg, impeding his flight. He bent to rip it free and a familiar scent washed over him, masking the stink of his own fear.
Vicki.
She said she would be there when the dawn reached out to take him. She would fight with him. For him. Would not let him burn.
Sanctuary.

The tension went out of his muscles and his fingers loosened where they crushed her shoulder. Tentatively, she let him go, ready to launch herself forward should he start to run again.

"The car's just back here." Actually, she'd kind of lost track of where the car was but hoped Henry would turn and see it. "Come on. Can you drive?"

"I—I think so."

"Good." Other questions could wait. Not only did the echoes of her skull hitting the sidewalk make it difficult to hear the answers, but from the sounds that had preceded his flight, Henry had just left a house full of police officers by way of a closed window. They'd be playing the chase scene any second and that would lead into a whole new lot of questions there were no answers for.

Ms. Nelson, can you tell us why your friend turned into a smoldering pile of ash in the holding cell at dawn?

One hand held tightly to his jacket as Henry surged toward the car, continuing to grasp it until her other hand touched familiar metal. She scrambled to get into her own seat the moment she figured out where it was, then watched him anxiously—or rather watched his shadow against the lights of the dash—as he started the engine and pulled carefully out of the parking space. She had no idea why people weren't boiling out of the Solicitor General's house like wasps out of a disturbed nest, but she certainly wasn't going to complain about a clean getaway.

"Henry . . . ?"

"No." Most of the raw terror had faded, but even Vicki's presence wasn't enough to completely banish the fear. *I can feel the sun. It's hours to dawn and I can feel the sun.* "Let me get home first. Maybe then . . ."

"When you're ready. I can wait." Her voice was deliberately soothing even though she really wanted to grab him, and shake him, and demand to know what had happened in there. *If this is Henry's reaction to the mummy, we're in a lot more trouble than we thought.*

"Do I go after him, Master?"

"No. You are tied into the spell and the spell is not yet finished." He spat the words out, the power of his anger crackling almost visibly around him.

"But the others . . ."

"They can hear nothing that happens within this room. They did not hear the window break. They will not interrupt." With an effort, he forced his attention back to the multilayered spell of coercion he had been in the middle of evoking. "When I have finished with the Inspector, then you may search the grounds. Not before."

Inspector Cantree tossed his head and sweat began to soak through the armpits of his costume. His eyes rolled back and the muscles of his throat worked to produce a moan.

"It didn't hurt the others, Master."

"I know."

The ka that had touched him earlier with its magnificent, unending potential for power, had been within his grasp and he had been forced by circumstance to let it get away.

That did not please him.

But now he knew of its existence, and, more importantly, it knew of him. He would be able to find it again.

That pleased him very much.

When Vicki finally saw Henry's face in the harsh fluorescent glare of the elevator lights, it gave nothing away. Absolutely nothing. He might as well have been carved from alabaster for all the expression he wore. *This isn't good . . .*

Three teenagers—in what might or might not have been costumes—got on in the lobby, took one look at Henry and stood quietly in their corner, not a word, not a giggle until they got off on five.

And every cloud has a silver lining, Vicki mused as they filed silently out.

The last, finding courage in leaving, paused in the doorway and stage-whispered back. "What's he supposed to be?"

Why not?

"A vampire."

Hennaed curls bounced on sequined shoulders. "Not even close," was the disdainful judgment as the elevator door slid closed.

Vicki used her keys to let them into the condo, then followed close on Henry's heels as he strode down the hall and into the bedroom. She flicked on the light as he flung himself on the bed.

"I can feel the sun," he said softly.

"But it's hours until dawn."

"I know."

"Colonel Mustard, in the library, with a mummy. . . ."

Henry glared at her from under knotted brows. "What are you talking about?"

"Huh?" Vicki started and lowered her arm. She'd been doing a painful fingertip investigation of the goose egg on the back of her head. Fortunately, it appeared that her little meeting with the pavement outside the Solicitor General's house had done no lasting damage. *And a concussion would be just what I need right now.* "Oh. Nothing. Just thinking out loud." The party had put them ahead only in that they now *knew* what they'd only suspected before: the mummy was ensorcelling the people who controlled the police forces of Ontario, acquiring its own private army. No doubt it intended to set up its own state with its own state religion. It had, after all, brought its god along.

They had a name, Anwar Tawfik, the man she'd helped out of the elevator at the Solicitor General's office. She couldn't prevent a twinge of sympathy; after three thousand years in a coffin, she'd be violently claustrophobic, too. *Still, I should've dropped the son of a bitch down the elevator shaft when I had the chance.*

She banged her fist against her thigh. "I don't think it can succeed at what it's attempting, but a lot of people are going to die proving that. And no one's going to believe us until it makes its move."

"Or a good while after it makes its move."

"What do you mean?"

"Who does the average citizen call when there's trouble?" Henry pointed out.

"The police."

"The police," Henry agreed.

"And it controls the police. Shit, shit, shit, shit."

"*Very* articulate."

Vicki's smile was closer to a snarl as she shifted position on the edge of the bed. "It looks like it's up to us."

Henry threw his forearm up over his eyes. "A lot of help I'll be."

"Look, you've been dreaming about the sun for weeks now and you're still functioning fine."

"Fine? Diving through that library window wasn't what I'd call fine."

"At least now you know you're not going crazy."

"No. I'm being cursed."

Vicki pulled his arm off his face and leaned over. The spill of light from the lamp just barely reached his eyes but, in spite of the masking shadows, she thought they looked as mortal as she'd ever seen them. "Do you want to quit?"

"What?" His laugh had a hint of bitter hysteria. "Life?"

"No, you idiot." She wrapped one hand around his jaw and rocked his head from side to side, hoping he couldn't read through her touch how frightened she was for him. "Do you want to quit the case?"

"I don't know."

Eleven

The absence of shadows against the wall told him he had slept late, his body trying vainly to regain some of the energy spent on spell-casting the night before. His tongue felt thick, his skin tight, and his bones as though they had been rough cast in lead. *Soon, a slave will wait at my bedside, a glass of chilled juice ready upon my awakening.* But *soon*, unfortunately, did him no good at the moment. He looked over at the clock—eleven fifty-six, oh three, oh•four, oh five—and then tore his glance away before it could trap him further in the progression of time. Only half the day remained for him to feed and find the ka that burned so brightly.

Moving stiffly, he swung out of bed and made his way to the shower. The late Dr. Rax, who over the course of a varied career had been familiar with the sanitary facilities, or lack thereof, along the banks of the Nile, had considered North American plumbing to be the eighth wonder of the world. As gallons of hot water pounded the knots from his shoulders, he was inclined to agree.

By the time he finished a large breakfast and was lingering over a cup of coffee—an addiction every adult ka he had absorbed seemed to share—he no longer felt the weight of his age and was ready to face the day.

For a change, a cloudless blue sky arced up over the city, and, although the pale November sun appeared to shed little warmth, it was still a welcome sight. He took his cup to the wall of windows that prevented the other, more solid walls from closing in around him and looked down at the street. In spite of laws that forced most businesses to remain closed on the day known as Sunday, a number of people were taking advantage of the weather and spending time outside. A number of those people had small children in hand.

The series of individually tailored spells he had worked last night, each with its own complicated layering of controls, had drained him and the power he had remaining would barely be enough to keep him warm as he chose the child whose ka would replenish his. He was using power in a way he would never have dared when unsworn souls were few and even slaves had basic protections but, with nothing to stand in the way of his feeding, he saw no reason to hold back. Not one of the deaths could be traced to him—necessity had taught him millennia ago to take the mundane into account—and very shortly even that would cease to be a consideration. When the police and their political masters gave themselves to Akhekh, he, as High Priest, would be inviolate.

He had no idea how many sworn acolytes his lord needed in order to gain the strength to create another such as he. Forty-three had been the greatest number he had ever been able to gather in the past but, as that had been just before Thoth's priests had been instructed to intervene, he suspected that forty-four or forty-five would be enough. That the thirty ka to be gathered up in this time had been coerced would make only a minimal difference. He had used the smallest pieces of their ka necessary to convince them—in two cases those had been very small pieces indeed—and enough truth had been spoken during the spellbinding that their pledges would hold. The thirty coerced would be equivalent to no less than twenty free; a respectable beginning.

After the ceremony, he would not need to be as magically involved and would, therefore, need to feed less often.

"And when I find you, my bright and shining one . . ." He placed his empty cup down with the rest of the breakfast dishes and scooped up the opera cloak the Solicitor General had found outside the library door. ". . . I may never need to feed again." As the satin folds slid across his fingers, he basked in the remembered glow. This ka would stand out like a blaze of glory against the others in this city; now that he had touched it, it would not be able to hide from him. He was mildly curious about what kind of a man—for it had been only a man, there had been no mark of god or wizard about the presence—would carry such a ka, but curiosity paled beside his desire.

The opera cloak pooled about his feet. Perhaps he would return the young man's forgotten garment, and as their fingers touched he would look into his eyes and . . .

With such power at his command there would be nothing he could not do.

Tony wasn't sure what had driven him from his basement room this morning, but something had nagged him up out of sleep and onto the street. Two coffees and a double chocolate chip muffin in Druxy's had brought him no closer to an answer.

Hands shoved deep into the pockets of his jacket, he stood on the corner of Yonge and Bloor and waited for the light, effortlessly eavesdropping on the conversations around him, filtering out the yuppie concerns, paying close attention to a cluster of street kids complaining about the cold. At this time of the year, those who lived in parks and bus shelters worried first about surviving the coming winter and then about their next meal, their next smoke, their next bit of cash. They talked about the best places to pan-handle, to turn tricks, what doorways were safe, what cop would cut a little slack, who'd been picked up, who'd died. Tony had survived on the street for almost five years and knew what talk had substance behind it and what talk was just wind. No one seemed to be saying anything that would clue him into whatever it was that had him so jumpy.

He walked west on Bloor, thin shoulders hunched high. The new jacket he wore, bought with money from a real honest-to-God steady job, kept him plenty warm enough, but old habits took time to break. Even after two months, he was still a little unsure about the job, afraid that it would vanish as suddenly as it had appeared and with it the room, the warmth, the regular meals . . . and Henry.

Henry trusted him, believed in him. Tony didn't know why, didn't really care why. The trust and the belief were enough. Henry had become his anchor. He didn't think it had anything to do with Henry being a vampire—although he had to admit that was pretty fucking awesome and it certainly didn't hurt that the sex was the best he'd ever had and just remembering it made him hot—he thought it had more to do with Henry just being a . . . well, being Henry.

The feeling that had driven him out and onto the street had nothing to do with Henry, not specifically at least. Henry feelings, he could always reconize.

Dropping down onto the low wall in front of the Manulife Center, Tony rubbed at his temples and wished the feeling would go away. He had better things to do with his Sunday afternoon than wander about trying to find where the ants between his ears came from.

He kicked his heels against the concrete and watched the parade of people pass by. A baby in a backpack, barely visible under a hat and mittens and a scarf and a snowsuit, caught his attention and he grinned up at it, wondering if it could even move. *Jeez, the kid's gonna spend the first few years of its life only seeing where it's been. Probably grow up to be a politician.*

The baby appeared to be gazing in happy fascination at the man who walked along behind its parents although, as far as Tony could tell, he wasn't doing anything to attract its attention. He wasn't a bad looking man either; quite a bit of gray in the hair and a nose that hooked out into tomorrow but with a certain something that Tony found attractive.

Guess he likes kids. Sure is staring at that . . . that . . . Jesus, no.

Under the pale blue hat with its row of square-headed yellow ducks, the baby's face had gone suddenly slack. The bulk of its clothing held it upright, arms reaching out over the carrier but Tony knew, without the shadow of a doubt, that the baby was dead.

Cold fingers closed around his heart and squeezed. There was now no gray in the hair of the man who followed.

He killed it. Tony was more certain of that than he'd ever been of anything in his life. He didn't know how it had been done, nor did he care. *Jesus God, he killed it.*

And then the man turned, looked right at him, and smiled.

Tony ran, instinct guiding his feet. Horns sounded. A voice yelled protest after a soft collision. He ignored it all and ran on.

When even terror could no longer keep him moving, he collapsed in a shadowed doorway and forced great lungfuls of air past the taste of iron in the back of his throat. His whole body trembled and every breath drove a knife blade, barbed and razor sharp, up under his ribs. Exhaustion wrapped itself shroudlike around what he'd seen, dulling the immediacy, allowing him the distance to look at it again.

That man, or whatever he was, had killed the baby just by looking at it.

And then he turned and looked at me. But I'm safe. He can't find me here. I'm safe. No footsteps sounded in the alley, nothing threatened, but his scalp prickled and the flesh between his shoulder blades twisted into knots. *He didn't need to follow. He's waiting for me. Oh, God. Oh, Jesus. I don't want to die.*

The baby was dead.

They'll think the baby's asleep. They'll laugh about the way babies sleep through anything. Then they'll get home and they'll take it out and it won't be sleeping. Their baby will be dead and they won't know when or how or why it happened.

He scrubbed his palms across his cheeks.

But I know.

And he knows I know.

Henry.

Henry'll protect me.

Except that sunset wouldn't be for hours and he couldn't stop thinking of the baby's parents arriving home and finding . . . He couldn't just let that happen. He had to tell someone.

The card he pulled from his pocket had seen better days. Limp and stained, the name and number on it barely legible, it had been for years his link to another world. Clutching it tightly in a sweaty hand, Tony moved cautiously from his hidey-hole and went looking for a pay phone. Victory would know what to do. Victory always knew what to do.

"Nelson Investigations. No one is available to take your call, but if you leave your name and number, as well as a brief reason for your call, after the tone, I'll get back to you as soon as possible. Thank you."

"Shit." Tony slammed the receiver down and laid his forehead against the cool plastic of the phone. "Now what?" There was always the number scrawled on the back of the card, but somehow Tony doubted that Detective-Sergeant Michael Celluci would appreciate having this kind of thing dumped in his lap. "Whatever kind of thing it is. Jesus, Victory, where are you when I need you?"

He shoved the card back in his pocket and, after a cautious examination of the passing crowds, slipped out of the phone booth. Squinting at the sky, he began making his way back to Yonge and Bloor. He knew where Henry was and the hours between now and sunset would only seem like they were taking up the rest of his life. With any luck.

The boy had seen him feed; or been aware, at least, that he had fed. Apparently, there *were* a few in this age who had not built barriers of disbelief around their lives. The incident was of interest but placed him in no danger. Who would the boy tell? Who would believe him? Perhaps later he would search him out and, if he could not be used, he was young enough still that his life would be an adequate source of power.

At the moment, he had all the power he needed. He felt wonderful. An infant's life, so very nearly entirely unrealized potential, was a pleasure to absorb. Occasionally, in the past, when his fortunes were high, he would buy a female slave, have her impregnated by an acolyte, and devour the life of the child at the moment of its birth. The slave's birth pains and then the despair at the loss of her child became a sacrifice to Akhekh. Such nourishment took careful purchasing and then constant monitoring, however, as the children of some women could be claimed by the gods while still in the womb. Perhaps, with so few gods active, when Akhekh's temple had been built anew, he would be able to feed in such a way as a matter of course.

He raised his personal temperature another two degrees just because he had the power to spare. It was too lovely a day to return to the enclosure of his hotel room. He would walk to the park, ward a small area, and *soak up a few rays* while he searched for the ka·that blazed so brightly.

*   *   *

"Mike, it's Vicki. It's about two-ten, Sunday afternoon. Call me when you've got time to talk." She hung up the phone and reached for her jacket. Now they *knew* high-ranking police officers were involved and, given those same officers had already pulled him off the case, a tap on Celluci's phone line was a possibility; a slim one, granted, but Vicki saw no reason to discount it just because the odds were ridiculously high. After all, they were hunting down an ancient Egyptian mummy and who'd want to figure the odds on that?

"An ancient Egyptian mummy named Anwar Tawfik." She hoisted her shoulder bag up into position. "How much do you want to bet that's not its real name." Still, it was the only name they had, so she planned on spending the afternoon checking the hotels clustered around the Royal Ontario Museum. Everything pointed to it having remained in that area and, from what Henry had to say, Mr. Tawfik apparently preferred to travel first class. She wondered briefly how it paid for such a lifestyle and muttered, "Maybe it has a platinum Egyptian Express card. Don't be entombed without it."

Henry.

Henry wanted to get as far away from this creature and its visions of the sun as was humanly possible. He didn't have to say it, it was painfully obvious. She doubted he'd be willing, or even able, to face the mummy again.

"So I guess that means it's up to me." Her glasses slid forward and she settled them firmly back on the bridge of her nose. "Just the way I like it best."

The vague, empty feeling, she ignored.

His ka swept over the city and found no trace of the life he had touched so briefly the night before. A ka with such potential should shine like a beacon and searching for it should only be a matter of following the blaze of light. He knew it existed. He had seen it, felt it. It should not be able to hide from him!

Where was it?

The connection between them had lasted less than a searing, glorious instant before the young man threw himself backward through the library window and away but even such a slight touch would enable him to gain access into the young man's ka. If he could find it.

Had the young man died in the night? Had he taken one of the miraculous traveling devices of this age and flown far away? His frustration grew as he brushed over a thousand kas that together burned less brightly than the one he desired.

And then he felt his own ka gripped by a greater power and, for a moment knew a sudden, all-encompassing fear. Recognition lessened the fear only slightly.

Why have you not given me the suffering of the one I claimed?

Lord, I . . . He had walked through the woman's ka and gathered all the information he needed for his lord's pleasure. He had intended to set it in motion the night before. Had he done so, the suffering would have begun. The touch of the intruder's ka had driven it right out of his mind.

No excuses.

It made no difference that the pain existed on the spiritual level only. His ka screamed.

"Are you all right?"

He felt strong hands around his arm, lifting him back into a sitting position, and knew the wards had broken. Slowly, because it hurt, he opened his eyes.

At first, while he fought his way free of the webs of pain, he thought the young man standing so solicitously by resembled the young man who had escaped him; who had been responsible for the delay in the working of his god's desire. Who had been responsible for the agony his god had seen fit to twist around him. A moment later, he saw the hair was lighter, the skin darker, the eyes gray rather than pale brown, but by then it didn't matter.

"You tipped over." The young man smiled tentatively. "Is there anything I can do?"

"Yes." He forced his throbbing head up enough to meet the other's gaze. "You can throw yourself in front of a subway."

Eyes widened and face muscles spasmed.

"Your last word must be Akhekh."

"Yes." Legs moved jerkily away. Body language screamed no.

He felt better. There had been nothing subtle about the coercion, but there had been no need. The young man would live such a short time that laying on an appearance of normalcy would be a waste. He could feel his lord following close behind, drinking in the despair and panic. The young man knew what he was about to do, he just couldn't stop himself from doing it.

Hopefully, his lord would be appeased until the chosen one could be delivered.

Vicki paused outside the Park Plaza Hotel and looked down at what she was wearing. Sensible shoes, gray cords, and a navy blue duffle coat were fine for most places in this city, but she had a feeling that when she walked through the door and into the lobby she was going to feel underdressed. The hotels she usually searched for suspects did not have a doorman; if someone was stationed out front, he was there as a lookout in case the police arrived. Adjoining shops sold cigarettes and condoms, not seven thousand dollar diamond and emerald necklaces. The windows would be opaque because of plywood, not because the glass had been impregnated with gold.

And I am not *being intimidated by a building*. The Park Plaza was directly across Bloor Street from the museum and therefore the logical place to begin a search for Anwar Tawfik. She strode past the doorman, swung through the revolving door at a speed that would have swept any other occupants off their feet, and paused again in the echoing quiet of the green marble lobby.

Some things, however, were universal to hotels. The registration desk had two harried clerks behind it and eleven people—eleven very well-dressed people, Vicki noted—attempting to check in. She sighed silently and got into line, mourning the loss of the badge that would have made waiting unnecessary.

His stride had nearly steadied by the time he reached the hotel. The vast amount of power he had absorbed from the infant's ka had acted as a buffer between the anger of his lord and any lasting damage. There had been times in the past when he had crawled away from such an encounter on his belly and it had taken days of pain and fear to recover his strength. Thankfully, the new acolytes would soon be sworn and his lord's attention would not then be directed so exclusively at him.

Akhekh, while not one of the more powerful gods, was still very conscious of services owed in return for immortality.

The liveried doorman scurried to open the door and he swept past the tinted glass and into the lobby, stopping abruptly at the touch of a familiar ka.

She looked much as she perceived herself although in truth was a little less tall, a little less blonde, and rather more determined of jaw. What was his lord's chosen doing here, however? He reached out and gently stroked the surface of her thoughts. After the nights he had spent mapping it, her ka could hold no secrets from him.

He frowned as he uncovered the reason for her presence. She searched for him? She was no wizard to be aware of his wandering in her . . . ah, she searched at the request of another. Apparently, he had not been as thorough at the museum as he had thought. No matter. He smiled. His lord would have twice the pleasure for the plans he had made for the suffering of Ms. Nelson could be adapted to include Detective-Sergeant Michael Celluci as well, without even the need to search the detective's ka.

But, in the meantime, it would not do for the chosen one to disrupt his sanctuary. Without so much as touching her awareness, he laid a false memory over the parameters of her search.

What am I doing back in line? Vicki wondered, shaking her head and turning for the door. *They're not going to have any more information now than they did a moment ago.* Computer listings could be changed, Anwar Tawfik might not be the name he was registered under, and if the manager had never heard of him, there wasn't much else she could do but check the rest of the hotels in the area.

Maybe she'd think of another angle to hit later.

"Yes, it was a very pleasant evening, Mrs. Zottie. Thank you. Now, if I could speak with your husband . . ." He looked out over the city as he waited for the Solicitor General to pick up the phone. When he stood close to the wall of windows, the rest of the suite seemed less enclosing.

"You wished to speak with me, Master?"

"I assume you are alone?"

"Yes, Master. I took the call in my study."

"Good." It had become necessary to ask for the effect of the control spell had Zottie's mental abilities deteriorating at an unanticipated pace. Fortunately, his assistance would be necessary only until the others were pledged.

"Pay attention, there's something important I want you to arrange . . ."

Henry had faced enemies before, faced them and conquered them, but his nature denied him the ability to face the sun. Vicki had offered him a chance to leave—she'd understand if he ran from this creature he had no chance of defeating.

She'd understand. But would I?

Forcing his muscles to respond, he swung his legs off the bed and sat up, golden afterimages of the sun still dancing across the periphery of his vision.

When I face this wizard-priest, I face the sun. When I face the sun, I face death. So when I face him, I face death. I've faced death before.

Except he hadn't. Not when he truly thought he was going to die. Deep in his heart he had always known he was stronger and faster. He was the hunter. He was Vampire. He was immortal.

This time, for the first time in over four hundred and fifty years, he faced a death he believed in.

"And the question becomes, what am I going to do about it?"

It was one thing to endure the dreams when he had no knowledge of how or why they came, it was another to let them continue knowing they were sent. *He must have become aware of me from the moment he woke at the museum.* But even knowing who, the question of why still haunted him. Perhaps the dream of the blazing sun was a warning, a shot fired across his bow saying, *"This is what I can do to you if I choose. Do not interfere in what I plan."*

"So it all returns to running. Do I let him have his way

or do I face him again?" He leapt to his feet and strode across the room, head high, eyes blazing. "I am the son of a King! I am Vampire! I do not run!"

With a loud crack, the closet door ripped off in his hands. Henry stared at it for a moment, then slowly let the pieces fall. In the end, the anger and the fine words meant nothing. He didn't think he could face Tawfik again, not knowing he had to face the sun as well.

The sudden ringing of the phone slammed his heart against his chest in a very mortal reaction.

"All right, Mr. Fitzroy says you can go up."

Tony nodded, brushed his hair back off his face with a hand that still trembled, and hurried for the inner door. The old security guard disapproved of him, could see the street kid lurking just below the surface; thought thief, and addict, and bum. Tony didn't give a rat's ass what the old guy thought, especially not tonight. All he wanted was to get to Henry.

Henry would make it better.

Greg watched the boy run for the elevator and frowned. He'd fought in two wars and he knew bone-deep terror when he saw it. He didn't approve of the boy—part of his job as security guard included keeping that type out of the building—nor did he approve of his relationship, whatever it was, with Mr. Fitzroy, but he wouldn't wish that kind of fear on anyone.

Henry could smell the fear stink from across the apartment and when Tony launched himself into his arms it became almost overwhelming. Keeping a tight grip on the Hunger that had risen with a body so vulnerably presented, he set his own fears aside and held the younger man silently until he felt muscles relax and the trembling stop. When he thought he'd get an answer, he pushed Tony gently an arm's length away and asked, "What is it?"

Tony rubbed his palm across lashes spiked with moisture, too frightened to deny there had been tears. The skin around his eyes looked bruised and he had to swallow, once, twice, before he could speak.

"I saw, this afternoon, a baby . . . he just . . ." The

shudder ran the length of his body, Henry's presence finally allowing him release. "And now, he'll . . . I mean I saw him kill the baby!"

Henry's mouth tightened at the suggestion that someone would threaten one of his. He pulled Tony, unresisting, over to the couch and sat him down. "I will not allow you to be harmed," he said in such a tone Tony had no choice but to believe it. "Tell me what happened. From the beginning."

As Tony spoke, slowly at first, then faster as though he were racing his fear to the end of the story, Henry had to turn away. He walked to the window, spread one hand against the glass, and looked out over the city. He knew the dark-haired, dark-eyed man.

"He's killing children," Vicki told him.

"He'll come for me," cried Tony.

"Because we're all there is." Even Mike Celluci had a voice in his head.

I feel the sun. It's hours to dawn and I feel the sun.

"Henry?"

Slowly, he turned. "I'll go to where you saw him last, and try to track him." He had no doubt he would recognize the scent, pick it out of a hundred scents laid across concrete on a November afternoon. And if he found the creature's lair, what then? He didn't know. He didn't want to know.

Tony sighed. He knew Henry wouldn't let him down. "Can I stay here? Until you come back?"

Henry nodded and repeated, "Until I come back," as if it were some sort of mantra that would ensure his return.

"Do you, do you need to eat before you go?"

He didn't think he could; not eat, not . . . "No. But thank you."

Brushing his hair back off his face, Tony managed a shaky grin and the shadow of a shrug. "Hey, it's not like I mind or anything."

Because he could do no less than this mortal boy, Henry drew up a smile in return. "Good."

The shrilling of the phone snapped both heads around wearing almost identical expressions of panic. Henry quickly slid a mask in place so that when Tony glanced over at him and asked, "You want me to get it?" he appeared under control and could calmly answer, "No. I'll take care of it."

He lifted the receiver before the second ring had quite finished sounding, having moved from the window to the phone in the space between one heartbeat and the next. It took him almost as long to find his voice.

"Hello? Henry?"

Vicki. No mistaking the tone split equally between worry and annoyance. He didn't know what he'd expected. No, that wasn't true; he knew exactly what he'd expected, he just didn't know why. If Anwar Tawfik decided to contact him, he would *not* be using the phone.

"Henry?"

"Vicki. Hello."

"Is something wrong?" The words had been given a professional shading that told him she knew something was wrong and he might as well tell her what.

"Nothing's wrong. Tony's here." Behind him, he heard Tony shift his weight on the couch.

"What's wrong with *Tony*?"

The obvious conclusion; he should've known she'd jump to it. "He has a problem. But I'm going to take care of it for him. Tonight."

"What kind of problem?"

"Just a minute." He covered the mouthpiece, half turned, and raised a questioning eyebrow.

Tony emphatically shook his head, fingers digging deep into a cushion. "Don't tell her, man. You know what Victory's like; she'll forget she's only human, just charge out there and challenge the guy and the next thing we'll know, she's history."

Henry nodded. *And I am not only human, I am the night. I am Vampire. I want her with me. I don't want to face this creature alone.* "Vicki? He doesn't want me to tell you. It's uh, trouble with a man."

"Oh." He didn't dare read anything into the pause that followed. "Well, *I* want to spend some time with Mike this evening; fill him in on what we know is happening. Warn him." Again the pause. "If you don't need me . . ."

What did she sense? The half lie? His fear? "Will you be here for the dawn?" Regardless of what happened to-

night, if he was to have another dawn, he wanted her there
for it.

"I will." It had the sound of a pledge.

"Then give my regards to the detective."

Vicki snorted. "Not likely." Her voice softened. "Henry?
Be careful." And she was gone.

A little of the horror lost its effect. It was amazing how
much *"be careful"* could sound like *"I love you."* Holding
her words—her tone—like a talisman, he went over the
location with Tony one more time, shrugged into his coat,
and went out into the night. He took dubious comfort in
the knowledge that now, at least, he could be sure he
wasn't going crazy.

Many of the spells he had spent long years learning
would have to be adapted to this new time and place. Unfortunately, as he now found himself in a culture that held
few things sacred, finding substitutions would not be easy.
The ibex had been revered to the extent that sacred had
become a part of its name and that made beak and blood
and bone very powerful agents for magic. Somehow he
doubted that rendering up a Canada goose would have the
same effect.

Suddenly he sat bolt upright in the chair and twisted to
face the windows. It was out there. And it was close. He
scrambled to his feet and began to throw on street clothes.
His ka would not need to search again; simple awareness
of the young man would be enough to find him.

He didn't know how that glorious light had been hidden
during the day, although he expected he'd soon find out.
One way or another.

Henry had traced the scent to the southeast corner of
Bloor and Queen's Park Road where it split, one track
going north, the other south. Slowly he stood, brushed off
the knee that had been resting on the concrete, and considered what he should do next. He knew what he wanted to
do, he wanted to go back to Tony, say he couldn't find the
creature, and deal with the younger man's fear instead of
his own.

Except that wasn't the way it worked. He had made Tony

his responsibility. Honor had driven him out onto the streets and honor would not let him return.

Night had followed day, cold and clear, the kind of weather where the scent clung to the ground and the hunt rode out behind the hounds.

His best friend, the brother of his heart, Henry Howard, the Earl of Surrey, rode beside him, their geldings tearing across the frozen turf neck and neck. Ahead, the staghounds bayed and just barely ahead of the pack the quarry raced in a desperate attempt to outrun the death that closed upon its heels. Henry didn't see the exact moment the dogs closed in, but there was a scream of almost human pain and terror and then the stag thrashed on the ground.

He pulled up well back from the seething mass of snarling dogs who darted past striking hooves and tossing antlers to worry at the great beast, but Surrey took his horse as close as it would go, leaning forward in the stirrups, eyes on the knife and the throat and the hot spurt of blood that steamed in the bitter November air.

"Why?" he asked Surrey later, when the hall was filled with the smell of roasting venison and they were sitting bootless, warm before the fire.

Surrey frowned, the elegant line of his black brows dipping in toward the bridge of his nose. "I didn't want the death of such a splendid animal to be wasted. I thought I might find a poem . . ."

His voice trailed off so Henry prodded, "Did you?"

"Yes." The frown grew thoughtful. "But a poem too red for me I think. I will write the hunt and keep the stag alive."

Four hundred and fifty odd years later, Henry answered as he had then. "But there is always death at the end of a hunt."

The track to the south had almost been buried beneath the other footsteps of the day. The track to the north seemed better defined, as though it had been taken more than once; to and from a hotel room perhaps. Henry crossed Bloor, drew even with the church on the corner, and froze so completely motionless that the stream of Sunday night pedestrians flowed seamlessly around him.

He knew the dark-haired, dark-eyed man approaching.

Twelve

Henry waited, motionless, while the other man drew closer. He felt like a rabbit caught in headlights, fully aware that death and destruction bore down on him but unable to move. The sun grew brighter and brighter behind his eyes until he struggled to see around it.

I have no way to fight this. . . .

And then, suddenly, he recognized what he faced. His kind could sense the lives around them, not only through scent and sound but also with an awareness peculiar to those who hunted the night. What he felt approaching was a life, ancient, unlike any life he had ever felt before, and the sun only a symbol created to deal with it.

I have been aware of his life from the moment he awoke, most aware in the times I am most vulnerable. Blessed Christ, he has driven me almost to death just by existing.

Brows down and teeth clenched, he fought to drive this life from the foreground of his mind, finally managing to push it back and dim the light although he could not banish it entirely. It existed now as a background to all he did, but at least it no longer blinded him.

The night returned, Henry blinked, and found himself sinking into irises so deep a brown they looked black. Just before this darkness closed over him, he snarled and pulled free.

"I will not go unresisting like a lamb to the slaughter!"

Force of will slammed at the spell of absorption and shattered it. In all the centuries since his god had changed him, he had never felt such raw power.

He should have known it would not be so easy and he

would not have even made the attempt had he not been
blinded by the glory of the other's ka. This one had protections; not only personal strength but also strong ties to the
one God who had swept the old ways down. Each alone
might be enough to stop him from taking what he so deeply
desired, together they were very nearly an impenetrable
barrier.

But I will *have this ka. I must.*

He touched only the very outermost edges of the other's
thoughts. In them, he could feel himself and he could feel
fear. Both would give him, if not a way through, a way
around. He probed for other weaknesses but saw only the
blaze of unlimited potential.

"What are you?"

Henry, muscles twisted into knots across his shoulders,
hands clenched so tightly into fists that his nails cut cres-
cents into his palms, saw no reason not to answer. He
pitched his voice so that it traveled across the distance between them but no further and threw it like a challenge.

"I am Vampire."

The ka he had absorbed since awakening gave him a
confusing pastiche of images not many of which seemed to
have much to do with the young man standing before him.
He sifted through the information until he recognized what
he faced. His people had called them by another name.

No wonder the young man's ka burned so brightly; as
long as the Nightwalkers fed on the blood of the living,
they were immortal. As immortal as he was himself. Did
his own ka burn like a beacon? A pity he would never
know, for it was the one ka he could not see.

What power would be his if he fed on the ka of an immortal being! It would no longer be necessary to work
through pitiful human tools. He would rule from the beginning in his own name.

Perhaps . . . perhaps a seat in the council of the gods
would not be beyond him. He saw himself surrounded by
glory, no longer the servant of a petty minor deity but a
master in his own name. Quickly, as much as he thrilled to
it, he buried the thought deep. It would not do for Akhekh
to find it.

But to devour an immortal ka—he had been so blinded by the life remaining, he had never even looked at the life lived, never even noticed it was far longer than the normal human span. He was, he discovered, the elder by a good many centuries, even discounting the millennia he had spent imprisoned. Still, he would have to move carefully, for if he was to finally feast, the Nightwalker's protections must be lowered. He did not have the power to break them down, even considering the fear woven through them.

Why do you fear me, Nightwalker?

Although it was an emotion he would use, it was a question he could not ask. So he asked another.

"Why do you search me out, Nightwalker?"

Why indeed?

"You hunt in my territory."

Ambiguous enough to hide a multitude of motives and also, Henry discovered as he spoke, the truth.

Again he attempted to read the other's ka, to enter past the surface, but he got no further this time than he had before.

"I would talk with you, Nightwalker. Shall we walk together for a time?"

Henry wanted to say no, torn between a desire to run and a desire to rip out the creature's throat and drink deeply of the blood he could hear surging beneath the smooth column of throat. The first would bring him no closer to a solution. The second . . . well, even if he could get past the defenses all wizards wore, which he doubted, it was Sunday evening at a major intersection in downtown Toronto and committing a violent murder in front of hundreds of witnesses, while it would be a solution of sorts, would not be one he himself would likely survive.

So, because it seemed the best, if not the only choice, he turned and fell into step at the other's side, trying to ignore the sun that continued to blaze in one corner of his mind.

They walked south down Queen's Park Road and the power that walked with them turned more than a few heads as they went.

"What shall I call you?" Henry asked at last.

"I use the name Anwar Tawfik. You may call me that."

"That's not the name you were born with."

"Of course not." He laughed gently, an elder chiding an errant pupil. "I took the name upon awakening. I am not likely to give you the power of my birth name." He had not heard his birth name spoken since before the joining of Egypt into a single country. "And I am to call you . . . ?"

"Richmond." Although he had answered to it in the past it had been a title, not a name, and so should be safe from whatever magics could be wrapped around it.

They walked a short distance further, until the sounds of Bloor Street faded and then, in mutual agreement, crossed over to the park. After dark on a November evening, they walked alone on paths damp with fallen leaves, under trees nearly bare. No one would overhear the words to be spoken; no one would have to die because they had heard.

The scattering of lights pushed back the darkness only in isolated areas; in the rest of the park the night stretched unbroken from infinity to the ground. Little light of any kind reached the bench they chose and as Henry watched Tawfik lower himself carefully down, he realized that the other had no better than mortal vision.

So I hold the advantage of sight. For all the good it will do.

Tawfik smelled of excitement, not fear, and his heart beat only a fraction faster than human norm. The movement of his blood called to the Hunger even as the weight of his life overwhelmed any desire Henry had to feed. Henry could smell the fear on himself and his own heart, while still ponderously slow by mortal measuring, beat faster and harder than it had in years.

Tawfik spoke first, his voice sounding mildly amused. "You have a hundred questions, why not begin?"

Why not? But where? Perhaps with the question he himself had answered. "What are you?"

"I am the last remaining priest of the god Akhekh."

"What are you doing here?"

"Do you mean how do I come to be here, in this century, in this place? Or do you mean what am I doing now I am here?"

"Both."

Tawfik shifted on the bench. "Well, that is, as they say, a long story and as you have only until dawn . . ." He saw no reason to lie to the Nightwalker about how and what he was and, although he would chose his words carefully, he was also willing to speak of his plans. After all, he wanted to win young Richmond's trust.

Fortunately, Dr. Rax provided him with a twentieth century framework to hang his story on.

"I was born about 3250 BC, in Upper Egypt just before Meri-nar, who had been King of Lower Egypt, created one empire that stretched the length of the Nile. I was, at the time of the conquest, a high-ranking priest of Set—not the Set that common history remembers, he was then a benevolent god, unfortunately on the losing side. After the conquest, Horus the elder, the highest of the gods of Lower Egypt, cast Set down and declared him unclean. Set, still very powerful, merely worked his way into the new pantheon." Tawfik's tone grew slightly dry. "Egyptian gods were, if nothing else, flexible.

"I, as a ranking priest, had been cast down with my god, stripped and scourged and thrown out of my temple. Only mortal and already middle-aged, I hadn't the luxury of concerning myself with Set's long-term plans. I wanted immediate revenge and I was willing to do . . ." He paused and Henry saw him frown as he remembered. "I was willing to do anything to regain the power and prestige I had lost.

"To me came Akhekh, a minor and dark deity, who in the confusion of the heavens had managed to get hold of more power than usual. *'Swear to me,'* said Akhekh, *'dedicate your life to my service, and I will give you the time you need for your revenge. I will make you more powerful than you have ever been. Become my priest and I will give you the power to destroy the ka of your enemies. You will feed on their souls and with such nourishment live forever.'* " Tawfik turned to face Henry and smiled tightly. "Now do not for a moment think that Akhekh made this offer out of regard for me. The gods exist only as long as belief exists. A change in those who believe means a change in the gods. When no one believes any longer, the gods lose definition, their sense of self if you will, and are absorbed back into the whole." He caught a powerful negative flare from the Nightwalker's ka and inclined his head politely toward the other man. "You wanted to say . . . ?"

Henry hadn't intended to say anything, but he found that when challenged he couldn't hold back. *I will not be like Peter and deny my lord.* "There is only one God."

"Richmond, please." Tawfik didn't bother to keep the amusement out of his voice. "You, at least, should know better. Perhaps there may someday be only one god, when all people dream and desire alike, and there are certainly less gods now than there were before I was entombed. But one god? No. I can . . . introduce you to my god, if you wish."

The night seemed to grow a little darker.

"No." Henry ground the word through clenched teeth.

Tawfik shrugged. "As you wish. Now then, where was I? Oh, yes. Of course, I accepted Akhekh's offer; that it came from a dark god meant little to me under the circumstances. I discovered that not only could I extend my life and power my magics with the life remaining in the ka I absorbed, but I also gained the life knowledge that ka held. An invaluable resource for those necessary moves between cultures that occur over a long, a very long life."

"So when you killed Dr. Rax . . ."

"I absorbed the power of his remaining life and came to know everything he knew. The younger the life the less knowledge but the greater potential for power."

"Then the infant you killed earlier today . . ."

That jerked Tawfik out of his relaxed posture. "How did you know?" he demanded and knew the answer before the question had quite left his mouth. The young man who had been watching, fully aware of what had occurred—the young man who had fled in terror—must have fled to the protection of the Nightwalker. He had heard they sometimes gathered mortals about them, a ready food source when hunting became unsure. *So, another pawn has entered the game.* Tawfik let nothing but the question show on his face or in his voice. If the Nightwalker thought he had forgotten the young man, his protection would be less extreme and easier to circumvent.

Henry heard Tawfik's heart speed up, but the wizard-priest made no mention of Tony. Perhaps Tony had been wrong and he hadn't been spotted. Given Tony's terror, that seemed unlikely. Perhaps Tawfik played a deeper game and had no wish to tip his hand. Tawfik no doubt had his own reasons for denying a witness; Henry's were simple, he would not betray a friend. He let the beast show in his voice as he repeated, "You've been hunting in my territory."

Tawfik recognized the threat, and countered with one of his own, playing on the Nightwalker's barely controlled fear of him. "As you were about to observe, the infant I killed earlier today made me *very* powerful." Stalemate again. "Now then, if I may continue with my history . . . ?"

"Go on."

"Thank you." Akhekh's offer had come with a condition: he could not devour the ka of one already sworn. For the first hundred years after the conquest, while the pantheon settled, the unsworn were easy to find and he had risen in power—which he discovered he desired much more than revenge—and the cult of Akhekh had grown strong. But the more stable and prosperous Egypt was, the fewer the people were content with their gods and the fewer unattached ka were available, so his power and Akhekh's waxed and waned in counterpoint to Egypt's. *This* age had a decadence he recognized and had every intention of exploiting—they were ripe for rituals Akhekh had to offer. Tawfik saw no reason to mention any of that to the Nightwalker.

"Because of me, my lord, in spite of his relatively subordinate position in the pantheon, was never absorbed into the greater gods like so many of the lesser deities had been and so in every age, in a thousand places along the Nile, I raised a temple to Akhekh." Occasionally, he was the only worshiper, but no need to mention that either. "Now and then, other priests objected to my having stepped out of the cycle of life, but the centuries had made me a skilled wizard—and had taught me when to cut my losses and leave town—so they could not take me down. As I only destroyed those who had no allegiance to a god, the other gods refused to get involved."

"But you were taken down, in the end."

"Yes. Well, I made a slight error in judgment. It could have happened to anyone." In the darkness, Tawfik smiled.

"Shall I tell you what it was? It is completely irrelevant to this time and place so even if you wished to, you couldn't use it against me. During what you now call the Eighteenth Dynasty, although things were extremely prosperous for Egypt, most nobles had very large families which meant that a number of the younger nobility had nothing to do. In such a social climate, the temple of Akhekh grew and flourished. My lord had more sworn acolytes than at any time since the conquest. Unfortunately, although I didn't see it as unfortunate at the time, two of the Pharoah's younger sons joined our number. This finally attracted the attention of the greater gods."

He paused, sighed, and shook his head. When he began to speak again, his voice had lost its lecturing tone and had become only the voice of a man sharing painful memories.

"The sons of the Pharoah were the sons of Osiris reborn and Osiris would not have them corrupted by what he termed an abomination. So Thoth, god of wisdom, came to one of his priests in a dream and told them how I might be overcome. My protections were shattered and once again I was dragged from my temple. The first time, I was left alive because my life had no meaning. This time, they were afraid to kill me because my life had gone on for so long. Even the gods were wary of what might happen should my ka be released into Akhekh's keeping with so many acolytes still performing the rituals. I was not to be slain, I was to be entombed alive. All this I was told as the priests of Thoth prepared me for burial.

"Three thousand years later, my prison was brought here to this city and I was freed."

"And you destroyed the man who gave you your freedom."

"Destroying him gave me my freedom. I needed his knowledge."

"And the other. The custodian."

"I needed his life. I had been entombed for three thousand years, Nightwalker. I had to feed. Would you have done any differently?"

Henry remembered the three days he had spent beneath the earth, hunger clawing at him until hunger became all he was. "No," he admitted, as much to himself as to Tawfik, "I would have fed. But," he shook free of the memory, "I would not have killed those others, not the children."

Tawfik shrugged. "I needed their power."

"So you took their lives."

"Yes." He shifted on the bench, linking his fingers together and leaning his forearms across his thighs. "I told you all this, Nightwalker, so you would learn you cannot stop me. You are no wizard. Thoth and Osiris are long dead and cannot help you. Your god does not interfere."

First the stick. "If you oppose me, I will be forced to destroy you."

And then the carrot. "As I see it, you have two choices; live and let live, as *I* am willing to do with you, or join me."

"Join you." Henry was not quite in control of the repetition.

"Yes. We have much in common, you and I."

"We have nothing in common."

Tawfik lifted his brows. "Of course we don't." The sarcasm had a razor edge. "This city has many more immortal beings."

"You murder the innocent."

"And you have never killed to survive?"

"Yes, but . . ."

"Killed for power?"

"Not the innocent."

"And who declared them guilty?"

"They did, by their own actions."

"And who appointed you as judge and jury and executioner? Have I not as much right to appoint myself to the position as you did?"

"I have never destroyed the innocent!" Henry held tightly to that while the sun grew brighter behind his eyes.

"There are no innocents. Or do you deny your church's position on original sin?"

"You argue like a Jesuit!"

"Thank you. I am as immortal as you are, Richmond. I will never grow old, I will never die, I will never leave you. Not even another Nightwalker can promise you that."

Vampires were solitary hunters. Humans were pack animals. In order to survive in a human world, the vampire could not surrender all humanity—those who did were quickly destroyed by the terror they evoked—and this double nature found itself constantly at war with itself. But to find a companion, one who would neither cause instinctive bloody battles over territory nor die just when he had become an intrinsic part of life. . . .

"No!" Henry leapt to his feet and flung himself forward into the darkness, trying to outdistance the sun. Halfway across the park, he managed to stop himself and, fingers dug deep into the living bark of a tree, old and gnarled and half his age, he fought back.

"I have lived, knowing I was immortal, for thousands of years." Tawfik continued to speak, sure that the Nightwalker could hear him. He watched the reaction of the other's ka and chose his words accordingly. "I am perhaps the only man you will ever meet who can understand you, who can know what you go through. Who can accept you entirely for what you are. I, too, have seen the ones I love grow old and die."

Listening, in spite of himself, Henry saw the years take Vicki from him as the years had taken the others.

"I am asking you to stand by my side, Nightwalker. A man should not go alone through the centuries; neither of us need ever stand alone again. You need not go blindly forward. I have lived the years you will live, I can be there to guide you." Tawfik couldn't quite hide the gasp as the Nightwalker was suddenly, silently, beside him again.

"You never told me what you plan to do now." The answer wasn't as important as shutting off the words, banishing the specter of isolation they invoked. He couldn't just walk away, so he had to change the subject.

"I plan to build a temple, as I have always done when I start a new life, and I will gather acolytes to serve my god. This is my only concern at this time, Nightwalker, for the acolytes should be sworn as soon as possible—a god deserves worshipers, rituals, all the little things that make being a deity worthwhile."

"Then why try to control the police and the justice system?"

"New religions are often persecuted. I have a way to prevent that and so I do. With no need to hide, I will shout AKHEKH from the top of the highest mountain. And once the temple is large enough to provide me with the power

I need, your innocents will be safe." Tawfik stood and held out his hand. "You live like a mortal, searching for immediate solutions, immediate answers. Why not plan for eternity? Why not plan with me?" He now had enough of a key to the Nightwalker's ka that if Richmond would just voluntarily reach out and take his hand, that act of trust would plant hooks that the younger man would never shake loose. In time those hooks would pull him closer and, in time, he would feed.

Scent and sound told Henry that Tawfik had not lied once since he began to speak.

Henry felt young, confused, afraid. For the seventeen years he had lived as a mortal he had fought to gain his father's love and approval. Tawfik—older, wiser, incontestably in control—made him feel the way his father had. Four hundred and fifty years hunting the night alone should have erased the bastard who only wanted to belong. It hadn't. He didn't know what to think. He stared down at the offered hand and wondered how it would feel to be able to plan for more than just a part of one mortal lifetime. To be part of a greater whole. But if Tawfik hadn't lied . . .

"Your god is a dark god. I want no part of him."

"You need have nothing to do with my god. Akhekh asks nothing of you. *I* ask for your companionship. Your friendship."

"*You* are more dangerous than your god!" On the last word, Henry launched himself forward. Red lines flared and he found himself flat on his back two meters away.

Tawfik let his hand drop slowly to his side. "Foolish child," he said softly. "I will not destroy you now as I could, nor will I take back the offer. If you grow tired of an eternity alone, come to the corner where we met tonight and I will find you." He felt the Nightwalker's gaze on him as he turned and walked away, not entirely displeased with the evening's work. The surface of the other's ka boiled with emotions too tangled for even millennia of experience to sort out but all of them, eventually, came back to him.

The evening mass was nearly over when Henry slipped into the church and settled into one of the empty pews at the back. Confused and frightened, he had come to the one place that had, through all the years and all the changes, stayed the same. Well, almost the same. He still missed the cadences, the grandeur of the Latin and occasionally murmured his responses in the language of the past.

The Inquisition had driven him from the church for a time but needing, at the very least, the continuity of worship, he had returned. Sometimes he saw the church as an immortal being in its own right, living much as he did during carefully prescribed hours, surviving on the blood of the mortals who surrounded it. And often the blood was less than metaphorical, for more had been shed in the name of a god of love . . .

He stood with the rest, hands lightly holding the warm wood of the pew in front of him.

Over the centuries there had been compromises, of course. The church declared he had no soul. He disagreed. He had seen men and women without souls—for a soul can be given up to despair or hatred or rage—but did not count himself among them. Confession had been a trial in the beginning, until he realized that the sins the priests would understand, gluttony, anger, lust, sloth applied as much to him as to mortals and that the specific actions were unimportant. He did the penance prescribed. He came away feeling part of a greater whole.

Except that he could not, since his change, take communion.

So once again I am set to one side, different from the closest thing to community I have known.

He found it interesting that Tawfik—the only other immortal being he had met since Christina and he had parted—came complete with a god of his own. Perhaps immortals *needed* that kind of continuity outside themselves. He found himself thinking of discussing the theory with Tawfik and thrust the thought away.

The pew back groaned under his grip and he hurriedly forced his hands to relax.

If not for the promises he had made to Tony, he would have run before he had the chance to be tempted. And if not for Vicki, the temptation would not have been so great. Vicki offered him friendship, perhaps even love, although she seemed to be frightened of what that implied, but her mortality sounded in the song of her blood and every beat of her heart took her one heartbeat closer to death. In time, in a very short time relative to the time he had already lived, she would be gone and soon after her, Tony, and then the loneliness would return.

Tawfik promised an end to the loneliness, a place to belong for longer than the length of a mortal life.

Why not *plan for eternity?*

The sun blazed up behind his eyes. It seemed he could no longer be completely unaware of Tawfik's existence.

If I die, I would have the eternity the church promises. It would be so easy to take that way out, come the dawn. *Except that suicide is a sin.*

The greater sin would be the pain he would leave behind. If he wanted to take that way out, he would have to wait. With a sudden lightening of his heart, he realized that for the first time in weeks, for the first time since the dreams had started, he could face the dawn without fear. The sun that Tawfik pushed at him could no longer push him in that direction. Whatever else happened—desire and fear and identity were still a tangled mess he could not sort—that would not.

The priest lifted one hand, his eyes nearly shut above the curves of his cheeks. "Go in peace," he said softly, and it sounded as though he meant it.

The mass over, the congregation of mostly elderly immigrants began to file out. Henry hung behind, waiting, while the priest greeted each of them at the door. When the last black-clad body was on its way down the path, he stepped forward and captured the priest's gaze.

"Father, I need to talk to you."

·More than vocation made it impossible for the priest to refuse that request.

It was seven ten when he got back to the condo, barely eighteen minutes before sunrise. Vicki met him at the door, grabbed his hands, and practically dragged him inside.

"Where the hell have you been," she snarled, worry twisting into anger now he was safe.

"I had an encounter with our mummy."

The flatness of his tone penetrated. *You can deal with this only if you deny the effect it had.* Over the years Vicki had seen enough of the effects of major trauma to recognize this particular defense mechanism in her sleep. With an effort, she damped her own emotions to suit. "So you found it. Tony called me about midnight, he was afraid the creature had sucked up your life the way it had the baby's. Mike drove me over. I'll have to call him after sunrise and let him know what happened." *Provided* you *let me know what happened.*

Henry could hear a slow and quiet heartbeat coming from the living room.

"Tony finally fell asleep on the couch about four," she continued. "I'll get him out of here after I've got you safe."

The grip that pulled him purposefully through the apartment would have been painfully tight around a mortal's hand; even Henry found it a bit uncomfortable. He made no effort to break it though; it was a welcome anchor.

Not until they reached the bedroom and the door had been closed behind him and the blackout curtain drawn, did Vicki release him. Leaving him standing in the middle of the room, she sat down on the end of the bed and slid her glasses back up the bridge of her nose.

"If you had died out there," she said slowly, because if she didn't speak she was going to explode, "you would have left a hole in my life impossible to fill. I've always hated the thought of putting conditions on . . ." She wet her lips. ". . . on love but if you ever go off to face an enemy whose strengths we don't know, who we know can kill with a look, who just the night before sent you running from him in panic, and don't come back looking at least a little the worse for wear . . ." Her head jerked up and she met his eyes. ". . . I'm going to wring your fucking vampiric neck. Do I make myself clear?"

"I think so. You went through hell, so I better have?" He sat down beside her on the bed. "If it makes you feel any better, I did."

"Fuck off, Henry, that's not what I meant." She wiped viciously at the tear that traced a line down her cheek. "I was scared spitless you'd taken on more than you could handle . . ."

"I had." He raised a hand to cut her off. "But not because I had to prove something after last night. I grew out of stupid displays of machismo three centuries ago. I went because Tony needed me to."

Vicki took a deep breath, and her shoulders straightened

as though a weight had lifted. God knows, she'd taken impossible risks in her time, and, thank God, he'd had a reason she could live with. "You are such an idiot."

Henry leaned forward and drew the flavor of her mouth deep into his. "And you have such interesting ways of saying *I love you*," he murmured against her lips. He realized just how frightened for him she'd been when she made no protest, merely returned his embrace with an intensity that held a hint of desperation. When she finally drew back, he got to his feet and began to strip off his shirt. If he didn't hurry, he'd be spending the day in his clothes.

She watched him, the soft, anxious expression she'd worn for a moment hardening into something a little closer to, *All right, let's get on with this.* "Are you okay?"

"Well, to begin, I didn't find him, he found me." He tossed the shirt to the floor. "And I discovered that the sun that I've been dreaming about has been nothing more than a manifestation of his life-energy."

"What?"

"Apparently there were times I was more susceptible than others. And now I've met him, I can't completely tune him out."

"You can always see the sun?"

"It hovers on the edge of my consciousness."

"Jesus Christ, Henry!"

"He frightens me, Vicki. I can't see any way we can beat him."

Her brows drew down. "What did he do to you?"

"He talked." Henry flipped the covers back and got into the bed. The sun, the other sun, trembled on the horizon. "He twisted me into knots and left me to sort myself out."

She shifted around until she faced him again. "Did you?"

"I think so. I don't know." *I won't know until I face him again.* "I spent the night trying to redefine myself. The church. The hunt." He reached out and laid two fingers against her wrist. "You."

I'm worried sick and he's out having a prayer, a snack, and a fuck? The smell of sex that clung to him was faint but unmistakable now she'd been made aware of it. *Calm down. Everyone deals with trauma his own way. At least he made it home.* "And what about you do I define?"

"My heart."

She laid her palm gently on his bare chest, stroking the soft red-gold curls with her thumb. "I really hate this mushy stuff."

"I know." He almost smiled, then quickly sobered again. "I tried to attack him. I couldn't even get close. He's dangerous, Vicki."

He obviously wasn't referring to the deaths that had occurred since the mummy disentombed itself and the faint shadow of pain that slipped into his voice was far more disturbing than out and out panic would have been. "Why?"

"Because I can't reject his offer out of hand."

"His offer?" Vicki's brows snapped down so hard that her glasses trembled on the very tip of her nose. "What offer? Tell me!"

He began to shake his head . . .
. . . then the motion slowed . . .
. . . then the day took him.

"When he wakes up, I'm going to grab him and shake him and he's going to tell me everything he knows and we're going to go over what happened second by second." Vicki stuffed another handful of cheese balls into her mouth. "This is what comes of letting your hormones interfere with your caseload," she muttered savagely, but indistinctly to an uninterested pigeon. Because she'd been so worried about Henry, first she'd babbled then she'd let him babble and nothing, absolutely nothing of any use had been passed on before he'd passed out.

"If I'd ever done anything half so stupid with a witness while I was on the force I'd have been up on charges of gross incompetence." Sucking the virulent orange stain from her fingers, she shook her head, growling around them, "And they wonder why I won't get mushy romantic." All right, that was unfair. Neither of them wondered. Celluci understood and Henry accepted. This screwup she could lay at no one's door but her own.

"Good lord. Celluci." She shoved the half-eaten package of cheese balls into her shoulder bag and checked her watch. He'd be going into headquarters for eleven and he'd told her to call him before he left. Vicki figured she owed him that much; not, given her lack of relevant information, that she was looking forward to it. To her surprise it was only eight fifty-three. Why did she feel like it should be later? *Time flies when you're having fits.* . . .

With Henry safely and infuriatingly tucked away, she'd roused Tony, reassured him, and popped him onto a subway heading toward his current job site, shoving five bucks into his hand so he could buy breakfast when he got there. Then she'd taken transit in the other direction, paused only long enough to pick up a snack and a short lecture on nutrition from Mrs. Kopolous at the store, and had just rounded the corner onto Huron Street and home. They left Henry's condo at ten to eight, it was now ten to nine. An hour seemed about right . . .

"Daylight savings time. My body thinks it's ten to ten." She sighed. "My body is an idiot. My emotional state is completely unreliable. Damn, but it's a good thing I'm so smart."

The legal side of Huron Street was, as usual, parked solid, so Vicki paid less than no attention to the brown sedan that had pulled over illegally in front of her building. She moved onto the walk, heard a car door open behind her, and froze when a familiar voice called out, "Good morning, Nelson."

"Good morning, Staff-Sergeant Gowan." She pivoted around to face him, the smile she wore completely unconvincing. Staff-Sergeant Gowan had resented everything about her while she'd been on the force, his resentment growing with every promotion, every citation, every bit of praise she got until it had festered into hate. To be fair, she despised him in turn. "Oh, and I see you brought Constable Mallard." She'd once turned Mallard into the Police Review Board for conduct unbecoming a human being. As far as she was concerned, the uniform meant responsibility; it didn't excuse the lack of it.

Her palms began to sweat. They were both out of uniform. Whatever was going to happen, it didn't look good.

"So, what unexpected pleasure brings you two out so early in the morning?"

Gowan's smile spread all over his face. It was the happiest she'd ever seen him. "Oh, a pleasure indeed. . . . We have a warrant for your arrest, Nelson."

"A what?"

"I knew if I waited long enough, you'd go one step too far and piss off the wrong person."

She backed away as Mallard approached.

"Looks like resisting arrest to me," he murmured and swung out with the nightstick he'd been holding, hidden, behind his leg.

The blow came too fast to avoid. It hit her hard across the solar plexus and she folded, gasping for breath. *He always was a fucking hotshot with that thing.* Each man grabbed an arm and the next thing she knew, she'd been tossed across the back seat of the car. Mallard climbed in with her. Gowan scurried around to the front.

The whole operation, from the time Gowan had first spoke, had taken less than a minute.

Vicki, her face pressed hard against musty upholstery, struggled to breathe. As the car began to move, Mallard yanked her arms back and forced the cuffs around her wrists, closing them so tightly the metal edges dug into the bone. The pain jerked her head up and his fist slammed it down.

"Go ahead, fight." He snickered and she felt him drive his forearm across the small of her back, immobilizing her with his weight.

Her glasses were hanging off one ear and losing them frightened her more than anything Mallard or Gowan could do. Although it wasn't going to be fun . . . she'd seen prisoners both men had released into holding cells. Apparently, they'd fallen down a lot.

When he started fumbling with the waistband of her jeans, she got one leg free and attempted to drive the heel of her sneaker through his ear. He grabbed her foot and twisted.

Goddamned, fucking son of a bitch!

The pain gave her something new to think about for a few seconds and the lesser pain of the needle almost got lost in it.

Needle?

Oh, shit . . .

The drug worked quickly.

Thirteen

"Nelson Investigations. No one is available to take your call, but if you leave your name and number as well as a brief outline of your problem . . ."

"*You're* my problem, Nelson," Celluci growled as he dropped the receiver back into the cradle. He glared at the clock on the kitchen wall. Ten twenty-five. Even at this hour of the morning, theoretically well past rush hour, driving from Downsview to the center of town was going to take just about all of that thirty-five minutes. He couldn't afford to wait any longer; Cantree had an understandable objection to his detectives wandering in to work when it suited them.

Of course, there was another number he could call. Fitzroy himself would have long ago crawled back into his coffin for the day, but Vicki might still be at his apartment.

Celluci snorted. "No, at his *condominium.*" God, that was such a yuppie word. People who lived in condominiums ate raw fish, drank lite beer, and collected baseball cards for their investment potential. Granted Fitzroy did none of those things, but he still played at the lifestyle. And romance novels? Bad enough for a man to write the asinine things but for a . . . a . . . for what Fitzroy was . . .

No. He wasn't calling Fitzroy's place. It was a big city, Vicki could be anywhere. Very likely she was taking young Tony home and tucking him in. The thought of Vicki in such a maternal role brought a sardonic smile and the thought that followed lifted his eyebrows almost to his hairline.

Tucking Tony in?

No. Celluci shook his head emphatically. Thinking about

Fitzroy was driving his mind right into the gutter. He shrugged into his jacket, grabbed his keys up off the kitchen table, and headed for the door. Vicki no doubt had a good reason for not calling. He trusted her. Maybe Tony's fears hadn't been completely unfounded—Fitzroy *had* been hurt facing the mummy, and she'd taken him wherever one took a hurt . . . romance writer. He trusted her innate good sense not to have used the information Fitzroy may have brought back and gone out after the mummy herself. . . .

"And if there isn't a message waiting for me at the office, I'm going to take her innate good sense and beat her to death with it."

The phone rang.

"Great timing, Vicki, I was just on my way out the door. And where the hell have you been anyway? I told you to call me first thing!"

"Celluci, shut up for a minute and listen."

Celluci blinked. "Dave?" His partner didn't sound like a happy man. "What's wrong. It's not the baby, is it?"

"No, no, she's fine." On the other end of the line, Dave Graham took a deep breath. "Look, Mike, you're going to have to lay low for a while. Cantree wants you picked up and brought in."

"Say what?"

"He's got a warrant for your arrest."

"On what charge?"

"There doesn't appear to be one. It's a special . . ."

"It's a fucking setup." Celluci grinned, suddenly relieved. "You didn't actually believe it, did you?"

"Yeah. I believed it. And you'd better, too." Something in Dave's voice wiped the grin off his face. "I don't know what's going on around here today, but they've shuffled a couple of departments around, no warning, and that warrant'll stand. I've never seen Cantree so serious about anything."

"Shit." It was more of an observation than an expletive.

"You can say that again, buddy-boy. I'm not sure I should ask, but just what have you done?"

"I was in the wrong place at the wrong time and I found out something I shouldn't have." Celluci considered what Vicki had told him about the Solicitor General's Halloween party. *Cantree. God damn it! The son of a bitch has sub-*

verted one of the few honest cops in the city. He had to assume that Fitzroy had been an accurate witness, but the thought of Cantree, of all people, blindly dancing to another man's tune made him feel physically ill. *And he's dancing right over me. The next time I think there's a mummy on the rampage in Toronto, I'll keep my fucking mouth shut.* "Are you calling from headquarters?"

"Do I look like an idiot?" Dave's voice was dry. "I'm at the Taco Bell around on Yonge Street."

"Good. Look, Dave, this is bigger than just me. Watch your back and, for the next little while, keep a very, very low profile."

"Hey, you don't need to tell me. There's something majorly weird going down around here and I've never been keen on being strip searched. How do I stay in touch?"

"Uh . . . good question." He could access messages off his machine by remote and as long as the messages were short enough there wouldn't be time to trace the line back; but they'd be monitoring and that would put Dave right in the toilet with him. Odds were good they'd also be monitoring Vicki's line. Cantree was well aware how close the two of them had been and how close they'd stayed. Best to keep away from Vicki's place completely and that included keeping Dave away from Vicki's answering machine.

"You could call me."

"No. Even if they don't suspect you warned me, they'll be monitoring your lines. You're the logical person for me to call. Damn it all to hell anyway!" He slapped his palm against the table and stared at the scrap of pink memo paper that fluttered down to the floor. Fitzroy? Why not? "I've got a number you can leave a message at. I can't guarantee I'll get it until after dark, but it should be safe. Memorize it, don't write it down, and use . . ."

"A public phone line. Mike, I know the drill." Dave repeated the number three times to be sure he had it, then warned, "You better get out of there. Cantree might not have wanted to wait until you came in. He may have sent a car up."

"I'm gone. And Dave? Thanks." Partners who could be depended on when the chips were down—or sideways—had saved the lives of more cops than a thousand fancy pieces of equipment. "I owe you one."

"One? You still owe me for a half a dozen meals, not to mention getting that asswipe from accounting off your back. Anyway, be careful." He hung up before Celluci could reply.

Be careful. Right.

Accompanied by a fine libretto of Italian swearing, Celluci threw a few clothes, some papers, and a box of ammunition in a cheap Blue Jays' gym bag. He had no time to change out of his suit, but the moment he could he'd ditch it for the uniform of the city—jeans and a black leather jacket worked better around Toronto than a cloak of invisibility. Not counting a pocket load of change, he had twenty-seven bucks in his wallet and another hundred in emergency money taped under the seat of the car. He'd take the money; he'd have to leave the car.

On his way out the door, he stopped and glanced back at the phone. Should he leave a message on Fitzroy's machine for Vicki? A second thought decided him against it. Cantree was likely to have a check run on all the numbers he'd called in the last couple of days and if Fitzroy's number showed up on the list . . .

"Good thing I didn't call it earlier." It appeared his ego was looking out for him.

He slipped the chain on, pulled the door closed, and heard the deadbolt click. His security system had been designed by one of the best break and enter boys in the city. Cantree would probably have the door smashed—the police were often less subtle than those they arrested—but it ought to slow the bastards down.

Very faintly, through the steel-reinforced oak, he heard the phone ring. It might be Vicki. He couldn't afford the time it would take to go back and answer it. If it *was* Vicki . . . well, Vicki had always been able to take care of herself and besides, she was safe enough for now; Cantree wanted him, not her.

The holding cell smelled of vomit and urine and cheap booze sweated out through polyester layered over years of too many desperate people and far too little money. A half dozen tired looking whores, waiting for their morning trip to court, huddled in one corner and watched Vicki forced down on the bench.

"What's she in for?" asked a tall brunette, adjusting what was either a very wide belt or a very short skirt.

"None of your damned business," grunted Mallard struggling with the cuffs, his shoulder pressing Vicki hard against the wall.

The hooker rolled her eyes. The other nodded.

"What was that?" Gowan asked. His position outside the cage had allowed him to see the expression Mallard had missed. "You got a problem with the officer's answer?"

"No." Her voice dropped just to one side of servile. "No problem."

Gowan smiled. "Glad to hear it, ladies."

Her expression supplicating, she gave him the finger, the gesture carefully hidden behind one of her companions. Working girls learned fast that cops came in two basic varieties. Almost all of them were just regular guys doing a job, but a nasty few would like nothing more than an excuse to pull out their sticks and apply a personal judgment. If fate threw them the latter, maintaining the merchandise dictated ass-kissing as hard and as fast as necessary.

Swearing softly, Mallard yanked the cuffs around on Vicki's wrists to give him a better angle with the key. "Goddamned things are stuck a . . . there." They dropped into his hands and he straightened. Without his support, Vicki sagged away from the wall and toppled sideways off the bench.

Although voluntary motor functions seemed to be under someone else's control and all the crevices of her brain had been filled with mashed potatoes, she was completely aware of everything that was going on. This was the Metro East Detention Center on Disco Road. Mallard and Gowan had tossed her bag at the Duty Sergeant and dragged her past saying, "Wait until you hear the story on this one . . ." They were now, obviously, going to leave her in the holding cell. Locked up. They said they had a warrant.

What the hell is happening?

She managed to focus on Mallard's face. The son of a bitch was smiling.

"Such a pity when a cop goes bad," he said clearly.

Cop? God damn it, don't say I'm a cop. Not here!

He reached down and pinched her cheek, hard enough for her to feel it through the drug, and gently resettled her glasses on her nose. "Wouldn't want you to miss any of this."

Don't leave me here! You can't just leave me here, you bastard! The thought slammed around inside her head but all that made it out was a kind of stuttering moan.

"I'll always remember you like this." His smile broadened, then he turned and moved back out of her line of sight.

She couldn't turn her head fast enough to watch him go. *NO!*

Heels rang against the concrete floor and Vicki struggled to focus on the young woman now standing over her.

Oh, Christ . . .

"Fucking cop."

The toes of her boots were dangerously pointed. Fortunately, she didn't know where use them to their best advantage. Nothing broke.

Vicki made an effort to remember the face behind the garish makeup before pain squeezed her eyes shut.

"Leave her alone, Marian. She's too stoned to feel it anyway."

She could feel snot running over her upper lip. She could feel something damp soaking through her jeans where her hip pressed against the floor. She'd never felt so desperately helpless in her entire life.

Somewhere else.
Eyes glowed red and Akhekh fed.

"How long do you figure the drug will last?"

Gowan shrugged. "I dunno, a few hours. It's the same stuff the animal control people use to bring down bears. Doesn't really matter how long it lasts. After the story we spun, they're not going to believe a word she says."

"But what if she gets a lawyer?"

"Not where she's going."

"But . . ."

"Chill out, Mallard." Gowan pulled carefully out of the parking spot and waved at the driver of a wagon just coming in. "Cantree said he needed a couple of days to get the evidence to nail the bitch and we've given it to him. It's his problem now."

"And hers."

Staff Sergeant Gowan nodded. "And hers," he repeated in pleased agreement.

The whores had been taken away. Vicki didn't know when. Time moved so slowly she might have been in the holding cell for days.

Inch by inch, she crawled one arm up the wall far enough for her hand to grab the edge of the bench. It took four tries for her grip to finally hold and another three before she could remember how to bend her elbow. Finally she was sitting, still on the floor but a definite improvement.

The massive physical effort needed to get this far had held panic at bay but now she could see—thank God, they hadn't taken her glasses—it rolled over her in turgid red waves that crashed against the backs of her eyes, receded and crashed down again. The only coherent word in the surging tide was *NO!* so she clutched at it and used it to keep from being pulled under.

NO! I will not surrender!

A sharp slap on her right cheek gave her a new focus and she managed to drag herself partially free.

"Hey? I said, can you walk?"

Vicki blinked. A guard. The panic receded further and relief flooded in to take its place. They'd realized what had happened and come to get her. She tried to smile and nod at the same time, couldn't do both so achieved neither, and threw everything she had into a struggle to get to her feet.

"Atta girl, upsa daisy. Christ," the guard grunted as she ended up lifting most of Vicki's weight. "Why are the stoners always so fucking big?"

The second guard, standing at the door of the cage, shrugged. "At least this one doesn't stink. I'll take a head over a drunk any day. Drugs don't make you puke on your shoes."

"Or my shoes," the first guard agreed. "Okay, you're up. Now then, left foot, right foot. *None* of us will enjoy it if we have to carry you."

It was more of a threat than an encouragement, but Vicki didn't notice. She could walk. It was shuffling, unsure, and slow, but it was forward locomotion and while both guards seemed merely satisfied, Vicki was overjoyed. She could walk. The drug must be wearing off.

Her relief grew when they took her straight to the Duty Sergeant and pushed her down onto a wooden chair.

I'm on my way out of here. . . .

"So," he said when the door closed and they were alone, "the two officers who brought you in suggested I book you myself."

Book me?

He patted the warrant with his fingertips. "They've left me a number to call for the official explanation. I can't wait. Cops who take advantage of their position to molest little kids don't go down very well with my people, or the inmates either for that matter. The officers seemed to think it would be better if no one else knew what you'd done."

I haven't done anything!

"Now they had no idea what drug you'd taken and I can't wait for it to wear off—if it's going to wear off—so we'll just enter your information off the warrant."

Okay. Don't panic. My name goes into the system, someone'll recognize it.

"Terri Hanover . . ."

Oh, God.

". . . age, thirty-two . . . five-foot ten . . . one hundred and forty-seven pounds . . ." He clicked his tongue. "Shaved a few pounds off there, did we?"

It's me, but it's not my name. Detectives were issued fake ID all the time and her specs were probably still on file. *What the hell is going on?*

The sound of his fingers against the keyboard began to sound like nails pounding into a cage being built around her. She couldn't just sit there and let it happen.

"I am not who they say I am!"

Except her mouth refused to form the words. Nothing came out except guttural noises and a trickle of saliva that ran off her chin to drip slowly into the hollow of her collarbone.

"Now then," he set the keyboard to one side and reached for the phone, "let's see what headquarters has to say."

"The Solicitor General's office. One moment please, he's expecting your call."

The phone on Zottie's desk buzzed but the Solicitor General just stared at it, a puzzled smile on his face.

"Pick it up," Tawfik commanded softly. The man would not last much longer. Fortunately, he wouldn't have to.

"Zottie here. Ah, yes, Sergeant Baldwin. Well, actually, it's not me you should be talking to. Hold on . . ." He passed the receiver to Tawfik, then lapsed back into semi-awareness as Tawfik began to speak.

The Solicitor General? Oh, God, then that means . . .

After his initial enthusiastic greeting, the Duty Sergeant said little. Finally, even the monosyllables faded into a blank stare.

This time the panic came with words.

The mummy put me here. Not Mallard and Gowan. The mummy. Christ. I should have remembered Cantree is under its control. But why? How? It doesn't know about me. Henry. Henry talked to it. Did Henry betray me? Without meaning to? Meaning to? Henry? Or Mike. It found out about Celluci. He was there. At the museum. It got Celluci. Took what it needed to know. I'm just another loose end. Mike? Are you dead? Are you dead? Are you dead?

She couldn't breathe. It hurt to breathe. She couldn't remember how to breathe.

The . . . mummy . . . has . . . to . . . be . . . stopped. And if Mike Celluci was dead? His death must be avenged. *A . . . venged.* She breathed in the first syllable and breathed out the second. *A . . . venged. A . . . venged. Avenged.*

"I understand."

Understand what?

"It will be done."

Eyes wide, unable to look away, Vicki watched him hang up the phone, pick up the warrant, her warrant, and walk over to the shredder.

NO!

She'd been entered into the system and as far as the system was concerned she now belonged here until they pulled her for a court appearance. Court appearances were booked by warrant. Without a warrant, she would rot here forever.

I could jump the sergeant. Hold him hostage. Call the newspapers! Call . . . call someone. I can't just disappear! But her body still refused to obey. She felt muscles tense, and then go slack, and then she began to tremble, unable to stop it or control it.

Sergeant Baldwin looked down at the shredder, frowned, and brushed one hand over the gray fringe of his hair. "Dickson!"

"Sarge?" The guard who had lifted Vicki to her feet back in the holding cell, opened the door and stuck her head into the office.

"I want you to search Ms. Hanover and then take her down to Special Needs."

"To the nut bars?" Dickson's brows rose. "You sure she shouldn't go to the hospital? She doesn't look so good."

The Sergeant snorted. "Neither did the kid when she got through seeing to him."

"Right."

Vicki heard the guard's voice pick up an edge; skinbeefs against children were universally despised. Strong fingers closed around her upper arm and heaved her up and out of the chair. Shoved toward the door, she struggled to remember how to walk.

"Oh, and Dickson? I want it to be a thorough search."

"Aw, come on, Sarge!" The guard's grip loosened a little as she turned to protest the order. "I had to do the last one."

"And you get to do this one, too. Here."

Vicki heard Dickson grunt as she caught something heavy and managed to get her head turned enough to see that it was her black leather shoulder bag.

The guard looked down at the huge, bulging bag in disbelief. "What am I supposed to do with this?"

"It came with her. When you've got her put away, you can enter the contents in her file."

"It'll take days."

"All the more reason to get started."

"Why me?" Dickson muttered, throwing the bag over her shoulder and dragging Vicki out of the office.

The grip on her arm had not been retightened. While going through the crowded doorway, Vicki attempted to twist free, reaching for her bag. If she could get her hands on it, it would make a decent weapon. She shouldn't be here. Anything to attract attention . . .

"Don't do that," Dickson sighed, effortlessly bouncing

her off the wall and then propelling her forward. "I'm not having a very good day."

The strip search was worse than Vicki could have imagined although, as she'd regained some gross motor control on the walk down the hall, it wasn't as bad as it could have been. Trapped inside her own head, there wasn't anything she could do but endure. She didn't blame Dickson, the guard was just doing her job, but when she got out of there Gowan and Mallard were going to be having their balls for breakfast. The image helped sustain her.

Dickson peeled off the rubber glove and tossed it into the trash. "These things only come in two sizes," she said, replacing the clothing Vicki had removed with jail issue. "Too big and too small. Can you dress yourself, Hanover?"

"Yuh . . ." *My God, that was almost a word!* She tried it again, humiliation wiped out in that one small victory over her body. "Yuh, yuh, yuh."

"Okay, okay, I get the picture. Jesus, you're drooling again."

With every article of clothing a small measure of control returned. Her movements were still jerky and unsure, but somehow she struggled into the jail blues, oblivious to the bored stare of the guard, oblivious to anything but the battle she fought with her body. Hands worked. Fingers didn't. Her sense of balance was still skewed and large movements nearly tipped her over but she leaned against the wall and got into the underwear, the jeans, and the shoes. The T-shirt nearly defeated her. She couldn't find the opening for her head and began to panic. Outside hands yanked it down, nearly taking her nose with it.

"Come on, Hanover. I haven't got all day."

The cotton overshirt with its wide v-neck was a little easier.

The drug's wearing off. Thank God. As soon as I can talk, someone's going to get one hell of an earful. As carefully as if she were threading a needle, Vicki reached for her glasses. Dickson reached them first.

"Forget that. You'll just have to squint."

It had never occurred to her that they wouldn't let her keep her glasses. Of course they wouldn't. Not in Special Needs. Glasses could be used as weapons.

But I can't see without my glasses.

All the composure she'd managed to gain with the control over her muscles fled.

I'll be blind.

It was what she'd been terrified of since the retinitis pigmentosa had been diagnosed.

Blind.

"Nuh!" Using her arm like a club, she knocked the other woman's hand away and attempted to snatch her glasses up off the pile of discarded clothing. But her fingers wouldn't close fast enough and a sharp shove from the guard sent her lurching back against the wall.

"Here, none of that! You show fight and you wear the restraints. Understand?"

You don't understand. My glasses . . .

Something of Vicki's fear must have shown on her face. Dickson frowned and said brusquely, "Look, Hanover, you convince the shrink you don't belong in Special Needs and we'll give you your glasses back."

Hope. The psychiatrist would listen to her. Probably even recognize the drug.

"Now come on, I haven't got all day. Christ, it'll probably take me the rest of the shift just to list what you've got in that bag."

The world had condensed into a fuzzy tunnel. Vicki shuffled along it, heart leaping as doors and furniture and people loomed up without warning. She cracked her knee on the edge of something and slammed her shoulder into a corner she couldn't see.

Dickson sighed as she steered her charge through the first of the locked doors and onto the range. "Maybe you'd do better if you just closed your eyes."

The noise was overwhelming; the clatter of a busy cafeteria with the volume control gone and so many women's voices that all individual sound was lost. The smell of food overpowered the smell of prison. Vicki suddenly realized that she hadn't eaten since about nine o'clock the evening before. Her mouth flooded with saliva and her stomach growled audibly.

"Great timing, Dickson," called a new voice. "We're just counting the spoons. You'll have to keep her out here until we finish and lock 'em in for cleanup."

"Oh, joy, oh, bliss," Dickson muttered. Vicki tensed as

the guard pushed her back until her shoulder blades pressed against the concrete wall. "Stay there. Don't move. You've missed lunch, but considering the food in here, that might be a good thing."

Vicki could feel people staring. The bars were a hazy grid at the edge of her vision and beyond that she could make out only a shifting sea of blue.

The hair on the back of her neck rose. *You're only in there until you talk to the shrink. You don't need to see anything.*

To her right, she could hear the clatter of spoons against a plastic tray and then the new guard's voice rising above the noise. "So, what've you got?"

"Skinbeef. Brain-fried, too."

"Violent?"

"Barely mobile."

"Can she piss in the pot?"

"Probably."

"Well, thank God for small mercies. I've already got four that have to be hosed down. Where the fuck am I supposed to put her though, that's the question. I'm three down in fifteen out of eighteen cells now."

"Put her in with Lambert and Wills."

During the long pause that followed, Vicki realized the two guards were talking about her. As though she wasn't there. As though she didn't matter. Because she didn't.

"Skinbeef, eh?" The second pause had a more ominous sound. "How old was the kid?"

"Don't know."

"Well, I think Lambert and Wills will make her feel real welcome." She raised her voice. "All right, you lot, get inside, you know the drill. Oh, for Christ's sake, Naylor, take Chin with you. You know she gets lost. . . ."

Gradually the sea of blue receded, turned into separate shapes, then disappeared. Vicki heard the sound of steel doors closing.

"Shu . . . shu . . . shu . . . ?"

"What the hell are you muttering about?" Dickson's face swam into focus as she grabbed Vicki's arm above the elbow and tugged her toward the set of double doors that led into the cell block.

"Shink . . ."

"Oh, the *shrink*. Hey, Cowan, the shrink been in yet today?"

"Yeah. Came and left before lunch."

"You heard her. Looks like you're in here until Wednesday at least."

Wednesday. Monday's half over. Then Tuesday. Then Wednesday. But the shrink came in the morning. So really only two days. Half of Monday, Tuesday, and half of Wednesday. I can do two days. I can make it. Even without my glasses.

They stopped in front of one of the cells and Vicki was willing to take any odds that the two women inside were watching her suspiciously from their bunks. The cells were built for two, a third meant the beginning of crowding that often went as high as five. She intended to move quietly into the cell, but her legs froze at the threshold and the panic started to rise again.

"Come on, Hanover, move it!"

A shove in the small of her back catapulted her forward and after three wild steps she crashed to her knees.

It's okay. It's only two days. Once the drug is gone, I'll be fine. These people are crazy. I'm not. Slowly, carefully, she got to her feet. Behind her, she heard the cell door locked and Dickson moving away. *Even if the mummy got to Henry, or Celluci*—and dealing with that possibility would have to wait—*it can't have gotten to the psychiatrist. Two days. I'll be out of here in two days.*

The bunk to her right squealed a protest as the woman reclining on it swung to her feet. Hands held out from her sides, Vicki turned to face her cell mate. *Remember, she's crazy. Probably confused. Lost. You're not. Two days.*

Cropped gray hair and a tiny, whippet-thin frame. Large dark eyes in a face that seemed all points. Something familiar . . . but Vicki couldn't see well enough to determine what.

"Well, well, well. Will wonders never cease."

The voice sound low and clear and frighteningly sane.

"Isn't it amazing the people you meet in these places, Natalie?"

The grunt from the other bunk could've meant anything.

Vicki felt a dry palm and fingers wrap around her right hand. Her knuckles began to rub painfully. She tried to return the pressure without much effect.

"It's *so* nice to see you again, Detective Nelson . . ."

Lambert. Angel Lambert. What the hell is she doing in Special Needs?

". . . you can't imagine."

Oh, yes, I can . . .

"Nelson Investigations. No one is available to take your call, but . . ."

"Damn it, Vicki, where the fuck are you?" Celluci slammed down the receiver and slammed out of the phone booth. Vicki never used her answering machine when she was home. So she wasn't home. So where was she? He'd left a message on Fitzroy's machine and called Vicki's apartment half a dozen times from half a dozen different areas in the city.

She was probably out working; tracking the mummy, gathering information; maybe even doing her laundry or the grocery shopping. He had no reason to believe she might be in danger.

Cantree's looking for me. Dave would've mentioned it if she'd been pulled into this as well. Trouble was, Cantree, not to mention a good part of the force, knew about their relationship. And if Fitzroy had found something out about the mummy that Vicki thought she could use, and then she had, Cantree and the Metro Police could be the least of her worries. *She was a good cop. One of the best. You don't get to be one of the best without learning not to throw yourself at a superior force.*

So that takes care of Cantree and the mummy, Celluci told himself. *Vicki's fine. There's no reason to believe she's in any danger just because she didn't call you when she said she was going to.* You're *the one up shit creek without the paddle.*

He lit a cigarette, shoved his hands back into his pockets, and slouched down the street, trying not to inhale—a haze of cigarette smoke made an almost impenetrable camouflage when people thought they were looking for a non-smoker. It had been one of Vicki's tricks for going undercover and he suddenly realized how much he'd been counting on her help. *Sure, she rushes right over when Fitzroy needs her, but when my balls are in the fire where is she . . . ?*

Fourteen

There were four messages on Henry's answering machine. Two were from Mike Celluci for Vicki. One was from someone named Dave Graham for Celluci; apparently nothing had changed. With a growing sense of unease, Henry wondered just what nothing referred to. The fourth message was from Tony, for him.

"Look, Henry, I know Victory says you're okay, but I want to hear it from you. Call me. Please."

He'd barely hung up after reassuring the younger man when the phone rang.

"Fitzroy? Celluci. Have you heard from Vicki?"

Henry's grip tightened on the receiver. The plastic groaned. "No," he said quietly, "I haven't. Why?"

"I've been trying to get her all day. When she contacts you, warn her to lay low. Cantree's got a warrant out for my arrest and he might have one for her."

Cantree. The man Henry had watched ensorcelled. According to Vicki, Celluci had been vocal about his belief in the mummy around the station so it wasn't surprising Tawfik had decided to silence him. Henry frowned. Tawfik had no contact with Vicki though.

"What does Vicki have to do with this?" he demanded.

"Cantree knows how close we are, Vicki and I." The emphasis was unmistakably a deliberate dig. "He won't believe for a minute that I didn't give her all the details on something I felt that strongly about."

Henry fought his way through a wave of jealousy and barely made it out the other side. "How do we know he doesn't already have her?"

"I gave Dave Graham, my partner, your number. If she's picked up, he'll let me know."

"Graham left a message. He says nothing's changed."

"Okay. Cantree doesn't have her. You stay put in case she calls. I'll stay in touch. Once we know she's safe, we can make plans."

"Do not presume, mortal . . ."

"And don't bullshit me, Fitzroy. Can you find her?"

Could he track the call of her blood, with so many other lives around? "No."

"Then stay put! Look," Henry heard the effort it took for Celluci to force reason into his voice, "if you hit the streets, we'll have no way to pull together again. Vicki can take care of herself."

"Not against Tawfik."

"God damn it, Fitzroy, she's not up against Tawfik. He's using Cantree now to . . ."

"What about Trembley?"

"He didn't have his bully boys in place then. I know how these guys work. Once they have an organization set up, they don't dirty their own hands anymore."

"Tawfik is not some petty crime boss, Detective." Henry bit the words off and spat them into the phone. "And you have no idea of how the mind of an immortal works." Ignoring anything further Celluci had to say, and that seemed to be a great deal, Henry very carefully hung up the phone. Vicki lived. He would have felt the absence of her life.

Come to the corner where we first met, Tawfik had told him. *And I will find you.*

Find me, Henry thought back at the memory, *give yourself up into my hands, and you will tell me where she is.*

The world had taken on a tint of red.

For a few hours at least, it was over. Vicki lay back on her mattress and tried to relax her muscles enough to sleep. Although she regained more control with every hour, the twisted ridges across her back refused to unknot. She didn't blame them.

Angel Lambert was pretending to have slipped a few gears in order to get out of a trip to Kingston and the Women's Penitentiary. The right diagnosis would send her to the relative comfort of a hospital and a short time later back out on the streets. Her bragging had been very explicit. Of course, the bragging had come after Lambert had assured herself that Vicki hadn't been placed on the range as a police spy.

"Maybe they figure'd that 'cause you aren't on the force no more you'd be safe." Arms crossed, Lambert had walked a slow circle around her new cell mate. Vicki tried to keep her in sight, nearly fell over, and gave up. " 'Course, druggin' you seems to be goin' just a bit far." Making sure Vicki saw what she was about to do, she lashed out, kicking Vicki hard in the calf, the toe of her sneaker sinking deep into the muscle.

Vicki tried to avoid the blow but couldn't get her leg to respond in time. She grunted in pain and made a grab for Lambert's throat.

Lambert leaned easily back out of the way. "Well, well, well. Got doped up and got yourself in trouble, eh? Heard the guard say you were in on a juvie skinbeef. You know what that means, don't you? They're not gonna care if you pick up a few bruises. In fact, they're hopin' you will. That's why you're in with us. We got us a bit of a rep for playin' rough." She leaned back against the wall and crossed her arms, scratching a little at her biceps. "I saw your eyes when you recognized me, so I know you're in there. And I know what you're thinkin'. You're thinkin' that as soon as that drug wears off you're gonna clean my clock. Not a bad plan, you're bigger than me and you got all that fancy training, but," she smiled, "I got something you don't. Natalie, come around where our new friend can see you."

At five ten, Vicki didn't look up at many women, but Natalie Wills was huge. Even slouched she had to top six feet; if she ever straightened up, she'd probably hit six six or six seven. Her frizzy halo of blonde hair emphasized the rounded curves of her face and her pale blue eyes bulged slightly out of the sockets. At some point in the past, her nose had been broken, at least once, and improperly set. Through the space between her slack lips, Vicki could hear heavy adenoidal breathing. Her breasts and belly stretched the limits of the jail uniform. It looked and moved like fat but Vicki wasn't willing to give any odds that it actually was.

"Natalie's my friend," Lambert purred. "Aren't you, Natalie?"

Natalie nodded slowly, the corners of her mouth twisting up in what Vicki assumed was a smile.

"Natalie's very strong. Aren't you, Natalie?"

Natalie nodded again.

"Why don't you show our new roommate how strong you are, Natalie. Pick her up."

Enormous hands closed around Vicki's upper arms with a grip that painfully compacted muscle down onto bone. Her shoulders rose first, but the rest of her body soon followed until her feet were six inches off the floor.

Oh, great, Darth Vader in drag.

"Very good, Natalie. Now, shake her."

After the first few seconds, it seemed as though Vicki's brain had broken free of its moorings and was slamming around independently inside her skull.

"Drop her, Natalie."

The floor seemed much farther away than she knew it was. Her knees cracked painfully hard against the concrete and she fell forward, just barely managing to get an arm between her face and the floor. If she'd had anything in her stomach, she'd have lost it.

"You puking down there?" Lambert inquired, squatting down and grabbing Vicki's hair. "You puke in my cell and you lick it up."

"Uck uf." Her voice still wasn't clear, but she figured Lambert got the point when her fist twisted around, nearly removing the handful of hair.

"Once that drug wears off, you'll be out of here next time the shrink's by. That'll be Wednesday at the earliest. You and me and Natalie, we're gonna have a fun two days."

Two days. I can take two days of anything.

But lying there, listening to Natalie's moist breathing, Vicki wondered if she could. It wasn't the physical abuse—if that got too bad, the guards would intervene, even for a skinbeef, and by morning she should be in better shape to defend herself—it was the sheer hopelessness of the situation. She'd been swept up and slotted neatly into the system and the system didn't like to admit it had made a mistake. The shrink would get her out of Special Needs, but that would only land her in another cell just like this one in another part of the jail. From there she could talk all she wanted, but her court date would never come up and like Lambert said, *"Who the hell's gonna believe you? A cop gone bad; a juvie skinbeef, a doper. In here, I've got more credibility."*

It was almost as if she'd been dropped into her worst nightmare.

Two days in here, but how long until I'm out?

And what about Henry and Celluci? Had Henry betrayed her? Had Celluci been taken? Not knowing made everything worse.

Her eyes filled with moisture and she angrily blinked them dry. Then she frowned. Refracted in a tear, she seemed to see two tiny pinpoints of glowing red light. That was impossible. She couldn't see anything.

Although the cells went no darker than a gray and shadowed twilight, lights out for Vicki had meant the end of what little sight she had without her glasses. Lambert had quickly recognized the handicap and set about taking full advantage of it. Surprisingly enough, when there was no longer any point in struggling to see, Vicki found things a little easier. Sound and smell, and the movement of air currents against her skin were a lot more useful than her deteriorating vision had been although, unfortunately, not useful enough to avoid the constant attacks. Natalie could have played the game all night, but Lambert had soon gotten bored and ordered the larger woman to bed.

Natalie liked hurting people—her strength was the only power she had—and Lambert liked seeing people hurt. Vicki sighed silently. *How nice for them that they've found each other.*

She knew she needed sleep, but she didn't think she'd be able to find it; she ached in too many places, supper had congealed into a solid lump just under her ribs, the mattress seemed to be deliberately digging into her shoulders and hips, and the smell of the place coated the inside of her nose and mouth, making it hard to breathe. Mostly she didn't think she could sleep because despair kept chasing its tail around and around in her head.

Finally exhaustion claimed her and she drifted off to the sound of plastic against concrete as two cells down a woman struggled against padded shackles and banged the hockey helmet she wore over and over against the wall.

Henry's fingers tightened where they rested against the concrete light standard and under the pressure the concrete began to crumble.

Tawfik! Here I am!

"Hey, buddy, can you spare a . . ."

Who dared? He turned.

"Holy Mary, Mother of God." Under stubble and dirt, the drunk paled. His nightmares often wore that expression. One filthy arm raised to cover his eyes, he staggered away, muttering, "Forget it, man. Forget me."

He was already forgotten.

Henry had no time to spare on thoughts of mortals. He wanted Tawfik.

He could feel the Nightwalker's anger. The brilliance of his ka was aflame with it.

Find me!

He stood at the window and stared down at the street. Although the angle of the hotel cut through his line of sight, he knew exactly where young Richmond waited. His passion thrust his ka forward with such force that Tawfik barely had to reach out to touch it. Surface thoughts were still all that were open to him, but those thoughts boiled with enough raw emotion that, for tonight, the surface was entertaining enough.

"Such a small city this turns out to be," he murmured, lightly touching the glass. "So you know my lord's plaything *and* the police officer who sent her to find me—who appears to be giving my hunting dogs a good run." Tawfik suddenly remembered the doors he had been maneuvered past on his walk through the chosen one's mind and he smiled. Two of the doors had just given up their secrets. How noble that she had tried to protect those close to her. "I imagine all these little interconnections have twisted her up far worse than I ever could. My lord must be pleased." If his lord even noticed; very often subtleties were ignored in favor of blind gorging. Tawfik sighed. He had realized long, long ago that he had sworn himself to a god without grandeur.

FIND ME!

"You can rant and rave all you like, Nightwalker. I am not going down there. You're not thinking right now, you're only reacting. Thoughts can be twisted. Reactions, especially from one with your physical power, should be avoided."

The Nightwalker, he was amused to note, had not grown beyond the possibility of love. How foolish, to love those who were fed upon. Like a mortal declaring himself for a cow or a chicken . . .

He took one last look at the burning, brilliant ka that he so desired and then closed his mind to it, removing temptation. "We'll straighten things out later," he promised softly. "We have the time, you and I."

"Graham. What?"

"Any word on Vicki?"

Dave Graham raised himself up on his elbow and peered at the illuminated numbers of the clock. "Jesus Christ, Mike," he hissed, "it's two o'clock in the fucking morning. Can't it wait?"

"What about Vicki?"

Curling around the receiver so as not to wake his wife, Dave surrendered. "There's no warrant in the system. No one's got orders to pick her up. They're keeping an eye on her place, but they're watching for you."

"Then they've already got her."

"They who? Cantree?"

"That's who he seems to be using."

"He?"

"Never mind."

Dave sighed. "Look, maybe she's got nothing to do with this. Maybe she just went to Kingston to visit her mother."

"We were working on the same case."

"A police case?" Dave took the long silence that followed his question as an answer and sighed again. "Mike, Vicki's not on the force anymore. You're not supposed to do that."

"Have you talked to Cantree?"

"Yeah, right after I talked to you this morning."

"And?"

"And like I said in my message, nothing's changed. He still wants you. I don't know why. He said it had something to do with internal security, that I wasn't to ask questions, and all would be made clear later on. He's got me doing scut work out in Rexdale."

"Did he seem strange?"

"Fuck, Mike, this whole thing is strange. Maybe you should just come in and straighten it out. Cantree'll listen."

The bark of laughter held little humor. "The only hope the whole city, maybe the whole world has is that I don't get picked up and I don't go anywhere near Frank Cantree."

"Right." It was two o'clock in the morning; he had no intention of getting into conspiracy theories. "I'll keep ears and eyes open, but there's not much I can do."

"Anything you see or hear . . ."

"I'll leave a message. Not that I'm likely to see or hear anything out west of God's country, I mean, we're talking Rexdale here. You'd better get going in case they've got a trace on this call . . . Mike? I was joking. Celluci? Christ . . ." He stared down at the receiver for a moment, then shook his head, hung up and wrapped himself around the soft, warm curves of his wife.

"Who was that?" she murmured.

"Celluci."

"What time is it?"

"Just after two."

"Oh, God . . ." She burrowed deeper under the covers. "They catch him yet?"

"Not yet."

"Pity."

By breakfast, Vicki had regained most of her muscle control; arms and legs moved when and where she wanted them to although the fine-tuning still needed work. Attempting to use her fingers for more than basic gripping of utensils was chancy and stringing more than two or three words together tied her tongue in knots. Thinking beyond her present situation, trying to analyze or plan, continued to wrap her brain in cotton, and thinking *about* her present situation did no good at all.

Without her glasses, breakfast was a heap of yellow and brown at the end of a fuzzy tunnel. It tasted pretty much exactly the way it looked.

She couldn't avoid eating sandwiched between her two cell mates, nor could she miss noticing how the other women on the range steered well clear of them, allowing them to move to the front of the food line as well as claim an entire pitcher of coffee. Natalie's strength combined with Lambert's viciousness placed them firmly on the top of the pecking order. The more coherent of the other inmates regarded Vicki with something close to relief, their expressions proclaiming not so much *better you than me* as *at least when it's you it isn't me.*

Protecting her food as well as herself turned out to be more than Vicki was capable of. Egged on by Lambert, Natalie lifted most of Vicki's breakfast and, under the cover of the rickety picnic table—that tilted alarmingly under every shift in weight—pinched her thigh black and blue. Natalie thought the whole thing was pretty funny. Vicki didn't, but the attacks came in from the side and she couldn't fight what she couldn't see. The meal became a painful and humiliating lesson in helplessness.

Locked back in the cell during cleanup, she kept her back against the wall and tried to force her eyes to function. Unfortunately, it didn't take Lambert long to map the limits of her vision. Trying to duck away from the wet end of a towel dipped in the toilet, Vicki felt a sudden kinship with those kids in school yards whom everyone picked on just because they could.

When they were let back out into the range, she groped her way past the row of tables and tried to talk to the guard. She knew where the duty desk should be even though she couldn't actually see it.

"Hey?"

"Hey what?" The guard's voice offered nothing.

"I ne . . ."

"No. No! NO! NO! NO! NO! NOOOOOO!"

Natalie. Standing right behind her. Although she knew what the result would be, Vicki tried again. "You go . . ."

"NO! NO! NO! NOOOOOO!"

She didn't think of this on her own. Lambert put her up to it. Teeth clenched so tightly her jaw ached, Vicki was willing to bet that the noise would go on indefinitely.

"Look!" she finally screamed, as she shoved impotently at the woman bellowing a hundred and twenty decibel accompaniment to everything she said. "I don' belon' he'!"

All at once iron rods slammed up against Vicki's face as

Natalie shoved her, and for an instant the guard loomed into focus. It wasn't Dickson. It wasn't anyone Vicki knew.

"So tell the shrink," she suggested. Her expression teetered between boredom and annoyance. "And back away from those bars."

"Mine for two days," Lambert told her as Natalie led Vicki back to her side.

They spent the morning watching game shows. Vicki sat in a kind of stupor, thankful, given what she could hear over the noise of forty women in an area designed for eighteen, that she couldn't see the televisions. Middle America rejoicing in the glory of frost free refrigerators would've pushed her over the edge.

Lunch was a repeat of breakfast, although Natalie moved to her other side and therefore pinched her other thigh. A woman with a bad case of the d.t.'s threw her plate against the bars and two others began screaming random profanity. Someone began to howl. Vicki kept her gaze locked firmly on her plate. Misery seasoned every mouthful.

After lunch, things quieted down as the soap operas came on. Lambert sat enthroned by the best of the four televisions with Natalie enforcing at least a localized silence.

"That's my husband, you know. That's my husband," an elderly woman called pointing at the screen. "We have thirteen children and a dog and two . . . ." A squawk of pain cut off the litany.

For the moment, Vicki appeared to have been forgotten. Moving carefully, she headed for the showers. Maybe if she scrubbed the stink of the place off she'd feel less wretched.

The concrete barricade that separated the showers from the common area rose from the floor to waist height and dropped from the ceiling to just above her shoulders. Everything in between was exposed to inmates and guards.

No one's going to be looking at your tits, Vicki, she told herself running one hand along the damp cement. *You're just another piece of meat. No one cares.*

A number of the stalls near the entrance were already full. In one, the flesh-colored blur separated itself out into two people. Anything that happened below the level of the barricades happened in as close to privacy as was available.

Stripping off shoes and pants and underwear wasn't so bad, but the flesh on Vicki's back crawled as she shrugged out of the shirt, and pulling the T-shirt up over her head left her feeling more exposed and vulnerable than she ever had in her life. She hurried in under the minimal protection the water offered.

Lost in the heat and the pounding of the spray, she almost convinced herself that she was safe at home and just for that moment things didn't seem so hopeless.

"Good idea, Nelson, but you shouldn't be by yourself. You're still unsteady on your pins and sometimes people fall in the shower. Terrible place. So easy to get hurt."

Lambert. And, as usual, not alone.

Vicki tried to twist her arm out of Natalie's grip. Natalie's answering twist nearly dislocated her elbow. The pain shot scarlet flames up behind her eyes and burned the fog away. Despair turned suddenly to anger.

She didn't stand a chance. She didn't care.

It didn't last long.

"What the hell is going on in there?"

"Nothing, boss," Lambert purred. "My buddy fell down." Below the guard's line of sight, her foot pressed lightly on Vicki's throat.

"She okay?"

"Fine, boss."

"Then pick her up and get out of there."

Natalie giggled, reached down, and pinched Vicki's stomach. Hard.

Vicki flinched but ignored it. Her head still rang from its violent contact with the tiles, but for the first time in what seemed like centuries, she was thinking clearly. Lambert and Wills were minor annoyances, no more. Her enemy was a three-thousand-year-old mummy who'd taken the law and twisted it and trapped her in the spiral he'd created. He was going to pay for that. She didn't know who he'd hurt to find her, Henry or Celluci, but he was going to pay for that, too. In order to make him pay, she had to be free and if the system wouldn't free her, then she'd have to do it herself.

"Thank you," she muttered absently, as Natalie dragged her upright.

People had broken out of detention centers before.

"Another beautiful day in the Metro West Detention Center. Thanks, guys, we can take her from here."

The young woman fought against the shackles, hissing and spitting like a large cat. The guards ignored her, hooked their hands under her arms and dragged her away.

"Fucking pigs!" she shrieked. "You're nothing but fucking pigs and I hope I fucking knocked your goddamned tooth out!"

Dave Graham sighed and turned to face his temporary partner. "Did she?"

"Nah," Detective Carter Aiken dabbed at the corner of his mouth and winced as his palm came away covered in blood, "but she split my lip."

"Not a bad right cross."

Aiken snorted. "Easier to appreciate it from your angle. There's a crapper at the end of the hall, I'll be right back."

"What're you going to do, stick your head in the toilet?"

"Who said anything about my head?" Aiken sucked the blood off his teeth and his brows rose dramatically. "I've had to piss since we left division."

Dave laughed as the other man disappeared around the corner and leaned back against the wall. He liked Aiken. He wished they'd met under better circumstances. He wished he knew what the hell was going on.

"Well, hello, stranger."

He straightened and turned. The Auxiliary Sergeant with her arms full of computer printout looked familiar but . . . "Hania? Hania Wojotowicz? Hot damn! When did you make sergeant?"

She laughed. "Six weeks ago. Actually, six weeks, two days, four hours and," she checked her watch, nearly losing the pile of papers, "eleven minutes. But who's counting. What are you doing way out here? Where's Mike?"

Obviously, she hadn't heard about Celluci. Fine with him, he was getting tired of talking about it. "Temporary duty. You know how it is. What about you?"

"Detention's having a little trouble with the OMS. Their computer program," she continued when he looked blank, "the Offender Management System. I've come to try and straighten it out."

"If anyone can do it . . ." When they'd first met, Hania had been brought in to crunch the data gathered as part of a massive manhunt after a homicide down in Parkdale. As far as he was concerned, what she could do with a computer should be filed somewhere between magic and miracle. Even Celluci, who'd been heard to suggest that all silicon should go back to the beach where it belonged, had been favorably impressed. "How bad is it?"

Hania shrugged. "Not very. In fact, I've done my part, all that's left is for someone to enter all this," a nod of her head indicated the printouts she carried, "back into the system."

"Good lord, that'll take days."

"Not really, most of this paper is blank. It's all personal possession lists and not many people book in here with luggage. Well, there are exceptions . . . ." She flipped a page back and grinned. "Listen to this. Four pens, four pencils, a black magic marker, a plastic freezer bag containing six folded empty plastic freezer bags, a brush, a comb, a cosmetic case containing a lipstick and two tampons, seven marbles in a cotton bag, a set of lock picks in a leather folder, a magnifying glass in a protective case, three notebooks half full, one notebook empty, a package of tissues, a package of condoms, a package of birth control pills, a screwdriver, a Swiss Army knife, a fish-shaped water pistol, cotton swabs, tweezers, a pair of needlenose pliers, a pair of wrapped surgical gloves, a small bottle of ethyl alcohol, a high-powered flashlight with four extra batteries, two u-shaped nails, $12.73 in assorted change, and a half-eaten bag of cheese balls. Now I ask you, what kind of weirdo carries all that in her purse?"

It took Dave a moment to find his voice. "No ID?" he managed at last.

"Not a thing. Not so much as a Visa statement. Probably pitched it just before she got picked up. They do sometimes, but you know that."

"Yeah." They did sometimes. He didn't think they had this time. "Who do they say belongs to all this?"

"They don't. But I can find out for you." She started down the hall. "Come on, there's a terminal in here we can use."

He followed blindly. He knew exactly what kind of weirdo carried all that in her purse.

"Dave? Detective-Sergeant Graham? Are you listening to me?"

"Yeah. Sorry." Except he wasn't. He couldn't hear anything over Celluci's voice saying, *"Then they've already got her."*

"Fitzroy? Celluci. I'm assuming that if you'd managed to find Vicki last night you'd have changed your message to let me know." *And if you found her and didn't change the message,* the tone continued, *I'm going to rip your head off.* "Stay put tonight. At least until I call. I'm going to try to get into her apartment and have a look around—no one disappears without leaving some kind of evidence—but after that we need to talk. We're going to have to work together to find her." The last statement landed like a thrown gauntlet even through the tiny speaker of the answering machine.

In spite of everything, Henry smiled. *You need my help, mortal man. Time you admitted it.*

"Hi, Henry, it's Brenda. Just a reminder that we need *Love's Labor Lashed,* or whatever you've decided to name it, by the fifteenth. We've got Aliston signed to do the cover on this one and he promises no purple eye shadow. Call me."

"Celluci? Dave Graham. It's quarter after four, Tuesday, November third . . ."

It was now six twelve, eight minutes after sunset.

". . . Call me the instant you get this message; I'll be home all evening." His voice grew strained, as though he couldn't really believe what he was saying. "I think I've found her. It isn't good."

Henry's fingers closed around the chair back and with a loud crack the carved oak splintered into a half dozen pieces. He stared down at the wreckage without really seeing it. This man on the phone, this David Graham, knew where Vicki was. If he wanted the information, he would have to take the message to Michael Celluci.

The police in the unmarked car were easy to avoid. They appeared to have little interest in the job they were doing and paid the shifting shadows just back of the sidewalk no attention at all. As for getting into the apartment itself, well, he had a key. The door opened quietly before him and closed as quietly behind. He stood silently in the entryway and listened to the life that moved about at the end of the hall. The heartbeat pounded faster than it should and the breath was short and almost labored. The blood scent dominated, but fear and anger and fatigue layered over it in equal proportions.

He walked forward and paused at the edge of the living room. Although it was very dark, he could see the kneeling man clearly.

"I have a message for you," he said, and took a perverse pleasure in the sudden jump of the heartbeat.

"Jesus H. Christ," Celluci hissed, surging to his feet and glaring down at Henry. "Don't do that! You weren't there a second ago! And besides, I thought I told you . . ."

Henry merely looked up at him.

Celluci pushed the curl of hair back off his forehead with a trembling hand. "All right, you have a message." His eyes widened. "Is it from Vicki?"

"Are you ready to hear it?"

"God damn you!" Celluci grabbed the lapels of Henry's leather trench coat and tried to drag him off his feet. He couldn't budge the smaller man although that took a moment to sink in. "Damn you!" he swore again, anchoring his grip more firmly in the leather. "If it's from Vicki, tell me!"

The pain in the detective's voice got through where anger alone wouldn't have and shame followed close behind. *What am I doing?* Almost gently, Henry pulled Celluci's hands off his coat. *She won't love me more for hurting you.* "The message was from Dave Graham. He wants you to call him at home. He says he thinks he's found her."

One breath, two, three; Celluci groped blindly for the phone, the darkness no longer a protection but an enemy to be fought. Henry reached out and guided his hands, then moved quickly to the extension in the bedroom as he dialed.

"Dave? Where is she?"

Dave sighed. Henry heard the soft flesh of his lower lip compressed between his teeth. "Metro West Detention Center. At least, I think it's her."

"Didn't you check?"

"Yeah, I checked." From the sound of his voice, Detective-Sergeant Graham still didn't believe what he'd found. "I better start at the beginning. . . ." He told how he'd run into Hania Wojotowicz and how she'd listed the contents of the purse, how she'd called up the inmate file, how the description had fit Vicki Nelson even though the name had said Terri Hanover. "They picked her up on a skinbeef, Mike, against a twelve-year-old boy. You've never read such a crock of shit. She was on something, they don't know what, so they stuck her in Special Needs."

"They drugged her! The bastards drugged her!"

"Yeah. *If* it's her." But he didn't sound like he had any doubts. "Who are *they,* Mike? What the fuck is going on?"

"I can't tell you. Where is she exactly—now?"

The pause said Dave knew exactly why Celluci asked. "She's still in Special Needs," he said at last. "D Range. Cell three. But I didn't actually see her. They wouldn't let me onto the range. I don't *know* it's her."

"I do."

"This has gone too far." He swallowed, once, hard. "I'm talking to Cantree tomorrow."

"No! Dave, you talk to Cantree about any of this and you'll be ass deep in it with the rest of us. Just keep your mouth shut for a little while longer. Please."

"A little while longer," Dave repeated and sighed again. "All right, partner, how long?"

"I don't know. Maybe you should take that vacation time you've got coming."

"Yeah. Maybe I should."

The quiet click as Dave Graham hung up his end of the line sounded through the apartment.

Henry came out of the bedroom and the two men stared at each other.

"We have to get her out," Celluci said. He could see only a pale oval of face in the darkness. *I'll do anything I must to get her out no matter how little I like it. I'll even work with you because I need your strength and speed.*

"Yes," Henry agreed. *The "detention centers" I know are centuries in the past. I need your knowledge. My feelings here are not important; she is.*

The silent subtext echoed so loudly between them it was amazing it didn't alert the police watching the building and bring them racing inside.

Fifteen

"All right, when the lights go out, you go over the wall, across the yard, in the emergency exit and . . ."

"Up three flights of stairs and through the first emergency door on my left. I remember your instructions, Detective." Henry stepped back from his BMW and looked down at Celluci who still sat in the driver's seat. "Are *you* certain you can get near enough to the generator?"

"Don't worry about me, you just be ready to move. You won't have much time. The moment the power goes off, all four guards will move to A Range to start emergency lockup. Vicki's in D; they'll do that last. You'll also have to deal with the other women on the range; it's just turned eight, so they won't be in the cells yet. . . ."

"Michael."

Celluci started. Something in the sound of his name stopped the flow of words and brought his head up. Although he knew the other man's eyes were hazel, they seemed much darker than hazel could be as if they'd absorbed some of the night.

"I want her out of there as much as you do. We will be successful. She will be freed. One way or another."

The words, the tone, the man himself, left no room for argument, no room for doubt. Celluci nodded, comforted in spite of himself and, as he had once before in a farmhouse kitchen, he thought that he would be willing to follow . . . *a romance writer. Yeah, sure.* But the protest had little force behind it. He wet his lips and dropped his gaze, aware as he did that Fitzroy had allowed it and, strangely enough, found himself not resenting the other's strength. "You won't have much time before the emergency system kicks in, so you'll have to be fast."

"I know."

He put the car into gear. "So, uh, be careful."

"I will." Henry watched the car drive away, watched until the taillights disappeared around a corner, then walked slowly across the street toward the detention center. His pants and crepe-soled shoes were black, but his turtleneck sweater was a deep, rich burgundy; no point in looking more like a second story man than necessary. He carried a dark wool cap to pull over his hair the instant he started over the wall as he'd learned early after his change that a pale-haired vampire was at a disadvantage when it came to moving through the darkness.

From not very far away came the sound of traffic, of a radio, of a baby crying; people who paid no attention to the knowledge that other people were locked in cages only a short distance from where they lived their lives. *Or perhaps they've forgotten they know.* Henry reached out and lightly touched the outer wall, sensitive eyes turned away from the harsh glare of the floodlights.

Dungeons, prisons, detention centers—there was little to choose between them. He could feel the misery, the defiance, the anger, the despair; the bricks were soaked in it. Every life that had been held here had left a dark impression. Henry had never understood the theory that torture by confinement was preferable to death.

"They're given a chance to change," Vicki'd protested when a news article on capital punishment had started the argument.

"You've been inside your country's prisons," he'd pointed out. *"What chance for change do they offer? I have never lived in a time that so enjoyed lying to itself."*

"Maybe you'd rather we followed good King Hal's example and chained prisoners to a wall until it was time to cut off their heads?"

"I never said the old ways were better, Vicki, but at least my father never insulted those he arrested by insisting he did it for their own good.

"He did it for his *own good,"* she'd snorted and had refused to discuss the matter further.

Having found the place he'd go over the wall, Henry moved on until he crossed the line between the floodlights and the night, then he turned and waited. He had faith in Celluci's ability to cut the power, more faith he suspected than Celluci had in his ability to go into the detention center and bring Vicki out—but then, he'd had a lot more time to learn to see around the blinkers jealousy insisted be worn.

They were very much alike, Michael Celluci and Vicki Nelson, both wrapped up in their ideas of The Law. There was one major difference Henry had noticed between them; Vicki broke The Law for ideals, Celluci broke it for her. *She,* not justice, had kept him silent last August in London. It was her personally, not injustice, that drove him tonight—however little he liked what they were about to do.

It probably wouldn't have helped, Henry reflected, if he'd told Celluci that he had attempted this sort of thing before. . . .

Henry had not been in England when Henry Howard, Earl of Surrey, had been arrested, and between the time it took for news to reach him and the complications laid on travel by his nature, he didn't arrive in London until January eighth; two days before the execution. He spent that first night frantically gathering information. An hour after sunset on the ninth, having quickly fed down by the docks, he stood and stared up at the black stone walls of the Tower.

Originally, Surrey had been given a suite overlooking the river, but an attempt to escape by climbing down the privy at low tide had ensured his removal to less congenial, interior accommodations. From where he stood, Henry could just barely see the flicker of light in Surrey's window.

"No," he murmured to the night, "I don't imagine you can sleep, you arrogant, bloody fool, not with the block awaiting you in the morning."

All things considered, he decided there was no real need to go over the wall—although he rather regretted the loss of the flamboyant gesture—and moved, a shadow within the shadows, past the guards and into the halls of the Tower. At Surrey's door, he raised the heavy iron bar and slipped silently inside, pulling the door closed behind him. Unless things had changed a great deal since his days at court, the guards would not bother them before dawn and by dawn they would be far away.

He stood for a moment drinking in the sight and scent of the dearest friend he had had in life, realizing how much he had missed him. The slight figure, dressed all in black, sat at a crude table by the narrow window, a tallow candle his only light, a heavy iron shackle locked around one slim ankle and chained in turn to a bolt in floor. He had been writing—Henry could smell the fresh ink—but he sat now with his dark head pillowed on his arm and despair written across the line of his shoulders. Henry felt a fist close around his heart and he had to stop himself from rushing forward and catching the other man up in a near hysterical embrace.

Instead, he took a single step away from the door and softly called, "Surrey."

The dark head jerked erect. "Richmond?" The young earl spun around, eyes wide with terror and when he saw who stood within his cell he threw himself against the far wall with a rattle of chain and strangled cry. "Am I so near to death," he moaned, "that the dead come calling?"

Henry smiled. "I'm as flesh and blood as you are. More so, you've lost a lot of weight."

"Yes, well, the cook does his poor best but it's not what I'm used to." One long-fingered hand brushed the air with a dismissive gesture Henry well remembered and then rose to cover Surrey's eyes. "I'm losing my mind. I make jokes with a ghost."

"I am no ghost."

"Prove it."

"Touch me then." Henry walked forward, hand outstretched.

"And lose my soul? I will not." Surrey sketched the sign of the cross and squared his shoulders. "Come any closer and I'll call for the guards."

Henry frowned, this was not going the way he'd planned. "All right, I'll prove it without your touch." He thought a moment. "Do you remember what you said when we watched the execution of my father's second wife, your cousin, Anne Boleyn? You told me that although her con-

demnation was an inevitable matter of state business, you
pitied the poor wretch and you hoped they'd let her laugh
in hell for you'd always thought her laugh more beautiful
than her face."

"Richmond's spirit would know that, for I said it while
he lived."

"All right," Henry repeated, thinking, *it's a good thing I
came early, this could take all night.* "You wrote this after
I died and, trust me, Surrey, your poems are not yet read
in heaven." He cleared his throat and softly recited, "The
secret thoughts, imparted with such trust,/The wanton talk,
the diverse change of play,/The friendship sworn, each
promise kept so just,/Wherewith we passed the winter
night away . . ."

" '. . . That place of bliss,/the graceful, gay companion,
who with me shared,/the jolly woes, the hateless short
debate . . .' " Surrey stepped away from the wall, his body
trembling with enough force to vibrate the chain he wore.
"I wrote that for you."

"I know." He had copies of nearly everything Surrey had
written; the earl's flamboyant lifestyle meant his servants
often waited for their pay and were, therefore, open to
earning a little extra.

" 'Proud Windsor, where I, in just and joy/With a King's
son my childish years did pass . . .' Richmond?" Eyes welling, Surrey flung himself forward and Henry caught him
up in a close embrace.

"You see," he murmured into the dusky curls, "I have
flesh, I live, and I've come to get you out of here."

After an incoherent moment of mingled joy and grief,
Surrey pushed away and, swiping at his cheeks with his
palm, he looked his old friend up and down. "You haven't
changed," he said, fear touching his expression again. "You
look no different than you did when you . . . than you did
at seventeen."

"You look very little different yourself." Although eleven
years had added flesh and he now wore the mustache and
long curling beard fashionable at court, Surrey's face and
manner were so little changed that Henry had no difficulty
believing he'd gotten himself into the mess he had. His
beloved friend had been wild, reckless, and immature at
nineteen. Mere months short of thirty he was wild, reckless,

and immature still. "As to my lack of change, well, it's a long story."

Surrey flung himself down on the bed and with difficulty lifted the shackled leg up onto the pallet. "I'm not going anywhere," he pointed out with a sardonic lift of ebony brows.

And he wasn't, Henry realized, not until his curiosity was satisfied. If he wanted to save him, he'd have to tell him the truth. "You'd gone to Kenninghall, to spend time with Frances, and His Majesty sent me to Sherifbutton," he began.

"I remember."

"Well, I met a woman . . ."

Surrey laughed, and the laughter held, in spite of his outward calm, a hint of hysteria. "So I'd heard."

Henry was thankful he could no longer blush. In the past that tone had turned him scarlet. This was the first time he had told the story since his change; he'd not expected it to be as difficult as it was and he walked over to the desk so he could look out into the night as he talked, one hand shuffling the papers Surrey had left. When he finished, he turned and faced the rude bed.

Surrey was sitting on its edge, head buried in his hands. As though he felt the weight of Henry's gaze, he slowly looked up.

The force of the rage and grief that twisted his face drove Henry back a step. "Surrey?" he asked, suddenly unsure.

"Vampire?"

"Yes . . ."

Surrey stood and fought to find his tongue. "You gained immortality," he said at last, "and you let me believe you were dead."

Taken completely by surprise, Henry raised his hands as though the words were blows.

"The death you allowed me to believe in dealt me a wound that still bleeds," Surrey continued, his voice shredding under the edge of his emotion. "I loved you. How could you betray me so?"

"Betray you? How could I tell you?"

"How could you not?" His brows drew down and his tone grew suddenly bitter. "Or did you think you couldn't trust me? That *I* would betray *you?*" He read the answer on Henry's face. "You did. I called you the brother of my heart and you thought I would give your secret to the world."

"I called you the same, and I loved you just as much as you loved me, but I knew you, Surrey; this is a secret you would not have been able to keep."

"Yet after giving me eleven years of sorrow you trust me with it now?"

"I've come to get you out. I could not let you die . . ."

"Why? Because my death would cause you the same grief that I've carried for so long?" He took a deep breath and closed his eyes, his throat moving in an effort to suppress the tears that trembled on the edge of every word. After a moment he said, so softly that had Henry still been mortal he would not have heard, "I'll keep your secret. I'll carry it to my grave." Then his head came up and he added, a little louder. "Tomorrow."

"Surrey!" Nothing Henry said would change his mind. He begged; he pleaded; he went down on his knees; he even offered immortality.

Surrey ignored him.

"Dying to have revenge on me is foolishness!"

"The Richmond I knew, the boy who was my brother, died eleven years ago. I mourned him. I mourn him still. You are not here."

"I could force you," he said at last. "I have powers you can't defend against."

"If you force me," Surrey said, "I will hate you."

He had no answer to that.

He stayed and argued until the coming sun forced him away. The next night, he entered the chapel of the Tower, opened the unsealed coffin that held the severed head and trunk of Henry Howard, Earl of Surrey, kissed the pale lips, and cut free a lock of hair. His nature no longer allowed him tears. He wasn't sure he would have shed them if it had.

" '*Sat Superest,* it is enough to prevail.' " Henry shook himself free of the memories. "I should have taken Surrey's motto as my own, shoved it down his throat, and carried him out of there flung over my shoulder." Well, he was older now, more sure of himself, more certain that his way was the right way, less likely to be swayed by hysterical reactions. "I should have let him hate me, at least he'd have been alive to do it." Vicki, he knew, would not have been so foolish. Had she been in the tower in Surrey's place, first she would have worried about getting free, *then* she would have hated him.

And she was unlikely to protest against this rescue tonight.

If she were in her right mind.

As Henry tried not to think of what the drugs might have done, the floodlights went out.

Vicki had spent the afternoon using sound and touch to discover the boundaries of her confinement. Surprisingly enough, with her eyes removed from the general equation and used only to peer at specific close-ups, she seemed to get around better, not worse. She hadn't realized how much she'd come to rely on other senses over the last year until they were all she had to rely on. Without her glasses, her vision—or lack of it—had become more of a distraction than a help.

After the incident in the showers, Lambert had returned triumphant to the soap operas, but Natalie followed close on Vicki's heels, her adenoidal breathing occasionally drowning out the constant roar of the four televisions and intermittent roar of the women who watched them. Commercials seemed to have the greatest effect—Vicki wondered if maybe it was because the plots of commercials were understood by the greatest number of the inmates.

Every now and then, Natalie would reach out and viciously pinch a hunk of Vicki's flesh. Her muscle control still affected by the residue of the drug, Vicki hadn't the speed or coordination to avoid the snakelike strikes. The fifth time it happened, she slowly turned and beckoned her tormentor closer.

"The nect time you do tha'," she said, forming the words as carefully as she could, "I'm gona' grab you' wris', pull you close, and rip you' ear off. Then I'm gona' feed it to you. You unnerstand?"

Natalie giggled, but the intervals between the pinches became longer and finally she wandered away to watch Family Feud. Vicki wasn't sure if her threat had worked or if the large woman had just become bored and moved on to another victim.

By suppertime Vicki had decided there was only one way out. Back in behind the shower there was an emergency exit; it wasn't particularly visible from the inside and most of the inmates weren't even aware it existed, but nine years spent on the police force gave Vicki an advantage. The Metro West Detention Center was the only detention center for women in the city, and while the numbers were climbing every year there were still far fewer female police officers than male. Female cops spent a disproportionate amount of time at Metro West.

Trouble was, the door opened in, there wasn't a handle or any real way to get hold of it, and the lock was a huge solid metal presence.

That any half decent cracksman could have open in a heartbeat and a half, Vicki decided after a quick fingertip examination. *Of course, lock picks and opportunity might prove a little difficult.*

After supper, during cleanup while they were locked back in the cells, Vicki sat cross-legged on her mattress and probed thoughtfully at the cotton ticking. The mattresses on the bunks were slabs of solid foam, absolutely useless for anything except as a barrier between body and boards, but the extras, the ones thrown on the floor were old army surplus issue. They weren't very thick, they weren't very comfortable, but they did appear to have metal springs. In time, she could work a piece free and . . .

Except, she didn't have time. The shrink would be doing examinations tomorrow afternoon and she'd be sent off Special Needs to one of the regular ranges—with the mummy in control she had no hope of being set free. It wouldn't be as easy to escape a regular range—or for that matter, to survive one. More of the inmates were likely to recognize her and fatal "accidents" were not unknown when cops found themselves on the other side of the system. She'd obviously have to convince the shrink she belonged right where she was.

Vicki grinned. Her playing crazy would drive Lambert crazy for sure.

"What the fuck are you grinnin' about?"

Vicki turned toward Lambert's side of the cell and her

grin broadened. "I was just thinking," she said, carefully maintaining control of each word, "how in the country of the blind, the one-eyed man, or in this case, woman, is king."

"You're fuckin' crazy," Lambert growled.

"Glad you think so." She didn't see Lambert's expression, but she heard Natalie come off her bunk and felt the air shift as the large woman moved toward her. *Oh, shit . . .*

She fought the nearly overwhelming urge to scramble away. It wouldn't prevent the inevitable. *And I am not going to give Lambert the satisfac . . .* The open-handed blow flung her head back and almost knocked her over. Vicki rolled with it and came up facing the fuzzy column of blue that was Natalie, trying to ignore the ringing in her ears.

Off to her left, she heard Lambert laugh. "So she's showin' fight, eh? This is gonna be interestin'. Hurt her, Natalie."

Natalie giggled.

"All right, cleanup's over!" The cell doors opening added percussion to the guard's announcement. "Everybody out! Roberts, put your clothes back on."

"Itchy, boss."

"I don't care. Get dressed."

Natalie paused and Lambert joined her in Vicki's limited field of vision. "Later," she promised, patting a massive biceps. "You can hurt her later. Meanwhile, I think she should sit with us to watch Wheel of Fortune."

Oh, God . . . "I'd rather be beaten unconscious," Vicki growled, trying to free her arm from Natalie's sudden crushing grip.

Lambert leaned close so Vicki could see her smile. "Later," she promised again.

Billy Bob Dickey from Tulsa, Oklahoma, had just bought a vowel when the lights went out, cutting Vanna off as she turned the first of four e's. The range erupted into complete and utter pandemonium.

"Everyone just stay calm!" The bellowing of the guard could barely be heard over the sounds of terror, rage, and hysterical glee. "Get back in your cells. Now!"

Vicki had no idea how much the others could or couldn't

see, but from the sound of it even those with normal night sight were nearly blind. The guards, she knew, would be racing for A Range where all four of them would be needed to coordinate a manual lockup. D Range would be unobserved for the next few minutes.

My kingdom for a set of lock picks. A God-given chance and I can't use it for anything . . . Jesus! She scrambled backward as the picnic table lurched sideways under the sudden shifting of weight across from panicked inmates. *This thing's being held together with spit and prayers.*

"And where the fuck do you think you're goin'?" Lambert demanded. "*I* say when we leave. Natalie, bring her back!"

"Can't see!" Natalie protested, wood groaning with relief as she stood.

"So what? Neither can she!"

Vicki felt the surge of air and stepped sideways out of the way. " 'Trust me, he said, and come. I followed like a child—a blind man led me home.' "

"What the fuck are you talking about?"

"It's a poem," Vicki told her, easily avoiding Natalie's next rush; the large woman displaced a tropical storm's worth of air. "By W. H. Davies. He was saying, I believe, that when everyone's blind, the people with the practice have the advantage." She smiled, bent, and used Natalie's momentum to heave her up and across her shoulders and into the air.

The crash of splintering wood told Vicki her enormous tormentor had just smashed through the abused table. "I hope . . . that . . . hurt," she panted as her knees buckled and she collapsed to the floor trying to get her breath. *Good God, she's got to weigh close to four hundred pounds; isn't it amazing what adrenaline can do.*

Her fingers brushed against a six-inch sliver of wood and, still fighting for breath, she picked it up. Given the spread of the debris, the table had been completely destroyed by the impact. *Jesus H. Christ. This thing could've killed somebody!* She sat back on her heels and tried to break the fragment across the grain. It bent but it didn't even crack. *I don't think this is pine. . . . Just like the city to buy oak picnic tables for a detention center and then let them fall apart.* Her heart suddenly began to slam against her ribs, her heartbeat drowning out the chaos around her. Oak. Hardwood. A splinter with a thin, flexible tip.

No. No way. That lock's big and clumsy, sure, but only an idiot would try to pick it with a chunk of wood. No.

Why not?

It's not like I've got a lot of options.

As Vicki stood, she brushed up against another body standing so close they were all but breathing the same air. Small, powerful fingers dug into her forearm.

"Natalie's going to fucking rip you apart!"

The emergency generator would be kicking in soon and Vicki knew she didn't have much time, but there were some temptations it would take a saint to resist.

"You shouldn't have come this close," she said, yanked Lambert's hand loose, twisted the arm up and around, and kicked her, hard, in the direction of her enforcer. A strangled grunt, a curse, and a cry of pain told her the target had been hit as she hurried toward the showers.

She found the concrete privacy barrier by crashing into it, and, limping a little, groped her way along its rough edge.

They're finished with A Range by now, probably well into B. So little time . . .

The area between the barrier and the wall was less than ten feet wide. Vicki launched herself across the gaping chasm it represented in the dark with no thought of caution. Preventing a few more bruises wouldn't pay for another night spent behind bars. She hit the wall with enough force to bounce back, then began searching frantically for the hidden exit.

The crash of steel doors sounded over the confusion behind her and she jumped, almost dropping her sliver of wood.

If they've already moved onto C Range . . .

Finally her fingers found the lock and she dropped to her knees in front of it.

And while I'm down here, I might as well say a prayer as I don't have a hope in hell of . . . son of a bitch. The first tumbler fell.

Christ, I could practically pick this thing with my fingernails. I get out of here and I'm going to have a long talk with someone. Those picnic tables are death traps and this lock is a joke. Odds are good the men's *detention center gets decent upkeep.*

The second tumbler fell.

This is a disgrace.

She could hear one of the guards yelling something about tranquilizers. He sounded close.

Oh, shit . . . Her hands were slick with sweat and she could feel the wood beginning to splinter.

Okay.

The guards were definitely in C Range. It suddenly got harder to breathe.

Almost.

Someone appeared to be putting up a fight.

Give 'em hell, slow them down, and . . .

That wasn't Natalie she could hear breathing behind her? No. Just the echo of her own desperate sucking in of air that tasted of shower mold.

There . . .

Although unlocked, the heavy door stayed securely closed and Vicki realized she had no way to pull it open.

"NO!" One knuckle split with the force of the blow and then she had to scramble back out of the way as the door flew open toward her.

She couldn't mistake the arm that wrapped around her and kept her from falling, nor the embrace she suddenly found herself enfolded in. With adrenaline sizzling along every nerve, she fought to get free.

"Goddamnit, Henry!" Something started her trembling violently. It felt like anger. "What the fuck took you so long?"

The sound of the shower had been going on for a long time. When it finally shut off, the two men looked at each other across the width of the living room.

"You've known her longer," Henry said softly. "Is she okay?"

"I think so."

"It's just she doesn't seem to be . . ." He spread his hands.

"Feeling anything?"

"Yes."

"It's all there. It's just all locked in behind the anger."

"She has every right to be angry."

Celluci scowled. "I didn't say she didn't have."

During the ride back to Henry's condo, Vicki had spat out the bare bones of what had happened to her. Both men had listened quietly, both recognizing that interrupting with either questions or passions would stop the flow of words completely. When she'd finished, Celluci had immediately begun making plans to take care of Gowan and Mallard, but Vicki had glared through the spare pair of glasses he'd brought for her and said, *"No. I don't know how or when, but the pay back's mine. Not yours. Mine."*

Her tone left little doubt that Gowan and Mallard would get exactly what they had coming.

And then she'd added, *"I want Tawfik,"* in such a voice that even Henry had found himself chilled by it.

They turned toward her as she limped into the living room, wet hair slicked back, the bruise that discolored one side of her face a sharp contrast to the pallor of the other cheek. The hand smoothing the front of her sweatshirt was wrapped in gauze.

I've seen holy fanatics, Henry thought, as Vicki crossed over to the window, *wearing exactly that expression.* Again, the two men exchanged worried glances. She moved, not as if she might break at any second, but as if she might explode.

"Before we begin," she said to the night, "order a pizza. I'm starving."

"But we still don't know," Celluci pointed out, waving a piece of gnawed crust for emphasis, "how Tawfik found out about Vicki."

"Once Cantree told him about you, it wouldn't have been difficult for Tawfik to have lifted the information from his mind." Henry paused in his slow pacing and looked down at Celluci. "Cantree would believe that anything you knew, you would have told Vicki and Tawfik must have decided to tie up the loose end."

"Yeah? Then why such an elaborate scenario?" Celluci tossed the crust into the box and straightened, wiping his hands. "Why not get rid of her the way he got rid of Trembley? Kapow and it's over."

"I don't know."

"It seems to me that you spent at least as much time talking with him as Cantree did. How do we know you didn't say anything?"

"Because," the pause filled with something very close to menace, "I wouldn't."

Celluci fought a nearly irresistible urge to drop his gaze and continued, his voice beginning to rise. "We know he can mess with people's thoughts—the staff at the museum are proof of that. How do we know he didn't lift her from your mind?"

"No! I would never betray her."

Celluci's eyes narrowed as he realized the source of the pain that shadowed Henry's protest. *No, he wouldn't betray her. He loves her. He really loves her. The son of a bitch. And he's afraid he might have done it. That Tawfik might have lifted Vicki out of his head.* "Would you have even noticed him doing it?" The question needed to be asked. He wasn't just twisting the knife. At least he didn't think he was.

"No one walks uninvited through my mind, mortal." But Tawfik had touched him just by existing and Henry had no real idea what the wizard-priest might have picked up. For all his declared certainty, this showed in his voice. Celluci heard it and Henry knew he did.

"Enough." Vicki threw herself up out of the armchair, wiping grease off her mouth with the palm of her hand. "It doesn't matter how he knew about me. It's over. The only thing that matters now, and I mean the *only* thing, is finding Tawfik and taking him out. Henry, you said that the woman who left the Solicitor General's library before Cantree went in said she'd meet him at the ceremony."

"Yes."

"And Tawfik himself told you it was essential for the gathered acolytes to be sworn to his god as soon as possible."

"Yes."

"Well, since we know that his first group of acolytes have been pulled—at the very least—from the upper ranks of both the metro and the provincial police forces, we'd better stop him before this ceremony happens."

"How do we know it hasn't?"

Vicki snorted. "You tell me. I've been a little out of touch the last couple of days."

"The party was Saturday. Tawfik spoke with me Sunday." Had it only been two days ago? "Monday . . ." Was that why he hadn't come, Henry wondered. Were they already too late?

"For what it's worth," Celluci offered, "Cantree was home last night."

"How do you know?"

"I watched his house for a while."

"Why?"

"I thought I might ask him what the fuck was going on."

"Did you?"

"No."

"Why not?"

"Because I remembered what happened to Trembley and it occurred to me that lying low might be a healthier plan. All right?" Celluci threw the question at Henry, then followed it with, "Might have been more useful if you'd done as thorough an interrogation on Tawfik during your little stroll. Or were you too busy being creatures of the night together that you forgot the s.o.b.'s a killer?"

"I am as immortal as you are, Richmond. I will never grow old. I will never die. I will never leave you."

Celluci read the thought off Henry's face. He flung himself up out of the chair and across the living room. "You bastard, that's exactly what happened, isn't it?"

Henry met the rush with an outstretched hand and Celluci rocked to a halt as though he'd hit a wall. Just for a moment, Henry wanted to make him understand. And then the moment passed. "Never presume," he said, catching the other man's gaze and holding it, forcing him to stand and listen, "that you know what I do or why I do it. I am not as you are. The laws I follow are not the laws that master you. We are very, very different, you and I; in two things only we are the same. Whatever Tawfik and I spoke of, whatever my reaction to him, all that has changed. He has hurt one of mine and I will not have that."

As Henry dropped his hand, Celluci staggered forward. He had the strange feeling he would have fallen had Henry not continued to hold his gaze until he steaded. "And the second thing," he demanded, stepping back and shoving the curl of hair back off his face.

"Please, Detective," Henry purposefully lowered his lids, allowing Celluci to look away if he chose, "do not attempt to convince me you have no knowledge of the other . . . interest we share."

Brown eyes stared into hazel for a moment. Finally, Celluci sighed.

"If you two have finished," Vicki snapped, leaning back against the windows and crossing her arms, "can we get on with it?"

"Finished?" Celluci snorted quietly, turning and walking back to the couch. "Something tells me we're just getting started." He pushed the pizza box out of the way and dropped down, the couch springs protesting the sudden weight. "Look, ceremonies don't usually happen on a whim. Most religions have schedules to keep."

Vicki nodded. "Good point. Henry?"

"He said, *soon.* Nothing more definite."

"Damnit, there's got to be somewhere we can find out about ancient Egyptian religious rituals." Her eyes narrowed. "Mike . . ."

"Uh-uh. The closest I ever got to ancient Egypt was doing a little overtime at the Tut exhibit. And that was years ago."

"Oh, you've been a lot closer to ancient Egypt than that." Vicki smiled. She never thought she'd be grateful he'd cultivated the woman. "What about your friend, Dr. Shane?"

"Rachel?"

"If there's anyone left in the city who'll know," Vicki pointed out, handing him the phone. "It's her."

Celluci shook his head. "I don't want to bring more civilians into this. The danger . . ."

"Tawfik is at his weakest now," Henry said quietly. "If Dr. Shane can't help us stop him before he completes his power base, then you won't be able to keep her safe, not from what's likely to come."

"Rachel? It's Mike. Mike Celluci. I need to ask you a couple of questions."

She laughed and doodled a sarcophagus in the margin of

the acquisition report she'd been spending the evening with. "What? Don't I even get dinner this time?"

"Sorry, but no."

Something in his voice drew her up straight in the chair. "It's important?"

"Very. Did the ancient Egyptians have specific dates when the priests of dark gods would perform important ceremonies?"

"Well, there were very specific dates set during the calendar year for the rites of Set."

"No, we're not looking for their version of Christmas or Easter . . ."

"Hardly that, Set is a *dark* god."

"Yeah. Well, it's not Set we're concerned about. If one of the lesser dark gods needed to hold an unscheduled rite, when would it happen?"

"It might help if you gave me some idea of why you needed to know."

"I'm sorry, I can't tell you."

Why did she know he was going to say that? "Well, it could happen any time, I suppose, but a dark rite would most likely be held during the dark of the moon, when the eye of Thoth is out of the sky. And probably at midnight, when Ra, the sun god, has been out of the world for the longest time, and will still be gone for an equal amount of time."

"Where?"

She blinked. "I beg your pardon?"

"Where would the rite be held?"

"Does this god of yours not have a temple?"

"The rite involves creating a temple."

Involves creating a temple? Present tense? Police work in Toronto was stranger than she thought. "Then the rite would have happened wherever the priest wanted the temple to be."

From the sound of his voice, his teeth were clenched. "I was afraid you were going to say that. Thanks, Rachel. You've been a help."

"Mike?" The pause before he answered told her she'd barely caught him before he hung up. "Will you tell me why you needed to know this when you've finished whatever you're working on?"

"Depends."

"On?"

"On who wins."

Rachel laughed at the melodrama as she settled the receiver back on the phone. Perhaps she should see Detective-Sergeant Celluci again; he was certainly more interesting than academics and bureaucrats.

"Depends on who wins," she repeated, bending back over the report. "He even sounded like he meant it." The sudden chill that brushed against the fine hair on her neck, she credited to an overactive imagination.

Vicki turned to look out the window and frowned. "It's the dark of the moon tonight."

"How do you know?" Celluci asked. "Maybe the moon's behind a cloud?"

"I start my period two days after the dark of the moon. It's Tuesday. I start Thursday."

Hard to argue with. "Yeah, but the dark of the moon happens once a month," Celluci pointed out.

"Tawfik said soon." She wrapped her arms around her body and winced as the motion pulled one of her multiple bruises into a painful position. "It's tonight."

"We're in no shape to take him on tonight."

"You mean I'm not. *We* don't have a choice."

Celluci knew better than to argue with that tone. "Then we still have to find him."

"He must have told you something, Henry." The city stretched out below her, offering a thousand possibilities. "What else did he say?"

"Nothing about the location of a temple."

"Wasn't there something about a mountaintop?" Celluci asked.

"In a manner of speaking. He said, 'With no need to hide, I will shout Akhekh from the top of the highest mountain.' "

"Well, we're a little short of mountains in this part of the country. High or low."

"No." Both of Vicki's hands pressed flat against the glass as she suddenly realized what had caught her attention. "No. We aren't. Look."

Her tone pulled both men to her side without questions.

Her eyes were wide, her breathing labored, and her heart beating so hard, Henry was almost afraid for her.

"What are we looking at?" he asked softly.

"The tower. Look at the tower."

The CN Tower rose at the foot of the city, a shadow against the stars. As they watched, a section of the revolving disk lit up as though a giant flashbulb had gone off inside. It only lasted for an instant, but the light left an afterimage on the eye like a film of grease.

"It could be anything." Not even Celluci believed the protest, but he felt he had to make it. "There're often lights on the tower."

"It's him. He's up there. And I'm going to bring him down if I have to bring the whole goddamned tower down with him."

Up above the observation deck, two of the red airplane safety lights hovered strangely close together.

Almost like eyes.

Sixteen

"What the hell are you doing?"

Henry slipped the BMW into neutral. "I'm stopping at a yellow light."

"Why?"

"Detective, contrary to popular belief, a yellow light does not mean speed up, there's a red light coming."

"Yeah? Well, contrary to what you seem to believe, we haven't got all night. Rachel said this thing'll go down at midnight and it's eleven thirteen now."

"And being pulled over for a minor traffic violation with a wanted felon in the car would slow us down a lot more than obeying the rules of the road."

"Why don't I drive?"

Vicki leaned forward. "Why don't we compromise? Mike, shut up. And, Henry, speed up. Neither of you are proving a damned thing."

They left the car on Front Street and pounded up the stairs and onto the walkway that led over the railway tracks to the base of the CN Tower. Although Henry could have quickly outdistanced the two mortals, he matched his speed to Vicki's; just in case.

Without the crowds of people that filled the area during the day, the acres of concrete had a surreal, deserted look and even rubber-soled shoes echoed. Flashing their messages at empty space, neon advertisements blazed along the path to the tower—for the restaurant, for the disco, for the Tour of the Universe.

"Actually only takes you to Jupiter," Vicki panted as they passed under the last sign. "Half a solar system. Some universe." She ran with one hand touching the wall for both guidance and support and didn't bother worrying about not being able to see her feet. The path was smooth and obvious, and after what she'd been through, she wasn't going to let a little lack of light stop her.

"If he's up there," Celluci yelled as they flung themselves down the stairs at the other end of the walkway and rounded the corner to the main entrance. "I bet he's locked the elevators at the top with him."

"No bet." Vicki threw herself against a glass handle with no more effect than if she'd been the wind. "Not when the son of a bitch has locked the doors at the bottom."

Henry wrapped both hands under Vicki's and pulled. With a crack that echoed up the tower and back from the Sky-dome, the handle snapped off.

"Shit!" She glared at the tinted glass door and then at Henry. "Can you break through it?"

He shook his head. "Not without some kind of weapon. That's three-quarter-inch solid glass. Even I'd break bones first."

It almost seemed as though the tower designers had thought ahead to such a possibility; nothing in the immediate neighborhood could be used to shatter the door. Even the various levels were joined by solid masses of poured concrete, no metal banisters, no steel safety rails.

"Don't bother," Vicki snapped as Henry squatted and attempted to pry up a paving block. "We're wasting our time trying to get in here when Celluci's most likely right about the elevators."

Henry straightened. "We have to get him tonight, now. Before those people are sworn. We have to stop his god from gaining enough power to create more of him."

"I know. We take the stairs."

Celluci shook his head. "Vicki, that door's going to be locked, too."

"But it's a metal door with a metal handle—not likely to pull off in Henry's hand." She was moving before she finished speaking, limping around the reflecting pool and up to the back of the tower. "I am not," she snarled as they arrived at the entrance to the stairwell, "going to have this place turned into the world's tallest freestanding Egyptian fucking temple. Henry—!"

The heavy metal door bowed on his first pull, layers of paint cracking and dropping to the ground, a battleship gray avalanche of paint flakes. The second pull ripped it free of its hinges and dragged the very expensive security system out through the door frame nearly intact.

It made surprisingly little noise, all things considered.

"Why no alarms?" Celluci demanded suspiciously, frowning at the tangle of ripped wires.

"How should I know?" Muscles protesting, his strength tested to its limit, Henry leaned the door against the tower. "Perhaps Tawfik's providing burnt offerings and he doesn't want to set off the sprinkler system."

"Or it's silent and there's a fleet of patrol cars on the way."

"Also possible," Henry agreed.

"Then maybe you'd better stop wasting time talking about it." Although the ambient light did Vicki little good, it provided contrast between the concrete giant and the jagged black hole that was their only entrance. She charged toward it only to be brought to a rocking halt by Celluci's grip on her arm.

"Vicki, wait a minute."

"Let go of me." The edge on her voice threatened to remove his arm if he didn't.

He took the chance. "Look, we can't just go charging up there without a plan. You're letting your emotions do the thinking for you. Hell, *we're* letting your emotions do the thinking for *us.* Just stop and consider for a second—what happens when we get to the top?"

She glared at him and twisted free. "We take out Tawfik, that's what happens."

"Vicki . . ." Henry moved forward into her line of sight. "We probably won't be able to get close to him. He has protections."

Her eyes narrowed. "If you're still afraid of him, Henry, you can wait down here."

Henry took another step toward her, his silence nearly deafening.

"I'm sorry." She reached out and touched him lightly on the chest. "Look, how hard can it be? Mike'll shoot him from the doorway. I doubt he has a protection up against that. You *do* have your gun?"

"Yeah, but . . ."

"It does have a certain simplicity that appeals," Henry admitted. "But I doubt he'll let us get that close. He'll have warded the temple area and the moment we cross those wards . . ." His voice trailed off.

"So you distract him and Mike shoots him," Vicki ground out through clenched teeth. "As you said, simple. And surprise is essential and *we are wasting time!*" She started for the tower again and again Celluci stopped her.

"You wait down here," he said. He'd already nearly lost her once this week. He wasn't going through that hell again.

"I *what*?"

"You're in no shape to face natural opposition let alone supernatural. I doubt you can even make it to the top; you're at the end of your resources, you're already limping, you're . . ."

"You. Just. Let. Me. Worry. About. Me." Each word emerged as a separate, barely controlled explosion.

Henry laid a hand on her shoulder. "You know he's right. I distract Tawfik and he shoots him; you didn't include yourself in your simple plan."

"*I* am going up there to watch him die."

"*You* are putting yourself at unnecessary risk," Celluci growled. "And what happens if we fail? Who's left to take a second shot?"

Vicki yanked her arm out of his hands and shoved her face up close to his. "What? Did I forget to mention plan B? If you two screw up, I'm there to pick up the pieces. Now either give me your gun and I'll shoot him myself, or get the fuck up those stairs."

"She has the right to be there," Henry said after a second that lasted several lifetimes, and it was obvious from his tone he liked it no more than Celluci did.

Vicki turned on him. "Thank you *very* much. *You* could have been at the top of the goddamned tower by now!" She stomped into the stairwell and groped for the first stair. Then the second. The emergency lights were a distraction so she closed her eyes. *Two down, one thousand, seven hundred and eighty-eight left to go.*

"Vicki?"

She hadn't heard Henry come up behind her, but she

could feel his presence just back of her left shoulder. She didn't want to listen to apologies or explanations or whatever he had to say. "Just go."

"But you're going to need help getting to the top. I could carry . . ."

"You could worry about Tawfik and not about me. Get moving." Through gritted teeth, she added, "Please."

The presence moved past, touched her lightly on the wrist, just at the spot where the vein lay closest to the surface, and was gone.

"He's right. You've barely got that drug out of your system not to mention the overt physical abuse. You won't make it to the top without help."

She glared at the vaguely man-shaped bit of dark on dark. "Fuck you, too, and stop worrying about *me*."

Celluci knew better than to say anything further although she heard him snarl something under his breath as he brushed by.

She tried to match his speed, and anger actually kept her to it for a while, but the distance between them gradually grew. Finally, the sound of single footsteps blended into a staccato background to the pounding of her heart.

Ten steps and a landing. Ten steps and a landing. It was going to take her a little longer than nine minutes and fifty-four seconds this time. Her lack of vision made no difference—after establishing the pattern, her feet were well able to find their own way—but with each movement the last two days made themselves felt on her body. Everything ached.

Ten steps and a landing.

Her lungs began to burn. Each breath became purchased with greater denominations of pain.

Ten steps and a landing.

Her left knee felt as though a spike had been driven up under the bone.

Ten steps and a landing.

Lift the right leg up, pull the left leg forward. Lift the right leg up, pull the left leg forward.

She peeled out of her jacket and let it lie where it fell.

Ten steps and a landing.

Unnecessary risk, my ass.

Ten steps and a landing.

Of course I wasn't part of my plan. Did they actually think I wasn't aware of the shape I'd be in at the top of this thing? I'm going to be lucky if I can stand.

Ten steps and a landing.

"She has a right to be there." Jesus H. Christ.

Ten steps and a landing.

Damned right I'm going to be there. And I'm going to spit on Tawfik's corpse.

Ten steps and a landing.

She'd read an article once about an American Medal of Honor winner who'd been hit twenty-three times by enemy fire and still managed, despite his injuries, to run across a bridge to save another member of his unit. She'd wondered at the time what he'd been thinking of when he did it. She suspected now that she had a pretty good idea.

You can fall down when this is over, not before.

Ten steps and a landing.

Leg muscles began to tremble, then jump. Every step became an individual battle against pain and exhaustion. She stumbled, lost the rhythm, and slammed her shin into a metal fronting.

Eight, nine, ten steps, and a landing.

With so much of her weight pulled ahead by hands and arms, the gauze wrapped round her split knuckle sagged— wet with sweat or blood, she neither knew nor cared. When it became more hindrance than help, she ripped it off and dropped it.

Ten steps and a landing.

Lesser angers burned away until only the anger at Tawfik remained. He'd drugged her and jailed her, but worst of all, he'd perverted something she believed in. *That* stretched between them like the rope she'd hang him with and she dragged herself toward him on it.

Ten steps and a landing.

Henry felt the wards as he crossed them, a faint sizzle along the surface of his skin that jerked every hair on his body erect. He had no idea what information they conveyed back to Tawfik, whether general or specific, but either way time now became critical. He raced up the last two flights of stairs. Far below he could hear Celluci laboring, and below that, Vicki's crippled progress. Their heartbeats echoed in the stairwell, their breathing so loud it sounded as if the whole structure inhaled and exhaled with them. It seemed he'd be on his own for some time.

Only one in four of the fluorescents were on in the hall that wrapped around the central pillar of the tower, and Henry, exiting out of the dim confines of the stairwell, gave thanks. Very often the level of light that mortals preferred placed him at a handicap and tonight he'd need every advantage.

Silently, he moved around the sweeping curve, following the hum of chanting. The background murmur in at least a dozen voices, consisted of nothing more than the name *Akhekh* repeated over and over with a kind of low-key intensity that worked its way beneath the surface and throbbed in bone and blood. Senses extended, Henry wasn't surprised to hear one single, all encompassing heartbeat where there should have been a multitude.

Rising over the chanting, a single voice spoke in a language that Henry didn't know, using cadences that sounded strange even to ears that had heard four and a half centuries of changes. Whatever else they were—and Henry had no doubt they held layers of meaning wrapped around each syllable, each tone—the words were a calling. Only the outermost edges brushed against him and he could feel himself urged closer.

He burst through the disco's main entrance, past an arc of empty tables. The background chanting grew louder.

Tawfik stood on the raised platform, inside an arc of padded rail where the dee jays usually sat, arms raised in the classic high priest pose. He wore a pair of khaki colored pants and an open necked linen shirt—not exactly the style of ancient Egypt, but then he didn't need a costume to declare what he was. Power crackled around him in an almost visible aura.

Crowded to either side of the dance floor, gazes riveted on Tawfik, were high-ranking officers from both the Metro and the Ontario Provincial police, two judges, and the publisher of the most powerful of the three Toronto daily newspapers. Henry had thought he'd heard a dozen voices, now, if he'd had to rely on hearing alone, he'd have said six although there were clearly more than twenty people involved. Individual tones and timbres were dissolving into the chant.

The most incongruous part of the entire scene had to be the giant silver disco ball that hung from the ceiling and spun slowly, flinging multicolored points of light over both Tawfik and his acolytes.

All this, Henry took in between one heartbeat and the next. Without breaking stride, he gathered himself up to spring forward at Tawfik's apparently unprotected back.

"AKHEKH!"

For a single voicing of the name, Tawfik joined the chant, the points of light began to coalesce, the silver ball stopped spinning, and Henry barely got his arm up over his eyes in time. He staggered, almost fell, and tried to blink away the afterimages left by the tiny fraction of the brilliance that had actually gotten through.

The volume of the chanting rose, then fell to a nearly subliminal murmur, almost easy to ignore, and Henry realized that the overlay of spell-casting had stopped.

"You are interfering in things you have no understanding of, Nightwalker." The voice was cold, distant, a counterpoint to the golden sun now burning in Henry's mind, larger and more brilliant than it had been only two days before.

Teeth clenched, Henry ignored the pain and wrapped the sun in his anger, dimming the overpowering life of the wizard-priest to the point where he could function. Through dancing patterns of light he saw Tawfik frown, an elder disturbed by the actions of a youth; those actions not a threat but merely an annoyance.

"Fortunately," Tawfik continued, still parent to child, teacher to student, "we have reached a point in the ceremony where a short pause will not affect the final outcome. You have time to explain your presence here before I decide what to do about you."

For an instant, Henry felt himself sliding into the role the wizard-priest defined. Snarling, he thrust it aside. He was Vampire, Nightwalker. He would not be made subordinate again by mere words. The confusion Tawfik had used and twisted before had all been burned away in his rage at Vicki's disappearance and the elder immortal's part in it. *He has hurt one of mine. I will not have that.*

He'd nearly gained the edge of the platform, less than an arm's reach away from Tawfik's throat, when red lines flared and slammed him back against the wall of the disco.

"I told you when we first met that you couldn't destroy me. You should have listened." The words stood out flat and uncompromising against the background chant as Tawfik realized that the Nightwalker's relative youth could no longer be manipulated and dropped the pose of bored disdain. After the challenges he had ignored the night before, he had known this confrontation would come, but tonight, when all his attention should be focused on Akhekh, tonight was not the time he would have chosen.

Not even the ceremony of sanctification had blocked the approaching glory of the Nightwalker's ka. He wanted it, wanted it more than he had ever wanted anything in his long life, and he had known from the moment the wards were shattered that tonight, at this moment, he held enough power to take what he so desperately desired. But the power he held wasn't his and Akhekh, for all he named his lord a petty godling, had painful ways of claiming ownership. The centuries had taught caution. After the ceremony, when Akhekh would be in a mood to grant favors, there would be power to spare and no risk of angering his lord. And once he had the Nightwalker's ka, he need never fear his lord's anger again.

If words were not enough to hold the Nightwalker, then other steps had to be taken. With a curt gesture, he raised the volume of the chant a fraction and then carefully, so as not to disturb the magical structures already in place and using only his own power, he began to weave a spell of binding. The mortals, still in the stairwell, could be ignored until they arrived, then their destruction would become part of the ceremony.

Stunned and bruised, Henry struggled to his feet. He had no idea how far behind him Celluci was as the scent and sound of the acolytes blocked the scent and sound of the detective's approach.

So you distract him and Mike shoots him. Simple.

Not so simple. Although if a physical attack had no effect, perhaps the wizard-priest could be distracted in other ways. He was fond enough of the sound of his own voice. Henry moved away from the wall. There was only one thing he was interested in hearing about. "Why did you attack Vicki Nelson?"

Tawfik smiled, fully aware of what the Nightwalker attempted, for the accumulated power gave him access to all but the deepest levels of that glorious immortal ka. It didn't matter. In a moment he would invoke the binding spell and the moment after begin the third and final part of the calling. And the moment after that, he would feed. Answering the Nightwalker's question would serve to fill the time. "Your Vicki Nelson was chosen by my lord. To use an analogy you might understand, he occasionally orders a specific meal rather than taking what's offered on the buffet. As the gods may not directly interfere except in the lives of those sworn to their service, I prepare the meal for him, placing the chosen one in a situation of optimum hopelessness and despair. That she happened to be the mortal you cared for was pure coincidence, I assure you. Did you go to a great deal of trouble getting her out of jail?"

"Not really." Henry stopped at the edge of the platform, at the point where the ambient power surrounding the wizard-priest brushed against him, throbbing in time with the single heartbeat of the chorus. "She'd nearly gotten herself out when I arrived."

"Almost a pity that she came along with you tonight." The Nightwalker's ka flared and Tawfik nearly lost himself in desire. "You didn't think I was unaware of your companions, did you? I'll have to kill her, of course."

"You'll have to kill me first."

Tawfik laughed, but Henry's expression didn't alter and his ka burned high and steady. Slowly, he realized that the statement, as unbelievable as it was, came from those guarded, innermost regions of the ka and that the younger immortal had meant exactly what he'd said. Shock and confusion destroyed his control of the binding spell. Ebony brows drew down to meet in a painfully tight vee. "You would lay down your immortal life for her? For one whose entire existence should mean no more to you than a moment's nourishment?"

"Yes."

"That's insane!" With the binding spell in tatters, Tawfik saw his options slip from his grasp. From the time the two mortals had entered the tower, their deaths had been woven into the ceremony of sanctification. The woman had to die. Her death was promised to Akhekh. But in order for the woman to die, he must kill the Nightwalker as well. If he killed the Nightwalker, all the power of that glorious ka would be lost.

No! I will not lose his ka! It is mine!

Henry had no idea what caused Tawfik to scowl so, but the wizard-priest certainly looked distracted. He pushed against the power barrier. It pushed back.

I could take the ka. Take it now. Use the power generated by the first two-thirds of the spell of sanctification. Use the power bled from the acolytes. Pay the price . . .

But would there be a price? Surely the devouring of an immortal life, would give him power equal to Akhekh's. Perhaps greater.

The chant began to rise in volume. The time had come to begin the third and final part of the spell of sanctification. He had no time to create another binding spell. He had no intention of losing the Nightwalker's magnificent, glorious ka.

Decision made between one heartbeat and the next, Tawfik wrapped his will around the accumulated power and threw all of it into the spell of acquisition. This would be rape, not the seduction he had initially planned, but the end result would be the same.

The sun flared white-gold behind Henry's eyes and he felt himself begin to burn. He could feel the strength that fed the flames, feel his edges consumed, feel . . . something familiar.

Hunger. He could feel Tawfik's Hunger.

Then he felt Tawfik's hands cup his face, lifting his head so their eyes met. Ebony eyes with no bottom to stop his fall.

The heartbeat of the acolytes roared in his ears. No. Not the acolytes. Not the heartbeat he had heard since he reached the top of the tower. Another heartbeat, a little faster than human norm, sound carried through the contact of skin against skin. Tawfik's heartbeat. Driving Tawfik's blood. For all his stolen centuries of life, Tawfik's scent was mortal. Had been mortal that night in the park. Was mortal now.

Henry set his own Hunger free, loosing the leash of restraint survival in a civilized world forced it to wear.

Steel fingers clamped down on Tawfik's shoulders and he cried out, forcing focus past the ecstasy to find the threat. He recognized the Hunter snarling out at him from the face between his hands.

"Nightwalker," he whispered, suddenly realizing what he held, what the legends meant when they were not legends any longer. During the time it took him to say the name, he felt the ka he sought to devour pull almost clear of the spell and just for that instant he slid beneath the surface of hazel eyes gone agate hard.

The grip on his shoulders tightened. The bone began to give. Desperately, Tawfik sucked yet more power from the acolytes and fed it into the protection spell—so stupid to have touched him and rendered all but the most basic defense useless. If he released the spell of acquisition, he had power enough to break free, but the spell of acquisition was all he had left. There could be no turning back.

He wrenched his gaze free of the Nightwalker's and dropped his hands down to the corded column of throat. An instant later, an answering band of flesh closed tightly around his own throat, only his magic keeping the crushing thumbs from his windpipe.

I will not loose this ka! He slammed the spell of acquisition against the Nightwalker's strength.

The sun became a holocaust of flame, but the Hunger dragged Henry through it to answer the blood that called from the other side.

How the fuck am I supposed to shoot at that? Celluci leaned panting against the wall of the disco, one hand shielding his eyes from the painfully bright lights scattering off the spinning silver ball. *Goddamned son of a bitch was supposed to distract him, not fucking dance with him.*

From where he stood, Celluci could see Fitzroy's back and, just above that, long golden fingers wrapped around Fitzroy's throat. A slight shift to his right showed him that Fitzroy's fingers were in turn locked around the throat of a tall dark man; probably good-looking under more normal circumstances. Although he couldn't say why, Celluci had the strangest feeling that the attempt at mutual strangulation was merely window dressing, that the real struggle was taking place somewhere else.

Maybe I should let them throttle each other and then shoot what's left. Gun cocked, he stepped out onto the dance floor. The new angle moved the combatants into unobstructed profile. Although their upper bodies swayed back and forth barely a hand's span apart, both sets of feet were firmly planted with nearly a meter between them. *Well, I'm no Barry Wu, but I think that I can at least guarantee not to hit the wrong legs.* He took his stance, braced his service revolver with his left hand, and tried to steady his breathing. He'd probably have a better chance if he waited until his lungs stopped heaving air in and out like asthmatic bellows, but it was coming up on midnight, and if Rachel Shane was right, the world didn't have much time. *Once in the knee to get his attention and then a second round to finish him.*

In such a small, enclosed space the sound of the gunshot expanded to touch the walls then slam back. And forth. And back. The shot itself went wide.

"Shit goddamnit!"

Ears ringing, Celluci raised the gun to shoot again, but unfortunately, although he'd done no damage, he had gotten the wizard-priest's attention.

The sound nearly jerked his grip from the Nightwalker's ka and only centuries of practice kept the spell of acquisition from shattering. He tightened his grip, slammed his rage at the interruption against the younger immortal's will, and, in the instant of breathing space that bought, sucked yet more power from the acolytes in order to snarl, "Stop him!"

"Stop him?" Celluci stepped back a step and then another. "Oh, fuck." He'd been so intent on the battle between Fitzroy and the mummy that he'd completely ignored the semicircles of chanting men and women that lined both sides of the dance floor. He had, in fact, passed right through one group in order to gain his current position, their presence never even registering. *Look, it's been a long day, I've got a lot on my mind.* But that kind of inattention to detail could get a man killed. *I can't believe I did that.*

Somewhere between twenty and thirty people shuffled out of the shadows, placing their bodies between their master and the threat. Still chanting, they moved slowly toward Celluci, faces frighteningly blank.

He backed up another few steps and raised his gun. Although he recognized a number of the group as senior police officers, they didn't seem to recognize the weapon and kept advancing. In another two or three feet, he'd be at the edge of the dance floor, his back against the wall. Fif-teen years on the force allowed him to maintain a patina of calm, but he could feel panic beginning to lap at the edges.

Almost frantically he searched for something to shoot, something that would get their attention, force them to acknowledge that *he* was the one with the gun. Unfortunately, the spinning disco ball, the most obvious target, was providing over half of the available light. Backing up another step, he made his decision and squeezed the trigger.

The ceiling tile exploded, throwing compressed foam and sound insulation down over the chanting crowd. Ignoring the echos battering the inside of his skull, Celluci lowered the gun.

Some instinct of self-preservation seemed to kick in and they stopped advancing, but the living barrier between him and Tawfik remained.

Okay. Now what?

A single man shuffled forward out of the front rank. In spite of the bad light, Celluci had no trouble recognizing . . .

"Inspector Cantree."

His hand grew sweaty around the pistol grip as his immediate superior shuffled closer. While there were any number of high-ranking police officers Celluci could've cheerfully shot, Cantree wasn't one of them. He'd been a black man on the force long before affirmative action programs and, in spite of all the bullshit thrown at him, he'd risen through the ranks with both his belief in the law and his sense of humor intact. That Tawfik could take a decent man, who had survived so much, and strip him of free will and honor twisted Celluci into knots, and to his horror he felt his eyes grow damp.

"Inspector, I don't want to shoot you."

One massive hand came up, palm outstretched, miming, "Give me the gun," very clearly over the continuing chant.

The roaring in his ears made it nearly impossible to think. "Inspector, don't make me do this."

Vicki heard the gunshot as she fell out of the stairwell and onto her knees, forehead pressed against the pale gray carpet. *Shooting should've been over ages ago. What the hell's going on up here?*

She had very little memory of how she'd managed to climb the last few flights of stairs although she knew that every movement had been imprinted on muscle and sinew and that her body would collect payment later, with interest, for the layers of abuse. She'd fallen twice and the second time, sprawled writhing on a concrete landing, only the thought of Celluci, already at the top, had given her the strength to move again. Her howl of desperate denial still echoed up and down the length of the tower.

Teeth clenched against the agony in her calves, she crawled to the wall and inched her way along it, not bothering, not able, to stand. Having been the native guide for her mother on numerous occasions, she ignored the disco's main entrance and continued around the curve of the hall as quickly as tortured muscles and bones could take her. All she could hear was her own labored breathing—in with the taste of blood, out with the taste of defeat.

You can't have won, you antique son of a bitch. I won't allow it.

Almost a quarter of the way around the arc of the tower was a window, designed so tourists could stand and watch the gyrations inside on the dance floor. The disco side of the window had been heavily tinted—apparently the management assumed the dancers had no interest in watching the tourists.

Just beyond, a dark line of shadows advanced toward Celluci.

Backing carefully away from the window, one hand still clamped to the frame for support, Vicki jammed her glasses back onto the bridge of her nose. *Looks like it's time for plan B.*

Close by, tucked discreetly into an angle in the wall, was an emergency exit; beside it, a glass-fronted cabinet of fire-fighting equipment. Vicki fell toward the cabinet, hung off the latch for a heartbeat, and finally managed to get it open. Clamping the nozzle under her arm, she turned the water on full force, then let her weight drop against the bar-latch on the door. She figured she had between five and ten seconds before the water reached the end of the hose and the pressure blew her off her feet.

Three seconds to drag the door toward her far enough to let her pass.

There's got to be a light here. You can't deal with emergencies in the dark. Two further seconds while logic actually answered and groping fingers closed on a familiar plastic switch.

One final second for her to take in Celluci backed against the wall, gun out; Inspector Cantree crawling on his stomach toward him, dragging blood across the parquet from a wounded thigh; a crowd of two dozen terrifyingly blank-faced men and women shuffling forward, fingers curled into claws.

For the first time, she could hear the chanting over the protests of her own body.

And then the water exploding from the nozzle nearly jerked the hose out of her hands. Knuckles white, thrown against the wall and held upright between the irresistible force and the immovable object, Vicki fought to keep the stream spraying across the dance floor, slamming Tawfik's puppets off their feet.

The chant abruptly shut off and with it the power he pulled from the acolytes. He felt thumbs press harder against his windpipe and his will drawn into the trap of agate eyes. To dissolve the spell of acquisition was no longer an option. In order to win, in order to live, his will must prove stronger and he must absorb the Nightwalker's ka. All or nothing. He released his personal power into the spell.

On a platform on the far side of the dance floor, Vicki saw Henry locked in combat with a tall, dark-haired man. Tawfik. It had to be. She felt Celluci push up against her side and shoved the hose into his hands, bellowing, "Keep . . . them down." Then she staggered back out into the hall for the fire ax.

"Vicki? Goddamnit, Vicki, what are you doing?"

She ignored him. It was all she could do to drag herself across the dance floor using the heavy ax as a kind of wedge-headed cane. Leg muscles had begun to spasm by the time she reached the platform and Tawfik's hair had gone from black to gray.

Teeth locked down on her lower lip, desperately fighting for enough air through flared nostrils, she stepped up behind the wizard-priest. It took her two tries to lift the ax over her head.

The sun became a burning weight, a thousand, a hundred thousand lives bearing down on him. The smell of his own flesh burning began to bury the blood scent. Ebony depths promised a cooling, an end. Henry pushed past the Hunger to reach them.

The ax went into the center of Tawfik's back with a meaty thunk and sank haft deep. Vicki'd put everything she had left into the blow. Fingers with no strength in them slid off the handle and the weight of her arms falling drove her back an involuntary step. Her hips slammed into the platform rail, her legs folded, and she dropped straight down to sit, more or less upright, against a padded support.

Tawfik's head jerked up and his mouth opened, but no sound came out. His hands released their hold on Henry's throat and groped behind him. He spun around, pulling free of Henry's grip, staggered, and fell, back arched against the pain, mouth still silently working.

Henry's shoulders straightened and his lips came up off his teeth. Now, finally, he would feed. . . .

"No, Henry!"

Snarling, he lifted his head toward the voice. Dimly, through the Hunger, he recognized Vicki, and turned to see what she stared at with such terror.

Two red eyes burned in the air at the edge of the platform. A faint crimson haze hinted at a bird's head, strangely winged, and an antelope's body.

Tawfik lifted one hand toward his god, trembling fingers spread, silently begging to be saved.

The red eyes burned brighter.

Gray hair turned white, brittle, and then fell to expose a yellowed dome of skull. Cheeks collapsed in upon themselves. Flesh melted away and skin stretched tight, tighter, gone. One by one, the tiny bones dropped from Tawfik's outstretched hand as tendons rotted and let go.

Finally, there were only clothes and the ax and a fine gray powder that might have been ash.

And the red eyes were gone.

"You guys okay?"

Henry reached across the remains and touched Vicki lightly on the cheek. In four hundred and fifty years, he had never felt the Hunger less. Vicki managed to nod. Together they turned to face Celluci.

"We're okay." Henry's throat closed around the words and they emerged with all the highs and lows scraped off. "What about you?"

Celluci snorted. "Fine. Just fine." He looked down at the powder, his movements jerky and tightly controlled. "All things considered. Why didn't . . ." The pause filled with a common memory of glowing red eyes. ". . . it save him? I mean, it made him."

Henry shook his head. "I don't know. I guess we'll never know. But I could feel Tawfik's life right until the last second. He was aware the whole time he was . . . was . . ."

"Dying. Jesus H. Christ." It was more a prayer than a profanity.

A collective moan that broke down into a babble of near hysteria drew their attention back out onto the dance floor. Most of Tawfik's ex-acolytes appeared to be in a state of shock. Most but not all.

Shirt wrapped in a makeshift bandage around his leg, supported by one of the two judges and the Deputy Chief of the OPP, Cantree dragged himself out of the crowd and scowled at the three on the platform.

"What the hell," he demanded, "has been going on here?"

"Go ahead, Mike." Vicki's head lolled back against the rail as she tried to decide whether she'd rather puke or cry, and if she had the energy to do either. "He's your boss. You tell him. . . ."

Celluci showed up at Henry's condo about an hour before dawn. He'd spent an uncomfortable two hours with Cantree in the emergency ward at St. Michael's Hospital telling him as much as he seemed willing to hear.

"You realize what this sounds like, don't you?"

"Yeah, I realize."

"I'd say you were the biggest liar of my acquaintance if it weren't for two things. I had no reason to have you arrested, yet I can remember giving the order and, just before you shot me, kind of hovering over your head . . ." He wet his lips. *". . . I saw a pair of red glowing eyes."*

"Apparently, it feeds on despair."

Cantree shifted position on the gurney and winced. "Nice to hear you weren't looking forward to pulling the trigger. . . ."

Moving carefully, he crossed the living room, threw himself down on the couch, and rubbed his face with his hands. "Christ, Vicki, you stink of liniment. You should've gone to the hospital yourself." Behind her glasses her eyes narrowed in warning and he let it drop. Again. He had to believe she was too smart to allow machismo to cripple her. "So how did the rest of it go?"

Henry turned away from the city. The night was his again. He'd almost lost it, would have lost it had Vicki not used the ax when she had. For all he had meant nothing by it, Tawfik had been right when he'd said a man shouldn't travel alone through the years. *You were the one traveling alone, old man,* he told the memory of ebony eyes. *And that's what killed you in the end. I have companions on the road. I have someone to guard my back. You gave up humanity for your immortality. I only gave up the day.* There would be no more dreams of the sun.

He leaned back against the window, arms folded across his chest, his gaze caressing Vicki lightly on its way to Celluci's face. "Fortunately, the various ex-acolytes remembered enough of what they'd agreed to—including rather explicit hallucinations during the chanting that none of them wanted to talk about—that 'it's over, it never happened' seemed to be explanation enough. Your Inspector Cantree was the only one involved who wanted to know what was really going on. By morning, the rest of them will have convinced themselves that they were at a wild party that got a little out of hand."

"All except George Zottie," Vicki added from the armchair. "Tawfik had taken over so much of his mind that when Tawfik died he didn't have anything left. The doctors say it was a massive stroke and he probably won't live long."

"A massive stroke," Celluci repeated, his eyes narrowing suspiciously, and he peered across the room at Henry. "What would make them think that?"

Henry shrugged. "Well, they were hardly likely to think his brain had been magically destroyed by a five-thousand-year-old Egyptian wizard-priest trying to sanctify a temple to his god."

"Yeah? And what about that god? Tawfik's dead. Is it?"

"Of course it isn't," Vicki snapped before Henry could speak. "Or Tawfik wouldn't *be* dead."

"Look, Vicki," Celluci sighed, "pretend it's very late and that I've been up for almost forty-eight hours, which it is and I have, and explain that to me."

"Tawfik's god allowed Tawfik to die. Therefore Tawfik was no longer necessary for its survival."

"But Tawfik told me that his god only survived because of him," Henry objected. "That a god with no one to believe in it is absorbed back into good or evil."

Vicki rolled her eyes. "Tawfik's god has people who believe in it," she said slowly and distinctly. "Us. Worship isn't necessary. Only belief."

"No, Tawfik worshiped."

"Sure he did; he sold his soul for immortality and that was his part of the bargain. But he also spent a few thousand years out cold in a sarcophagus and he sure as shit wasn't worshiping then. His god seems to have survived just fine." She slid her glasses back up her nose. "So tonight, Tawfik does something to piss off his god. We don't know what. Maybe it didn't approve of the venue for the temple—although any god that feeds off hopelessness and despair should find itself right at home in that meat market—maybe it didn't like the taste of the acolytes, maybe it didn't like Tawfik's attitude. . . ."

"Tawfik wanted to be seen as all powerful," Henry said thoughtfully, remembering.

"Well, there you have it." Vicki spread her hands. "Maybe it was afraid of a temple coup. Whatever the reason, it chose to trade Tawfik in. It'd never get a better opportunity because you," she jabbed an emphatic finger in Henry's direction, "are as immortal as Tawfik was."

Celluci frowned. "Then Henry's in danger."

Vicki shrugged. "We all are. We know its name. The moment we give in to hopelessness and despair, it'll be on us like—like politicians at a free bar. It may not need worshipers to survive, but it certainly needs them to get stronger. All it has to do is convince one of us and then we tell two friends and they tell two friends and so on and so on and here we go around the mulberry bush again. It'll want Henry, he'll last longer. But it'll settle for you or me."

"So basically what you're saying," Celluci sighed, "in your own long-winded way, is that it isn't over. We've beaten Tawfik, but we've still got Tawfik's god to fight."

To his surprise, Vicki smiled. "We've been fighting the god of hopelessness and despair all our lives, Mike. Now, we know it has a name. So what? It's the same fight."

Then her expression changed and Celluci, who recognized trouble, shot an anxious look at Henry who apparently recognized it, too.

"And now, I have something to say to you both." Her voice should've been registered as a lethal weapon. "If either of you ever again pull the patronizing bullshit you pulled on me tonight at the base of the tower, I'm going to rip your living hearts out and feed them to you. Do I make myself clear?"

The answering silence spoke volumes.

"Good. You can spend the next few months making it up to me."

BLOOD PACT

For Mrs. Mac, who helped me through a rough time without having a clue of what she was getting into and never really got thanked. Thank you.

Thanks also to Michael Humphries of Wattam's Funeral Home in Picton, Ontario, who gave generously of his time and expertise.

One

"Mrs. Simmons? It's Vicki Nelson calling; the private investigator from Toronto?" She paused and considered how best to present the information. *Oh, what the hell . . .* "We've found your husband."

"Is he . . . alive?"

"Yes, ma'am, very much so. He's working as an insurance adjuster under the name Tom O'Conner."

"Don always works in insurance."

"Yes, ma'am, that's how we found him. I've just sent you a package, by courier, containing a copy of everything we've discovered, including a number of recent photographs—you should receive it before noon tomorrow. The moment you call me with a positive ID, I'll take the information to the police and they can pick him up."

"The police thought they found him once before—in Vancouver—but when they went to pick him up he was gone."

"Well, he'll be there this time." Vicki leaned back in her chair, shoved her free hand up under the bottom edge of her glasses and scrubbed at her eyes. In eight years with the Metropolitan Toronto Police and nearly two years out on her own, she'd seen some real SOBs; Simmons/O'Conner ranked right up there with the best of them. Anyone who faked his own death in order to ditch a wife and five kids deserved exactly what he got. "My partner's going to talk to him tonight. I think your husband will decide to stay right where he is."

The bar was noisy and smoky, with tables too small to be useful and chairs too stylized to be comfortable. The beer was overpriced, the liquor over-iced, and the menu a tarted-up mix of at least three kinds of quasi-ethnic cooking plus the usual grease and carbohydrates. The staff were all young, attractive, and interchangeable. The clientele were a little older, not quite so attractive, although they tried desperately hard to camouflage it, and just as faceless. It was, for the moment, the premier poser bar in the city, and all the wannabes in Toronto shoehorned themselves through its doors on Friday night.

Henry Fitzroy paused just past the threshold and scanned the crowd through narrowed eyes. The smell of so many bodies crammed together, the sound of so many heartbeats pounding in time to the music blasting out of half a dozen suspended speakers, the feel of so many lives in so little space pulled the Hunger up and threatened to turn it loose. Fastidiousness more than willpower held it in check. In over four and a half centuries, Henry had never seen so many people working so hard and so futilely at having a good time.

It was the kind of place he wouldn't be caught dead in under normal circumstances, but tonight he was hunting and this was where his quarry had gone to ground. The crowd parted as he moved away from the door, and eddies of whispered speculation followed in his wake.

"Who does he think he is . . ."

". . . I'm telling you, he's somebody . . ."

Henry Fitzroy, bastard son of Henry VIII, onetime Duke of Richmond and Somerset, Lord President of the Council of the North, noted, with an inward sigh, that some things never changed. He sat down at the bar—the young man who had been on the stool having vacated it as Henry approached—and waved the bartender away.

To his right, an attractive young woman raised one ebony brow in obvious invitation. Although his gaze dropped to the pulse that beat in the ivory column of her throat and almost involuntarily traced the vein until it disappeared beneath the soft drape of magenta silk clinging to shoulders and breasts, he regretfully, silently, declined. She acknowledged both his glance and his refusal, then turned to more receptive game. Henry hid a smile. He wasn't the only hunter abroad tonight.

To his left, a wide back in a charcoal gray suit made up

most of the view. The hair above the suit had been artfully styled to hide the thinning patches just as the suit itself had been cut to cover the areas that a fortieth birthday had thickened. Henry reached out and tapped lightly on one wool-clad shoulder.

The wearer of the suit turned, saw no one he knew, and began to scowl. Then he fell into the depths of a pair of hazel eyes, much darker than hazel eyes should have been, much deeper than mortal eyes could be.

"We need to have a talk, Mr. O'Conner."

It would have taken a much stronger man to look away.

"In fact, I think you'd better come with me." A thin sheen of sweat greased the other man's forehead. "This is just a little too public for what I plan to—" slightly elongated canines became visible for an instant between parted lips— "discuss."

"And?"

Henry stood at the window, one hand flat against the cool glass. Although he seemed to be looking down at the lights of the city, he was actually watching the reflection of the woman seated on the couch behind him. "And what?"

"Henry, stop being an undead pain in the ass. Did you convince Mr. O'Conner/Simmons to stay put until the police arrive?"

He loved to watch her; loved to watch emotions play across her face, loved to watch her move, loved to watch her in repose. Loved her. But as that was a topic not to be discussed, all he said was, "Yes."

"Good. I hope you scared the living shit out of him while you were at it."

"Vicki." He turned, arms crossed on his chest, and frowned in what was only partially mock disapproval. "I am not your personal bogeyman, to be pulled out of the closet every time you think someone needs to have the fear of God . . ."

Vicki snorted. "Think highly of yourself, don't you?"

". . . put into them," he continued, ignoring the interruption.

"Have I ever treated you like my 'personal bogeyman'?" She raised a hand to cut off his immediate reply. "Be honest. You have certain skills, just like I have certain skills, and when I think it's necessary, I use them. Besides," she pushed her glasses back into place on the bridge of her nose, "you said you wanted to be more involved in my business. Help out with more cases now that you've handed in *Purple Passion's Pinnacle* and aren't due to start another romantic masterpiece until next month."

"Love Labors On." Henry saw no reason to be ashamed of writing historical romances; it paid well and he was good at it. He doubted, however, that Vicki had ever read one. She wasn't the type to enjoy, or even desire, escape through fiction. "Tonight—it wasn't what I had in mind when I said I wanted to be more involved."

"Henry, it's been over a year." She sounded amused. "You should know by now that most private investigating consists of days and days of boring, tedious research. Thrilling and exciting life-threatening situations are few and far between."

Henry raised one red-gold brow.

Vicki looked a little sheepish. "Look, it's not my fault people keep trying to kill me. And you. And anyway, you *know* those were the exceptions that prove the rule." She straightened, tucking one sneakered foot up under her butt. "Tonight, I needed to convince a sleazebag—who deserved to be terrified after what he put his wife and kids through— to stay put until the police arrive. Tonight, I needed you. Henry Fitzroy, vampire. No one else could've done it."

Upon reflection, he was willing to grant her that no one else could have done the job as well, although a couple of burly mortals and fifty feet of rope would have had the same general effect. "You really didn't like him, did you?"

"No. I didn't." Her lip curled. "It's one thing to walk out of your responsibilities, but it takes a special kind of asshole to do it in such a way that everyone thinks he's dead. They mourned him, Henry. Cried for him. And the son of a bitch was off building a new life, fancy-free, while they were bringing flowers, every Saturday, to an empty grave. If he hadn't gotten into the background of that national news report, they'd still be crying for him. He owes them. In my book, he owes them big."

"Well, then, you'll be happy to know that I did, as you so inelegantly put it, scare the living shit out of him."

"Good." She loosened her grip on the throw pillow. "Did you . . . uh . . . feed?"

"Would it matter if I had?" Would she admit it if it mattered? "Blood's blood, Vicki. And his fear was enough to raise the Hunger."

"I know. And I know you feed from others. It's just . . ." She dragged one hand through her hair, standing it up in dark blonde spikes. "It's just that . . ."

"No. I didn't feed from him." Her involuntary smile was all he could have asked, so he crossed the room to see it better.

"You're probably hungry, then."

"Yes." He took her hand and gently caressed the inner skin of her wrist with his thumb. Her pulse leapt under his touch.

She tried to stand, but he pushed her back, bent his head, and ran his tongue down the faint blue line of a vein.

"Henry, if we don't go soon, I won't be able to . . ." Her voice faded out as her brain became preoccupied with other things. With a mighty effort, she forced her throat to open and her mouth to work. "We'll end up staying on the . . . couch."

He lifted his mouth long enough to murmur, "So?" and that was the last coherent word either of them spoke for some time.

"Four o'clock in the morning," Vicki muttered, digging for the keys to her apartment. "Another two hours and I'll have seen the clock around. Again. Why do I keep doing this to myself?" Her wrist throbbed, as if in answer, and she sighed. "Never mind. Stupid question."

Muscles tensed across her back as the door unexpectedly swung fully open. The security chain hung loose, unlocked, arcing back and forth, scraping softly, metal against wood. Holding her breath, she filtered out the ambient noises of the apartment—the sound of the refrigerator motor, a dripping tap, the distant hum of the hydro substation across the street—and noted a faint mechanical whir. It sounded like . . .

She almost had it when a sudden noise drove off all hope of identification. The horrible crunching, grinding, smashing, continued for about ten seconds, then muted.

"I'll grind his bones to make my bread . . ." It was the closest she could come to figuring out what could possibly be happening. *And all things considered, I'm not denying the possibility of a literal translation.* After demons, were-wolves, mummies, not to mention the omnipresent vampire in her life, a Jack-eating giant in her living room was less than impossible, no matter how unlikely.

She shrugged the huge, black leather purse off her shoulder and caught it just before it hit the floor. With the strap wrapped twice around her wrist it made a weapon even a giant would flinch at. *Good thing I hung onto that brick . . .*

The sensible thing to do would involve closing the door, trotting to the phone booth on the corner, and calling the cops.

I am way too tired for this shit. Vicki stepped silently into the apartment. *Four in the morning courage. Gotta love it.*

Sliding each foot a centimeter above the floor and placing it back down with exaggerated care, she made her way along the short length of hall and around the corner into the living room, senses straining. Over the last few months she'd started to believe that, while the retinitis pigmentosa had robbed her of any semblance of night sight, sound and smell were beginning to compensate. The proof would be in the pudding; although she knew the streetlight outside the bay window provided a certain amount of illumination in spite of the blinds and the apartment never actually got completely dark, as far as her vision was concerned, she might as well be wearing a padded blindfold.

Well, not quite a blindfold. Even she couldn't miss the blob of light that had to be the television flickering silently against the far wall. She stopped, weapon ready, cocked her head, and got a whiff of a well-known aftershave mixed with . . . cheese?"

The sudden release of tension almost knocked her over.

"What the hell are you doing here at this hour, Celluci?"

"What does it look like?" the familiar voice asked mockingly in turn. "I'm watching an incredibly stupid movie with the sound off and eating very stale taco chips. How long have you had these things sitting around, anyway?"

Vicki groped for the wall, then walked her fingers along it to the switch for the overhead light. Blinking away tears as her sensitive eyes reacted to the glare, she gently lowered her purse to the floor. Mr. Chin, downstairs in the first floor apartment, wouldn't appreciate being woken up by twenty pounds of assorted bric-a-brac slamming into his ceiling.

Detective-Sergeant Michael Celluci squinted up at her from the couch and set the half-empty bag of taco chips to one side. "Rough night?" he growled.

Yawning, she shrugged out of her jacket, tossing it over the back of the recliner. "Not really. Why?"

"Those bags under your eyes look more like a set of matched luggage." He swung his legs to the floor and stretched. "Thirty-two just doesn't bounce back the way thirty-one used to. You need more sleep."

"Which I had every intention of getting." She crossed the room and jabbed a finger at the television control panel. "Until I came home to find *you* in my living room. And you haven't answered my question."

"What question?" He smiled charmingly, but eight years on the force with him, the last four intimately involved— *Now* that's *a tidy label for a complicated situation,* she mused—had made her pretty much immune to classical good looks used to effect.

"I'm too tired for this shit, Celluci. Cut to the chase."

"All right, I came by to see what you remembered about Howard Balland."

She shrugged. "Small-time hood, always looking for the big score but would probably miss said big score if it bit him on the butt. I thought he left town."

Celluci spread his hands. "He's back, in a manner of speaking. A couple of kids found his body earlier tonight behind a bookstore down on Queen Street West."

"And you've come to me to see if I remember anything that'll help you nail his killer?"

"You've got it."

"Mike, I was in fraud for only three short months before I transferred to homicide and that was a good chunk of time ago."

"So you don't remember anything?"

"I didn't say that . . ."

"Ah." The single syllable held a disproportionate weight

of sarcasm. "You're tired and you'd rather screw around
with your little undead friend than help get the bastard who
slit the throat of a harmless old con man. I understand."

Vicki blinked. "What the fuck are you talking about?"

"You *know* what I'm talking about. You've been off
playing Vlad the impaler with Henry Fucking Fitzroy!"

Her brows drew down into a deep vee, the expression
making it necessary for her to jab her glasses back up onto
the bridge of her nose. "I don't believe this. You're
jealous!"

They were chest to chest and would've been nose to nose
accept for the difference in their heights. Although Vicki
was tall at five ten, Celluci was taller still at six four.

"JEALOUS!"

Over the years Vicki had learned enough Italian to get
the gist of what followed. The fight had barely begun to
heat up when a soft voice slid through a pause in the
screaming.

"Excuse me?"

Expressions ludicrously frozen in mid-snarl, they turned
to face the wizened concern of Mr. Chin. He clutched a
burgundy brocade bathrobe closed with one frail hand and
had the other raised as though to snare their attention.
When he saw he had it, he smiled into the silence.

"Thank you," he told them. "Now, shall we see if we
can maintain this situation?" At their puzzled frowns, he
sighed. "Let me make it a little simpler for you. It's 4:22
a.m. Shut up." He waited for a moment, nodded, and left
the apartment, gently pulling the door closed behind him.

Vicki felt her ears grow hot. She jerked around as a
cross between a sneeze and a small explosion sounded from
Celluci's direction. "What are you laughing at?"

He shook his head, arms waving as he searched for the
words.

"Never mind." She reached up and pushed the curl of
dark brown hair back off his face, her own mouth twisting
up in a rueful grin. "I guess it was pretty funny at that.
Although I'm going to spend the rest of the day with this
vaguely unfinished feeling."

Celluci nodded, the thick curl dropping back down into
his eyes. "Like not remembering if you've eaten the last
bite of doughnut."

"Or drunk the last swallow of coffee."

They shared a smile and Vicki collapsed into the black leather recliner that dominated the small living room. "Okay, what do you need to know about the late Mr. Balland?"

Vicki moved away from the warm cliff of Celluci's back and wondered why she couldn't sleep. Maybe she *should* have told him to go home, but it'd seemed a little pointless making him drive all the way out to his house in Downsview when he was expected back downtown at headquarters in barely six hours. Or less. Maybe. She couldn't see the clock unless she sat up, turned on the light, and found her glasses, but it had to be nearly dawn.

Dawn.

In the center of the city, eighteen short blocks away from her apartment in Chinatown, Henry Fitzroy lay in his sealed room and waited for the day; waited for the rising sun to switch off his life; trusted that the setting sun would switch it on again.

Vicki had spent the day with Henry once, held captive by the threat of sunlight outside the bedroom door. The absence of life had been so complete it had been a little like spending the day with a corpse. Only worse. Because he wasn't. It wasn't an experience she wanted to repeat.

She'd run from him that night, the moment the darkness had granted her safe passage. To this day she wasn't sure if she'd run from his nature or from the trust that had allowed him to be so helpless before her.

She hadn't stayed away for long.

In spite of late nights, or occasionally no nights at all, Henry Fitzroy had become a necessary part of her life. Although the physical attraction still tied her stomach in knots and caught the breath in her throat—even after a year of exposure—what bothered her, almost frightened her, was how much he had invaded the rest of her life.

Henry Fitzroy, vampire, bastard son of Henry VIII, was Mystery. If she spent a lifetime trying, she could never know all he was. And, God help her, she couldn't resist a mystery.

Now Celluci—she rolled onto her side and layered herself around the curve of his body—Celluci was the yin to her yang. She frowned. Or possibly the other way around. He was a shared joke, shared interests, a shared past. He fit into her life like a puzzle piece, interlocking and completing the picture. And now she thought of it, *that* frightened her, too.

She was complete without him.

Wasn't she?

Lord, oh Lord, oh Lord. When did my life start resembling country and western music?

Celluci stirred under the force of her sigh and half roused. "Almost forgot," he murmured. "Your mother called."

The late morning sun had nearly cleared Vicki's bay window when she sat down at the kitchen table and reached for the phone. Returning her mother's call while Celluci was dressing would make it easier to deal with the questions she knew she was going to have to answer. Questions that would no doubt start with, *Why was Michael Celluci in your apartment when you weren't?* and escalate from there to the perpetual favorite, *When will you be coming to visit?*

She sighed, fortified herself with a mouthful of coffee, and wrapped her fingers around the receiver. Before she could lift it out of the cradle, the phone rang. She managed, just barely, to keep the coffee from going out her nose but it took a half a dozen rings to get the choking under control.

"Nelson Investigations."

"Ms. Nelson? It's Mrs. Simmons. I was beginning to think you weren't there."

"Sorry." She hooked a dish towel off the refrigerator door and swiped at the mess. "What can I do for you?"

"The photographs came. Of my husband."

Vicki checked her watch. Nearly noon in Toronto meant nearly eleven in Winnipeg. *Hot damn. Truth in advertising; I've found a courier who can tell time.*

"It *is* my husband, Ms. Nelson. It's him." She sounded close to tears.

"Then I'll take the information to the police this afternoon. They'll pick him up and then they'll get in contact with you."

"But it's the weekend." Her protest was more a whimper than a wail.

"The police work weekends, Mrs. Simmons. Don't worry." Vicki turned up the reassurance in her voice. "And even if they can't actually bring him in until Monday, well, I personally guarantee he's not going anywhere."

"You're sure?"

"I'm sure."

"I need to ask him why, Ms. Nelson; why he did such a horrible thing to us?"

The pain in the other woman's voice tightened Vicki's fingers on the receiver until her knuckles went white. She only just managed to mask her anger with sympathy during the final few moments of the call.

"God-damned, fucking, son of a BITCH!"

Her notepad hit the far wall of the apartment with enough force to shatter the spine and send loose paper fluttering to the floor like a flock of wounded birds.

"Anyone I know?" Celluci asked. As he'd come into the living room barely a meter from the impact point, he supposed he should be thankful she hadn't thrown the coffee mug.

"No." She surged up out of her chair, slamming it back so hard it fell and bounced twice.

"Something to do with your found missing person?" It wasn't that difficult a guess; he knew the bare bones of the case and he'd heard her use the name Simmons during the phone conversation. Also, he knew Vicki and, while she was anything but uncomplicated, her reactions tended to be direct and to the point.

"Lousy bastard!" Her glasses slid to the end of her nose and she jabbed them back up the slope. "Doesn't give a shit about what he put his family through. You should have heard her, Mike. He's destroyed everything she ever believed in. At least when she thought he was dead, she had memories, but now he's fucked those, too. He's hurt her so badly she hasn't even hit anger yet."

"So you're getting angry for her."

"Why not?"

He shrugged. "Why not, indeed." Intimately familiar with Vicki's temper, he thought he saw something more than just rage at a woman wronged. Lord knew she'd seen enough of that during her years on the force and had never—all right, seldom—reacted with such intensity. "Your mother, did she ever get angry when your father left?"

Vicki came to a dead stop and stared at him. "What the hell does that have to do with anything?"

"Your father walked out on your mother. And you."

"My father, at least, had the minimal decency not to hide what he was doing."

"And your mother had to support the two of you. Probably never had time to get angry."

Her eyes narrowed as she glared across the apartment at him. "What the fuck are you talking about?"

He recognized the danger signs but couldn't let the opportunity pass. Things had been working toward this for a long time and with her anger for Mrs. Simmons leaving her so emotionally open he knew he might never get a better chance. *What the hell, if it comes to it, I'm armed.* "I'm talking, whether you like it or not, about you and me."

"You're talking bullshit."

"I'm talking about how you're so afraid of commitment that you'll barely admit we're anything more than friends. I understand where it's coming from. I understand that because of the way your father left and because of what happened afterward with your mother that you think you need to put tight little parameters on a relationship . . ."

She snorted. "Did the force just send you to another sensitivity seminar?"

He tightened his grip on his own temper and ignored her. ". . . but all that happened over twenty years ago and, Vicki, it has to stop."

Her lip curled. "Or else?"

"Or else nothing, God damn it. I'm not making threats here."

"This is about Henry, isn't it? You *are* jealous."

No point in forcing her to face the truth if he didn't. "You're god-damned right I'm jealous of Henry! I don't want to share that much of you with *anyone* else. Especially not with someone who . . . who . . ." Mike Celluci didn't have the words to explain how he felt about Henry Fitzroy and even if he had, it was none of Vicki's business. The edge of his hand chopped off the thought. "We're not talking about Henry, we're talking about us."

"There's nothing wrong with *us.*" She looked everywhere but at the man standing across the room. "Why can't we just go on the way we have been?"

"Because we're not going anywhere!"

She jerked at each staccato word.

"Vicki, I'm tired of being nothing more than your buddy. You've got to realize that I . . ."

"Shut up!" Her hands had curled into fists.

"Oh, no." He shook his head. "You're going to hear it this time."

"This is *my* apartment. I don't have to hear *anything.*"

"Oh, yes you do." He crossed to stand directly in front of her, balancing on the balls of his feet, his hands a careful distance away. As much as he wanted to grab her and shake her, he didn't want to deal with the return violence he knew would follow. A quick game of *Who's more macho?* would add nothing to the situation. "This isn't going to be the last time I say this, Vicki, so you'd better get used to it. I love you. I want a future with you. Why is it so hard for you to accept that?"

"Why can't you just accept me, us, the way I am? We are?" The words were forced out through clenched teeth.

He shoved the lock of hair back off his forehead and unsuccessfully tried to calm his breathing. "I've spent five fucking years accepting you and *us.* It's time you met me halfway."

"Get out."

"What?"

"Get out of my apartment! NOW!"

Trembling with the need to hold himself in check, he pushed past her and grabbed his coat off the hook by the door. Jabbing his arms into the sleeves, he turned. His own anger made it impossible for him to read her expression. "Just one more thing, Vicki. I am *not* your fucking father."

The door closed behind him with enough force to shake the building.

A heartbeat later it opened again.

"And don't forget to call your mother!"

The coffee mug exploded into a thousand pieces against the wood.

                              *   *   *

"And did you?"

"Did I what?" Vicki snapped. Giving Henry the gist of the fight had put her in nearly as bad a mood as the fight had. It didn't help that she *knew* she should've kept her mouth shut, but when Henry had asked what was bothering her, she couldn't seem to stop a repeat of the whole infuriating conversation from pouring out.

"Did you call your mother?"

"No. I didn't." She turned to face the window, jabbed at her glasses, and glared out at the darkness. "I wasn't exactly in the mood to talk to my mother. I went down to Missing Persons and nailed Mr. Simmons/O'Conner to the wall instead."

"Did that make you feel better?"

"No. Although it might have if they'd let me use real nails."

A facetious comment spoken with complete and utter sincerity. Even from across the room Henry could feel pulsing waves of anger radiating off of her. He wished now that he hadn't asked, that he'd ignored her mood and never been subjected to Detective-Sergeant Michael Celluci's all-too-accurate analysis of Vicki's inability to commit. But now that he'd heard it, he couldn't let it rest. Vicki would continue to think about what Celluci had said, had obviously been thinking of little else since Celluci had slammed out of her apartment, and, now that her nose had been rubbed in it, would in time see it for the truth. At which point she would have to choose.

He wouldn't lose her. If that meant taking the day as well as the night, his love gave him a right equal to Celluci's to assert a claim.

You raised the stakes, mortal, he told the other man silently. *Remember that.*

He stood and crossed the carpet to stand at her side, glorying for a moment in her heartbeat, savoring her heat, her scent, her life.

"He was right," he said at last.

"About what?" The words were forced out through clenched teeth. No need to ask which *he* was meant.

"We can't, any of us, go on the way we have."

"Why not?" The final consonant carried the weight of a potential explosion.

"Because, like Mike Celluci, I want to be the most important person in your life."

She snorted. "And what about what I want?"

He could see the muscles working beneath the velvet surface of her skin, tensing around her eyes and the corners of her mouth and so he chose his next words with care. "I think that's what we're trying to discover."

"And what if I decide I want him?"

Her tone held a bitter, mocking edge. Henry couldn't help but respond.

"Could you give *me* up?"

The power in his voice pulled her around to face him. He heard her swallow hard as she met his gaze, heard her heartbeat quicken, saw her pupils dilate, tasted the change in her scent on the air. Then he released her.

Vicki jerked back, furious at Henry, furious at herself. "Don't ever do that again!" she panted, fighting to get enough air into her lungs. "I give nobody power over my life. Not you. Not him. Nobody!" Barely in control of her movements, she whirled and stomped across the living room. "I am *out* of here." She snatched her coat and bag up off the end of the couch, "And you can just play Prince of fucking Darkness with somebody else."

He hadn't moved from the window. He knew he could call her back, so he had no need to make the attempt. "Where are you going?"

"I'm going for a long walk in the sleaziest neighborhood I can find in the hope that some dickweed will try something stupid and I can break his fucking arms! *Don't* follow me!"

Even a security door can be slammed if enough force is applied.

"Vicki? It's your mother. Didn't Mike Celluci give you my message? Well, never mind, dear, I'm sure he has a lot on his mind. While I'm thinking of it though, I *did* wonder why he was in your apartment while you were out. Have you two been getting more serious? Call me when you get a chance. There's something I have to tell you."

Vicki sighed and rubbed at her temples as the answering machine rewound. It was ten after twelve and she was just not up to a heart-to-heart with her mother, not after the day she'd had. "Have you two been getting more serious?" Jesus H. Christ.

First Celluci.

Then Henry.

The powers-that-be had really decided to mess up her life.

"Whatever happened to men who just want to get laid on a regular basis?" she muttered, flicking off the light and making her way to the bedroom.

The pitcher of draft she'd downed in the gay bar on Church Street—the one place in the city safe from testosterone cases—churned uneasily in her stomach. All she wanted to do was go to sleep. Alone.

She'd call her mother in the morning.

The night had been filled with dreams, or more specifically, dream—the same images occurring over and over. People kept coming into her apartment and she couldn't get them to leave. The new staircase to the third floor bisected her kitchen and a steady stream of real estate agents moved up it, dragging potential tenants. The back of her closet opened into Maple Leaf Gardens and the post-hockey crowds decided to leave through her bedroom. First she tried the voice of reason. Then she yelled. Then she physically picked up the intruders and threw them out the door. But the door never stayed closed and they wouldn't, any of them, leave her alone.

She woke up late with a splitting headache and an aching jaw, her mood not significantly better than when she'd gone to sleep. An antacid and an aspirin might have helped, but as she'd run out of both she settled for a mug of coffee so strong her tongue curled in protest.

"And why did I *know* it would be raining," she growled, squinting out through the blinds at a gray and uninviting world. The sky looked low enough to touch.

The phone rang.

Vicki turned and scowled across the room at it. She didn't have to answer to know it was her mother. She could feel mother vibes from where she stood.

"Not this morning, Mom. I'm just not up to it."

Her head continued ringing long after the bell fell silent. An hour later, it rang again.

An hour of conscious thought had done nothing to improve Vicki's mood.

"I said *no,* Mom!" She slammed her fist down on the kitchen table. The phone rocked but continued to ring. "I don't want to hear about your problems right now and I sure as shit don't want to tell you about mine!" Her voice rose. "My personal life has suddenly collapsed. I don't know what's going on. Everything is falling apart. I can stand on my own. I can work as part of a team. I've proved that, haven't I? Why isn't that *enough!*"

It became a contest in volume and duration and Vicki had no intention of letting the phone win.

"Odds are good Celluci's about to propose and this vampire I'm sleeping with—Oh, didn't I tell you about Henry, Mom?—well he wants me as his . . . his . . . I don't *know* what Henry wants. Can you deal with that, Mom? 'Cause I sure as shit can't!"

She could feel herself trembling on the edge of hysteria, but she wouldn't quit until the phone did.

"Celluci thinks I'm angry about the way dear old Dad walked out on you. Henry thinks he's right. How about that, Mom? I'm being fucking double-teamed. You never warned me about something like this, did you, Mom? And we never, ever discuss Daddy!"

The last word echoed around a silent apartment and seemed to take a very long time to fade.

With a trembling finger, Vicki slid her glasses back up her nose. "I'll talk to you tomorrow, Mom. I promise."

An hour later, the phone rang again.

Vicki turned on the answering machine and went for a walk in the rain.

When she got back, late that evening, there were seven messages waiting. She wiped the tape without listening to any of them.

The phone rang.

Vicki paused, one foot into the shower, sighed, and got back into her robe. Welcome to Monday.

"Coming, Mom." No point putting it off. She'd have to

face the music sooner or later and it might as well be sooner.

Today things didn't seem so bad. Yesterday was an embarrassing memory of self-indulgence. Tomorrow, well, she'd deal with tomorrow when it arrived.

She dropped into one of the kitchen chairs and scooped up the receiver. "Hi, Mom. Sorry about yesterday."

"Is this Victoria Nelson?"

Her ears grew hot. It was an elderly woman's voice, strained and tight and most definitely not her mother.

Let's make a great impression on a potential client there, Vicki. "Uh, yes."

"This is Mrs. Shaw. Mrs. Elsa Shaw. I work with your mother. We met last September . . .?"

"I remember." Vicki winced. *Mom must really be pissed if she's getting coworkers to call. This is going to cost me at least a visit.*

"I'm afraid I have some bad news for you."

"Bad news?" *Oh, God, don't let her have caught the early train to Toronto. That's all I need right now.*

"Your mother hasn't been feeling well lately, and, well, she came into work this morning, said how she'd been trying to get in touch with you, made the coffee like she always does, came out of Dr. Burke's office and . . . and, well, died."

The world stopped.

"Ms. Nelson?"

"What happened?" Vicki heard herself ask the question, marveled at how calm her voice sounded, wondered why she felt so numb.

"Dr. Burke, the head of the Life Sciences Department— well, you know who Dr. Burke is, of course—said it was her heart. A massive coronary, she said. One minute there, the next . . ." Mrs. Shaw blew her nose. "It happened about twenty minutes ago. If there's anything I can do . . ."

"No. Thank you. Thank you for calling."

If Mrs. Shaw had further sympathy or information to offer, Vicki didn't hear it. She set the receiver gently back in its cradle and stared down at the silent phone.

Her mother was dead.

Two

"Dr. Burke? It's about number seven . . ."

"And?" Receiver tucked under her chin, Dr. Aline Burke scrawled her signature across the bottom of a memo and tossed it into the out basket. Although Marjory Nelson had been dead for only a couple of hours, the paperwork had already begun to get out of hand. With any luck the university would get off its collective butt and get her a temporary secretary before academic trivia completely buried her.

"I think you'll want to see this for yourself."

"For heaven's sake, Catherine, I haven't got the time for you to be obscure." She rolled her eyes. Grad students. "Are we losing it?"

"Yes, Doctor."

"I'll be right over."

"Damn." The surgical glove hit the wastebasket with enough force to rock the container from side to side. "Tissue decomposition again. Just like the others." The second glove followed and Dr. Burke turned to glare at the body of an elderly man lying on the stainless steel table, thoracic cavity open, skull cap resting against one ear. "Didn't even last as long as number six."

"Well, he was old to start with, Doctor. And not in very good physical condition."

Dr. Burke snorted. "I should say not. I suppose I'm moderately surprised it lasted as long as it did." She sighed as the young woman standing by the head of the cadaver looked crushed. "That was *not* a criticism, Catherine. You did your usual excellent job and were certainly in no way responsible for the subject's deplorable habits when alive. That said, retrieve the rest of the mechanicals, salvage as much of the net as you can, be very sure *all* of the bacteria are dead, and begin the usual disposal procedures."

"The medical school . . ."

"Of *course* the medical school. We're hardly going to weight it with rocks and drop it into Lake Ontario— although I have to admit that has a certain simplicity that appeals and would involve a lot less additional work for me. Let me know when it's ready, I should be in my office for the next couple of hours." Hand on the door, she paused. "What's that banging noise?"

Catherine looked up, pale blue eyes wide, fingers continuing to delve into the old man's skull cavity. "Oh, it's number nine. I don't think he likes the box."

"It doesn't *like* anything, Catherine. It's dead."

The younger woman shrugged apologetically, accepting the correction but unwilling to be convinced. "He keeps banging."

"Well, when you finish with number seven, decrease the power again. The last thing we need is accelerated tissue damage due to unauthorized motion."

"Yes, Doctor." She gently slid the brain out onto a plastic tray. The bank of fluorescent lights directly over the table picked up glints of gold threaded throughout the grayish-green mass. "It'll be nice to finally work with a subject we've been able to do preliminary setup on. I mean, the delay while we attempt to tailor the bacteria can't be good for them."

"Probably not," Dr. Burke agreed caustically and, with a last disapproving look in the direction of number nine's isolation box, strode out of the lab.

The pounding continued.

"Where to, lady?"

Vicki opened her mouth and then closed it again. She didn't actually have the faintest idea.

"Uh, Queen's University. Life Sciences." Her mother would have been moved. Surely someone could tell her where.

"It's a big campus, Queen's is." The cabbie pulled out

of the train station parking lot and turned onto Taylor Kidd Boulevard. "You got a street address?"

She knew the address. Her mother had shown her proudly around the new building just after it opened two years ago. "It's on Arch Street."

"Down by the old General Hospital, eh? Well, we'll find it." He smiled genially at her in his rearview mirror. "Fifteen years of driving a cab and I haven't gotten lost yet. Nice day today. Looks like spring finally arrived."

Vicki squinted out the window beside her. The sun was shining. Had the sun been shining in Toronto? She couldn't remember.

"Winter's better for business, mind you. Who wants to walk when the slush is as high as your hubcaps, eh? Still, April's not so bad as long as we get a lot of rain. Let it rain, that's what I say. You going to be in Kingston long?"

"I don't know."

"Visiting relatives?

"Yes." *My mother. She's dead.*

Something in that single syllable convinced the cabbie his fare wasn't in the mood for conversation and that further questions might be better left unasked. Humming tunelessly, he left her to relative silence.

An attempt had been made to blend the formed concrete of the new Life Sciences Complex in with the older, limestone structures of the university, but it hadn't been entirely successful.

"Progress," the cabbie ventured, as Vicki opened the back door, his tongue loosened by a sizable tip. "Still, the kids need more than a couple of Bunsen burners and a rack of test tubes to do meaningful research these days, eh? Paper says some grad student took out a patent on a germ."

Vicki, who'd handed him a twenty because it was the first bill she'd pulled out of her wallet, ignored him.

He shook his head as he watched her stride up the walk, back rigidly straight, overnight bag carried like a weapon, and decided against suggesting that she have a nice day.

"Mrs. Shaw? I'm Vicki Nelson . . ."

The tiny woman behind the desk leapt to her feet and

held out both hands. "Oh, yes, of course you are. You poor dear, did you come all the way from Toronto?"

Vicki stepped back but couldn't avoid having her right hand clutched and wrung. Before she could speak, Mrs. Shaw rushed on.

"Of course you did. I mean you were in Toronto when I called and now you're here." She laughed, a little embarrassed, and let go of Vicki's hand. "I'm sorry. It's just . . . well, your mother and I were friends, we'd worked together for almost five years and when she . . . I mean, when . . . It was just . . . such a terrible shock."

Vicki stared down at the tears welling up in the older woman's eyes and realized to her horror that she didn't have the faintest idea of what to say. All the words of comfort she'd spoken over the years to help ease a thousand different types of grief, all the training, all the experience—she could find none of it.

"I'm sorry." Mrs. Shaw dug into her sleeve and pulled out a damp and wrinkled tissue. "It's just every time I think of it . . . I can't help . . ."

"Which is why I keep telling you, you should go home."

Thankfully, Vicki turned to face the speaker, the calm, measured tone having dropped like a balm over her abraded nerves. The woman standing just inside the door to the office was in her mid-forties, short, solidly built, and wearing an almost practical combination of gray flannel pants and white, lace-edged blouse under her open lab coat. Her red-brown hair had been cut fashionably close, and the heavy frames of her glasses sat squarely on a nose well dusted with freckles. Her self-confidence was a tangible presence, even from across the room, and in spite of everything, Vicki felt herself responding.

Mrs. Shaw sniffed and replaced the tissue in her sleeve. "And I keep telling you, Dr. Burke, I'm not going home to spend the day alone, not when I can stay here, be surrounded by people, and actually accomplish something. Vicki felt small fingers close around her arm. "Dr. Burke, this is Marjory's daughter, Victoria."

The department head's grip was warm and dry and she shook hands with an efficiency of motion that Vicki appreciated.

"We met briefly a few years ago, Ms. Nelson, just after

your first citation, I believe. I was sorry to hear about the retinitis. It must have been difficult leaving a job you cared so deeply about. And now . . ." She spread her hands. "My condolences about your mother."

"Thank you." There didn't seem to be much left to say.

"I had the body taken over to the morgue at the General. Your mother's personal physician, Dr. Friedman, has an office there. As we didn't know exactly when you'd be arriving or what the arrangements would be, that seemed best for all concerned. I did have Mrs. Shaw call to let you know, but you must have already left."

The flow of information carried no emotional baggage at all. Vicki found herself drawing strength from the force of personality that supported it. "If I could use one of your phones to call Dr. Friedman?"

"Certainly." Dr. Burke nodded toward the desk. "She's already been informed and is waiting for your call. Now, if you'll excuse me." She paused at the door. "Oh, Ms. Nelson? Do let us know when the service is to be held. We'd . . ." Her gesture included Mrs. Shaw. ". . . like to attend."

"Service?"

"It *is* customary under these circumstances to hold a funeral."

Vicki barely noticed the sarcasm, only really heard the last word. *Funeral* . . .

"Well, she doesn't look asleep." There was no mistaking the waxy, gray pallor, the complete lack of self that only death brings. Vicki had recognized it the first time she'd seen it in a police cadet forensic lab and she recognized it now. The dead were not alive. It sounded like a facetious explanation but, as she stared down at the body her mother had worn, she couldn't think of a better one.

Dr. Friedman looked mildly disapproving as she drew the sheet back up over Marjory Nelson's face, but she held her tongue. She could feel the restraints that Vicki had placed around herself but didn't know the younger woman well enough to get past them. "There'll be no need for an autopsy," she said, indicating that the morgue attendant should take the body away. "Your mother has been having heart irregularities for some time and Dr. Burke was practically standing right beside her when it happened. She said it had all the earmarks of a massive coronary."

"A heart attack?" Vicki watched as the door swung shut behind the pallet and refused to shiver in the cold draft that escaped from the morgue. "She was only fifty-six."

The doctor shook her head sadly. "It happens."

"She never told me."

"Perhaps she didn't want to worry you."

Perhaps I wasn't listening. The small viewing room had suddenly become confining. Vicki headed for the exit.

Dr. Friedman, caught unaware, hurried to catch up. "The coroner is satisfied, but if you're not . . ."

"No autopsy." She'd been to too many to put her mother—what was left of her mother—through that.

"Your mother had a prepaid funeral arranged with Hutchinson's Funeral Parlour, up on Johnson Street, just by Portsmouth Avenue. It would be best if you speak to them as soon as possible. Do you have someone to go with you?"

Vicki's brows drew down. "I don't *need* anyone to go with me," she snarled.

"According to your mother's arrangement, Ms. Nelson, Vicki . . . Ms. Nelson"—the funeral director blanched slightly as his client's expression returned him to last names but he managed to continue smoothly—"she wanted to be buried as soon as possible, with no viewing."

"Fine."

"As she also wanted to be embalmed . . . perhaps the day after tomorrow? That would give you time for a notice in the local paper."

"Is the day after tomorrow as soon as possible, then?"

The younger Mr. Hutchinson swallowed. He found it difficult to remain completely calm under such hard-edged examination. "Well, no, we could have everything ready by tomorrow afternoon . . ."

"Do so, then."

It wasn't a tone that could be argued with. It wasn't even a tone that left much room for discussion. "Is two o'clock suitable?"

"Yes."

"About the casket . . ."

"Mr. Hutchinson, I understood that my mother prearranged *everything.*"

"Yes, she did . . ."

"Then," Vicki stood, slung her bag over her shoulder, "we will do exactly as my mother wanted."

"Ms. Nelson." He stood as well, and pitched his voice as gently as he could. "Without a notice in the paper, you'll have to call people."

Her shoulders hunched slightly and the fingers that reached for the doornob shook. "I know," she said.

And was gone.

The younger Mr. Hutchinson sank back down into his chair and rubbed at his temples. "Recognizing there's nothing you can do to help," he told a potted palm with a sigh, "has got to be the hardest part of this business."

The old neighborhood had gotten smaller. The vast expanse of backyard behind the corner house at Division and Quebec Streets that she'd grown up envying had somehow shrunk to postage stamp size. The convenience store at Division and Pine had become a flower shop and the market across from it—where at twelve she'd argued her way into her first part-time job—was gone. The drugstore still stood at York Street but, where it had once seemed a respectable distance away, Vicki now felt she could reach out and touch it. Down on Quebec Street, not even the stump remained of the huge maple that had shaded the Thompson house and not even the spring sunlight could erase the shabby, unlived in look of the whole area.

Standing in the front parking lot of the sixteen-unit apartment building they'd moved to when her father's departure had lost them the house in Collins Bay, Vicki wondered when it had happened. She'd been back any number of times in the last fourteen years, had been back not so long before and had never noticed such drastic changes.

Maybe because the one thing I came back for never changed. . . .

She couldn't put it off any longer.

The security door had been propped open. *A security door protects nothing unless it's closed and locked. If I told her once I told her . . . I told her . . .* The reinforced glass trembled but held as she slammed it shut and stumbled down the half flight of stairs to her mother's apartment.

"Vicki? Ha, I should've known it was you slamming doors."

"The security door has to be kept closed, Mr. Delgado." She couldn't seem to get her key into the lock.

"Ha, you, always a cop. You don't see me bringing my work home." Mr. Delgado came a little farther into the hall and frowned. "You don't look so good, Vicki. You okay? Your mother know you're home?"

"My mother . . ." Her throat closed. She swallowed and forced herself to breathe. So many different ways to say it. So many different gentle euphemisms, all meaning the same thing. "My mother . . . died this morning."

Hearing her own voice say the words finally made it real.

"Dr. Burke? It's Donald."

Dr. Burke pulled her glasses off and rubbed at one temple with the heel of her hand. "Donald, at the risk of sounding clichéd, I thought I told you not to call me here."

"Yeah, you did, but I just thought you should know that Mr. Hutchinson has gone to get the subject."

"Which Mr. Hutchinson?"

"The younger one."

"And he'll be back?"

"In about an hour. There's no one else here, so he's going to start working on it immediately."

Dr. Burke sighed. "When you say no one else, Donald, do you mean staff or clients?"

"Clients. All the staff are here: the *old* Mr. Hutchinson *and* Christy."

"Very well. You know what to do."

"But . . ."

"I'll see to it that the interruptions occur. All you have to worry about is playing your assigned role. This is vitally important to our research, Donald. It could bring final results and their accompanying rewards practically within our grasp."

She could hear his grin over the phone as he broadly returned the cliché circumstances demanded. "I *won't* let you down, Dr. Burke."

"Of course you won't." She depressed the cutoff with her thumb and contacted the lab. "Catherine, I've just heard from Donald. You've got a little more than an hour."

"Well, I've got number eight on dialysis right now, but he shouldn't take much more than another forty minutes."

"Then you'll have plenty of time. Call me just before you arrive and I'll have Mrs. Shaw begin making inquiries about flowers and the like. The state she's in, she'll probably be able to keep the lines tied up for most of the afternoon. Has number nine quieted?"

"Only after I cut the power again. He's barely showing life signs."

"Catherine, it is *not* alive."

"Yes, Doctor." The pause obviously contained a silent sigh. "It's barely showing wave patterns."

"Better. Did all that banging damage it?"

"I haven't really had time to examine him, but I think you'd better come and take a look at the box."

Dr. Burke felt her eyebrows rise. "The box?"

"I think he dented it."

"Catherine, that's im . . ." She paused and thought about it for a moment, knowing Catherine would wait patiently. With natural inhibitors shut down and no ability to feel pain, enhanced strength might actually be possible. "You can run some tests after you get the new lot of bacteria working."

"Yes, Doctor."

My, my, my . . . Dr. Burke gave the receiver a satisfied pat as it settled into its cradle. It sounded like they could actually have made a breakthrough with number nine. *Now, if we can only keep it from decomposing* . . .

Breakfast dishes were still out on the drying rack and the chair with the quilted cushion sat out a little from the table. The makeup case lay open on the bathroom counter, the washcloth beside it slightly damp. The bed had been made neatly, but a pair of pantyhose with a wide run down one leg lay discarded in the center of the spread.

Vicki sat at the telephone table, her mother's address book open on her lap, and called everyone she thought should know, her voice calm and professional as though she were speaking of someone else's mother. *Mrs. Singh?*

I'm Constable Nelson, from the Metro Police. It's about your son . . . I'm afraid your husband . . . The driver had no chance to avoid your wife . . . Your daughter, Jennifer, has been . . . The funeral will be at two tomorrow.

When the funeral home called, Mr. Delgado took her mother's favorite blue suit from the closet and delivered it. When he returned, he forced her to eat a sandwich and kept insisting she'd feel better if she cried. She ate the sandwich without tasting it.

Now, there was no one left to call and Mr. Delgado had been convinced to go home. Vicki sat, one foot dangling over the arm of the old upholstered rocking chair, one foot pushing back and forth against the floor.

Slowly, the room grew dark.

"I'm telling you, Henry, she looked wrecked. Like *Night of the Living Dead.*"

"And she didn't hear you when you called to her?"

Tony shook his head, a long lock of pale brown hair falling into his eyes. "No, she just kept walking, and the guard wouldn't let me go up the stairs after her. Said only ticket holders were allowed and wouldn't believe me when I said I was her brother. The motherfucking bastard." A year under Henry's patronage hadn't quite erased five years on the street. "But I copied down all the places the train was going." He dug a crumpled and dirty piece of paper out of the front pocket of his skintight jeans and passed it over. "She was carrying a bag, so I guess when she gets there she's gonna stay."

The names of nine towns had been scrawled onto the blank spaces of a subway transfer. Henry frowned down at them. Why had Vicki left town without telling him? He thought they'd moved beyond that. Unless it had something to do with the fight they'd had on Saturday night. However great the temptation to prove his power, he knew he shouldn't have coerced her as he had and he intended to apologize as soon as she cooled down enough to accept it. "Her mother lives in Kingston," he said at last.

"You think you did something, don't you?"

He looked up, startled. "What are you talking about?"

"I like to watch you." Tony blushed slightly and dug his toe into the carpet. "I watch you all the time we're together. You've got your Prince-of-Men face, and your Prince-of-Darkness face, and your sort of not-there writer face, but when you think about Victory . . . about Vicki . . ." His blush deepened but he met Henry's gaze fearlessly. "Well then it's like you're not wearing a face, you're just you."

"All the masks are gone." Henry studied the younger man in turn. A number of the hard edges had softened over the last year since Vicki and a demon had brought them together. The bruised and skittish look had been replaced by the beginnings of a calm maturity. "Does that bother you?"

"About you and Victory? Nah. She means a lot to me, too. I mean, without her, I wouldn't have . . . I mean, we wouldn't . . . And besides—" he had to wet his lips before he could continue—"sometimes, like when you feed, you look at me like that." Abruptly, he dropped his gaze. "You going after her?"

There really wasn't any question. "I need to know what's wrong."

Tony snorted and tossed his hair back out of his eyes. "Of course you do." His voice returned to his usual cocky tones. "So call her mom."

"Call her mother?"

"Yeah, you know. Like on the telephone?"

Henry spread his hands, willing to allow Tony this moment. "I don't have the number."

"So? Get it out of her apartment."

"I don't have a key."

Tony snorted again. "*You* don't really need one. But," he laced his fingers together and cracked the knuckles, "if you don't want to slip past the lock, there's always our old friend Detective-Sergeant Celluci. I bet he has the number."

Henry's eyes narrowed. "I'll get it from Vicki's apartment."

"I've got Celluci's number right here, I mean if you . . ."

"Tony." He cupped one hand around Tony's jaw and tightened the fingers slightly, the pulse pounding under his grip. "Don't push it."

From the street, he saw the light on, recognized the shape visible between the slats of the blinds, and very nearly de-

cided not to go in. Tony had seen Vicki leave the city in
the early morning. Overnight case or not, she could very
easily have returned and, if so, she obviously wasn't spending the evening alone. Standing motionless in the shadow
of an ancient chestnut, he watched and listened until he
was certain that the apartment held only a single life.

That changed things rather considerably.

There were a number of ways he could get what he
wanted. He decided on the direct approach. *Out of sheer
bloody-mindedness,* honesty forced him to admit.

"Good evening, Detective. Were you waiting for someone?"

Celluci spun around, dropped into a defensive crouch,
and glared up at Henry. "Goddamnit!" he snarled. "Don't
do that!"

"Do what?" Henry asked dryly, voice and bearing proclaiming that he did not in any way perceive the other man
as a threat. He moved away from the door and walked into
Vicki's living room.

As if he has every right to. Celluci found himself backing
up. *Son of a bitch!* It took a conscious effort, but he dug
in his heels and stopped the retreat. *I don't know what
game you're playing, spook, but you're not going to win it
so easily.* "What the hell are you doing here?"

"I might ask you the same thing."

"I have a key."

"*I* don't need one." Henry leaned against the wall and
crossed his arms. "My guess is, you've come back to apologize for slamming out of here on Saturday." He read a
direct hit in the sudden quickening of Celluci's heartbeat
and the angry rush of blood to his face.

"She told you about that." The words were an almost
inarticulate growl.

"She tells me about everything." No need to mention
the argument that followed.

"You want me to just back off right now, don't you?"
Celluci managed to keep a fingernail grip on his temper.
"Admit defeat."

Henry straightened. "If I wanted you to back off, mortal,
you would."

*So if I'm a good eight inches taller than he is, why the
hell do I feel like he's looking down at me?* "Think pretty

highly of yourself, don't you. Look, Fitzroy. I don't care what you are and I don't care what you can do. You should've been dust four hundred years ago. I am *not* letting you have her."

"I think that should be her choice, not yours."

"Well, she's not going to choose you!" Celluci slammed his fist down onto the table. A precariously balanced stack of books trembled at the impact and a small brown address book fell onto the answering machine.

The tape jerked into motion.

"Ms. Nelson? It's Mrs. Shaw again. I'm so sorry to bother you, but your mother's body has been moved over to the General Hospital. We thought you should know in case . . . well, in case . . . I expect you're on your way. Oh, dear . . . It's ten o'clock, April ninth, Monday morning. Please let us know if there's anything we can do to help."

Celluci stared down at the rewinding tape and then up at Henry. "Her mother's body," he repeated.

Henry nodded. "So now we know where she is."

"If this call came in at ten, we can assume she got the original call about nine. She didn't tell you . . ." Celluci broke off and pushed the curl of hair back out of his eyes. "No, of course, she couldn't, you'd be . . . asleep. She didn't leave a message?"

"No. Tony saw her boarding the 10:40 train for Kingston so she must have left the apartment just before that call. She didn't leave a message for you either?"

"No." Celluci sighed and sat back on the edge of the table. "I'm getting just a little tired of this 'I can handle everything myself' attitude of hers."

Henry nodded again. *I thought we'd gone beyond this, she and I.* "You and me both."

"Don't get me wrong, her strength is one of the things I . . ." .

The pause was barely perceptible. A mortal might have missed it. Henry didn't. *Well, he's hardly going to tell me he loves her.*

". . . admire about her, but," his expression seemed more weary than admiring, "there's a difference between strength and . . ."

"Fear of intimacy," Henry offered.

Celluci snorted. "Yeah." He reached behind him for the

address book. "Well, she's just going to have to put up with a little fucking intimacy because I'm not going to let her stand alone in this." The binding barely managed to survive the force of his search. "Here it is, under M for Mother. Christ, her filing system . . ." Then, suddenly, he remembered who he was talking to. He wasn't, however, prepared for how fast Henry could move—didn't, in fact, see Henry move.

Henry looked down at the address and handed the book back to the detective. "I assume I'll see you in Kingston," he said and headed for the door.

"Hey!"

He turned.

"I thought you couldn't leave your coffin?"

"You watch too many bad movies, Detective."

Celluci bristled. "You've still got to be under cover by dawn. I can see to it that you aren't. One phone call to the OPP and you'll be in a holding cell at sunrise."

"You won't do that, Detective." Henry's voice was mild as he caught Celluci's gaze with his own and let the patina of civilization drop. He played with the mortal's reaction for a moment and then, almost reluctantly, released him. "You won't do it," he continued in the same tone, "for the same reason I don't use the power *I* have on you. *She* wouldn't like it." Smiling urbanely, he inclined his head in a parody of a polite bow. "Good night, Detective."

Celluci stared at the closed door and fought to keep from trembling. Patches of sweat spread out under each arm and his palms, pressed hard against the table, were damp. It wasn't the fear that unnerved him. He'd dealt with fear before, knew he could conquer it. It was the urge to bare his throat that had him so shaken, the knowledge that in another instant he would have placed his life in Henry Fitzroy's hands.

"Goddamnit, Vicki." The hoarse whisper barely shredded the silence. "You are playing with fucking fire. . . ."

"Geez, Cathy, why'd you bring *them*?"

"I thought they could carry the body."

"Oh." Donald stepped back as Catherine helped two shambling figures out of the back of the van. "The program

I wrote for them is pretty basic; are you sure they can do something that complicated?"

"Well, number nine can." She patted the broad shoulder almost affectionately. "Number eight may need a little help."

"A little help. Right." Grunting with the effort, he dragged a pair of sandbags out of the van. "Well, if they're so strong, they can carry these."

"Give them both to number nine. I'm not sure about eight's joints."

Although living muscles strained to lift a single bag off the ground, number nine gave no indication that it noticed the weight, even after both bags had been loaded.

"Good idea," Donald panted. "Bringing them along, that is. I'd have killed myself getting those things inside." Fighting for breath, he glanced around the parking lot. The light over by the garage barely illuminated the area and he'd removed the light over the delivery entrance that afternoon. "Let's just make sure nobody sees them, okay. They don't look exactly, well, alive."

"Notices *them?*" Catherine moved number eight around to face the door, then turned and discovered number nine had moved without help. "We better be sure that no one notices *us.*"

"People don't look too closely at funeral homes." Still breathing heavily, Donald slipped his key into the lock. "They're afraid of what they might see." He shot a glance at number nine's gray and desiccated face perched above the collar of a red windbreaker and snickered as he pushed the door open. "Almost makes you wish someone *would* stumble over Mutt and Jeff here, doesn't it?"

"No. Now get going."

Long inured to his colleague's complete lack of a sense of humor, Donald shrugged and disappeared into the building.

Number nine followed.

Catherine gave number eight a little push. "Walk," she commanded. It hesitated, then slowly began to move. Halfway down the long ramp to the embalming room, it stumbled. "No, you don't . . ." Holding it precariously balanced against the wall, she bent and straightened the left leg.

"What took you so long," Donald demanded as the two of them finally arrived.

"Trouble with the patella." She frowned, tucking a strand of nearly white-blond hair back behind her ear. "I don't think we're getting any kind of cell reconstruction."

"Yeah, and it's starting to smell worse, too."

"Oh, no."

"Oh, yes. But hey—" he threw open both halves of the coffin lid—"let's not stand around sniffing dead people all night. We've got work to do."

Number eight's fingers had to be clamped around the corpse's ankles, but number nine took hold of the shoulders with very little prompting.

"I'm telling you, Donald," Catherine caroled as they guided the two bodies back up the ramp, "number nine has interfaced with the net. I'm sure we're getting independent brain activity."

"What does Dr. Burke say?"

"She's more worried about decomposition."

"Understandable. Always a bummer when your experiments rot before you can gather the data. Stop them for a second while I get the door."

The two grad students did the actual loading of the van. Not even Catherine could figure out a series of one-word commands that would allow number eight to carry out the complicated maneuvers necessary. And, as Donald reminded her, both speed and silence were advisable.

"Because," he added, settling number eight into place, "what we're doing *is* illegal."

"Nonsense." Catherine's brow drew down. "It's science."

He shook his head. He'd never met *anyone* who came close to being so single-minded. As far as he'd been able to determine, she had almost as little life outside the lab as their experimental subjects did—and considering that they were essentially dead, that was saying something. Even stranger, she honestly didn't seem to care that what they were doing would result in fame and fortune all around. "Well, in the interest of science, then, let's try to stay out of jail." He gave number nine a push toward the vehicle.

Number nine lowered his head and the reflection of the stars slid off the artificially moist surface of his eyes.

Three

"That is *not* a healthy heart."

Donald peered over the edge of his surgical mask and into the chest cavity. "Not now it isn't," he agreed. "Didn't smoke, didn't drink, and just look at it. Almost makes you want to go out and party."

With a deft stroke of the scalpel, Dr. Burke exposed the tricuspid valve and began to remove the shredded membrane. "I wasn't calling for moral commentary, Donald. Pay attention to what you're doing."

Not noticeably chastened, Donald emptied the hypodermic he held, drew it out of the corner of the eye socket, and picked up a smaller needle. The liquid in the chamber appeared almost opalescent in the glare of the fluorescent lights. "All right, boys." He carefully slid the point through the cornea. "Time to go to work. Lift that curve, tote that bale, if you don't repair the iris, then you're in the pail."

"We can do without the poetry, thank you." Tight sutures closed up the incision in the heart. "If you've hydrated both eyes, help Catherine in the abdominal cavity. We've got to get those blood vessels tied off as soon as possible so we can get the nutrient fluid circulating.

"Time is vitally important in work of this nature . . ." The lecture continued as Donald placed soaked cotton swabs over each staring eye and moved around to the side of the table. "Fortunately, the first step in the embalming process toughens the vessels, making them easier to work with at speed and enabling us to . . ."

"Uh, Doctor, this is our tenth cadaver," Donald reminded her, suctioning away the sterile solution they used to force the embalming fluid out of the body. Catherine, who'd been suturing under water, shot him a grateful smile, the corners of her eyes crinkling up above her mask. "I mean, we know all this. And we *did* do six of the previous nine with our own little fingers."

"And you *did* do an excellent job. I only wish my schedule had allowed me to give you more assistance." Dr. Burke was more than willing to give credit where credit was due as, at the moment, it didn't mean anything. She reached behind her for a tiny motor and an electric screwdriver. "That said, it never hurts to be reminded of how important the proper balance of moisture is to healthy tissue."

Donald snickered and in a nearly perfect imitation of the sultry voice in the commercial intoned, "How dead do you think I am?"

Dr. Burke stopped working and turned to stare at him. "I must be more tired than I thought. I actually found that funny."

Catherine shook her head and fished out the end of another artery.

A few moments later, they settled the bag of gel replacing the digestive system into place. Pearly highlights quivered across the thick agar coating.

"We've got bacteria to spare this time," Dr. Burke pointed out as she finished attaching the artificial diaphragm's second motor. "I want those organs saturated."

"Saturated it is," Donald agreed. He accepted the liver culture from Catherine, frowned, and glared over her shoulder. "Stop that!"

"Stop what?" she asked, bending to work on a kidney.

"Not you. Number nine. He's staring at me."

She straightened and checked. "No, he isn't. He's just looking in your direction."

"Well, I don't like it."

"He isn't hurting anything."

"So?"

"Children." Had Dr. Burke's voice been any dryer it would have cracked. "If we could keep our minds on the matter at hand?" She waited, pointedly, until they both began working before she released the rib spreader. "If it bothers you that much, Donald, Catherine can put it in its box."

Donald nodded. "Good idea. Make her put her toys away when she's done playing with them."

Catherine ignored him. "He'd be better left out, Doctor. He needs the stimuli if we want him interfacing with the net."

"Good point," the doctor acknowledged. "Sloppily put, but a good point. Sorry, Donald. It stays out."

Catherine shot him a triumphant look.

"When you finish there, one of you can close while the other starts the pump and begins replacing the sterile solution. I want that circulatory system up and running ASAP. Now, if you think you can manage without my having to act as referee, I'm going to open up the skull."

"He's still looking at me," Donald growled a moment later, his voice barely audible over the whine of the bone saw.

"Hopefully, he's learning from you."

"Yeah?" One latex-covered finger lifted in salute. "Well, learn this."

Across the room, three of the fingers on number nine's right hand curled slowly inward and tucked under the support of the folded thumb. Although the face remained expressionless, a muscle twitched below the leathery surface of the skin.

Henry guided the BMW smoothly around the curves of the highway off-ramp at considerably more than the posted speed. Two hours and forty-two minutes, Toronto to Kingston—not as fast as it could be done, but considering the perpetual traffic congestion he'd faced leaving the city and the high number of provincial police patrolling the last hundred kilometers, it was a respectable time.

Although he enjoyed high speeds and his reflexes made possible maneuvers that left other drivers gaping, Henry had never understood the North American love affair with the automobile. A car to him was a tool, the BMW a compromise between power and dependability. While mortal drivers blithely risked their lives straining the limits of their machinery, he had no intention of abruptly ending four hundred and fifty years because of metal fatigue or design flaws—but then, unlike mortal drivers, he had nothing to prove.

Vicki's mother's apartment was easy enough to find. Not only did Division Street run directly from the 401, but even from a block away there was no mistaking the man emerging from the late model sedan parked in front of the building. Henry swung into the tiny parking lot and settled the BMW into the adjoining space.

"You made good time," he remarked as he got out of his car and stretched.

"Thanks." The word had left his mouth before Celluci realized he had no reason to feel so absurdly pleased by the observation. "*You* obviously broke a few laws," he snarled. "Or don't you feel our speed limits apply to you?"

"No more than you feel they apply to you," Henry told him with an edged smile. "Or don't the police have to follow the laws they're sworn to uphold?"

"Asshole," Celluci muttered. Nothing dampened righteous anger faster than forced recognition of shaky ethical ground. "And I don't see why you came anyhow. Vicki needs the living around her, not more of the dead."

"I am no more dead than you are, Detective."

"Yeah, well, you're not . . . I mean, you're . . ."

"I am Vampire." Henry spread his hands. "There, it no longer hangs between us. The word has been said." He caught Celluci's gaze and held it but this time used no force to keep the contact. "You might as well acknowledge it, Detective. I won't go away."

Curiosity overcame better judgment and Celluci found himself asking, "What were you?"

"I was a Prince. A royal bastard."

The corners of the detective's mouth twitched. "Well, you're a royal bastard, that's for sure." He fought his way back to a more equal footing, ignoring the suspicion that a more equal footing was allowed him. "Why isn't anyone ever a fucking peasant?"

"Anyone?" Henry asked, brows rising.

"You, Shirley MacLaine . . . Never mind." He leaned back against his car and sighed. "Look, she doesn't need both of us."

"So why don't I just go home? I don't think so."

"What can you give her?"

"Now? In her grief? The same things you can."

"But I can give them night *and* day. You only have the night."

"Then why are you so worried about me being here? Surely you have the advantage. Mind you," Henry continued, his tone thoughtful, "I left sanctuary for her, risked the sun in order to be at her side. That should count for something."

"What do you mean, count for something?" Celluci snorted. "This isn't a contest! Man against . . ." His eyes narrowed. ". . . romance writer. We're supposed to be here for *her*."

"Then maybe," Henry starting moving toward the building, "we'd better work a little harder at remembering that."

Goddamned patronizing son of a bitch! Fortunately, longer legs allowed Celluci to catch up without having to run. "So we concentrate on her until this is over."

Henry half turned and looked up at him. "And after?"

"Who the hell knows about after?" *Stop looking at me like that!* "Let's get through this, first."

Listening to the pounding of Celluci's heart, Henry nodded, satisfied.

It took Vicki a moment to realize what the pounding meant.

The door.

Bang. Bang. Bang.

The police at the door. The pattern was unmistakable. She frowned at the dark apartment and stiffly stood up. *How long?* Eyes useless, in spite of the spill of light from the street, she groped her way to the phone desk, then along the wall to the door.

Celluci scowled down at Henry and raised his hand to knock again. "You're certain she's in there?"

"I'm certain. I can feel her life."

"Yeah. Right."

Bang. Bang. Bang.

Her fingers scraped across the light switch and she flicked it on, her eyes watering in the sudden brilliance. Her mother always used hundred watt bulbs.

"I don't care how much more energy it burns, it's more important that you can see when you come home. I can well afford it and the environment can go hang."

Her mother *had* always used 100 watt bulbs.

The lock stuck, halfway around.

"I told her to get this fixed," she growled as she fought to force the tumblers down. "God-damned stupid piece of junk."

Bang. Bang. Bang.

"Keep your fucking pants on!"

Celluci lowered his hand. "She's in there."

The lock finally gave. Vicki took a deep breath, adjusted her glasses, and opened the door.

"What the hell are you doing here?" she asked after a long pause.

"We came to help," Henry told her quietly.

She looked from one to the other, confusion the only emotion she could readily label. "Both of you?"

"Both of us," Celluci agreed.

"I didn't *ask* for your help."

They exchanged identical expressions and Celluci sighed. "We know," he said.

"Vicki?"

All three of them turned.

Mr. Delgado stood just outside his door, weight forward on the balls of his feet, shoulders back, arms loose at his sides, trousers pulled on under a striped pajama top. "Is there a problem?"

Vicki shoved at her glasses. The completely truthful answer would be, *Not yet.* "No," she said. "No problem. These are friends of mine from Toronto."

"What are they doing here?"

"Apparently," her voice grew less vague with every word, "they came to help."

"Oh." His gaze swept over Celluci from head to toe and then began on Henry. For Vicki's sake, Henry kept a grip on his annoyance and let the old man finish. "Well, if there's any trouble," the last two words were a warning, "you let me know."

"I can handle these two, Mr. Delgado."

"I don't doubt it. But you shouldn't have to. Not right now." His chin jutted forward. "You boys understand?"

Celluci's patience showed signs of wear. "We understand, Mr. Delgado."

"Both of you?"

Henry turned a little farther until he faced down the hall. "We both understand."

Mr. Delgado squinted at Henry then almost seemed to come to attention. "Had to ask . . ."

"I know."

"Well, goodnight."

Henry inclined his head in dismissal. "Good night."

The three of them watched as the door closed and then Vicki stepped back out of the way. "You might as well come in."

". . . did it never occur to either of you that maybe I wanted to handle this myself?" Vicki paced the length of the living room, reached the window, and glared out into the night. The apartment was half a story below ground, not exactly basement, not exactly first floor. The windows looked out over a narrow strip of grass, then the visitor's parking, then the sidewalk, then the road. It wasn't much of a view. Vicki's mother had invested in both blinds and heavy drapes to keep the world from looking back. Vicki hadn't bothered closing either. "That maybe," she continued, her throat tight, "there isn't anything for you to help with?"

"If you want both of us, or either of us, to go back to Toronto, we will," Henry told her quietly.

Celluci shot him a look and his mouth opened, but Henry raised a cautionary hand and he closed it again without speaking.

"I want both of you to go back to Toronto!"

"No, you don't."

Her laugh held the faintest shading of hysteria. "Are you reading my mind, Henry?" She turned to face them. "All right, you win. As long as you're here, you might as well stay." One hand sketched surrender in the air. "You might as well both stay."

*　　*　　*

"How did you convince Mike to go to sleep?"

"I merely told him that you'd need him rested tomorrow, that I was the logical choice to keep watch over the night."

"Merely?"

"Well, perhaps I persuaded him a little."

She sat on the edge of the twin bed in the room she'd grown up in and smoothed nonexistent wrinkles out of the pillow with the fingers of one hand. "He won't thank you for that in the morning."

"Perhaps not." Henry watched her carefully, not allowing the full extent of his concern to show lest it cause her to bolt. "But I did explain that it was a little difficult for either of us to give comfort when both of us were there. He seemed to agree." He had, in fact, grunted, *"So leave."* but Henry saw no need to mention that to Vicki.

"All of that while I was in the bathroom?"

"Should it have taken longer?"

"I guess not."

He'd been prepared for her to be angry at his highhandedness—would have preferred the bright flame of her anger to the gray acceptance he got. He reached out and gently captured the hand that still stroked the pillow. "You need to sleep, Vicki."

The skin around her eyes seemed stretched very tight.

"I don't think I can."

"I do."

"If you need to feed, I don't think . . ."

Henry shook his head. "Not tonight. Maybe tomorrow. Now get some sleep."

"I can't . . ."

"You can." His voice deepened slightly and he lifted her chin so that her eyes met his.

They widened as she realized what he was doing and she pushed ineffectually at his fingers.

"Sleep," he told her again.

Her inarticulate protest became a long, shuddering sigh, and she collapsed back on the bed.

Frowning thoughtfully, Henry tucked her legs up under the covers and moved her glasses to safety on the bedside table. In the morning, the two of them could trade stories about the unfair advantage he'd taken over mortal minds. Perhaps it would bring them closer together. It was a risk

he'd had no choice but to take. But for the moment . . .
He reached up and flicked off the light.

"For the moment," he murmured, tucking the blankets
around the life that glowed like a beacon in the darkness.
"For the moment, I will guard your dreams."

"Henry . . ." She raised herself up on one elbow and
groped for her glasses. The room was gray, not black. It
couldn't be dawn because she could feel his presence even
before she managed to find the deeper shadow by the door.

"I can't stay any longer." He spread his hands in apology. "The sun is very close to the horizon."

"Where are you going?"

She could hear the smile in his voice. "Not far. The walk-
in closet in your mother's room will make an adequate
sanctuary. It will take very little to block the day."

"I'm going with you." She swung her legs out of the bed
and stood, ignoring the lack of light. Her mother had made
no real changes in the room since she'd left—she'd have to
be more than blind to lose her way.

At the door, Henry's cool fingers wrapped around her
arm just above the elbow. She turned, knowing he could
see her even though she could barely see the outline of
his body.

"Henry." He moved closer as she reached out and laid
her palm against his chest. "My mother . . ." The words
wouldn't come. She could feel him waiting and finally had
to shake her head.

His lips brushed very lightly against her hair.

"You were right," she said instead. "Sleep helped.
But . . ." Her fingers twisted in his shirt and she yanked
him slightly forward. ". . . don't ever do that again."

His hand covered hers. "No promises," he told her
quietly.

Yes, promises, she wanted to insist. *I won't have you
messing with my head.* But he messed with her head just
by existing and under the circumstances, she wouldn't believe any promises he made. "Get going." She pushed him
toward the door. "Even *I* can feel the sun."

Celluci lay stretched out on top of her mother's bed,
shoes off but otherwise dressed. She started, seeing him so
suddenly appear in the glare of the overhead light and she

had to stop herself from shaking him and demanding to know what he was doing there. On her mother's bed. Except her mother wouldn't be sleeping in it any more so what difference did it make?

"He won't wake," Henry told her as she hesitated by the door. "Not until after I'm . . . asleep."

"I wish you hadn't done that."

"Vicki."

The sound of her name pulled her forward until they stood only a whisper apart by the closet door.

He reached up and gently caressed her cheek. "Michael Celluci has the day; I cannot share it with him. Don't ask me to give him the night as well."

Vicki swallowed. His touch drew heated lines across her skin. "Have I ever asked that of you?"

"No." His expression twisted and slid a little into sadness. "You've never asked anything of me."

She wanted to protest that she had, but she knew what he meant. "Not now, Henry."

"You're right." He nodded and withdrew his hand. "Not now."

Fortunately, the closet had plenty of room for a not so tall man to lie safely hidden away from the sun.

"I'll block the door from the inside, so it can't be opened accidentally, and I brought the blackout curtain you hung in my bedroom to wrap around me. I'll be back with you this evening."

With memory's eyes she could see him, rising with the darkness after a day spent . . . lifeless.

"Henry."

He paused, half through the door.

"My mother is dead."

"Yes."

"You'll never die."

The four-hundred-and-fifty-year-old bastard son of Henry the VIII nodded. "I'll never die," he agreed.

"Should I resent you for that?"

"Should I resent you for the day?"

Her brows snapped down and the movement pushed her glasses forward on her nose. "I hate it when you answer a question with a question."

"I know."

His smile held so many things that she couldn't hope to understand them all before the closet door closed between them.

"Vicki, you can't possibly agree with what Fitzroy did!" When she suddenly became engrossed in sponging a bit of dirt off her good shoes, he realized she did, indeed, agree. "Vicki!"

"What?"

"He knocked me out, put me to sleep, violated my free will!"

"He just wanted the same time alone that you're getting now. Guaranteed free of interruption."

"I can't believe you're defending him!"

"I'm not. Exactly. I just understand his reasons."

Celluci snorted and jammed his arms into the sleeves of his suit jacket. A few stitches popped in protest. "And what did the two of you do during that time alone free of interruption?"

"He put me to sleep as well. Then sat and watched over me until dawn."

"That's it?"

Vicki turned to face him, both brows well above the upper edge of her glasses. "That's it. Not that it's any of your damned business."

"That won't wash this time, Vicki." He stepped forward, took the shoe from her hand, and dropped to one knee with it. "Fitzroy made it my business when he pulled that Prince of Darkness shit."

She sighed and let him guide her foot into the plain black pump. "Yeah, I suppose he did. I needed to sleep, Mike." She reached down and brushed the long curl of hair back off his face. "I couldn't have done it without him. He gave me the night to sleep when he could have taken it for himself."

"Very noble of him," Celluci grunted, sliding her other foot into the second shoe. *And it was very noble,* he admitted to himself as he stood. *Noble in the running-roughshod I-know-best-so-don't-bother-expressing-an-opinion sort of a way that went out with the fucking feudal system.* Still, Fitzroy *had* acted in what he considered to be Vicki's best interests. And he honestly didn't think that he *could* have left them alone together—as Fitzroy had no choice but to do come morning. *So I suppose I might have done the same thing under similar circumstances. Which doesn't excuse his royal fucking undead highness one bit.*

What bothered him the most about it was how little Vicki seemed to care, how much she seemed to be operating on cruise control, and how little she seemed to be interacting with the world around her. He recognized the effects of grief and shock—he'd seen them both often enough over the years—but they were somehow harder to deal with because they were applied here and now to Vicki.

He wanted to make it better for her.

He knew he couldn't.

He hated having to accept that.

All right, Fitzroy, you gave her sleep last night, I'll give her support today. Maybe together we can get her through it.

He got her to eat but eventually, when even trying to start an argument failed, he gave up trying to get her to talk.

About noon, Mr. Delgado arrived to ask if Vicki needed a lift to the funeral home. She looked up from where she sat, silently rocking, and shook her head.

"Humph," he snorted, stepping back out into the hall and once again looking Celluci over. "You one of her friends from the police?"

"Detective-Sergeant Michael Celluci."

"Yeah. I thought so. You look like a cop. Louis Delgado." His grip was still strong, his palm hard with a workman's calluses. "What happened to the other guy?"

"He sat up with her all night. He's still sleeping."

"He's not a cop."

"No."

To Celluci's surprise the old man chuckled. "In my day two men fighting over one woman, there would have been blood on the street, let me tell you."

"What makes you think . . ."

"You think maybe I shut my brain off when I retired? I saw the three of you together last night, remember?" His face grew suddenly somber. "Maybe it's a good thing people got more civilized; she doesn't need fighting around her right now. I saw her grow up. Watched her decide to be an adult when she should have been enjoying being a child.

Tried to take care of her mother, insisted on taking care of herself." He sighed. "She won't bend, you know. Now that this terrible thing has happened, you and that other fellow, don't you let her break."

"We'll do our best."

"Humph." He snorted again and swiped at his eyes with a snowy white handkerchief, his opinion of their best obviously not high.

Celluci watched him return to his own apartment, then quietly closed the door. "Mr. Delgado cares about you a great deal," he said, crossing the room to stand by Vicki's side.

She shook her head. "He was very fond of my mother."

She didn't speak again until they were in the car on the way to the funeral home.

"Mike?"

He glanced sideways. She wore her courtroom face. Not even the most diligent of defense attorneys could have found an opinion on it.

"I didn't call her. And when she called me, I didn't answer. And then she died."

"You know there's no connection." He said it as gently as he could. He didn't expect an answer. He didn't get one.

There wasn't anything else to say, so he reached down and covered her left hand with his. After a long moment, her fingers turned and she clutched at him with such force that he had to bite back an exclamation of pain. Only her hand moved. Her fingers were freezing.

"It really is for your own good." Catherine finished fastening the chest strap and lightly touched number nine on the shoulder. "I know you don't like it, but we can't take a chance on you jerking the needles free. That's what happened to number six and we lost her." She smiled down into the isolation box. "You've come so much farther than the rest, even if your kidneys aren't working yet, that we'd hate to lose you, too." Reaching behind his left ear, she jacked the computer hookup into the implanted plug, fingertips checking that the skin hadn't pulled out from under the surgical steel collar clamped tight against scalp and skull.

"Now then . . ." She shook her head over the shallow

dents that marred the inner curve of the insulated lid. "You just lie quiet and I'll open this up the moment your dialysis is over."

The box closed with a sigh of airtight seals and the metallic snick of an automatic latch.

Frowning slightly, Catherine adjusted the amount of pure oxygen flowing through the air intake. Although he'd moved past the point where he needed it and he could have managed on just regular filtered air, she wanted him to have every opportunity to succeed. Later, when the muscle diagnostics were running, she'd give him a full body massage with the estrogen cream. His skin wasn't looking good. In the meantime, she flicked the switch that would start the transmission through his net and moved to check on the other two boxes.

Number eight had begun to fail. Not only were the joints becoming less responsive but the extremities had darkened and she suspected the liver had begun to putrefy, a sure sign that the bacteria had started to die.

"Billions of them multiplying all over the world," she said sadly, stroking the top of number eight's box. "Why can't we keep these alive long enough to do some good?"

At the third box, recently vacated by the dissected number seven, she scanned one of a trio of computer monitors. Marjory Nelson's brain wave patterns, recorded over the months just previous to her death, were being transmitted in a continuous loop through the newly installed neural net. They'd never had actual brain wave patterns before. All previous experiments, including numbers eight and nine, had only ever received generic alpha waves recorded from herself and Donald.

"I've got great hopes for you, number ten. There's no reason you . . ." A yawn split the thought in two and Catherine stumbled toward the door, suddenly exhausted. Donald had headed for his bed once the major surgery had been completed and Dr. Burke had left just before dawn. She didn't mind finishing up on her own—she liked having the lab to herself, it gave her a chance to see that all the little extras got done—but if she wasn't mistaken, she was rapidly approaching a day and a half on her feet and she needed to catch a nap. A couple of hours lying down and she should be good as new.

Fingers on the light switch, she paused in the doorway, looked back over the lab, and called softly, "Pleasant dreams."

They weren't dreams, nor were they quite memories but, outside the influence of the net, images stirred. A young woman's face in close proximity, pale hair, pale eyes. Her voice was soothing in a world where too many lights were too bright and too many sounds only noise. Her smile was . . .

Her smile was . . .

Organic impulses moved turgidly along tattered neural pathways searching for the connection that would complete the thought.

Her smile was . . .

Kind.

Number nine stirred under the restraints.

Her smile was kind.

"Ms. Nelson?"

Vicki turned toward the voice, trying very hard not to scowl. Relatives and friends of her mother's were milling about the reception room, all expecting her to be showing their definition of grief. If it hadn't been for Celluci's bulk at her back, she might have bolted—if it hadn't been for his quick grip around her wrist she'd have definitely belted the cousin who, having driven in from Gananoque, remarked that earlier or later would have been a better time and he certainly hoped there'd be refreshments afterward. She didn't know the heavyset man who'd called her name.

He held out a beefy hand. "Ms. Nelson, I'm Reverend Crosbie. The Anglican minister who usually works with Hutchinson's is a bit under the weather today, so they asked me to fill in." His voice was a rough burr that rose and fell with an east coast cadence.

A double chin almost hid the clerical collar but, given the firmness of his handshake, Vicki doubted that all of the bulk was fat. "My mother wasn't a churchgoer," she said.

"That's between her and God, Ms. Nelson." His tone managed to be both matter-of-fact and sympathetic at the same time. "She wanted an Anglican service read to set her soul at peace and I'm here to do it for her. But"—

bushy white brows drew slightly in—"as I didn't know your mother, I've no intention of speaking as if I did. Are you going to be doing your own eulogy?"

Was she going to get up in front of all these people and tell them about her mother? Was she going tell them how her mother had given up the life a young woman was entitled to in order to support them both? Tell them how her mother had tried to stop her from getting her first job because she thought childhood should last a little longer? Tell them about her mother, a visible beacon of pride, watching as she graduated from high school, then university, then the police college? Tell them how after her promotion her mother had peppered the phrase, "My daughter, the detective," into every conversation? Tell them how, when she first got the diagnosis about her eyes, her mother had taken a train to Toronto and refused to hear the lies about being all right and not needing her there? Tell them about the nagging and the worrying and the way she always called during a shower? Tell them how her mother had needed to talk to her and she hadn't answered the phone?

Tell them her mother was dead?

"No." Vicki felt Celluci's hand close over her shoulder and realized her voice had been less than clear. She coughed and scanned the room in a near panic. "There. The short woman in the khaki trench coat." To point would expose the trembling. "That's Dr. Burke. Mother worked for her for the last five years. Maybe she'll say something."

Bright blue eyes focused just behind her for a second. Whatever Reverend Crosbie saw on Celluci's face seemed to reassure him because he nodded and said quietly, "I'll talk to Dr. Burke, then." His warm hand engulfed hers again. "Maybe you and I'll have a chance to talk later, eh?"

"Maybe."

Celluci's grip on her shoulder tightened as the minister walked away. "You all right?"

"Sure. I'm fine." But she didn't expect him to believe her, so she supposed it wasn't exactly a lie.

"Vicki?"

This was a voice she recognized and she turned almost eagerly to meet it. "Aunt Esther." The tall, sparse woman opened her arms and Vicki allowed herself to be folded into them. Esther Thomas had been her mother's closest friend. They'd grown up together, gone to school together, had been bride and bridesmaid, bridesmaid and bride. Esther had been teaching school in Ottawa for as long as Vicki could remember, but living in different cities hadn't dimmed the friendship.

Esther's cheeks were wet when they pulled apart. "I thought I wasn't going to make it." She sniffed and dug for a tissue. "I'm driving Richard's six-cylinder tank, but they're doing construction on highway fifteen. Can you believe it? It's only April. They're still likely to get snow. Damn, I . . . Thank you. You're Mike Celluci, aren't you? We met once, about three years ago, just after Christmas when you drove to Kingston to pick Vicki up."

"I remember."

"Vicki . . ." She blew her nose and started again. "Vicki, I have a favor to ask you. I'd . . . I'd like to see her one last time."

Vicki stepped back, trod on Celluci's foot, and didn't notice. "See her?"

"Yes. To say good-bye." Tears welled and ran and she swiped at them without making much impact. "I don't think I'll be able to believe Marjory's actually dead unless I see her."

"But . . ."

"I know it's a closed coffin, but I thought you and I might be able to slip in now. Before things start."

Vicki had never understood the need to look at the dead. A corpse was a corpse and over the years she'd seen enough of them to know that they were all fundamentally alike. She didn't want to remember her mother the way she'd been, stretched out on the table in the morgue, and she certainly didn't want to remember her prepared like a mannequin to go into the earth. But it was obviously something Esther needed.

"I'll have a word with Mr. Hutchinson," she heard herself saying.

A few moments later, the three of them were making their way down the center aisle of the chapel, shoes making no sound on the thick red carpet.

"We did prepare for this eventuality," Mr. Hutchinson said as they approached the coffin. "Very often when the casket is closed, friends and relatives still want to say one

last good-bye to the deceased. I'm sure you'll find your
mother much as you remember her, Ms. Nelson.''

Vicki closed her teeth on her reply.

"The service is due to start momentarily," he said as he
released the latch and began to raise the upper half of the
lid, "so I'm afraid you'll have to . . . have to . . ."

Her fingers dug deep into satin cushioning as Vicki's
hands closed over the padded edge of the coffin. In the
center of the quilted pillow lay the upper end of a large
sandbag. A quick glance toward the foot of the casket determined that a second sandbag made up the rest of the
necessary weight.

She straightened and in a voice that ripped civilization
off the words asked, "What have you done with my
mother?''

Four

"This would probably go a lot easier if you'd get Ms. Nelson to go home." Detective Fergusson of the Kingston Police lowered his voice a little further. "It's not like we don't appreciate your input, Sergeant, but Ms. Nelson, she hasn't been a cop for a couple of years. She really shouldn't be here. Besides, you know, she's a woman. They get emotional at times like these."

"Get a lot of body snatching, do you?" Celluci asked dryly.

"No!" The detective's indignant gaze jerked up to meet Celluci's. "Never had one before. Ever."

"Ah. Then which times like these were you referring to?"

"Well, you know. Her mother dying. The body being lifted. This whole funeral home thing. I hate 'em. Too damn quiet. Anyway, this'll probably turn out to be some stupid prank by some of those university medical school geeks. I could tell you stories about that lot. The last thing we need scrambling things up is a hysterical woman—and she certainly has a right to be hysterical under the circumstances, don't get me wrong."

"Does Ms. Nelson look hysterical to you, Detective?"

Fergusson swept a heavy hand back over his thinning hair and glanced across the room where his partner had just finished taking statements. A few months before, he'd been given the opportunity to handle one of the new high-tech assault rifles recently issued to the special weapons and tactics boys. Ex-Detective Nelson reminded him a whole lot of that rifle. "Well, no. Not precisely hysterical."

While he wasn't exactly warming to the man, Celluci

wasn't entirely unsympathetic. "Look at it this way. She was one of the best police officers I ever served with—probably ever will serve with. If she stays, think of her as an added resource you can tap into and recognize that because of her background she will in no way disrupt your handling of the case. If she goes," he clapped the older man lightly on the shoulder, "you're telling her. Because I'm not."

"Like that, eh?"

"Like that. It'd be convenient that you're already in a funeral home. Trust me. Things will probably go a lot easier if she stays."

Fergusson sighed, then shrugged. "I guess she'll feel better if she thinks she's doing something. But if she goes off, you get her out of here."

"Believe me, *she* is my first concern." Watching Vicki cross the chapel toward him, Celluci was struck by how completely under control she appeared. Every muscle moved with a rigid precision, and the intensity of suppressed emotion that moved with her made her frighteningly remote. He recognized the expression; she'd worn it in the past when a case touched her deeply, when the body became more than just another statistic, when it became personal. Superiors and psychologists warned cops about that kind of involvement, afraid it would lead to burnout or vigilantism, but everyone fell victim to it sooner or later. It was the feeling that kept an investigation going long after logic said give it up, the feeling that fueled the long and seemingly pointless hours of drudge work that actually led to charges being laid. When "Victory" Nelson wore that expression, people got out of her way.

At this point, under these circumstances, it was the last expression Celluci wanted to see. Grief, anger, even hysterics—". . . *and she certainly has a right to be hysterical under the circumstances*—" would be preferable to the way she'd closed in on herself. This wasn't, couldn't be, just another case.

"Hey." He reached out and touched her arm. The muscles under the sleeve of her navy blue suit jacket felt like stone. "You okay?"

"I'm fine."

Yeah. Right. It was, however, the expected response.

* * *

"Now then." The elder Mr. Hutchinson sat forward, placing his forearms precisely on the charcoal gray blotter that protected his desk and linking his fingers. "I assure you all that you will have our complete cooperation in clearing up this unfortunate affair. Never in all the years that Hutchinson's Funeral Parlour has served the needs of the people of Kingston has such a horrible thing occurred. Ms. Nelson, please believe you have our complete sympathy and that we will do everything in our power to rectify this situation."

Vicki limited herself to a single tight nod of acknowledgment, well aware that if she opened her mouth she wouldn't be able to close it again. She wanted to rip this case away from the Kingston police, to ask the questions, to build out of all the minute details the identity of the scum who dared to violate her mother's body. And once identified . . .

She knew Celluci was watching her, knew he feared she'd start demanding answers, running roughshod over the local forces. She had no intention of doing anything so blatantly stupid. Two years without a badge had taught her the value of subtlety. Working with Henry had taught her that justice was often easier to find outside the law.

"All right, Mr. Hutchinson." Detective Fergusson checked his notes and shifted his bulk into a more comfortable position in the chair. "We already spoke to your driver and to your nephew, the other Mr. Hutchinson, so let's just take it from when the body arrived."

"Ms. Nelson, you'll likely find this distressing . . ."

"Ms. Nelson spent four years as a homicide detective in Toronto, Mr. Hutchinson." Although he might have his own doubts about her being there, Fergusson wasn't about to have an outsider pass judgment on an ex-member of the club. "If you say something that distresses her, she'll deal with it. Now then, the body arrived . . ."

"Yes, well, after she arrived, the deceased was taken down to our preparation room. Although there was to be no viewing, her arrangement with us made it quite clear that she was to be embalmed."

"Isn't that unusual? Embalming without viewing?"

Mr. Hutchinson smiled, the deep wrinkles across his face falling into gentle brackets. "No, not really. A number of people decide that while they don't wish to be stared at after death, neither do they wish to, well, not look their best. And many realize, as happened in this instance, that friends and relatives will want one last look regardless."

"I see. So the body was embalmed?"

"Yes, my nephew took care of most of that. He did the disinfecting, massaged the tissue to bring pooled blood out of the extremities, set the features, drained the body and injected the embalming fluid, perforated the internal organs with the trocar . . ."

Fergusson cleared his throat. "There's, uh, no need to be quite so detailed."

"Oh, I am sorry." The elder Mr. Hutchinson flushed slightly. "I thought you wanted to hear everything."

"Yes. But . . ."

"Mr. Hutchinson." Vicki leaned forward. "That last word you used, trocar, what is it?"

"Well, Ms. Nelson, it's a long steel tube, hollow, you know, and quite pointed, very sharp. We use it to draw out the body fluids and inject a very, very astringent preserving fluid into the cavity."

"Your nephew didn't mention it."

"Well," the old man smiled self-consciously, "he was probably being a little more concise. I tend to ramble on a bit if I'm not discouraged."

"He said," she caught his gaze with hers and held it, "that he'd just placed the incision sealant into the jugular vein when he was called upstairs."

Mr. Hutchinson shook his head. "No. That's not possible. When I came down to finish—as the young woman in the office was most insistent she speak with David—the trocar button had already been placed in the abdomen, sealing off the entry wound."

The silent sound of conclusions being drawn filled the small office.

"I think," Detective Fergusson said slowly, "we'd better speak with David again."

David Hutchinson repeated what he'd said previously.

The elder Mr. Hutchinson looked confused. "But if you didn't aspirate the body cavity, and I certainly didn't, who did?"

The younger Mr. Hutchinson spread his hands. "Chen?"

"Nonsense. He's only here on observation. He wouldn't know how."

"That would be Tom Chen?"

Both of the Mr. Hutchinsons nodded.

"Before you're accepted into a program to become a funeral director," the younger explained, "you have to spend four weeks observing at a funeral home. This isn't a job everyone can do. Anyway, Tom has been with us for the last two and a half weeks. He was in the room while I prepared the body. He helped a little. Asked a couple of questions . . ."

"And was in the room when I came down to finish. He certainly seemed to indicate that you'd done the aspirating, David."

"Well, I hadn't."

"Are you sure?"

"Yes!" The word cracked the quiet reserve both men had been trained to wear and they turned identical expressions of distress on the police office sitting across the desk.

"And Tom Chen is where?"

"Unfortunately, not here. He did work through the weekend," the elder Mr. Hutchinson explained, regaining control. "So when he asked for the day off, I saw no harm in giving it to him."

"Hmmm. Jamie . . ."

Fergusson's partner nodded and quietly left the room.

"Where is he going?"

"He's going to see if we can have a talk with Mr. Chen. But for now," Fergusson leaned back and tapped lightly on his notebook with his pen, "let's just forget who did the aspirating, eh? Tell me what happened next."

"Well, that was about it. We dressed the body, applied light cosmetics, just in case, placed the body in the casket and, well, left it there. Overnight. This morning, we brought the casket upstairs to the chapel."

"Without checking the contents?"

"Nothing's ever happened to the *contents* before," the younger Mr. Hutchinson declared defensively.

"It must've happened during the night." The elder Mr. Hutchinson shook a weary head. "After the casket comes upstairs, there's no possible way anyone could remove the body without being seen."

"No sign of a forced entry," Fergusson mused aloud. "Who has keys?"

"Well, we do, of course. And Christy Aloman, who does all our paperwork and has been with the company for years. And, of course, there's a spare set here, in my drawer. That's strange." He opened a second drawer and a third. "Oh, here they are."

"Not where you usually keep them?"

"No. You don't think that someone took them and made copies, do you, Detective?"

Detective Fergusson glanced back over his shoulder at the corner where Vicki and Celluci sat and lifted an eloquent brow. Then he sighed. "I try not to think, Mr. Hutchinson. It's usually too depressing."

"All right." Celluci turned onto Division Street, one hand palming the wheel, the other grabbing air for emphasis. "Why would Tom Chen steal the body?"

"How the hell should I know?" Vicki snarled. "When we find him, I'll ask him."

"You don't know he had anything to do with it."

"No? We're talking fake address and total disappearance the morning after the crime—that sure as shit sounds incriminating to me."

"Granted."

"Not to mention the did-we-or-didn't-we shuffle that went on in the embalming room. That girl who insisted on talking to the younger Mr. Hutchinson was probably a planned distraction."

"Detective Fergusson and his partner are looking into it."

Vicki turned to face him as they pulled into the parking lot at the apartment building. "So?"

"So let them do their job, Vicki." Celluci parked and reached over the back of the seat for the bag of take-out chicken. "Fergusson's promised to keep you completely informed."

"Good." She got out of the car and strode toward the building, the heels of her pumps making emphatic statements in the gravel. "It'll make *my* job easier."

"And your job is?" He had to ask. He didn't need to, but he had to.

"Finding Tom Chen."

Celluci took three long strides to catch up and then one more to cut in front and pull open the door to the apartment building. "Vicki, you do realize that Tom Chen—the name, the person, the body snatcher—is probably as fake as his address. How the hell are you going to find him?"

"When I find him . . ." Her voice made the finding a fact not a possibility, and Celluci strongly suspected she hadn't heard a word he'd said. ". . . I find my mother's body."

"Of all the lousy luck."

Catherine frowned as she unbuckled number nine's restraints and stepped back so he could climb out of his box. "I suppose it is unfortunate," she said doubtfully, "but it doesn't actually have anything to do with us."

"Yeah, right." Donald snorted. "Earth to Cathy: try to remember that we're the ones who walked off with the body they're looking for. Try to remember that body snatching is a crime." His voice rose. "Try to remember that you'll get bugger all amount of research done if they throw your ass in jail!" He jumped back as number nine suddenly lurched toward him. "Hey! Back off!"

"Stop shouting! He doesn't like it." Catherine reached for an undead arm. It took another two steps for the pressure of her fingers to register, but when it did, number nine obediently stopped. "It's okay," she said softly. "It's okay."

"It is *not* okay!" Donald threw both hands up into the air and whirled to face Dr. Burke. "Tell her, Doctor. Tell her it's not okay!"

Dr. Burke looked up from the alpha wave pattern undulating across the monitor. "Donald," she sighed, "I think you're overreacting."

His eyes bulged. "Overreacting! Try to remember that *I'm* the one they can identify!"

"No, you're not." While not exactly soothing, Dr. Burke's tone was so matter-of-fact that it had the same effect. "They can identify Tom Chen, not Donald Li. But as Tom Chen doesn't exist and there's nothing to tie him to Donald Li, I think we can assume you're safe."

"But they know what I look like." His protest had died to a near whine.

"Yes, the others at the funeral home could pick you out of a lineup, but you have my personal guarantee it will never go that far. What kind of a description can they give the police? A young Oriental male, about five-six; short dark hair; dark eyes; clean-shaven . . ." Dr. Burke sighed again. "Donald, there are hundreds of students just at this university that fit that description, let alone those in the rest of the city."

Donald glowered. "You saying we all look alike?"

"Just as alike as young Occidental males about five-eight; short brown hair; light eyes; clean-shaven, of which there are also hundreds at this university. I'm saying the police will never find you." She bent over the electrocardiograph. "Just stay close for a few days and everything will be fine."

"Stay close. Right." He paced the length of the room and back, unwrapping a miniature chocolate bar he'd taken from his jacket pocket. "I was a grade A idiot to let you talk me into this. I knew this was going to be trouble, right from the start."

"You knew," Dr. Burke corrected, straightening, "this was going to make us all a great deal of money, right from the start. That the applications for the work we're doing are infinite and the implications are staggering. That we might be talking Nobel Prize . . ."

"They don't give the Nobel Prize to body snatchers," Donald pointed out.

Dr. Burke smiled. "They do when they've conquered death," she said. "Do you know what people would be willing to do for the information we're discovering?"

"Well, I know what I've done for it." Donald watched as across the lab Catherine guided number nine to a chair. Mere weeks ago, the ex-vagrant had been lying unclaimed on a slab. *And now, if death hasn't been reversed, well, it's certainly been given a kick in the teeth.* "Look, why wait any longer? With the tricks we've got Cathy's bacteria to do already, not to mention old number nine's apparent brain-computer interface, we could easily cop the prize now."

"We've been through this, Donald. If we publish before we finish, we'll never be permitted to finish."

"Government," Catherine interjected, "has no business regulating science."

Donald looked from the doctor's stern features to his

fellow grad student's obstinate stare. "Hey! I'm on your side, remember? I want my share of the profits not to mention a shot at a Nobel Prize. I just don't want my butt getting tossed behind bars where some lowlife built like a gorilla will no doubt bend me over and ram . . ."

"You've made your point, Donald, but I honestly doubt that the police are going to put that much effort into finding young Mr. Chen. All too soon, there'll be indignities performed on living bodies that will need their attention."

"Yeah? Well what about that Vicki Nelson, the daughter? I hear she's hot shit."

Dr. Burke's brows drew down. "While I find this sudden affection of yours for scatological references distasteful, you have a point. Not only was Ms. Nelson previously a police detective, but she's now a private investigator, and not, by all reports, the sort of person to give up easily. Luckily, there's exactly the same lack of information for her as there is for the police and while it might take her longer to grow discouraged, she still won't find anything because we've been very careful to leave nothing for her to find. Haven't we?"

"Well, yeah."

"So stop worrying. It was unfortunate that they decided to open the casket, but it's hardly the disaster you're making it out to be. Don't you have a tutorial this afternoon?"

"I thought you wanted me to stay close?"

"I want you to behave exactly as you normally do."

He grinned, unable to worry about anything for long. "That is to say, badly?"

Dr. Burke shook her head and half-smiled. "Go."

He went.

"*Is* he in any danger, Dr. Burke?"

"Didn't I just say he wasn't?"

"Yes, but . . ."

"Catherine, I have never lied to Donald. Lies are the easiest way to lose the loyalty of your associates."

Apparently unconvinced, Catherine gnawed on her lower lip.

Dr. Burke sighed. "Didn't I promise you," she said gently, "back when you first approached me, that I'd take care of everything? That I'd see to it you could work without interference? And haven't I kept my promise?"

Catherine released her lip and nodded.

"So you needn't worry about anything but your work. Besides, Donald's dedication to science isn't as strong as ours." She patted the isolation box that held the remains of Marjory Nelson. "Now then, if you could set up the muscle sequences, I'd best get back to my office. With Mrs. Shaw home having hysterics, God only knows what's going on up there."

Alone in the lab, Catherine crossed slowly to the keyboard and sat, staring thoughtfully at the monitor for a few moments. *Donald's dedication to science isn't as strong as ours.* She'd always known that. What she was just beginning to realize was that perhaps Dr. Burke's dedication to science wasn't as strong as it might be either. While there'd always been a lot of talk about the purity of research, this was the first she'd heard of infinite applications and profit sharing.

Behind lids that had lost the flexibility to completely open or completely close, filmy eyes tracked her every movement.

Number nine sat quietly, content for the moment to be out of the box.

And with her.

"So, how is she?"

Celluci stepped out of the apartment and pulled the door partially closed behind him. "Coping."

"Humph. Coping. This evil thing has happened and all you can say is she's coping." Mr. Delgado shook his head. "Has she cried?"

"Not while I've been with her, no." It took an effort, but Celluci managed not to resent the old man's concern.

"Not other times either, I bet. Crying is for the weak; she isn't weak, so she doesn't cry." He thumped a gnarled fist against his chest. "I cried like a baby—like a baby, I tell you—when my Rosa died."

Celluci nodded slowly in agreement. "I cried when my father died."

"Celluci? Italian?"

"Canadian."

"Don't be a smart ass. We, my Rosa and young Frank

and me, we came from Portugal just after the second World War. I was a welder."

"My father's family came just before the war. He was a plumber."

"There." Mr. Delgado threw up both hands. "And if the two of us can cry, you'd think she could manage a tear or two without losing machismo."

Vicki's voice drifted into the hall. "Mr. Chen? Perhaps you can help me, I'm looking for a young man, early twenties, named Tom Chen . . ."

Mr. Delgado's shoulders sagged. "But no. No tears. She holds the hurt inside. You listen to what I'm saying to you, Officer Celluci. When that hurt finally comes out, it's going to rip her to pieces."

"I'll be there for her." He tried not to sound defensive—Vicki's inability to deal with this wasn't his fault—but he didn't entirely succeed.

"What about the other guy? Will he be there, too?"

"I don't know."

"Humph. None of my business? Well, maybe not." The old man sighed. "It's hard when there's nothing to do to help."

Celluci echoed the sigh. "I know."

Back inside the apartment, he leaned against the closed door and watched Vicki hurl the Kingston phone book across the room. "No luck?"

"So he doesn't have a listed number, or a family in town." She jabbed at the bridge of her glasses. "He's probably a student. Lives in residence. I'll find him."

"Vicki . . ." He took a deep breath and exhaled slowly. "You're looking for a fake name. Anyone with the brains to pull this off also had the brains to work under an alias." That he had to keep telling her this was a frightening indication of how deeply she'd been affected both by the death and the loss of the body. It was a conclusion any first-year police cadet would come to and should never have had to be pointed out to "Victory" Nelson. "Tom Chen is . . ."

"All we've got!" A muscle jumped in her jaw as she spat the words at him. "It's a name. It's something."

It's nothing. But he didn't say it because behind the challenge he could hear her desperate need for something to hold onto. *I suppose I should be happy she's clutching at this instead of at Fitzroy.* What would it hurt to go along with her? At least it would keep him close and in time she might decide to hold onto him. "All right, if he lives in residence, where's he keeping . . ." Not *your mother.* There had to be something better to call it. ". . . the body?"

"How the hell should I know? First thing tomorrow, I get my hands on the university registration lists."

"How?" Celluci crossed the room and dropped onto the couch. "You don't *have* a warrant and you can't *get* a warrant. Why don't you let the local police take care of it? Detective Fergusson seems to be positive it's med students so I'm sure he'll check the university."

"So? I don't care what Detective Fergusson checks. I don't care if the whole fucking police force is on the case." She stood and stomped into the tiny kitchen. "I'm going to find this son of a bitch and when I do I'll . . ."

"You'll what?" He surged up off the couch and charged into the kitchen after her, forgetting for the moment that Tom Chen was a name and nothing more. "Why do you want to find this guy before the police do? So you can indulge in a little more participatory justice?" Grabbing her shoulder, he spun her to face him, both of them ignoring the coffee that arced up out of the mug in her hand. "I closed my eyes last fall because there wasn't a way to bring Mark Williams to trial without causing more damage than he was worth. But that isn't the case here! Let the law deal with this, Vicki!"

"The law?"

"Yeah, you remember, what you used to be sworn to uphold."

"Don't bullshit me, Celluci. You know just how much manpower the law is going to be able to allot to this. I'm *going* to find him!"

"All right. And then?"

She closed her eyes for a second and when she opened them again they were shadowed, unreadable. "When I find him, he's going to wish he'd never laid a finger on my mother's body."

The calm, emotionless tone danced knives up Celluci's spine. He knew she was speaking out of pain. He knew she meant every word. "This is Fitzroy's influence," he growled. "*He* taught you to take the law into your own hands."

"Don't blame this on Henry." The tone became a warning. "I take responsibility for my own actions."

"I know." Celluci sighed, suddenly very, very tired. "But Henry Fitzroy . . ."

"Doesn't know what you're talking about." The quiet voice from the doorway pulled them both around. Henry looked from Vicki to Celluci then settled himself on a kitchen chair. "Why don't you tell me what went wrong?"

Henry stared at Celluci in some astonishment. "Why on earth do you think I would know the reason the body is missing?"

"Well, you're . . . what you are." It might have been said, but Celluci still wasn't going to say it. Not right out. "It's the sort of thing you should know about, isn't it?"

"No. It isn't." He turned to Vicki. "Vicki, I'm so sorry, but I have no idea why anyone in this day and age would be body snatching."

She shrugged. She really didn't care why, all she wanted to know was who.

"Unless it wasn't body snatching." Celluci frowned, turning over a new and not very pleasant idea.

Henry's eyes narrowed. "What do you mean?"

"Suppose Marjory's body wasn't taken." He paused, working at the thought. "Suppose she got up and walked out of there."

Vicki's coffee mug hit the floor and shattered.

"You're crazy!" Henry snapped.

"Am I?" Celluci slammed both palms down on the table and leaned forward. "A year ago, some asshole tried to sacrifice Vicki to a demon. I *saw* that demon, Fitzroy. Last summer, I met a family of werewolves. In the fall, we saved the world from the mummy's curse. Now I may be a little slow, but lately I've come to believe that there's a fuck of a lot going on in this world that most people don't know shit about. *You* exist; you tell me why Marjory *couldn't* have got up and walked out of there!"

"Henry?"

Henry shook his head and caught one of Vicki's hands

up in his. "They embalmed her, Vicki. There's nothing that could survive that."

"Maybe they didn't." Her fingers turned until she clutched at him. "They were confused about the rest. Maybe they didn't."

"No, Vicki, they did." Celluci touched her gently on the arm, wondering why he couldn't learn to keep his big mouth shut. He'd forgotten about the embalming. "I'm sorry. I should've thought it through. He's right."

"No." There was a chance. She couldn't let it go. "Henry, could you tell?"

"Yes, but . . ."

"Then go. Check. Just in case."

"Vicki, I assure you that your mother did not rise . . ."

"Henry. Please."

He looked at Celluci, who gave the smallest of shrugs. *Your choice,* the motion said. *I'm sorry I started this.* Henry nodded at the detective, apology accepted, and pulled his hand free of Vicki's as he stood. She'd asked for his help. He'd give it. It was a small enough thing to do to bring her at least a little peace of mind. "Is the casket still at the funeral home?"

"Yes." She began to rise as well, but he shook his head.

"No, Vicki. The last thing you need right now is to be picked up by the police while breaking and entering. If they're watching the place, I can avoid them in ways you can't."

Vicki shoved at her glasses and dropped back in her chair, acknowledging his point but not happy about it.

"If I thought you suggested this merely to remove me," Henry said quietly to Celluci at the door as he pocketed the directions, "I would be less than pleased."

"But you don't think it," Celluci replied, just as quietly. "Why not?"

Henry looked up into the taller man's eyes and smiled slightly. "Because I know an honorable man when I meet one."

An honorable man. Celluci shot the bolt behind his rival and let his head drop against the molding. *Goddamnit, I wish he'd stop doing that.*

If the embalming had been done, the blood drawn out and replaced by a chemical solution designed to disinfect and preserve, to discourage life rather than sustain it—and from both Vicki's and Celluci's reports, the younger funeral director was certain it had—then there was no way that Marjory Nelson had risen to hunt the night. Nor did the manner of her death suggest the change.

Henry parked the BMW and stared into the darkness for a moment, one hundred percent certain that he would find nothing at the funeral home that the police had not already found. *But I'm not going for information, I'm going for Vicki.* Leaving her to spend the night alone with Michael Celluci.

He shook his head and got out of the car. Whether or not Celluci would take advantage of the time was irrelevant—Vicki had shut everything out of her life except the need to find the person or persons who had taken her mother's body and the need to be comforted had been buried with the grief she hadn't quite admitted. Because he loved her, he wouldn't lie to her. He'd go to the funeral home, discover what he already knew, and let her delete one possible explanation beyond the shadow of a doubt.

But first, he had to feed.

Vicki hadn't had the energy to spare and while he'd been tempted to prove his power to Celluci, that was a temptation he'd long since learned to resist. Besides, feeding required an intimacy he was not yet willing to allow between them and feeding from Celluci would take subtleties they hadn't time for.

Head turned into the wind, he searched the night air. Half a block behind him, a dog erupted in a frenzied protest. Henry ignored it; he had no interest in the territory it claimed. There. His nostrils flared as he caught a scent, held it, and began to track it to its source.

The open window was on the second floor. Henry gained it easily, becoming for that instant just another shadow moving against the wall of the house, flickering too fast for mortal eyes to register what they saw. The screen was no barrier.

He moved so quietly that the two young men on the bed, skin slicked with sweat, breathing in identical tormented rhythms, had no idea he was there until he allowed it. The blond saw him first and managed an inarticulate exclamation before he was caught in the Hunter's snare. Warned, the other whirled, one heavily muscled arm flung up.

Henry let the wrist slap against his palm, then he closed his fingers and smiled. Held in the depths of hazel eyes, the young man swallowed and began to tremble.

The bed sank under the weight of a third body.

·He became an extension of their passion, which quickly grew and intensified and finally ignited, racing up nerve endings until mere mortals became lost in the burning glory of it.

He left the way he came. In the morning, they'd find the catch on the screen had been broken and have no idea of when it had happened. Their only memory of his participation would keep them trying, night after night, to recreate what he had given them. He wished them joy in the attempt.

The casket had not been moved from the chapel. Henry stared down at it in distaste. He could no more understand why they'd covered the wood with blue-gray cloth than he could the need to enshrine empty flesh in expensive, beautiful cabinets, sealed against rot and protected from putrefaction. In his day, it was the ceremony of interment that had been important, the mourning, the declarations of grief, the long and complicated farewell. Massive monuments to the dead were placed so people could appreciate them, not buried for the pleasure of the worms. *What was wrong,* he wondered, stepping closer, *with a plain wooden box? He'd* been buried in a plain wooden box.

The sandbags had been taken away, but the imprint still showed in the satin pillow. Henry shook his head and leaned forward. There was no comfort for the dead and he couldn't see how denying that comforted the living.

Suddenly, he hesitated. The last time he'd bent over a coffin that should not have been empty he'd ended up nearly losing his soul. But the ancient Egyptian wizard who called himself Anwar Tawfik had never been dead and Marjory Nelson assuredly had. He was being foolish.

There was a hint of Vicki's mother about the interior. He'd spent the day surrounded by her scent and he easily recognized the trace that still clung to the fabric under the patina of odor laid on by the day's investigation. Straightening, he was certain that whatever else she'd done in her life, or her death, Marjory Nelson had not risen as one of his kind.

But there *was* something.

Over the centuries, he'd breathed in the scent of death in all its many variations, but this death, this faint suggestion that clung to the inside of nose and mouth, this death he didn't know.

Five

"Dr. Burke, look at this! We're definitely picking up independent brain wave patterns."

"Are you certain we're not just getting echos of what we've been feeding in?"

"Quite certain." Catherine tapped the printout with one gnawed nail. "Look at this spike here. And here."

Donald leaned over the doctor's shoulder and squinted down at the wide ribbon of paper. "Electronic belching," he declared, straightening. "And after thirty hours of this-is-your-life, I'm not surprised."

"You may be right, Donald." Dr. Burke lightly touched each peak, a smile threatening the corners of her mouth. "On the other hand, we might actually have something here. Catherine, I think we should open the isolation box."

Both grad students jerked around to stare at their adviser.

"But it's too soon," Catherine protested. "We've been giving the bacteria a minimum of seventy-two hours . . ."

"And it hasn't been entirely successful," Dr. Burke broke in. "Now has it? We lost the first seven, number eight is beginning to putrefy, and according to this morning's samples, even number nine hasn't begun any cellular regeneration in muscle tissue. The near disaster with number five proved that we can't continue isolation much past seventy-two hours, so let's see what happens when we cut it short."

Catherine ran her hand over the curved surface of the box. "I don't know . . ."

"Besides," the doctor continued, "if these spikes do indicate independent brain wave activity, then further time in what is essentially a sensory deprivation chamber will very likely . . ."

"Squash them flat."

The two women turned.

"Inelegant, Donald, but essentially correct."

Pale eyes scanned the array of hookups: monitors and digital readouts and one lone dial. "Well, except for the continuous alpha wave input, she isn't actually doing anything in there," Catherine admitted thoughtfully.

Dr. Burke sighed and decided, for the moment, to let Catherine's terminology stand. "My point exactly. Donald, if you would do the honors. Catherine, keep an eye on things and if there are any changes at all, sing out."

The seal sighed open, the hint of formaldehyde on the escaping oxygen-rich air surely an illusion, and the heavy lid rose silently on its counterweights. The body of Marjory Nelson lay naked and exposed on what had been a sterile pad, huge purple scars stapled shut. Hair, already becoming brittle, fell away from the clips that held the top of the skull in place. A faint trace of burial cosmetics painted an artificial blush across cheekbones death-mask prominent.

At her station by the monitors, Catherine frowned. "I'm not sure. It could be a loose connection. Dr. Burke, could you please check the jack."

Pulling on a pair of surgical gloves, Dr. Burke bent over and reached to roll the head a little to the left.

Gray-blue eyes snapped open.

"Holy shit!" Donald danced backward, crashed into number nine's box, and clutched at it for support.

Dr. Burke froze, one hand almost cradling the line of jaw.

One second. Two seconds. Three seconds. An eternity.

As suddenly as they opened, the eyes closed.

Her view of the body blocked by equipment, Catherine ignored Donald's outburst—in her opinion they came too often to mean anything—and sighed. "Just a wiggle. Probably something in the wire."

"In the wire!" The stethoscope around Donald's neck swung in a manic arc. "We didn't get a wiggle, partner, we got recognition."

"What?" Catherine shot to her feet and stared from Donald to Dr. Burke. "What happened?"

"We opened the lid, she opened her eyes, and bam!" Donald punched at the air. "Just for an instant, she knew who was standing over her. I'm telling you, Cathy, she recognized Dr. Burke!"

"Nonsense." Dr. Burke calmly checked the implant before straightening. "It was an involuntary reaction to the light. Nothing more." The peeled gloves slammed into the garbage. "Switch off the oxygen supplement—we've only got three full tanks left and I'm not sure when we can get more from the departmental supplies—and run a complete check on the mechanicals. Draw the usual samples."

"And the alpha waves?"

"Keep recording." A little pale under the glare of the fluorescents, Dr. Burke paused at the door. "But at the first sign of any agitation, cut the power. I have things to catch up on, so I'll see you both later."

Catherine's puzzled gaze traveled from the lab door to Donald.

"Sure as shit looked like recognition to me," he repeated, wiping his palms on his pants. "I think the good doctor's spooked and I don't blame her. Spooked me, too, and I barely knew the woman."

Catherine chewed her lip. "Well, it didn't register electronically."

He shrugged. "Then maybe we've got activity going on outside the net."

On cue, number nine began banging on the inside of his box.

Donald jumped and swore, but Catherine looked suddenly stricken.

"Oh, no! I promised him he wouldn't have to spend more time in there than absolutely necessary to maintain the integrity of the experiment."

Watching her hurry across the lab, Donald fished a candy from his pocket and methodically unwrapped it. *Now that's a person who doesn't get out enough.*

Usually, Dr. Burke considered the sound of her footsteps, leather soles slapping against tile, nothing more than background noise, acknowledged then forgotten. Today, the sound chased her through the empty halls of the old Life Sciences building, across the connecting walkway, and up into the sanctuary of her office. Even tucked into the comforting depths of her old wooden chair, she thought she could still hear the echoing trail she'd left. After a moment, she realized she was listening to the rapid pounding of her heart.

You're being ridiculous, she told herself firmly, palms flat on the desk. *Take a deep breath and stop overreacting.*

Marjory Nelson's heart condition, not to mention her accessibility, had made her the perfect candidate for the next phase of the experiment. Brain waves had been recorded, tissue samples has been taken, bacteria had been specifically tailored to her DNA—all in preparation for her death. Or rather for the attempted reversal of it. Marjory, knowing nothing of what they'd been doing, submitted to the tests she'd been told might help, and died right on schedule.

Right on schedule. A second deep breath followed the first. *It was fast and painless when it otherwise might not have been.* Not to mention that her presence at the collapse had ensured they wouldn't have to worry about the tissue destruction inherent in an autopsy.

Squaring her shoulders, Dr. Burke pulled the morning's mail across the desk. They were reversing death. Catherine might have created the bacteria, but without her involvement this application would still be years, if not decades, in the future. She had made possible the logical progression of Catherine's experiments and she would reap the rewards.

If recognition *had* flashed just for that instant in Marjory's eyes, then they trembled on the brink of success long before empirical data suggested they should.

If recognition had occurred then . . .

Then what?

Marjory Nelson is dead and I'm truly sorry about that. She was an essential member of my staff and I'll miss her. With a deft movement, Dr. Burke slid the letter opener the length of the envelope. *The body in the lab is experimental unit number ten. Nothing more.*

"I already spoke to the police about this, Ms. Nelson." Nervously, Christy Aloman shuffled the papers on her desk. "I don't know if I should be speaking to you."

"Did the police tell you not to speak to anyone else?"

"No, but . . ."

"You have to admit, if anyone has a right to know, it's me." Vicki felt the pencil dig deep into the callus on her second finger and forced her hand to relax.

"Yes, but . . ."

"My mother's body was stolen from these premises."

"I know, but . . ."

"I should think you'd want to do what you could to help."

"I do. Truly I do." She made the mistake of looking at Vicki's face and found she couldn't look away. Gray-blue eyes were like chiseled bits of frozen stone and she felt as she had when, so many winters ago, she'd responded to childish dares and touched the metal gatepost with her tongue—foolish and trapped.

"Then tell me everything you can remember about Tom Chen. How he looked. What he wore. How he acted. What he said. What you overheard."

"Everything?" It was complete surrender and they both knew it.

"Everything."

"I don't suppose you ever wore anything like this when you were alive." Catherine pulled the Queen's University sweatpants up over number nine's hips. Grayish skin glistened with the most recent application of estrogen cream. "I mean all things considered, you were in pretty good shape, but you didn't look like a jock. Sit."

Number nine obediently sat.

"Raise your arms. Higher."

A bit of agar oozed out between incision staples over the sternum as number nine's arms lifted into the air.

Catherine ignored it and tugged a matching sweatshirt down over the arms and head. "There you go. A pair of shoes and you're fit for polite company."

"Cathy, I hate to say this, but you're looney tunes." Donald pushed away from the microscope and rubbed his eyes. "You're talking to an animatronic corpse. It doesn't understand you."

"I think he does." She slid one bony foot into a running shoe, pressing the velcro closed. "And if maybe he doesn't understand all of it now, he'll never learn to understand if we don't talk to him."

"I know. I know. Necessary stimulus. But we're not getting anything back—brain wave wise—that we haven't put in. Granted—" he held up a hand to cut off her protest—"we're getting some evidence of interfacing with gross motor skills. You don't need to give every muscle fiber a separate instruction and that's fucking amazing, but face it"—he tapped his head—"there's nothing upstairs. The tenant is gone."

Catherine snorted and patted number nine reassuringly on the shoulder. "Great bedside manner. I can see why you got kicked out of med school."

"I didn't get kicked out." Donald set another slide under the microscope lens. "I made a lateral move into graduate studies in organic chemistry."

"Not an entirely voluntary move from what I heard. I heard Dr. Burke had to save your ass."

"Catherine!" Miming shock and horror, Donald spread both hands wide. "I didn't know you knew such words." He shook his head and grinned. "You've spent too much time with single-celled orgasms . . ."

"Organisms!"

". . . you need to get a life."

Catherine moved to number eight's box and adjusted the power. "Somebody has to stay here and take care of them."

Donald sighed. "Better you than me."

Touch.
Her touch.
As electronic impulses continued to move out from the net, more and more words were returning. Hold. Want. Have. Number nine didn't know what to do with those words, not yet.
Wait.

"Is she asleep?"

"Yes." Henry sank down onto the sofa and rested his arms across his knees, the scattering of red-gold hair below his rolled-up sleeves glittering in the lamplight.

"Did you have to . . . convince her?"

"Very nearly, but no. I merely helped her to calm and exhaustion did the rest."

Celluci snorted. "Helped her to calm?" he growled. "Is

that a euphemism for something I don't want to know about?"

Henry ignored the question. "It's late. What are you doing up?"

Lifting his feet up onto the coffee table and stretching long legs, Celluci grunted, "Couldn't sleep."

"Do you want to?"

It was asked innocently enough. *No. Not innocently. Nothing Fitzroy did came under the heading of innocent.* Neutrally enough. "No." Celluci tried to keep his response equally neutral. "I just thought that if you had any idea of what we're supposed to do next, well, I'd like to hear it."

Henry shrugged and threw a quick glance back over his shoulder toward the bedroom where Vicki's heart beat slow and steady, finally free of the angry pounding it had no doubt taken all day. "I honestly have no idea." He turned to look through the shadows at the other man. "Don't you have a job to go back to?"

"Compassionate leave," Celluci told him shortly, eyes half closed. "Shouldn't you be out, oh, I don't know, stalking the night or something?"

"Shouldn't you be out detecting?"

"Detecting what? It hardly makes sense to stake out the scene of the crime and you can bet that asshole Chen, or whatever his real name is, has vanished. All the profiles in the world won't help us identify a perp we can't find."

Henry reached down and fanned the papers on the coffee table by Celluci's feet. Vicki had spent the evening compiling the day's data and when he'd risen, just before eight, she'd presented her results.

"I spoke to everyone who might have had contact with him—except one of three bus drivers, and I'll speak to him tomorrow. Clothes and hairstyles may change, but tiny habits are harder to break. He smiles a lot. Even when he's alone and there's nothing apparent to smile about. He drinks Coke Classic exclusively. He usually has some kind of candy in his pocket. He most often sits in the seat in front of the rear door next to the window. He'd get on the Johnson Street bus at Brock and Montreal with a ticket, not a transfer. That probably means he lives downtown."

Henry had been impressed; and equally concerned. "Victory" Nelson appeared to have no room in her investigation for grieving. A steady emotional diet of rage, especially at this time, couldn't be healthy. He scanned the pages of notes and shook his head. "She's got everything here but a picture."

Reluctantly, Celluci agreed. Years of training seemed to have gained a foothold in Vicki's emotional response and she was now searching for the person instead of just blindly clutching at the name. "Detective Fergusson says he'll try to free up the police artist tomorrow."

"Why do I get the feeling that Detective Fergusson doesn't think that's necessary?"

"It's not that. It's resources. Or specifically *lack* of resources. As he pointed out, and this is a quote, 'Yeah, it's a terrible thing, but we can't hardly keep up with indignities done to the living.' " Celluci's lips thinned as he remembered various "indignities" he'd witnessed done to the living that had gone unpunished due to lack of manpower, or departmental budget cuts, or just plain bad management. He didn't, by any means, approve of Vicki's recent conversion to vigilantism, but, by God, he understood it. The satisfaction of *knowing* that Anwar Tawfik was dust and this time would stay dust, of *knowing* Mark Williams had paid for the innocents he'd slaughtered, of *knowing* that Norman Birdwell would loose no further horrors on the city, all of that weighed heavily against law in the scales Justice held.

He peered blearily at Henry Fitzroy from under heavy lids. How many others had there been? Hundreds? Thousands? While he'd been busting his butt and walking his feet flat, had Fitzroy and others like him been spending the night methodically squashing the cockroaches of humanity? Celluci snorted silently. If they were, they were doing a piss poor job.

Vampires. Werewolves. Demons. Mummies. Only for Vicki would he even consider accepting such a skewed view of reality. Maybe he should've listened to his family, married a nice Italian girl, and settled down. Much as Henry had done earlier, he shot a glance over his shoulder toward the bedrooms. *No. A nice girl, Italian or otherwise, couldn't hope to compete.* Vicki was a comrade, and a friend, and, as asinine as it sounded, the woman he loved. He'd stand by her now when she needed him, regardless of who, or what, stood by her other side.

He didn't want to have anything to do with Henry Fitzroy. He didn't want to respect him. He sure as shit didn't want to like him. He appeared to have no choice regarding the first point, had months ago lost the second, and strongly suspected, in spite of everything, that he was losing the third. *Jesus. Buddies with a bloodsucker.* Responses had to be filtered through the memory of power he'd been shown in Vicki's living room. *Safer to play with a pit bull.*

Henry felt the weight of Celluci's gaze and tried to remember the last occasion on which he'd spent this much time alone with a mortal he hadn't been feeding from. Or hadn't intended to feed from. The situation was, to say the least, unusual.

In all his long life, Henry had seldom felt so frustrated. "We can't resolve this," he said aloud, "until the body is found and interred, and her grieving is over."

Celluci didn't bother pretending to misunderstand what *this* referred to, although he was tempted. "So find the body," he suggested, a yawn threatening to dislocate his jaw.

Henry arched a brow. "So easy to say," he murmured.

"Yeah? What about that funny smell Vicki says you ran into last night?"

"I am not a bloodhound, Detective. Besides, I traced it as far as it went—to the parking lot."

"What did it smell like?"

"Death."

"Not surprising. You were in a body parlor." He yawned again.

"Funeral homes go to a great deal of effort *not* to smell like death. This was something different."

"Oh, lord, not again," Celluci groaned, dragging a hand up through his hair. "What is it this time? The creature from the Rideau Canal? The Loch Ness fucking monster? The Swamp Thing? Godzilla? Megatron? Condor? Rodan?"

"Who?"

"Didn't you ever watch Saturday afternoon monster movies?" He shook his head at Henry's expression. "No, I guess you didn't, did you? Every weekend thousands of kids were glued to their sets for badly dubbed, black and white, Japanese rubber monsters stomping on Tokyo. Not to mention *Jesse James Meets Frankenstein's Daughter, Ab-*

bott and Costello Meet the Mummy, The Curse of the Were-wolf."

A car door, slamming in the parking lot, suddenly sounded unnaturally loud.

"Jesus H. Christ." Celluci's eyes were fully open. Still tired, he no longer had any desire to sleep. He sat up and swung his feet to the floor. "A motive. You don't think . . ."

"That Tom Chen was playing Igor to someone else's Dr. Frankenstein?" Henry smiled. "I think, as I said before, that you watch too many bad movies, Detective."

"Oh, yeah? Well, you know what I think? I think . . ."

Bam. Bam. Bam.

They faced the door, then they faced each other.

"The police," Celluci said, and stood.

"No." Henry blocked his way. He could feel the lives, hear the singing blood, smell the excitement. "Not police although I suspect they'd like us to think so."

Bam. Bam. Bam.

"A threat?"

"I don't know." He crossed the room. When he stopped, Celluci moved up to stand behind his left shoulder. It had been a very long time since he'd had a shield man. He opened the door.

The flash went off almost before he could react. A mortal would have recoiled—Henry's hand whipped out and covered the lens of the camera before the shutter had completely fallen. He snarled as the brilliant light drove spikes of pain into sensitive eyes and closed his fingers. Plastic and glass and metal became only plastic and glass and metal.

"Hey!"

The photographer's companion ignored both the sound of a camera disintegrating and the accompanying squawk of protest. Sometimes they got a great candid shot when the door opened, sometimes they didn't. She wasn't going to worry about it. "Good evening. Is Victoria Nelson at home?" Elbows primed, her notebook held like a battering ram, she attempted to push forward. Most people, she found, were just too polite to stop her.

The slight young man never budged; it felt like she'd hit a not very tall brick wall. Time for plan B. And if that didn't work, she'd go right through the alphabet if she had to. "We were so sorry to hear about what happened to her mother's bo . . ." Her train of thought derailed somewhere in the depths of hazel eyes.

Henry decided not to be subtle. He wasn't in the mood and they wouldn't understand. "Go away. Stay away."

Darkness colored the words and became threat enough.

Not until they were safely in the car, cocooned behind steel and locked doors, did the photographer, cradling the ruins of his camera in his lap, finally find his voice. "What are we going to do?" he asked, primal memories of the Hunt trembling in his tone.

"We're going to do . . ." With an icy hand and shaking fingers, she jammed the car into gear, stomped on the gas, and sprayed gravel over half the parking lot. ". . . exactly what he said."

Together they'd been threatened a hundred times. Maybe a thousand. Once, they'd even been attacked by an ex-NHL defenseman swinging a hockey stick with enraged abandon. They'd always gotten the story. Or a version of the story at least. This time, something in heart and soul, in blood and bone recognized the danger and overruled conscious thought.

Inside Marjory Nelson's apartment, Celluci glared enviously at the back of Henry's red-gold head. If he hated anything, it was the press. The statements they insisted on were the bane of his existence. "I wish I could do that," he muttered.

Henry wisely kept from voicing the obvious and made sure all masks were back in place before turning. This was not the time for Michael Celluci to see him as a threat.

Celluci rubbed at the side of his nose and sighed. "There'll probably be others."

"I'll deal with them."

"And if they come in the daytime?"

"You deal with them." Henry's smile curved predator sharp. "You're not on duty, Detective. You can be as rude as . . ." Just how rude Celluci could be got lost in a sudden change of expression and a heartbeat later he was racing for the bedroom.

To mortal eyes, one moment he was there, the next gone. Celluci turned in time to see Vicki's bedroom door thrown open, swore, and pounded across the living room. He hadn't heard anything. What the hell had Fitzroy heard?

*   *   *

How could she have forgotten?

She dug frantically at the tiles in the kitchen. As they ripped free, she flung them behind her, ignoring the fingernail that ripped free with them, ignoring the blood from her hands that began to mark its own pattern on the floor. Almost there. Almost.

The area she cleared stretched six feet long by three feet wide, the edges ragged. Finally only the plywood subfloor remained. Rot marked the gray-brown wood and tendrils of pallid fungus grew between the narrow boards. Fighting for breath, she slammed her fists against this last barrier.

The wood cracked, splintered, and gave enough for her to force a grip on the first piece. She threw her weight against it and it lifted with a moist, sucking sound, exposing a line of gray-blonde curls and perhaps a bit of shoulder.

How could she have forgotten where she'd left her mother?

Begging for forgiveness, she clawed at the remaining boards. . . .

"Vicki! Vicki, wake up, it's only a dream."

She couldn't stop the first cry, but she grabbed at the second and wrestled it back where it came from. Her conscious mind clung to the reassurances murmured over and over against her hair. Her subconscious waited for the next board to be removed. Her hands clung of their own volition, fingers digging deep into the shoulder and arm curved protectively around her.

"It's all right, Vicki. It's all right. I'm here. It was only a dream. I'm here. I've got you . . ." The words, Henry knew, were less important than the tone and as he spoke he drew the cadence around the fierce pounding of her heart and convinced it to calm.

"Henry?"

"I'm here."

She fought the terror for control of her breathing and won at last. A long breath in. A longer breath out. And then again.

Henry almost heard the barriers snap back into place as she pushed away, chin rising defiantly.

"I'm okay." *It was only a dream. You're acting like a*

child. "Really, I'm okay." The darkness shifted things, moved furniture that hadn't been moved in fifteen years. *Where the hell is the bedside table?* "Turn on the light," she commanded, struggling to keep new panic from touching her voice. "I need my glasses."

A cool touch against her hand and her fingers closed gratefully around the heavy plastic frames. A second touch helped her settle them on her nose just as the room flooded with light. Squinting against the glare, she turned to face the switch and Michael Celluci's worried frown.

"Jesus. Both of you."

"I'm afraid so." Henry shifted his weight on the edge of the bed and asked, without much hope of success, "Do you want to talk about it?"

Her lip curled. "Not likely." Talking about it would mean thinking about it. Thinking about what she'd have found, what she'd have seen, if she'd managed to tear up just one more piece of floor. . . .

"Celluci? Fergusson. Med school's got three Chens. One of them's even a Tom Chen—Thomas Albert Chen. And guess what, the kid's got an airtight alibi not only for that night but for the whole two and a half weeks our boy was at the body parlour. Rough luck, eh?"

Celluci, receiver pinned between shoulder and ear, washed down a forkful of scrambled eggs with a mouthful of bitter coffee. He hadn't thought Fergusson a subtle enough man for sarcasm. Obviously, he'd been wrong. "Yeah, rough. You take his picture around to Hutchinson's just in case?"

"Give it up, Celluci, and stop wasting my fucking time. You and I both know that we're not looking for any Tom Chen." Fergusson sighed at Celluci's noncommittal grunt, the sound eloquently saying *give me a break.* "Tell Ms. ex-Detective Nelson that I'm sorry about her mother, but I know what the fuck I'm doing. I'll get back to you if we get any *real* information in."

Celluci managed to hang up and shovel another pile of eggs into his mouth before he succumbed to Vicki's glare and repeated the conversation. *She* might have dropped off, reassured by Fitzroy's supernatural protection but *he'd* spent a restless night stretched out in the next room, straining to hear any sound that might make its way through the wall, wondering why he'd so easily surrendered the field. *You've got the day,* he reminded himself, reaching for another piece of toast. Which was really no answer at all. *Goddamn Fitzroy anyway.* Hopefully, massive quantities of food would make up for lost sleep.

Vicki pushed her plate away. She knew she had to eat, but there was a limit to how much she could choke past the knots. "I want you to check that alibi."

Oh, God, not again. He'd really thought that she'd shaken her obsession that Tom Chen could be the actual name of their suspect. The profiling she'd done had been good solid police work and he'd taken it—*prematurely as it turns out*—as an indication that she was beginning to function. Hiding concern she wouldn't appreciate, he reached across the table and covered one of her hands with his. There was no point in restating the obvious when she refused to hear him, so he tried a different angle. "Vicki, Detective Fergusson *knows* his job."

"Either you check it or I do." Pulling her hand free, she regarded him levelly. "I won't let this go. You can't make me. You might as well help; it'll be over sooner."

Her eyes were too bright and he could see the tension twisting her shoulders and causing her fingers to tremble slightly. "Look, Vicki . . ."

"I don't need a babysitter, Mike. Not you. Not him."

"All right." He sighed. She'd asked for his help. While it wasn't exactly the kind of help he wanted to give, it was something. "I'll check the alibi and I'll run a picture over to Hutchinson's. I don't think you should be alone, but you're an adult and you're right, this will go faster with both of us working on it."

"All three of us."

"Fine." Too much to expect she'd want Fitzroy to butt out. "What'll you be doing?"

She set her empty coffee mug down on the table with a sharp crack. "Tom Chen wanted my mother's body specifically. In the time he was at that funeral home, he passed up two other women of roughly equal age and condition. I'll be finding out why." As she stood, she knocked her knife to the floor. It bounced once, then slid across the kitchen floor, across tiles still whole, still covering . . .

How could she have forgotten where she'd left her mother?

The eggs became a solid lump the size of her fist, shoved up tight against her ribs. Eyes up, she stepped over the knife. Another two steps took her off the tiles.

Gray-blonde curls and perhaps a bit of shoulder.

Just one more board. . . .

"Raise right leg." As Donald spoke, he fed the stored brain wave pattern corresponding to the command directly into the net.

In the open isolation box, the right leg trembled and slowly lifted about four inches off the padding.

"Hey, Cathy, we've got a fast learner here. Remember how ol' number nine's leg flew up? Like he was trying to kick the ceiling?"

"I remember how Dr. Burke was worried he might have damaged his hip joint," Catherine replied, continuing to adjust the IV drip that nourished the rapidly deteriorating number eight. "And at least we didn't have to manipulate his leg for the first hundred times like we had to on all the others."

"Hey, chill out. I wasn't saying anything against super-corpse. I was only pointing out that number ten seems to have quantitative control."

"Well, we are using *her* brain wave patterns."

"Well, number nine used *my* brain wave patterns for gross motor control." He echoed her supercilious tone. "So *he* should've had the advantage."

"I'm amazed he learned how to walk."

"Ow." Donald dramatically clutched at his heart. "I am cut to the quick." Rolling his eyes at her non-responsive back, he tapped another two computer keys. "And it's painful going through life with a cut quick, let me tell you. Lower right leg."

Surrendering to gravity, the right leg dropped.

"Raise left leg. I've got a feeling that number ten's going to be the baby that makes our fortune."

Catherine frowned as she moved to check on number nine. There's been too much talk of "making fortunes" lately. The discovery of new knowledge should be an end in itself; the consideration of monetary gains clouded research. Granted number ten represented a giant step forward as far as experimental data was concerned, but she was by no means as far as they could go.

There was something she had to do.
The need began to force definition onto oblivion.

"Frankly, Vicki, I'm amazed your mother didn't tell you all this." Adjusting her glasses, Dr. Friedman peered down at Marjory Nelson's file. "After all, we had a diagnosis about seven months ago."

Vicki's expression didn't change, although a muscle twitched in her jaw. "Did she know how bad it was?" *She* could refer to anyone's mother, not that the illusion of distance helped. "Did she know that her heart could give out at any time?"

"Oh, yes. In fact, we'd agreed to try corrective surgery but, well . . ." The doctor shrugged ruefully. "You know how these things keep getting put off, what with hospitals having to trim beds."

"Are you saying budget cutbacks killed her?" The words came out like ground glass.

Dr. Friedman shook her head and tried to keep her tone soothing. "No. A heart defect killed your mother. She'd probably had it all her life until, finally, an aging muscle couldn't compensate any longer."

"Was it a usual condition?"

"It wasn't a *usual* condition . . ."

Vicki cut her off with a knife-edged gesture. "Was it unusual enough that her body may have been stolen in order to study it?"

"No, I'm sorry, but it wasn't."

"I'd like to see the file."

Brow furrowed, Dr. Friedman studied the plain brown folder without really seeing it. Technically, the file was confidential, but Marjory Nelson was dead and beyond caring. Her daughter, however, was alive, and if the contents of the file could help to bring healing out of dangerously strong denial, then confidentiality be damned. And it wasn't as if the file contained anything she hadn't already divulged during the last hour's interrogation—details had been lifted out of her memory with a surgical precision both frighten-

ing and impressive. Reaching a decision she pushed the
folder across the desk and asked, "If there's anything else
I can do?"

"Thank you, Doctor." Vicki slid the file into her purse
and stood. "I'll let you know."

As that hadn't been exactly what she had in mind, she
tried again. "Have you spoken to anyone about your loss?"

"My loss?" Vicki smiled tightly. "I'm speaking to everyone about it." She nodded, more a dismissal than a farewell, and left the office.

Loss, Dr. Friedman decided, as the door swung shut, had
been an unfortunate choice of words.

She almost had it. Almost managed to grab onto memory. There was something she *had* to do. Needed to do.

"Cathy. She made a noise."

"What kind of a noise? Tissue stretching? Joints cracking, what?"

"A vocal noise."

Catherine sighed. "Donald . . ."

"No. Really." He backed away, still holding the
sweatshirt he'd been about to pull over electronically raised
arms. "It was a kind of moan."

"Nonsense." Catherine took the shirt out of his hands
and gently tugged it down into place. "It was probably just
escaping air. You're too rough."

"Yeah, and I know the difference between a belch and
a moan." Cheeks pale, he crossed to his desk and dropped
into the chair, fingers shredding the wrapper off a mint.
"I'm going to start running today's biopsies. *You* can finish
dressing Ken and Barbie."

"Your mother was a pretty everyday sort of person."
Mrs. Shaw smiled sadly over the edge of her coffee mug.
"You were probably the most exotic thing in her life."

Vicki let the sympathy wash past her—waves over a
rock—and pushed at her glasses. "You're certain she wasn't
involved in any unusual activities over the last few
months?"

"Oh, I'm certain. She would've told me about it if she
had been. We talked about everything, your mother and I."

"You knew about the heart condition."

"Of course. Oh." Flustered, the older woman cast about for a way to erase her last words. "Uh, more coffee?"

"No. Thank you." Vicki set what had been her mother's cup down on what had been her mother's desk, then reached over and gently laid her academy graduation portrait facedown.

"An investigation must not become personal." The voice of a cadet instructor echoed in her head. *"Emotions camouflage fact and you can charge right past the one bit of evidence you need to break the case."*

"Actually, if anything, well, unusual was going on with your mother, Dr. Burke might know." Mrs. Shaw set her own mug down and leaned forward helpfully. "When she found out about the heart condition, she convinced your mother to have a whole lot of tests done."

"What kind of tests?"

"I don't know. I don't think your mother . . ."

Stop saying that! Your mother! Your mother! She had a name.

". . . knew."

"Is Dr. Burke available?"

"Not this afternoon, I'm afraid. She's in a departmental meeting right now, but I'm sure she'll be able to make time for you tomorrow morning."

"Thank you." Moving carefully, Vicki stood. "I'll be back." Lips twisted in a humorless smile. She felt more like Charlie Brown than Arnold Schwarzenegger.

"Goddamn, look at the time. It's almost 8:30 p.m. No wonder I'm so hungry."

Catherine carefully set the petri dish in the incubation chamber. "Hungry? I don't see why, you've been eating sugar all day."

"Cathy. Cathy. Cathy. And you a scientist. Sugar stimulates hunger, it doesn't satisfy it."

Pale brows drew in. "I don't think that's exactly right."

Donald shrugged into his jacket. "Who cares. Let's go for pizza."

"I still have work to do."

"*I* still have work to do. But I doubt I'll be capable of working to my full potential if all I can think of is my stomach. And," he crossed the room and punched her on the shoulder, brows waggling, "I'm sure I heard your tum demanding attention mere moments ago."

"Well . . ."

"Doesn't your research deserve to have your full attention?"

She drew herself up indignantly. "Without question."

"Distracted by hunger, who knows what damage you could do. Come on." He picked up her coat. "I hate to eat alone."

Recognizing truth in the last statement at least, Catherine allowed herself to be herded to the door. "What about them?"

"Them?" For a moment, he had no idea of who she was referring to, then he sighed. "We'll bring them back a pepperoni special, pop it in a blender, and feed it to them through the IV, okay?"

"That's not what I meant. They're just sitting there, out of the boxes. Shouldn't we . . ."

"Leave them. We're coming right back." He pulled her over the threshold. "You're the one who said they needed the stimulation."

"Yes. I did."

With Catherine safely in the hall, Donald reached back and flicked off the overhead lights. "Don't do anything I wouldn't do," he caroled into the room, and pulled the door closed.

One by one, the distractions ceased. First the voices. Then the responses she couldn't control or understand. Finally, the painful brightness. It grew easier to hold on to thought. To memory.

There was something she had to do.

Raise your right leg.
Raise your left leg.
Walk.

She remembered walking.

Slowly, lurching to compensate for a balance subtly wrong, she crossed the room.

Door.

Closed.

Open.

It took both hands, fingers interlaced, to turn the handle—not the way memory said it should work, but memory lay in shredded pieces.

There was something she had to do.

Needed to do.

Number nine watched. Watched the walking. Watched the leaving.

This new one was not like the other. The other had no . . .

No . . .

The other was empty.

This new one was not empty. This new one was like him.

Him.

He.

Two new words.

He thought they might be important words.

He stood and walked, as he'd been taught, toward the door.

Six

"This isn't the eighteenth century, Fitzroy. Medical schools stopped hiring grave diggers some time ago."

Henry tugged at the lapels of his black leather trench coat, settling it forward on his shoulders. "You have a better idea, Detective?"

Celluci scowled. He didn't, and they both knew it.

"Historical precedents aside," Henry continued, "Detective Fergusson seems certain that there were medical students involved; an opinion based, no doubt, on local precedents."

"Detective Fergusson blames Queen's students for everything from traffic jams to the weather," Celluci pointed out acerbically. "And I thought your opinion of Detective Fergusson wasn't high."

"I've never even met the man."

"You said . . ."

"Enough," Vicki interrupted from her place on the couch, the tap, tap, tap of her pencil end against the coffee table a staccato background to her words. "Logically, all the storage facilities in the city should be searched. Also logically, for historical reasons, if nothing else, the medical school is the place to start."

"Those who refuse to learn from history," Henry agreed quietly, "are doomed to repeat it."

"Spare me the wisdom of the ages," Celluci muttered. "These places don't do public tours at midnight, you know; how are you planning on getting in?"

"It's hardly midnight."

"At twenty to nine, it's hardly open house either."

"It's April, the end of term, there'll be students around, and even if there aren't, it isn't easy to deny me access."

"Don't tell me. You turn into mist?" He raised a weary hand at Henry's expression. "I know; I watch too many bad movies. Never mind, I meant it when I said don't tell me. The less I know about your talents for B&E the better."

"You have the photograph?" Vicki asked. Tap. Tap. Tap. "You'll be able to make an identification?"

"Yes." Henry doubted Marjory Nelson still looked much like her picture, but it was a place to start.

Tap. Tap. Tap. "I should go with you."

"No." He crossed the room and dropped to one knee by her side. "I'll be able to move faster on my own."

"Yes, but . . ." Tap. Tap.

Henry covered her hand with his, stopping the pencil from rising to fall again. Her skin felt heated and he could feel the tension sizzling just under the surface. "I'll be able to move faster," he repeated, "on my own. And the faster I move, the sooner you'll have the information."

She nodded. "You're right."

He waited a moment, but when she said nothing further, he stood, reluctantly releasing her hand.

Tap. Tap. Tap.

Very lightly, he brushed his fingertips across her hair then turned.

Celluci met him at the door. Together, they glanced back at the couch. Vicki had removed the shades from both end-table lamps and, in the harsh light, the area around her mouth and eyes looked both bruised and painfully tight.

"Don't leave her alone," Henry murmured, and left before the detective could decide on a reply.

The sound of the pencil tapping followed him out of the building.

The door almost stopped her; the latching mechanism was almost beyond her abilities. The line of stitches just above the hairline gaped as her brows drew in and she forced her fingers to push and pull and prod until finally the door swung open.

There was something she had to do. Perhaps it was on the other side of the door.

Most of the overhead lights were off and she shuffled along from shadow to shadow. She was going somewhere. The halls began to look familiar.

She passed through another doorway and then into a room so well known that, for an instant, chaos parted and she knew.

I am . . .

Then the maelstrom swept most of it up again and she was left with only scattered fragments. For a single beat of her mechanically enhanced heart, she was aware of what she'd lost. Her wail of protest throbbed against the walls, but even before the last echo died, she'd forgotten she'd ever made it.

She crossed the room to a pair of desks, pulled one of the chairs out, and sat. It felt right. No, not quite right. Frowning, she carefully moved the *World's Greatest Mother* coffee mug from the center of the blotter over to the far right side. It always sat on the right side.

Something was still wrong. After a moment of almost thought, she scrabbled at a silvery frame lying facedown, finally managing to grab hold and lift it. With trembling fingers, she gently touched the face of the uniformed young woman whose photograph filled the frame. Then she stood.

There was something she had to do.

She shouldn't be here.

She had to go home.

He didn't know where the other one was, so he walked, following the path of least resistance, until he bumped up against a tiny square of reinforced glass that showed him the stars.

Outside.

He remembered outside.

Face pressed to the glass, eyes on the stars, he pushed at the barrier, sneakers pedaling against the tile floor. More by luck than design, his hands clutched at the waist-high metal bar. Another push, and the fire door swung open.

The alarm drove the stars from his head. He moved away from the hurting as fast as he was able, onto the dark and quiet pathways that ran between and behind the university buildings. He would find her. Find the kind one. She would make it better.

* * *

"Now, then, don't you feel better?"

"I suppose so."

"You suppose so?" Donald sighed and shook his head. "The best pizza in Kingston, not to mention my congenial company, and you'd probably rather have stayed in the lab, munching on a stale sandwich, if you'd remembered to eat at all, exchanging wisecracks with the dead stooges."

"Did you leave the door open?"

"Did I what?" He peered down the dimly lit hall at the door angled out into the corridor. "You sure that's ours?"

"Of course, I'm sure."

"Well, I closed it when we left *and* I heard the lock catch."

Catherine broke into a run. "If something's happened to them, I'll never forgive myself."

Donald followed considerably more slowly, half inclined to bolt. Although Security kept an eye on entrances and exits, they didn't bother to patrol the interior. The old Life Sciences building was a rabbit warren of halls and passageways and strangely subdivided rooms and, had the university budget extended to demolition, it would have long ago been turned into a much more useful three-story parking garage. While Donald had occasionally wondered if they were the *only* clandestine lab operating, he'd never been worried about discovery.

Except that he knew he'd closed the door.

And Dr. Burke, who carried the only other set of keys, would never leave it open.

So it appeared they'd been discovered.

The question is, he mused, bouncing on the balls of his feet, uncertain whether he should go forward or back, *have we advanced far enough that the end will justify the means in the eyes of the authorities?* Numbers one through nine, after all, had been bodies donated for research purposes. Unfortunately, he didn't think that even Dr. Burke could talk her way around body number ten, not without the final payoff of death overcome, and they were a while away from that.

Right. He had no intention of going to jail. Not for science. Not for anything. *I'm out of here.*

"Donald! They're gone!"

He froze, half-turned. "What do you mean they're gone?"

"Gone! Not here! They left!"

"Cathy, get a grip! Dead people don't just get up and walk away."

Her glare, anger and exasperation equally mixed, burned through the shadows between them. "You taught them to walk, you idiot!"

"Oh, lord, we're fucked." He ran for the lab. "You sure somebody didn't break in and steal them?"

"Who? If someone found them, they'd still be here waiting for an explanation."

"Or off calling the cops." He waved aside her protest and pushed past her. A quick glance at the monitors showed number eight remained in its isolation box, refrigeration units humming at full capacity in an attempt to prevent further decomposition. The chairs where they'd left numbers nine and ten were empty. The other two boxes were empty. He checked under the tables, in the closet, in the storeroom, around and below every bit of machinery in the lab.

If no one had found them, and logic pointed to that conclusion, then they had to have left on their own.

"It's impossible." Donald sagged against the doorframe. "They don't *have* abstract thought processes."

"They saw us leave." Catherine grabbed his arm and dragged him back out into the hall. "It was imitation if nothing more." She shoved him to the left. "You go that way!"

"Go where that way?"

"We have to search the building."

"Then call out the Mounties," he snapped, rubbing at his forehead with trembling fingers, "because it'll take you and me alone years to search this place."

"But we have to find them!"

He couldn't argue with that.

Voices.

Number nine moved toward the sound, drawn by almost familiar cadences.

Was it her?

"Cathy!" Donald pounded the length of the hall and rocked to a panting stop beside the other grad student.

"Thank God I found you. We've got bigger trouble than we thought. I went over to talk to the guys at the security desk in the new building, just to see if they might have heard something. Well, they did. They heard the fire alarm. Someone went out the fire door at the back."

"Outside?" Pale skin blanched paler. "Unsupervised?"

"At least one of them. Where's your van?"

"In the lot behind the building." She turned and raced toward the exit. "We've got to find them before someone else does!"

Hand pressed tight against the stitch in his side, Donald followed. "Brilliant deduction, Sherlock," he gasped.

The voices were closer. He stopped at the border between soft ground and hard, head turning from side to side.

"I'm telling you, Jenny, sweetheart, no one ever comes back here. It's perfectly safe."

"Why can't we park by the tower, like everyone else?"

"*Because* everyone else parks there and I have a moral objection to cops shining flashlights in my face at delicate moments."

"At least let's close the windows."

"It's a beautiful night, let's celebrate spring. Besides, steamy windows are a sure sign that something naughty is going down if anyone happens to pass. And speaking of going down . . ."

"Pat! Wait, I'll put the seat back. Be careful . . . oh . . ."

His soles scuffed as he lurched forward, aiming for the deeper shadows where two buildings joined. He didn't understand the new noises, but he followed them to a metal bulk he recognized as *car*.

He didn't know what car meant. Was it hurting her?

Bending carefully, he peered inside.

Pale hair.

Her face but not her face.

Her voice but not her voice.

Confused, he reached out and touched the curve of her cheek.

Her eyes snapped open, widened, then she screamed.

It hurt.

He began to back away.

Another face rose out of the darkness.

Hands grabbed for him.

His wrist caught, he clutched at air. He only wanted to get away. Then his fingers closed on something soft and kept closing until the screaming stopped. The second face lolled limp above his grip. Her face, not her face, gazed up at him. Then she screamed again.

He turned and ran.

He remembered running.

Run until it stopped hurting.

Soft ground under his feet.

He slammed hard against a solid darkness and pulled himself along it until he reached a way through. There were lights up ahead. She—the real she, the kind one—was where there were lights.

"There! Coming around that building!"

"Are you sure?"

"For chrissakes, Cathy, how many dead people are walking around this city tonight? Get over there!"

The van hadn't quite stopped when Donald threw himself out onto the road. He stumbled, picked himself up, and raced toward the shambling figure just emerging from the shadows.

He ignored the sound of screaming rising from behind the building. Catching sight of number nine's face under the streetlights, he figured he could pretty much guess what had caused it. Some of the sutures holding the scalp in place had torn and a grayish-yellow curve of skull was exposed above a flapping triangle of skin.

Dr. Burke's going to have my balls on a plate! He skidded to a stop, took a deep, steadying breath, and, as calmly as he was able, said, "Follow."

Follow.

He knew that word.

"Donald, I can hear screaming. And a car horn."

"Look, don't worry about it. Number nine's in, so just drive."

"Well, we should check to see if he's all right. They might have hurt him."

"Not *now,* Cathy. He's safe for the moment, but number ten isn't. We've got to find her. It."

Catherine glanced back over her shoulder at number nine lying strapped in place, nodded reluctantly, and pulled out into the street. "You're right. First we find number ten. Where to?"

Donald sank back against the passenger seat, sighed, and spread his hands. "How the hell should I know?"

Marjory Nelson had not been in the university's medical morgue; not in whole nor in part. Motionless beside the trunk of an ancient maple, ridding himself of the scent of preserved death, Henry considered how best to spend the remainder of the night. The city's two large hospitals were close. If he checked both their morgues before dawn, and he saw no reason why he shouldn't be able to, it would leave him available to . . . to . . . to what?

Over the last year, he'd learned that private investigators spent most of their time pulling together bits of apparently unconnected information into something they hoped would resemble a coherent whole—a little like first doing a scavenger hunt for jigsaw puzzle pieces and then constructing it with no idea of the final picture. They were more likely to spend time in libraries than in car chases and results were about equally dependent on training, talent, and luck. Not to mention an obstinate determination to get to the bottom of things that bordered on obsession.

Obsession. Vicki's obsession with finding her mother's body blocked the grief she should be feeling, blocked getting on with the rest of her life. Henry leaned back against the tree and wondered how long he was going to let it continue. He knew he could break through it, but at what cost. Could he do it without breaking her? Without losing her? Without leaving Detective-Sergeant Michael Celluci to pick up the pieces?

Suddenly he smiled, the moon-white crescent of his teeth flashing in the darkness. *You measure your life in centuries,* he chided himself. *Give her some time to work through this. It's only been a couple of days.* Too much of the twentieth century's preoccupation with getting through unpleasantness as quickly and as tidily as possible had rubbed off on

his thinking. Granted, repressing emotions was unhealthy
but . . . *two days hardly deserves to be called an obsession.*
It was, he realized, the presence of Michael Celluci that
had made it seem so much longer. *He can do no more for
her than you can. Trust in her strength, her common sense,
and the knowledge that as much as she is able, she loves you.*

Both, added a small voice.

Shut up, he told it savagely.

Straightening, he stepped away from the tree, and froze,
the hair rising on the back of his neck. A second later, the
screaming started.

The sound echoed around the close-packed buildings,
making it difficult for him to locate its source. After chasing
down a number of false leads, he arrived at the small se-
cluded parking lot just as the campus police screeched to
a stop, their headlights illuminating a terrified teenage girl
backing away from a rust-edged car and the body of an
equally young man sprawled half out of it onto the pavement. The boy had obviously been dead when the car door
was opened—only the dead fall with such boneless disre-
gard for the landing.

Eyes narrowed against the intrusive glare, Henry slid into
a patch of deep shadow. While it wouldn't be unusual for
a passerby to be drawn by the screams, anonymity when
possible ensured a greater degree of survival for his kind.
With less noise than the wind made brushing up against
the limestone walls, he began to move away. The girl was
safe and although he would have intervened had he been
in time, he had no interest in the myriad ways that mortals
killed mortals.

"Like the guy looked like he was dead! Like all rotten
and dead! I am *not* hysterical! Like I've seen movies, you
know!" The last word trailed off into a rising wail.

The guy looked like he was dead.

And a corpse gone missing.

Henry stopped and turned back. There was probably no
connection. He moved silently forward, around the edge of
a building, and almost choked. The scent of the death he'd
touched at the funeral home lay so thick on the grass that
he had to back away. Skirting the edges, and *that* was closer
than he wanted to go, he traced it to a pothole-shattered
access road and lost it again.

At the sound of approaching sirens, he pulled the night around him once more and made his way back to the parking lot. He would watch and listen until the drama played itself out. The girl could very well be hysterical, terror painting a yet more terrifying face on murder. The police would surely think so. Henry didn't.

If Henry comes up empty at the morgue, I'll have him start riding the buses. A young Asian male sitting just in front of the back door eating candy shouldn't be too hard to spot. Celluci can do the day shift. Vicki circled the Brock Street transfer point on her bus map. It wasn't much of a lead, but it was the only one they had and she knew it was one the police would have neither time nor manpower to follow. If Tom Chen—or whatever his name was—was still in Kingston, and still riding the buses, they'd find him eventually.

Eventually. She sat back on the couch and rubbed her eyes under her glasses. *That is,* if *he's still in Kingston, and* if *he's still riding the buses.*

And if he wasn't?

What if he'd thrown her mother's body into a car and driven away? He might not only have left the area but the country as well. The Ivy Lea Bridge over the Thousand Islands to the States wasn't far, and with the amount of traffic that crossed daily, the odds of his car being searched by Customs were negligible. He could be anywhere.

But he knew her mother. There was no other reason for him to pass over the other bodies that had come through the funeral home and then run off with hers. Specifically hers. So the odds were good he had his base in the area.

That took care of who and where. Or, at least, that assembled as much information as they had.

Vicki dug her fingers into the back of her neck, trying to ease the knots of tension that tied her shoulders into solid blocks, then bent over the coffee table again, ignoring the knowledge that she'd be more comfortable in the kitchen. Stacking her notes on Tom Chen neatly to one side, she spread the contents of Dr. Friedman's file over the table. *Who* and *where* and *when* and even *how;* she had notes on all of these, a sheet of paper for each with the heading written in black marker at the top of the page.

Only *why* remained blank. Why steal a body? Why steal her mother's body?

Why didn't she tell me she was so sick?

Why didn't I answer the phone?

Why didn't I call her?

Why wasn't I there when she needed me?

The pencil snapped between her fingers and the sound drove Vicki back against the sofa cushions, heart pounding. Those questions weren't part of the investigation. Those questions were for later, for *after* she'd gotten her mother back. Left hand pressed against the bridge of her glasses, Vicki fought for control. Her mother needed her to be strong.

All at once, the lingering smell of her mother's perfume, cosmetics, and bath soap coated nose and throat with a patina of the past. Her right fist dug into her stomach, denying the sudden nausea. The ambient noise of the apartment moved to the foreground. The refrigerator motor gained the volume of a helicopter taking off and a dripping tap in the bathroom echoed against the porcelain. An occasional car sped by on the street outside and something moved in the gravel parking lot.

Gradually, the other sounds faded back into the distance, but the footsteps dragging across the loose stones continued. Vicki frowned, grateful for the distraction.

It could be Celluci returning from the fish and chip store across the street, his footsteps hesitant because . . . well, because both he and Henry had been hesitant around her since they'd arrived. It wasn't that she didn't appreciate their help, because she did, but she wished they'd get it through their mutually thick heads that she could take care of herself.

Something brushed against the living room window.

Vicki straightened. The large ground level windows of the basement apartment had always been a tempting target for neighborhood kids and over the years had been decorated with soap, paint, eggs, lipstick, and, once, with Smurf stickers. Standing, she walked over and flicked on the floor lamp with its three, hundred-watt bulbs. With luck, enough of the brilliant white light illuminating the living room would spill out into the night and she'd actually be able to see the little vandals before they ran.

She paused at the window, one hand holding the edge of the curtain, the other the cords of the Venetian blind that ran behind. This close, she could hear that something was definitely rubbing against the other side of the glass. With one smooth, practiced motion, she threw the curtain aside and yanked the length of the blind up against its top support.

Pressed up against the glass, fingers splayed, mouth silently working, was her mother. Two pairs of eyes, an identical shade of gray, widened in simultaneous recognition.

Then the world slid sideways for a second.

My mother is dead.

Fragmented memory fought to become whole. Desperately, she grabbed at the pieces.

This is my . . .

This is my . . .

She couldn't find it, couldn't hold it.

A teenager, legs pumping, a ribbon breaking across her chest. A tall, young woman standing proudly in a blue uniform. A tiny pink mouth opening in what was surely the first yawn in creation. A child, suddenly grown serious, small arms reaching out to hold her while she cried. A voice saying, "Don't worry, Mother."

Mother.

This is my daughter. My child.

She knew now what it was she had to do.

The window was empty. No one moved in the parking lot as far as the spill of light and Vicki's vision went.

My mother is dead.

Around the corner, out of sight on the gravel path that lead to the entrance of the building, the same faltering footsteps sounded.

Vicki whirled and ran for the apartment door.

She'd turned the lock behind Celluci, a habit ingrained after years spent in a larger, more violent city. Now, as trembling fingers twisted the mechanism, the lock jammed.

"GODDAMNED FUCKING SON OF A BITCH!"

She couldn't hear the footsteps any longer. Couldn't hear anything but the blood roaring in her ears.

She'll be on the step now . . . The metal pushed bruises

into her hands. . . . *opening the outer door* . . . Had the
security door been locked when Celluci left? Vicki couldn't
remember. *If she can't get in, she'll go away.* The whole
door shuddered as she slammed the lock with her fists.
Don't go away! Through fingers white with strain, she felt
something give.

Don't go away again. . . .

The hall was empty.

The security door open.

Over the scream of denial that slammed echoes up
against the sides of her skull though no sound passed teeth
ground tight together, Vicki heard a car door slam. Then
tires retreating across gravel.

Adrenaline catapulted her up the half flight of stairs and
flung her out into the night.

"That was close, Cathy, too close. She was inside the
building!"

"Is she all right?"

"What do you mean, is she all right? Don't you mean,
did anyone see you?"

"No." Catherine shook her head, the flying ends of hair
gleaming ivory under the passing street lights. "The repairs
we did aren't designed for so much activity. If any of those
motors have burned out . . ."

Donald finished strapping the weakly struggling body in
and made his way to the front of the van. "Well, everything
seems to be working," he sighed, settling into his seat. "But
it sure didn't want to come with me."

"Of course not, you interrupted the pattern."

"What pattern?"

"The body was responding to leaving the Life Sciences
building by retracing a path followed for years."

"Yeah? I thought it was going home."

"Her home is with us now."

Donald shot an anxious glance over his shoulder into the
back of the van. Number nine lay passively by, but number
ten continued to push against the restraints. It had followed
on his command, but he'd be willing to bet his chances for
a Nobel Prize that it hadn't wanted to.

"Lie still," he snapped, and was only mildly relieved
when it followed the programming.

*   *   *

Mike Celluci stepped out of the tiny fish and chip shop, inhaling the smell of french fries and greasy halibut overlaid on a warm spring night. Just at that particular moment, things didn't look so bad. While finding Marjory Nelson's body as soon as possible would be best for all concerned, Vicki was an intelligent adult, well acquainted with the harsh reality that some cases never got solved. Eventually, she'd accept that her mother was gone, accept that her mother was dead, and they could return to solving the problem all of this had interrupted.

He'd be there to comfort her, she'd realize Fitzroy had nothing to offer, and the two of them would settle down. Maybe even have a kid. *No.* The vision of Vicki in a maternal role, brought revision. *Maybe not a kid.*

He paused at the curb while a panel van pulled out of the apartment building's driveway, turning south toward the center of the city. A moment later, the food lay forgotten in the gutter as he sprinted forward to catch hold of the wild-eyed figure charging out onto the road.

"Vicki! What is it? What's happened?"

She twisted in his grip, straining to follow the van. "My mother . . ." Then the taillights disappeared and she sagged against him. "Mike, my mother . . ."

Gently, he turned her around, barely suppressing an exclamation of shock at her expression. She looked as though someone had ripped her heart out. "Vicki, what about your mother?"

She swallowed. "My mother was at the living room window. Looking in at me. The lock stuck, and when I got outside she was gone. She went away in that van. It's the only place she could have gone. Mike, we have to go after that van."

Cold fingers danced down Celluci's spine. Crazy words tucked in between shallow gasps for breath, but she sounded like she believed them. Moving slowly, he steered her back toward the apartment. "Vicki." His voice emerged tight and strained, her name barely recognizable, so he started again. "Vicki, your mother is dead."

She yanked herself free of his hands. "I know that!" she snarled. "Do you think I don't know that? So was the woman at the window!"

*   *   *

"Look, I only left her alone for a few minutes." Even as he spoke, Celluci heard the words echoed by a thousand voices who'd returned to find disaster had visited during those *few minutes* they were gone. "How was I supposed to know she was so close to cracking? She's never cracked before." He leaned his forearm against the wall and his face against the cushion of his arm. After that single outburst, Vicki had begun to shake, but she wouldn't let him touch her. She just sat in her mother's rocking chair and rocked and stared at the window. Years of training, of dealing with similar situations, seemed suddenly useless. If Mr. Delgado hadn't shown up, hadn't cajoled her into swallowing those sleeping pills—"And how can you be strong tomorrow if you don't sleep tonight, eh?"—he didn't know what he would have done; shaken her probably, yelled certainly, definitely not done any good.

Henry rose from his crouch by the window. There was no mistaking the odor that clung to the outside of the glass. "She didn't crack," he said quietly. "At least not the way you think."

"What are you talking about?" Celluci didn't bother to turn his head. "She's having hallucinations, for chrissakes."

"No. I'm afraid she isn't. And it seems I owe you an apology, Detective."

Celluci snorted but the certainty in Henry's voice made him straighten. "Apology? What for?"

"For accusing you of watching too many bad movies."

"I don't need another mystery tonight, Fitzroy. What the hell are you talking about?"

"I'm talking about," Henry stepped away from the window, his expression unreadable, "the return of Dr. Frankenstein."

"Don't bullshit me, Fitzroy. I'm not in the . . . Jesus H. Christ, you're not kidding, are you?"

He shook his head. "No. I'm not kidding."

Impossible not to believe him. *Werewolves, mummies, vampires; I should've expected this.* "Mother of God. What are we going to tell Vicki?"

Hazel eyes met brown, for once without a power struggle between them. "I haven't the faintest idea."

Seven

"I think we should tell her."

Arms crossed over his chest, Henry leaned against the wall near the windows. "Tell her that we think someone has turned her mother into Frankenstein's monster?"

"Yeah. Tell her exactly that." Celluci rubbed at his temples with the heels of his hands. It had been a very long night and he wasn't looking forward to morning. "Do you remember that little *incident* last fall?"

Henry's brows rose. There could be little doubt what the detective was referring to, although he'd hardly describe the destruction of an ancient Egyptian wizard as an *incident*. "If you're speaking of Anwar Tawfik, I remember."

"Well, I was thinking of something Vicki said, after it was all over, about there being a dark god out there who knows us and that if we give in to hopelessness and despair it'll be on us like a politician at a free bar." He sighed, a long, shuddering exhalation, and was almost too tired to breathe in again. "If it hasn't noticed her yet, it'll be on her soon. She's on the edge."

"Vicki?"

"You didn't see her."

Henry had difficulty believing Vicki would ever give in to anything, least of all to hopelessness and despair, but he recognized that under the present circumstances even the strongest character might succumb. "And you think that if we tell her what we suspect? . . ."

"She'll be furious and there's nothing that wipes out hopelessness and despair faster than righteous anger."

Henry thought about it, arms crossed, shoulder blades pressed against the wall. Tawfik's dark god continued to exist because the emotions it fed on were part of the human condition, but the three of them—he, Celluci, and Vicki— knew its name. If it wanted acolytes, and what god didn't, it would have to go to one of them. If Celluci was right about Vicki—and Henry had to admit that the years the mortal had known her should make him a fair judge— giving her anger as a protection would be the best thing they could do. There was also one other factor that shouldn't be ignored. "She'd never forgive us if we didn't tell her."

Celluci nodded, lips pursed. "There is that."

Silence reigned for a moment as they considered the result of having Vicki's fury directed at them. Neither figured their odds of survival would be particularly high, at least not as far as maintaining a continuing relationship went. Henry spoke first. "So, we'll tell her."

"Tell her what?" Vicki stood in the entrance to the living room, clothing creased, eyes shadowed, cheek imprinted with a fold from the pillowcase. Stepping forward carefully, she swayed and grabbed for the back of a chair, bracing herself against its support. She felt distant from her own body, an effect of the sleeping pills she'd barely managed to fight off. "Tell her that she's out of her mind? That she couldn't have seen her dead mother at the window?" Her voice rode crazy highs and lows; she couldn't seem to keep it steady.

"Actually, Vicki, we believe you." Henry's tone left no room for doubt.

Taken by surprise, Vicki blinked then tried to focus a scowl on Celluci. "You *both* believe me?"

"Yes." He met her scowl with one of his own. "We *both* believe you."

Celluci flinched as the Royal Dalton figurine hit the far wall of the living room and smashed into a thousand expensive bone china shards. Henry moved a little farther away from the blast radius.

"Goddamn, fucking, shit-eating bastards!" The rage that turned her vision red and roared in her ears, stuck in Vicki's throat, blocking the stream of profanity. She scooped up another ornament and heaved it as hard as she could across the room. As it shattered, she found her voice again. "How DARE they!"

Breathing heavily, she collapsed back onto the couch, teeth clenched against waves of nausea, her body's reaction to the news. "How can someone do that to another human being?"

"Science . . ." Celluci began, but Vicki cut him off—which was probably for the best as he wasn't entirely certain what he was going to say.

"This isn't science, Mike. This is my *mother.*"

"Not your mother, Vicki," Henry told her softly. "Just your mother's body."

"Just my mother's body?" Vicki shoved at her glasses with her fist so they wouldn't see her fingers tremble. "I might not have been the world's best daughter, but I know my own mother, and I'm telling you that was my *mother* at the window. Not just her fucking body!"

Celluci sat down beside her on the couch and caught up one of her hands in both of his. He considered and discarded four or five comforting platitudes that didn't really seem to have any relevance and wisely decided to keep his mouth shut.

Vicki tried halfheartedly to pull her hand away, but when his fingers only tightened in response, she let it lie, saving her strength to throw into the anger. "I *saw* her. She was dead. I *know* dead. Then I saw her again at the window. And she was . . ." Again, a wave of nausea rose and crested and sullenly retreated. "She was *not dead.*"

"But not alive." As the words themselves denied consolation, Henry offered them as they were, unadorned by emotion.

Once again, her mother's face rose up out of the darkness, eyes wide, mouth working silently. Celluci's grip became a warm anchor and Vicki used it to drag herself out of the memory. "No." She swallowed and a muscle jumped in her jaw. "Not alive. But up, and walking." For a moment, the thought that there'd been only a pane of glass between them, made it impossible to go on. *I want to scream and cry until all of this goes away and I don't have to deal with it. I want it to be last Saturday. I want to have answered the phone. I want to have talked to her, to have told her I love her, to have said good-bye.* Her whole body ached with the effort of maintaining control but of all the maelstrom barely held in check by will, she could only release the anger. "Someone did that to her. Someone at that university has committed the ultimate violation, the ultimate rape."

Celluci flinched. "At the university? Why at the university?"

"You said it yourself, science. It's hardly going to be someone at the fucking grocery store." She knuckled her glasses again, then bent forward and swept her notes off the coffee table, the force of the blow scattering them as far as the apartment door. Her voice, in contrast, had gained rigid control. "This changes everything. We can find her now."

Reluctantly, Celluci released her hand; she'd accepted all the comfort she was going to. He watched in silence as she pulled a blank sheet of paper toward her, wanting to shake her but not entirely certain why.

"All right. We know the body is still in the city, so we know where to look for the lowlife, sons of bitches who've done this to her." The pencil point snapped off against the paper, and she fought against the urge to drive it right through the table. "She's in the city. They're in the city."

"Vicki." Henry crossed the room to kneel by her side. "Are you sure you should be doing this now?" When she raised her head to look at him, the hair on his arms lifted with the tension in the air.

"What am I supposed to do? Go to sleep?"

He could hear her heart pounding, hear the effects of the adrenaline pumping through her system. "No . . ."

"I need to do this, Henry. I need to put things together. Build some sort of a structure out of this. I need to do it now." The alternative was implicit in her tone. *Or it will eat away at me until there's nothing of me left.*

The hand that settled on his, just for an instant, was so hot it nearly burned. Because he could do nothing else, Henry nodded and moved to the rocker by the door, from which he could watch her face. For the moment, he would let her deal with her horror and her anger in her own way.

He found it interesting that Celluci looked no happier about it than he felt. *We want to ride to her rescue and instead we find ourselves* allowed *to help. Not exactly a comfortable position for a knight errant to be in.* But then, Vicki wasn't exactly a comfortable woman to love.

"All right, shifting the emphasis from finding my mother's body to finding the people who did this to her, what are we looking for?" With a new pencil, she etched "What?" across the top piece of paper. "Someone who can raise the dead. Discounting the Second Coming, as I doubt it was as simple as *pick up your bed and walk,* we turn to science." She wrote "A scientist" under the heading, then shuffled out a fresh page and wrote "Where?"

Celluci leaned forward, old patterns winning out over his concern. "All signs point to the university. One, it's where you find scientists. Two, who can afford a private lab these days, especially containing the equipment they'd have needed to . . ."

"Three," Vicki interrupted. The last thing she wanted to deal with right now were the details of what had actually been done.

"Not the last thing," said a little voice in the back of her head.

"Three," she said again, slamming it over the certain knowledge that somehow, if she'd just answered the phone, all of this could have been prevented. "We've already determined it had to be someone who knew she was going to die. She worked at the university. Her friends were at the university. She had tests done at the university. Four, the campus is less than ten blocks south on Division Street. We're close." Her laugh held more hysteria than humor. "Even a dead woman could walk it."

"And five," Henry added softly, while Vicki fought to bridle her reactions again and Celluci's arm hovered helpless behind her back, certain that she'd refuse sympathy, unable not to offer it. "There is another, and it was *on* the campus tonight."

Vicki's chin came up, Henry's reminder that it wasn't strictly personal helping her to regain a little distance. Celluci's arm dropped back to his side. She wrote down his words verbatim, took another sheet, wrote "Why?" and had to fight for distance again. "At least we know what they wanted the body for. But why *my* mother? What was so special about her?"

"They knew she was going to die." Celluci couldn't find a way to finish the thought that wouldn't rub salt in emotions already raw and bleeding, so he drew in a fortifying breath and said instead, "Vicki, why don't you let me deal with this?"

"While I do what? Pour ashes on my head? Fuck you, Celluci. They knew she was going to die and they needed a fresh body. There. It's been said. Now let's go on."

His own nerves rubbed raw, Celluci shot a glance across the room at someone who might understand. *I didn't want to hurt her!*

I know. Henry's gaze flicked to Celluci's left and back, adding as clearly as if he'd spoken aloud, *And she knows.*

"There wasn't an autopsy done." Vicki's pencil began to move again. "I expect that if you're going to get the body up and around, that's important. With a diagnosis of death in six months from heart failure, there'd be no need to do an autopsy when my mother had her heart attack. I wonder." She looked up and frowned. "Did they wait around for this other guy to die as well? We can check personnel, find out who else died recently, see if there's a connection to my mother, and trace it back."

With one hand she fanned the three sheets of paper. The other bounced the eraser end of the pencil on the tabletop. "Okay. That's what, where, why . . ." The pencil stilled. "I don't think we need to worry about *how*."

A body stretched out on a slab, its grotesque shadow thrown upon a rough, rock wall. In the background, strange equipment. In the corners, darkness, broken by the faint gray tracery of a spider's web. Up above, a Gothic dome open to the night. Thunder cracks and lightning arcs down from the heavens. And Death is pushed aside.

"Vicki?"

"What!" She whirled on Celluci, eyes wide.

"Nothing." Now that he had her attention, he wasn't sure what to do with it. "You just looked a little . . ." *haunted.* He closed his teeth on the last word.

"Tired." Henry stepped smoothly into the pause. "Don't you think you should get some sleep?"

"No. We're not done. I'm not going to sleep until we're done." She knew she sounded a bit frantic, but she'd gone past the point where she cared. "So, what do we have for *who*. A scientist, or a group of scientists, at the university, who knew my mother was going to die, who has the knowledge to raise the dead and the arrogance to use that knowledge."

"Most criminals are arrogant." Celluci sagged back against the sofa cushions. "It's what makes them criminals. They think society's laws don't apply to them."

Vicki shoved at her glasses. "Very profound, Detective, but this is hardly like ripping off a corner store for beer money. We need a motive."

"If you had the ability to raise the dead, wouldn't that be motive enough?" Henry asked, his eyes suddenly very dark. "They're doing this because they *can* do it. They probably don't even see it as a crime—this godlike ability puts them above such petty concerns."

"Well," Celluci snorted, "you should know."

"Yes."

The single syllable lifted the hair on the back of Celluci's neck and he realized, belatedly, that no one understood the abuse of power quite so well as those who shared the potential.

Vicki ignored them both, shuffling her notes into a tidy pile, her movements jerky. "So we're looking at the university for an arrogant scientist with a medical background who knew my mother was about to die. That'll be like finding the needle in the proverbial haystack."

Celluci fought his attention free of Henry Fitzroy and back to the matter at hand. "What about your mother's boss?"

"Dr. Burke? I don't think so. My mother said she was the most gifted administrator she'd ever worked for, and that doesn't leave a lot of time to put into raising the dead."

"So? If she signed the death certificate she must be a medical doctor, whatever else she is. She knew your mother was going to die and, as department head, she's sure as shit in a position to acquire equipment for a secret lab." He shoved both hands up through his hair and tried to force his tired brain to function for just a while longer. "She's a place to start."

"I have an appointment to see her in the morning. I'll see what I can find out." Her tone made it clear she didn't expect to discover much.

"*We'll* see what *we* can find out."

"No, Mike." She shook her head, and wished she hadn't as the room spun. "I want you to tie up a few loose ends with Mr. Chen."

"Vicki, Tom Chen is a dead end."

She swiveled around to face him, bracing herself against the back of the couch. "He still may be the only end we've got. I don't need you with me, Mike."

"You shouldn't be doing this alone."

"I'm not. Unless you want to go home."

He looked across the room at Henry. Who was no help. "Of *course* I'm not going home," he snarled. Surrender might be his only option, but nothing said he had to do it graciously. "So what do we do now?"

To his surprise, it was Henry who answered. "We sleep. I have no choice. It's very nearly dawn. I can feel the sun. You, Detective, have been up all night. And, Vicki, I can smell the drugs in your system—you need to sleep to clear the clouding from your mind."

"No, I . . ."

Henry cut her off with the lifting of an imperious brow. "A few hours will make no difference to your mother and a great deal to you." Crossing the room, he extended a hand. "I can make you forget for a time, if you like."

"I don't want to forget, thank you." But she took his hand and pulled herself to her feet, a piece of broken china shattering further under the sole of her shoe. His fingers were as cool as Celluci's had been warm. An anchor of a different sort. "And, in spite of what *both* of you think, I'm fully aware that self-abuse will contribute nothing at all toward finding the shit eaters who did this. I will sleep. I will eat. And then . . ." Anger and exhaustion, equally applied, destroyed the rest of the thought before she had it barely formed. She gripped Henry's arm and stared intently into his face. "I won't be able to wait for you. Sunset's just too damned far away."

He touched her cheek with his free hand and repeated, "Too damned far away. I couldn't have said it better, myself. But be careful while I'm not with you." His gaze lifted over her shoulder to meet Celluci's. "*Both* of you be careful."

Donald secured the slide, stared down at the spread of purple stain for a moment, sighed, and turned. "Cathy, I don't like what we're getting into here."

"Trouble with number eight?" Catherine glanced up from her dissection, brow furrowed, hands buried under one of number eight's decomposing organs.

"Number eight's past the point where it can give us any trouble," Donald snorted. "I'm more concerned with the dynamic duo over there."

Puzzled, Catherine peered over her mask at the two working isolation boxes. "I'm sure all the damage they took last night was superficial. You stitched number nine's lacerations closed. We both checked for mechanical overload. I adjusted their nutrient levels to compensate for the strain on the bacterial restructuring . . ."

"That's not what I meant." He ripped the paper off a candy, balled it up, and threw it in the general direction of a waste basket. "Don't you think those two have gone just a tad outside the parameters of the experiment?"

"Of course not." Catherine set a kidney down on a sterilized tray. "We're going to need tissue samples from the others for comparison."

"Yeah, yeah, I know. I'll break out the biopsy needle in a minute, but first we're going to have a chat about last night's little walkabout. *It* had nothing to do with Organ Regeneration through Tailored Bacteria or even Reanimation of the Human Body by Tailored Bacteria and Servomotors."

"What are you talking about? If last night wasn't animation I don't know what is; you want them any more animated, you'll have to call in Disney."

"Was that a joke?" Donald demanded. "Because if it was, it wasn't very funny. She—" he pointed at Marjory Nelson's box— "wasn't supposed to go home and he . . . well, he wasn't supposed to go anywhere."

Catherine shrugged, her hands once again buried to the wrist. "Obviously, feeding her own brain wave patterns through the neural net stimulated buried memories. Considering that when she was alive she walked home from the

Life Sciences building every night for years, it was only logical that she follow that programming. We should've anticipated it happening and taken precautions." Her voice dropped into a fair approximation of Dr. Burke's lecturing cadence. "The more impulses are sent along a given memory trace, the easier it becomes for later impulses to follow the same circuit. *And* considering the pains we've taken to teach number nine to follow us, I should think you'd be pleased that he followed her. After all, you're the one who said he wasn't learning anything."

"Yeah, well, I'm also the one who says he doesn't like this." He bit down hard on the candy in his mouth and it crunched between his teeth. "I mean, suppose we're not just re-creating physical responses."

Catherine laid the second kidney beside the first. "I don't know what you're talking about."

"I'm talking about souls, Cathy!" His tone grew a little shrill. "What if, because of what we've done, Marjory Nelson has come back to her body?"

"Don't be ridiculous. We're not bringing back an old life, we're creating new ones, like—putting new wine in old skins."

"You're not supposed to do that," Donald pointed out acerbically. "The old wine taints the new." He swiveled around on his stool and bent over the microscope. He could see there was no point in discussing this; souls had no place in Cathy's world. And maybe she was right. She was the certified genius, after all, and it was her experiment. He was just in it for curiosity's sake—and for the final payoff, of course.

Still, he mused, the edge of his lower lip caught between his teeth, uncomfortably conscious of the questions that lay in the isolation boxes behind him, *I'd be happier if I knew we were remaking* Frankenstein *instead of* Night of the Living Dead. A moment's reflection reminded him that Frankenstein had not exactly had a happy ending. *Or a happy middle, for that matter.*

He could hear voices. Her voice and *his* voice. He couldn't hear what they were saying, but he could hear the tone.

They were arguing.

He remember arguing. How it ended in hitting. And pain.

He often argued with her.

Number nine didn't . . .

. . . didn't . . .

. . . didn't like that.

"Good morning, Dr. Burke. The coffee's ready."

"Good." Dr. Burke dropped her briefcase at the door to the inner office and circled back to the coffeepot. "You are a lifesaver, Mrs. Shaw."

"It's probably not as good as when Marjory made it," Mrs. Shaw sighed. "She always had such a way with coffee."

Her back to the room, Dr. Burke rolled her eyes and wondered how long the melodrama of office grieving would continue. Two days of every report, every memo, every little thing delivered with a eulogy was about as much as she could take. She lifted her mug off its hook and dropped three heaping spoonfuls of sugar into the bottom of it. If the university would just come through with the promised temporary—or better still, a permanent replacement for Marjory Nelson's position—she'd tell Mrs. Shaw to take a few days off. *Unfortunately,* Dr. Burke topped up her mug and glared down into the dark liquid, *the wheels of academia grind geologically slow.*

Behind her, Mrs. Shaw turned on the radio. The Village People were just finishing up the last bars of "YMCA."

Dr. Burke turned and transferred her glare to the radio. "If they're doing another '70s retrospective, we're changing stations. I lived through disco once, I shouldn't have to do it again."

"This is CKVS FM, it's nine o'clock, and now the news. Police still have no leads in the vicious murder last night of a QECVI student on the Queen's University campus. The only witness to the crime is under observation at Kingston General Hospital and has not yet been able to give police an accurate description of the murderer. While the young woman was not physically hurt in the incident, doctors say she is suffering from shock. Both police and medical personnel report that until she was sedated she continued to scream, 'He looked dead. The guy looked dead.' Anyone with information concerning this tragic incident is asked to contact Detective Fergusson at Police Headquarters.

"Elsewhere in the city . . ."

"Isn't it awful." Mrs. Shaw dabbed at her eyes with the back of her hand. "That poor young man, cut down in his prime."

The guy looked dead. Dr. Burke's fingers tightened around the handle of her mug. *The girl obviously has an overactive imagination. This has nothing to do with . . .*

"The other stations had a much more complete report. She said that he lurched when he walked, that his skin was gray and cold, and that his expression never changed even while he was strangling her boyfriend. Terrifying. Just terrifying."

It was impossible. "Did she say what he was wearing."

"Some kind of athletic clothing. A tracksuit I think. Dr. Burke? Where are you going?"

Where was she going? She stared down at her coffee, then set the mug firmly down on the filing cabinet, the fingers of her other hand already taking a white-knuckled grip on the door handle. Thank God no one around the office *expected* her to smile. "I just remembered, I had a grad student running a program last night and I promised I'd check it this morning. Don't know why I bothered, he keeps getting it wrong."

Mrs. Shaw smiled and shook her head. "You bothered because you always hope they'll get it right. Oh, my." The smile disappeared. "Marjory's daughter will be coming by this morning."

Marjory Nelson's daughter, the ex-detective, the private investigator, was the last person she wanted to talk to right now. "Give her my apologies and . . . No. If she comes while I'm gone, ask her to wait. I'll be back as soon as I can." Better to know the direction Ms. Nelson was heading in the search for her mother's body. Information was knowledge; ignorance, a potential for disaster.

"There was a young man killed on campus last night. Do either of you know anything about it?"

Donald spun around so fast he nearly threw himself off the stool. "Dr. Burke! You startled me!"

She took another step into the lab, a muscle jumping in

her jaw and her eyes narrow behind her glasses. "Just answer the question."

"The question?" He frowned, heart still racing, and sorted the words out of the fear. *There was a young man killed last night.* "Oh, fuck." In his memory, number nine staggered out into the light while screams sounded behind a building. "What, what makes you think we'd know anything?"

"Don't bullshit me, Donald." Dr. Burke used the voice that could command attention from the back row of a seven-hundred-and-fifty-seat lecture hall. Donald tried not to cringe. "There was a witness. Her description drew a pretty accurate picture of number nine, and what I want to know"—her palm slapped down on the table, the crack of flesh against metal echoing like a gunshot—"is what the hell was going on down here."

"He didn't do it on purpose." Catherine rose gracefully from behind number nine's isolation box and stood, both hands resting lightly on the curved lid.

"I was wondering where you were." Dr. Burke turned, nostrils flaring, the younger woman's calm acting as a further goad. Her gesture toward the box had a cutting edge. "As it has no purpose, being dead, it needs no defense. The two of you, however, have no such excuse. So let's *begin* with an explanation of why the experiments were taken from the lab."

"Uh, they weren't." Donald cleared his throat as she directed her basilisk gaze back at him but continued. He had no intention of being blamed for something that wasn't his fault. "They left on their own."

"They left on their own?" Her quiet repetition was less than reassuring. "They just decided to get up and go out on an evening constitutional, did they?" A sudden rise in volume slapped her words against the walls. "What kind of an idiot do you take me for?"

"He's right." Catherine raised her chin. "We locked the door behind us. When we came back, the door was unlocked, from the inside, and they were gone. We found number nine wandering on campus." Her fingers stroked the box comfortingly. "We found number ten just outside the apartment building she lived in when she was Marjory Nelson."

"She went home," Donald added.

Catherine sighed. "She merely followed old programming."

"You didn't see her face, Cathy."

"I didn't need to. I *know* the parameters of the experiment."

"Well, maybe they've changed!"

· "Shut up, both of you." *Gray eyes suddenly snapped open, widening with an instant of recognition.* Dr. Burke closed her own eyes for a moment and when she opened them again, muttered. "Maybe this has gone too far."

Catherine frowned. "What has?"

"All of this."

"But, Dr. Burke, you don't understand. If number nine killed that boy, he acted on his own. It wasn't anything we programmed in. It means he *can* learn. He *is* learning."

"It means he—it—killed someone, Catherine. That boy is dead."

"Well, yes, and that's too bad, but nothing we can do will bring him back." She paused, weighing possibilities, frowned, and shook her head. "No. It's too late." Her eyes refocused. "But we *can* explore and develop this new data. Don't you understand? Number nine must be thinking. His brain is functional again!"

"Cathy!" Donald jumped down off his stool and came over to her, incredulity written across his face. "Don't *you* understand? Some guy is *dead.* This bit of your experiment," he whacked number nine's box, "is a killer and the other is, is . . ." He couldn't find the words. No, that wasn't exactly true. He knew the words. He just couldn't say them. Because if he said them, he might have to believe them. "Dr. Burke, you're right. This has gone too far. We've got to close down and get out of here before the police track number nine back to his lair!"

"Donald, be quiet. You're hysterical. The police do not now believe, nor are they likely to, that a dead man is out roaming around committing homicide."

"But . . ."

Dr. Burke silenced him with a look, her own crisis of conscience pushed aside in the light of new information. She hadn't actually considered the incident from the perspective of experimental results. This could indicate a giant step forward. "If number nine is thinking, Catherine, I *don't* like what it's thinking about."

Two spots of color appeared on Catherine's cheeks. "Well, yes, but he's thinking. Isn't that the important thing?"

"Perhaps," the older woman allowed. "If it is actually thought and not merely reaction to stimuli. We may have to devise a new series of tests."

Donald swallowed and tried again. "But, Dr. Burke, that kid is dead!"

"Your point?"

"We have to do something!"

"What? Give ourselves up?" She caught his gaze with hers and, after a moment, half smiled. "I didn't think so. Terminate the experiment? That wouldn't bring him back to life." She squared her shoulders. "That said, I am very annoyed about your carelessness. You will make certain it doesn't happen again. Remove them from their boxes only when absolutely necessary. Never leave them alone and unconfined. Have you run an EEG on number nine since it happened?"

Catherine's color deepened. "No, Doctor."

"Why not?"

"Number eight died in the night, and we had to begin . . ."

"Number eight has been dead for some time, Catherine, and isn't going anywhere. Run the EEG now. If there's a brain wave pattern in there, I want it recorded."

"Yes, Doctor."

"And for heaven's sake, keep them under control. I will not have my career destroyed by premature discovery. If anything like this happens again, I will not hesitate to pull the plug. Do you understand?"

"Yes, Doctor."

"Donald?"

He nodded toward the second box. "What about her? What if . . . what if . . ."

What if we've trapped Marjory Nelson's soul? She read the words off his face. Heard them whispered in the silence. And refused to share his fear. "We're here to answer *what ifs,* Donald; that's what scientists do. And now," Dr. Burke glanced at her watch. "I have an appointment with Marjory

Nelson's daughter." She paused at the door and turned to face the lab again. "Remember. Anything else goes wrong and we're cutting our losses."

As her footsteps faded down the corridor, Donald drew a long and shaky breath. Things were getting just a little too deep for him. Maybe it was time he started thinking about cutting his own losses. "Can you believe that, Cathy? Some guy gets offed and she's *annoyed*."

Catherine ignored him, her full attention on the muffled pounding coming from the box in front of her. She didn't like the way things were going. Surely Dr. Burke realized the importance of number nine acquiring independence and how vital it was to protect the integrity of the experiment. What did careers have to do with that? No, she didn't like the way things were going at all. But all she said was, "He doesn't like being confined."

Daughter.

The word filtered through the hum of machinery and the sound-deadening properties of the box itself. She used it to pick an end of thread from the tangled mass of memory.

She had a daughter.

There was something she had to do.

Eight

Unable to remain still, Vicki paced the outer office, uncomfortably conscious of Mrs. Shaw's damp and sympathetic gaze following her every move. She didn't need sympathy, she needed information.

All right, so she hadn't reacted particularly well to being presented with a box of her mother's personal effects, but that was no reason for Mrs. Shaw to assume anything. If the last notation in the date book hadn't been, *Call Vicki,* she would've been fine.

"Would you like a cup of coffee, dear?"

"No. Thank you." Actually, she'd love a cup of coffee, but she couldn't face using her mother's mug. "Will Dr. Burke be long?"

"I don't think so. She just had to check on one of her grad students."

"Students? What does she teach?"

"Oh, she doesn't actually teach, she just takes a few of the grad students under her wing and helps them along."

"Medical students?"

"I'm not sure." Mrs. Shaw reached for a fresh tissue and dabbed at her eyes. "Your mother would know. She was Dr. Burke's *personal* secretary."

My mother isn't here. Vicki tried not to let the thought show on her face, given that the accompanying emotion was annoyance, not grief.

"Your mother really respected Dr. Burke," Mrs. Shaw continued with a wistful glance across the room at the empty desk.

"She sounds like a person worth respecting," Vicki broke

in before a flood of teary memories began. "She's got, what, two degrees?"

"Three. An MD, a doctorate in organic chemistry, and an MBA. Your mother always said hiring her to run this department was the smartest thing the university ever did. Most academics are not particularly good administrators and most administrators are completely insensitive to the needs of academia. Your mother called Dr. Burke a bridge between two worlds."

Why the hell does it have to keep coming back to my mother? Vicki wondered, as Mrs. Shaw fielded three phone calls in quick succession.

"Yes, Professor Irving, I'll see that she gets the message as soon as she comes in." Mrs. Shaw dropped the receiver back into the cradle and sighed. "That's how it goes all day. They *all* want a piece of her."

"I guess she doesn't have much time for lab work."

"Lab work? She barely has time to grab a bite to eat before someone needs her again." Patting the pile of memos, already impressive before the addition of the latest three, Mrs. Shaw's voice grew sharp. "They've got her running from meeting to meeting, solving this problem, solving that problem, burying her under forms and surveys and reports, annual this and semiannual that and biweekly the other . . .

"And God only knows how I'm going to dig myself out without your mother's help."

Mrs. Shaw colored and Vicki turned to face the door.

"Sorry to keep you waiting, Ms. Nelson." Dr. Burke crossed the room and held out a hand for her memos. "But as you've already heard, I'm quite busy."

"No problem at all, Doctor." Something about that sturdy figure in the starched white lab coat had a calming effect, and Vicki followed her gesture into the inner office feeling more under control than she had in days. She suddenly remembered her mother describing her new boss—just after Dr. Burke had taken over the department—as being so completely self-assured that the urge to question anything became lost in her vicinity. Vicki'd laughed at the time, but now she thought she could see what her mother had meant. She'd felt a bit of the effect herself, earlier in the week. It had been Dr. Burke who'd grounded her and sent her to the hospital morgue and Dr. Burke she'd turned to for a eulogy.

Before they'd discovered a eulogy would be unnecessary.

As Vicki settled into one of the almost comfortable wood and leather chairs, Dr. Burke moved around behind the desk and sat down, dropping the dozen or so pink squares of paper into a tidy pile. "I'm not usually in quite this much demand," she explained, shooting an annoyed glare at the pile. "But it's end of term and bureaucratic nonsense that could have been taken care of months ago has to be dealt with immediately."

"You can't delegate?"

"Science and Administration speak two different languages, Ms. Nelson. If I delegate, I end up having to translate. Frankly, it's much easier just to do it myself."

Vicki recognized the tone; she'd used it herself once or twice. "I imagine you'd rather be, oh, fiddling about with test tubes or something?"

"Not at all." Dr. Burke smiled, and there was no mistaking the sincerity behind her words. "I very much enjoy running other people's lives, seeing that each cog in a very complicated machine continues to run in its appointed place." It might have been more accurate to say, *in the place I appoint,* but Dr. Burke had no intention of allowing that much insight into her character. *Now that we have established I enjoy my job, shall we get on with the investigation, Ms. Nelson?* "Mrs. Shaw tells me you want to ask about the tests I ran on your mother."

"That's right." An early call to Dr. Friedman had determined that her mother's doctor had known about the tests, so they probably had nothing to do with . . . with the end result. But they were a place to start. Vicki pulled a pad of paper and a pen from the depths of her shoulder bag. "I assume they had to do with her heart condition?"

"Yes. Although I haven't practiced medicine for some time, I am a medical doctor and your mother, understandably upset, wanted a second opinion."

"And you told her?"

"That she had perhaps six months to live without corrective surgery. Pretty much exactly what her own doctor told her."

"Why didn't she go in for the surgery?"

"It's not that easy," Dr. Burke said, leaning back in her chair and lacing her fingers across her stomach. "There are always waiting lists for major surgery, especially transplants, which is what your mother would have needed, and with budget cuts . . ."

Vicki's pen gouged through the paper and her voice emerged through clenched teeth. "So Dr. Friedman said." *My mother could've died from god-damned fucking budget cuts.* "I'd like to see copies."

"Of the tests? I didn't keep any. I gave copies to your mother, who, I assume, gave them to her doctor, but I saw no point in keeping a set myself." Dr. Burke frowned. "I did what I could for her. Do you doubt my diagnosis, Ms. Nelson?"

"No. Of course not." *So you were there for her and I wasn't. That's not the issue now.* "Who else knew about the tests?"

"Why?"

The question came as no surprise, and Vicki realized it came primarily in response to her aggressive tone. She'd have asked it herself if someone slammed a question at her with that amount of force. *Brilliant interrogation technique, Nelson. Forgotten everything you ever learned?* Maybe she should've brought Celluci. Maybe she wasn't thinking clearly. *No. I don't need him holding my hand. I've worked through anger before.* She'd been one of the best; top of her class; the fair-haired girl of the Metro Police. She took a deep breath and fought for some semblance of professionalism. "My mother's body is missing, Dr. Burke. I intend to find it and any information you might be able to give me can only help."

Dr. Burke leaned forward, both hands flat on the desk. "You think that the body was taken by someone who knew she was going to die?"

Celluci'd always said she was a lousy liar. Vicki looked Dr. Burke in the eye and decided not to even make the attempt. "Yes. That's exactly what I think."

Dr. Burke held her gaze for a moment, then sat back again. "Besides myself and Dr. Friedman, I can only be certain of Mrs. Shaw, although it's likely Dr. Friedman's nurse knew. I didn't tell anyone, Mrs. Shaw might have, and your mother could have mentioned it to friends, of course."

"She never mentioned it to me," Vicki snarled and then pressed her lips tightly shut, afraid of what else might slip out. She hadn't intended to say that.

"Given that we were using university equipment," Dr. Burke continued, graciously ignoring the outburst, "I can't guarantee that no one else knew about the testing, you understand."

"Yes." A single word seemed safe enough. Pity she had to use more; every syllable carried more heat than the last and there didn't seem to be anything she could do about it. "I need to speak with those members of your department my mother came into frequent contact with."

"That would be all of them," Dr. Burke told her dryly.

"But surely you don't believe that someone in my department is responsible?"

"They do seem to be the first people I should check, don't they?"

Answering a question with a question. Nice try, Ms. Nelson, but I have no intention of surrendering control. "I'd certainly be interested in your reasons for thinking so."

As her reasons for thinking so were based solely on a midnight visit she had no intention of mentioning, Vicki found herself momentarily at a loss. "The members of your department are scientists."

"And why would a scientist take your mother's body?" Dr. Burke kept her expression outwardly neutral while inwardly she kicked Donald's careless butt. She knew Catherine couldn't be counted on to consider the more mundane aspects of the situation, but she'd expected better of him. It was obvious that last night's side trip had been observed. Nothing else but the knowledge that a dead woman was up and walking around could logically account for the sudden obstinate certainty that someone at the university had to be responsible. "It could just as easily," she continued, "have been taken by a spurned lover. Have you looked into that possibility?"

"She had no lover," Vicki ground out, "spurned or otherwise."

Behind a mask of polite apology, Dr. Burke enjoyed the

reaction. Of course she didn't. Mothers never do. Aloud she said, "That brings us back to my scientists, then. Shall I have Mrs. Shaw make some phone calls for you, set up appointments?" It was a large university and there were ways to make it larger still.

"If you would. Thank you." Well aware that Dr. Burke's assistance could cut through the time-consuming tangle of academic red tape, Vicki had been about to ask. That Dr. Burke remained on the list of potential suspects devalued that assistance not at all. The manner of the assistance, could, in fact, be used as further evidence. "I need to talk to the faculty in the school of medicine." She'd start with the obvious. Later, if necessary, she'd widen the circle. If necessary, she'd tear the bloody university apart, limestone block by limestone block.

"I'll do what I can. If I might make a suggestion, your mother was quite friendly with a Dr. Devlin, a cellular biologist." *And talking with that old Irish reprobate should keep you busy sorting fact from fancy for days.* "In fact, he comfortably covers both our theories as I believe he was very fond of her."

"*Both* our theories?"

"The scientist and the spurned lover."

Just for a moment, Vicki wondered if her mother *had* gotten involved with someone who'd refused to surrender to death; wondered if a twisted love had tried to force a return of life and created the travesty of her mother she'd seen at the window. *No. Impossible. Henry said there was another one. And besides, she'd have told me if she'd met someone new.*

The way she told you about her heart condition? asked a small voice.

Dr. Burke watched the emotional storm playing out across her visitor's face and decided the experiment was in no immediate danger. Although last night's unfortunate lapse in security had brought Ms. Nelson closer to the truth, when it came right down to it, close didn't count. *And now I've given her something new to think about. Dr. Devlin should be in for an interesting interview.* When that played out, another wild goose could always be found.

In the meantime, it was obvious to even the most casual

observer—which she most certainly was not—that Marjory Nelson's daughter rode a precarious balance between rigid control and a complete breakdown. An emotional teeter-totter that could only get in the way of an objective investigation and a situation easy to exploit.

"It's amazing," she murmured, almost as though she were speaking to herself, "how much you resemble your mother."

Vicki started. "Me?"

"You're taller, of course, and your mother wore no glasses, but the line of your jaw is identical and your mouth moves very much the way hers did."

Did . . . Her mother's face rose up in memory, a sheet of glass between them, eyes wide, mouth silently working.

"In fact, you have many of the same mannerisms."

Vicki desperately tried to banish the horror her mother had become and replace it with an earlier memory. The sheet lifted, the gray and waxy pallor of death, the chemical smell of the hospital morgue . . . In the memory before that, a phone rang on, unanswered.

"Ms. Nelson? Are you all right?"

"Fine." The word was a warning.

Dr. Burke stood, satisfaction covered with polite regret. "If you have no further questions, I'm afraid I have a list as long as my arm of meetings to attend. I'll have Mrs. Shaw set up those appointments for you."

Vicki shoved her notes into her bag and stood as well, jabbing at her glasses. "Thank you," she said, forcing her mouth to form the conversational phrases. "And thank you for your time this morning." Throwing the bag up onto her shoulder, she headed quickly toward the door. She neither knew nor cared if she'd covered all she'd intended to. She wanted out of that office. Of that building. She wanted to be somewhere where no one knew her mother. Where no one could see reflections of the dead in her face.

"Ms. Nelson? We miss your mother around here." Intended to be a parting dig at damaged defenses, Dr. Burke found to her surprise that she meant what she was saying and instead of twisting the knife, finished simply with, "The office seems empty without her."

Halfway out the door, Vicki turned and acknowledged

the observation with a single nod. She couldn't trust herself to speak and wished, just for that instant, that she'd listened to Celluci and not come here alone.

Dr. Burke spread her hands and her voice picked up the cadence of a benediction. "I guarantee, she didn't suffer at the end."

"No. I'm sorry, Detective, but none of these photographs are of the Tom Chen that we employed."

Celluci pulled the shot of Tom Chen, medical student, out of the pile. "You're sure about this one?"

"Quite. Our Mr. Chen had slightly longer hair, more prominent cheekbones, and a completely different eyebrow line. We reshape a lot of faces in this business, Detective," the younger Mr. Hutchinson continued in response to Celluci's silent question. "We become used to observing dominant characteristics."

"Yeah, I suppose you do." Celluci slid the grainy black and white photographs back into the large manila envelope. Tom Chen, or whatever his name actually was, was not now attending medical school at Queen's, nor had he graduated from the program over the last three years.

Detective Fergusson had been more than willing to call the registrar's office on campus and suggest they release the pictures.

"No problem," the Kingston police officer had declared with complete insincerity. "I'm more than willing to humor ex-Detective Nelson and her wild corpse chase." The distinctive sound of hot coffee being slurped from a cardboard cup echoed over the line. "You catch the news this morning? Half the fucking force goes out with some kind of spring flu and some asshole starts strangling young lovers. We got a hysterical witness—who's seen Michael Jackson's 'Thriller' video one too many times, if you ask me—and no suspects. And I don't need to tell *you* that the fresher the corpse, the higher the priority. If a phone call will keep your girlfriend happy and off my back while I deal with this new situation, it's worth the two minutes it'll take."

Celluci'd been tempted to tell him that the two were connected in one final attempt at enlisting law and order against whatever it was that Vicki and Fitzroy were dispensing but at the last minute decided he'd better not. *Your*

*murderer is a reanimated corpse, Detective. How do I know?
A vampire told me.* Kingston had a large psychiatric facility
and he had no intention of ending up in it.

Meanwhile, the search for Igor moved no further ahead.

"All right, Mr. Hutchinson." Time to try another angle.
"You said that all funeral directors have to serve a four-
week observation period at a funeral home before they're
accepted into a training program."

The younger Mr. Hutchinson leaned back in his chair.
"That's correct."

"Well, where do these observers come from?"

"From the applicants to the program at Humber College
in Toronto."

"So this young man, whoever he was, had to have applied to that program?"

"Oh, yes, *and* gone through an interview. The Health
Sciences people try very hard to weed out unsuitable candi-
dates before they're placed for observation."

Celluci frowned. "So, it was just chance that Ig . . . Tom
Chen, for lack of a better name, ended up here?"

"No, not at all. He asked to come here. Said he'd been
impressed by the way we handled the funeral of his aunt
some years before and wanted to work with us." Mr.
Hutchinson sighed. "All fabricated, I presume, but at the
time we were flattered and agreed to take him on. He was
a very pleasant fellow and everyone liked him."

"Yeah, well everyone makes a bad call now and then."
Celluci finished scrawling a note to call Humber College,
shoved his notebook in his pocket and stood, glad to be
leaving. Funeral homes, with their carpets and flowers and
tastefully arranged furniture, gave him the creeps. "I
wouldn't worry about it. I don't suppose you get much opportunity to practice character assessment."

Mr. Hutchinson rose as well, his expression stony. "Our
services are for the benefit of the living, Detective," he
snapped. "And I assure you, we are quite as capable of
character assessment as, say, the police department. Good
day."

As he had nothing more to ask, Celluci accepted the
dismissal. Once outside, he snorted and headed for the
nearest bus stop—with the suspect's transit habits still their
only concrete clue, he'd left his car at the apartment build-

ing. "Quite as capable of character assessment as the police department," he repeated, digging for change. "Just a little sensitive there, aren't we?" Still, he supposed that funeral directors were as sick of stereotypes as, well, police officers, so the comment hadn't been entirely undeserved.

Swinging up onto the Johnson Street bus, he glanced back at the seat just in front of the rear door, hoping for a young, Oriental male, eating candy. The seat was empty.

"Of course it is," he muttered, sitting in it himself. "Or it would be too easy."

"Violent Crimes. Detective-Sergeant Graham."

"Why the hell aren't you out working? Jesus, I can't take my eyes off you for a second."

"Hello, Mike. I miss you, too."

Celluci grinned and braced the phone against his shoulder. "Listen, Dave, I need you to do me a favor."

On the other end of the line, his partner sighed with enough force to rattle the wires between Toronto and Kingston. "Of course you do. Whey else would you call?"

"I want you to call Humber College and talk to someone in Health Sciences about a Tom Chen who applied recently to their funeral director's program."

"Humber . . . Health Sciences . . . Tom Chen . . . Okay. What do you want to know?"

"Everything they know."

"About this Chen?"

"No, about life in general." Celluci rolled his eyes at his reflection in the etched mirror over the couch. "The name's an alias, but that shouldn't make any difference to your inquiries. And I need the info ASAP."

The wires rattled again. "Of course you do. How's she holding up?"

"Vicki?"

"No, her mother, asshole."

"About as well as can be expected, all things considered."

"Yeah. Well . . ." There was a pause while things were considered. "So, you going to be at Vicki's mother's place for the next couple of days?"

Celluci looked around the apartment. "Far as I know. You got the number?"

"Yeah. I'll call collect."

"Cheap Scots bastard," Celluci muttered and hung up, smiling. Dave Graham was a good cop and a loyal friend. Except in their dedication to their work, they were nothing alike, and their partnership was both successful and uncomplicated.

"Uncomplicated; I could use a little of that right now." Celluci headed for the kitchen and the coffee maker. "Vicki's dead mother is paying house calls. Some joker who's equally dead is murdering teenagers. And there's a vampire in the closet."

He froze, a step half taken.

"A completely helpless vampire in the closet."

Even with the door braced from the inside, it would still be so easy to remove his rival. To have Vicki to himself. To let in just enough sunlight . . .

He finished the step and picked up the coffeepot. Fitzroy was too smart, had lived too long, to be in that closet if he thought he was in any danger. Celluci shook his head at the subtlety of trust and lifted a mug of coffee in salute.

"Sleep well, you son of a bitch."

Rubbing at her temples with both hands, Vicki exhaled noisily. Adrenaline had run out some time before and she was mind-numbingly tired. The physical exhaustion she could cope with—had coped with many times in the past— but emotionally she felt as though she'd spent the day being flayed and then salted.

Dr. Burke had begun it, with her sudden sympathy, and then Dr. Devlin had finished the job. He had been more than fond of her mother and, still devastated by her death, had, in typical Irish fashion, poured out his grief. Vicki, unable to stop him, had sat dry-eyed while the middle-aged professor railed against the cruelties of fate, told of how universally Marjory Nelson had been liked and respected, and went on in detail about how proud Marjory Nelson had been of her daughter. Vicki knew how to stop him. "Sometimes," the cadet instructor had told them, "you want to give the person you're questioning their head. Let them talk about whatever they want, we'll teach you how to separate the gold from the dross. But sometimes, you have to cut it short and take control." She just couldn't do it.

She didn't want to hear what a wonderful person her mother had been, how much they'd all depended on her, how much they missed her, but not listening felt like a betrayal. And she'd done enough of that already.

The box of personal effects she'd taken from the office sat accusingly at the end of the coffee table. She hadn't been able to do more with it than get it back to the apartment and even that hadn't been easy. It had weighed a lot more than it looked like it should.

All at once, she became aware that Celluci had just asked her a question and she had no idea what it had been. "Sorry," she said, shoving her glasses back into place with enough force to drive the plastic bridge into her forehead.

He exchanged a look with Henry and, although she didn't catch the content, she didn't like the possibilities. Separately, she could barely handle them. At this point a united front, on any issue, would be beyond her.

"I asked," he repeated levelly, "about Dr. Burke's grad students. You told us she had some. Any chance they could be doing the work under her supervision?"

"I doubt it. According to Mrs. Shaw, when I went back for that appointment list, one's into bacteria, a couple have something to do with computers, and one—and I'm paraphrasing here—is a fuck-up who can't make up his mind. I'll . . ." Celluci opened his mouth but she corrected herself before he could speak, "we'll check them out further tomorrow."

Henry sat forward in his chair, his expression one she'd begun to recognize as his hunting face. "So you *do* suspect Dr. Burke?"

"I don't know what I think about Dr. Burke." Looking back on the interview, all Vicki could hear was the doctor's voice saying quietly, *"It's amazing how much you resemble your mother."* Which was an irrelevant observation at the best of times and doubly so now; her mother was dead. "She's got the necessary arrogance, that's for damned sure, and the intelligence and the background, but all anyone can talk about is what a brilliant administrator she is." She shrugged and wished she hadn't; her shoulders felt as though they were balancing lead weights. "Still, until we know she *didn't* do it, she stays on the list. I think, though, we can safely ignore Dr. Devlin."

"Why?"

"Because he could never have kept the research secret. If he were doing *this*," she made the innocuous pronoun sound like a curse, "he wouldn't be able to keep from telling the world. Besides, I gather he's a devout Irish Catholic and until recently, they weren't even keen on autopsies."

"He's also a scientist," Celluci pointed out. "And he could be acting."

"All the world's a stage," Henry added quietly, "and we but players on it."

Celluci rolled his eyes. "What the hell is that supposed to mean."

"That if you do talk to the person responsible, they're going to lie."

"That's why you build a body of evidence, Fitzroy. To catch the liars. We know more tonight than we did last night and we'll know more tomorrow than we do now. Eventually the truth will out. Nothing stays hidden forever."

We haven't got forever. Henry wanted to say. *Every moment that passes eats into her. How long before there's nothing left but a cause?* "We need a smoking gun," he said instead.

Celluci snorted in disbelief. The phrase sounded ridiculous coming from Henry's mouth. "You *have* been reading the literature."

Henry ignored him. "I'm going to track the other one; the male who killed the teenager. There were too many police around to do it last night. If I find him, I'll find your mother's body as well."

"And then?" Vicki demanded. "What do we do then?"

"We give them to Detective Fergusson. Lead him to the laboratory. Let him deal with the . . ."

"Wait a minute," Celluci interrupted. "You're actually suggesting we let the police handle this?"

"Why not? We have no one to protect this time, except me, and unlike ancient Egyptian gods of darkness or demons summoned up out of hell, mad scientists should fall within the capabilities of the law."

Celluci closed his mouth. Wasn't that *his* argument?

"Henry, you can't go to the police," Vicki began.

Henry smiled and cut her off. "I won't. I'll deliver the

information to you. You'll deliver it to the police. Detective Fergusson will be so happy to have his murderer, I think he'll let you be a bit vague as to where and how you found it.''

Vicki's lips almost curved. "You know, most guys just give a girl flowers or candy.''

"Most guys," Henry agreed.

The air in the apartment seemed suddenly charged and Celluci felt the hair on his arms rise. Fitzroy's eyes had darkened and even from across the room he thought he could see Vicki's reflection gazing out of their depths. The sudden flash of understanding snapped the pencil he held. Neither of them noticed.

Vampire.

How often do vampires have to feed?

Had Fitzroy fed at all since they'd come to Kingston?

Yeah, well you're not feeding in front of me, boyo. And you're not sending me off to never-never land again while you . . . while you . . .

While you offer her a comfort she won't take from me.

Another look at Henry's face and he knew the offer wouldn't be made at his expense. Somewhere, somewhen, they'd gone beyond that.

"I've got to get out of here." His voice brusk but determined, Celluci stood. *I can't believe I'm doing this.* "I need a nice long walk to clear my head. Help me think." Half a dozen long-legged strides took him to the door. He yanked his jacket off the coat stand and charged out into the hall before they had a chance to try and stop him. *'Cause I sure as shit can't offer this more than once.*

Safely outside, door closed behind him, he sagged against the wall and closed his eyes for a second, amazed at what he'd just done. *Yes, ladies and gentlemen, see a man act like a fool completely of his own free will.*

But he had the day.

Was it fair to deny Fitzroy the night?

And anyway, he shoved both hands up through his hair. *It should be Vicki's choice. Not a choice forced on her by my presence.*

If you love something, let it go. . . .

"Jesus H. Christ. What kind of idiot takes advice from a fucking T-shirt?"

*   *   *

Vicki stared across the room at the apartment door and then turned to stare at Henry. "Did he just? . . ."

"Leave?" Henry nodded, more than a little amazed himself. "Yes."

She couldn't get her brain around it. "Why?"

"I believe he is removing himself as an obstacle between us."

"Between us? You mean so we can? . . ."

"Yes."

"Why that arrogant shit!" Her brows snapped down, but she was so tired the exclamation had little force. "Didn't he think I might have something to say about that?"

Henry spread his hands, the fine red-gold hairs glinting in the lamplight. "No one's stopping you from saying it, Vicki."

She glared at him for a moment longer, then sighed. "All right. Valid point. But I think you two are getting along too goddamned well."

"Wouldn't it make things easier for you if Detective-Sergeant Celluci and I got along?"

"That depends." She sank back against the sofa cushions and added dryly, "On how *well* you get along."

"Vicki!" Her name dripped with exaggerated shock. "Surely you don't think . . ."

It took her a moment to catch the implication and when she did, she couldn't stop herself from giggling. It had to be the exhaustion; she never giggled. "You wish. Michael Celluci is straight enough to draw lines with."

Henry's smile changed slightly and his eyes darkened, enough of the hunter showing to make his desire plain. "Then I shall have to find someone else."

Vicki swallowed, if only to move her heart down out of her throat. He was making no attempt to catch her gaze, to draw her into his power. If she said no, and she could taste the word on her tongue, he would hunt elsewhere. *But he needs me.* Even from across the room, she could feel his Hunger. It wouldn't be a betrayal. There was nothing more she could do for her mother tonight. More important, his needs covered hers and behind their camouflage, she could, if only for the duration, let go.

He needs me. Repeated, it drew attention from the more dangerous *I need him.*

"Vicki?"

His voice stroked heat into her skin. "Yes."

Celluci watched Henry cross the parking lot, and worked at unclenching his teeth. There was nothing in the way the other man—*vampire-slash-romance writer,* Celluci savagely corrected the thought—moved to give any indication of what had gone on in the apartment. *Well, he doesn't brag. I'll give the little fucker that.*

"Detective."

"Fitzroy."

"Be quiet when you go into the apartment. She's asleep."

"How is she?"

"Some of the knots have loosened. I wish I could say they'll still be that way in the morning."

"You shouldn't have left her alone." *I left her alone and look what happened.* They both heard the corollary. They both ignored it.

"I'm listening to her heartbeat, Detective. I can be at her side in seconds. And this is as far as I'll go until you're ready to take over."

Celluci snorted and wished he could think of something to say.

Henry lifted his face and breathed deeply of the night. "It's going to rain. I'd best not linger."

"Yeah." Hands shoved into his jacket pockets, Celluci pushed himself up off his car. All right, so he hadn't walked far. He hadn't said he was going to. He wanted to believe that Fitzroy had left her no choice but he knew better; he wouldn't have left if that had been even a possibility.

"Michael."

Pulled around by his name, he tried not to let any of what he was feeling show on his face. It wasn't hard. He didn't *know* exactly what he was feeling.

"Thank you."

Celluci started to ask, *For what?* But he bit it back. Something in Henry's tone—he'd call it honesty if forced to put a name to it—denied a facetious response. Instead, he nodded, once, and asked, "What would you have done if she'd said no?" Even before the last word left his mouth, he wondered why he was asking.

Henry's gesture seemed to move past the overlapping

yellow-white of the streetlights. "We're in the middle of a small city, Detective. I'd have managed."

"You'd have gone to a stranger?"

Red-gold brows, darkened by shadow, rose. "Well, I wouldn't have had time to make friends."

Sure, take the cheap shot. "Don't you know there's a fucking epidemic on?"

"It's a disease of the blood, Detective. I *know* when someone is infected and am therefore able to avoid it."

Celluci tossed the curl of hair back off his forehead. "Lucky you," he grunted. "I still don't think that you should . . . I mean . . ." He kicked at the gravel and swore when a rock propelled by his foot clanged off the undercarriage of his car. Why the hell was he worrying about Fitzroy anyway? The son of a bitch had lasted centuries; he could take care of himself. *Trusting him is one thing. And I'm not sure I do. I am certainly* not *beginning to like him. Uh-uh. No way. Forget it.* "Look, even if you can sense it, you shouldn't be . . ." *Be what? Jesus, normal vocabulary is not up to this.* ". . . doing it with strangers," he finished in a hurry.

Henry's lips curled up into a speculative smile. "That could be difficult," he said softly, "if we stay here for very long. Even if she were willing, I can't feed off Vicki every time the Hunger rises."

The night air suddenly got hard to breathe. Celluci yanked at his collar.

"And after all," Henry continued, the corners of his eyes crinkling with amusement, "there's only one other person in this city whom I can't consider a stranger."

It took Celluci the same moment it had taken Vicki. "You wish," he snarled, whirled on one heel, and stomped toward the apartment building.

Smile broadening, Henry watched him go, listening to the angry pounding of Celluci's heart as he charged around the corner and out of sight. It had been less than kind to tease the mortal when he'd been honestly concerned, but the opportunity had been impossible to resist.

"And if I wished," he reminded the night when he had it to himself again. "I would."

Nine

The night held countless different kinds of darkness, from the wine-dark sky arching over the Mediterranean, to the desert cut into sharp relief by edged moonlight, to cities that broke it into secret pieces with a kaleidoscope of bright lights. Henry knew them all. He was never certain whether the night had more faces than the day or if he'd merely had more time to find them—four hundred and fifty years rather overshadowed barely seventeen. Were those faces each, in their own way, truly beautiful, or was he finding beauty in inevitability?

Walking south along Division Street, toward the university, he drank in yet another night. The return of a sun he would never see had warmed the earth and the scent of new growth nearly overwhelmed asphalt and concrete and several thousand moving bits of flesh and blood. Infant leaves, still soft and fragile, danced tentatively on the wind, the whispers of their movement a counterpoint to the hum of electrical wires and the growl of automobiles and the never-ending sounds of humanity. He knew if he took the time to look in the shadowed places of the city, he would find others pulled back to the hunt by the rising temperatures; some on four legs, most on two.

He crossed Princess Street, eyes hooded against the blaze of light bracketing the intersection. A young woman waiting for the opposing green studied him as he passed and he acknowledged her interest with a slow smile. The heat of her reaction followed him for several paces. When it came right down to it, cities and their people, were very much the same the world over.

And thank God for that, he conceded with a silent salute to the heavens. *It makes* my *night so much easier.*

Division Street spilled him out onto the actual campus and he slid into the shadow of a recessed doorway as a police car drove by. Twenty-four hours after a murder, they were likely to ask a number of questions he didn't want to answer. Questions like, *where are you headed* and *why.* Over the centuries, he'd found that the easiest way to deal with the police was not to deal with them at all.

By the time he reached the tiny hidden parking lot where the murder had actually occurred, he'd avoided that same cruiser twice more. The Kingston constabulary were taking their media-delivered promise of increased patrols very seriously.

Senses extended, Henry ducked under the yellow police tape and slowly crossed the asphalt. At the blurry chalk lines that isolated the victim's final resting place, he crouched and laid his fingers lightly on the pavement. The boy's death lingered; the scent of his terror, the imprint of his body, the instant of change when flesh became meat. Layered over it, layered over the whole area, was the other death; the scent of putrefaction, of chemicals, of machines, of death gone very, very wrong.

Straightening, trying not to gag, Henry's hand traced the sign of the cross. Abomination. The word lodged in his brain and he couldn't shake it loose. He supposed it was as good a word as any to describe the creature whose trail he had to follow. Abomination. Perversion. Evil. Not of itself perhaps, but evil in the creation of it.

When he tracked the creature to its sanctuary, if he found Marjory Nelson beside it, he would take steps to ensure that Vicki never saw what had been made of her mother. The one quick glimpse she'd already had was all that anyone should be required to live with.

"Geez, Cathy, don't you ever go home?"

Catherine looked up from the monitor and frowned. "What do you mean?"

"You know, *home.* "Donald sighed. "Home with a bed, and a television, and a refrigerator full of condiments and half a container of moldy cottage cheese." He shook his head and laced his voice with exaggerated concern. "I'm not getting through to you here, am I?"

It was Catherine's turn to sigh. "I know what home is, Donald."

"Can't prove it by me. You're always *here.*"

Catherine's gaze swept the lab and her expression smoothed into contentment. "This is where my work is," she said simply.

"This is where your life is," Donald snapped. "Don't you even go home to sleep?"

"Actually," pale cheeks darkened, "I have a bit of a place set up down in the subbasement."

"What? Here? In this building?"

"Well, sometimes the experiments can't be left or they have to be checked three or four times in the night and my apartment is way out on Montreal Street by the old train station and, well, it just seemed more practical to use one of the empty rooms here." The explanation spilled out in a rush of words. She watched, lower lip caught between her teeth, as Donald propped a buttock on the corner of a stainless steel table, pulled a candy from his pocket, unwrapped it, and popped it in his mouth.

"I'll be damned," he said at last, grinning broadly. "You never struck me as the squatting type."

"It's not squatting!" she protested hotly. "It's . . ."

"Caretaking." When she continued to scowl, he tried again. "Behaving in a responsible manner toward your experiments?"

"Yes. That's it exactly."

Donald nodded, his grin returned. "Squatting." She could rationalize any way she liked, but that's still what it was, not that he disapproved. In fact, he considered it an amazing show of initiative from someone he considered too tied to her test tubes. "Why the subbasement?"

She glared at him for a moment before she answered. "There aren't any windows to seal off." They both glanced at the plywood covered west wall. "And I'm less likely to be disturbed."

"Disturbed?" His brows jumped for his hairline. "What are you doing down there besides sleeping?"

"Well . . ." Catherine rubbed the top edge of the monitor with the ball of her thumb, her eyes on the screen.

"Come on, Cathy, you can tell me."

"You won't mention it to Dr. Burke?"

He traced an X across his chest. "Cross my heart and hope to die."

"I've got a small lab set up down there."

Rolling his eyes, Donald pulled out another candy. "Why am I not surprised? You've got yourself a secret hideout, a perfect opportunity for debauchery, and what do you do in it? You work." He dropped off the table and walked across the room to a clutter of microscopes and chemicals and a small centrifuge. "You work all the time, Cathy. That's *not* normal. I can't remember even being in this lab without you being here, too."

"Like you said, I have a sense of responsibility to my work."

"Like I said, you're looney tunes."

Her chin rose. "It's late. What are *you* doing here?"

Instead of answering, he began to wander around the room, fidgeting with the laser array, peering at a readout, finally drumming his fingers down the length of one of the isolation boxes. "Hey! Hang on!" He jerked a thumb at the shadowed cubbyhole between the isolation box and the wall. "What's he doing out? Dr. Burke said . . ."

"To remove them from their boxes only when absolutely necessary. To never leave them alone and unconfined. He isn't alone, I'm here with him. And I think that it's absolutely necessary for him to be out of his box as much as possible. He's *got* to have the stimulus. He's *thinking*, Donald."

"Yeah, right." But for all the bravado in his voice, Donald couldn't meet number nine's gaze. "So why don't you let them both out and they can play rummy or something. Look, Cathy," he came around the bank of monitors and threw himself down on the other chair at the computer station, legs straddling the back, arms folded across the top, "can we talk?"

She swiveled her own chair around to face him, her expression confused. "We *are* talking."

"No, I mean *talk*." Staring down at his hands, he picked at a hangnail beside his left thumb. "Talk about what we're really doing here. I've got to tell you, Cathy, I'm getting kind of concerned. This has gone way beyond the stuff Dr.

Burke said we were going to be doing. I mean we're definitely doing more than just developing a repair and maintenance system."

"Is this about what happened last night?"

"Sort of, but . . ."

"It won't happen again. I'm going to be very careful to never leave them alone. We were so lucky they didn't damage themselves out walking around unsupervised."

Donald's gaze snapped up to meet hers. "Geez, Cathy, some guy died last night and all you can worry about is the effect of a little mileage on the Bobbsey Twins?"

"I'm sorry that happened," she told him earnestly, "but worrying about it won't bring him back. Number nine made an amazing breakthrough last night and that's what we should be concentrating on."

"What if he was just reacting?"

She smiled. "Then it wasn't a programmed reaction and he had to have learned it on his own."

"Yeah? From where?" Donald twisted around and stared at number nine sitting impassively against the wall. "Those are my brain wave patterns bouncing around in there and I certainly never strangled anyone."

"That's a very good point." Catherine considered it for a moment, brow furrowed. "Perhaps we should bring a psychologist in?"

"Sure. Great." Donald faced her again, arms waving. Behind him, number nine tracked his movement. "Put him into therapy. The answer of the decade. Time for a reality break here, Cathy. This guy was dead and I don't think he is anymore. It's time to ask ourselves—what have we created?"

"Life?"

"Full points. Now then," his gestures grew broader as his voice rose, "what does that actually *mean?* Besides getting up and walking around and all that scientific bullshit about interfacing with the net, and ignoring for the moment whether it's an old life or a new one. It means we've got a person here. Just like you or me. Except," he flung a hand back in number nine's direction without turning, "he's rotting on his feet."

On his feet.

It was almost the command. Slowly, number nine stood.

He liked to hear her talk. Liked to listen to her voice. He didn't like the other one. The other one was loud.

Moving carefully, a hand braced against the container he recognized as his, he walked forward quietly.

"So what you're saying is that we have a live man in a dead body?"

"Yes! And what are we going to do about it?"

Catherine regarded him calmly. "The bacteria are keeping the body functional."

"Yeah, but only for a limited time. He's alive and he's decomposing, and doesn't that bother you just a little bit? I mean, ethical considerations about grave robbing aside, that's one hell of a thing to do to somebody!"

"Of course it bothers me." She brushed her hair back off her forehead and noted how well number nine was controlling his movements. Any residual lurching probably resulted from mechanical failure in the knees and hips. "What I really think we need are fresher bodies. I have high hopes for number ten."

"Fresher bodies!" Donald almost shrieked the words. "Are you crazy?"

"I've come to believe that the sooner the bacteria are applied the better they do." Her fingers danced over the keyboard. A moment later she offered him the printout. "I've graphed the time factor against the life of the bacteria and the amount of repair they were able to do. I think you'll find my conclusions to be unquestionable. The fresher the body, the longer it will last, the greater the chance of complete success."

Donald looked from the papers to Catherine and his eyes widened with a sudden realization. He didn't know why he hadn't seen it before. Maybe the money and recognition Dr. Burke kept talking about had interfered. Maybe the whole godlike concept of raising the dead had clouded his judgment. Maybe he just hadn't wanted to see.

When he looked number nine in the eyes, he saw a person and that was pretty terrifying. When he put Catherine under the same scrutiny, he didn't recognize what he saw and that was more terrifying still. Heart pounding, he stood and began to back away. "You *are* crazy."

His shoulder blades slammed up against number nine. He whirled and screamed.

* * *

The sound hurt.
But he had learned how to make it stop.

Donald clawed at the hand wrapped around his throat, fingernails digging into dead flesh.

Catherine frowned. It looked very much as though number nine had merely responded to Donald's scream. The sound appeared to hurt him, so he stopped it. Without further data, the obvious conclusion was that the young man last night had also screamed. Still, number nine *was* applying last night's lesson to a new situation and *that* was encouraging.

The wet noises were better. Quiet would be better still. He tightened his grip.

Release! Release! The command had been implanted. Number nine would have to obey. The word roared inside Donald's skull, but he couldn't force it out. His vision went red. Then purple. Then black.

Number nine looked down at what he held, then up at her. Slowly, he straightened his arm, offering the body.
She also looked down. Then up. Then she nodded, and he knew he had done the right thing.

"Put him on the table." As number nine moved to obey, Catherine saved the program she'd been working on and loaded Donald's brain wave patterns into the system. She'd needed a fresher body to test her hypothesis and now she had one. The perfect one. Even the bacteria had already been tailored.
Except the bacteria were in her other lab down in the subbasement because Dr. Burke had told her to stop wasting valuable experimental time on something that wouldn't be used.
She could put the net in now and then go for the bacteria or she could go for the bacteria and leave Donald where he was or . . .
Moving quickly—whatever she did, time was of the

essence—she opened the isolation box that had held number eight. If she put him in here, she could at least keep him cold while she ran downstairs. Decision made, she touched number nine lightly on the arm.

"Put him in here."

Number nine knew the box.
The head went so.
The feet went so.
The arms lay straight at the sides.

"Good." Catherine smiled her approval, lowered the lid, then switched on the refrigeration unit. She didn't bother latching the box. She wouldn't be gone long. Pushing him gently, she guided number nine up against the wall and out of the way. "Stay here. Don't follow."

Her rubber soled shoes made no sound against the tile as she sprinted for the door.

Stay here. Don't follow.
He wanted to be with her, but he did as she said.

Henry glared at the fire door. Obviously, he couldn't go into the building the same way the creature had come out. Although he might be able to work his way around the lack of an external handle, he could do nothing about the alarm. From the outside, he couldn't even destroy it. Somewhere, there had to be another way in.

Plywood covered the first floor windows between the wire grilles and the glass and a quick tour of the entrances showed them to have been similarly barricaded and wired besides. Frustrated and back by the fire door, Henry shoved his fingers behind the lower edge of a grille and gave an experimental tug. *If the direct approach is necessary . . .*

The bolts pulled out of the concrete and the side bars began to bend, metal screaming.

Bad idea. He froze, listening for reaction. In the distance, he heard leather soles slap against concrete and felt two lives, coming closer. Stepping away from the building, he became part of the night and waited.

". . . so he said, 'Chicago? In four? You've got to be out of your mind. I'll bet you twenty bucks they don't even make it out of the quarterfinals.' So I took the bet and in a couple of days, I'll take the twenty."

"Ah, man, how can you think of hockey at a time like this?"

"A time like what?"

"Baseball season, man. Opening day was the sixth. You got no business thinking about hockey, talking about hockey, playin' hockey, after baseball season starts."

"But hockey season isn't over."

"Maybe not, but it should be. Shit, this keeps up they'll be giving out ol' Stanley's cup in June."

They wore the uniform of university Security; two men bracketing forty, both with flashlights, both with billies in their belts. One of them carried his weight forward on his feet, daring the world to try something. The other balanced an impressive gut with enormous shoulders and arms. They passed inches from the shadow where Henry stood and never knew they were observed.

"This the door?"

"Yeah." The steel rattled under a slap from a beefy hand. "Some asshole genius student probably cutting through from the new Life Sciences building."

"Cutting through? In the dark?"

"What dark? They keep one in four lights on in there just in case."

"Just in case what?"

"Beats the hell out of me, but the place still has power."

"What a friggin' waste of money."

"No shit. Maybe if they turned off the lights and saved the dough they could afford to tear this ratbox down and build that parking garage."

"A parking garage? Now, man *that's* a building we could use around here."

From the Parthenon to the parking garage; how much further can civilization deteriorate? Henry wondered as the patrol moved on. Hands shoved into his pockets, he turned toward the new Life Sciences building, a brightly lit contrast to the dark and boarded structure it had replaced. *So the buildings are connected. The creature went into the old and Dr. Burke works in the new—along with a couple of hundred other people. Just exactly the sort of not quite information that Vicki and Celluci have been collecting all day.*

Let's see if the night can find some answers for them.

The guard at the front entrance noticed only the brief touch of a breeze that ruffled her newspaper but missed the movement that had made it. Once inside, Henry headed silently for the lower levels at the north end of the building. As the connection had not been visible, it had to be underground.

In the basement, he crossed a scent he knew. Or rather, the perversion of a scent he knew. He'd spent the last three days in the dark of Marjory Nelson's closet surrounded by her clothes and the stored bits and pieces of her life. The scent of her death, robbed of its peace and twisted back into a grotesque existence, clung to the tiles and paint much the way it had clung to the apartment window.

It led him to the passage, through it, up a flight of stairs, down a hall, up another flight of stairs, across an empty lecture hall with scars in the floor where the seats had been. Finally, it led him to a corridor, so thick with the stench of abomination, he could no longer separate individual paths.

Halfway down the corridor, a razor's edge of light showed under a door.

He could hear the low hum of electronic equipment, he could hear motors, and he could hear a heartbeat. He couldn't sense a life.

When he tried to step forward, his legs refused to obey.

Henry Fitzroy, Duke of Richmond and Somerset, bastard son of Henry VIII, had been raised to believe in the physical resurrection of the body. When the Day of Judgment came and the Lord called the faithful to Him, they would come not only in spirit, but also in flesh. He had gone to chapel nearly every day of his seventeen years, and this belief had been at the core of his religious upbringing. Even when his royal father had split from Rome, the resurrection of the body had remained.

Four and a half centuries had changed his views on religion but he had never been able to fully rid himself of his early training. He had been raised a sixteenth-century Catholic and, in some ways, a sixteenth-century Catholic he remained.

He couldn't go into that room.

And if you're not going to do it, who is? A bit of wood trim splintered beneath his fingers. *Michael Celluci? Will*

*you give him that much? Give him the opportunity to ride
to the rescue while you cower in superstitious terror? Vicki,
then? What of the vow you made to keep this from her?*

He managed a step, a small one, toward the door. Had
his nature allowed him to sweat, his hand would have left
a damp signature on the wall. As it was, his fingertips imprinted the plaster.

Legend named his kind undead but, in spite of how it
had appeared to the medical establishment of his time, he
had changed, not died. In that room, the dead were up and
walking. Robbed of their chance for eternal life. Removed
from the grace of God. . . .

I will not be ruled by my past at Vicki's expense.

The door was unlocked.

The room it bisected was enormous, stretching half the
length of the hall. Henry raised a hand to shield sensitive
eyes from the brilliant white glare of the fluorescents, noting as he did how the windows had been carefully blocked
to prevent any of that light from escaping and marking the
room as in use. He recognized almost none of the equipment that filled much of the available space. Fictional prec-
edent aside, the working of the perversion obviously
involved more than a scalpel and a lightning rod.

*Perhaps I'd recognize it if I wrote science fiction instead
of romance,* he mused, moving silently forward accompanied by the demons of his childhood.

The stench of abomination had become so pervasive it
coated the inside of his nose and mouth and lungs and
spread like a layer of scum across his skin. He could only
hope he could eventually be rid of it, that he wouldn't be
forced to carry it throughout eternity like an invisible mark
of Cain.

There were brass tanks lined up below the windows,
shelves of chemicals, two computers, and a door leading to
a small and mostly empty storeroom. The door leading out
the other side of the storeroom was locked.

Finally, unable to avoid it any longer, Henry turned
toward the slow and steady beat that he'd been all too
aware of since he'd entered the room.

The creature stood behind a row of metal boxes, eight
feet long and four feet wide. Too large to be coffins, they
reminded Henry of the outer sarcophagus that had kept

an ancient Egyptian wizard imprisoned, undying, for three millenia. Most of the electrical noise that Henry could hear came from the boxes. The mechanical noise came from the creature.

Cautiously, Henry slid along the wall, never in its direct line of sight. When he drew even with the creature, he paused and forced himself to acknowledge what he saw.

Unkempt dark hair fell back from a long line of face where green-gray skin wore the look of fine-grained leather and a black-threaded seam stitched a flap of forehead down. A nose that had obviously been broken more than once folded back on itself above purple-gray lips no longer able to close over the ivory curve of teeth. Even taking the desiccation of death into account, the muscles were wiry and the bones prominent through the navy blue tracksuit. It had been a man. A man who had not been very old when he died.

The narrow chest rose and fell, but it gave no indication it was aware.

Sweet Jesu! Henry took a step forward. And then another. Then he turned to face it.

Its eyes were open.

Number nine waited. She would be back soon.

He saw the strange one enter the room and he watched the strange one come closer.

The strange one looked at him.

He looked back.

Snarling, Henry broke contact and jerked away.

It was alive.

The body was dead.

But *it* was alive.

Whoever has done this thing should be damned for all eternity and beyond!

Trembling with anger and other emotions less easily defined, Henry dropped his hands to the lid of the box in front of him. Marjory Nelson, Vicki's mother, had to be in one of these. He no longer knew what he would do when he found her.

We give them to Detective Fergusson. So easy to decide in the abstract.

And what will Detective Fergusson do?

He opened the box.

The smell of recent death, free of any taint, rose with the lid and for an instant Henry hoped—but the body in the box had never belonged to Marjory Nelson. A young Oriental male wearing a band of purple finger marks around his throat, eyes bulging, tongue protruding, lay stretched out in the padded plastic hollow. He'd been dead for such a short time that the flush of blood caused by strangulation had not yet left his face.

Marjory Nelson suddenly became of lesser importance. She had already been lost and he could do no more for her than find her. This boy he could save.

Moving quickly, he closed the staring eyes then slid his arms behind knees and shoulders and lifted the chilled body free. The weight meant nothing but the load was awkward and he had to shuffle sideways until he cleared the row of boxes and could turn.

"What do you think you're doing?"

Drowning in the stink of abomination, Henry hadn't scented her approach nor, with ears tuned only to a heart that should be making no noise, had he heard her. In no mood to be subtle, he raised his head to meet her eyes, to order her away, and found behind a surface veneer of normalcy nothing he could touch. Her thoughts spiraled endlessly; starting nowhere, going nowhere.

Pale eyes narrowed. Pale cheeks flushed. "Stop him," she said.

Hands clamped onto Henry's shoulders and yanked him back. Across the top of his head, he could feel death breathing. *This is not life!* his senses screamed. His skin crawled in revulsion. He lost his grip on the boy, felt himself lifted and slammed down onto a surface that gave beneath the force of the blow. He twisted and looked up in time to see the lid coming down.

"NO!"

·

"He's not back yet."

Celluci jerked away, head snapping up painfully, muscles suddenly tense. "Wha . . .?"

"He's not back yet," Vicki repeated from the center of

the living room, arms wrapped tightly around herself. "And it's nearly dawn."

"Who's not back? Fitzroy?" Shoving his fist in front of a jaw-cracking yawn, Celluci glanced down at his watch. "6:12. When's the sun due up?"

"6:17," Vicki told him. "He's got five minutes." She kept her face and voice expressionless, reporting the facts, just the facts, because if she gave the screaming panic clawing at her from inside any chance to get free she was horribly afraid she'd never be able to control it again.

Celluci recognized the defense. There wasn't a cop on the planet who hadn't used police training to cover a personal terror at least once. The ones who cared too much used it frequently. Occasionally, it started to use them. Joints protesting, he heaved himself up out of the armchair he'd fallen asleep in, muttering, "How the hell do you know when the sun comes up?"

All at once, a terrifying possibility hit him. Had Fitzroy been . . . been . . . his mind shied away from the whole concept of sucking blood, of feeding. Had Fitzroy been *with* her long enough that she was becoming like him? Wasn't that how it worked? He shot an anxious glance at the mirror over the couch and was relieved to see her reflection still in it. Then he remembered that it had reflected Fitzroy just as clearly. "You're not turning into a . . . a . . . one of them, are you?" he snarled.

Vicki pushed at her glasses with the back of one hand. "What the hell are you talking about?"

"How do you know that sunrise is at 6:17?" He wanted to cross the room and shake the answer from her and barely managed to hold himself back.

"I read it in the paper last night." Her brows drew in, confused by the unexpected attack. "What is your *problem, Mike?*"

She read it in the paper last night. "Sorry, I, uh . . ." The surge of relief was so intense it left him feeling weak and a little dizzy. He spread his hands in apology and sighed. "I thought you were becoming like him," he said quietly, "and I was afraid I was going to lose you."

Drawing her lower lip between her teeth, Vicki stared at him for a long moment, although in the dim dawn light she could barely make out individual features. With no resources left to throw at denial, she could sense his caring, his fear, his love—and knew he put no conditions on it, no conditions on her. To her surprise, rather than diminishing her sense of self, it added to it and made her feel stronger. Even the panic over Henry calmed a little. Her eyes grew damp.

I am not *going to cry.*

Shoving the words past the lump in her throat, she said, "It doesn't work like that."

"Good." He heard, if not acceptance, at least acknowledgment in her tone and was content for the time to leave it at that.

The room grew perceptibly lighter.

Vicki turned toward the windows, arms wrapped tightly around herself once more. "Open the curtains."

They both heard the silent corollary. *You open them because I can't. Because I'm afraid of what I might see.*

"Who was your slave last year," Celluci grumbled to cover it.

It was going to be a beautiful day. Several dozen birds were noisily welcoming the dawn and the air had the kind of clarity that only occurred in the morning in spring.

His watch said 6:22. "How long can he last in the sun?"

"I don't know."

"I'm going to check outside. Just in case he almost made it home."

No twisted, blackened body crawled toward the door. No pile of ash spread man-shaped in the parking lot. When Celluci came back inside, he found Vicki standing where he'd left her, staring at the window.

"He isn't dead."

"Vicki, you have no way of knowing that."

"So?" Her teeth were clenched so hard her temples began to throb. "He *isn't* dead."

"All right." Celluci crossed the room to her side and gently turned her to face him. "I don't want to believe it either." It was true, he didn't. He didn't understand half the responses Fitzroy evoked in him, but he didn't want him gone. "So we won't believe it together."

Together. Face twisted into a scowl to stop the threat of

tears, Vicki nodded. Together sounded a whole lot better than alone.

He could feel the dawn. Even through the terror and the frenzy and the panic, he could feel the morning approach. For a moment he fought harder, slamming his whole body up against the lid of his prison, then he collapsed back against the padding and lay still.

The familiar touch of the sun trembling on the edge of the horizon brought sanity with it. For too long he had known only the all pervasive stench of abomination and the pain he inflicted upon himself to get free. Now he knew who he was again.

Just in time to lose himself to the day.

Working on her own, it took Catherine until after seven to finish preparing Donald's body and hook it up in number nine's box. She'd intended to use number eight's, but the intruder locked inside had forced her to change her plans. It wouldn't hurt number nine to stay out for a while. It might even be good for him.

She yawned and stretched, suddenly exhausted. It had been a long and eventful night and she was in desperate need of a couple of hours' sleep. The constant pounding from number eight's box had been very irritating and more than a little distracting during certain delicate procedures. She very nearly turned the refrigeration unit back on just to see if that would cool him down.

How unfortunate that, when the pounding finally stopped, she'd been nearly finished and able to appreciate the quiet for only a short time.

Ten

Vicki woke first and lay staring blindly at the ceiling, uncertain where she was. The room felt unfamiliar, the dimensions wrong, the patterns of shadow that made up the world without her glasses not patterns she recognized. It wasn't her bedroom, nor, in spite of the man still asleep beside her, was it Celluci's.

Then she remembered.

Just past dawn, the two of them had lain down on her mother's bed. Her dead mother's bed. Two of them—where there should've been three.

All three of us in my dead mother's bed? The edge on the sarcasm very nearly drew blood. *Get a grip, Nelson.*

She slid out from under Celluci's arm without waking him and groped on the bedside table for her glasses, the daylight seeping around the edges of the blinds providing barely enough illumination for her to function. Her nose almost touching the surface of the clock radio, she scowled at the glowing red numbers. Ten minutes after nine. Two hours' sleep. Add that to the time Henry had granted her and she'd certainly functioned on less.

Pulling her robe closer around her, she stood. She couldn't go back to sleep now anyway. She couldn't face the dreams—Henry burning and screaming her name while he burned, her mother's rotting body a living barrier between them. If she wanted to save Henry, she had to go past her mother. And she couldn't. Feelings of fear and failure combined, lingered.

My subconscious is anything but subtle.

Bare feet moving soundlessly over the soft nap of the carpet—it was still nearly new; Vicki could remember how

pleased her mother had been to have replaced a worn area
rug with thick wall-to-wall plush—she made her way to
the walk-in closet where Henry had been spending his
days. After a moment's groping to find the switch, she
flicked on the closet light and closed the door silently behind her.

It was, as Henry had said, just barely large enough for a
not-so-very-tall man. Or a not-so-very-tall vampire. A pad
of bright blue compressed foam, the sort commonly used
for camping, lay along one wall under the rack of woman's
clothes. On it, a neatly folded length of heavy blackout
curtain rested beside a leather overnight bag. Another
piece of curtain had been tacked to one side of the door
which itself had been fitted out with a heavy steel bolt.

Henry must've put it up, Vicki touched the metal slide
and shook her head. She hadn't heard hammering but,
given Henry's strength, hammering might not have been
necessary. *We'd better remember to take it down or it'll confuse the hell out of the next tenant.*

The next tenant. It was the first time she'd considered the
apartment as anything but her mother's. *Only reasonable, I
suppose.* She let her head fall back against the wall and
closed her eyes. *My mother's dead.*

The scent of her mother's cologne, of her mother, perme-
ated the small enclosure, and with her eyes shut it almost
seemed that her mother was still there. Another time, the
illusion might have been comforting—or infuriating. Vicki
was honest enough to admit the possibility of either reaction. At the moment, though, she ignored it. Her mother
wasn't the reason she was here.

Opening her eyes, she dropped to her knees beside the
pallet and lifted the makeshift shroud to her face, breathing
in the faint trace of Henry trapped in the heavy fabric.

He wasn't dead. She refused to believe it. He was too
real to be dead.

He *wasn't* dead.

"What are you doing?"

"I'm not entirely certain." With knuckles white around
the folds, she set the piece of curtain down and turned to
face Celluci, standing outlined in the doorway. He'd
opened the blinds in the bedroom and the morning sun
behind him threw his face into shadow. Vicki couldn't see

his expression, but his tone had been almost gentle. She didn't have a clue to what he was thinking.

He held out his hand and she put hers into it, allowing him to pull her to her feet. His palm was warm and callused. Henry's would have been cool and smooth. With her free hand resting on a crumpled expanse of shirtfront, she had the sudden and completely irrational desire to take that one extra step into the circle of Celluci's arms and to rest her head—not to mention the whole mess she found herself in—if only for a moment, on the broad expanse of his shoulders.

This is no time to be getting soft, Vicki, she told herself sternly, fighting the iron bands tightening around her ribs. *You've got far too fucking much to do.*

Celluci, who'd read both the desire and the internal response off Vicki's face, smiled wryly and moved out of her way. He recognized the growing strain that painted purple half-circles under her eyes and pinched the corners of her mouth and knew that some of it needed to be bled off before it blew her apart. But he didn't know what to do. Although their fights had often been therapeutic, this situation went a little beyond the relief that could come from screaming at one another over trivial disagreements. While he could think of a few nontrivial disagreements available for argument, he had no intention of hurting her by bringing them up. All he could do was continue to wait and hope he was the one in the right place to pick up the pieces.

Of course, if Fitzroy's actually bought it . . . It was a dishonorable thought, but he couldn't stop it from taking up residence.

"So." He watched her cross to the open bedroom door and wondered how long he'd have been content with the status quo had Fitzroy *not* come into their lives. "What do we do now?"

Vicki turned and stared at him in some surprise. "We do exactly what we *have* been doing." She jabbed her glasses up onto the bridge of her nose. "When we find the people who have my mother's body, we'll find Henry."

"Maybe he just went to ground, got caught out too late and had to take what shelter he could."

"He wouldn't do that to me if he could help it."

"He'd call?" Celluci couldn't prevent the mocking tone.

Vicki's chin went up. "Yeah. He'd call." *He wouldn't leave me to think he was dead if he could help it. You don't do that to someone you say you love.* "We find my mother. We find Henry." *He couldn't call if he was dead. He isn't dead.* "Do you understand?"

Actually, he did. After nine years, he'd gotten proficient at reading her subtext. And if his understanding was all she'd take . . . Celluci spread his hands, the gesture both conciliatory and an indication that he had no wish to continue the discussion.

Some of the stiffness went out of Vicki's stance. "You make coffee," she told him, "while I shower."

Celluci rolled his eyes. "What do I look like? Live-in help?"

"No." Vicki felt her lower lip tremble and sternly stilled it. "You look like someone I can count on. No matter what." Then, before the lump in her throat did any more damage, she wheeled on one bare heel and strode out of the room.

His own throat tight, Celluci pushed the curl of hair back off his face. "Just when you're ready to give up on her," he muttered. Shaking his head, he went to make the coffee.

Running her fingers through her wet hair, Vicki wandered into the living room and dropped onto the couch. She could hear Celluci mumbling to himself in the kitchen and, remembering what had happened on other occasions, decided it might be safer not to bother him when he was cooking. Without quite knowing how it happened, she found herself lifting the box of her mother's personal effects and setting it in front of her on the coffee table.

I suppose no day's so bad that you can't make it worse.

There was surprisingly little in it: a sweater kept hanging over the back of the office chair, just in case; two lipsticks, one pale pink, the other a surprisingly brilliant red; half a bottle of aspirin; the coffee mug; the datebook with its final futile message; her academy graduation portrait; and a pile of loose papers.

Vicki picked up the photograph and stared into the face of the smiling young woman. She looked so young. So confident. "I looked like I thought I knew everything."

"You still think you know everything." Celluci handed

her a mug of coffee and plucked the picture out of her grasp. "Good God. It's a baby cop."

"If I ignore you, will you go back into the kitchen?"

He thought about it for a second. "No."

"Great." Pulling her bathrobe securely closed, Vicki lifted out the loose paper. *Why on earth did Mrs. Shaw think I'd want a bunch of Mother's notes?* Then she saw how each page began.

Dear Vicki: You're probably wondering why a letter instead of a phone call, but I've got something important to tell you and I thought I might get through it easier this way, without interruptions. I haven't written a letter for a while so I hope you'll forgive . . .

Dear Vicki: Did I tell you the results of my last checkup? Well, I probably didn't want to bore you with details, but . . .

Dear Vicki: First of all, I love you very much and . . .

Dear Vicki: When your father left, I promised you that I'd always be there for you. I wish I . . .

Dear Vicki: There are some things that are easier to say on paper, so I hope you'll forgive me this small distance I have to put between us. Dr. Friedman tells me that I've got a problem with my heart and I may not have long to live. Please don't fly off the handle and start demanding I see another doctor. I have.

Yes, I'm afraid. Any sensible person would be. But mostly I was afraid that something would happen before I found the courage to tell you.

I don't want to just disappear out of your life like your father did. I want us to have a chance to say goodbye. When you get this letter, call me. We'll make arrangements for you to come home for a few days and we'll sit down and really talk.

I love you.

The last and most complete letter was dated from the Friday before Marjory Nelson died.

Vicki fought tears and with shaking hands laid the letters back in the box.

"Vicki?"

She shook her head, unable to push her voice past an almost equal mix of grief and anger. Even if the letter had been mailed, they still wouldn't have had time to say goodbye. *Jesus Christ, Mom, why didn't you have Dr. Friedman call me?*

Celluci leaned forward and scanned the top page. "Vicki, I . . ."

"Don't." Her teeth were clenched so tightly it felt as though there was an iron band wrapped around her temples. One more sympathetic word—one more word of any kind—would destroy the fingernail grip she had on her control. Moving blindly, she stood and hurried toward the bedroom. "I've got to get dressed. We've got to look for Henry."

At 10:20, Catherine lifted the lid of the isolation box and smiled in at the woman who had once been Marjory Nelson. "I know; it's pretty boring in there, isn't it?" She pulled on a pair of surgical gloves and deftly unhooked the jack and laid it, gold prongs gleaming, to one side. "Just give me half a sec and we'll see what we can do about getting you out of there." Nutrient tubes were tugged gently from catheters and tucked away in specific compartments in the sides of the box. "You've got amazingly good skin tone, all things considered, but I think that working a little estrogen cream into the epidermis might be in order. We don't want things to tear while you're up and moving around."

Catherine hummed tunelessly to herself as she worked, stopping twice to make notes on muscle resilience and joint flexibility. So far, number ten proved her theory. None of the others, not even number nine, had responded to the bacteria quite so well. She couldn't wait to see how Donald—number eleven—turned out.

Had she seen the girl before? Why couldn't she remember?

The girl was not the right girl, although she didn't understand why not.

Hooking her fingers over the side of the box, she pulled herself up into a sitting position.

There was something she had to do.

Catherine shook her head. Initiative was all very well but at the moment a prone, immobile body would be of more use.

"Lie down," she said sternly.

Lie down.

The command traveled deeply rutted pathways and the body obeyed.

But she didn't want to lie down.

At least she didn't think she did.

"You're trying to frown, that's wonderful!" Catherine clapped gloved hands together. "Even partial control of the zygomaticus minor is a definite advance. I've got to take some measurements."

Number nine watched closely as she moved about the other one like him. He remembered another word.

Need.

When she needed him, he'd be there.

Just for an instant, he thought he remembered music.

With number ten measured, moisturized, dressed, and sitting at the side of the room, Catherine finally turned her attention to the intruder. She'd heard no sounds at all from what had been number nine's box since she'd returned to the lab and she rather hoped he hadn't died. With no brain wave patterns and no bacteria tailored, it would be a waste of a perfectly good body, especially as, if he'd suffocated or had a heart attack, there wouldn't even be any trauma to repair.

"Of course, if he *has* died, we could use Donald's brain wave patterns and the generic bacteria," she mused as she lifted the lid. "After all, it worked on number nine and he wasn't exactly fresh. It'd be nice to have a little backup data for a change."

She frowned down into the isolation box. The intruder lay, one pale hand curled against his chest, the other palm up at his side. His eyes were closed and long lashes, slightly darker than the strawberry blond hair, brushed against the curve of pale cheeks. He didn't look dead. Exactly. But he didn't look alive. Exactly.

Head to one side, she pushed his collar back and pressed two fingers into the pulse point at his throat. His flesh responded with more resilience than she'd expected, far more than a corpse would have but, at the same time, it seemed his body temperature had dropped too low to sustain life. She checked to make sure that the refrigeration unit had, indeed, been shut off. It had.

"How very strange," she murmured. Then things got stranger still for just as she was about to believe his heart had stopped, for whatever reason, a single pulse throbbed under her fingertips. Frown deepening, she waited, eyes on her watch as the seconds flashed by. Just over eight seconds later, the intruder's heart beat again. And then eight seconds after that, again.

"About seven beats a minute." Catherine drummed the fingers of both hands on the side of the isolation box. "The alternation of systole and diastole occurs at an average rate of about seventy times per minute in a normal human being at rest. What we have here is a heart beating at one tenth the normal rate."

Brows knit, she carefully lifted an eyelid between thumb and forefinger. The eye had not rolled back. The pupil, rather than being protected under the ridge of brow bone, remained centered, collapsed to pinprick dimensions. There was no reaction of any kind to light. Nor, for that matter, to any other kind of stimuli by any other part of the body— and Catherine tried them all.

Accompanied by low level respiration, the heart continued to beat between seven and eight times a minute, undetectable had she not been specifically searching for it. These were the only signs of life.

She'd heard of Indian fakirs putting themselves into trances so deep they appeared to be in comas or dead and she supposed this was a North American variation on that ability; that when her intruder had found himself trapped, he'd lowered his metabolism to conserve resources. Catherine had no idea what he'd been hoping to accomplish as he seemed, at the moment, totally unable to defend himself, but she had to admit that, minor point aside, it was a pretty neat trick.

Finally, she had number nine help her remove his leather trench coat and, rolling up his shirtsleeve, she pulled two vials of blood. She'd intended to take three but, with the intruder's blood pressure so low, two used up all the time she was willing to allow. Closing the box, she headed for one of the tables at the other end of the lab. Running the blood work might give her some answers to this trance thing but, even if it didn't, she could always use the information later should the intruder happen to die.

"Look, Detective Fergusson, I'm aware that my mother died of natural causes before the crime was committed and I realize that this makes her a very low priority but . . ."

"Ms. Nelson." Detective Fergusson's voice hovered between exasperation and annoyance. "I'm sorry you're upset, but I've got a murdered teenager on my hands. I'd like to find the asshole who offed him before I've got another body bag to deal with."

"And you're the only detective on the force?" Vicki's fingernails beat a staccato rhythm against the pay phone's plastic casing.

"No, but I am the one assigned to the case. I'm sorry if that means I can't give your mother the attention you think she deserves . . ."

"The cases," she snarled, fingers curling into a fist, "are connected."

Behind her, leaning on the open door of the phone booth, Celluci rolled his eyes. Even without hearing the other end of the conversation, he had some sympathy for Fergusson's position. Although she could be surgically delicate with a witness, Vicki tended to practice hammer and chisel diplomacy on the rest of the world.

"Connected?" The exasperation vanished. "In what way?"

Vicki opened her mouth then closed it again with an audible snap. *My mother has been turned into a monster. Your boy was killed by a similar monster. We find my mother, I guarantee we find your perp. How do I know all this? I can't tell you. And he's missing anyway.*

Shit.

She shoved at her glasses. "Look, call it a hunch, ok..."

"A hunch?"

Realizing that she'd have had much the same reaction had their positions been reversed, her tone grew sharply defensive. "What's the matter? You've never had a hunch?"

Anticipating disaster should the current conversation continue, Celluci used a shoulder to lever Vicki back from the phone, then dragged the receiver from her grip. Scowling, she allowed his interference with ill grace and the certain knowledge that antagonizing the Kingston Police was a bad idea.

"Detective Fergusson? Detective-Sergeant Celluci. We've determined that one of Dr. Burke's grad students, a Donald Li, at least superficially fits the description of Tom Chen. We'd appreciate it if you could call the registrar's office and have them release a copy of his student photo so we can check his identity with the funeral parlor."

Detective Fergusson sighed. "I called the registrar's office yesterday."

"And they released the photos of the medical students. But Li isn't studying medicine and they won't release his picture without another call from you."

"Why do you think Li's involved?"

"Because he works for Dr. Burke, as did Marjory Nelson."

"So. What make you think Dr. Burke's involved?"

"Because she appears to have the scientific qualifications to raise the dead as well as access to the necessary equipment."

"Give me a break, Sergeant." Incredulity fought with anger for control of Fergusson's voice. "How did you come up with raising the fucking dead?"

Good question, Celluci admitted, ignoring a glare from Vicki so intense that he could almost feel its impact. Making a quick decision—given that the police were already involved—he pulled out as much of the truth as he thought Fergusson could swallow. "Ms. Nelson thought she saw her mother outside the apartment window, two nights ago."

"Her dead mother?"

"That's right."

"Walking around?"

g you're going to tell me," Fergusson growled, dead mother offed my teenie bopper."

". ."

"No buts, Sergeant." His voice clipped off the words. "And I've listened to as much of this crap as I'm going to. Go back to Toronto. Get a life. Both of you."

Celluci got the receiver away from his ear just barely fast enough to save his hearing from the force of Fergusson's disconnection. He hung up the phone with an equal emphasis. "I knew I shouldn't have let you talk to him."

Behind her lenses, Vicki's eyes narrowed. "And *you* did so much better? What the hell made you tell him about my mother? About Dr. Burke?"

Celluci pushed his way out of the phone booth. She stepped back, giving him *just* enough room to get by. "This is science, Vicki, not one of the weird supernatural situations your undead buddy has pulled us into over the last year. I thought he could handle it. I thought he should know."

"You didn't think we should discuss it first?"

"You brought it up. 'The cases are connected.' Jesus H. Christ, Vicki, you knew you couldn't support a statement like that."

"I didn't notice you supporting *your* statements with much, Celluci." With an effort, she unclenched her teeth. "I assume he's *not* going to make the call?"

Celluci's scowl answered the question. And then some.

"All right." She hoisted her bag off the sidewalk and threw it onto her shoulder. "I guess we do it the hard way."

"You're a lot more philosophical about this than I expected you'd be."

"Mike, my recently dead mother has been turned into some kind of grade B movie monster, my—*what word to use?*—friend who also happens to be a vampire is missing, in the daylight, and possibly captured. When I sleep, I have nightmares. When I eat, the food turns to rock and just sits there." She turned to face him and her expression closed around his heart and squeezed. "I find it difficult to give a shit that local police don't see things exactly my way."

"You've still got me." It was the best he could offer.

Her lower lip began to tremble and she caught it savagely

between her teeth. Unable to trust her voice, she reached up and pushed the long curl of dark brown hair back off his forehead then turned and strode away from the Administration buildings, heels hitting pavement with such force that they should have imprinted crescent moons into the concrete.

Celluci watched her for a moment. "You're welcome," he said quietly, his own voice not entirely steady. With a dozen long strides, he caught up and fell into step by her side.

"All right, Catherine, I'm here." Dr. Burke pushed the lab door shut behind her and walked purposefully across the room. "What is it you've found that's so important I had to see it immediately?"

Catherine came out from behind the computer console and offered a page of printout. "It's not that it's important, precisely, it's more that I don't understand what I've found. If you could just take a look at the results of this blood work."

Dr. Burke frowned down at the piece of paper. "Formed elements sixty percent of whole blood—that's high. Plasma proteins, twelve percent—high as well. Organic nutrients . . ." She looked up. "Catherine, what *is* this?"

Catherine shook her head. "Read the rest."

Although inclined to demand an immediate explanation, respect for the grad student's abilities—manipulating the younger woman's genius had, after all, been a main component of the plan from the beginning—dropped Dr. Burke's gaze back down to the printout. "Ten million red blood cells per cubic millimeter of blood? That's twice human norm." Her brows drew in as she continued. "If this data on the hemoglobin is correct . . ."

"It is."

"Then just what *is* this?" Dr. Burke punctuated her questions by shoving the paper back into Catherine's hands. "A replacement for the nutrient solution?"

"No, although . . ." Her eyes glazed and two spots of color began to come up on pale cheeks.

Dr. Burke recognized the signs, but she didn't have the time to allow genius to percolate. She'd had to reschedule an end of term meeting to come here and she had no intention of falling farther behind. "Think about it later. I'm waiting."

"Yes. Well . . ." Catherine took a deep breath and smoothed down the front of her lab coat. She hadn't even begun to consider the experimental applications yet. The ability to leap so far ahead, she mused, was what made Dr. Burke such a brilliant scientist. "We had an intruder in the lab last night."

"A what!"

Catherine blinked at both volume and tone. "An intruder. But don't worry, number nine took care of him."

"Number nine took care of him?" Dr. Burke suddenly saw her world becoming infinitely more complicated. She shot a disgusted glance across the room to where both number nine and Marj . . . and number ten sat motionless by the wall. "The way he, it, took care of that boy?"

"Oh, no! He captured the intruder, and with only the most basic of instructions. There really can be no more doubt that he's reasoning independently, although I haven't had time this morning to run a new EEG."

"Catherine, that's fascinating I'm sure, but the intruder? What did you do with him?"

"I locked him into number nine's isolation box."

"Is he still in there?"

"Yes. He made a horrible racket at first, very distracting while I was working—especially since I had to do the whole job alone—but he quieted around sunrise."

"Quieted." Dr. Burke rubbed at her temples where an incipient headache had begun to pound. Thank God, Catherine had been mucking about in the lab long after the rest of the world had gone to sleep. Had there been no one around to stop him, they would have all very likely been in a great deal of trouble. On the other hand, *Catherine* stopping an intruder was a mixed blessing, her grip on the world's standard operating procedures not being particularly strong. "He didn't die, did he? I mean you *did* check on him?" *And if he's alive, what the hell are we going to do with him?*

"Of course I did. His metabolic rate is extremely low, but he's alive." She held the printout higher. "This is a partial analysis of his blood."

"That's impossible," Dr. Burke snapped. With a captured

intruder to deal with, she didn't have time for the grad student's delusions.

Catherine merely shook her head. "No, it isn't."

"No one has blood like that. You had to have done something wrong."

"I didn't."

"Then the sample was contaminated."

"It wasn't."

Unable to break past Catherine's calm certainty, Dr. Burke snatched the printout back and glared down at it, scanning the data she'd already read, looking more closely at the rest. "What's this? This isn't blood work."

"I also did a cheek swab."

"Your intruder has thromboplastins present in his saliva? That's ridiculous."

"He's not my intruder," Catherine protested. "And if you don't trust my results, run the tests yourself. Besides, if you'll notice, they don't exactly register as thromboplastins although there is a ninety-eight-point-seven percent similarity."

"No one has that kind of clotting initiators in their sa . . ." Ten million red blood cells per cubic millimeter of blood . . . thromboplastins present in his saliva . . . he quieted around sunrise . . . his metabolic rate is extremely low . . . quieted around sunrise . . . around sunrise. . . . "No, that's impossible."

Eyes narrowed, Catherine squared her shoulders. She couldn't understand how Dr. Burke continued to deny the experimental results. Science didn't lie. "Obviously, it *isn't* impossible."

Dr. Burke ignored her. Heart pounding, she turned toward the row of isolation boxes. "I think," she said slowly, "I'd better have a look at your intruder."

"He isn't *my* intruder," Catherine muttered again as she followed the other woman across the room.

Palms resting on the curve of number nine's isolation box—apparently no longer only number nine's—Dr. Burke told herself she was letting fantasy get the best of both common sense and education. *He can't be what evidence suggests he is. Such creatures exist in myth and legend. They aren't walking around in the twentieth century.* But if the test results were accurate . . . *There's probably a perfectly*

normal, scientific explanation for all this, she told herself
firmly, and opened the lid.

"Good Lord, he's paler than you are. I didn't think that
was possible." She hadn't expected him to look so young.
Much as Catherine had done earlier, she pushed her fingers
up against the pulse point at the base of the ivory column
of throat. Thirty seconds passed while she stood silently,
eyes on her watch, then she wet her lips and said, "Not
quite eight beats a minute."

"I got the same," Catherine nodded, pleased to have her
figure corroborated.

She reached to check his pupils but instead, her hand
moving almost of its own volition, she peeled up a lip
barely tinted with color.

Catherine's brow furrowed. "What are you looking for?"

Her heart beat so loudly she nearly missed the question.
"Fangs," she said softly, realizing she was being one hundred sorts of an old fool. "Fangs."

Bending forward, Catherine peered down at the exposed
line of white. "Although the canines are somewhat prominent, I wouldn't go so far as to . . ."

"Son of a bitch! They're sharp!"

Together, the two women watched the drop of blood roll
from the puncture in Dr. Burke's finger. It splashed crimson against the barrier of the teeth, seeped into sculpted
crevices, drained into the mouth beneath. So slowly that
they would have missed the movement had they not been
staring so hard, the young man swallowed.

In the long moment that followed, Dr. Burke reviewed
a thousand rational reasons why this creature could not be
what it had to be. Finally, she said, "Catherine, do you
realize what we have here?"

"Incipient percutaneous infection. Better sterilize the
puncture."

"No, no, no. Do know what he *is?*"

"No, Doctor." Catherine rocked back on her heels and
shoved her hands deep into the pockets of her lab coat. "I
realized I didn't know what he was when I saw the results
of the blood work. That's why I called you."

"This," Dr. Burke's voice rose with an excitement she
didn't bother to suppress, "is a vampire!" She whirled to
face Catherine, who looked politely interested. "Good lord,

girl, don't you find that amazing? That this is a *vampire*? And *we* have him?"

"I guess."

"You guess?" Dr. Burke stared at the grad student in disbelief. "We have a vampire break into the lab and you *guess* it's amazing?"

Catherine shrugged.

"Catherine! Pull your head out of your test tubes and consider what this means. Up until this moment, vampires were creatures of myth and legend. We can now prove that they exist!"

"I thought vampires disintegrated in daylight."

"He hasn't been in daylight, has he?" An expansive gesture indicated the wall of boarded up windows. "The scientific community will go crazy over this!"

"If he *is* a vampire. So far we can only prove he has a hyperefficient bloodtype, clotting agents in his saliva, and sharp teeth."

"And doesn't that say vampire to you?"

"Well, it doesn't prove it. Sunrise may have caused his metabolic rate to drop, but we can't actually prove that either." She frowned. "I suppose we could push him up against an open window and see what happens."

"No!" Dr. Burke took a deep breath and leaned back against number eight's isolation box, allowing the soft vibration of the machinery to soothe her jangled nerves. "This is a vampire. I'm as certain of it as I've ever been of anything in my life. You saw how he reacted to my blood."

"That was pretty strange."

"Strange? It was incredible." With her left hand supporting the vampire's hip—he was heavier than she expected—she slid her right hand into his pants pocket and pulled out a slim, black leather wallet. "Now then, let's find out who you are."

"Would a vampire carry identification?"

"Why not? This is the twentieth century. Everyone carries identification of some kind. Here we are; Henry Fitzroy. I suppose they can't all be named Vladimir." Lips pursed and eyes gleaming, Dr. Burke turned over a gold patterned credit card. "Don't leave the crypt without it, as Donald would probably say. Speaking of Donald . . ." She paused and frowned. "Where is he, anyway?"

"Well, you see . . ." Catherine laid a gentle hand on number eight's isolation box. "He . . ."

"Has that damned tutorial this morning, doesn't he? And I expect he was long gone before our visitor showed up. It's his loss, you'll have to fill him in later. Now then, ownership, insurance, ah, driver's license. Apparently the myth that vampires show no photographic image is also false."

"I just can't believe we have vampires in Kingston."

"We don't. He's from Toronto." Gathering up the contents of the wallet, Dr. Burke tossed them onto a pile of clothes draped over a nearby chair. "We'll have to do something about his car . . . no, we don't. He'll just disappear. Become another tragic statistic. He's already living a lie; who's going to look for him?" She patted the back of one pale hand, fingers lightly stroking the scattering of red-gold hair. "Of all the laboratories in all the world, you had to stumble into mine."

"But, Dr. Burke, what are we going to do with him?"

"Study him, Catherine. Study him."

Head cocked to one side, Catherine examined the doctor. The last time she'd seen the older woman this excited had been the day number four had made the initial breakthrough with the neural net. Her eyes had held the same brilliant mix of greed and self-satisfaction then that they did now and, now that she thought about it, Catherine hadn't liked the expression that day either. "Dr. Burke, vampires are outside my experimental parameters."

Eleven

Vicki lifted her face into the wind blowing in off Lake Ontario and remembered how this slab of stone jutting into the water had once been both refuge and inspiration. All through her teens, whenever life got too complicated and she couldn't see her way clear, she'd come to the park, clamber out on the rock, and the world would simplify down to the lake and the wind. The city at her back would disappear and life would be back in perspective. Winter or summer, good weather or bad—it hadn't mattered.

The lake still crashed rhythmically against the rock below her feet, and the wind still picked up the spray and threw it at her but, even together, they were no longer strong enough to uncomplicate the world. Tightening her arm on the bulk of her shoulder bag, she blocked out the pounding of the waves and listened for the crackle of paper; heard her mother's words read from the letter in her mother's voice.

I don't want to just disappear out of your life like your father did. I want us to have a chance to say good-bye.

She swiped at the water on her cheeks before turning and climbing back up the bank to where Celluci waited, more or less patiently, by the car.

The detour had given her nothing but damp sneakers and the certain knowledge that the only way out of the situation she found herself in was going to be the hard way.

So we concentrate on finding my mother.

We find her, we find Henry.

And then we'll . . .

. . . we'll. . .

She shoved viciously at her glasses, jamming the plastic

bridge up into her forehead, ignoring the drops of water that spotted the lenses—refusing to acknowledge drops that were salt water not fresh and were on the inside of the lenses. *Let's just concentrate on finding them.* Then *we'll worry about what we do next.*

"Good morning, Mrs. Shaw. Is Dr. Burke in?"

"No, dear, I'm sorry, but you just missed her."

Vicki, who had been watching and waiting until she saw Dr. Burke hurry from the office, manufactured a frown.

"Is there anything I can do to help?"

She shifted the expression to hopeful. "I need to talk to Donald Li about my mother and I'm finding it impossible to track him down around the campus. I was wondering if Dr. Burke could give me his home address."

Mrs. Shaw smiled up at her and pulled an overflowing rolodex forward. "You don't need to bother Dr. Burke about that, I've got Donald's address right here."

"Uh, Mrs. Shaw . . ." The young woman temporarily assigned to the office shot an uneasy glance from Vicki to her coworker. "Should you be giving that out? I mean that's private information and . . ."

"Don't worry about it, Ms. Grenier," Mrs. Shaw instructed firmly, flipping through the cards with practiced fingers, "this is Marjory Nelson's daughter."

"Yes, but . . ."

Vicki leaned forward and caught the temporary's eye. "I'm sure Donald won't mind," she said quietly.

Ms. Grenier opened her mouth, closed it, and decided she wasn't being paid enough to interfere with someone who'd just made it quietly clear that any opposition would be removed from the field on a stretcher if necessary.

Mrs. Shaw copied the address onto the back of a message form and handed it to Vicki. "Here you go, dear. Has there been any news from the police about your mother's body?"

"No." Vicki's fingers crushed the small square of pink paper. "Not yet."

"You'll let me know?"

"Yes." She didn't bother attempting a smile. "Thank you for this." It was probably fortunate that the outer office door had been designed in such a way that it couldn't be slammed.

"First to have her mother die and then to find that the

body had been stolen." Mrs. Shaw sighed deeply and shook her head. "The poor girl was devastated."

Ms. Grenier made a silent but eloquent moue and bent back over her keyboard. As far as she was concerned, devastated might describe anything that got in that woman's way but it could hardly be applied to her emotional condition.

Celluci made no comment as Vicki slid into the passenger seat and slammed the car door. Although she'd insisted before going up that she could handle any sympathy expressed by her mother's ex-coworker, something had obviously gotten through. As nothing he could say would help, he merely started the engine and pulled carefully away from the curb.

"Make the next left," Vicki instructed tersely, yanking the seat belt into position then slamming it home. "We're heading for Elliot Street."

Three blocks later, she sighed deeply and said, "Odds are good that was a lot less trouble than breaking into the records office."

"Not to mention less illegal," Celluci pointed out dryly.

He got his reward in the quick flicker of a smile, there and gone so fast he would've missed it had he not been watching.

"Not to mention," Vicki agreed.

"Catherine." Dr. Burke turned to face the wall, cupping the mouthpiece of the receiver with her free hand. It wouldn't do to be overheard. "I thought I'd give you a quick call between meetings to see how those tests are going."

"Well, his leukocytes are really amazing. I've never seen white blood cells like these."

"Have you looked at any tissue samples?"

"Not yet. I thought you wanted the blood work done first. I've drawn another two vials as well as a sample of lymphatic fluid and, Doctor, his plasma cells are just as unique as the rest."

Dr. Burke ignored a gesturing colleague. They couldn't start the damned meeting without her anyway. "Unique in what way?"

"Well, I'm not an immunologist, but given a little time I may be able to . . ."

A sudden realization threw everything into sharp-edged relief. "Good lord, you might be able to develop a cure for AIDS." That would mean more than just a Nobel prize; an AIDS vaccine would practically net her a sainthood.

Catherine hesitated before replying. "Well, yes, I suppose that might be one result. I was thinking more along the lines of my bacteria and . . ."

"Think big, Catherine. Look, I've got to go now. Concentrate on the plasma cells, I think they're our best bet. Oh, for pity's sake, Rob, I'm coming." She hung up the phone and turned to the worried looking man hovering at her elbow. "What *is* your problem?"

"Uh, the meeting . . ."

"Oh, yes, the meeting. God forbid we shouldn't waste half our life in meetings!" She practically danced her way back across the hall. *I've got a vampire and he's going to give me the world!* An AIDS vaccine would be only the beginning.

As he followed her, Dr. Rob Fortin, associate professor of microbiology, found himself wishing he had an excuse to cut and run. When Aline Burke looked that cheerful, someone's ass was grass.

In the lab, Catherine stared at the phone for a moment, then somberly shook her head. "It's not like I don't have other things to do," she muttered.

Turning slightly, she shot a reassuring smile at number nine and number ten. She'd been shuffling them in and out of the one remaining isolation box all day as their physical needs had dictated but hadn't really been able to spend any quality time with them. "I'm not ignoring you," she said earnestly. "I'll just finish up this analysis for Dr. Burke and then we can get back to important things."

Donald, she could guiltlessly ignore for another twelve hours or so, but it wasn't fair to the others that all her time be taken up by Mr. Henry Fitzroy, vampire.

After all, he wasn't going anywhere.

The key had hardly entered the lock when the door to the next apartment opened and Mr. Delgado came out into the hall.

"Vicki, I thought it was you." He took a step toward her, the lines around his eyes deepening into worried grooves. "The police haven't found anything?"

"The police aren't exactly looking," Vicki told him tersely.

"Not looking? But . . ."

"The murder at the university has tied up their manpower," Celluci interjected. "They're doing what they can."

Mr. Delgado snorted. "Of course you'd say that, Mister Detective-Sergeant." He gestured at Vicki. "But she shouldn't have to be doing this. She shouldn't have to go out looking."

Vicki's fingers whitened around the key. "It's my responsibility, Mr. Delgado."

He spread his hands. "Why?"

"Because she's my mother."

"No." He shook his head. "She *was* your mother. But your mother isn't anymore. Your mother is dead. Finding her body won't bring your mother back to you."

Celluci watched a muscle jump in Vicki's jaw and waited for the explosion. To his surprise, it didn't come.

"You don't understand," she said through clenched teeth and moved swiftly into the apartment.

Celluci remained in the hallway a moment longer.

"I'm right. I watched her grow up." Mr. Delgado sighed, the deep, weary exhalation of an old man who'd seen more death than he cared to remember. "She thinks it's her fault her mother died and if she can just find the body it'll make amends."

"Is that such a bad thing?"

"Yes. Because it *isn't* her fault Majory died," Mr. Delgado pointed out, turned on his heel, and left Celluci standing alone in the hall.

He found Vicki sitting on the couch, staring down at her notes, all the lights in the apartment on even though it was barely mid-afternoon and the living room was far from dark.

"He doesn't know about Henry," she said without looking up.

"I know," Celluci agreed.

"And just because I've reacted to my mother's body being stolen by attempting to find it again, well, that doesn't mean I'm repressing anything. People grieve in different ways. Damn it, if *you* were in my situation, you'd be out looking for *your* mother's body."

"Granted."

"My mother's dead, Mike. I know that."

So you keep saying. But he closed his teeth on the words.

"And my mother isn't the fucking point anymore. We've got to find Henry before they turn him into . . . Christ!" She ripped off her glasses and rubbed at her eyes. "You think Donald Li's made a run for it?" she asked, somehow forcing the question to sound no different than it had on a hundred other occasions looking for a hundred other young men.

"I think that if a university student spends the night away from home it usually means he's gotten lucky." Celluci watched her closely but matched his tone to hers.

"On the other hand, if he *was* Tom Chen, he's probably aware we're looking for him and he's gone to ground. Maybe we *should* stake out his apartment."

"The little old lady on the first floor promised she'd call the moment he came home. My guess is she doesn't miss much."

"My guess is she doesn't miss anything." Her glasses back in place, Vicki scowled down at the pile of papers on the coffee table then jumped to her feet. "Mike, I can't just sit here. I'm going back to the university. I'm going keep poking around. Maybe I'll turn something up."

"What?"

"I don't know!" She charged toward the door and he had no choice but to get out of her way or be run down.

"Vicki? Before you go, can I ask you something?"

She stopped but didn't turn.

"*Do* you think you're responsible for your mother's death?"

He read the answer in the lines of her back, the sudden tension clearly visible even through shirt, sweater, and windbreaker.

"Vicki, it wasn't your fault when your father left and that didn't make your mother's life your responsibility."

He almost didn't recognize her voice when she answered. "When you love someone, they *become* your responsibility."

"Jesus H. Christ, Vicki! People aren't like puppies or kittens. Love isn't supposed to be that kind of a burden." He grabbed her shoulder and spun her around. Then wished he hadn't when he saw the look on her face. It was almost worse when that expression smoothed into one that told him nothing at all.

"If you are completely finished, Dr. Freud, you can get your god-damned hands off of me." A twist of her upper body, a step back, and she was free. "Now, are you going to help or are you going to sit around here all day with your psychoanalysis up your ass?"

She whirled, flung open the door, and stomped out into the hall before he had time to answer.

Well, Mr. Delgado. Celluci dragged both hands up through his hair and tried very hard not to grind the crowns off his teeth. *When you're right, you're really right. Still, she asked for my help. Again. I suppose that's progress of sorts.* Closing and locking the apartment behind him, he hurried to catch up. *Mind you, I'd feel better about that if it wasn't so obvious that she now feels responsible for Mr. Henry fucking Fitzroy.*

Dr. Burke acknowledged Mrs. Shaw's greeting but continued into her office without pausing. She couldn't decide what she hated more, bureaucracy itself or the sycophants that fawned around it. *Why,* she wondered, *does it have to be so difficult to end a term? Just send the students home and hose down the blackboards.*

The last thing that she needed, after not one but three meetings in which she valiantly attempted to impose logic onto rules and regulations, was to see Marjory Nelson's daughter wandering the halls of the Life Sciences building, peering through windows into labs and lecture halls and generally making a nuisance of herself. Watching the younger·woman's progress from the anonymity of a shadowed recess, she'd very nearly called Security and had her escorted out. The presence of the Toronto police officer—whom she'd been introduced to briefly at the truncated funeral—changed her mind. Arbitrary actions were just the sort of thing that tended to make the police suspicious.

Besides, the chances of Vicki Nelson stumbling onto the lab, and her mother's body, were slim. First, she'd have to find the access passage into the old building. Then, she'd have to negotiate through the rabbit warren of halls that crossed and recrossed the hundred-year-old structure—halls that had occasionally, in the past, defeated freshmen armed with maps—to find the one room in use.

No, Vicki Nelson had no chance of finding her mother's body, but that didn't mean Dr. Burke liked seeing her hanging around.

Why the hell doesn't she just go home? She dropped into her chair and fanned the pile of messages on her desk. *Without her prodding, the police would've back-burnered this before they'd even begun.*

If only the coffin hadn't been opened; no one would have been the wiser.

If only Donald hadn't allowed Marjory Nelson to walk out of the lab and home.

If only the sight of the mother reanimated hadn't convinced the daughter that the answer lay at the university.

Vicki Nelson was an intelligent woman; even allowing for maternal prejudices, the facts spoke for themselves. Eventually, in her search for her mother, she'd stumble onto something that would jeopardize Dr. Burke's position. Dr. Burke had no intention of allowing that to happen.

Slowly, the Director of Life Sciences smiled. The incredible circumstance that had dropped a vampire into her hands had also given her an easy answer to the problem. "If Ms. Nelson wants to find her mother so badly," she murmured, tapping out the number for the lab, "maybe she should."

Catherine answered the phone on the third ring with a terse, "What is it, Doctor? I'm busy."

"How are the tests going?"

"Well, you want rather a lot done and . . ."

"Isn't Donald helping?"

"No, he . . ."

"Has he even been in today?"

"Well, no, he . . ."

"I don't want to hear his excuses, Catherine, I'll deal with him myself later." This wasn't the first time Donald had taken an unscheduled holiday, but it *was* time she put her foot down about it. "Have you run into anything this afternoon that might prevent us developing an AIDS vaccine?"

"Well, actually, I've observed that certain nonphagocytic leukocytes have a number of specialized functions on a cellular level that might possibly be developed into just that." She paused for a moment, then continued. "We'd have to practically drain Mr. Fitzroy to acquire a serum, though, and his pressure's already awfully low. I keep having to take new samples because even a minute amount of ultraviolet light destroys the cell structure."

"For pity's sake, Catherine, don't let any ultraviolet light fall on him. We can always replenish his blood . . ." The thought brought an interesting evisceral response that could possibly be explored later when they had more time. ". . . but if he loses cellular integrity, even your bacteria won't be able to rebuild him."

"I am aware of that, Doctor. I'm being very careful."

"Good. Now, then, since Mr. Fitzroy so fortuitously fell into our hands, I've altered our plans somewhat. Here's what we're going to do: run one final analysis on numbers nine and ten—*no point in wasting data that might be useful later*—then terminate them, strip them of all hardware, do the usual biopsies, and process both of them out through the medical morgue. We'll work up the standard paperwork on number nine, but someone's sure to recognize Marjory Nelson. I'll see to it that she can't be traced back to us, everyone will claim ignorance, there'll be a six days' wonder, and then we'll be safely able to continue with no threat of discovery."

She could hear breathing so she knew Catherine was still on the line, but moments passed and there was no response. "Catherine?"

"Terminate numbers nine and ten?"

"That's right. We don't need them anymore." She felt a triumphant smile spread across her face and made no effort to stop it. "We have captured a creature who in and of himself can unlock the Nobel door."

Catherine ignored the triumph. "But that'll kill them!"

"Don't be ridiculous, they're already dead."

"But, Dr. Burke . . ."

Dr. Burke sighed and moved her glasses up on her head

so she could rub at her temples. "No buts, Catherine. They're becoming a liability. I was willing to overlook that when they were our best chance for success, but with Mr. Fitzroy under our control we have an unlimited potential to make scientific history." She softened her voice. Once again Catherine would have to be manipulated onto the most productive path. "If you can fuse the elements of Henry Fitzroy's blood into your bacteria, it will make everything we've done so far redundant. We're moving onto a new level of scientific discovery here."

"Yes, but . . ."

"Science moves forward, Catherine. You can't let yourself be trapped in the past. An opportunity like this doesn't come along every day." *Now,* that *was an understatement,* she mused as the triumphant smile returned. "You begin the termination. I'll be down as soon as I can. Sunset is at 7:47, see that Mr. Fitzroy is locked up tightly a good half an hour before then."

Sounding numb, Catherine murmured, "Yes, Dr. Burke," into the phone and hung up.

Shaking her head, Dr. Burke replaced the receiver. In a few days Catherine would be so immersed in new discoveries that she'd forget numbers nine and ten even existed as anything but collections of experimental data. *Which, of course,* she reminded herself acerbically, *is all they are.*

Catherine stared at the phone for a moment, turning Dr. Burke's words over and over in her head. Science had to keep going forward. It couldn't remain stuck in the past.

Science had to keep going forward.

She truly believed that.

The quest for knowledge, in and of itself, is of primary importance. Those were her own words, spoken to the doctor during her search for the funds and lab space necessary to develop her bacteria to their full potential. Dr. Burke had agreed and they'd taken the quest together.

Terminate numbers nine and ten.

She couldn't do it.

Dr. Burke was wrong. They were alive.

She wouldn't do it.

Taking a deep breath and smoothing the front of her lab coat, she turned. Sitting where she'd left them against the far wall, they were both watching her; almost as if they knew. They trusted her. She wasn't going to let them down.

Unfortunately, bundling them into the back of her van and disappearing into the sunset wasn't an option. In order to keep them functional, she needed the lab. Dr. Burke, therefore, had to be made to change her mind.

. . . with Mr. Fitzroy under our control we have an unlimited potential to make scientific history.

Suppose Mr. Fitzroy was no longer under her control?

Brow furrowed in thought, Catherine crossed the room to the isolation box that held the quiescent vampire. Essentially, it was operating as nothing more than a containment unit with none of its specialized functions working. It wasn't even plugged in. Theoretically, it was mobile. In actuality, its weight made it difficult to move.

Catherine placed both hands against one end and shoved as hard as she could. Nothing. Bracing her feet against the wall, she shoved again, straining until her vision went red.

The isolation box jerked forward six inches and stopped when she did.

It had taken all three of them, her and Donald and Dr. Burke, to move the empty boxes in. Catherine bowed her head over her folded arms, breath misting the cool metal, and admitted she couldn't move it out, not on her own.

Number nine stood and walked carefully forward, supporting himself once on the back of a chair as his left leg nearly folded beneath him. He had no way of knowing that inside the knee, tendons and ligaments were finally surrendering to rot.

He saw she was sad.

That was enough.

He stopped beside her and laid his hand on her shoulder.

Catherine turned at the touch and looked up. "If we hide the vampire," she said, "we'll have time to convince Dr. Burke that she's wrong."

There were many words number nine didn't understand, so he merely placed his palms where hers had been, and pushed.

*   *   *

The isolation box rumbled forward.

"Stop."

Number nine stopped pushing. The box moved a few inches farther, then ground to a halt under its own weight.

"Yes! We can do this together!" Catherine threw her arms around number nine in an impulsive hug, ignoring the way. tissue compacted under her touch, ignoring the smell that had begun to rise.

Number nine struggled to recognize what he felt.

It was . . .

It was . . .

Then her arms were gone and it was lost.

Stepping back, Catherine glanced around the lab. "We can hide the vampire and the other isolation box as well. That way, Dr. Burke won't be able to hold you hostage for his return. The dialysis machine is portable and an IV drip can replace the nutrient pump for a few days. We'll take one of the computers with us just in case Dr. Burke takes too long to come to her senses. You shouldn't suffer from lack of input just because she's being stubborn."

Then she paused. "Oh, no. Donald." Reaching out, she patted the box that enclosed the body of the other grad student. "I can't unplug you, Donald, it's too soon. I'm sorry, but we'll have to leave you here." She sighed deeply. "I only hope that Dr. Burke will allow you to finish developing. She's just not thinking straight, Donald. I've had this feeling lately that all she wants is fame and money, that she doesn't care about the experiments. I care. I know you'll understand."

Checking her watch, she hurried back across the room to the computer terminal, copied the day's work onto a disk, and then scrubbed it from the main memory. "Just in case," she murmured, slipping the copy into her lab coat pocket. "I can't leave her a way out."

On her way back to where number nine waited patiently, she picked up the vampire's trench coat and the shirt she'd had to remove as well. She didn't have time to dress him again, but she spread them neatly over the body before closing the lid and latching it.

"This is going to take all of us. Number ten, come here."

*   *   *

Released from the compulsion to stay, she rose to her feet. "Come here" was not an implanted command so, although she knew what it meant, she moved toward the door.

She had something she had to do.

"Stop." Catherine shook her head and circled around number ten until she could look her in the face. "There's something the matter, isn't there? I wish you could tell me what it was, maybe I could help. But you *can't* tell me and, right now, we've all got problems."

Taking hold of one gray-green wrist, Catherine led Marjory Nelson's body over to stand beside the front end of the box, wrapped dark-tipped fingers around a metal handle, and said, "Hold."

The fingers tightened.

With number nine pushing and number ten obeying rapid orders to push or pull, the massive piece of equipment, and the body it contained, rumbled across the lab and out into the hall.

. . . you could tell me what it was . . .
. . . you could tell me . . .
She remembered *talking*.

If vampires exist. . . Dr. Burke scribbled a question mark in the margin of an application for summer research funds that had been handed in at absolutely the last minute. *. . . and they very obviously do, then just think of what else might be out there. Demons. Werewolves. The Creature from the Black Lagoon.* Even though her cheeks were beginning to ache, she couldn't control the spreading grin. Hadn't been able to control it all afternoon. *Henry Fitzroy's blood will enable me to collect every accolade the scientific community possesses on a silver platter. In fact, they'll have to create new awards, just for me.*

They would have to take precautions, of course. The legendary vampire had been accredited with a number of abilities that could be a threat. While many of them could be discounted out of hand—as he hadn't been able to get out of the isolation box before sunrise, the actual vampire appeared incapable of becoming mist—he *was* very strong; the dents he'd added to number nine's pattern on the inside of the lid testified to that. *So it's probably best that he spend his nights locked in that box.*

He'd have to be fed, of course, if only to replace the fluids Catherine removed during the day. Fortunately, there were a number of small tubes available that blood could be passed through.

And as for the granting of eternal life. Dr. Burke drummed her fingertips on the desk. Henry Fitzroy's identification seemed to indicate that he lived a reasonably normal life, even considering that the day was unquestionably denied him, and nothing but legend indicated that he'd lived any longer than the twenty-four years his driver's license allowed him. She'd have to discuss his history with him later—not that it mattered much. What point in living forever if forever had to be lived in hiding? *Skulking about in the dark. Helpless in the day. Not, I think, for me.*

After years of being anonymously responsible for keeping the infrastructure of science running, she wanted recognition. She'd spent long enough tucked away out of sight, tilting with bureaucracy while others garnered the glory.

One lifetime, properly appreciated, would be long enough. Conquering death had always been merely a means to an end and she had no more intention of becoming a blood-drinking creature of the night than she did of allowing her body to be used to create one of those shambling monstrosities she'd told Catherine to destroy.

Although, perhaps when Catherine has all the bugs worked out . . .

Resisting the temptation to begin composing her acceptance speech for Stockholm, Dr. Burke forced herself to concentrate on the grant application. When she'd dealt with this last bit of unavoidable paperwork, she'd be free to spend a few hours in the lab. She was actually looking forward to the unavoidable conversation with their captured vampire.

Half an hour later, a tentative knock at the office door brought her up out of a projected balance sheet that proved at least one of the department's professors had taken a course in economics—and not paid much attention.

"Come in."

Mrs. Shaw leaned into the room. "I just wanted to let you know that I'm leaving now, Doctor."

"Is it as late as all that?"

The older woman smiled. "It's later. But Ms. Grenier and I pretty much cleared the backlog."

Dr. Burke nodded approvingly. "Good. Thank you for all the hard work." Appreciation made the best motivator regardless of where it was applied. "There'll be another stack out there tomorrow," she added, indicating the pile of folders on the corner of her desk.

"You can count on me, Doctor. Good night. Oh." The door, in the process of closing, opened again and Mrs. Shaw reappeared. "Marjory's daughter was around this morning. She wanted Donald Li's home address. I hope you don't mind."

"A little late now if I did, isn't it?" Somehow, she managed to keep the question light. "Did Ms. Nelson tell you *why* she wanted Donald's address?"

"She wanted to talk to him about her mother." Mrs. Shaw began to look worried at the expression on her employer's face. "I know it's against policy, but she *is* Marjory's daughter."

"*Was* Marjory's daughter," Dr. Burke pointed out dryly. "Never mind, Mrs. Shaw." There was no point in getting annoyed so long after the fact. "If Donald doesn't want to talk to her, I'm sure he can take care of it himself."

"Thank you, Doctor. Good night."

Dr. Burke waited a moment, to be certain that this time the door would stay closed, then pulled the phone across the desk and tapped in Donald's number. After four rings, his answering machine came on with a trumpet fanfare and the message that ". . . autographed pictures are available for twenty dollars plus a self-addressed, stamped envelope. For personal dedications, add five dollars. Those actually wishing conversation with Mr. Li can leave a message after the tone and he'll get back to you the moment he has a break in his too, too busy schedule."

"This is Dr. Burke. If you're there, Donald, pick up."

Apparently, he wasn't there. After leaving instructions that she be called at his earliest opportunity, Dr. Burke hung up and shoved the phone away.

"He's probably spent the day avoiding that woman. At least he didn't lead her to the lab."

The lab . . .

A memory nibbled at the edge of conscious thought. Something to do with the lab. She leaned back in her chair and frowned up at the ceiling tiles. Something not quite right that the incredible discovery of the vampire had distracted her from. Something so normal . . .

. . . leaned back against number eight's box, allowing the soft vibration of machinery to soothe her jangled nerves.

Number eight no longer existed. The vampire was in number nine's box but both number nine and number ten had been sitting passively against the wall.

Who was in number eight's box?

Then a second memory surfaced.

Gathering up the contents of the wallet, she tossed them onto a pile of clothes draped over a nearby chair.

It suddenly got very hard to breathe.

"Oh, lord, no . . ."

They could hear the phone ringing from the hall. As could be expected under the circumstances, the key jammed.

Four rings. Five.

"God*damn*it!" Her mood not exactly sunny, Vicki backed up and slammed the bottom of her foot against the door just below the lock. The entire structure shuddered under the impact. When she grabbed the key again, it turned.

"Nothing like the Luke Skywalker method," Celluci muttered, racing for the phone.

Nine rings. Ten.

"Yes? Hello?"

"Good timing, Mike. I was just about to hang up."

Celluci mouthed "Dave Graham" at Vicki, jammed the receiver between ear and shoulder, and readied a pen. "What've you got for me?"

"I had to call in a couple of favors—you owe me for this, partner—but Humber College finally came through. Your boy was recommended to the course by a Dr. Dabir Rashid, Faculty of Medicine, Queen's University. And as a bonus, they threw in the information that he requested young Mr. Chen serve his four-week observation period at Hutchinson's."

"No mention of a Dr. Aline Burke?"

"Nary a word. How's Vicki?"

Good question. "Damned if I know."

"Like that, is it? You gotta remember that death affects different people different ways. I know when my uncle died, my aunt seemed almost relieved, handled the funeral like it was a family reunion. Two weeks later, blam. Completely fell apart. And my wife's cousin, he . . ."

"Dave."

"Yeah?"

"Later."

"Oh. Right. Listen, Cantree says to take as much time as you need for this. He said we'll manage to muddle through somehow without you."

"Nice of him."

"He's a saint. Let me know how it shakes down."

"You got it, buddy." He turned from hanging up the phone to find Vicki glaring at him. "Our Tom Chen got his recommendation from a Dr. Dabir Rashid, Faculty of Medicine, Queen's University. I don't suppose that could be an alias for Dr. Burke?"

"No. I met Dr. Rashid briefly yesterday." Vicki stomped across the room and threw herself down onto the couch. "He's a year older than God and isn't sure if he's coming or going. I assume he has tenure."

Celluci dropped a hip onto the telephone table and shrugged. "Easy to confuse, then, if you wanted him to do you a favor you didn't want traced."

"Exactly." Vicki spit the word out. "He probably thought he was recommending the Tom Chen who's actually studying medicine." She jabbed at her glasses. "From what I saw, if he even remembers giving it, he'll never remember who asked him to do it."

"Then we'll have to stimulate his memory."

Vicki snorted. "The shock would probably kill him."

"You never know. The recommendation included a request that Chen serve his four-week observation period at Hutchinson's—the more details, more chance one of them stuck."

"Yeah. Maybe." Snatching up a green brocade cushion, she threw it against the far wall. "Jesus, Mike; why isn't it ever easy?"

Another good question. "I don't know, Vicki, maybe . . ."

His voice trailed off as he watched all the color suddenly drain out of her face. "Vicki? What's wrong?"

"It's a four-week observation period." Her hands were shaking so violently she couldn't lace the fingers together, so she curled them into fists and pressed the fists hard against her thighs. "My mother was given six months to live." She had to force the words out through a throat closed tight. "They couldn't keep placing people in that funeral home." Why hadn't she seen it before? "My mother had to die during those four weeks." She turned her head and met Celluci's gaze square on. "Do you know what that means?"

He knew.

"My mother was murdered, Mike." Her voice became steel and ice. "And who was with my mother seconds before she died?"

He reached behind him and scooped up the phone. "I think we've got something Detective Fergusson will listen to now . . ."

"No." Vicki got slowly to her feet, her movements jerky and barely under control. "First, we've got to rescue Henry. Once he's safe, she's history. But not until."

She wasn't going to fail Henry the way she'd failed her mother.

Twelve

As the day surrendered its power to hold him, Henry fought the panic that accompanied awareness—the steel coffin still enclosed him, wrapped him in the stink of death perverted and the acrid odor of his own terror. He couldn't prevent the first two blows that slammed up into the impervious arc of padded metal, but he managed to stop the third and the fourth. With full consciousness came greater control. He remembered the futile struggles of the night before and knew that mere physical strength would not be enough to free him.

His head swam with images—the young man, strangled, newly dead; the older man, long dead, not dead, not alive; the young woman, pale hair, pale skin, empty eyes. He swallowed, tasted the residue of blood, and was nearly lost as the Hunger rose.

It was too strong to force back. Henry barely managed to hold the line between the Hunger and self.

He had fed the night before. The Hunger should be his to command. Then he realized his struggles had tangled his arms in the heavy folds of his leather trench coat. Someone had removed both it and his shirt and not bothered to replace them. Bare to the waist, he found the marks of a dozen needles.

And I no more want to be strapped to a table for the rest of my life than to have my head removed and my mouth stuffed with garlic.

He'd made that observation, somewhat facetiously, just over a year ago. It seemed much less facetious now. Over the course of the day someone had obviously been conducting experiments. He was helpless during the oblivion of the day. He was captive in the night.

The panic won and a crimson tide of Hunger roared free with it.

Consciousness returned a second time that night, bringing pain and an exhaustion so complete he could barely straighten twisted limbs. His body, weakened by blood loss, had obviously set a limit on hysteria.

Can't say . . . as I blame it. Even thinking hurt. Screaming had ripped his throat raw. Bruising, bone-deep on knees and elbows, protested movement. Two of the fingers on his left hand were broken and the skin over the knuckles, split. With what seemed like the last of his strength, he realigned the fractures then lay panting, trying not to taste the abomination in the air.

They've taken so much blood, I have to assume they know what I am.

The Hunger filled his prison with throbbing crimson need, bound for the moment by his weakness. Eventually, the weakness would be devoured and the Hunger would rule.

In all his seventeen years, Henry had never been in a darkness so complete and, in spite of Christina's remembered reassurances, he began to panic. The panic grew when he tried to lift the lid off the crypt and found he couldn't move. Not stone above him but rough wood embracing him so closely that the rise and fall of his chest brushed against the boards.

He had no idea how long he lay, paralyzed by terror, frenzied need clawing at his gut, but his sanity hung by a . . .

"No." He could manage no more than a whispered protest, not quite enough to banish the memory. The terror of that first awakening, trapped in a common grave, nearly destroyed by the Hunger, would reach out to claim him now if he let it. "Remember the rest, if you must remember at all."

. . . he heard a shovel blade bite into the dirt above him, the noise a hundred thousand times louder than it could possibly have been."

"Henry!"

The Hunger surged out toward the voice, carrying him with it.

"Henry!"

His name. It was his name she called. He clutched at it like a lifeline, the Hunger a surrounding maelstrom.

"Henry, answer me!"

Although the Hunger tried to drown him out, he formed a single word. "Christina . . ."

Then, the nails shrieking protest, the coffin lid flew back. Pale hands, strong hands, gentle hands held him in his frenzy. Rough homespun ripped away from alabaster skin and a wound in a breast reopened so he could feed again on the blood that had changed him, safe behind a silken curtain of ebony hair.

He couldn't free himself.

Four hundred and fifty years ago, a woman's love had saved him.

He couldn't surrender to despair.

But it had taken Christina three days . . .

Vicki, come quickly. Please. I can't survive that again.

The halls had always been empty when she walked them, empty, echoing, and dimly lit. *And they are no different tonight,* Aline Burke told herself firmly, placing one foot purposefully before the other. *They are still empty. I am making the only sounds. Shadows are merely absences of light.*

But air currents moved where she'd never felt air currents before and the whole building exuded an aura of expectant doom.

Which is not only overly melodramatic, it's ridiculous. She dried moist palms against her pants and kept her eyes firmly focused on the next band of illumination. She would not give in to fear; she never had and she wasn't about to begin now.

Who was in number eight's isolation box?

There could be any number of very good reasons why Donald hadn't been around all day; Vicki Nelson's investigation was only the most obvious. Donald, charming, brilliant, and undisciplined, had never had any trouble in coming up with reasons to take a day off.

Who was in number eight's isolation box?

Memory continued to replay the fall of Henry Fitzroy's wallet onto the pile of clothes.

Who was in number eight's isolation box?

There was only one way to find out.

Rounding a corner, she could see the outline of the lab door. No light escaped, but then they'd gone to a great deal of trouble to ensure that none did.

They're probably both in there. Arguing about something trivial. Or he's watching her work, letting those damned candy wrappers fall on my floor.

She put her hand on the metal doorknob, the stainless steel cold under her fingers. Stainless steel. Like the isolation boxes.

Her heart began to pound. The metal warmed under her grip. Fifteen seconds passed. Twenty. Forty-five. A full minute. She couldn't turn the knob. It was as if the link between brain and hand had been severed. She knew what she had to do, but her body refused to respond.

Lips compressed into a thin line, she jerked her arm back to her side. This kind of betrayal could not be allowed. She drew in a calming breath, exhaled, and then in one continuous motion grabbed the knob, turned it, pushed the door open, and stepped into the room.

The lights were off. She could see a number of red and green power indicators at the far end of the room but nothing else. Stretching out her left arm, she groped along the wall, the sound of her breathing moving outward to meet the hum of working equipment. The light switches were just to the right of the door. Turning her back was out of the question.

Her fingers touched a steel plate, recoiled, then continued on until finally they hooked behind a protruding bit of plastic.

A heartbeat later, Dr. Burke blinked in the sudden bluewhite glare of the fluorescents.

At the far end of the room, number eight's isolation box—number eight's no longer—hummed in unattended solitude. The other two boxes were gone and with them the portable dialysis machine and one of the computers. A quick scan showed smaller pieces of equipment were missing as well and apprehension turned to anger as Dr. Burke stomped the length of the room to the remaining computer.

"That vindictive little bitch!"

The message on the screen was succinct and to the point.

I've hidden Mr. Fitzroy. You can have him back when you agree that numbers nine and ten can continue to their natural conclusions. I have the only copy of today's data. I'll be in touch. –Catherine.

Obviously, she'd not only hidden the vampire but numbers nine and ten as well.

"Damn her! She must've started the second I hung up the phone." This would ruin everything! If Catherine couldn't be brought round and quickly, the whole plan would be as dead as . . .

. . . as dead as . . .

She raised her head and bands of pressure settled around her temples. The distorted reflection of a small, warped figure in white stared back from the curved side of the only remaining box.

Why hadn't Catherine hidden this box as well?

Because it couldn't be unplugged.

Why couldn't it be unplugged?

Because the bacteria still worked on the body it contained.

Who was in number eight's isolation box?

The clothes remained on a chair on the other side of the lab, a pale brown windbreaker draped over the back.

Lots of people wear jackets like that in Kingston in April.

She made the largest circle around the box she could without admitting to herself that she was avoiding it. Desperately holding on to the anger, using it as a weapon against the rising fear, she reached out and lifted the jacket off the chair. It could still belong to anyone. Ignoring the damp smudges her fingers printed on the fabric, she reached into one of the front pockets and drew out two wrapped candies and a half-eaten chocolate bar, package neatly resealed with a bit of tape.

There's nothing that says Donald couldn't have left his jacket in the lab.

But she was losing the fight and she knew it.

Henry Fitzroy's identification lay where she'd tossed it.

Draping the jacket over one arm, she watched her free hand reach out and scoop the wallet and its contents up off a neatly folded pile of clothes. A jacket might be accidentally left behind but not jeans and a shirt, socks and underwear. These were Donald's clothes, no question of that, and beneath the chair, heels and toes precisely in line, were the black high-top basketball sneakers he'd been so absurdly proud of.

"But Donald, you don't play basketball."

Donald continued to vigorously pump the bright orange ball set into the tongues of his new shoes. "What does that have to do with anything?" he asked, grinning broadly. "We're talking the cutting edge of footwear here. We're talking high tech. We're talking image."

Dr. Burke sighed and shook her head. "The perception of athletics without the sweat?" she offered.

The grin grew broader. "The point exactly."

Still holding the jacket and the vampire's wallet, Dr. Burke slowly turned to face the isolation box. Numbers one through nine had been pulled from the medical school morgue already very dead. Marjory Nelson was dying. But Donald, Donald had been very alive.

She took a step forward, feeling so removed from reality that she had to concentrate on placing her foot down on the floor. Walking no longer seemed to be a voluntary movement. She could see Donald, dark eyes sparkling, completely unrepentant, as he sat in her office and listened to the reasons why he should not only be thrown out of medical school but brought up on charges. When she'd asked him why he'd done it, he'd actually looked thoughtful for a moment before answering. *"I wanted to see what would happen."* She'd gotten him off. The particulars were buried when the professor who'd uncovered the incident had moved out west the next semester.

She took another step. She could see Donald frowning over the neural net, clever fingers running along the gold strands, bottom lips caught between his teeth as he struggled with the design.

Another step. She could see Donald lifting a confused Catherine's hand aloft for a high-five when number four finally responded to their combined genius.

Another. She could see Donald joining her in a private

toast to fame and fortune, barely touching the single malt to his lips, for he never drank.

Another. She could see Donald agreeing that Marjory Nelson was the inevitable next step.

Her knee touched the box, the vibration burrowing into the bone. She flinched back, then froze.

Staring down at her reflection, she saw it become a progression of gray faces, contorted, robbed of rest, bodies disfigured by gaping incisions hastily tacked together with knotted railway lines of black silk. What would she see when she lifted the lid? How far had Catherine gone?

Forcing a deep breath past the constriction in her throat, she let Henry Fitzroy's wallet drop from her right hand to floor. It wasn't really important anymore. Anymore. Anymore . . .

She reached out, unable to stop the trembling but refusing to give in, and wrapped her empty hand around the latch. Her fingers were so cold, the metal felt warm beneath them.

"Knowledge is strength," she whispered.

The latch clicked open.

From inside the box came a sigh of oxygen rich air as the seal broke, then, following it, a noise that had nothing to do with electronics or machinery.

Dr. Burke froze. The muscles in her arm, already given the command to lift, spasmed and shook.

A moan.

"Donald?"

Vowels began to form. A tortured shaping. Still recognizable.

There was nothing even remotely human in the sound.

Sweat dribbled in icy tracks down her sides. Fingers fought to close the latch. Whatever was in there wasn't getting out.

"Doc . . . tor . . ."

She jerked back; panting, whimpering. Then she turned and ran.

Terror that couldn't be banished by intellect, or rationalizations, or strength of purpose ran beside her through the empty halls. The echoes mocked her. The shadows bulged with horror.

* * *

"What if she's not there?"

"She's not at home," Vicki replied through set teeth—they'd found Dr. Burke's address in the brown leather book beside her mother's phone. "She has to be somewhere."

"Not necessarily at the office."

Vicki turned to face him, even though the darkness left her blind. "You have a better idea?"

She heard him sigh. "No. But if she isn't there, what then?"

"Then we rip her office apart. We look for anything that might tell us where Henry is."

"And if we don't . . ."

"Shut up, Celluci." She spat the words in his direction. "We'll find him."

He drew in breath to speak again, then let it out silently.

Vicki twisted back around in the passenger seat, her grip on the dashboard painfully tight. *We'll find him.* All she could see through the windshield was the glare of the headlights, nothing of what they illuminated, not even the surface of the road. The lights of other cars appeared suspended, red and yellow eyes on invisible beasts. She felt the car turn, then slow, then finally stop. Silence fell, then darkness.

"I parked around beside the building," Celluci said. "A little less obvious if we have to slip past Security."

"Good idea."

For a moment, neither of them moved, then Vicki turned toward her door just as Celluci opened his. The interior light came on and for a heartbeat she saw herself reflected in the car window.

Pressed up against the glass, fingers splayed, mouth silently working, was her mother.

"Mike!"

He was at her side in an instant, the door mercifully closing as he slid across the front seat. She backed into the circle of his arms, squeezed her eyes so tightly shut they hurt, and tried to stop shaking.

"Vicki, what is it? What's wrong?" He'd never heard his name called in such a way before and he hoped like hell he'd never hear it called that way again. The pain in Vicki's voice not only gouged pieces out of his soul, it clutched at him in a way *she* wasn't able to. She had her back pressed so hard against his chest he could barely breathe, but her fingers were folded into fists and her arms wrapped tightly around herself.

"Mike, my mother is dead."

He rested his cheek against the top of her head. "I know."

"Yeah, but she's also up and walking around." A hint of hysteria crept into her tone. "So, it just occurred to me, when we find her, what are we supposed to do. I mean, how do we bury her?"

"Jesus H. Christ." The whispered profanity came out sounding more like a prayer.

"I mean," she had to gulp air between every couple of words, "am I going to have to kill her again?"

"Vicki!" He held her closer. It was all he could think of to do. "Goddamnit! You didn't kill her the first time! As much as it seems cruel to say it, her dying had *nothing* to do with you."

He could feel her fighting for control.

"Maybe not the first time," she said.

The Hunger clawed and fought to be free and it took almost all the strength he had left to contain it. Released, it would quickly drive his abused body back into unconsciousness, probably breaking more bones as it fought to feed. Henry had no intention of allowing that to happen. He *had* to remain aware in case his captors should actually be stupid enough to open the box between dusk and dawn.

With so little left to fuel fear, he was able to view his imprisonment almost dispassionately. Almost. Memories of being trapped in darkness flickered mothlike against the outside edges of his control but worse even than that were images of the experiments that would begin when sunrise made him vulnerable once more.

Henry had seen the Inquisition, the slave trade, and the concentration camps of World War II and knew full well the atrocities people were able to commit. He'd seen his own father condemn men and women to the pyre for no better reason than temper. *And these particular people,* he thought, *have already proven themselves less than ethically bound.* There had been three containers. He was in one of them. Vicki's mother was, no doubt, in one of the other two.

Turning his head slightly so that the flow of fresh air through the grille—through the unbreakable grille—passed over his mouth and nose, he concentrated on breathing. It wasn't much of a distraction, but it was one of the few he had.

A minor comfort that I don't have to worry about suffoca . . .

The stench of abomination suddenly engulfed him. He jerked back against the far side of his prison, shoulder blades pressed hard into the plastic, laboring heart pounding in his ears. The creature was right outside the box; it had to be.

Cupping his injured hand against his chest, Henry fought for calm. This might be his only chance for freedom; he couldn't allow blind panic to take it from him.

Something dragged across the top of the box, something large and soft. Henry had a sudden vision of an old Hammer film, where Dracula brought his pair of hungry brides a child to feed on.

Oh, lord, not that.

Given an opportunity to feed, he wouldn't be able to stop the Hunger. The child would die. He'd killed many times over the centuries; sometimes because he had to, sometimes only because he could. But never an innocent. Never a child.

The dragging stopped.

When the lid opens . . . Henry made himself as ready as he was able. But the lid remained closed and a moment later, muscles trembling, he sagged back against the padded bottom.

"If I call her in the morning, she'll have had time to think it over and she'll realize that I'm serious."

Although he could still smell nothing but abomination, Henry recognized the voice. It belonged to the pale young woman with the empty eyes.

"She's a reasonable person and I'm sure that as a scientist she'll come to see my position."

The young woman was crazy. Henry, who had touched her mind, had no doubt about that. But she was also on the outside of the box, capable of releasing him, and crazy or not, she was, at this moment, the only game in town. Ignoring the pain, he squirmed around until his mouth pressed up against the dented surface of the air vents and pitched his voice to carry, keeping his tone as matter-of-fact as he could.

"Excuse me? Would you mind opening the lid?"

For a very little while, he thought normalcy might have worked where an attempt at coercion or charm would've found no reaction. He caught a trace of her scent threaded through the stink of perverted death—not, he thanked God, enough to pull the Hunger out of his control—he heard her hands at the latch, then he heard her reply.

"Yes, I would mind actually, because I didn't have time today to take any tissue samples."

"If all you want are tissue samples, let me out and I'll stay around so you can take them." Henry swallowed, his throat working around the fear. *Just let me* out!

"Well, actually, I'm not very good at biopsies on living subjects. I think I'll wait until tomorrow."

Not very good at biopsies on living subjects? What the hell was she talking about? "But I'll still be alive!"

"Not exactly." She sounded as though she were pointing out something so obvious that she couldn't understand why he even brought it up.

He heard her move away. "Wait!"

"What is it now? I have a lot on my mind tonight."

"Look, do you know what I am?" All things considered, she *had* to know.

"Yes. You're a vampire."

"Do you know what that means?"

"Yes. You have fascinating leukocytes."

"What?" He couldn't stop himself from asking.

"Leukocytes. White blood cells. And your hemoglobin has amazing potential as well."

Much more of this and I'll be as crazy as she is. "If you know what I am, you know what I can give you." His voice reverberated inside the box; ageless, powerful. "Let me out and I can give you eternal life. You'll never grow old. You'll never die."

"No, thank you. I'm working on something else at the moment."

And he heard her move away.

"Wait!" He forced himself to lie quiet and listen, but all he could hear was the pounding of his own heart and Henry Fitzroy, bastard son of Henry the VIII, four-hundred-and-fifty-year-old vampire, became suddenly just Henry Fitzroy.

"DON'T LEAVE ME ALONE!"

"You know," Catherine said, pulling the heavy steel door closed behind her. "I hadn't realized he'd be so noisy. Good thing we put him in here." She slid a lock through the eye of the security bar and snapped it shut. "Dr. Burke will never be able to hear him."

Number nine stared at the door. The "Warning: High Voltage" meant nothing to him, but he remembered being locked in the box. In the same box. He hadn't liked it.

Slowly, the two fingers on his right hand that were still working closed around the security bar.

Already halfway across the room, Catherine turned at the noise as the lock jumped but held. "What is it? What's wrong?"

Without releasing the bar, he carefully turned to face her. He hadn't liked being locked in the box.

"You think I should have let him out?" She came back to his side, shaking her head. "You don't understand. If I can isolate the factors that result in his continuous cell regeneration, I can integrate them into a bacterium that will actually repair you." Taking hold of his wrist, she very gently pulled his hand from the door and smiled up at him. "You can stay with me forever."

He understood the smile.

He understood forever.

That was enough.

His walk had degenerated into a lurch and a shuffle as he followed her from the room.

He remembered joy.

The level in the bottle of single malt whiskey had dropped rather considerably over the last . . . Dr. Burke peered at her watch but couldn't quite make out the time. Not that it mattered. Not really. Not any more.

"Nothing can stop me from garnering the glory." Bracing her elbow, she poured a little more whiskey into her mug.

"I said that. Nothing can stop me." She took a long drink and sat back, cradling the mug against her stomach.

"Doc . . . tor . . ."

She couldn't hear him. He was locked in a stainless steel box in another building.

"Doc . . . tor . . ."

She took another drink to drown out the sound.

"Are you all right?"

Vicki slid into the outer office and started across the room. Why was he asking her now? She'd managed to regain control before they left the car. "I'm fine."

"Would you tell me if you weren't?"

Unable to see, she slammed her knee into the side of a desk and bit back a curse. Obviously, her memory of the office layout was less than perfect. "Fuck off, Celluci."

Aware she could no more see him than she could see anything else, he rolled his eyes. She certainly sounded a lot better.

Dr. Burke heard the impact of flesh against furniture even through the covering noise of the whiskey. Her heart stopped. She *had* latched the isolation box. It *couldn't* have climbed out and followed her.

Could it?

Then she heard the voices and her heart started beating again.

"How nice." The alcohol she'd consumed, while not yet enough to insulate her from the memory of what she'd left in the lab, was enough to make her feel removed from the rest of the world. "I've got company."

Bending carefully down from her chair so as not to put more stress on an already overloaded sense of balance, she lifted Donald's jacket from the carpet and laid it on the desk in front of her.

"Please come in, Ms. Nelson. I can't abide a person who lurks."

Celluci pivoted to face the door. "Sounds like we've found the doctor." Through the light grip around Vicki's biceps he felt her shudder, but her voice remained steady.

"So let's not keep her waiting."

Together they moved into the inner office.

The street lamp, outside the window and five stories down, provided enough illumination for Celluci to see the doctor sitting at her desk. He couldn't make out her expression, but he could smell the booze. Twisting around, he stretched back a long arm and flicked on the overhead light.

In the sudden glare, no one moved, no one said anything, until Vicki stepped forward, watering eyes squinted almost shut, and said with no trace of humor, "Dr. Frankenstein, I presume."

Dr. Burke snorted with laughter. "Good God, wit under stress. We could use a little more of that around here. Grad students are generally a boring, academically intensive bunch." One hand closed tightly around a fold of the jacket on her desk, the other lifted the mug to her mouth. "Generally," she repeated after a moment.

"You're drunk," Vicki snarled.

"A-plus for perception. C-minus for manners. As obvious as it obviously is, that's not the sort of thing you're supposed to point out."

Vicki charged the desk, barely stopping herself from going over it with a white-knuckled grip on the edge. "Enough bullshit! What have you done with Henry Fitzroy?"

Dr. Burke looked momentarily surprised. "Oh, good lord, is *that* what this is about? I should have realized he was too good to be an accident. I should have realized he was with you. You strike me as just the sort of person who'd keep company with vampires. Detective-Sergeant!" She swung her head around to face Celluci, who'd come up on her right side. "Do you know that your buddy here aids and abets the bloodsucking undead?" She set the empty mug carefully on the desk and reached for the bottle. Celluci was faster. Shrugging philosophically, Dr. Burke sat back in her chair. "So, what brought you to the conclusion that your Mr. Fitzroy was with me?"

"Realizing that you killed my mother." Behind her glasses, Vicki's eyes blazed. Although she remained motionless, every line of her body screamed rage.

"And what makes you say that?" The question could have concerned a thesis footnote for all the emotion Dr. Burke showed.

Vicki glared at her. Her voice trembled with the effort it took to keep from shrieking accusations. "My mother's death had to occur during the four weeks Donald was at the funeral home. Preferably near the end of those four weeks when the Hutchinsons had come to trust him."

"Donald was very charming," Dr. Burke agreed, her left hand continuing to work in the jacket.

"That kind of timing can't be left to chance," Vicki continued, a muscle jumping in her jaw. "You were with her just before she died! You killed her!"

"You forget that Mrs. Shaw was with her *when* she died. But, never mind." Dr. Burke held up her hand. "Why don't I just tell you what happened. I gave your mother vitamin shots every morning. You must have read that in Dr. Friedman's records?"

Vicki nodded, gaze locked on the other woman's face.

"These shots, they couldn't actually do anything to help, but they made your mother feel like she *was* doing something, so she felt better, was under less stress, and the last thing she needed in her condition was stress." She frowned and shrugged. "You'll have to bear with me if I'm less than usually coherent. As you pointed out earlier, I'm drunk. Anyway, I had a lovely talk with Dr. Friedman about stress. That last morning your mother didn't get a vitamin shot; she got l0ccs of pure adrenaline. Her heart slammed into action and the strain was too much for it."

"An autopsy would find that much adrenaline," Celluci pointed out quietly. "And there's be little difficulty in tracing it back to you."

Dr. Burke snorted. "Why the hell would anyone do an autopsy? Everyone was waiting for Marjory to die." She shot a smug look at Vicki. "Well, everyone but you."

"Shut up."

"She kept saying she was going to tell you. I guess she never got around to it."

"SHUT UP!"

Dr. Burke watched half the items from the top of her desk crash to the floor and turned to Celluci. "What are the chances of me getting that bottle back if I told you I needed it for medical reasons."

Celluci smiled unpleasantly. "Shut up," he said.

"You two have a decidedly limited vocabulary." Dr.

Burke shook her head. "Don't you even want to know why I did it?"

"Oh, yes," Vicki snarled. "I'd love to know why you did it. My mother thought you were her *friend!*"

"It's a good thing I'm not a melancholy drunk, or you'd have me in tears. Your mother was dying, no way out. I saw to it she died for a reason. No, don't bother." Again Dr. Burke raised her hand. "I know what you're going to ask. If she was dying anyway, why not wait and have her leave you her body in her will or something. Well, it doesn't work that way. We had tissue cultures, brain wave patterns, everything to go to the next experimental step and this was our only way to get the body."

"So she was just a body to you?"

Dr. Burke leaned forward. "Well, she was after she died, yes."

"She didn't *die*. You killed her."

"I expedited the inevitable. You're just angry because you seem to be the only person she didn't confide in."

"Vicki! No!" Celluci threw himself forward and managed to prevent Vicki's hands from going around the doctor's throat. He pushed her back and held her until blind rage faded enough for reason to return, then released her. When he was certain she had herself under control, he turned to Dr. Burke and said with quiet passion. "The next time you make a crack like that, I won't stop her and you'll get exactly what you deserve."

"What I deserve?" The smile was humorless, the tone bitter. "Detective-Sergeant, you have no idea."

Celluci frowned. His gaze dropped down to the jacket, then slowly lifted back to Dr. Burke's face. "You said Donald *was* charming. Why *was?* Why past tense? What's happened to Donald?"

Dr. Burke picked up the bottle from where Celluci had dropped it in order to restrain Vicki's charge and refilled her mug. "I expect that Catherine killed him."

"Catherine's your second graduate student? . . ."

"Go to the head of the glass." She took a long swallow and sighed in relief; the world had been threatening to return. "Perhaps I'd better start at the beginning."

"No." Vicki slapped both palms down on the desk. "First, we get Henry back."

Dr. Burke met Vicki's gaze and sighed again. "You need to save him because you couldn't save your mother." Her voice held so much sympathy that Vicki lost her reaction in it. "I think you'd better know about Catherine."

Celluci swiveled his attention from one woman to the other but held his tongue. It was Vicki's call.

"All right," she said at last, straightening. "Tell us what's going on."

Dr. Burke took another drink, then visibly slipped into lecture mode. "I am a good scientist but not a great one. I just don't possess the ability to devise original concepts that greatness requires. I *am* a great administrator. Probably the best in the world. Which means diddley squat. I make a reasonable amount of money, but do you have any idea what a couple of biological patents with military applications could net you? Or something that the pharmaceutical companies could really sink their teeth into? Of course you don't. This is where Catherine comes in.

"She's a genius. Did I mention that? Well, she is. As an undergraduate she'd patented the prototype of a bacterium that should, with further development, be able to rebuild damaged cells. When I became her adviser, it soon became obvious that she was, like many geniuses, extremely unstable. About to suggest that she seek professional help, I realized that this was my chance. Her research was the only thing that she related to and I was her only touchstone with reality. The whole situation begged to be exploited.

"Pretty soon I realized we weren't just heading toward monetary rewards but that there was a distinct possibility of a Nobel prize. Once we actually managed to defeat death, of course. Sounds insane, doesn't it?" She took another drink. "Let's not rule it out; it might be a valid defense. Anyway, Catherine came up with some pretty amazing possibilities and we began working out experimental parameters."

"Don't you guys usually work with rats," Celluci growled.

"Usually," Dr. Burke agreed. "Are you familiar with the theory of synchronicity? Just as Catherine finished working out the theory, someone in Brazil published a paper involving roughly the same ideas. There was only one way to guarantee we'd win the race. We went directly to experimentation on human cadavers. I set up a lab and rerouted the freshest bodies from the medical morgue—you'll excuse me if I don't go into the tedious bureaucratic details of how that was accomplished with no one the wiser, but if you'll remember I did say I was a great administrator. . . ." Confused, she stared down into the mug. "Where was I?"

"Human cadavers," Vicki snarled.

"Oh, yes. That was when I realized we needed someone else. Donald had gotten himself in a little trouble at medical school and I'd smoothed things over for him. Mostly because I liked him. Also a genius, he was charming and pretty much completely unethical." With exaggerated care, she smoothed out the wrinkles she'd folded into the jacket. "After a while, we began to have some success. We'd been using nonspecific bacteria and brain wave patterns, but if we wanted to move on we had to get our hands on a body we'd been able to type before death. That turned out to be Marjory Nelson. When I was certain she was going to die anyway, under the cover of tests on her condition, we took tissue samples and recorded her brain wave patterns."

"Then you brought her back to life."

Gray eyes opened with a flash of recognition. "More or less. We brought back the mechanics of life, that was all." That *was* all. "Organic robots, if you like. Trouble was, the bacteria are very short-lived and we had a problem with rot. Which, in case you were wondering, was why I wanted your mother partially embalmed." She finished the whiskey remaining in the mug, then lifted it to Vicki in a mocking salute. "If you'd just left that casket closed, no one would have been the wiser."

"You seem to be forgetting that you murdered my mother!"

Dr. Burke shrugged, refusing to argue the point any further. "So now you know the whole story, or at least the edited for television version. There'll be a test in the morning. Any questions?"

"Yeah, ignoring for the moment a teenage boy whose death you're also directly responsible for, I've got two." Vicki shoved at her glasses. "Why are you telling us all this?"

"Well, there are theories that say confession is a human compulsion, but mostly because our little experiment has now moved completely out of my control. Catherine slipped

into the abyss and I have no intention of following her."
Although just for a moment, with her hand on the latch of
the casket, she'd come close. How far, she'd wondered,
would they be able to go with a really fresh corpse? And
then Donald had told her. But that was personal and no
one's business but hers. "And because Donald's dead."

"So's that kid and so's my mother!"

"The kid was an accident. Your mother was dying. Donald had everything to live for." For an instant her face
crumpled then it smoothed again. "What's more," she continued, pouring the final dregs from the bottle, "I liked
Donald."

"You *liked* my mother!"

Dr. Burke looked placidly across the desk at Vicki. "You
said you had two questions. What's the second?"

How could this creature sit there so calmly and admit to
such horror? Caught up in an emotional maelstrom, Vicki
was unable to speak. Realizing that the next time she
broke, Celluci wouldn't be able to stop her, she spread her
hands and stepped back from the desk.

He recognized the signs and moved forward.

"Where," he asked, "is Henry Fitzroy?"

"With Catherine."

He took a deep breath and ran both hands up through
his hair. "All right. Where is Catherine?"

Dr. Burke shrugged. "I haven't the faintest idea."

Thirteen

"All right. Let's see if I understand what you're saying." Vicki drew in a deep breath and exhaled slowly. Screaming and throwing things would contribute nothing to the situation. "Your graduate student, Catherine, who is crazy, has murdered your other graduate student, Donald. When you went back to the lab, late this afternoon, you discovered she'd hidden Henry and you don't know where she is—they are."

Dr. Burke nodded. "Essentially."

So much for good intentions. "WHAT THE FUCK DO YOU MEAN, ESSENTIALLY?"

Alcohol-induced remoteness cracked as Vicki grabbed the lapels of Dr. Burke's lab coat and nearly dragged her over the desk. "If you could loosen your grip," she gasped, "I might find it easier . . . to answer your question."

Vicki merely snarled inarticulately.

"Detec . . . tive!"

Celluci shifted his gaze to a point about six inches over the doctor's head, expression aggressively neutral.

Collar cutting into her windpipe, Dr. Burke realized further hesitation would only make things worse. "She's in the old Life Sciences building. Your vampiric friend is locked in a big metal box. Trying to maneuver that out the door and into her van would've attracted a bit of attention. *Where* in the building . . ." Considering her position, the shrug was credible. ". . . I have no idea."

Vicki didn't so much release her hold as shove the older woman back into the chair. "Your lab is in there? In the old building?"

"Yes." Rubbing the back of her neck where the fabric

had dug in, Dr. Burke snapped, "And so is your mother. Somewhere." She shot a superior look up over the edge of her glasses. "Your dead mother. Walking around."

My dead mother. Walking around. Anger couldn't stand under the weight of that pronouncement.

"Vicki?"

She fought free of the image of her mother flattened against the window and met Celluci's worried gaze.

"We have a confession. We can call in Detective Fergusson now. You don't have to have anything more to do with this."

"Nice try, Mike." She swallowed, trying to wet a throat gone dry. "But you're forgetting about Henry."

"Mustn't forget Henry." Above the hand still rubbing at her throat, Dr. Burke almost grinned. "I'd love to hear you explain *him* to the local police. Until you find Henry, you've got to keep this quiet. And after? What about after?" She shook her head at their expressions and sighed, placing both hands flat on her desk. "Never mind, I'll tell you. There won't *be* an after. Until Catherine contacts me, you haven't a chance of finding your friend. There's a million stupid, useless cubbyholes in that building and she could've stuck him in any of them. You're just going to have to sit here with me and wait for her phone call."

"And then?"

"Then I play along, she tells me where she's stashed him, you get him out, call the police, and she pays for Donald."

Vicki's eyes narrowed. "And *you'll* pay for my mother."

"Ms. Nelson, if it makes you happy, I'll even pay for dinner."

"What if she doesn't call?" Celluci demanded, cutting off Vicki's response.

"She said she would."

"You said she's crazy."

"There is that."

"Mike, I can't wait." Vicki took four steps toward the door, turned on one heel, and took three steps back. "I can't base everything on what a crazy woman may or may not do. I'm going to find him. *She* . . ." A toss of her head indicated the doctor. ". . . can take us to the lab. We'll work a search pattern from there."

"Not on your life." *She* wasn't going near the lab. Bad

enough she could still hear him calling her in spite of half a bottle of Scotch. "You'll have to drag me. Which might alert Security. There'll be a brouhaha. Your Henry Fitzroy ends up confiscated by the government. You want to go to the lab, you can find it on your own."

Vicki leaned forward, laying her hands on the desk, fingertips not quite touching the doctor's, her posture more of a threat than her earlier actions had been. "Then you'll give us very precise directions."

"Or you'll what? Try to pay attention, Ms. Nelson—you can't do *anything* until you rescue your friend."

"I can beat your fucking face in."

"And what will that accomplish? If you beat the directions out of me, I can guarantee they won't be accurate. Try to be realistic, Ms. Nelson, if you can. You and your flat-footed friend here can go and try to find Mr. Fitzroy, but you'll have to leave me out of it." Not even in words would she trace the path to the lab again. "But just to show there's no hard feelings, I'll let you in on a nonsecret. There's a way into the old building from the north end of the underground parking lot. Security's supposed to have video cameras down there, but they ran out of money. Don't say I never gave you anything. Happy trails."

Celluci took hold of Vicki's shoulder and pulled her gently but inexorably away from the desk. "And what will you be doing while we're searching?"

"The same thing I was doing when you showed up." Dr. Burke bent and opened the bottom drawer of her desk, pulling out an unopened bottle of Scotch. "Attempting to drink myself into a stupor. Thank God, I always keep a spare." It took three tries before the paper seal tore. "I assure you, I'm not going anywhere."

"Why not, when at the very least you'll be facing a murder charge?" Vicki asked, shaking free of Celluci's hold.

"You're still on about your mother, aren't you?" The doctor sighed and stared for a moment into the pale depths of the amber liquid before continuing. "I lost interest in the game when Donald died." The bottle became a silver casket. She shuddered and raised her head, looking past Vicki's glasses, meeting her eyes. "Essentially—and I beg your pardon, Ms. Nelson, if the word offends you, but it's the only one that fits—essentially, I just don't care any more."

And she didn't. Even through her own grief and rage and confusion, Vicki could see that. "Come on." Pulling her bag up onto her shoulder, she jerked her head toward the door. "She's not going anywhere right now."

"You believe her?"

Vicki took another look into Dr. Burke's eyes and recognized what she saw there. "Yeah. I believe her." She paused at the door. "One more thing; you may not care now but don't think you'll be able to use your knowledge of Henry as a bargaining chip later . . ."

"Later," Dr. Burke interrupted, both hands around the bottle to keep from spilling any of the Scotch as she refilled her mug, "without an actual creature to run tests on, I can scream vampire until I'm blue in the face and no one will believe a word I say. Grave robbing does not help to maintain credibility in the scientific community."

"Not to mention murdering one of your grad students," Celluci pointed out dryly.

Dr. Burke snorted and raised the mug in a sarcastic salute. "You'd be surprised."

"Jesus H. Christ." Celluci slammed the flat of his hand against the wall in frustration. "This place is like a maze; hallways that don't go anywhere, classrooms that lead to hidden offices, labs that suddenly appear . . ."

Vicki played the powerful beam of her flashlight down the hall. With the one in four emergency lighting on in the old building, she could see well enough to keep from crashing into things but not well enough to identify the things she wasn't crashing into. Only the area starkly illuminated by her flashlight held any definition. It was like she was moving through the slides of a bizarre vacation, stepping into a scene just as it was replaced by the next. Her nerves were stretched so tightly she could almost hear them twang with every movement.

Her dead mother was walking around in this building.

Every time she moved her circle of sight she wondered, *Will this be the time I see her?* And when all that showed was another empty room or bit of hall, she wondered, *Is she standing in the darkness beside me?* Under her jacket and sweater, her shirt clung to her sides, and she had to keep switching the flashlight from hand to hand to dry her palms.

"This isn't going to work." Her arm dropped to her side and the hall slid into darkness except for the puddle of illumination now spilling over her feet. "The layout of this place defeats any kind of a systematic search. "We've got to use our heads."

"Granted," Celluci agreed. He tucked himself up against her left shoulder; close enough, he judged, for her to see his face. "But we've got a crazy woman who's run off with a vampire. That doesn't exactly lend itself to logical analysis."

"It has to." Adjusting her glasses, more for the comfort of a familiar action than from necessity, she gave half her mind over to searching the scant information they had for clues. The other half of her mind filtered the noises of an old building at night, listening for the approach of shuffling footsteps. Suddenly, she turned to squint up at Celluci. "Dr. Burke said Henry was in a large metal box."

"So?"

"And she implied it was heavy."

"Again, so?"

Vicki almost smiled. "Look at the floor, Celluci."

Together, they bowed their heads and stared at the pale, institutional gray tile, dulled by the passage of thousands of feet. A number of nicks and impressions dimpled the surface with shadow and darker still were a half-dozen signatures of black rubber heels.

"If the box is as massive as Dr. Burke implied," Vicki said, raising her head and looking Celluci in the eyes, "one way or another it'll have left its mark. Rubber wheels will scuff. Metal wheels will imprint."

Celluci nodded slowly. "So we look for the tracks she left moving the box. It's still a big building. . . ."

"Yeah, but we know damn well she didn't take it up and down the stairs." Vicki raised her arm and shone the flashlight down the hall. "The power's on, so the elevators must be working. We check just outside them on every floor for the marks and then backtrack from there."

An appreciative grin spread over Celluci's face. "You know, that's practically brilliant."

Vicki snorted. "Thanks. You needn't sound so surprised."

For no reason other than that they had to start somewhere, they began working their way down from the eighth, and highest, floor. On three, they found what they were looking for—pressed not only into the tile but into the metal lip leading onto the elevator, were the marks of two pairs of wheels about four feet apart. Silently, they stepped out into the hall and let the door wheeze closed behind them.

No one appeared to investigate the noise.

Unwilling to risk the flashlight and a premature discovery, Vicki grabbed Celluci's shoulder and allowed him to lead her down the hall. To her surprise, moving in what was to her total darkness was less stressful than the peep show the flashlight had offered. Although she still listened for approaching footsteps, the accompanying tension had lessened. *Or maybe,* she conceded, her grip tightening slightly, *it's just that now I have an anchor.*

When they reached the first intersection, even she could see the way they had to go.

The harsh white of the fluorescent lights spilled out through the open door and across the corridor.

Vicki felt Celluci's shoulder rise as he reached beneath his jacket and she heard the unmistakable sound of metal sliding free of leather. Up until this moment, she hadn't realized he'd brought his gun. Considering the amount of trouble he could get into for using it, she couldn't believe he'd actually drawn it.

"Isn't that just a tad *American,*" she whispered, lips nearly touching his ear.

He drew her back around the corner and bent his head to hers. "What Dr. Burke neglected to mention," he said in a voice pitched to carry to her alone, "was that there's something else wandering around in here besides a mad scientist and your uh . . ."

"Mother," Vicki interjected flatly. "It's okay." Her feelings were irrelevant to the situation. *And I'll just keep telling myself that.*

"Yeah, well, something else killed that kid and we're not taking any more chances than we have to."

"Mike, if it's already dead, what good will shooting it do?"

His voice was grim as he answered. "If it died once, it can die again."

"So what am I supposed to use, strong language?"

"You can wait here."

"Fuck you." And under the bravado, fear. *Not alone. Not in the dark. Not here.*

They made their way to the open door. Vicki released her hold on Celluci's shoulder at the edge of the light. "Give it a five count." His breath lapped warm against the side of her face, then he darted across the opening.

The next five seconds were among the longest Vicki had ever spent as she closed her eyes, leaned her head back against the wall, and wondered if she'd have the courage to look. On five, she swallowed hard, opened her eyes, and peered around and into the room, conscious of Celluci across the doorway mirroring her movements.

Even with lids slitted against the glare, it took a moment for her eyes to stop watering enough for her to focus. It *was* a lab. It had obviously been in use recently. It had just as obviously been abandoned. Eight years with the police had taught her to recognize the telltale mess left behind when suspects had cut and run.

Cautiously, they moved away from the door, slowly turned, and simultaneously spotted the isolation box, humming in mechanical loneliness at the far end of the room.

Vicki took two quick steps toward it, then stopped and forced her brain to function. "If this is the original lab, we know Catherine moved Henry away . . ."

"So Henry's not in that box."

"Maybe it's empty."

"Maybe."

But neither of them believed it.

"We have to know for sure." Somehow, without her being aware of it, Vicki's feet had moved her to within an arm's length of the box. All she had to do was reach out and lift the lid.

. . . and lift the lid. Oh, Momma, I'm sorry. I can't. She despised herself for being a coward, but she couldn't stop

the sudden cold sweat or the weakness in her knees that threatened to drop her flat on her face.

"It's all right." It wasn't *all right*, but those were the words to say, so Celluci said them as he came around her and put one hand on the latch. This, at least, he could do for her. "You don't have to stay."

"Yes. Yes, I do." She could be a passive observer, if only that.

Celluci searched her face, swore privately that someone would pay for the pain that kept forcing its way out through the cracks in the masks she wore, and lifted the lid.

The release of tension was so great that Vicki swayed and would have fallen had Celluci not stepped back and grabbed her. She allowed herself a moment leaning on the strength of his arm, then shook herself free. From the beginning, she'd declared she was going to find her mother. *Why am I so relieved that we didn't?*

Thick purple incisions, tacked closed with coarse black thread, marked the naked body of the young Oriental male in an ugly "y" pattern. A collar of purple and green bruises circled the slender column of the throat. Plastic tubes ran into both elbows and the inner thigh. Across the forehead, partially covered by a thick fall of ebony hair, another incision appeared to have been stapled closed.

Over the years, both Vicki and Celluci had seen more corpses than they cared to remember. The young man in the box was dead.

"Mike, his chest . . . it's . . ."

"I know."

Two steps forward and she was close enough to reach over the side and gently touch her fingertips to the skin over the diaphragm. It was cold. And it rose and fell to the prompting of something that vibrated beneath it.

"Jesus . . . There's a motor." She withdrew her hand and scrubbed the fingers against her jacket. Raising her head, she caught Celluci making the sign of the cross. "Dr. Burke never mentioned this."

"No. Not quite." He shifted his gun to his right hand and slipped it back into the shoulder holster. It didn't look like he'd be needing it right away. "But something tells me we've finally found Donald Li."

The young man's eyes snapped open.

Vicki couldn't have moved had she wanted to. Nor could she look away when the dark eyes tracked from her to Celluci and back again.

A muscle shifted behind the purple bruises on the throat. Gray-blue lips parted.

"Kill . . . me . . ."

"Holy Mary, Mother of God, he's alive."

In the box, the dark eyes slid slowly back to Celluci. "No . . ."

"No? What the hell do you mean no?"

"He means he's not alive, Mike." Vicki could hear a part of herself screaming. She ignored it. "He's like my mother." *Hands splayed against the glass. Mouth moving soundlessly.* "He's dead. But he's trapped in there."

"Kill . . . me . . . please . . ."

Her fingers digging into the bend of Celluci's elbow, Vicki backed away, pulling him with her. She stopped when the high rim of stainless steel replaced Donald Li's face with her own. "We have to do something."

Celluci continued to stare in the direction of the box. "Do what?" he demanded harshly.

Vicki fought the urge to turn and run, thankful Celluci seemed frozen to the spot because she didn't have the strength to stop them both. "What he asks. We have to kill him."

"If he's alive, killing him is murder. If he's dead . . ."

"He's dead, Mike. He says himself he'd dead. Can you walk away and leave him like that?"

She felt the shudder run down the length of his body and barely heard his answer.

"Vicki, we're out of our·depth here." This was the stuff of nightmares. Not demons or werewolves or mummies or a four-hundred-and-fifty-year-old romance writer—this. He'd thought that thirteen years of police work had equipped him to deal with anything and that the events of the last year had covered everything else. He'd been wrong. "I can't . . ."

"We have to."

"Why?" Weighed down by horror, his voice hardly rose above a whisper.

"Because we found him. Because we're all he has."

There's a whole world out there. Let someone else deal

with it. But when he turned and looked down into Vicki's face, he couldn't say it. He recognized the look of someone very nearly at the end of her resources, someone who'd been hit too hard and too often, but he also recognized the determined set to her jaw. *She* couldn't walk away leaving Donald Li trapped in his prison of dead meat. He couldn't walk away and leave her. Although he had to force his mouth to form the words, he asked, "How do we do it?"

Speaking slowly—if she lost control even a little she'd lose it all—Vicki laid out what they knew. "He's dead. We know it. He says so. But his . . ." Twentieth-century attitudes added difficulty to expressing what was so terrifyingly clear. ". . . his soul is trapped. Why? The only difference between this corpse and any other . . ." *Except my mother's.* She felt herself begin to slide toward the edge. *No! Don't think of that now.* ". . . is that someone has given it an artificial resemblance to life. That has to be why he's trapped."

"So we unhook his life support?"

"Yeah. I guess."

"Vicki. One of us has to be *sure.*"

She lifted her head and met his gaze.

After a moment, he nodded. "Let's do it."

It didn't take long for them to unhook the tubes and hoses, training and practice shoehorning distance in between what had to been done and feelings about doing it. Neither of them touched the body any more than was absolutely necessary. When they'd finished, although Donald Li said nothing, they saw him still staring up out of dead eyes and knew it hadn't been enough.

"We should've known. The others are up and walking around."

Then Vicki found the input jack hidden under a thick fringe of hair and traced the cable back to the computer. She squinted at Catherine's message on the screen and tried to keep her hands from shaking just long enough to work the keyboard.

"It seems to be loading programming into . . ." There was only one place it could be loading programming. "Okay. Odds are good that if programming can be loaded, it can also be erased." Wiping her palms on her thighs, she dropped into the chair.

"You sure you know what you're doing?" Celluci asked, grateful for an excuse to walk away from the horror in the box. "This setup's more complicated than the gear you've got at home."

"How complicated can it be?" Vicki muttered, making a note of the destination file. "It all comes down to ones and zeros. Besides," she added grimly, hitting the reset button, "how could I possibly make it any worse?"

She scanned the main menu. "Mike, what does initialize mean to you?"

"Something to do with starting up?"

"That's what I thought." Under the list of things that could be initialized was the destination code the program had been downloading into.

"Well?"

"I just told it to reinitialize Donald's brain."

"And?"

"And that should wipe it clean."

"Are you sure?"

"No, but I wiped my hard drive that way once." Shoving the chair back from the desk, Vicki stood and pushed at her glasses. "Hopefully, it'll release him."

"And if it doesn't?"

She shook her head. "I don't know." If it didn't work, they'd have to leave him there and hope that as the body slowly decayed so would whatever held him to it. *To know you're dead. To watch your body rot. To have that be your only hope. . . .* She clamped down hard on the hysteria she could feel rising. *Later,* she told it. *Later, when Henry's safe and my mother's . . . my mother is . . ."*

Celluci's voice cut through the thought. "No change."

"Give it a minute." One step at a time, she managed to return to the box and to Celluci's side. If he hadn't gone back before her, she didn't think she could've made it. With her arm pressed up against the warm resilience of his, she looked down, at Donald Li's face.

Dark eyes caught her gaze and held it. Wrung dry, Vicki didn't even attempt to pull away. Suddenly, she realized that as all encompassing as her terror and revulsion might be it was *nothing* next to the terror that shrieked from behind the eyes of Donald Li.

She had nothing to be afraid of in comparison.

As the fear faded, anger rose to take its place.

What sort of a person could do this to another human being?

All at once, the dead man's eyes widened and just for an instant his expression changed to one of incredulous joy.

Then his face held no expression at all.

Vicki released a breath she didn't remember holding. "You see that?"

"Yeah."

"Any doubts that we did the right thing?"

"Not one."

Together they reached up and pulled the lid closed.

Alone in the dark, Henry wondered how much of the night he had left. Surely he'd endured a dozen hours or more since sunset. *Why can't I feel the dawn?* With the Hunger clawing for freedom and steel wrapped about him like a shroud, he yearned for oblivion even as he dreaded it.

He'd run through all the moments of Vicki he had. *Unfair that a year slips through memory so fast.* While some of what they'd shared had added to the Hunger, most had helped to force it back. Vicki had given him her life, not just her body and blood. Had forged friendship out of circumstance. Had helped him when he needed it. Had come to him for help. Had trusted him. Been trusted in return.

Passion. Friendship. Need. Trust.

Together, love. Considered in that light, he supposed it wasn't actually necessary for Vicki to *say* she loved him. *Although it would have been good to hear. . . .*

He tried to remember how many times he had heard the words. A hundred voices cried out; women's voices, men's voices—he quieted them all, searching the past for the glint of gold among the dross. A thousand nights slipped by, a hundred thousand, and out of all the shared passion and friendship and need there were only four, three women and a man, with whom there had also been trust enough for love.

"Ginevra. Gustav. Sidonie. Beth." He murmured their names into the darkness. So many others he'd let go of, forgotten, but those he still held. "Only four in all those years. . . ."

Two had been taken from him by violence, one by accident, one by time.

He could feel the melancholy gathering into a tangible presence, threatening to crush him under its weight.

"Vicki." A fifth name. A living name. "And as they say . . ." Although he knew it would do no good, Henry pressed his uninjured hand up against the lid as hard as exhaustion and pain allowed. ". . . where there's life, there's hope."

Muscles strained, the darkness developed a reddish hue, then the arm collapsed down across his chest and he was nearly deafened by the sound of his heart slamming up against his ribs. He had no idea what he'd been trying to prove.

One last effort for the sake of love? He shifted slightly, changing his position as much as he could, the plastic padding beneath him tugging at the bare skin of his back. *At least this time I won't be the one left behind to mourn.*

Melancholy turned to despair and closed icy fingers around him.

It would be so easy to surrender.

I am Henry Fitzroy, Duke of Richmond, the son of a king. I am Vampire.

He was too tired. It just wasn't enough anymore.

Vicki wouldn't quit.

Vicki won't quit. Not until she finds you. Find strength in that. Trust her.

She will come.

Christina had come. She had birthed him from the darkness, nourished him, guarded him, taught him, and finally let him go.

"Listen to what your instincts tell you, Henry. Our nature says we hunt alone. This is your territory, I give it to you, and I will not stay to fight you for it."

"Then stay and share it with me!"

She only smiled, a little sadly.

He paced the length of the room and back to throw himself down on his knees at her feet. Even a short time before, he would have finished the motion by burying his head in her lap but now, in spite of the position, he was unable to close the distance.

Her smile grew sadder still. "The bond of your creation

is nearly broken. If I stay," she added softly, *"one of us will very soon drive the other away and that will wipe out even the memory of what we shared."*

The voice of the Hunter growing louder in his head told him she spoke the truth. "Then why," he cried, "did you change me, knowing this would happen? Knowing we would have so little time together?"

Ebony brows drew down as she considered it. "I think," she said slowly, "I think I forgot for a while."

His voice rose, echoing off the damp, stone walls of the abandoned tower. "You forgot?"

"Yes. Perhaps that is why we are able to continue as a race."

He bowed his head, eyes squeezed shut, but his nature no longer allowed tears. "It hurts. As though you cut my heart out and take it with you."

"Yes." Her skirts whispered as she stood and he felt her fingers touch his hair in gentle benediction. "Perhaps that is why we are so few."

He never saw her again.

"And that," he told the darkness as despair's grip tightened, "is not helping." Surely there were pleasanter times to use as weapons against the knowledge that he was trapped, and alone. . . .

"No. There have been prisons and prisoners before," he snarled. "I can survive it."

You can survive the nights, despair whispered, *but what of the days? So much blood has been taken. How much more will they take? How much more can you lose and still have a night to return to? What else will they do that you will be unable to prevent?*

Lips drawn back from his teeth, Henry tried to twist away from the voice. It surrounded him, sounded within him, echoed against the metal that enclosed him. "Vicki . . ."

She doesn't know where you are. What if she doesn't find you in time? What if she doesn't come?

"NO!"

He released his hold on the Hunger and let the Beast take him as it clawed its way free.

It was all he had left to fight with.

* * *

"As long as these are working, we have no guarantee that she's going to leave Henry in one place." Vicki squinted in the brightly lit interior of the elevator and switched off her flashlight. "She can keep rolling him around this building with us two steps behind like some kind of bad Marx Brothers movie."

"So we jam them?" Celluci asked, stepping over the threshold and matching his companion's don't-fuck-with-me tone. That either of them was still functioning at all, he considered to be some sort of miracle. *Let's hear it for the human animal's ability to cope.*

Vicki shook her head and hit the button for the subbasement with enough force to nearly crack the plastic cover. "Not good enough. The elevators are in opposite ends of the building. She can unjam them as fast as we can jam them. We're going to shut them off."

"How?"

"By shutting off the power supply to the building."

"I repeat, how?"

Vicki turned to stare at him through narrowed eyes. "How the hell should I know? Do I look like an electrician? We'll find the electrical room and pull the plug."

"Metaphorically speaking."

"Don't give me any of your fucking attitude, Celluci."

"My attitude? Nelson, you've got one hell of a nerve."

"Nerve!"

"You want attitude?"

Their voice overlapped, the sound slamming up against the confining walls and crashing back. Words got tangled in the noise and were stripped of meaning. Toe to toe, they stood and screamed invective at each other.

The elevator reached the subbasement. Stopped. The door opened.

". . . patronizing asshole!"

The echoes changed. The words shot into the darkness and didn't come back.

They realized it together and together fell silent.

Vicki was trembling so violently, she wasn't sure she could stand. Her legs felt like cooked pasta and there was a metal band wrapped so tightly around her throat that breathing hurt and swallowing was impossible. Her glasses had slid so far down her nose they were almost useless.

She peered over them, through the tunnel the disease had pared her vision down to, and tried to focus on the face just inches from her own. Her hand came up to push them back into place but instead continued moving until it brushed the curl of hair off Celluci's forehead. She heard him sigh.

Slowly, he raised his arm and, with one finger against the bridge, slid her glasses back into place. "We okay?"

His breath was warm against her cheek. She nodded jerkily and stepped back, out of the range of that comfort.

"What about the tracks?" he asked.

She switched on her flashlight and walked out into the subbasement, a little amazed her legs would obey even such basic commands. "We look for tracks *after* we immobilize Catherine."

Celluci paused for a moment on the threshold of the elevator, his presence preventing the door from closing. "We turn off the power to the building," he said, "and we'll turn off any other experiments she might be running."

Vicki stopped and half turned to face him. "Yes."

He recognized the raw anger that spit the word out. Recognized it because he felt it himself. It had nothing to do with the contest in vitriol they'd held in the elevator—that had been nothing more than tension given voice—and everything to do with the horror they'd found in the lab. He wanted to find whoever had been responsible, take them by the throat and . . . Words didn't exist for what he wanted to do.

Over the last week, layer after layer of Vicki's control, of her protection, had been stripped away. He was afraid there was nothing left to keep her anger from being acted on.

He was afraid that if they found Henry the way they'd found Donald Li, she'd go right over the edge and he wouldn't be able to stop her.

He was more afraid that he wouldn't even try.

On the second floor, in a utility cupboard that shared a wall with the elevator shaft, Marjory Nelson worked the muscles of her face into the closest she could come to a frown. She heard voices.

Voices.

Voice.

She knew that voice.

She had been told to stay. It was one of the commands
enforced by the neural net. One of the commands that had
worn a rutted passage into memory.

Stay.

Trembling, she stood . . .

Stay!

. . . shuffled toward the door . . .

STAY!

. . . opened it and lurched out into the hall.

There was something she had to do.

Fourteen

"Radio room. Constable Kushner."

"This the police . . . stashun?"

"Yes, ma'am, it is."

Dr. Burke took a deep breath and, enunciating very carefully, said, "I'd like to speak to De-tective Fergusson, plead . . . please."

"I'll put you through to homicide."

"You do that." Eyes nearly closed, Dr. Burke sagged against the receiver.

"Homicide. Detective Brunswick."

"Right. De-tective Fer-gusson, please."

"Detective Fergusson's not here right now, can I help?"

"Not here?" She pivoted the receiver around on her mouth, just far enough so she could glare blearily at it. "Whadda you mean, not here?"

By the time she remembered that the other half had to stay against her ear, she'd missed the first part of Detective Brunswick's reply. ". . . But can I take a message?"

"A meshage?" Sipping at her Scotch, she took a moment to think about it. "Well, I was gonna . . . confesh. Theories say confeshun is necess . . . ary. But if he's not . . . there, maybe I won't."

Detective Brunswick's voice picked up a distinct, let's-humor-the-crazy-person inflection. "If you give me your name, I can tell him you called."

Heaving herself more-or-less erect in the chair, Dr. Burke declared in ringing tones, "*I* am the Director of . . . Life Sciencesh. He knows who I am. Everyone knows . . . who *I* am." Then she hung up.

"So much . . . for tha." She pulled Donald's jacket off

the desk and onto her lap. "I really feel . . . awful 'bout thish, Donald. I'm gonna make it up . . . to you. You'll see." An idea somehow forced its way through a bottle and a half of single malt. "You know, if the iso-lation box is running then the re-frigeration is running and you're prob-ly cold." With a desperate grip wrapped around the arm of her chair, she managed to get to her feet. "If you're cold, you're gonna want your jacket." Finishing the mouthful of Scotch in the mug nearly knocked her over. She swayed, steadied, and started for the door. "I'm gonna take you your . . . jacket."

Somewhere, far behind the layers of insulation provided by the alcohol, a terrified voice shrieked, *"No!"*

Dr. Burke ignored it.

"How many electrical rooms can one lousy building have?" Breathing heavily, Vicki backed out into the hall, trying to shine her flashlight in all directions at once. Her voice scraped across her teeth in a strained whisper. "Every time we open a door, I expect to see my mother behind it."

Celluci reached out and closed one hand over her shoulder, the other catching her wrist and directing the beam of light away from his eyes. The last thing they needed was for both of them to be wandering around blind. "Let *me* open the doors," he suggested quietly, turning her to face him.

"No." She shook her head. "You don't understand. She's *my* mother."

"Vicki . . ." Then he sighed because there really wasn't anything he could say that would change things and if the thought of opening a door and finding Marjory Nelson star-ing at them out of a corpse's eyes had him scared spitless, God only knew what it was doing to Vicki. Donald Li had been bad enough, but Marjory Nelson was, as Dr. Burke had so kindly reminded them, up and walking. Up and walking and dead. But if Vicki had the guts to face it, he'd face it beside her. Besides, as much as he might wish that Henry Fitzroy had never appeared on the scene, he couldn't abandon him to the kind of living death that Don-ald had been trapped in. "Let's shut that power off, find Fitzroy, and get out of here."

She nodded, head barely moving, the motion more intent

than actuality, and twisted out from under Celluci's hands. The shadows pressed against her, trying to undermine the precarious balance she maintained. *We're going to find Henry. To do that, we're going to confine him to one floor. So we're going to shut the power off. Then we're going to tear this place apart, one floor at a time. We're going to find Henry. I will not fail him. Like I failed my mother.* As long as she clung to that, she could function. Let the shadows push as they would.

The air in the subbasement tasted of damp concrete and rust and disuse and the building itself—creaking, settling, hiding secrets—made more noise than both of them; although the sound of their breathing seemed to linger where they passed. The rooms to the right of the corridor were up against the outside wall and so every one of them had to be checked; the door opened, the light shone in, the potential horror realized. They'd found two small electrical substations with panels labeled "labs three," "labs four," and "lecture one" but hadn't touched the breakers. *"All at once,"* Vicki had growled. *"So we don't warn her."*

One door remained before the corner; one door, one room and they'd finished the north side of the building. Celluci checked his watch as they hurried toward it. *11:17? Is that all?* They still had over half the night. Not so long, he amended as he realized it was probably *all* the time they had.

A square shadow of darker paint at eye level, metal dimpling all four corners, indicated a missing sign. A security bar resting loosely over a steel eye suggested that the room had once held something worth guarding.

"This could be it." Jerking the bar free, Vicki hauled the heavy door open. Stiff hinges shrilled a clichéd protest that scraped against the inside of her skull like nails on a blackboard. She gritted her teeth and scythed the flashlight beam across the darkness.

Something moved just beyond the edge of the light.

She froze. The circle of illumination froze with her.

Just past it, something moved again.

All she had to do was direct the flashlight less than a meter to the left. All she had to do . . .

The single, naked bulb hanging caged from the ceiling cut black silhouettes around a complex arrangement of pipes. About four feet off the ground, a humped brown body and naked tail disappeared down an impossibly narrow crevice.

Vicki remembered how to breathe. "Rat," she said, because she had to say something.

"Or a mouse trying out for the Olympics," Celluci allowed, his hand still covering the light switch. He wet his lips and tried to push his heart down out of his throat. "I'm beginning to think that finding her would be better than the constant fear that we will."

Wiping at her streaming eyes, Vicki battled the knot in her stomach. *You will not puke!* she commanded herself, swallowing bile. After a moment, she lifted her head and muttered, "I'm beginning to think you're right." She jabbed her glasses back into place. "This is obviously the sprinkler room. Not what we're looking for."

Out in the hall, she paused and said, before he could follow, "Leave the light on."

He caught up to her as she was about to check the first room on the west wall. Frowning, he squinted down the length of the corridor, attempting to isolate the sheen of polished metal that had caught his eye. "Vicki, there's a padlock on that door down there."

Vicki turned. The cone of light stretching out from her hand didn't quite stretch far enough. Not only could she not see a lock, she only had Celluci's word for it that there was a door.

"In my experience," he continued, "you lock rooms you don't want people to go into."

"Or get out of," Vicki added. "Come on."

Unlike the entrance to the room they'd just left, this door retained its sign. *Danger. High Voltage. Keep out.*

"Odds are good this is the electrical room." Handing Celluci the flashlight—"Here. Hold this. I'm going to need both hands."—Vicki rummaged her lockpicks out of her purse. "Keep it steady." Dropping to one knee, she flicked open the case and drew out the two largest picks.

Her hands were shaking so violently, she couldn't get either of them into the lock.

Her second attempt was no more successful.

On the third attempt, she dropped one of the probes. It bounced off her knee, chimed against the tile, and came to rest with the hooked end over the toe of Celluci's shoe. Vicki stared down at it. Then she scowled at the remaining pick, so tightly gripped that her fingertips had gone white behind the nails, spun suddenly, and flung it down the hall.

"God*damn*it!"

She couldn't stop her hands from shaking. There was no way she was going to be able to pick that lock. *So much for finding the fucking electrical room.* They were going to turn off the power. Prevent Henry from being moved from floor to floor. They were going to tear the building apart one floor at a time. They were going to find Henry. She had to hold onto that. It was all she had. *Except that it's all falling apart!* She wanted to beat her head against the door and scream with fear and frustration.

As if he'd read her mind, Celluci reached out and cupped her chin, gently drawing her around to face him. "Let me try."

Not trusting herself to speak, she nodded and stood, holding out the remaining picks.

"No. Not quite my style." Passing her back the flashlight, he added, "Wait here."

He disappeared before she could object and for one terrifying moment it seemed that the darkness had devoured him. By the time she'd swung the light around, he'd gone beyond its range. All at once, with a familiar squeal of metal, the far end of the hall leapt, if not into focus, at least into sight.

What the hell is he doing in the sprinkler room?

A moment later, not bothering to close the door behind him, he came back around the corner, both hands holding . . .

. . . a length of pipe?

She moved out of his way as he returned, jammed one end of the pipe down through the loop of the padlock and braced it against the metal covering the door. Taking a deep breath, he threw his weight against the other end.

The pipe bit into the door, metal buckling.

Face darkening, Celluci growled an inarticulate challenge, grateful for a place to finally throw all the terror-produced adrenaline of the night.

The security bar slowly bowed.

"Mike? . . ."

"Not. Now."

Bit by bit the screws dragged free.

"Just. A little. Fur . . ."

The sudden surrender flung him backward as the entire assembly crashed to the floor. He staggered, nearly fell, and leaned panting on the pipe.

Vicki stepped forward and retrieved her fallen lock-pick from under the mess. "Obviously, your break-and-enter specialist was a little more direct than mine," she muttered dryly.

Celluci gulped for air. "Obviously."

Caught by the sheer normalcy of the exchange, they stared at one another for a moment, then Vicki's mouth curved into almost a smile as she reached up and pushed the curl of hair back off his forehead. "Well, then," she stretched the words out, feeling some of the desperation go with them, "let's hear it for testosterone."

Celluci snorted, straightened, and let the pipe drop. "Personally, I'm amazed you didn't pull a package of plastique out of that suitcase you carry." Shoving the junked security bar out of the way, he pulled open the door and fumbled around the corner for the light.

They'd definitely found the electrical room.

And something else.

"Vicki . . ."

She struggled for command of her voice. "I see it."

The bloodscent drew him out of the pit where exhaustion had flung him and threw the Hunger loose again.

Someone, something, was banging on the inside of the box.

"Henry?" Vicki called, one foot moving in front of the other through no conscious decision she could remember.

There was no answer—only the continued banging.

She couldn't call for the other. In case there *was* an answer.

"Vicki, let me . . ."

"No. This is something *I* have to do."

"Of course it is," Celluci growled, fighting the paralysis that the sight of the stainless steel box invoked and moving up behind her left shoulder. *Goddamnit, Vicki, why can't you turn and run? So I can turn and run.*

She watched her reflection grow larger as she approached. The closer she got, the more distance her mind insisted on until, not quite touching the box, she stopped, stared into her own eyes, and straightened her glasses, feeling as though the whole experience had slid out of reality.

I don't even watch horror movies, she told herself. *What the hell am I doing starring in one?*

She watched her arm come up, her hand cover the latch, her fingers twist slightly sideways. . . .

The lid flew open, slapping her hand aside.

She caught a glimpse of a pale face under red-gold hair. Then, before she could react, something black and heavy swooped down upon her and she stumbled back, blind. Cold and clammy, it wrapped tightly around her head and draped over her shoulders with obscene familiarity. Her throat pumping out shrill sounds of incoherent terror, she tore at it in panicked frenzy.

Finally, as terror began to pick up some of the shading of rage, she wrenched it loose and flung it to the floor. Her glasses, secured over only one ear, began to fall, and the greater fear their loss roused brought her back to sanity as she shoved them back into place.

At her feet lay a pile of black leather.

Henry's trench coat.

All at once, as if recognition had thrown a switch, she became aware of snarling, cursing, and the impact of flesh on flesh. Looping the strap of her bag over her wrist—it was the only weapon she had—she whirled in time to see Celluci get a leg between his body and Henry's and use it to fling the smaller man across the room.

Naked to the waist, Henry's torso gleamed like alabaster, amethyst bruises marking the inside of both arms. He used the momentum of the blow to roll up onto his feet and, snarling, charged again.

Celluci grunted under the impact and slammed his elbow into the side of Henry's head—to no apparent effect.

Once or twice over the last year, Vicki had been given a glimpse of what lay behind the mask of civilization Henry wore. Had—even while cold sweat beaded her skin and

common sense screamed "Run!"—been aroused by so
much deadly power so lightly held in control.   ·

He had warned her once, *"The beast is much closer to
the surface in my kind."*

The beast was loose.

Celluci had barely registered that the box was open when
he found himself flat on his back and fighting for his life.
He'd hit the floor with Henry Fitzroy's hands around his
throat and had only survived those first few seconds because one hand, swollen and nearly useless, had not been
able to maintain its grip.

With his left forearm shoved up under Fitzroy's chin and
his right hand trying to rip the crushing fingers from his
windpipe, Celluci had a sudden, unavoidable epiphany
about vampires.

He'd caught a glimpse of the reality last August when
Mark Williams had died, but that had been easy to bury in
the tangled mix of reaction that Henry evoked. Even through
his jealousy, he'd recognized and responded to Fitzroy's personal power. Respect had been inevitable when stopping
Anwar Tawfik had thrown them together. Other emotions,
less easily defined, had been, for the most part, ignored.

Now, it all distilled down to survival.

He's stronger. Faster. The frenzy of the attack gave him
an opening. Hooking his foot into the top of Fitzroy's pel-
vis, Celluci heaved the smaller man across the room. Less
than a heartbeat later, the vampire charged him again.

"Fuck!"

Nails gouged into his cheek. He knew the skin had been
broken by the intensity of Fitzroy's response. Frantically
twisting his head to one side, he heard teeth snap beside
his ear. *I never noticed his fucking teeth were so god-
damned long!*

I'm meat to him.

I'm a dead man.

This isn't something they did to him. He's after the blood!
Emotional response insisted she throw herself into the battle, ripping Henry off Celluci's throat. A more visceral reaction suggested she run for her life. She stomped down hard

on both and stood trembling where she was. *Goddamnit, Vicki, think! Remember what he's told you!*

He'd talked about his desire to feed like it was a force separate from the rest of him—a force over which he had to exert a certain amount of conscious control.

All right. He's lost control. He's hungry. It wasn't a difficult deduction; his need was a tangible presence, beating against the walls of the small room. *Those bastards have probably been drawing blood for tests all day. Blood's all Henry has. He has to replace it. He'll rip Mike's throat out to get to it.*

So I give him an easier source. One he doesn't have to fight for.

Dropping to her knees, Vicki upended her purse, searching for her knife.

Mike Celluci was a large man in excellent physical condition, speed and strength enhanced by the certain knowledge that if he lost, he died.

Fortunately for him, Henry Fitzroy had been not only weakened by blood loss but also exhausted and injured by the Hunger's fight to get free.

Which only delayed the inevitable.

Bleeding from half a dozen small wounds, breath burning in his throat, joints popping as Fitzroy's teeth slowly descended in spite of everything, Celluci knew with cold certainty that he was losing. And there wasn't a damned thing he could do about it.

Blood trickling down into her hand, Vicki dove across the room, buried her fingers in Henry's hair and yanked his head up.

Celluci felt lips peel back against his skin and the lightest kiss of pain. Then the heated contact jerked away and teeth sheared the air in the hollow between jaw and neck.

Vicki straddled both men and yanked again, harder.

Howling, Henry reared back onto his knees.

Without the grip on his hair she would have lost her balance, but she managed to bring her arm around, blood soaking her cuff and dripping to the floor, and shove the wound against his face.

She cried out as his teeth cut deeper into flesh and the fingers of his good hand clutched almost to the bone. Then she cried out again as he began to suck, mouth working desperately at her wrist.

Vaguely aware of Celluci scrambling clear, she half slid down Henry's body until she knelt behind him, free hand moving from his hair to his shoulder. Eyes closed, she could feel the blood leave her body for his, feel his urgency catch her up and sweep her along, feel herself begin to be lost in his Hunger. He'd been a passive recipient the last time she'd forced her blood on him. While his need might be no greater now, it was far from passive.

This had a reality that burned, that consumed the memories of all the other times Henry had fed.

Her eyes snapped open as, snarling with frustration, he thrust her wrist aside and whirled to face her. She rocked back. He followed, lips and teeth stained crimson, eyes compelling her to offer her throat, to submit.

She felt her chin begin to rise and forced it back down. "Fuck that!" The hoarse whisper traveled just far enough. "You feed where *I* allow." She brought her left hand up between them, trailing scarlet streamers in the air.

It wasn't enough. The blood came too slowly.

He batted the wound aside, laid his teeth against the soft flesh of the throat, and breathed in the rich scent of life.

Life . . .

He knew this life.

Then the Hunger roared forward, out of control, and his teeth pierced skin.

A blow struck him hard in the side. He lost his hold, twisted as he fell and landed on his back, staring up at a dark-haired male who dared to take him from his prey.

Another blow. He grabbed at the leg and heaved it away, surging back onto his knees as part of the same motion.

Vicki winced as Celluci hit the wall but kept her eyes locked on Henry. Just for a second, she'd felt the Hunger falter. She *could* reach him. She *had* to reach him. It was the only chance for all three of them.

Right hand clamped tourniquet-tight above the wound—
from the pain involved she suspected his teeth had torn a
hole significantly larger than her initial incision—she again
offered her left.

He started to dive at her, checked, and slowly raised his
eyes up from the welling blood to her face.

The Hunger bucked and writhed, but he held it tight,
pulling strength from the blood he'd already taken. Pulling
strength from her blood.

"Henry?"

Henry. Yes. A name to leash the Hunger with. He forced
his lips to form a name to help recage it.

"Vicki."

She frowned as he swayed, and shuffled toward him, still
on her knees. "Henry, you've got to keep feeding. You
haven't taken nearly as much as you need. Besides . . ."
She glanced down at her wrist and looked quickly away
again. "Besides," she repeated, "we're just wasting it on
the floor."

Henry moaned and crumpled.

Vicki caught him, smearing his back with blood. Holding
him awkwardly, she dragged her legs out from under, and
gathered him onto her lap.

"No . . ." He pushed her wrist away as she laid it against
his mouth. The brief taste of her nearly catapulted the Hunger to freedom. The bloodscent alone tore at hastily erected
barricades. "I don't trust . . . myself."

She laid her wrist against his mouth again, blood drib-
bling down over lips clamped shut and staining his cheeks.
That he was too weak to stop her merely proved her point.
"Oh, for Christ's sake, Henry, stop being a martyr. *I* trust
you."

She felt him hesitate, then she felt his lips part. The torn
flesh wrapped barbed lines of pain around her arm as he
pressed against her and began to suckle. Muscles tensed,
but she managed not to pull away and slowly the familiar
rhythm pushed the pain to one side, her body responding
with something very like post-coital lassitude. Resting her
cheek against the top of Henry's head, she sighed.

"Isn't that nice," Celluci grunted, glaring down at the

tableau and wiping at the blood on his face. "Love conquers all." Sucking his breath through his teeth, he squatted beside them and peered into what he could see of Vicki's face. "Are you okay?"

Caught in the incessant pull of Henry's need, she didn't bother to raise her head, wouldn't have even bothered to answer except that the concern in his voice demanded a response. "I'm fine." And then, because she belatedly realized Celluci deserved more than that, added, "I *think* I'm fine."

"Great." He shifted position. Somehow, this was more intimate than watching them make love. He barely resisted the urge to grab Henry and violently stuff him back into the isolation box. "How do you know when he's had enough?"

"He'll know. He'll stop."

"Yeah? What if he needs more than you can spare?"

Vicki sighed again, but this time the exhalation had an entirely different sound. "He won't *take* more than I can spare."

Celluci reached up for the open lip of the box and hauled himself to his feet. "You'll excuse me if I don't put a lot of faith in that. A few minutes ago he was ready to kill both of us."

"That was then . . ."

"And this is now? Very deep, Vicki. Very deep bullshit. He stops in fifteen seconds or I'm yanking him off the tit."

"There'll be no need, Detective." The statement, although barely audible, left no room for argument. Henry, having pulled away just enough for speech, molded his mouth back over the wound, pressing the edges of the torn flesh together in order for the coagulant in his saliva to work. He could feel Vicki's life wrapped around his own and, while the last thing he wanted right at this moment was to break free of it, continuing to feed would only endanger them both. She would die from loss of blood and he would die from loss of her. He had taken all he was going to.

This was the second time she had saved him. The first time, she hadn't known the risks and, defeated by the demon, the Hunger had lain in darkness with him beyond the need for control. This time, she knew what she was offering and offered in spite of the Hunger raging free. *I wanted to hear her say I love you. I just heard it.*

And what had he given in return?

"I'm sorry, Vicki." He rested his head against her breast, conserving the little strength he'd regained. "I can stop most of the bleeding, but I can't repair the damage. You're going to need a dressing of some kind."

Vicki glanced down at her wrist and her stomach twisted. "Jesus H. Christ." She swallowed bile. "It looks like it should hurt a lot more than it does." Then suddenly, it did. "Oh, damn . . ."

Celluci grabbed Henry's shirt out of the box and dropped to his knees. "I think Jesus H. Christ about sums it up. Fuck, Fitzroy, you're a god-damned animal!"

Henry met the detective's stormy glare with a calm gaze of his own. "Not when I can help it," he said quietly.

"Yeah. Well." Celluci looked away first, burying his confusion—*He almost kills both of us. He chews a big fucking hole in Vicki. And I feel sorry for him?*—in the wrapping of Vicki's arm. "You're lucky," he grunted as he began to bind Henry's shirt around the wound. "It's messy, but I don't think there's any tendon damage. Move your fingers."

"It hurts."

"Move them anyway."

Muttering profanities under her breath, Vicki did as instructed, all three of them anxiously watching the digits perform.

"What did I tell you." Relief made Celluci's own fingers tremble as he tied off the thick bandage and held a sleeve up in each hand. "We'll use these as a sling, to immobilize it, but you're going to Emergency as soon as we get out of here." Vicki bowed her head as he knotted the cuffs at the back of her neck and he rested his cheek for a moment against her hair, much as she'd done earlier with Henry—who still reclined against the support of her good arm. "I thought . . ." He'd thought she was going to die when he'd kicked the teeth away from her throat. He'd thought she was suicidal when she'd presented herself again. And when it had actually worked, he'd thought . . . he'd thought . . . He didn't know what he thought anymore. "I thought it was all over," he finished lamely and sat back on his heels. *And if she asks me what I meant by* all, *I don't know what to tell her.*

Then his eyes widened, and he snickered.

Henry looked startled and pulled himself up into a shaky but nearly erect sitting position.

Vicki's brows snapped down. "What the hell are you laughing at?" she demanded.

Celluci waved a hand at the two of them and snickered again. "Just for a minute there I was reminded of Michelangelo's Pietà. You know, the statue of the Madonna holding the body of Christ across her lap?"

"And you think me an inappropriate Christ?" Henry asked.

Celluci took a good long look at the other man—at the bruising, at the horror that still lurked around hazel eyes, at the mixture of physical youth and spiritual age, at the nearly visible sense of self now firmly back in place—and shook his head. "Actually," he said, "as Christs go, I've seen worse. But the Madonna . . ." The snicker returned at Vicki's indignant stare. "But the Madonna has definitely been miscast."

Vicki's lips twitched. "You rotten bastard," she began. Then she lost it and howled with laughter.

Which pushed Celluci over the edge.

Henry hesitated, nerves scraped raw and unsure if he should be finding insult when Vicki didn't or blasphemy where none was intended—although honesty forced him to admit that Celluci had a valid point. Unable to withstand the purge of emotion, he joined in.

If some of the laughter had a slightly hysterical tone, they all agreed to ignore it.

"Hey, Fergusson! What are you doing back here, man?"

"Forgot something." Detective Fergusson picked a long narrow paper bag up off his desk and pulled a bottle of bubble bath shaped like a ninja turtle out far enough for the other man to identify it. "My daughter sent me back for it. Informed me on her way to bed that broken promises make blisters."

"How old is she now, four? Five?"

"Five."

Detective Brunswick shook his head. "Five years old and she's already got you asking how high on the way up. Man, when she becomes a teenager, she's going to run you ragged."

Fergusson snorted, cramming bag and bottle into his coat pocket. "By that time maybe her mother'll be slowing down." He leaned over and squinted at the piece of pink message paper topping a stack of reports like a square of icing. "What the hell's this?"

"Just some drunk calling you to confess."

"Confess to what?"

"The sinking of the Lusitania? The shooting of JFK? Repatriating the constitution? I don't know. She didn't want to confess to me."

"Geez, why do *I* always get them?"

Brunswick grinned and snapped his gun. "Because you're such a sweetie."

"Fuck you, too," Fergusson muttered absently, reading the actual message. "Director of Life Sciences? . . ."

"She seemed to think I should know who she was. In fact, she told me that *everyone* knew who she was." He watched the other man's face for a moment and his grin faded. "You don't think there's actually anything in this, do you?"

"I don't know." He crumpled the paper and stuffed it in the pocket with his daughter's bubble bath, his expression resembling that of a hound worrying at a bone. "Maybe." Then he shrugged and sighed. "Maybe not."

"You haven't even begun to convince me that we shouldn't haul ass out of here right now," Celluci growled. "You," he jabbed a finger at Henry, "are operating on half a tank. And you," the finger moved to wave in front of Vicki's nose, "are about three pints short."

"Not that much," Vicki protested, although from the way she felt, she wasn't going to bet on it.

Celluci ignored her. "We *all* look like we've been through the wars. Let's just clear out of here and leave the mopping up to the police."

"Mike . . ."

"Don't *Mike* me. And I want that wrist of yours looked at by a doctor before you get gangrene in it and have to have your fucking hand chopped off."

"The wound won't infect," Henry said with quiet assurance. "And *I* am going to the lab." He stretched out both arms. Although the bruising had faded from purple to green and the broken bones in his hand had begun to knit, the marks of needles were still very evident. "If, as you say, Catherine didn't move me until late afternoon, any samples, any test results, will be there. They have to be destroyed."

"Oh, come on, Fitzroy," Celluci sighed. "No one's going to believe anything these people say after their attempt to play Dr. Frankenstein has been discovered."

"I can't risk that."

Celluci looked from Henry to Vicki and back again, then he savagely shoved both hands up through his hair. "Jesus, there's nothing to choose between you. All right, all right, we'll go."

"I said *I* was going," Henry pointed out. "You don't have to come with me."

"Fuck that," Celluci told him bluntly. "We went through too much to find you. You're not moving out of our sight until we stuff you back in that god-damned closet come morning. Unless? . . ." He raised an eloquent brow.

Henry half smiled. "You're both perfectly safe. Although I still hunger, Vicki's blood was more than enough to return my control."

Celluci's hand rose involuntarily to the place on his throat that Henry's teeth had grazed. Angrily, he turned the motion into an abrupt gesture at the wall of wiring and electrical panels. "We still shutting off the power?"

Vicki nodded and instantly regretted the motion as her head seemed to want to keep on falling. "The reasons for doing it haven't changed. If there're any more of those . . . experiments in this building, I want them shut down." She paused and swallowed, hard. Dr. Burke had said her mother was up and walking around. It wouldn't be so easy to turn her mother off; to see that her mother died a second time. "We should have about forty-five minutes on the emergency lighting—not that it'll make any difference to me. Plenty of time to get to the lab, do what we have to, and get out. Then the police can handle the rest." She caught Celluci's gaze and held it. "I promise."

"Fine." He moved toward the corner of the room where a thick plastic pipe came through the wall and disappeared into a metal box about two feet square. "This is the main feed, so this must be the main disconnect box."

Close behind him, Vicki peered over his shoulder. "How do you know? I thought your father was a plumber?"

"It's a guy thing, you wouldn't under . . . Ow! Damn it. Vicki, that was the last bit of unbruised flesh I had."

"Had," Vicki repeated, flicking on her flashlight. "Just pull the switch."

The switch, about a foot long and rust-pitted down its entire length, refused to surrender so easily. "This thing," Celluci grunted, throwing his weight on it, "hasn't been moved since they wired the building." He managed to force it down to a forty-five-degree angle but could budge it no farther. "I need something to lever it with. The pipe we used on the door . . ."

"May I?" Henry reached past Celluci, wrapped long pale fingers around the switch, and slammed it down in one, fluid motion, snapping it off at the base.

The light in the electrical room went out.

"I thought you hadn't regained all your strength." Celluci squinted in the circle of illumination thrown by Vicki's flashlight.

Henry, who'd stepped back to shield sensitive eyes, shrugged, forgetting for the moment that he couldn't be seen. "I haven't."

"Jesus H. Christ. How strong *are* you?"

Resisting the urge to brag, to further advance himself over a rival who had somehow become much more, Henry settled for a diplomatic, "Not strong enough to get free on my own." Which was, after all, only the truth.

Catherine frowned down into the microscope. There had to be a way to use the regenerative properties of the vampire's cells to extend the limited life of her bacteria. Once found, she could tailor new bacteria for number nine and keep him from decomposing like all the rest. She looked up and shot a smile across the room to where he sat patiently watching her from the edge of the bed.

All at once, the lights went out and the constant hum of her computer was swallowed by the silence that swept in with the darkness.

"It's her!" Catherine gripped the table tightly with both hands until the world steadied. "She's done this. She wants you to die." Knocking over her stool, she stood and stumbled to the door, arms stretched stiffly out before her. A moment's fumbling with the lock and she stepped out into the hall.

At each bend of the corridor, battery-operated emergency lights provided enough illumination for movement.

"This has gone far enough. We have to get to the lab. Come on," she called back over her shoulder. "We'll stop her together."

Number nine could just barely see her outlined in the doorway. He stood and slowly shuffled toward her.

Together.

He wished he could see her better.

Gaze jerking from one shadow to the next, searching out the possibility of Dr. Burke, Catherine never noticed that number nine's eyes now shone in the darkness with the faint phosphorescence of rot.

Fifteen

The sudden darkness hurled Dr. Burke up against the wall, heart in her throat, palms prickling with sweat. She could feel the jolt of adrenaline eating away at the alcohol-induced distance and struggled to calm herself. Being sober, in *this* building, was no part of her plan.

"I knew, I knew, I knew I should've brought the resht . . . of the sec . . . ond bottle," she muttered, her voice very nearly lost in the passage of throat and teeth and lips it had to negotiate before it could clear her mouth.

The equally sudden appearance of light from the battery-operated floods at each end of the hall brought a victorious wave of Donald's jacket. "Ha, ha! Let's hear it for modern engin . . . eering! Power goes off, emer . . . gency lights . . . go on. Rah! Damn good thing they did, too," she continued, stumbling forward again. "Never find the damn lab . . . otherwise. Wander around here for . . . days. Maybe even . . . months."

She squinted down the length of the corridor. "Speaking of . . . which. Where the hell am I?" It took a moment's concentrated effort before she recognized the upcoming t-junction. The left wing, after crossing a lecture hall and going down a small flight of stairs, was a dead end, she thought, but the right, with a little luck, would eventually lead her to the back door of the lab. The small wooden door led into the storeroom; they'd never used it, but Dr. Burke had seen to it in the beginning that she carried the key.

"Maybe I knew something like this was . . . going to happen," she confided to a fire extinguisher. "Maybe I was just being . . . prepared for crazy-Cathy to pop her . . . cork."

And were you prepared, asked the voice of reason, *for what happened to Donald?*

Not even a bottle of single malt whiskey could shut the voice up, but it did make it very easy to ignore. So Dr. Burke did.

While Vicki could see the emergency lights as white pinpricks in a black shroud, her companions apparently found them more than sufficient illumination. Given that Henry needed so little light, he could probably see quite clearly, and she knew from experience that Celluci had better than average night vision. God, how she envied them; to be able to move freely without fear of misstep or collision, to be able to see movement in the shadows in time to . . .

To what?

Vicki pushed the question away and concentrated on not outpacing her circle of sight. Although she kept the flashlight beam trained closely on the floor in front of her so as not to blind the two men, she allowed a small part to overlap onto Henry. After everything they'd been through—everything all three of them had been through—she wasn't letting him slip into darkness just because of her lousy eyes.

Henry was safe.

They'd saved him.

Her mother was dead, but Henry was alive and he was safe with them.

That made up for a lot.

Breathing heavily, Celluci's hand tucked into the elbow of her good arm, she followed the little bit of Henry out of a stairwell and squinted up at the red pinprick in the darkness that had to be the exit sign. "You guys sure this is the right floor?"

"I'm sure." Henry's voice was flat and atonal. "The stink of perverted death is strongest here."

"Henry . . ." Shaking free of Celluci's grip, Vicki reached out and poked him gently in the hip with the side of the flashlight. "It's going to be worse in the lab." They'd told him about Donald down in the electrical room. All three of them had needed a moment to recover from the telling.

"You can wait in the hall if you think it's going to be too strong."

"It's only a difference of degree," Henry told her abruptly, not turning. He could see the outline of the door at the end of the hall. "I might as well go into the lab because I can't smell anything else even here." Then he reached back and brushed his fingers over the warmth of her hand, softening his tone. "We've all moved past the time for running. Now it's time to face those last few fears and . . ."

"And get the hell out of here," Celluci finished. "Which we won't do if we continue to stand here flapping our lips. Come on." He caught hold of Vicki again and dragged her forward, forcing Henry to move ahead or be run down. If they lost momentum, they'd never get this finished. He hadn't wanted to see anything finished quite so much in a very long time. "It can't possibly be worse than the last visit, for any of us."

Vicki tightened her hand around the barrel of the flashlight, giving thanks the grip was heavy ridged rubber. Her palm was so wet that a slicker surface would've squirted right out of her grasp. *Face our last few fears. Oh, God, I hope not.*

The lab—possibly because it was such a large room, possibly because after a century of renovation the building just generally defied logic—rated an emergency light of its own.

"Well, thank God for small favors," Celluci muttered as they entered. "I didn't much want to be in the dark with *that.*"

Vicki let her light lick over *that,* the stainless steel blazing momentarily then sliding into shadow again. All the horror lay in memory now for the body the isolation box contained was merely dead, and they'd all dealt with death before. *He's really most sincerely dead.* She bit back a giggle and stomped down hard on the thought. It would be frighteningly easy to lose control.

Henry ignored the box and strode quickly down the length of the room to the one remaining computer, trench coat flapping back from his naked torso. With the power off, he had no way to tell if it contained the files concerning him, but he had to assume that if Catherine did the tests in this lab then she entered the data into this machine.

"Fitzroy."

He turned, fingers already wrapped around a fistful of cables.

"You might want to clear this out of here as well." Celluci offered him the wallet he'd picked up off the floor, various pieces of ID stuffed loosely inside. "Let's not give Detective Fergusson a chance to cash in on the obvious."

"Thank you." A quick check, and Henry shoved it all into his coat pocket. "If the police managed to connect me to all of this, I'd have had to disappear." One corner of his mouth twisted in the detective's direction. "Maybe you should have left the wallet on the floor."

Celluci mirrored both expression and tone. "Maybe I should have."

Setting cables, monitor, and keyboard carefully to one side, Henry lifted the actual computer over his head and threw it into the corner as hard as he could.

Catherine jerked back at the sound of plastic shattering, eyes snapping open impossibly wide. "It's her. She's wrecking things." Her fingers wrapped around number nine's arm, molding imprints into the increasingly malleable flesh. "We've got to stop her!"

Number nine stopped moving, obedient to the pressure. He would do what she wanted.

From the lab up ahead came the sound of further destruction, small pieces being made smaller still until they were beyond all hope of repair.

"All right." Catherine rose on her toes and rested her forehead on number nine's skull just below where the staples held the cap of bone in place. "This is my plan. I'll distract her, get her to chase me, and lose her in the halls. You go in and get Donald. He should be viable outside the box by now. Don't let anything stop you."

He couldn't feel her breath, warm against his ear and neck—the nerves in the skin had never regenerated—but he could feel her closeness and that was enough. He reached up and awkwardly patted her arm.

"I knew I could count on you!" She squeezed his hand in return, never feeling the tiny bones shifting out of their moorings, tendons and ligaments beginning to let go. "Come on!"

* * *

While Henry smashed hardware into progressively smaller pieces and Celluci snapped disks, Vicki, flashlight tucked under her chin, flipped through reams and reams of printout.

"Finding anything?" Celluci asked, reaching for yet another plastic square.

Vicki shook her head. "Mostly EEG records."

He craned his neck and peered down at the paper bisected with a black ink trail of spikes and valleys. "How the hell do you know that?"

She snorted. "They're labeled."

"Stop it!"

All three of them jerked around.

"Stop it this instant!"

Vicki's flashlight just barely managed to pick out a pale circle of face and hair over a paler rectangle of lab coat in the doorway at the far end of the long room.

"Stop it! Stop it! Stop it!" Fury and madness were stridently obvious in her voice.

"Catherine." Leaping the wreckage at his feet, Henry charged forward.

The figure in the doorway disappeared.

"Fitzroy!"

"Henry!"

He ignored them, intent on the hunt. This madwoman had imprisoned him, tortured him, left him alone in the darkness; she was his. Knowing what she was, he would avoid sinking into the emptiness of her eyes. He would take her down. Her blood was not tainted even if her mind was. And she owed him blood.

In spite of his speed, not yet fully returned but still greater than mortal, she was out of sight when he reached the hall. Her scent lay buried under the clinging stench of death perverted, which not only filled the air but covered the inside of his mouth and nose like a noxious film of oil. He *could* hear her life so he sped after it.

But sound became a twisting and uncertain trail, easy to lose track of in the maze of rooms and passageways and, so long used to hunting by sight or scent, Henry found it more difficult than he'd believed possible to close the distance. Her life grew closer, but embarrassingly slowly.

Madness gives strength of limb even while it destroys strength of mind. He couldn't remember who had said that to him, so many years ago, but it appeared that madness gave fleetness of foot as well as strength for Catherine continued to elude him, using the peculiarities of the building to her advantage.

Around a corner and through a lecture hall and out a small door only someone with intimate knowledge of the building would know existed, her heartbeat led him on. The emergency lighting provided patches of too bright light alternating with bands of shadow much easier on his eyes. He was beginning to grow tired, his body protesting the demands he was making on it so soon after the punishment it had endured. Vicki's blood could only do so much.

In the instant before flight, Catherine had recognized the vampire and it hadn't taken her long to realize that she couldn't outrun him. Her knowledge of the building was her only advantage and while it prevented an immediate confrontation, she soon saw it wasn't enough to throw him off her trail.

She had no idea what he would do when he finally caught her, nor did she care. Her only thoughts were for number nine and how she'd been forced to leave him alone and outnumbered in the lab. She had to get back to him.

Rounding a corner, the angle of the emergency light caught her eye and she skidded to a stop. The heavy battery contained in the base had proved too much for the antique plaster and lath expected to hold the screws and the unit had sagged away from the wall. Chest heaving, she jumped for it and hooked her fingertips over a narrow metal lip.

Henry followed Catherine's life around another corner and down a corridor much darker than the rest had been. Her heartbeat grew louder. Then he saw her outlined against the institutional gray of the wall; cowering, cornered.

His lips drew off his teeth and the Hunter closed in on his prey.

She straightened, her body no longer blocking the object cradled in her arms.

Brilliant white light drove spikes of hot metal into night-sensitive eyes. Crying out in pain, Henry fell back, hands raised, an ineffectual barrier now that the damage had been done. He heard her go by, recoiled as her life brushed its shattered edges over him, and could not follow.

Celluci had taken three quick steps after the running vampire, saw he was fast being left behind and stopped. "God damn him!" He flung the disk he was holding at the wall, as hard as he was able, and found his feelings were not in the least relieved by its shattering. "After all we went through to haul his ass out of danger, that god-damned undead bastard runs off on us!"

Vicki merely shook her head, hand clutched tightly around the barrel of her flashlight. Although the sound of her own heartbeat nearly deafened her, she felt surprisingly calm. "It's not," she said softly, "like he's a tame lion."

Celluci turned on her, both hands driving up through his hair. "And what the hell is *that* supposed to mean?"

"It's a line from a children's book. I used it to describe him last spring, when we met."

"Great, just great. You're taking a literary trip down memory lane and Fitzroy's buggered off." He took another step toward the door, then changed his mind, whirled, and stomped back to her side. "Vicki, that's it. We're out of here." Feelings of betrayal outweighed worry and concern. "If Fitzroy's able to go running off like some kind of blood-sucking avenging angel, he can manage without us around and . . ."

All at once, he realized she wasn't listening to him. Which was, in itself, not particularly unusual but her expression, pointed fixedly down the flashlight beam, was one he'd seen on her face only once before—about an hour and a half before when they'd opened the metal coffin and Donald Li had opened his eyes.

The flesh between his shoulder blades crawling, he spun around.

Standing in the doorway was a parody of a man.

She had told him to rescue Donald. She had not mentioned the people standing beyond the box, so number nine ignored them.

He shuffled forward.

                                *   *   *

Celluci's right hand came up and sketched a quick sign of the cross. "That girl, the witness the night the boy was killed, she said that he was strangled by a dead man."

The creature continued to shuffle forward, the stink of it growing with every step.

A sane man would run. But his feet and legs refused to obey. "This has got to be the thing that killed the boy."

"Odds are good," Vicki agreed, her voice sounding as though she'd forced it through clenched teeth. "So what are you going to do? Arrest it?"

"Oh, very funny." Without taking his eyes off the lurching obscenity, he moved sideways until his shoulder came in contact with hers; the warmth of another life suddenly important. "What do you suppose it wants?"

He felt her shrug. "I'm afraid to guess."

It arrived at the isolation box and reached out for the latch.

"Fuck that!" Barely aware he was moving, Celluci charged forward. After what they'd gone through to save Donald Li—after what Donald Li had gone through—he'd be damned if he'd let the kid be dragged back into the ranks of the undead. *Ranks of the undead . . . Jesus! I sound like the cut line on a made-for-TV movie.* He rocked to a halt at the end of the box and bellowed, "Go on! Get away from there!"

It ignored him.

"God damn you, I said get away!" He didn't remember pulling his gun, but there it was in his hand. "Just back away from the box! Now!"

Finally recognizing some sort of threat, it turned its head and looked right at him.

Get Donald. Don't let anything stop you.

Number nine stared at the man by the box. The voice had held command, but the words had not been words he had to obey.

Don't let anything stop you.

The words were not enough to stop him. The man could be ignored.

He turned his attention back to the latch, trying to get his fingers to close.

* * *

The worst of it wasn't the grave-gray of the skin, lips and fingertips greenish-black, nor was it the line of staples across the forehead or even the obvious signs of the triumph of decay. The worst of it was that there was someone in there—that not only an intelligence but a personality existed within the ruin.

Trembling violently with horror and pity and revulsion in about equal proportion, Celluci braced his gun with his left hand and, whispering a "Hail Mary" through dry lips, pulled the trigger. The first shot missed. The second creased the back of the creature's skull with enough force to spin it around and throw it over the stainless steel curve of the isolation box. He never got the chance to fire a third.

The blow caught him just below the shoulder, knocking him into the trio of oxygen tanks lined up under the window. He lost his grip on the gun, was vaguely aware of it skittering away across the floor, and saw Vicki charging around the end of the box, flashlight raised like a club.

Vicki had watched Celluci advance on the creature with a curious detachment. It was as though, when she'd seen it appear in the doorway and realized both what it was and what it wasn't, an overload switch had been tripped and she could no longer react, only wait. Her mouth had moved in response to comments made, but her mind had been disconnected. After the last few days of constant internal turmoil, charges and countercharges and just general hysteria, the peace and quiet was kind of nice. She kept the flashlight beam trained on the creature as it shuffled along and refused to wonder what it was she waited for.

She thought she understood what motivated Celluci to try and prevent the opening of the box, but she couldn't seem to make it matter. She heard him speak, but the words got tangled and made no sense. When he pulled his gun, the only thing she felt was mild surprise.

Muscles spasmed with the first shot, her brain slamming back and forth between her ears. The crack of the second shot jerked her out of her retreat and shook her awake.

She saw the creature's arm come up and Celluci fly back. She started moving before he hit the floor. Keeping the beam pointed along her path until she got near enough to finish blind, she raised the heavy flashlight like a club and slammed it down. Contact had a strangely muffled feel.

Although she'd come so close that the slightly sweet stink of decomposing flesh wrapped around her, she couldn't actually see the creature she faced. *And thank God for small mercies.* It had been terrifying enough from a distance. Unfortunately, neither could she see the return blow.

With only one arm for balance, she went down hard, more concerned with hanging onto her only means of sight than with breaking her fall. She struck, rolled, and crushed her injured wrist against the floor.

Celluci heard her gasp of pain as he launched himself back at the creature. *What are you doing?* screamed the still rational part of his brain. But even while he recognized that the question had merit, the night had gone on too long for him to listen to it.

With a dull squelch, his shoulder drove into the creature's ribs, forcing it back toward the door. They went down together, grappled, rolled. He lost track of time, lost track of place, lost track of self until he found himself staring up at the hall ceiling as his spine smashed into the tile. He grunted as the heavy muscles of his back absorbed most, but not all, of the blow. He tried to kick free. Was lifted. Thrown against a wall of shelves. Slid down them. Saw a door closing. And was suddenly alone in darkness.

Number nine had put the last intruder in the box. She had been pleased with that. So he found a box for this intruder as well.

Pressing down with both hands, he bent the round metal thing until it would no longer turn.

Now the intruder would stay in the box.

It was undoubtedly a storage closet—not that it mattered. Celluci flung himself against the door. It didn't budge. And when, screaming Italian profanity, he finally found the knob, it didn't turn.

Vicki levered herself up onto her knees, head spinning. She assumed the sounds of impact she heard were Celluci and the creature, but at the moment she was physically incapable of going to his aid. Curled around her injured arm, she dry retched, fighting the waves of dizziness that threatened to knock her flat again.

Damn it, Vicki, get it together! Mike needs you! So you've lost a little blood, big fucking deal. It isn't the first time. Get UP!

Panting through locked teeth, she groped for the flashlight and suddenly realized she wasn't alone.

Her vision consisted of only a very narrow path along the floor, illuminated by the flashlight and bound by the disease that had destroyed her sight. Into that path shuffled a pair of feet wearing new track shoes with velcro tabs. Beyond horror, Vicki froze, unable to move, unable to think, unable to look away as the feet shuffled toward her. When they stopped, she could also see sweatpants covering the legs from knees to ankles. The creature by the box had been wearing sweatpants, but she could still hear the sounds of fighting. . . .

Finally, she got her fingers closed around the rubber grip and, clutching it like a talisman, she slowly forced herself to straighten.

Her mother looked down at her, much as her mother had looked down at her a thousand times before. Except this time, her mother was dead.

She felt reason slipping away and scrambled desperately for its edges. This was her mother. Her mother loved her. Dead or not, her mother would never harm her.

Then the dead lips parted and a dead mouth formed her name.

Too much.

Henry heard the scream, turned, and ran toward it. Still half blind, his sense of smell useless in corridors saturated with abomination, he raced back along the path of Vicki's terror and came up facing a dead end.

Howling with rage, he doubled back, senses straining for the touch of her life to guide him.

"VICKI!" Celluci threw himself against the door in impotent fury. Again, and again.

And again.

*   *   *

Mouth dry, heart pounding in the too-small cage of her ribs, Vicki slowly backed away. Hands reaching out for her, her dead mother followed. The harsh illumination of the flashlight accentuated the death pallor and threw tiny shadows beside each of the staples across Marjory Nelson's forehead.

Her feet continued moving for a moment before Vicki realized she wasn't going any farther, that the distance between them was closing. The cold metal curve of the isolation box pressed into the small of her back. *Go around!* she thought, but she couldn't remember how. She couldn't take her eyes off the approaching figure. Nor could she turn the light away in the hope that it would disappear in the darkness.

"Stop!"

Vicki jerked, the sound slapping at her.

The dead woman, who had been Marjory Nelson, dragged herself forward one more step, then had to obey.

"Stay!" Catherine, with number nine following close behind her, entered the lab, squinted as she crossed the beam of light, and glared around. "Just look at this place. It'll take days to get it all cleared up." She kicked at a fractured bit of circuit board and turned on Vicki, her movements nearly as jerky as her companion's. "Who are you?"

Who am I? Her glasses were sliding down her nose. She bent her head until she could push them up with the index finger of her injured hand. Who was she? She swallowed, trying to wet her mouth. "Nelson. Vicki Nelson."

"Vicki Nelson?" Catherine repeated, coming closer.

The tone sent a knife blade down Vicki's spine, although the grad student was still outside the boundary of her vision. *This person is insane.* Crazy just wasn't a strong enough word for the fractures in Catherine's voice.

Leaving number nine in the shadows, Catherine crossed into the cone of light and stopped just in front of where Marjory Nelson strained against the compulsion holding her in place. "Dr. Burke told me about *you.* You wouldn't stop snooping around." The pointed chin rose and the pale blue eyes narrowed. "She wouldn't have tried to terminate the experiments if it wasn't for you. This is all your fault!" The last word became a curse and she threw herself forward, fingers curved to claws, claws reaching for Vicki's throat.

Self-preservation broke the paralysis. Vicki threw herself sideways, knowing she wasn't going to be fast enough. She felt fingertips catch at her collar, had a sudden look into the pit of madness as, for an instant, Catherine's contorted face filled her vision, then all at once, found herself staggering back, no longer under attack. Sagging against the support of the box, she raised the light, searching for an explanation.

Catherine dangled from her mother's hands, then was tossed, with no apparent effort, to one side.

It was the sort of rescue that small children implicitly believed their mothers could perform. In spite of everything, Vicki found herself smiling.

"Way to go, Mom," she muttered, trying to catch her breath.

Number nine had not understood what the other who was like him was about to do.

Then he heard *her* cry out as she struck the floor.

She was hurt.

He remembered anger.

Number nine's first blow shattered ribs, the crack of breaking bone gunshot loud, splinters driven into the chest cavity.

That first blow would have killed her, had she not already been dead. She staggered under the impact but managed to remain standing. The second blow knocked uplifted arms aside, the third threw her halfway across the lab.

Vicki struggled to keep the battle in sight, bracing herself on the box and playing the flashlight beam over the room like some kind of demented spotlight operator at a production more macabre than anything modern theater had to offer.

Nutrient fluid dripped from the ruin of number nine's hands, violence having finished what rot had begun. Glistening curves of bone showed through the destruction of his wrists. He used his forearms like clubs, smashing them down again and again.

Vicki watched as her mother's body slammed into a metal shelving unit, shelves and contents crashing to the floor. A number of the glass containers seemed to explode on contact with the floor, spewing chemical vapor into the air to mix with the smell of decay. As number nine lurched forward, Vicki could stand it no longer.

"For chrissakes, Mom!" she screamed. "Hit the bastard back!"

Her mother turned, head lolling on a neck no longer capable of support, met her daughter's gaze for a moment, then bent and ripped free one of the shelves' flat metal struts. Holding it like a baseball bat, she straightened and swung.

The ragged end of the steel bar caught number nine in the temple, shearing through the thin bone and into the brain. Gold gleamed for a second as the neural net tore loose, then number nine reeled back and collapsed.

The bar rang against the tile. Marjory Nelson swayed and crumpled, as though invisible strings had been cut.

"MOM!" Vicki stumbled forward and threw herself to her knees. She couldn't hold her mother and the flashlight both, so she shoved the latter in under her sling and dragged the limp body up onto her lap. The diffuse light, shining through the thin cotton of Henry's shirt, wiped away all the changes that death and science had made and gave her back her mother.

"Mom? Don't be dead. Oh, please, don't be dead. Not again. . . ."

Too much damage. She could feel the binding letting go. But there was something she had to do.

"Mom? God*damn*it, Mom . . ." Pale gray eyes, so like her own, flickered open and Vicki forgot how to breathe. She shouldn't have been able to see their expression, but she could, could see it clearly, felt it wrap around her and for one long moment keep her safe from the world.

". . . love you . . . Vic . . . ki . . ."

Tears pooled under the edge of her glasses and spilled down her cheeks. "I love you, too, Mom." Her vision blurred and when it cleared she was alone. "Mom?" But the gray eyes stared up at nothing and the body she held was empty. Very, very carefully, she slid it off her lap and stroked the eyes closed.

Her mother was dead.

She started to shake. The pressure grew, closing her throat, twisting her muscles into knots, tossing her back and forth where she knelt. The first sob ripped huge burning holes in her heart and held as much anger as grief. It hurt so much that she surrendered to the second, curled around the pain, and cried.

Cried for her mother.

Cried for herself.

Number nine lay where he had fallen. The anger was gone. Although he had no way of knowing that the neural net had stopped functioning, he dimly understood that the part that was body and the part that was *him* were now separate.

He stared up at the ceiling, wanting . . .

. . . wanting . . .

Then the view shifted and *she* was there.

Catherine gently turned number nine's head to face her.

"I can't fix you," she whispered, drawing her finger softly around the curve of his jaw, alternately tracing flesh and bone. "You were going to stay with me forever. I wouldn't have let her shut you down." She smiled and tenderly pushed a flap of skin back into place.

"You were," she told him, voice catching in her throat, "the very best experiment I ever did."

He wanted her to smile.

He liked it when she smiled.

Then she was gone.

He wanted her to come back.

Slowly, every movement precisely performed, Catherine got to her feet. Every step carefully planned, she advanced across the lab. She paused at the jagged length of steel, still lying where it had been dropped, bent, and lifted it from the floor.

The end torn from the shelf gleamed, polished and pointed by the force that had ripped it free.

She held it up and smiled at it.

*   *   *

The flat metal bar cracked across Vicki's bent shoulders and smashed her to the floor. The world tilted and instinct took over as, gasping in pain, she managed to squirm around to face the assault, shoving her glasses back into place.

The flashlight twisted in the folds of cloth and somehow finished pointed straight up, a miniature searchlight. It lit the gleaming end of steel descending toward Vicki. But not in time.

Sixteen

Henry heard the pounding as he raced down the corridor leading to the lab, heard it and would have ignored it had it not been accompanied by a fine libretto of Italian profanity. He rocked to a stop in front of an old paneled door, saw that the doorknob had been bent down in such a way as to render it nonfunctional, and solved the problem by bracing one hand against the wall and yanking the entire mechanism out of the wood.

The door crashed back and Celluci exploded out into the hall, the force of his exit throwing him to his knees.

Grabbing him by the collar, Henry hauled him to his feet, blocking the resulting flurry of blows with his other arm.

Celluci's snarled challenge broke off as he finally recognized the vampire. "Where the hell were you?" he demanded.

"Finding my way back," Henry answered coldly. "What were you doing in there?"

"Trying to get out." The tone matched exactly. "I heard Vicki scream."

"So did I."

Together they turned and ran toward the lab.

As they raced through the doorway, the bloodscent hit Henry an almost solid blow, too close now to be masked by either decay or the alcohol vapor still seeping into the air. Far from replete, the Hunger rose. For Vicki's sake Henry held it and forced it back; he couldn't help her if he lost control. While he struggled to maintain reason, Celluci pulled ahead.

It seemed there were bodies all over the room, but Celluci only saw one that mattered. Sprawled on her back to one side of the isolation box, Vicki lay motionless except for the purely kinetic jerk that occurred when a blow landed. He saw the steel bar go up and come down, then, howling in inarticulate rage, he grabbed the pale-haired woman by the shoulders and flung her behind him.

"Your fault, too!" Catherine screamed, launching herself back, the jagged end of the bar dripping crimson.

There was no time for Celluci to prepare himself for the attack. Then, all at once, there was no attack.

His arm darting out faster than mortal eye could follow, Henry caught Catherine by the back of the neck, wrapped his other hand around the top of her head, and twisted.

The pale eyes rolled up. For the second time that night the metal strut rang against the tile as it fell from fingers suddenly slack.

Tossing the body aside, Henry threw himself to his knees, his hands joining Celluci's as they frantically searched for the wounds below Vicki's blood-soaked clothing.

The iron bar had torn a chunk of flesh from her left shoulder and had scored the right side of her ribs in two places. Ugly wounds, all three, but hardly fatal.

Then they lifted her fingers out of the puddle between hip and thigh.

"Jesus!" Henry pressed his hand down on the spot and met Celluci's wild gaze. "Arterial," he said quietly and strained to hear her heart above the painful pounding of his own.

The blood spattered across the flashlight lens made Rorschach patterns on the ceiling.

Number nine lay, head to one side as she had left him, waiting for her to come back.

And then she was there.

But she didn't see him and she didn't smile.

"Fifteen minutes. It takes fifteen minutes to bleed to death from that kind of wound."

"I know that!" Henry snapped. He had her heartbeat now, but it was frighteningly faint.

"Of course you do." His fingers trembling, Celluci looped the arm of her glasses back over the curve of her ear. "You're a fucking vampire. You know bleeding. So do something about it!"

Henry glared at him. There was no way to do a tourniquet in the joining of torso and leg. No way but direct pressure to stop the bleeding and he was already doing that, even if he did it too late. "Do what?" he demanded, sure there was nothing else he could do.

"How the fuck should I know! You're the fucking . . . Jesus!"

Pulled by the intensity of Celluci's terrified stare, Henry twisted around. Across the lab, by the wall of boarded up windows, one of the bodies rose slowly to its feet.

One of them had killed her.

Killed her dead.

The anger number nine had known before was less than nothing in comparison to what he felt now.

My gun? Where the hell is my gun? Swatting aside panic, Celluci scanned the floor and finally spotted it almost under the cavader's feet. *Fucking great. . .*

Scrambling to his feet, he launched himself forward, dove, got both hands around the weapon, rolled, and pulled the trigger at almost point-blank range.

The bullet plowed through the putrefying tissue with almost no loss of velocity and rang against the brass casing of the oxygen tank directly behind. It ricocheted up the curve, hit the next tank, and sprayed bits of the valve across the room. Oxygen began to hiss free.

"Jesus H. Christ!" Still on the floor, Celluci crabbed back. Although pus and fluid and God-knew-what poured from the hole, the dead man continued to shuffle forward. "What the fuck do you think this is? A fucking James Cameron movie?" His hands were shaking too hard to try a head shot. He watched his second round blow a chunk from the outside curve of the thing's thigh without any noticeable effect. "Goddamnit, stay dead!"

The third round passed through the abdomen again, rang against brass and sparked.

All hell broke loose.

Henry threw himself over Vicki.

Celluci flattened.

The explosion sent chunks of the oxygen tank flying through the air like shrapnel. Several of the larger chunks slammed into number nine, cutting him into pieces.

He remembered dying.
The last time, she had been there when it was over.
He hoped she'd be there again.

With a whoosh, the alcohol vapor in the air ignited, then the alcohol, then the desk.
Then the emergency light shut off.
Celluci picked his way back to Vicki's side. "Fucking place is on fire. At least we can still see." He squinted at Henry, the pale skin of the vampire's face and chest just barely visible in the flickering light. "You okay?"
"Yes."
"Vicki?"
Henry hesitated, praying he'd hear something different, knowing he wouldn't. "She's dying."
"Fuck that!" Ripping off jacket and shoulder holster, Celluci yanked his shirt over his head, ignoring the buttons. Folding most of the fabric into a rough pad, sleeves dangling, he shoved it at Henry. "She said your saliva causes clotting."
"Yes, but . . ."
"Spit on this and tie that wound off. We're practically on top of a fucking hospital. You get the bleeding stopped and we move her."
"It's too . . ."
"Do it!"
Although he knew it would make no difference, Henry took the shirt and bent over the jagged hole. Michael Celluci had lived less than forty years and still thought death could be fought. Four and a half centuries had taught a different lesson. In a battle between love and death, death always won. He could feel Vicki's life ebbing, knew that nothing they could do would change that.
His fingers maintaining pressure, he covered the still bleeding gash with his mouth. At least when she died, he would have contact with her blood. He pulled the touch, the taste, the scent of her into memory. *You are mortal,*

*my love, I always knew you'd die, but I never dreamed we'd
have so little time. . .*

Suddenly, Celluci's fingers were in his hair and the contact broken.

"I said wrap it, Goddamnit. Not fucking take what she
has left!"

Henry drew bloodstained lips back off his teeth. "Get
your hands off me, mortal!"

The explosion had jerked Vicki back out of the twilight
zone of pain and darkness she'd sunk into. She hadn't
thought it was possible to hurt so much and still be alive.
She could hear the two men arguing and fought against the
weight hanging from her tongue.

"Mi . . ."

"Vicki?" Henry forgotten in the sound of her voice, Celluci twisted around and cupped her face in his hands. The
fire licked at the plywood over the windows. Celluci ignored it. The high ceiling drew the smoke up and away.
The path to the door remained clear. As long as the fire
posed no immediate danger, it could be ignored for more
important concerns. The highly polished metal of the isolation box reflected the orange glow of the flames out into
the room. In its light, Celluci saw Vicki's eyelids flicker,
once, twice. "Hang on, we're going to get you to the
hospital."

The hospital? She wanted to tell him there wasn't any
point but couldn't figure out how.

"Michael." The pain in the detective's voice damped
Henry's anger and drew his own grief to the fore. With one
hand still foolishly, hopelessly holding pressure on Vicki's
leg, he gently grasped Celluci's shoulder with the other.
"There isn't enough time."

"No."

"She'll be dead even before you get her out of this
building."

"No!"

"I can feel her life ebbing."

"I said, NO!"

Listen to him, Mike. He's right. She thought she was still
breathing but she couldn't be certain. *I'm still here, I must
be breathing.*

"Damn it, Vicki, don't die!"

Oh, God, Mike, don't cry. She'd thought it couldn't hurt anymore. She'd been wrong.

"There has to be _something_ we can do!"

Henry felt a vise close round his heart and squeeze. "No." One word, two letters, somehow carried all he felt.

Pulled by the sound of suffering as great as his own, Celluci looked up and met hazel eyes washed almost gold by the firelight. They held a truth too bitter to deny. Vicki was dying.

I'm cold. And it's dark. And it isn't fair. I could tell you I love you now. Could tell both of you. Love was enough to bring my mother back. I guess I'm not as strong. Her body didn't seem to be a part of her anymore. The flesh wrapped around her like a badly fitting suit of clothes. _Oh, shit. I can't feel anything. This sucks. This really sucks. I DON'T WANT TO DIE!_

Her eyes snapped open. She could see a familiar shadow bending over her. Her fingers trembled, aching to brush the curl of hair back from his face.

"Vicki?"

She pulled enough strength from him to form a single word. "Hen : . . ry."

The name pierced into Celluci's soul and ripped it to shreds with barbed hooks. She wanted Henry. Not him. Wanted to die in Henry's arms. He bit his lip to keep from crying out and tried to jerk his head away. He couldn't. Something in her eyes held him. Something that insisted he understand.

She saw the sudden white slash of his smile and carried it with her into darkness. She'd done what she could. Now it was up to him.

Henry had heard his name and was bending forward when Celluci lifted his head. He froze. He'd expected to see on the other man's face the pain of Vicki's choice written over the pain of her dying. He hadn't expected to see a wild and insane hope.

"Change her!"

Henry felt his jaw drop. "What?"

"You heard me!" Celluci reached across Vicki's body and grabbed a fistful of leather coat. "Change her!"

Change her. He'd fed from her deeply only a short time

before. And fed from her the night before that. His blood held enough of the elements of hers that her system might accept it, especially as she had so little blood of her own left to replace. But considering his condition, did *he* have enough for them both?

Change her. If he changed her, he'd lose her. They'd have a little over a year but no more before her new nature drove them apart.

"Do it," Celluci begged. "It's her only chance."

Henry suddenly realized that Celluci had no idea of what the change would mean. That he, in fact, believed the exact opposite of the truth. Believed that if Vicki changed she was lost to him. Henry could read the knowledge of that loss in the other man's face. Could read how he was willing to surrender everything to another for Vicki's sake.

You think I've won, mortal. You're so very wrong. If she dies, we both lose her. If she changes, I lose her alone.

"Henry. Please."

And if you can give her up for love, wondered Henry Fitzroy, vampire, bastard son of Henry VIII, *can I do any less?* His heart would allow only one answer.

Lifting his own wrist to his mouth, Henry opened a vein. "It might not work," he said as he pressed this smaller wound into the hole in her leg, forcing the flow of his blood to act as a barrier for hers. A moment later, he lifted his arm and threw Celluci back his shirt, the motion flinging a single crimson drop across the room like a discarded ruby. "Bind it. Tightly. This could still kill her in spite of everything I do."

Celluci did as instructed, lifting his eyes in time to see Henry open a vein over his heart with Vicki's Swiss army knife. Even with so prosaic a tool, it held the shadow of ancient ritual and he watched, unable to look away, as blood welled out of the cut, appearing almost black against the alabaster skin.

Sliding his arm behind Vicki's shoulders, Henry lifted her and pressed her mouth to his breast. Her life had dropped away to a murmur in the distance; not dead, not yet, but very, very close.

"Drink, Vicki." He made it a command, threw all he was into it, breathed it against the soft cap of her hair. "Drink to live."

He was afraid for a moment that she could not obey him even if she wanted to; then her lips parted and she swallowed. The intensity of his reaction took him completely by surprise. He could vaguely remember how it had felt when Christina had fed from him. It was in no way comparable to the near ecstasy he felt now. He swayed, wrapped his other arm around her body, and closed his eyes. This rapture wasn't enough to make up for the eventual loss of her, but, by God, it was close.

Celluci tied off the makeshift pressure bandage, his hands operating independently of conscious direction. There was something both so blatantly sensual and so extraordinarily innocent about the scene that he couldn't have looked away had he wanted to. Not that he wanted to. He wanted every second of Vicki he could have before he had to face the rest of his life without her.

The firelight turned Vicki's hair the color of spilled honey, danced orange highlights down the black leather enveloping her, and reflected crimson in the puddles of her blood spilled on the floor.

Jesus H. Christ! The fire! All at once, as though it had been waiting to be remembered, he could feel the heat licking against his back. He turned. The entire wall of boarded windows was aflame. The smoke had a greenish tinge and an unpleasant taste—spilled chemicals or burning plastic, it was irrelevent at the moment. They had to get out.

"Fitzroy!"

The voice seemed to come from a long way away, but it held an urgency difficult to ignore. Henry opened his eyes.

"We've got to get out of here before this whole place goes up! Can you move her?"

It took a moment for Henry's eyes to clear, but gradually he, too, became aware of the danger. He glanced down at Vicki, still nuzzling like a blind kitten at his breast, and pulled free enough to find his voice. "I've never done this before, Detective." He had no energy left for anything but the truth and the touch of her life was still so tenuous. "She's dying slower than she was, but she's still dying."

"Christ! What more will it take!"

"More, I'm afraid, than I have right now to give." He

swayed, Vicki's head rising and falling with the motion. "I told you it might not work."

Fucking great. Vicki was still dying, Fitzroy looked like hell, and the building was burning down around them. He coughed and scrubbed his forearm across his face. *Goddamned cup's not half empty if I say it's half full.* Grabbing jacket and holster and gun up off the floor, Celluci stood. "If she's still dying, she's not dead. Let's try to keep it that way. Come on!"

Shifting his grip, cradling Vicki in his arms as though she were a child, Henry tried to stand. The room tilted.

Eyes streaming from the smoke, Celluci shoved his free hand into a leather-covered armpit and helped heave Henry and his burden off the floor. "Can you hold her?"

"Yes." He didn't actually think he could let her go but he didn't have enough strength for the explanation. Henry leaned on the larger man's strength as his knees threatened to buckle and, together, they staggered toward the door. Unable to see where he was placing his feet, he stumbled over a piece of something wet—he didn't want to know what—and nearly fell.

"Oh, no, you don't." Muscles popping, sweat streaming down his chest, Celluci somehow kept all three of them up and moving. "After everything we've been through tonight, we aren't fucking quitting yet."

Arms locked around Vicki, holding her life with his own, Henry dredged up the ghost of a smile. "Never say die, Detective?"

Celluci tossed the curl of hair back off his face and led the way out of the lab. "Fucking right," he growled.

As they disappeared down the hall, the door to the store-room slowly swung open and, coughing, Dr. Burke stumbled out into the lab.

"Now that," she declared, "was a most edi . . . fying evening. Who says eaves . . . droppers never hear anything good?" She wiped her streaming eyes and nose on her sleeve and picked her way carefully through the smoke and debris toward the door.

From the sound of it, Marjory Nelson's daughter and her companions had problems of their own. Problems that could easily be used to convince them that Dr. Aline Burke might be better left alone, that her involvement in this whole sordid affair was nothing more than chance.

Donald was dead. She didn't want Donald to be dead, but upon consideration there wasn't anything she could do about it. Why should she suffer just because Donald was dead?

Catherine was dead, too, and therefore a convenient, nonprotesting scapegoat.

"I had no idea what was going on, your honor." She started to giggle and gagged instead. Whatever chemicals were burning were undeniably toxic. "Go ahead, burn!" she commanded. "Let's give Catherine and her friends a fine Viking send-off and in the pro-shess . . ." A fit of coughing doubled her over. She staggered to the isolation box and sagged against it, stomach heaving.

"And in the proshess," she repeated when she'd caught her breath and swallowed a mouthful of bile, "destroy as much evidence as possible. A little vampiric blackmail, a little—what's the word?—con . . . fla . . . gration and I'll be out of this with no major career damage done." Her flame-bordered reflection appeared smugly satisfied and she smiled down at it, patting herself on the cheek. The box was becoming warm to the touch and the skin of her face and hands was beginning to tighten in the growing heat. Time to go.

Head lowered to avoid the worst of the smoke now billowing down from the ceiling, coughing almost continually, she started for the door, lifting her feet with alcohol-exaggerated caution over bodies and parts of bodies.

Then she spotted the disk. Spilled half out of Catherine's lab coat pocket, very blue against the bloodstained white, it could contain only one thing: the copies of the tests made that afternoon on the vampire. What else would be important enough for Catherine to carry around with her?

Only this afternoon. Seems so long ago. With one hand resting against the end of the isolation box, her balance not being exactly stable, Dr. Burke bent to pick it up. It didn't seem to be damaged. Having been sheltered in the curve of Catherine's body, it didn't even seem to be very hot. She shoved it into her own pocket, suddenly realizing that not only would she come out of this with her career essentially undamaged, but with information the scientific community would award high honors for.

A few simple experiments, she thought, grinning broadly, *and that Nobel prize is . . .*

One of the oxygen tanks had remained amazingly undamaged after the earlier explosion had flung it out into the lab. It had lain, partially under the far side of the isolation box, safely away from the main heat of the fire. But temperatures were rising. The plastic valve finally began to melt. The metal collar below it expanded a very, very small amount. It was enough.

The blast slammed Dr. Burke to the floor where she watched in horror as a giant, invisible hand lifted the isolation box and dropped it to fall, impossibly slowly, across her legs. She heard bones shatter, felt the pain a moment later, and slid into darkness.

When the light returned, it was the orange-red of the approaching fire and almost no time had passed. She couldn't feel what was left of her legs.

"That's all right. Don't need legs."

Catherine's extended hand had begun to sizzle.

"Don't need legs. Need to get out of here." The isolation box was on its side. The curve would give her a little room. If she could just push against it, she could pull her legs free and crawl out of the room. Crawl away from the flames. She didn't need legs.

Dragging herself up into a sitting position, she shoved at the box. Nestled on an uneven surface, it rocked. Something squelched beneath it but that didn't matter.

The flames were licking at the sleeve of Catherine's lab coat. Over the stink of chemical-laden smoke came the smell of roasting pork.

Swallowing saliva, she pounded at the box.

It rocked again.

The latch that number nine had partially turned gave way.

The lid fell open, knocking Dr. Burke back to the floor as it rose into the air on silent hinges, spilling the body thrown up against it by the explosion out onto her lap.

The naked, empty shell of Donald Li rolled once and came to rest in the circle of her arms, his head tucked back so that it seemed his face stared up into hers.

The flames stopped the screaming when they finally came.

"Christ on crutches!" Detective Fergusson ducked behind his car as the explosion flung pieces of burning wood and heated metal out into the street. "Last time I investigate drunken confessions in the fucking morning!" Snatching up his radio, he ignored the panicked shouts of the approaching security guards and called in the fire with a calm professionalism he was far from feeling.

". . . *and* an ambulance!"

He thought he could hear screaming. He hoped like hell he was wrong.

"Now what?"

"It's just after two. I need to feed. In about an hour, if she's still alive, I need to feed her. And then I need to get her back to Toronto before dawn."

"Why Toronto? Why can't she just stay here?"

Henry sank down onto the end of the bed. His head felt almost too heavy to lift. "Because if she changes, I need to have her in a place I know is secure." He waved a weary, bloodstained arm at the apartment. "This isn't. And if she . . . if she . . ."

"Dies," Celluci said emotionlessly, staring down at Vicki's unconscious form. He felt as though the world had skewed a few degrees sideways and he had no choice but to try to keep his balance on the slope.

"Yes." Henry matched the detective's lack of expression. If the facade cracked now, it would sweep them all away. "If she dies, I'll need to dispose of the body. I'll need to be in a city I know in order to do that."

"Dispose of the body?"

"Her death is going to be a little difficult to explain if I don't, don't you think? There'll be an autopsy, an inquest, and questions you don't have the answer to will be asked."

"So she just disappears . . ."

"Yes. Yet another unsolved mystery."

"And I'll have to act as though I have no idea if she's dead or alive."

Henry lifted his head and allowed a hint of power to touch his voice. "Mourn her as dead, Detective."

Celluci didn't bother to pretend that he misunderstood. He jerked his gaze from Vicki and recklessly met the vampire's eyes. "Mourn her regardless? Fuck you. You tell me what happens, Fitzroy. If she disappears because she's dead, I'll mourn her. If she disappears into the night with you, I'll . . ." A muscle jumped in his jaw. "I'll miss her like I'd miss a part of myself but I won't mourn her if she isn't any more dead than you are."

Since they'd found her dying in the lab, Henry had been measuring time by Vicki's heartbeat. He let three go by while he studied Mike Celluci's soul. "You really mean that," he said at last. He found it difficult to believe. Found it impossible not to believe.

"Yeah." The word caught in Celluci's throat. "I really mean it." He swallowed and fought for control. Then his eyes widened. "What do you mean, you have to feed?"

"You should know what that means by now."

"On who?"

"I could hunt." Except that he was so incredibly tired. The night had already lasted longer than any night he could remember. It seemed a pity to hunt when there was . . . He allowed the power to rise a little more.

"Stop it. I know what you're trying." With an effort, Celluci wrenched his gaze away and back to the woman on the bed. She was still alive. All that really mattered was keeping her that way. He'd made that decision back in the lab. He'd stand by it now. "If it includes anything but sucking blood, you can fucking well order takeout."

Astounded by the offer, Henry felt his brows rise. "It needn't include anything but sucking blood, Detective. It's not nourishment I need so much as refueling."

"All right, then." Celluci shrugged out of his jacket, dropping it carefully inside out so as not to stain the carpet, and began to roll up his sleeve. "Wrist, right?"

"Yes." Henry shook his head, wonder and respect about equally mixed in his voice. "You know, in four and a half centuries, I've never met a man quite like you. In spite of everything, you offer me your blood?"

"Yeah. In spite of everything." With one last look at Vicki, he turned and lowered himself onto the end of the bed. "At the risk of offending, after what went down tonight," he sighed, "this doesn't seem like much. Besides,

I'm doing it for her. Right now, as far as I'm concerned, you're just a primitive branch of the Red Cross. Get on with it."

Henry lifted the offered arm, then looked up at Celluci, his eyes dark, the smallest hint of a smile brushing against the outside corners of his lips. "You know, it's a shame there's so much between us, Detective."

Celluci felt the heat and tossed the curl of hair back off his forehead. "Don't press your luck, you undead son of a bitch."

As he carried her out the door, her life still balanced on the razor's edge, Henry paused. "Doesn't it gnaw at you," he asked at last, unable to leave with knowing, "that at the end she chose me?"

Celluci reached out and gently tucked her glasses into the pocket of her coat. Her purse and her suitcase had already been loaded in Henry's car.

"She didn't choose you," he said, stepping back and rubbing at the bandage on his wrist. "She chose the one chance she had to live. I refuse to feel bad about that."

"She could still die."

"See that she doesn't."

A thousand thoughts between one faltering heartbeat and the next. "I'll do my best."

Celluci nodded, acknowledging truth; then he bent forward and kissed her gently on lips that felt less warm than they had.

"Good-bye, Vicki."

And there wasn't anything more he could say.

He dealt with Detective Fergusson. Explained Vicki had had a bit of a breakdown, perfectly understandable under the circumstances, and gone back to Toronto with a friend. "I'll let her know what happened . . ."

He dealt with the contents of her mother's apartment, calling an estate auctioneer and putting everything in his hands. "Just sell it. The money goes to the lawyer until the will clears probate, so what's the problem."

He dealt with Mr. Delgado.

"I saw her leave in his car, through my window." The

old man looked up at him and shook his head. "What happened?"

Just for a moment, Celluci wanted to tell him—just for a moment, because he desperately needed to tell somebody. Fortunately, the moment passed. "There's an old saying, Mr. Delgado: 'If you love something, let it go.' "

"I know this saying. I read it on a T-shirt once. It's bull-shit, if you'll excuse my language." His head continued to shake like it was the only moving part of an ancient clock-work. "So she made her choice."

"We all made a choice."

He dealt with driving back to Toronto not knowing. He wouldn't call Fitzroy. He'd bent as far as he could. Let Fitzroy call him.

He dealt with the message when it finally came and thanked God he only had to deal with Fitzroy's voice on the machine. Even that was disturbing enough. He tried to be happy she was still alive. Tried very hard. Almost managed it.

He found out what was happening next by accident. He hadn't intended to walk by her apartment. It was stupid. Ghoulish. He knew she wasn't there. He'd gone in once, the night he'd arrived from Kingston, cleared out his stuff, and without knowing why, had taken a picture of the two of them that he hated off her dresser. When he got home, he shoved it up on the shelf in his hall closet and never looked at it again. But he had it.

"Hey, Sarge." A slender shadow detached itself from the broad base of the old chestnut tree and sauntered out onto the sidewalk. "There's no point in going in, her stuff's all gone. New tenants coming next week, I expect."

"What are you doing here, Tony?"

The young man shrugged. "I was dropping off the key and I saw you coming around the corner, so I figured I'd wait. Save me a trip later. I got a message for you."

"A message," he repeated, because he couldn't ask who from.

"Yeah. Henry said I was to tell you that you were one of the most honorable men he ever met and that he wished things could've been different."

"Different. Yeah. Well."

Tony shot the detective a glance out of the corner of his eye and hid his disappointment. Henry wouldn't tell him what he meant by *different,* if he meant with Vicki or what, and now it looked like Celluci was going to be just as closedmouthed. Although he'd been given the overall story behind that last night in Kingston, he had none of the details and curiosity was almost killing him. "Henry also wanted me to tell you that a year is a small slice of eternity."

Celluci snorted and started walking down Huron Street, needing the distraction of movement. "What the hell does *that* mean?" he asked as Tony fell into step beside him.

"Beats me," Tony admitted. "But that's what he wanted me to tell you. He said you'd understand later."

Celluci snorted again. "Fucking romance writer."

"Yeah. Well." When they reached the corner at Cecil Street, and the detective hadn't spoke again, Tony sighed. "Mostly she sleeps," he said.

"Who sleeps?" A muscle jumped in Celluci's jaw.

"Victory. Henry's still pretty worried about her, but he thinks things are going to be all right now that the hole in her leg finally healed up. We're moving to Vancouver."

"We?"

"Yeah. She's pretty helpless right now. They need someone who can deal with the sun. And . . ."

"Never mind." Vancouver. All the way across the country. "Why? For the sea air?"

"Nah. So nobody recognizes her when she starts to hunt. Apparently they're pretty messy at first."

They'd eaten a thousand meals together. Maybe two thousand. "Tell him she's not likely to get a lot neater."

Tony snickered. "I'll tell him. Anything you want me to tell her?"

"Tell her . . ." His voice trailed off and he seemed to be staring at something Tony couldn't see. Then his face twisted and, lips pressed into a thin, white line, he spun on one heel and strode away.

Tony stood and watched him for a moment, then he nodded. "Don't worry, man," he said softly. "I'll tell her."

He dealt with everything until Detective Fergusson called from Kingston about the inquest.

"Look, she's moved to Vancouver, all right. Other than that, I don't know where the fuck she is."

Detective Fergusson jumped to the obvious conclusion. "Dumped you, eh?"

In answer, Celluci ripped the phone off his kitchen wall and threw it out the back door. A few days later, after he'd been brought in by a couple of uniforms for racing a jet down the runway at the Downsview Airport, the backseat of his car rattling with empties, the police psychologist suggested that he was suppressing strong emotions.

Still painfully hung over, Celluci barely resisted the urge to suppress the police psychologist.

"I hope she's worth you flushing your career down the toilet, because that's what you're doing." Inspector Cantree's chair screeched a protest as he leaned back and glared at Celluci. "You know what I've got here?" One huge hand slapped down on the file folder centered on his blotter. "Never mind. I'll tell you. I've got a report from the department shrink that suggests you're dangerously unstable and that you shouldn't be allowed out on the street carrying a gun."

Lips compressed into a thin, white line, Celluci started to shrug out of his shoulder holster.

"Put that the fuck back on!" Cantree snapped. "If I was going to listen to the pompous quack, I'd have had your badge days ago."

Celluci shoved the curl of hair back off his face and tried to ignore how much the motion reminded him of her. "I'm fine," he growled.

"Bullshit! You want to tell me what's wrong?"

"Nothing's wrong." His tone dared Cantree to argue the point and Cantree's expression did just that. Celluci had heard the rumors making the rounds about ex-Detective Vicki Nelson's hasty relocation to the West Coast— although he'd heard them second or third hand because no one had the guts to speculate to his face. Obviously, Cantree had heard them, too. "It's personal."

"Not when it affects your job, it isn't." The Inspector leaned forward and held Celluci's gaze with his. "So here's what you're going to do. You're going to take a leave of absence for at least a month and you're going to get out

of the city and you're going to find wherever it is you've
left your brains and then you're going to come back and
have another little talk with Dr. Freud-enstein."

"What if I don't want to go?" Celluci muttered.

Cantree smiled. "If you don't take a leave of absence,
I'll suspend you for a month without pay. Either way,
you're out of here."

Betting in headquarters had three to one odds that Mike
Celluci's leave of absence would begin on the first available
flight to Vancouver. Several people lost some serious
money.

A week after the interview in Cantree's office, Celluci
found himself escorting his ancient grandmother onto a
plane bound for Italy and a family reunion.

"Jesus, Mike it's good to have you back." Dave Graham's grin threatened to dislodge the entire lower half of
his face. "I mean, one more temporary partner like the last
one and *I'd* have taken six weeks off."

"Who the fuck left coffee rings all over my desk!"

"On the other hand," Dave continued thoughtfully as
Celluci began accusing coworkers of messing with his stuff,
"it *was* a lot quieter while you were gone."

"You buying one of those, Mike?"

"What?" Celluci looked up from the paperback book
display and scowled at his partner.

"Well, you've been staring at it for the last five minutes.
I thought that maybe you were in the mood for a little light
reading." Dave reached past his head at the blond giant
cradling a half-naked brunette on the cover. "*Sail into Destiny* by Elizabeth Fitzroy. Looks like a winner. You think
you know a guy . . ." He flipped the book over ". . . think
you know his tastes, and then you find out about something
like this. You figure Captain Roxborough and this Veronica
babe are going to get together in the end or is that a
given?"

"Jesus H. Christ, we're in a mall! Someone might see
you." Celluci grabbed the book and shoved it back on
the shelf.

"Hey, you were the one who stopped to browse," Dave

protested as the two detectives started walking again. "You were the one . . ."

"I know the author, all right? Now drop it."

"You know an author? I didn't even think you knew how to read." They watched a crowd of teenage boys saunter past and into a sports store. "So what's she like? Does she live in Toronto?"

He's a vampire. He lives in Vancouver. "I said, drop it."

There were bits of Vicki scattered all over the city and whenever he ran into one—her old neighborhood, her favorite coffee shop, a hooker she'd busted—it gouged the scabs off his ability to cope. Now, he was finding bits of Fitzroy as well and every copy of the book he saw ground salt into the wounds. Fortunately, he'd gotten better at hiding the pain.

He'd even convinced the police psychologist that he was fine.

". . . and the Stanley Park murders continue in Vancouver. Another known drug dealer has been found by the teahouse at Ferguson Point. As in the three previous cases, the head appears to have been ripped from the body and sources in the Coroner's Office report that, once again, the body has been drained of blood."

Celluci's grip tightened around the aluminum beer can, crushing the thin metal. His attention locked on the television, he didn't notice the liquid dripping over his hand and onto the carpet.

"The police remain baffled and one of the officers staking out the teahouse during the time the murder occurred freely admitted having seen nothing. Speculation in the press ranges from the likelihood of a powerful new gang arriving in the Vancouver area and removing competition, to the possibility of an enraged sasquatch roaming the park.

"In Edmonton . . ."

Drained of blood. Celluci shut off the sound and stared unblinkingly at the CBC news anchor who silently continued the National without him. *Not a sasquatch. A vampire.* A new, young vampire learning to feed. Rip off the heads to hide the first frenzied teeth marks. Fitzroy was strong enough. Leave dead drug dealers in the park to make a point. He could see Vicki all over that.

"God-damned vampire vigilantes," he muttered through teeth clenched so tightly his temples ached. Back before Fitzroy, Vicki had realized that law was one of the few concepts holding chaos at bay. As much as she might have wanted to behead a few of the cockroaches that walked on two legs in the city's gutters, she'd never have taken matters into her own hands. Fitzroy had changed that even before he'd changed her.

Vicki was alive, but what had she become? And why didn't he care?

Celluci didn't want to face the answer to either question. The TV continued to flicker silently in the corner as he cracked open a bottle of Scotch and methodically set about searching for oblivion.

Time passed but only because there was nothing to stop it.

She stood outside for a while and watched his shadow move against the blinds. There was a tightness in her chest, and, if she didn't know herself better, she'd say she was frightened. "Which is ridiculous."

Wiping her palms against the thighs of her jeans, the movement dictated no longer by need but by habit, she started up the driveway. Waiting would only make it worse.

Her knock, harder than she'd intended, for she still didn't have complete control of her strength, echoed up and down the quiet street. She listened to him approach the door, counted his heartbeats as he turned the knob, and tried not to flinch back from the sudden spill of light.

"Vicki."

She felt as though she hadn't heard her name spoken for a very long time and couldn't hear his reaction over the sound of her own. With an effort, she kept her voice more or less even. "You don't seem especially surprised to see me."

"I heard about what happened last night to Gowan and Mallard."

"No more than they deserved. No more than I owed them."

"The paper says they'll both live."

The night flashed for an instant in her smile. "Good. I

want them to live with it." She rubbed her palms against her jeans again, this time wiping clean old debts. "Can I come in?"

Celluci stepped back from the door. She was thinner, paler, and her hair was different. It took a moment for the most obvious change to sink in.

"Your glasses?"

"I don't need them anymore." This smile was the smile he remembered. "Good thing, too."

Closing the door behind her, he felt like an amputee who'd woken up to find his legs had grown back. He couldn't seem to catch his breath and it took a moment to identify the strange sense of loss he was feeling with an absence of pain. He almost heard the click as the piece that had been gouged from his life slid back into place.

"You know, the potential problems with the RP never even occurred to me that night in the lab," she continued, leading the way into the kitchen. "Can you imagine a vampire with no night sight? Biting by braille—God, what a mess that would be."

"You're babbling," he said shortly as she turned to face him.

"I know. Sorry."

They stared at each other for a long moment and a number of things that needed to be said were discussed in the silence.

"Henry owes you an apology," Vicki told him at last. "He never mentioned to you that vampires can't stay together after the change is complete."

"It's been fourteen months."

She spread her hands. "Sorry. I got off to a slow start."

Celluci frowned. "I'm not sure I understand. You *can't* ever see him again?"

"He says I won't want to. That we won't want to."

"The bastard could've told me." He dragged a hand up through his hair. *"Henry wanted me to tell you that a year is a small slice of eternity."* Taking a deep breath, he wondered what he would've done had their positions been reversed. "Never mind. Henry doesn't owe me anything. And the son of a bitch already apologized."

Vicki looked doubtful. "Yeah? Well, I'm not buying into his tragic separation bullshit even if we can't share a territory." Brave words, but she wasn't so sure that they meant anything, that her new nature would allow a bond to remain without the blood.

"I'm not giving you up without a fight."

Henry turned away from the lights of a new city and sadly shook his head. "You'll be fighting yourself, Vicki. Fighting what you are. What we are."

"So?" Her chin rose. "I don't surrender, Henry. Not to anything."

"He's got a cellular phone and he just bought a fax machine, for chrissake; I think we'll manage to stay in touch."

"Really?" Celluci propped one hip on the counter and crossed his arms over his chest. "You never called *me*."

"I wasn't able to until just recently—things were a little chaotic at first. And then . . ." She rubbed a pale finger along the edge of his kitchen table, glad she'd lost the ability to blush. "And then I was afraid."

He'd never heard her admit to being afraid of anything before. "Afraid of what?"

She looked up and he found his answer in the desperate question in her eyes.

"Vicki . . ." He made her name a gentle accusation. *Couldn't you trust me?*

"Well, I'm *different* now and . . . What are you laughing at?"

How long had it been since he laughed like that? About fourteen months, he suspected. "If *that's* all you're worried about; Vicki, you've *always* been different."

The question faded, replaced by hope. "So you don't mind?"

"I'd be lying if I said it won't take getting used to, but, no, I don't mind." Mind? There wasn't much he couldn't get used to if it meant having her back beside him.

"It won't be the same."

"No shit."

"Henry says it can be better."

"I don't care what Henry says."

"It won't be settling down and raising a family like you wanted."

He slid off the counter. "Don't tell me what I wanted. I wanted you."

She opened her arms, her teeth a very white invitation against the curve of her mouth.

He met her halfway.

They hit the floor together.

Two hours and twenty-three minutes later, Vicki pillowed her head on his shoulder and stared up at the kitchen ceiling. She'd thought that over the last fourteen months she'd come to terms with what she'd become—vampire, child of darkness, nightwalker—but she hadn't, not really, not until her teeth had met through a fold of Mike Celluci's skin and she'd drawn his life back into hers. She licked at a drop of sweat and could feel his breath, warm against the top of her head, his scent wrapped around her.

"What're you thinking of?" he asked sleepily.

Vampire. Child of Darkness. Nightwalker.

Reaching up, she brushed the curl of hair back off his forehead and smiled. "I was just thinking about the next four hundred and fifty years."

Tanya Huff

The Finest in Fantasy

To Order Call: 1-800-788-6262

DAW 21